12.12   104   £5.00

GW00384580

Worlds Apart

An Antholgy of Russian Fantasy and Science Fiction

Worlds Apart

An Antholgy of Russian Fantasy and Science Fiction

EDITED AND WITH COMMENTARY BY

ALEXANDER LEVITSKY

Translated by Alexander Levitsky and Martha T. Kitchen

OVERLOOK DUCKWORTH

NEW YORK • WOODSTOCK • LONDON

First published in 2007 by
Overlook Duckworth, Peter Mayer Publishers, Inc.
New York, Woodstock, and London

NEW YORK:
141 Wooster Street
New York, NY 10012

WOODSTOCK:
One Overlook Drive
Woodstock, NY 12498
www.overlookpress.com
[for individual orders, bulk and special sales, contact our Woodstock office]

LONDON:
90-93 Cowcross Street
London EC1M 6BF
inquiries@duckworth-publishers.co.uk
www.ducknet.co.uk

Portions of this book are from the author's earlier volumes: *Life Class,
Hotel Splendide, Small Beer,* and *I Love You, I Love You, I Love You*

Cataloging-in-Publication Data is available from the Library of Congress

Book design and type formatting by Bernard Schleifer
Manufactured in the United States of America
ISBN-10 1-58567-819-8 / ISBN-13 978-1-58567-819-8 (HC)
ISBN-10 1-58567-820-1 / ISBN-13 978-1-58567-820-4 (PB)
ISBN-13 978-0-7156-3733-3 (UK PB)

1 3 5 7 9 10 8 6 4 2

CONTENTS

PART II
MODERN RUSSIAN FANTASY, UTOPIA
AND SCIENCE FICTION

TABLE OF TRANSLITERATION

The Library of Congress system of transliteration with the diacritical marks omitted is used in this anthology, with the following exceptions: a. commonly used spellings of place-names or personal names (Moscow rather than Moskva, and Maria rather than Marriia); b. well-known writers (e.g. Fyodor Dostoevsky rather than Fiodor Dostoevskii; Boris Pilniak rather then Boris Pil'nik); c. certain well-know first names (but not patronymics) are spelled by their common published practice (such as Yuri rather than Iurii, Evgeny rather than Evgenii, and Alexander rather than Aleksandr); d. surnames ending with "-skii" are given throughout as "sky" (for example, Zabolotsky rather than Zabolotskii).

A NOTE ON THE TRANSLATIONS

In compiling an anthology, space considerations always impose difficult choices. This is true even for collections dealing with fairly narrow or self-limiting themes—perhaps the works of a single author or literary school, or of a particular historical period. The present volume has broader ambitions. We hop to provide the general reader with an introduction to the incredibly rich trove of fantasy and science fiction produced over the span of many centuries by Russia's folk singers, fabulists, poets, novelists, and masters of other genres more difficult to pigeonhole.

About half of the works in this volume have been newly translated, with the remainder borrowed from previous publications. By necessity and choice, ours was not a unified method. Ideally every work would be presented in its entirety, but this is rarely possible and in fact was not practicable for us: some works are here in full form, and a few have been cut.

Naturally, shorter poetic works, such as the poems of Blok, Briusov and Zabolotsky were kept intact. But long verse narrative like Lermontov's *The Demon*, or a lengthy text like Blok's *The Twelve*, for example, are represented by selected excerpts. Our approach has been flexible in other ways as well. Pushkin's *The Bronze Horseman* is also a narrative poem: although the work is brief enough to appear here in its entirety, our new translation renders only the prologue in rhymed verse. For the remainder we chose instead unrhymed but rhythmical prose (metered in iambic octameter), which we feel presents the imagery and themes of this seminal text to the general reader in a more accessible form, with paragraphs corresponding to the irregular stanzas by Pushkin. The same method was applied to Derzhavin's folkloric *Zlogor*.

It is not really the case that translating prose is less demanding than translating poetry. Master prose writers—19th century "giants" like Dostoevsky, Gogol, and Turgenev, or 20th century classics like Bulgakov, Remizov, Pilniak, and Olesha—work with subtleties and shadings as complex as any poet's. To convey some sense of this in English was a challenge that deepened our appreciation of their varied narrative genius.

Moreover, whenever possible we have been at great pains to match the scansion of an English line with its Russian original: our poetry translations are rhymed and retain their original meter, as we have taken seriously Joseph Brodsky's axion: "Meter is everything."

ALEXANDER LEVITSKY
MARTHA T. KITCHEN

WORLDS OF RUSSIAN FANTASY

(In lieu of an introduction)

The poet's eye, in a fine frenzy rolling,
Doth glance from heaven to earth, from earth to heaven;
And, as imagination bodies forth
The forms of things unknown, the poet's pen
Turns them to shapes, and gives to airy nothing
A local habitation and a name.

—WILLIAM SHAKESPEARE

Imagination is more important than knowledge.
Knowledge is limited. Imagination encircles the world.
—ALBERT EINSTEIN

The New York Times headline of October 5, 1957 read:

SOVIET FIRES EARTH SATELLITE INTO SPACE;
IT IS CIRCLING THE GLOBE AT 18,000 M. P. H.;
SPHERE TRACKED IN 4 CROSSINGS OVER U.S.

MY AGE-WORN and yellowed copy of this issue has someone's inscription pencilled in red block letters over the headline. It reads: A NEW WORLD HAS BEEN BORN. "Astonished" is the first verb in the lead article conveying the reaction of the directors of the United States' earth-satellite program. Such were indeed the feelings around the globe about this date, or rather about the previous day (October 4 of the International Geophysical Year), when the first man-made object capable of defying gravity was actually hurled into space. Beeping by radio signals at regular intervals from the blackness of the star-studded skies, it inspired excitement and awe—of a kind that previously had only been dreamed of in works of literature, especially science-fiction.[1]

---

1. Without entering into a lengthy elaboration of its possibly multiple and lengthy definitions, the term *Science Fiction* will be used here simply as a subgenre of literary *Fantasy*, which deals with an impact of imaginary or real science or technology upon an imagined society or an individual. As opposed to the unlimited worlds of imagination in *Fantasy*, perhaps best expressed by the Shakespeare passage quoted at the outset of this essay, all works termed *science fiction* in our volume will require some degree of plausibility with respect to empirical thought or technological progress. In spite of this limiting factor, *Sci-Fi* is regarded here as part of the fantastic in literature, since it—just as fantasy—always relies on an element of *dislocation* regarding the expected time, place or a set of preconceived ideas, normative at the time of its writing. In this way, I agree with Philip K. Dick's general belief that it is very hard to separate fantasy from science fiction, except in the degree of their respective *plausibility* from the vantage point of the general reader (cf. *The Shifting Realities of Philip K. Dick: Selected Literary and Philosophical Writings*. Ed. by Lawrence Sutin I. NY: Dutton, 1995, pp. 99-100).

The launch of this first *Sputnik*—the Soviet Space Program had chosen the name, which in Russian denotes "*a fellow traveler*"—was deemed by some a unifying expression of mankind's universal desire to explore the heretofore uncharted zones of space. But the same date also marked the brutal police suppression of student demonstrations in Poland—the Soviet Union's political satellite *on terra firma*—a story which also appeared on the front page of that day's *Times*. In this sense the date served to remind realists of how divided the globe still was; indeed, it sent the American government, unwilling to be included as a Soviet "fellow traveler" in the political sense, into a funding frenzy. Dozens upon dozens of new Russian Studies programs were created at American universities, with the express purpose of educating their students to avoid this fate. For the same social system, which had finally accomplished the technological marvel of a space flight—formerly found only in utopias of imagined future worlds—was in itself derived from earlier Russian utopian dreams. These dreams, however, had gone terribly wrong and had caused the extermination of Russia's own citizens—by tens of millions—in concentration camps scattered all across the eleven time zones of the Soviet Union's geographic space.

Time seemed to accelerate for mankind at an ever increasing pace after *Sputnik* was launched into space. It was only a few years later that a man within another metallic sphere was hurled into orbit and felt for himself the vastness of the universe surrounding his Earth. As if tied to it by an umbilical cord, he was still held in orbit by gravity, but within several years more he felt confident enough to tear himself from Earth and walk for the first time on another celestial body—the Moon. Dizzying advances in technology, particularly computer technology, led some to believe during these years that the moment had come in which technology itself, with its power to expand man's mind, could transcend Mankind and assure us of a computer-android Eden—not only on the Earth, but eventually throughout interplanetary space.

But as we chart our course in a new century and contemplate its unknowable unfolding, a future governed by technology and predicated on rational thought seems a rather less desirable proposition than it did in 1957. The centrifugal forces of globalism, bolstered by rapid advances in information technology, could potentially free mankind to participate in a new world without borders—some even maintain to create a brave new world without material want. Yet such developments threaten other needs of man. Irrational or undesirable these needs might appear to some, stemming as they do from human experiences gained in more limited polities: nation, tribe, family, cultural roots, and native tongues. Nonetheless they are respected by those who define man in broader terms than simply by his ability to reason. We stand on the threshold of the third millennium, in which the diversity of human languages is declining at a rate that outstrips even the notoriously swift decline in bio-diversity. At such a moment it might behoove us to reflect on the roots of culture, and of Russian culture in particular, considering the fact that it has just celebrated a millennium of its own rich and continued growth. Such a turn seems to be especially warranted since Russia and the vast Soviet Union it created and dominated for the last seventy years of that *millennium*, has in our recent past conducted social experimentation on the most grandiose scale—anticipating "global village" advocates—experimentation which failed miserably after decades of tinkering with the concept of Man.

Of course, Russia has offered the world not only a technological realization of a man's dream to fly. Indeed, our volume attempts within its modest confines to chart a reflection of Russian cultural history as it moved through its works of literature often in defiance of any commonplace notions of conquering so-called *objective reality*. These include escapes to the worlds generated by fantasy-making, which—along with idealistic visions of futures founded on advances in science and technology—offer their rejection as well by those who scoff at any kind of imposed social order. Beginning with folk tales and folk epics, the volume charts all kinds of imaginative scapes on a path between the netherworld and the stars, both in their physical and spiritual manifestations. It offers literary dreams and other-worldly visitations, satires, as well as the utopias merging science and fiction, chronologically ending roughly at the time when *Sputnik* was launched into space.

Let us note that the term "utopian literature" is subject to many definitions and can incorporate many separate genres. It thus becomes not very useful, unless one speaks only of literature closely resembling the content and the rhetorical departure of a much earlier work, Sir Thomas More's *Utopia*, or at least his understanding of the word itself (which he derived from the Greek *ou* and *topos*, denoting literally "no place"). If understood in More's usage (he sometimes employed the term *Nusquama* derived from the Latin *nusquam* or "nowhere" when he referred to his book), and if, in addition, one keeps in mind that the story of *Utopia* is told by Raphael Hytloday (his family name derived from the Greek *hutlos* meaning "nonsense" and loosely translated as *Raphael the Nonsense-speaker*, then at least one half of More's design implies any other but a "real" place, that is a truly fictional place for the setting of his Book Two. Book One, on the other hand, consists of an unveiled satire on 16th-century England and as such constitutes a narrative with a "real" place as its implied setting. It is important to note that More's respective settings *coexist* in the same time frame; a prospective "future," if any, is only implied for England in the sense that it might imitate some of the customs of Utopians, including their communal living, moneyless economy, etc., which, if adopted, could turn England (also an island society) into Utopia almost overnight. More's narrator does not expect this to happen as he ends the book. In other words, *Utopia* represents for More primarily a mental projection of a moral ideal attainable *at any time*, should the inhabitants of any commonwealth choose to embrace the ways of *Utopia*. The Renaissance's second most famous utopia, Tommaso Campanella's poetical dialogue, *La Citta del Sole* (The City of the Sun)— though different from More's in many striking aspects—is nearly identical to it in its formal design, describing an island communal society, surrounded by a wall, *coexisting in time* with the narrative dialogue describing its ways. For that reason and for clarity's sake, we shall employ the word *utopia* throughout our text as having a *neutral* sense in terms of its time displacement or value judgement as to the desirability of its imagined world. *Eutopia, desired* or *positive utopia* will be the terms used to describe "the good place" from the vantage point of its author, whereas *dystopia, admonitory* or *cautionary* utopia will denote the converse.

N. V. Gogol (1809-52) was one of the few Russian writers in the 19th century to have kept intact More's basic elements: satire, temporal displacement, a fantastic setting, and the nonsensical narrator (not so much in his name, but in the manner of his narration). Of course, at first glance, Gogol's fiction is not anything like More's, and if More intended by his choice of the word *utopia* a possible pun on another Greek compound *eutopos* (or "good place") then the crux of Gogol's writings is rather the portrayal of the obverse, or *dystopia* (a term introduced in the 1950s). Moreover, as opposed to More, Gogol in his mature fiction (*The Nose, The Overcoat* or *Dead Souls*) often fused the two worlds, the "real" and the fantastic," in such a manner that the two became indivisible in his reader's mind, with the resultant effect of a colossal farce hardly suggesting the possibility of attainment of any utopia. Yet neither the content nor the quality of Gogol's fiction is at issue here (as it will be commented upon later); rather it is the interpretation it received from the then-rising "civic school" of literary criticism, headed by V. G. Belinsky (1811-48). Gogol's literary practice was understood by Belinsky as a perfect "cleansing medicine" for Russia to embark on a path toward a society rather resembling the utopia of More (although More was not mentioned in his critical essays of the forties).

It should not come then as a surprise that it was a pupil of Belinsky, N. G. Chernyshevsky (1828-89), who succeeded in molding, while in prison, an extremely important work of utopian character for the second half of the 19th century, the novel *What Can Be Done* (1862). Chernyshevsky's novel, however, represents a new brand of utopian literature, one with a definite *future* in mind, a future predicated by the newly discovered "laws" of historical process as posited by Marx (who derived his theory from Hegel's philosophical system). Most 20th-century definitions of *utopia* are far more indebted to Marx than to More and imagine a social order set in the future, and coming about as a result of "predictable" advances in science and technology. Chernyshevsky's novel fulfills this definition. With the major theme centered on the emancipation of women and the rational division of labor, it is ultimately the woman protagonist's "dream" that provides a vision of future discoveries in science and technology. As is shown in our anthology, among the images employed is that of the *Crystal Palace* which the new, classless society inhabits. Chernyshevsky obviously modeled this image on the real *Crystal Palace*, an architectural wonder of glass and steel erected at Sydenham for the Great London Exposition of 1852 (the year of Gogol's death).

Chernyshevsky's novel is hardly a work with primarily literary concerns, but rather a work of agitational and sociophilosophical character. At best, it is a second-rate work of fiction. Chernyshevsky did not set out to create a work in which sociopolitical concerns replaced literary ones; on the contrary, Chernyshevsky's novel was written to advance *a priori* political ideas camouflaged in a literary form. The fact that one of the most important political pamphlets of V. I. Lenin (1870-1924) bears the title of Chernyshevsky's work is not an accident of history, but a historical indication that the study of Chernyshevsky's "novel" belongs more to the history of political ideas than to literary inquiry. On the other hand—despite Marx's protestations to the contrary, and his reliance on the so-called scientific method of social history—much of Marxist idealism belongs to the realm of fictional future "reality," where the word fictional denotes precisely the primitive mechanism of literary fantasy as opposed to the scientific method. Since the popular mind is not particularly bothered by the conceptual opposition of good science vs. good literature, this bridging of disciplines was highly successful in its time, and the work proved to be one of the most important political documents leading to the victory of the Bolshevik revolution in twentieth-century Russia and to the division of the world on the eve of the *Sputnik* era.

Setting aside for the moment such oppositions as free market vs. directed forms of economy, democratic vs. controlled forms of elections and other major differences which divided humanity in the twentieth century, both socialist and capitalist societies were in complete agreement on one thing, namely that man is a *rational entity* capable of choosing what is naturally advantageous to his well-being. Both schools of thought defined well-being primarily in terms of the acquisition of material wealth, e.g. how many cars, televisions, computers, or metric tons of agricultural products were made *per capita* in their respective societies, and the desirability of living in one or the other was often measured simply in terms of an algebraic addition of such wealth. Both furthermore held that human ability to reason was best exemplified by science and that human progress was best measured by man's advances in science. Both, therefore, put great store in supporting science and its attendant technology and, at least in the pure sciences, their constructive dialogue continued relatively unabated and shared.

The fundamental conceptual similarity uniting socialism and capitalism—popularly perceived as antithetical ideologies—was perhaps most cogently expressed by *existentialism,* one of the twentieth-century's most influential philosophical and literary movements. Existentialist thought posed an effective and troubling challenge to the basic assumptions that underlay both philosophical camps. Though international in scope, it is important to note that the movement found productive roots in the writings of at least one major Russian writer, F. M. Dostoevsky (1821-81), whose works were for decades proscribed by the Soviet regime. The eminent critic Irving Howe—writing a few years after *Sputnik* was put into orbit and on the eve of the date when the new world it had created was close to being annihilated by the Cuban missile crisis—had the following to say of Dostoevsky's connection to existentialism:

> The assumption that man is rational, and the assumption that his character is definable—so important to western literature—are both threatened when the underground man appears on the historical scene. <. . .> As rebel against the previously secure Enlightenment, he rejects the claims of science, the ordered world-view of the rationalists, the optimism of the radicals. He is tempted neither by knowledge, like Faust, nor glory, like Julien Sorel; he is beyond temptation of any sort. The idea of ambition he regards as a derangement of ego, and idealism as the most absurd of vanities. He hopes neither to reform nor cure the world, only to escape from beneath its pressures.
>
> A creature of the city, he has no fixed place among the social classes, he lives in holes and crevices, burrowing beneath the visible structure of society. Elusive and paranoid, he plays a great many parts yet continues to be recognized as a type through his unwavering rejection of official humanity: the humanity of decorum, moderation and reasonableness. Even while tormenting himself with reflections upon his own insignificance, the underground man hates still more—more than his own hated self—the world above ground.
>
> Brilliantly anticipated in Diderot's fiction, *Rameau's Nephew,* the underground man first appears full face in Dostoevsky's novels. Here he assumes his most exalted guise, as a whole man suffering the burdens of consciousness. In *Notes from the Underground* he scrutinizes his motives with a kind of phenomenological venom; and then, as if to silence the moralists of both Christianity and humanism who might urge upon him a therapeutic commitment to action, he enters a few relationships with other people, relationships that are commonplace yet utterly decisive in revealing the impossibility of escape from his poisoned self.

In the 20th Century the underground man comes into his own and, like a rise of pus, breaks through the wrinkled skin of tradition. Thus far, at least, it is his century. He appears everywhere in modern literature, though seldom with the intellectual resources and intensity of grandeur that Dostoevsky accorded him.[2]

Although most works present in our volume involve travel, whether real or imagined, including even interstellar flight (glancing *from heaven to earth, from earth to heaven,* as Shakespeare has it), we must elaborate the underground man's musings even further, since he probably best defines the lack of movement of any kind, or an absolute stalemate.[3] It would of course be an injustice to Dostoevsky—who, incidentally, nearly deified Shakespeare—to consider his views as *pre-existentialist,* as some have posited, or lacking in idealism of his own. Rather, we shall regard the pathos of the underground man's plight as an implicit companion to our volume, as its most necessary shadow.[4] The underground man—imprisoned within himself—would be indeed a most unwilling companion on any quest. His diary occupies that pole which is inimical to travel, especially mathematically calculated travel, like that described in the *Diaries* of K. E. Tsiolkovsky who—while an occupant of a different kind of prison—was first in the twentieth century to provide a technological solution to the concept of flight in interplanetary space, and who was fondly remembered during the *Sputnik* era. As if to underscore the underground man's lack of élan for any idealism—either for a future made fantastic by advances in technology, or one simply predicated on human love—Dostoevsky leaves his protagonist standing at a cross-roads, at the end of a novel which had forever changed the world's understanding of Man.

Let us note that the underground man spends a great deal of time defending his need to create an irrational world, in which 2x2 could equal 5. It would seem, therefore, that he should be the first to defend that capacity in man which makes other worlds of fantasy possible—the irrational and energetically anti-empirical—or those worlds in which, as Alice learns from the Queen, "it takes all the running one can in order to stand in one place." Yet he would not enter the Queen's world either, because he is forever caught in his self-styled definition of the *paradox of being,* revolving

---

2. Howe, Irving. "Celine: The Sod Beneath the Skin—I." *The New Republic* (July 20, 1963), 19-22.

3. Although Fantasy and Utopia often overlap, they are in fact two antagonistic forms of the literary enterprise. Fantasy almost always involves movement—travel, heroic journey or quest—and consequent abrupt shifts in the narrative. Utopias are essentially static, needing no movement at all in the eternal bliss already achieved.

4. Due to the ease with which this work can be acquired its text will not be included in this volume.

around the following syllogism: Man, he posits, is both a "rational animal" and an "irrational human," e.g. man may recognize by reason what is to his advantage, but, at the same he may—by free will—deliberately choose to contravene what reason dictates. Man's free will, he argues, therefore consists not in his ability to exercise judgement or make reasoned choices (a view posited by the Enlightenment and alive today), but rather in his ability to exercise *caprice*, hence to be irrational. Of course, contravening self-interest (or any Crystal Palace society) leads to suffering, and for that reason "suffering is the sole cause of consciousness," he tells his readers. If "suffering is the sole cause of consciousness," and if to be conscious is to be one's self, then to be one's self is indeed to be a man. In short, to be a man, rather than "an ant, a piano key, or an organ stop" (in his terms) is to be trapped on a continuous treadmill of logic which brings the aforementioned series to a complete circle—to the paradox of man as both a "rational animal" *and* an "irrational human," caught in his subterranean and sub-social existence. It is then due to his fixation on a man's need to savor "his own toothache" so as to prove his individuality, as he puts it, that the underground man rejects even those other, non-empirical worlds of fancy, which are nearly always founded on a heroic quest for the betterment of one's own or the human condition. Battling giants or dragons, facing the unknown and mystical obstacles, overcoming the minions of dark armies, or leaping through black holes—all these are quests in which pain or any kind of suffering is to be overcome by the promise of a greater good to be achieved.

The underground man's argument might have been different had he been born a creature of the *steppe*, the typical setting of Old Russian literary quests. Perhaps he might have defended his precious sense of *freedom*—after all, his principal goal—in an open combat as a legendary hero. As Howe importantly observes, however, the underground man is "a creature of the city," and in a Russian context, a creature of St. Petersburg. In Dostoevsky's eyes the semi-utopian city founded by Peter the Great had degenerated into an unnatural and terrifying setting for human habitation, in which such miracles of nature as the purity of powder-white snow—normally falling as *manna* from the skies—turns "wet, yellow and dingy." Perhaps when Dostoevsky himself looked up into the skies, he hoped that the suffering he considered so necessary for the development of the human self would also prove redemptive. Through it, perhaps, man would be led to another city, akin to St. Augustine's *City of God*, or—following the path of some medieval saints—to a monastery. Such are at least the indications from his other writings, but this hope is certainly not offered to the underground man. In a world with no God and no Heaven to reproach for his condition, he vents his spite against those well-wishers of mankind who posit utopian city-society settings which would eliminate *suffering*—his last vestige of freedom—and lay the foundations for dehumanizing mankind. In their ideal world, composed of even more accurate geometrical spaces than his Petersburg offered, 2x2 would always equal 4, it would never snow and the skies would always be clear. In fact it is in just such a sanitized city-scape that Evgeny Zamiatin was to set his seminal dystopian novel, *We*.

Whatever Dostoevsky's philosophical views ultimately became—and for Russia at least he predicted an escape from the dead-end of absolute rationalism in the form of a return to its Christian roots—as an artist he never accepted a stalemate. Enduring one of the most trying periods of his life, beginning in 1864 when he completed *Notes from Underground*, Dostoevsky was nevertheless able to churn out novels at the approximate rate of one per year, each work lengthier and more complex than the one before. It should perhaps not come as a surprise that the writer who laid the foundations of Russian psychological *realism* theorized toward the end of his life that the ultimate work of realism would be one which expressed the most unimaginable and fantastic states of being. He might have been guided in this regard by Cervantes and the fantastic journeys of *Don Quixote*. Or he might have wished simply to establish a quasi-paradoxical link between *realism* and *fantasy*, but chose to express the thought indirectly, because Russian 19th-century fiction—despite tremendous achievements in the representation of the fantastic—did not enshrine *fantasy* as a genre. The equivalent Russian term *fantasia* normally connoted only that which is meant in English by the slightly archaic term "fancy." He was certainly aware of a centuries-old western tradition (from *Beowulf*, Chaucer, and Shakespeare to the modern day), which accords distinct generic status to works of fantasy. Such texts usually posit a universe in which the author has made a conscious break with ordinary experienced reality, and engaged with the Other. But Dostoevsky also knew that Russian culture, enriched by a millennium of spiritual growth interweaving the pagan and the Christian worlds, never quite shared the west's certainty as to the exact locus of boundaries separating empirical experience from that other realm. In any case, his infrequently cited claim as to the ultimate goal of realism is well represented by the texts included in this volume. Presenting some of the best examples of Russian literature in the fantastic mode, the collection supplies a matrix of texts rooted in the familiar *topoi* of fairylands, utopias, and dreamscapes—all feeding the notion that fantasy-making might be the very essence of art.

The Russian reading public of Dostoevsky's day knew western literary traditions well, but much of Russian literature was largely unknown to the western reader before it burst upon the European scene with stunning impact in the prose of I. S. Turgenev (1818-83), Dostoevsky, and L. N. Tolstoy

(1828-1910). Each was a "realist" with prodigious gifts, and each was decidedly unlike the others in matters of style. Yet all three—to a greater or lesser degree—allowed the fantastic to intersect with the real, often with no conscious break from reality. *The Double* (1846), one of Dostoevsky's earliest published works, is just one example. Their realism, as opposed to its western counterpart, was far more profoundly weighted toward depicting events best characterized as improbable or even impossible.

For any further discussion of the premise of the fantastic it is important to note that Shakespeare designates *the poet* as the namer of uncharted places. Neither Dostoevsky nor his two great realist compatriots, were principally poets (though Turgenev wrote some poetry). Yet the genius of these masters of prose was born and nurtured at a time when poetry was indeed the principal and choice form of literary expression—a period which Russians universally feel was their literature's *Golden Age*. In retrospect, the period is dominated by the figure of A. S. Pushkin (1799-1837), whom Russians consistently view as their greatest *poet*, and the years of his short life frame in their minds the Golden Age as a whole. But during his own time Pushkin was regarded as one of a whole pleiade of incredibly gifted older and younger poets—all participating in poetic discourse as their principal vehicle of literary creativity. Such names as I. A. Krylov (1769-1844), V. A. Zhukovsky (1783-1852), N. I. Gnedich (1784-1833), D. V. Davydov (1784-1839), F. N. Glinka (1786-1880), K. N. Batiuskov (1787-1855), P. A. Viazemsky (1792-1878), K. F. Ryleev (1795-1826), V. K. Kiukhelbeker (1797-1846), A. A. Bestuzhev (1797-1837), A. A. Delvig (1798-1831), E. A. Baratynsky (1800-44), to list but a few, mean very little today to a western reader, but many of these contemporaries of Pushkin wielded at least as much influence as Pushkin and themselves had a profound effect on his own craft.

Some of these, such as Bestuzhev (pseud. Marlinsky), and even Pushkin himself, turned to prose at the end of their lives. It was, for instance, the ultra-romantic prose of Bestuzhev (rather than that of Pushkin) that Turgenev later acknowledged as his first love and a formative influence. But with the notable exception of N. M. Karamzin (1766-1826) who was the single most influential Russian prose writer before the 1830s, and whose stylistic innovations in both prose and poetry paved the way for the Golden Age, Russia did not have a single prose writer whose artistic impact could rival that of Dostoevsky or Tolstoy later on. This was not due to any lack of native talent, but rather to Russia's peculiar literary history, which had no notion of literature as *belle-lettres* prior to the eighteenth-century. Russia's medieval system of literary genres—rich as it was, and embodying a profound interest in the unexpected or the unexplained—gave place in the eighteenth century to the *neoclassicist* system, which signified Russia's major embrace of the rational, utilitarian world-view offered by the Enlightenment. Nevertheless, Shakespeare's under-standing of the poet's reason defying role was also on the ascendant, since in the years roughly from 1735 to 1835—the period from which we draw our initial selections—poetry was clearly elevated as the supreme form of literary endeavor.

It was in 1735 that V. K. Trediakovsky (1703-69) published his cele-brated treatise, *A New and Concise Handbook for Russian Versification.* Much of poetry composed before Trediakovsky, and for some time after him, was of translational nature and based on western literary models (just as the preceding seven hundred years of Medieval Russia's literature had been principally focused on translating Byzantine texts). But Trediakovsky's 1735 application of the syllabotonic system of versification facilitated a remarkably rapid assimilation of western poetry's broad spectrum in Russia—from Homer, Pindar and Ovid to Shakespeare, Boileau, Racine, and Pope. One hundred years later, in 1835, N. V. Gogol first published *Arabesques,* a seminal work of experimental Russian prose. Gogol's imme-diate influence on prose was no less profound than Trediakovsky's had been on poetry, and the Petersburg stories from *Arabesques,* such as *The Portrait, Nevsky Prospect* and *The Diary of a Madman,* had a similar formative effect on Russian literature. The intervening century thus can safely be called the period of the dominance of poetry over prose. The priv-ilege enjoyed by the former over than latter was deep and pervasive. Trediakovsky, for example, felt compelled to render Fancois Fénelon's novel *Les Aventures de Télémaque* (*Telemakhida,* 1766) into hexameter verse. And A. P. Sumarokov (1717-1777), one of Russia's foremost neo-classicist poets—indeed the first to translate Shakespeare into Russian— had such disdain for the novel (the principal prose genre) that he vowed never to write one himself even if he were dying of hunger. There were other vows that he did not keep, but he kept this one despite being desti-tute toward the end of his life.

Sumarokov, of course, had in mind the most popular reading material among literate Russians who did not quite belong to the elite circles of his day—the *picaresque novel.* Fantastic elements, sudden shifts of fate, and rapid transformations of geographic settings, all typical of the fantastic mode, abounded in the narrative plots of these early Russian prose works. But most of these pre-Gogolian novels were dominated by migratory motifs borrowed from their western antecedents and will not be discussed here. Rather the emergence of highly original Russian *poets* began the long process by which Russian literature itself developed into a model for west-ern emulation. The foremost of those who achieved such acclaim was G. R. Derzhavin (1743-1816), whose ode *God,* composed roughly at the mid-point of this period, had the distinction of being translated into a dozen world languages during the poet's own life, and it is with Derzhavin's craft that our main body of texts will unfold.

The aim of this introduction is thus to provide a new angle from which to view Russian literature as it ascends to universal esteem, but within the realm of the fantastic. Russia's *Golden Age* coincided with the reign of *Romanticism* in Europe. The Grimm brothers, Herder, and other Romantic theorists stressed the importance to every nation of its own unique folkloric heritage. Russian Romantic poets, most of whom will not enter the main body of our anthology, must nevertheless be alluded to at this juncture, for they were among the first to turn in full force to the folklore heritage of their homeland, as well as to the very notion of *Fantasy*, the crux of this volume.[5] Of these, the name of the aforementioned V. Zhukovsky, a most important literary figure of the early nineteenth century, comes certainly to mind. His fame rests largely on adaptations and translations into Russian of an almost dizzying variety of texts, including parts of the *Mahabharata* as well as *The Odyssey* and many works of his European contemporaries. Principal among them was the ballad—a poetic narration usually with a gothic or folk-tale backdrop featuring supernatural or occult overtones. Most of Zhukovsky's ballads were translations from such poets as Goethe, Schiller, and Scott, although it might be more accurate to call them transformations. Before turning to these, let us note that in one of his original poems, *To Myself*, Zhukovsky elects to speak of the "Phantom of Phantasy" as a self-defining concept:

> You that now mourn for the days borne away past recalling,
> Ruefully pondering, hopelessly longing still to revive them—
> Take but the Present to serve as your comfort and *daimon*!

---

5. *Fantasy*, as intimated earlier, is understood for the purposes of this publication to be a most inclusive term and to denote any genre characterized by an element of *dislocation* with respect to the time, place, or set of preconceived ideas, normative at the time of its creation. At its most minimal form, such as in poetry for instance, *the fantastic* may begin by any non-hackneyed use of rhyme, figure of speech, or even simple syntactic inversion. In its full-fledged guise, the term is used to denote the creation of any *imaginative world* other than tangible (uncharted shores in an epic, utopia, fairy-land, futuristic space-flight, dream, etc.) and synonymous with the Greek sense of *phantasía*, which is made "visible," or "present" to the spectator's (reader's) mind by the artistry of the poet or the creator. Fantasy always involves *imagination* and depends on *a shift of ground rules,* which are in force for the reader or the general audience—even on such a basic mechanism of time displacement, as in most folk tales: "once upon the time. . . ." Though some works may be deemed less fantastic in a sense that they involve such shifts more sparingly after the initial displacements in time or place are made (much of science-fiction) or highly fantastic (most dream journeys), no assumptions are made in this volume as to which are better. Thus, though I agree with Eric Rabkin that "a true Fantasy such as *Alice* continues to reverse its ground rules time and again," (*The Fantastic in Literature*, 37), my agreement holds in the sense that is a more complex narrative than, let us say, an average fairy tale.

Trusting the moment, live your life free from vexation!
Light are the pinions that bear Life's precipitate passage!
Having no sooner attained to the ripeness of full understanding,
Having but glimpsed in the distance a goal worth our striving,
All of our time is fled like a wraith of our dreaming—
Phantom of Phantasy—now to the vision which offers
Bloom-studded meadows, with frolicsome mountains and valleys;
Now clad in sorrow's dark raiment which rises, ascending
Over wild steppelands, forests and horrid abysses.
Follow the Sages! Be ever unchanging in spirit;
All that blind Fate may allot you, accept without murmur! 'Tis fruitless,
Filled with vain sorrow and grieving o'er bliss gone forever,
Thus to disdain the gifts we receive from the minute![6]

This Romantic idea of a mysterious gap between the physical and the metaphysical, of man caught between two worlds, and of the enigma of human life within the flow of history, resembles the musings of Derzhavin's poetic persona in the *Magic Lantern*, which is entered into our main body of texts. The two worlds are shown from another angle in Zhukovsky's *Lesnoi Tsar* (literally "The Forest Tsar"), an original rendering of Goethe's familiar anthology piece *Der Erlkönig*. Here subtle but telling departures from the original transform the Germanic *Elf King* into a Slavic forest deity. Sung to Schubert's setting for the original, Zhukovsky's *Lesnoi Tsar* enjoyed great popularity in nineteenth-century Russia, and is mentioned as a subtext in another work in this volume, namely *Shtoss* by M. Iu. Lermontov (1814-41). For this reason we cite it here in its entirety in our new rhymed translation:

Who knifes through the chill and the mist at a run?
A horseman rides late and he clasps his young son.
Atremble, the boy holds his kind father's arm,
The old man enfolds his child, keeping him warm.

"My child, you cling close—why this timid despair?"
"The Tree King, dear father, I saw his eyes flare:
His beard is a thicket, he wears a dark crown."
"Ah no, 'tis the pale mist that covers the tarn."

My child, glance behind you! Come boy, take my hand:
There's much of delight you will find in my land.
There blossoms of lapis fringe streams pearly-cold,
The halls that I dwell in are cast of pure gold.

---

6. The translation of Zhukovsky's "Phantom of Phantasy," and all other texts in the introduction are ours, A.L. & M.K.

"Dear father, the Tree King calls me to his lair:
He promises joy and much gold to me there."
"Ah no, my dear young one. Your hearing's deceived:
The wind has awakened, it rustles the leaves."

Come boy, come and enter my oak-grove with me,
My daughters you'll meet there, all lovely to see.
By moonlight they'll play with you, teach you to fly,
'Mid playing and flying they'll sing lullaby.

"Dear father, the Tree King his daughters has called,
They nod to me where the dark branches unfold!"
"Ah no, all is calm in the depth of the night,
There's naught but the grey-tressed dry forest in sight."

My child, I'm enslaved by your features so fine,
And will you or nill you—I'll have you for mine!
"My father, the Tree King will catch us at last,
I labor for air and my breath comes so fast!"

Fear hastens the rider, how swiftly he flies
As anguish now seizes the boy midst his cries;
Yet faster he darts—then at once halts his steed . . .
His arms bear a dead child, now silent to plead.

A less morbid tone permeates *Svetlana,* one of Zhukovsky's two famous adaptations of Gottfried Bürger's *Leonore.* In the German original a dead man rises from the tomb and carries his betrothed off to the underworld. Zhukovsky's first version, entitled *Liudmila,* preserves this plot but gives the tale an atmosphere more mournful than horrific. *Svetlana,* arguably one of his most successful creations, strikes off in a more original direction. *Svetlana* is a *ballad*—the defining genre of European Romanticism ever since J. Macpherson (1736-96) published in 1760 his famous forgery, *Fragments of Ancient Poetry Collected in the Highlands of Scotland and Translated from the Gallic or Erse Language,* claiming that his texts were based on the works of the third-century Gaelic poet Ossian (orig. Oisín). Enchanted by the newly "discovered" worlds of magic visitations, monster-slayings, and heroic combat from ancient Scots-Irish lore, the developing Romantic movement sought inspiration in the medieval oral traditions of individual nations. Challenging the classicist notion of the supreme value of the Greco-Roman heritage, European cultures (German, Czech, etc.) aspired to a universal recognition of their distinct national traditions. Russian Romantics, such as Zhukovsky, were soon to follow with the rediscovery of their country's medieval past—sampled in our introductory section—

and learned that Russia possessed a particularly rich folk literature, large-ly dominated by poetic genres. The world of this *ballad* is entirely Russian, depicting the fortune-telling practiced by young girls on the eve of Epiphany:

> Once, upon Epiphany, maidens told their fortunes:
> Off her foot each slipped a shoe—past the gates they cast them;
> Drew their sigils in the snow, listened at the window;
> Fed the hen with numbered grains, scried the hot wax cooling;
> In a bowl of water clear placed the ring of purest gold,
> And the emerald earrings; spread the spotless kerchief out;
> O'er the bowl then sweetly sang magic chants and carols.

Falling asleep in the expectation of prescient visions, Svetlana dreams she is riding in a sleigh with her corpse-like groom over snow-clad Russia:

> They get in—the team's away! Steam spouts from their nostrils;
> From their hoofbeats rises up whirlwinds 'neath the runners.
> Swift their gait . . . Naught 'round about, steppes her eyes encompass;
> Darkly is the moon eclipsed, meadows faintly shimmer,
> Trembles her prophetic soul; timidly Svetlana speaks,
> "Why so silent, sweeting?" Not one word does he reply,
> Fixed upon the moon his gaze—Pale and full of sorrow.

> O'er the hillocks speed the jades, trampling down the snowdrifts;
> To one side a distant kirk stands a lonely vigil.
> Now a gale blows wide the doors, throngs the congregation;
> From the censers brightest light is obscured by incense;
> In the nave—a black-draped bier, and the priest goes droning on:
> "May the grave receive you!" All the more she trembles now,
> As they pass. Her love is mute—Pale and full of sorrow.

> Suddenly a circling storm, snow in masses heaping;
> Wings a-whistle, o'er the sleigh soars a night-black raven.
> "Sorrow!" is the raven's cry—Now the fleet-foot horses
> Scan the dark with whitened eyes, and their mane-crests shiver.
> Flickers in the field a light, there a quiet berth they spy,
> 'Neath the snow, a cottage. Swifter now the horses run,
> Breast the snow, make straight the way, rushing there together.

Zhukovsky ultimately chooses in *Svetlana* to transmute Bürger's demon-lover theme into a joyful celebration of life and the protective power of love (of the poem's twenty fourteen-line stanzas we have cited here the contents of four, but contracted for economy into septains in our translation). A different take on the subject of love is given in Russia's most accomplished *Novel-in-verse*, Pushkin's *Evgeny Onegin*, in which each protagonist is fated to love—but never to possess—the other. Pushkin's nuanced portrait of the novel's heroine, Tatiana, has been hailed as an unsurpassed depiction of the ideal Russian female. Her terrifying dream (contributing a great deal to her psychological profile in Chapter 5, stanzas X-XXI of the novel) owes much to Zhukovsky's earlier representation of Svetlana's winter dream-scape, and is translated below into metered prose:

Tatiana, as her Nurse advises, prepares a night of sorcery; gives quiet orders that the bathhouse table be laid out for two. But suddenly Tatiana's frightened . . . And I—just thinking of Svetlana—I'm frightened too. So be it, then . . . Tatiana's spells are not for us. Tatiana now removes her silken sash, undresses, goes to bed. The love-god Lel' now floats above her, while underneath her downy pillow, the maiden mirror lies secure. The world grows still. Tatiana sleeps.

An eerie dream comes to Tatiana. And in this dream it seems that she is walking through a snow-clad meadow, a somber gloom surrounding her; before her through the looming snow-banks there gushes in a steaming spate a seething freshet, dark and bleak, that winter chain's could not subdue; two slender poles, cased in an ice-floe, a perilous and shifting bridge, were laid across the flowing stream; and she, before the freshet's roar, her mind now full of doubt and fear, has hesitated and then stopped.

As if this obstacle annoyed her, Tatiana grumbles at the stream, sees no one on the other bank who might have offered her his arm; but then a heap of snow's in motion, and who appears from underneath? A large and shaggy-coated Bear; Tatiana—"*Ah!*"—He starts to roar: his paw, its dewclaws sharp and pointed, he stretches out to her. She steels herself, with trembling hand she leans on it. With steps then hesitant and timid, she makes her way across the brook, walks on—what's this? The Bear comes too!

She never dares a glance behind her, proceeds with still more hasty gait, but from her shaggy-coated footman cannot escape by any means. With grunts the horrid bruin lumbers, the wood's ahead, the pine-trees stand unmoving, beautiful but dour. Their branches all are weighted down with clumps of snow, and through the tops of aspen, linden, bare-limbed birch, the rays of Night's own torches beam. There is no path; the shrubs, the slopes are drifted over by the storm, and buried deep beneath the snow.

Now Maid and Bear are in the forest; the unpacked snow's above her knees. A trailing branch, now of a sudden, scores her neck, and from her ears a golden earring rips by force. Deep in the snow she leaves behind the soaking slipper from her foot, and lets her silken kerchief fall. No time to pick it up, in dread she hears the bear still coming after her, and with her trembling hand she even fears to raise her hem. She runs, but he still follows close, and now her strength to run is gone.

Into the snow she falls. The Bear at once then deftly snatches her. She is near swooning now, and docile. She does not move and does not breathe. They rush along a forest pathway. Then—through the trees—a humble hut stands overgrown. The wild, bleak snow has covered it on every side. A tiny pane is brightly glowing, and in the hut are shouts and din. The Bear: "My kinsman lives inside: come in and warm yourself a little." Straight through the entry-hall he goes, and on a threshold sets her down.

Tatiana stirs and looks around her: The bear is gone, she's in a hall. Beyond the door she hears some shouting, and glasses clink, as at a wake. She makes no sense of this at all. With stealth she peers in through a cranny, and sees there . . . what? A table's there, with monsters seated all around: One horned and with a dog-like muzzle, another bears a rooster's head, a witch that sports a goatish beard, a skeleton, both prim and haughty, a dwarfish imp with tiny tail, and there—a thing half-crane, half-cat.

Still more to fear, and more to marvel: A crab there rides a spider-steed, a skull atop a goose's neckbone there twirls, with scarlet cap adorned. A wind-mill does the Russian squat-jig, its wings are creaking now and flailing. Loud barks and laughter, whistling, claps; now humans sing and horses stamp! But what thoughts came to our Tatiana when, there among the guests, she spies the one most dear and dread to her—the hero of this very novel! Onegin sits there at the table and slyly glances through the door.

He gives a sign—the creatures bustle; he drinks, they all drink too, and shout; he laughs, and they all break out laughing; he frowns, and all are mute at once. He is the Master here, that's certain. And Tania, somewhat less dis-heartened and pricked by curiosity, has opened up the door a bit... A sudden wind-gust, and the night-lights' flames are snuffed out all at once. The goblin-horde's in disarray. Onegin, eyes now burning brightly, forsakes the table with a roar: all rise, he's heading for the doors.

Afraid again and in a flutter, Tatiana tries her best to run. But she's unable. Thus impatient, she twists about and wants to scream. She can't—Evgeny's at the door-side, he swings it wide. The Maid's now standing revealed to all the hellish crew. Ferocious laughter sounds—their eyes devour her; their trunk-like noses, their hoofs, long tufted tails and fangs, mustaches, bloody lolling tongues, their horns and skeleton-like fingers—all point as one at her alone, and all shout out: it's mine, it's mine.

It's mine, exclaimed Evgeny fiercely, and all the gang was gone at once. The youthful maid, in frost and darkness, remained with him now *tête-à-tête*. Onegin gently draws Tatiana into a corner; down he lays her upon a shaky bench. He rests his head upon her shoulder. Then comes Olga brusquely, Lensky follows, and suddenly— a flash of light— Onegin lifts his arm to strike, his eyes in frenzy, wildly roaming, he chides his uninvited guests; Tatiana lies there half alive.

The brawl grows louder. Then Evgeny takes up a knife, and in a trice he cuts down Lensky. Horrid shadows loom thickly; then a piercing cry has broken forth . . . The hut is reeling . . . And Tania, horrified, awakens . . . She looks: it's light now in her room, and through the window's frosted glass a crimson ray of dawn is dancing. Her door has opened . . .

This passage is included here at such length because it provides the necessary backdrop for a fuller understanding of such later writers as A. Remizov and B. Pilniak. At the same time it shows that Pushkin's roots in the Russian mythic tradition, which incidentally incorporated bear worship, run deeper than Zhukovsky's. Also, it is not for naught that the country girl Tatiana falls in love, yet has such a horrid dream about a city *dandy*. On the one hand, *Evgeny Onegin* pays thematic homage to Karamzin's sentimental elegy in prose, *Poor Lisa* (1792), which shows the impossibility of lasting love between a city slicker and a country girl. On the other, Pushkin's novel-in-verse involves themes a great deal more complex than love doomed by social inequality (for one thing, Tatiana and Evgeny are both aristocrats). Pushkin's Evgeny is one of the first characters in Russia to sound a pre-existentialist note: he rejects human civilization as expressed by city life, but as a product of that life is powerless to imagine an alternative. Since the times of the Roman poet Horace rural life had been priviledged over the artificiality of urban life. The punning Latin epigraph to the novel's second chapter which equates rural Russia with Horatian rusticity offers Evgeny a fundamental choice, but, tragically, he is too corrupted by the city to take advantage of it. Fortunately for his readers Pushkin succeeds in reinvesting the Russian countryside with the Horatian ethos, without the putrid idealizations of the concept of "natural man," as advanced by J. J. Rousseau (1712-1778).

The theme of an individual's alienation from the city is strengthened by the tale of another Evgeny, in Pushkin's *The Bronze Horseman* (included in our Pushkin section). The protagonist of this work is literally crushed by the march of civilization as envisioned by Peter the Great who decided to build a new capital for Russia on a par with the great cities of the West. For strategic reasons, he chose a spot on the north-western border of Russia on the banks of the River Neva and Gulf of Finland. The area was marshy and boggy and also quite a distance from the center of civilization, in short, a very difficult place on which to build a city. Nevertheless Peter went ahead with his plan and created what has indeed become a magnificent city, today's St. Petersburg, but he did so at a great human cost: thousands of workers and craftsmen died of disease and over-work in this remote marshland. Ever since then St. Petersburg has been regarded as a special order of city and symbol—a magnificent edifice raised on the misery and agony, indeed the bones, of common men.

The city then began to evoke in Russia very powerful and ambivalent feelings. Even during Peter's own lifetime, Old Believer schismatics (the heirs of Archpriest Avvakum) regarded the Petersburg as an "unnatural" city, and its founder to be the *Antichrist*. But the literature of the ruling class—now transplanted from the ancient capital of Moscow—viewed St. Petersburg for the most part with awe and admiration. Following Peter's death in 1725, the eighteenth century witnessed Russia's rise to an unprecedented level of recognition by Europe, and nowhere else was this rise more evident than in the incredibly swift development of St. Petersburg, which soon came to challenge the most advanced cities on the European continent. Successive Russian rulers invited the most pioneering 18th-century architects to oversee the building of Russia's new capital, which soon grew to prominence as a technological and artistic marvel of its time, deserving the epithet "The Venice of the North." As the century came to a close, St. Petersburg's newly founded, lasting enchantment was recorded by Derzhavin, in the prologue to his exquisite poem, *The Murza's Vision*. Here, through the persona of an Eastern sage Derzhavin delivers the first poetic apostrophe to Russia's new and enigmatic Western-style capital:

> Within the ether's dark-blue ocean,
> Down casting silver from on high,
> The golden moon was floating lonesome;
> She, gleaming from the northern sky,
> Brought light to my house through its windows,
> And with the palest of her beams
> Traced down the glazing's golden sheen-glow
> Flat on my lacquered flooring seams;
> Sleep, with its languorous, silent hand
> Poured forth the dew of dreams engendered
> In douce oblivion's distant land,
> Enchanting thence my family members;
> Now sunk in slumber was the district:
> Petropolis amidst its spires,
> Neva in granite urn, all glistened,
> The Baltic coast bore twinkling fires;
> And Nature, in her silent twilight,
> Sunk deep into her mighty dream,
> Seemed dead to hearing and to eyesight;
> Yet from the heights and depths unseen
> Cool zephyrs wafted 'round blue ether,
> And brought refreshment to my heart.

As he does in other areas, Derzhavin—with whom we start the main body of texts in our collection—stands at the core of modern fantasy-weaving in Russia. Significantly, he identifies within a very short space in this prologue the thematic locus of a dichotomy between the City (the domain of Man), and Nature (as created by God). This dichotomy was to plague much of 19th-century Russian fiction, including fantasy fiction. The two domains are held in a delicate balance in the poet's waking dream, which obliterates any sharp borders separating them, and in this poem Peter's creation is not threatening. Indeed Peter's grand-daughter by marriage, Catherine II, appearing in goddess form to the poet later on, firmly unites all man-made and divine aspects of human existence in this city in one utopian vision of emotional and material plenitude.

A far more qualified depiction of Petersburg is given by Russia's greatest 19th-century poet, A. S. Pushkin, with whom we continue unfolding our volume. In one of his most accomplished narrative poems, *The Bronze Horseman*, Peter the Great appears both as a historical personage and also as an active participant in a dream which drives the poem's only human protagonist to madness. Peter's image, represented concretely by the equestrian statue which Catherine II had erected in his honor in 1782, is transmuted into the image of the City itself: Petersburg, Peter's town, his creation and achievement. This feat is sung by Pushkin in his famous *apostrophe* which begins with the celebrated line "I love Thee, Peter's true creation . . ." and continues for many more, all of which practically every Russian knows by heart. But if Derzhavin in *A Murza's Vision* introduced a similar and sustained notion of Petersburg as a *eutopic dreamscape*, accessible through his poetry, in Pushkin's *The Bronze Horseman* the city is also seen as an eerily unnatural construct, the product of one man's obsession (in *Notes from Underground* Dostoevsky termed it "the most intentional city in the world").

While not a direct participant in any sense, Petersburg does function as an important setting in another Pushkin masterpiece entered in this anthology, *The Queen of Spades*. In contrast to *The Bronze Horseman*, it explores the ramifications of an obsession of a different kind—that of cards and money—but an obsession which is inseparably linked to the society inhabiting Peter's city over a century later. This superbly crafted *mock society-tale*, which subtly parodies within a short narrative space a plethora of social and literary conventions, is certainly Pushkin's best known prose work. It also served as a source for many literary types and themes developed by later Russian authors and as a stimulus for an opera by Chaikovsky, a film, and several TV productions. In all of these, just as at its very inception, St. Petersburg becomes a kind of mythological city, a city fraught with symbolic meaning which will be re-explored in Gogol's, and above all in Dostoevsky's and Bely's fiction. Bely in particular will restate Petersburg's enigma in terms very different from Derzhavin's or Pushkin's.

The first Russian writer after Pushkin to leave a lasting legacy regarding the Petersburg myth was N. V. Gogol, with his most accomplished cycle of stories, known as *Petersburg Tales*. This cycle began with the publication of a book entitled *Arabesques* (1835), a miscellany of essays on art and literature combined with occasional examples of fictional prose. The latter consisted of the famous stories, *The Portrait, Nevsky Prospect*, and the *Diary of a Madman,* which were subsequently revised, published and discussed as separate works, deriving their unity from the Petersburg setting common to all. There is much to be gained, however, when their original context—the entire set of entries published in book called *Arabesques*—is kept in focus. It is during their writing that Gogol began seriously tinkering with the romantic notion of *genius*. Perhaps on account of his growing fame from his earlier literary accomplishments, but certainly connecting to turn-of-the century Germany's fascination with the topic, he freely supplied in the *Arabesques* his own views on the role of the exceptional in painting, architecture, design, music and dance. But in 1834—as his *Arabesques* were being stitched together—Gogol's personal world was a world in crisis, which stemmed from Gogol's inordinate wish to fuse the ideal with everyday reality. On the one hand, he contemplated (a-la-Wackenroder and Tieck in Germany) the world of ideal existence, while on the other, and quite unlike his German models, he wished to represent its relevance for the "real" world as well. Whenever he did—and this happened in the aforementioned "fictional" segments of *Arabesquess*—his excursions into the Sublime shifted tonality and portrayed a world grotesquely warping such sublimity, a world of darkness, fog and blurred vision. The perfectly rectilinear streets of Petersburg became modern-day *labyrinths* for its inhabitants and perfectly average clerks in this city began to imagine themselves to be the Kings of Spain and heard dogs talking in human voices. Such characters, by the very setting they inhabited, hardly fitted into the scheme of things imagined from the sublime world and, significantly, all Gogol's fictional representations of the "little folk" were originally presented as cases of *wasted genius* (the first two tales depicting poor artist-painters, the protagonist of the third was initially a musician). Indeed, the discrepancy between the real and imagined worlds became so patent, so insistent, for Gogol in these years that he could no longer accept the Romantic imagery which contemplated the ideal world imagined in the essayistic component of *Arabesques*. At the same time, he was extremely loath to give it up and accept the real world. A tension developed in his imagery between the two worlds on which he formerly focused as separate, the ideal and the real: they ceased to interact and began to merge and fuse. Brilliantly anticipated in the fictional parts of his *Arabesques*, most importantly in "Diary of a Madman," a new alternate world arose from these polarities: a mixed-up world in which the motivation of the fantastic and the real became the same—a world of the *absurd*.

Gogol's fiction and drama single-handedly shaped the themes and images which were to infuse most of Russia's literature until well after the era of *Sputnik*. Moreover, much of Gogol anticipates the characteristic fictional worlds of other writers from Dostoevsky to Andrei Bely and Franz Kafka, and, later on, to Jorge Luis Borges and the magic realism of Gabriel Garcia Marquez. With the advent of the symbolist epoch, literature dealing with apparitions, time-travel, and excursions into altered states of reality became a commonplace in Russian literary culture and often formed a conscious return to some of the preoccupations of Russian and Western romanticism. Nonetheless, the *fin de siècle* fascination with the romantic past harbored in some cases the seeds for the "romanticization" of possible futures, as in S. Belsky's *Under the Comet* (*Pod kometoi*, 1910), a book which could be said to be a thematic return to V. F. Odoevsky's *The Year 4338*. Similarly, A. Kuprin's *Liquid Sunshine* (1913) is based on the presumed technological feasibility of capturing the energy of the sun in order to secure the future for the inhabitants of a cooling Earth. The project fails due to an insignificant but fatal mistake of its creator—a perfectly romantic touch of irony at the ending of the story. Kuprin's work is also significant in the sense that it is one of the first Russian literary creations bearing the unmistakable influence of *The Time Machine* by H. G. Wells, whose works were to be imitated in the Soviet Union particularly during the twenties.

A curious blend of *fantasy*, *science fiction* and *fairy tale* was provided for Russian readers of the 1910s in F. K. Sologub's *Created Legend* (*Tvorimaya legenda*) where the protagonist Trirodov succeeds in raising dead children from the grave to a zombie-like state, reducing his enemies to prisms, and transforming his gothic estate into a spaceship capable of defying gravity. Sologub's fiction will be represented in this volume with the short story *A Little Man*, a masterpiece blending fantasy, social satire and literary humoresque. In it Sologub gives a tongue-in-cheek treatment of topics with eminently literary significance. Set very much in a neo-Gogolian universe, it deals a final blow to the theme of the little man with which Russian literature had been obsessed ever since Gogol's *The Overcoat*.

Ultimately, it could be said that the arrival of the 20th century brought about two conceptually opposed forms of depicting the future. For some adherents of a materialistic doctrine, the future offered nearly limitless possibilities due to advances in science, and often implied the conquest of space. The planet Mars seems to have been a particularly fascinating subject at the time. A. Bogdanov's utopia *Red Star* is perhaps the most accomplished work on this theme, incorporating the aforementioned view of the future. First published in 1908, it was followed by a less successful sequel, *Menni, the Engineer* (Inzhener Menni), five years later. Bogdanov utilized his novel to foreshadow the Earth's future by presenting his readers with an account of Mars' past (a fairly transparent rehashing of Earth's history from the Marxist viewpoint) and present, using the context of the novel as a guide to social institutions of the future. At the same time the book raised the possibility of space flight to Mars. Interestingly enough this was reinforced several years later by K. E. Tsiolkovsky's famous first theoretical designs for rocket propulsion, which made interplanetary flight plausible.

On the other hand, as early as the middle of the second half of the 19th century, some important Russian writers and philosophers were taken by the apocalyptic notion of the future particularly evident in the work Vladimir Solovyov, Russia's famous philosopher of the time. In some of his prophecies Solovyov was amazingly on the mark. He envisioned a United Nations Organization (the name in Russian for the United Nations is nearly identical to the one used by Solovyov), the creation of the state of Israel prior to the Antichrist's arrival, and an Ecumenical World Council of Churches (Solovyov in fact envisioned the erection of a monumental church in which churches of various rites would pray in different rooms to one Deity). The last days would be characterized by a world conflict on such a grandiose scale and with such advanced weapons as only likely in an all-out nuclear war. It is from Solovyov's cup that many well-known Russian symbolists such as V. Briusov and A. Bely drank in their own assessments of plausible futures.

Bely's famous novel *Petersburg* exploits the ambiguities and uncertainties of Russian life in the first decade of the 20th century. The author does not make clear the actual future he foresees as the outcome of the cataclysm about to engulf the Petersburg society of 1905. But it is patently obvious that physical actions within his fictional world will have metaphysical consequences along the lines envisioned by Solovyov. Briusov also views the future with the profoundest misgivings in works such as *The Republic of the Southern Cross* published in a volume entitled the *Earth's Axis* (1907). As opposed to Bely's veiled portrayal of the future, Briusov provides us with an outright anti-utopia in *The Republic of the Southern Cross*, set at the South Pole, as scientific advances have enabled the population to be protected from the rigors of the Antarctic climate. The society is living in a controlled climate with an arching dome above it—that same "Crystal Palace" which Dostoevsky had rejected some forty years earlier. Like Dostoevsky's *Notes from Underground*, Briusov's work expresses his belief that material conditions alone are insufficient for human happiness.

The inhabitants of the republic become possessed by a disease which forces them to exhibit anti-social tendencies and the entire population abandons its controlled environment.

The allusion to the crystal palace forcefully re-emerges after the Bolshevik Revolution in Zamiatin's dystopia *We*, perhaps the most famous Russian work on the subject in that century. For Zamiatin, imagination is one of the prime ingredients of the human personality, with or without metaphysical connotations. The protagonist is a representative of another *Crystal Palace* society which to a large measure has succeeded in reducing its members to the level of robots. They work, sleep, and make love according to a prescribed schedule, punching their time cards; they do not have names, only numbers. They live in transparent quarters. The protagonist, a representative of the society and an engineer on a futuristic space-ship that is meant to conquer other worlds, experiences a personality split under the influence of love. His object of desire is a female member of a "free" society settled beyond the wall that surrounds and confines the so-called *Integral* society within, and is one of the subversive elements intent on destroying the *Integral*. The plot proves abortive, and at the end of his diary, the protagonist undergoes an operation that surgically removes his faculty of imagination. As in More's *Utopia*, we are introduced to two coexisting forms of social order, but neither is portrayed as desirable.

Needless to say, *We* did not sit well within the framework of the future promised to the masses by the Bolshevik government which took control of Russian society in 1917. While it can be said that literary history rarely coincides with the official history of any state, in the genre of literary utopia the year 1917 marks a clear caesura. Although the new regime overwhelmed the populace with the promises of political Utopia in the near future, it could not tolerate any expression of a view challenging its own promises. In other words, the political reality of Soviet Russia made it soon impossible for Russian writers to publish works of fiction with a gloomy view of the future because any admonitory utopia would simply undercut the very foundation of Soviet rhetorical persuasion. While it is true that some writers too much respected to be touched by the regime, such as Bulgakov, were successful in writing science fiction of dystopic character in the twenties (in Bulgakov's case particularly *The Heart of a Dog* and *Fatal Eggs*), their voices were stifled by the early 1930s.

A number of minor science-fiction writers, too numerous to list here, appeared on the literary scene in the mid-twenties and science fiction began to be published in such special science-fiction journals as *Bor'ba Mirov*, *Mir prikliuchenii*, *Vokrug sveta*, *Vsemirnyi sledopyt*, and *Znanie—Sila*. It is interesting, however, that the period did not produce a great number of utopias *par excellence*. In fact only a handful, such as Ya. Okuniev's *Future*

World or Nikol'sky's *In a Thousand Years*, can be mentioned. The great majority of futuristic fiction at the time featured the fantastic adventure story in the form of a scientific or pseudo-scientific romance. This trend was heralded by Alexei Tolstoy's *Aelita*, a humorous return to the Martian theme begun in Russia by Bogdanov. Perhaps for its description of love affairs with blue-skinned Martian women, the novel was an instant success and served as a model for the adventure-type science fiction prevalent in those years, particularly the so-called *Red Detective* (Krasnyi detektiv) popular in the second half of the twenties. V. Shklovsky's and V. S. Ivanov's *Iprit*, M. Shaginian's *Mess-Mend or Yankees in Petrograd* may serve as illustrations of the latter. In such fiction the socialist state was invariably threatened by the futuristic imagination of representatives of capitalist societies. Perhaps ironically, the period also allowed for numerous translations of Western science fiction titles (over a hundred of them, as counted by V. Liapunov, appeared in translation between 1923 and 1930) with Verne and Wells by far the most popular.

While many pro-Soviet writers produced some samples of futuristic fiction at the time (*Ruler of Iron* by V. Kataev, *Trust D.E.*, by I. Erenburg; etc.), the second half of the twenties was dominated particularly by Alexander Beliaev who introduced as his common literary material the phenomenon of biological change in human beings. His protagonists are usually scientists, surgeons capable of adapting men to unusual biological environments such as water (*The Amphibian Man*) or air (*Ariel*); they also succeed in adjusting the human brain to various forms of ESP and in performing cranial transplants.

With the beginning of the thirties and the rise of the "cult of personality," it became increasingly more dangerous to "err" in any predictions of the future, and until the mid-fifties the former élan for science-fiction writing subsided, with periods of total disappearance of science-fiction books from circulation. Yet there were almost heroic attempts in the thirties by major Russian writers to question Soviet present-day reality and its future. Among these, M. Zoshchenko's *Youth Restored* (Vozvrashchennaya molodost', 1933), is an interesting attempt to combine fantastic fiction with the format of a scientific treatise and "scholarly" footnotes. The work provides a tongue-in-cheek treatment of the "elixir of life" theme revolving around the elderly protagonist's attempt to regain his youth. M. Bulgakov's *Master and Margarita*, first published in an excerpted form almost thirty years after its completion (1966-67), is perhaps the most provocative and pioneering work of this period. Certainly one of the masterpieces of 20th-century Russian fiction, it is related to both More's and Gogol's fiction in being a merciless *satire* of Soviet reality, as well as in using duplex settings for its plot development. Unlike earlier attempts, however, Bulgakov complicates his plot by shifting the plane of narration from present-day Moscow to the

time of Christ's crucifixion in Jerusalem and finally to the eternal, metaphysical plane, a re-working of More's "no-place", where his major protagonists finally find peace from their earthly troubles. Bulgakov sees no
possible utopia in physical reality, filled with the greed and pettiness which
he so deftly portrays. In this sense, Bulgakov's novel is also a return to the
philosophical precepts of Dostoevsky.

The first post-war Soviet writer of almost legendary fame among
younger science fiction buffs was Ivan Efremov. His *Andromeda Nebula*
(Tumannost' Andromedy, 1956) a large-scale utopian novel set in the far
future of interstellar travel, not only provided impetus for the cosmic theme
to become the prevalent subject of post-war science fiction, but in itself
started the period of the "THAW" for science fiction. At the same time
Efremov is one of those writers who express an unwavering view that societies of the distant future cannot have any other than the Communist form
of social organization. At times, as in his novelette *The Heart of a Serpent*,
Efremov takes up a situation formerly explored by a Western writer and
transforms the plot to fit his preconceived idea of a more advisable resolution of the problem stated. Efremov also began in a serious way to explore
another facet of post-Stalin futuristic fiction, namely that of contact with
an alien civilization. Invariably, as opposed to the fears frequently posited
by Western writers in their stories, such contact has a happy resolution for
Efremov.

The Soviet sixties witnessed a rapid rise in the quantity of science-
fiction stories. Among the most able writers one should mention the brothers Arkady and Boris Strugatsky, Ilya Varshavsky, Valentina Zhuravlyova,
E. Parnov, M. Emtsev, and a host of others. These years also witnessed the
appearance of a most impressive twenty-five-volume anthology of contemporary science fiction (*Biblioteka sovremennoi fantastiki*) which included
selections from both Western and Soviet science-fiction writers, a publishing feat perhaps unrivaled in any language in its size and inclusiveness. For
some strange reason the Soviet government decreased the volume of science
fiction publications in the late seventies by about ten-fold in comparison
with the sixties and early seventies. One of the reasons may be that science
fiction was used by some Soviet writers for shrewd and often ingenious
allusions to the present form of Soviet society, and for implicit criticism of
Marxist doctrine. Such is the case with many of the writings of the
Strugatsky brothers, whose contribution to science fiction is by far the most
productive when compared with any other Soviet writer—as well as being
the most satisfying from a literary point of view. On the other hand, even
those writers who were seemingly innocent vis-à-vis the Soviet regime found
in the sphere of science fiction productive avenues for interesting literary
experimentation, often far removed from the precepts of Socialist realism.

With the fall of the Soviet Union, future-oriented utopian fiction began to fare rather poorly. It was supplemented instead by a rediscovery of a pure fantasy realm, especially by rekindling a Tolkien craze promoted both by new translations of his books and by dozens of native novelistic elaborations of the Tolkien universe. Shunning the future, Russian readers began—as their Romantic ancestors had done—to revel in a rediscovery of Russia's forgotten past, that is those elements of it which were formerly either forbidden by the Soviet censorship or simply not stressed. Russia's pull toward the non-empirical universe is clearly evident in the revival of its religious faith—a new baptism of Orthodox Russia. Even Vladimir Putin, a former KGB member, often parades on TV with a retinue of Orthodox hierarchs and is consistently shown making the sign of the cross. Others, skeptical of religious fervor, still seem to support the kind of fiction that appeals to deeds based on myth, rather than science. *Conan the Barbarian*, for instance, exists not only in translation, but also in dozens of native sequels.

Regrettably, we will not be able to cover these developments, as they would require another volume and another setting. Let us just note that the current quest to reunite with the native past was begun two centuries ago by poets like Zhukovsky, one of the principal harbingers of the Romantic sensibility in Russia, and that a volume tracing the developments in Russian literature in the fantastic mode is needed before we can comment on the present. Even such early practitioners of weaving fantasy worlds as Pushkin and Lermontov (whose poetry Russians regard as second in importance only to Pushkin, and who brought Russian Romanticism to a close) are little known to our readers. At the same time, Pushkin and Lermontov are *prima facie* examples of Russia's turn to prose as a vehicle for fantasy-making, and their works stand on the threshold of the time when Russian literature did become an equal partner in shaping western literature. Their prose selections are still presented together with their poetry at the outset of the volume, while prose is nearly the exclusive narrative mode of all other authors selected.

These include Gogol, whose surreal universe easily represents the single greatest achievement of Russian fantasy; Turgenev, the first Russian writer to use the term *fantasy* as a generic label in his story *The Phantoms*; and Dostoevsky, generally known for his ability to fashion some of the bulkiest tomes in Russian literature, yet who is a master in the realm of short fiction, far less well-known in the West, and offers splendid examples of fantasy-making. The collection includes neglected works of some less well-known but excellent writers, such as B. A. Pilniak, A. M. Remizov, and A. P. Platonov, who have productively contributed to the formation of the fantastic realm in Russian literature. Also represented are the Russian

Symbolists, whose *ouevre* can be considered equally as a reflex of Russian Romanticism and as a harbinger of an entirely new literary conscious-ness—*Modernism*—which privileges fantasy as one of its key vehicles of expression. Russian authors are represented here, unlike in other anthologies, by at least two selections. Each will be introduced in his respective section, with the founders of Modern Russian Literature given a separate foreward. This rich sampling gives the reader an unmistakable sense of each writer's individual literary voice as they set about their task, and thereby *give to airy nothing a local habitation and a name.*

—Alexander Levitsky, Providence, 2007

PART I
Russian Early-Modern Fantasy
and Utopian Thought

PART I OF THIS book samples Russia's leap into the fantastic within its first millennium. With the exception of the first section which surveys the first 900 years of Russian literature, the genesis of nearly all other works in Section A can be traced back to Romanticism. The Neo-Classicist School, preceding it, had idealized and paid obligatory homage to the "unsurpassed" literary achievements of Greece and Rome, but the Romantics found this notion stultifying to the imagination. The very notion of a literary cannon, of compulsory rules, models and genres, was inimical to poets keen on creating new worlds in literature—to explore the individual *inner self*, rather than a rational or ideal model of Man, to celebrate the rich cultural heritage of nations the Greeks and Romans never knew, or had dismissed as merely barbaric. Adherents of this rising literary sensibility felt that the supreme guarantee of the quality of their craft rested in *inspiration*, a gift that comes to a small elect cast of men, chosen by Fate, Nature—or even by God Himself, speaking to those few as he did to Moses. Far from embracing the universal, the expected, or the normative forms of art, Romantic poets sought the bizarre, the wild, the exotic, the exceptional, the strange, or simply indescribable. A Romantic poet aspired to create entirely new, intensely individual monuments of verbal art, to render his own unique moment of inspiration paradoxically universal, as he shared with other mortals his vision of the true—though most often hidden—ways our world turns.

G.R. Derzhavin, with whose poetry our immersion into Russian nineteenth-century literature starts, in many ways embodies the Russian literary transition from Neo-Classicism to this new literary sensibility, though he was by no means a Romantic poet himself or an adherent of any "school." He was, simply put, the first major poet in Russia to channel all life's impressions through his persona; he valued inspiration and feeling above reason, he was the first to sing of the Russian countryside, its soul and folk customs; but above all else he was Russia's supreme metaphysical poet. Unlike the Romantics, he did not forsake the idea of God and did not replace him with the worship of Nature. Indeed, no other nineteenth-century Russian writer could ever replicate this organic balance in his relation to his immediate surroundings and to the deity, with which Derzhavin seems to have been blessed. After Derzhavin's death, the very existence of the divine meaning in human life was progressively put under question until awareness of it gradually dissipated from most works of popular literature.

But even in a world without God, the need to experience the miraculous or otherworldly was as strong as ever and was uniquely answered by nearly every major writer, whatever his teleology, throughout the century following Derzhavin, as is shown in the works selected from the *oeuvre* of some of the greatest masters of Russian pre-Symbolist literature, such as Pushkin, Lermontov, or Turgenev. They offer examples of confronting the fantastic—either luridly inviting or simply bizarre, in dreams or in worlds alternate to ours—in which protagonists are not offered an easy escape into a socially constructed utopia, or the bliss of never meeting the unknown. Romanticism found an appropriate vehicle for creative thought in poetry, and it is only with late Romanticism that Russian prose comes into its own, principally in the works of Gogol. A separate subsection is devoted to a major sampling of Gogol's fantastic art in prose.

Section B begins with a sampling of Russia's influential nineteenth-century utopias by Bulgarin, Odoevsky and Chernyshevsky. Displaced by centuries from present-day realities, these works offer visions of the future, in which *quest*—one of the principal agents of fantasy-making—is no longer necessary. The section ends with a selection of works by Dostoevsky. Less well-known than his major novels, they are just as intensely powerful in their tragic denial of utopia of any kind on this Earth. .

Section A
From Folk Myth to the Fantastic in Poetry and Prose

A1. *Foregrounding Travel in Space:*
Fantastic and Utopian Scapes of Bygone Years

Old Russia may appear static, but in general only to those who, for the comfort of their own cultural and historical assumptions, consign genuine knowledge of the past to a dusty shelf. Even to old Russia's most rooted people—the peasants—the cycles of the agricultural year, the human narratives of birth, courtship, marriage, and death were dynamic in themselves. They were marked by choral dances and songs, and hedged about with charms, spells and incantations. The whole complex of rituals surrounding betrothal and marriage, for example, was traditionally referred to as the wedding *igra,* a word suggesting the movements of a play or game. And the one thing that unites old Russia's *skomorokhi*—the minstrels who throughout Russia's vast territories kept alive such folk customs, as well as an entire corpus of heroic songs and verse tales—is that they traveled widely. Most of their songs remain unread by the English reader to this day. With our focus in mind, it should be noted that many of their songs touched the infinite worlds of fantasy-making, replete with dreams, visitations by devils, flights of chariots, miracles, visions, and, most notably, fantastic journeys. Russia itself was at times expressed as an enchanted realm, as can be seen in the following (newly translated) excerpt from what is arguably the most inspired quest of Old Russian Literature, *The Lay of Igor's Campaign*:

> O Boyan the Seer, elder days' nightingale, were you to sing of Igor's campaign, laying your vatic fingers upon the living strings, whilst pouring your Wisdom in the Great Tree, running as a gray Wolf over the land, gliding below clouds as a blue-ashen Eagle and, recalling the feuds of former times, you'd let loose ten Falcons upon a flock of Swans, and the first Swan overtaken would sing a Song to old Yaroslav < . . .> [to all great men of his kin, and to] Our Igor, who—having looked up at the Sun—saw all his warriors enveloped in darkness, and called on his brethren, summoned his troops to mount their swift steeds in defense of their land, to catch but a glimpse of the blue river Don [saying]: *"Far better it is to be slain in the battle than captured."*

> Then, weaving Paeans from both halves of time, you'd climb that Tree of Wisdom, and sing, soaring in your mind up to the clouds, roving the Troyan Trail o'er the meads and hills: *"No chance storm has swept falcons over the wide fields—swift jackdaws flock up, racing toward the great river Don; steeds neigh beyond the Sula—glory rings in Kiev; trumpets blare in Novgorod—banners fly in Putivl . . ."*

But the Sun blocks Igor's campaign by darkness, and night, moaning with thun-
derstorms, awakens the birds, the whistling of the beasts arises, as Div—the
bird-god Daeva—flutters up at the top of the Tree and cries out to all the
unknown lands by the Volga, the Azov Sea, the river Sula, the cities of Surozh,
Korsun and you, idol of Tmutorokan.—The while the Kumans hasten by
untrodden paths to the Don, their carts screech at midnight, as dispersed swans.

Igor leads his warriors to the Great Don: The birds in oak forests portend his
misfortunes, the wolves in ravines conjure the storms, the eagles' screeches bid
beasts to the bones, the foxes yelp at the vermilion shields. *"O Russian land!
Thou art now beyond the hills!"* <. . .> Very early on the next morn bloody
dawn heralds the light, ebony clouds arrive from the sea, wanting to cover the
four Suns, and in them throb blue lightnings: There is to be great thunder—the
rain of arrows will come from the great river Don.<. . .>.

As the introductory section of this twelfth-century epic clearly demon-
strates, old Russia possessed a unique ensemble of myths and images, on
which any modern work of fantasy could thrive. Its power resides in the
mastery with which it links events of recorded history (Igor's campaign,
the solar eclipse of May 1, 1185) with events that parallel the campaign in the
unrecorded history of nature. Personified, Nature becomes an active participant in history (the Sun's eclipse blocks Igor's campaign, birds portend misfortunes, wolves conjure up storms, foxes yelp at the shields). Igor's campaign is
further linked with the mythical universe (the bird-god Daeva), indeed, with
the cultural heritage of all mankind (the Wisdom Tree, the Trojan Trail).
    Even this short excerpt reveals that old Russia had a keen sense of poet-
ry, as the apostrophic turn to the semi-legendary poet, Boyan the Seer[1]
would suggest. Like Boyan, the anonymous author of *The Lay*, perhaps
more appropriately translated as *The Song of Igor's Campaign*,[2] is clearly a
poet in his own right. Although his narrative is replete with songs, laments,
and dreams—a rich ensemble of recognizable tropes, figures and sub-genres
of poetry—it lacks, as all Russian medieval texts do, a recognizable system
of prosody accessible to a modern reader. In fact, like all of the texts
(whether prosaic or poetic) that belong to the corpus of Old Russian
Literature, it shuns any kind of recognizable division, such as a verse line,
stanza, or end-rhyme. Even its punctuation and paragraphs cannot be fully
analyzed, counted, or commented upon. Rather, as if to underscore the very
indivisibility of its poetic universe, it weaves its own dynamic and ever-
changing world of fantasy-making, which is enriched by a deft use of tropes

---

1. A semi-historical bard, presumably living during the reign of Yaroslav the Wise, the
prince of Kiev from 1019 to 1054.
    2. Cf. Vladimir Nabokov's translation of the full text in *The Song of Igor's Campaign*
(New York: Vintage Books, 1960)

and figures—a technique, which one of the foremost scholars of this period (Czyzhevsky) has called "magic realism." Weaving "paeans from both halves of time", or expressing and celebrating the past as *coexistent* with the present, could not have been a talent possessed only by the semi-mythical poet Boyan the Seer. Consider the history behind the *Lay*. Igor, a minor prince, led his warriors on an expedition which ended in fiasco: his troops were defeated and he himself was imprisoned—the incident merits only the barest mention in Russia's medieval chronicles. Yet the *Lay's* anonymous author adroitly transforms and transmutes this material into a splendid victory of verbal craft, permanently fixed in the annals of Russian literature.

Other poets emerged as Russia itself underwent a cataclysmic defeat at the hands of the invading Mongolian hordes in 1237—a defeat which was recorded in practically all of her chronicles, and which meant her obliteration as an independent country for at least two centuries. And yet during this dark period of Russian history (commonly referred to as the *Mongol yoke*), when countless Russians were forcibly removed from their native soil and displaced to the East to serve as slave labor in building the Mongol empire, another unnamed poet enshrined in words the longing that the departing Russian men and women must have had for their now ruined homeland. Commonly referred to as *The Orison on the Downfall of the Russian Land*, this highly poetic, but still quite obscure, thirteenth-century Russian work was written shortly after the Mongol invasion. It opens with a passage depicting Russia as an enchanted world—a utopian, but clearly tangible vision of peaceful plenitude:

> *O radiant brightness—most finely adorned Thou art, Rus'!*
> *Magnificent Land art Thou, charmed with such myriad beauties:*
> *Countless deep lakes, cerulean rivers, and sacred clear springs,*
> *Mountains so tow'ring, steeply pitched slopes, and oak groves unnumbered,*
> *Dazzling wide meadows, teaming with creatures, abundant in birds,*
> *Many great cities, and beautiful boroughs, monastic sweet vineyards,*
> *Princes most feared, proud boyars of honor, and countless great lords.*
> *All wealth is contained in Thine heart—O Christian and Orthodox Faith!*

The manuscript, which returns the reader's mind to a time just prior to the Mongol invasion, is often regarded as second in importance only to *The Song of Igor's Campaign* in the Old Russian literary canon. Its extant text (only slightly longer than the passage quoted) consists of a fragment from what was most likely a much longer work, lamenting Russia's lost glory. Our passage is, however, rhetorically complete in the sense that it represents an organized verbal medium, with a recognizable beginning and closure: its last line provides a mirror-like restatement of its rhythmic and poetic opening. As mentioned earlier, Russian pre-sixteenth-century

prosody remains a mystery in that scholars working from surviving manuscripts have to this day been unable to derive its systemic unity.
Nevertheless, *On the Downfall of the Russian Land* is clearly a rhythmically executed text, which is transposed in our translation into eight verse
lines of irregular ternary meters. Thereby we give it a visual organization
lacking in the original, but which is implicit in its rhetorical design. It is
noteworthy that the author, lamenting a ravaged Russia, chose the present
tense to represent its natural beauty. In this sense the passage unscrolls a
bird's-eye-view fantasy of a recreated past—an Edenic utopia which for the
author and his generation is now irretrievably lost.

Many centuries were to pass before Russian literature would be able to
express such awareness of the land's intense beauty with comparable power.
That is not to say that during this period Russia had no literature. On the
contrary, forced by the tragic loss of its independence, Russia turned especially to holy writ for inspiration and produced wonderful translations of
countless hymns and books of the Bible. Yet no matter how groundbreak-
ing the various transpositions of the sacred texts may have been, translational
literature is rarely studied with an eye to the originality of the translator as a
poet in his own right. Moreover, since such texts had anonymous translators,
they are further neglected due to the post-Romantic notion of the pre-eminence
of the persona of the writer, and are usually not considered as literature
proper.[3] Although original in their transformations of the model texts, they
require their own explication and fall outside of the corpus of the present
anthology. Quite unfortunately, we are able to offer here only a snapshot of
a vast and self-contained medieval fantasy universe, which included many
other genres (lives, martyrions, travelogues, chronicles, orations, sermons,
etc.)[4] from which modern Russian writers drew productive motifs, images
and inspiration. Dostoevsky himself, for instance, found the *Lives of the
Saints* to be a rich trove.

Since our volume has space limitations, we should like to introduce here
only one additional work, namely *The Life of Archpriest Avvakum, Written
by Himself* (1682). This text, *The Lay of Igor's Campaign,* and *The Orison
on the Downfall of the Russian Land* are arguably the three most original

---

3. For example, *The Psalter*, indisputably a model many world cultures have emulated, does
transform itself in many individual translations. Yet the translations themselves are rarely assumed
to be exemplary carriers of literary value. Despite W. H. Auden's claim that English literature
would not exist without the rhymed translations of the *Psalms,* it is very rare that any particular
translation of the Psalms by a known poet, from the Metaphysicals onwards, is assumed to be his
or her principle contribution to the formation of the literary canon. Just as the celebrated King
James translation of the Bible, the work of forty-nine individual contributors, is not assumed to be
principally a literary monument as such, but rather a sacred text.

4. Many are available to an English reader in *Medieval Russia's Epics, Chronicles, and
Tales* , Edited, Translated, and with an Introduction by Serge A. Zenkovsky (New York: E. P.
Dutton, 1963; Revised and Enlarged Edition, 1974)

and most celebrated Russian works composed before Peter the Great. Avvakum (the Russian form of the Old Testament name Habbakuk) was born in 1621 and became a priest at the age of twenty. A zealot and a staunch traditionalist, for forty years Avvakum was a thorn in the side of Church authorities. A vociferous opponent of the ecclesiastical reforms imposed on the Russian Orthodox Church by the Patriarch Nikon, in 1653 Avvakum was exiled to Siberia with his family. Their wanderings through this vast, largely unexplored territory were to last nine years. In 1682 he was burned at the stake. His death, just as his uncompromising life, have left an indelible mark in Russian consciousness as supreme examples of an unbending spirit, which many Russians have grown to admire and emulate. But for our purposes, we should also remember that Avvakum was a sophisticated writer and that his *Life* is considered one of the most accomplished autobiographical journey "novels" ever composed in Russia.[5]

TITLE PAGE:

Avvakum,
the Archpriest,
hath been charged to write his Life
by the monk Epifanii—his personal confessor,
so that the works of GOD shall not pass into oblivion;
and to this end hath he been charged by his confessor
for the glory of Christ our GOD.
Amen!

Vision l:

In our Russia there was a sign: the Sun was dimmed in [7]162 (1654), a month or less before the plague. Simeon, the Archbishop of Siberia, was sailing along the Volga river, as darkness covered the light at midday, two weeks or so before St. Peter's day. Simeon and his crew lingered by the shore, weeping for three hours. The Sun grew black, as the Moon approached, gliding from the West.

---

5. Russia's religious history is unique and quite distinct from that of western Europe. The familiar terms "reformation" and "counter-reformation", for example cannot be applied here, even though the Russian Orthodox church also experienced a long period of dissent and unrest, culminating in a significant schism. Avvakum was a contemporary of John Bunyan and the west has often seen him as a Russian Protestant, although this is in many ways misleading. In the west, the intensely personal conversion narratives and spiritual autobiographies spawned by religious dissent had a significant effect on the development of the novel. Avvakum's influence in Russia was much less pervasive until he was "discovered" in the nineteenth century. But there is an interesting correspondence to our grounding of Russian fantasy literature in Avvakum's spiritual *picaresque*. Douglas Adams' phenomenally successful scifi/fantasy series *The Hitchhiker's Guide to the Galaxy* (1979) chronicles the misadventures of one Arthur Dent, a reluctant traveler through space and time. Adam's choice of name for his hero cannot have been accidental. One of John Bunyan's own favorite books was: *The Plain Man's Path-way to Heaven: Wherein Every Man May Clearly See Whether He Shall Be Saved or Damned, Set Forth Dialogue-wise for the Better Understanding of the Simple*, by Arthur Dent.

According to Dionysios, GOD thus reveals his wrath against men: at that time Nikon, the Apostate, was defiling the Faith and the laws of the Church, and for this GOD poured forth the vial of his wrathful fury upon the Russian land; a mighty plague it was—no time to forget—we all remember. The Sun grew dark once more about fourteen years later, during the Fast of St. Peter, on Friday during the sixth hour, when the Moon covered all by darkness—ebbing from the West—again revealing the wrath of GOD: at this time the hierarchs in a cathedral church were shearing the Archpriest Avvakum—that destitute and poor soul—along with some others, and after damning them, they cast them into a dungeon at the Ugresha river. The True Believer will understand what is happening to our Land due to the turmoil in the Church. Enough talk of it: On Judgment Day everyone will understand! Let us endure till then . . .

Vision 2:

[Upon hearing the confession of a young woman, burdened with many sins], I reached my *izba* home. The hour must have been nigh onto midnight. I wept before the icon of the Lord, so that my eyes swelled: I prayed in earnest that God might detach me from my spiritual children, since the burden was heavy and hard to bear. And I threw myself face-down on the ground, sobbing in grief. As I lay there, all unawares of my bitter weeping, the eyes of my heart beheld the river Volga, and this is what I saw: Two stately golden boats were sailing gracefully—their oars and masts were of gold—all was of gold. At the helm of each sat a man for the crew, and I said to them: "Whose ships are these?" They answered: "Luke's and Lawrence's." Now Luke and Lawrence had been my spiritual children; they set me and my house on the path to salvation, and their passing had been pleasing to God. And lo, I then saw a third ship, not adorned with gold, but decked out in varied hues—red, and white, and blue, and black, and ashen—so that the mind of man could not take in all its beauty and excellence. A radiant youth sat at the helm, steering so eagerly toward me from the Volga, as if he would want to devour me. And I called out to him: "Whose ship is this?" And he—sitting in it—replied: "Your ship. Sail in it with your wife and children, if you're going to pester the Lord." And I was seized with wonder and, having seated myself aboard, I pondered: "What is this vision? And what kind of voyage will it be?"

Vision 3:

Having fixed our boat, we let out our sails and made ready to cross the Baikal—the sea-lake. But midway the air grew eerily quiet, so we took up oars. In that place the sea is not very broad, maybe a hundred—or some eighty—versts (65-50 miles). Just as we were reaching for the shore a storm sprang up with mighty winds, and it was hard to find refuge sheltered from the waves. At the banks—ringed by steep mountains—the cliffs of rock stood fearfully high: I have wandered twenty thousand versts, and more, over the face of the earth, but never have I seen their like. Along their summits are pavilions and turrets, gates and pillars, walls and courtyards—all skillfully fashioned from stone and earth—all works of GOD. Onions grow there, and garlic, bigger than the Romanov onion and uncommonly sweet. Wild hemp grows there as well in the care of GOD; in the courtyards grow fine, red grasses and most colorful, exceedingly fragrant flowers. And there are great numbers of birds—geese and swans that drift over the lake like snow. The water is fresh, but huge seals and sea-lions live in it: I saw no such sea-calves and sea-hares all the time I lived on the shores of the ocean-sea Mezen. This lake swarms with fish—sturgeon and trout, sterlet, salmon and whiting and many other kinds. The sturgeon and taimen salmon are fat as can be; one can't fry them in a pan—nothing but fat would be left. And all this has been done through our Jesus Christ, our Light, for man, so that he—with a mind at last at rest—might lift his praise to God. But such is man that he is given "to vanity, and his days are as a shadow that passeth away." He capers like a goat; he puffs himself up like a bubble; he rages like a lynx; he seeks to devour others like a serpent; when he covets the beauty of his neighbor's mate, he neighs like a colt; he is fiendish as a devil; when he has gorged himself full he drops off to sleep like any heathen, without saying his prayers. He puts off repentance till his old age and then disappears—we know not where, to light or darkness. But all will be revealed on Judgment Day. Forgive me all: for I have myself sinned more than other men.

While neither *The Lay of Igor's Campaign* nor *The Life of Archpriest Avvakum* can properly be called a fantasy, let us note that both involve a *journey*—a subgenre considered a principal venue for fantasy-making, as, for example, in Lewis Carol's classics *Alice in Wonderland* and *Through the Looking Glass*. To be sure, Igor and Avvakum travel over real geography, but a geography so foreign to the average reader of their day as to take on the function of a fantastic topography akin to Tolkien's *Middle Earth*. At the same time, both the military tale and the spiritual narrative posit a universe replete with signs and wonders, natural and supernatural phenomena sent to guide, assist and admonish the human soul in its travels.

Travels to enchanted and mysterious places and the heroic deeds of protagonists embarking on such journeys characterize another major source of literary creativity, namely the oral narrative tradition. The two permanent sources of inspiration for the development of fantasy in Russia were *skazki* (folk tales) and *byliny* (folk epics). No written sources for either survive from earlier than the eighteenth century, while the major corpus Russian folk tales and epics was collected, transcribed, and edited in the nineteenth and twentieth centuries. In folk tales we find that fantastic journeys can successfully be undertaken by female protagonists, as well as by male, but the latter dominate almost exclusively the epic realm. The principal characteristics which allow a female protagonist to succeed in the world of magic transformations are usually perseverance, orderliness, and above all beauty, be it *Alionushka* whose youthful charms ultimately rescue both herself and her brother *Ivanushka* from poverty, or *Marya Morevna*, a warrior princess who—no matter how powerful her military exploits—is attractive to prince Ivan precisely because she is a "beautiful queen." A poor merchant's daughter has the success of her quest inscribed in her name, *Vasilisa the Beautiful*. Her story follows the typical plot of an ascent to the throne of a folk hero, who despite considerable obstacles succeeds in marrying beyond his/her social origins.

Vasilisa marries a prince at the end of the tale, but even she needs the help of magic agents and a great deal of self discipline and perseverance to be victorious in her struggle with her wicked step-mother. For the purposes of our discussion *Vasilisa the Beautiful* is remarkable on two counts. First, that her principal magic agent, a gift from her dying mother, is a fully animated talking, eating, and hard-working doll—rather than the magic beast typical of the folk mytho-poetic universe. The doll gives Vasilisa advice and comfort whenever she is in trouble, performs all the menial chores for her, weeds flower beds, sprays the cabbage, brings the water into the house, and fires up the stove; it even shows Vasilisa an herb that will protect her from sunburn. The wish for a magic agent in human form to accomplish daily tasks—so unambiguously expressed in this popular tale of Russia's pre-industrial folk culture—considerably predates the futurist concept of robots or androids, a theme which has defined much of modern science fiction ever since Karel Capek coined the word in his famous [1920] play RUR.[6] It is notable that the ultimate benefactor and protector in Vasilisa's fictional universe is a superhuman doll which allows her to triumph even over the all-powerful, villainous and deceptive female ruler of Russian forests, *Baba Yaga*.

The behavior of the latter provides second noteworthy aspect of this folk tale. Baba Yaga normally eats people, tricking them in uncanny ways to accomplish this. But because of the magic abilities of Vasilisa' doll, the witch here becomes yet another agent assisting the heroine to get the better of her vicious stepmother and her two step-sisters, the tale's true villains. Her role as a positive force in Vasilisa's quest is not immediately apparent, however, as the tale's magically shifting and mystifying setting is described:

> *Vasilisa thus made ready, tucked her doll into her pocket, crossed herself before the icon, headed off into the forest. Fearful, trembling, she walked onwards. Then she heard the sound of hoof-beats and a horseman galloped past her. White his visage and his raiment, white his steed and all his trappings—and the dawn came with his passage. She went further, and another horse was heard and soon passed near her. Red was he, and all his garments, and his jade was red as fire—pallid dawn gave way to sunrise. Just as evening fell the maiden came upon a little clearing where the witch's hut was nestled. Suddenly another horseman, black of visage and of raiment, mounted on a coal-black charger, galloped by where she was standing—night had fallen in the forest.*

6. The coining of the word *robot* is, in fact, attributed to his brother-collaborator, Josef, who is supposed to have derived it from the Old Czech (Church Slavic) word *robota*, which meant menial or hard toil.

As if the magic of these visions was not enough, Vasilisa must still face *Baba Yaga's* entry into the plot, accompanied by the usual paraphernalia surrounding the witch's dreadful persona: terrifying noises resounding through the woods, trees crackling and dry leaves rustling as she herself appears riding in a mortar, which she prods on with a pestle, sweeping up her tracks with a broom. The only way for Vasilisa to survive is to serve the witch in her hut for the next three days and nights. *Baba Yaga* is truly frightening when she instructs Vasilisa to perform next-to-superhuman tasks. Her power is restated as Vasilisa learns from her captor that the three horsemen, obviously embodiments of the sun's daily journey across the sky, are also "her faithful servants."[7] Yet after Vasilisa performs nearly impossible chores with the help of her untiring doll, *Baba Yaga* rewards the heroine by giving her a skull with burning eyes, whose rays consume the true villains in the tale by fire and turn them to ashes.

Marya Morevna, another very popular Russian folk tale, expresses three other major utopian folk themes. The first, man's primordial wish *to fly*, is magically realized at the very beginning of the tale. The male protagonist, Prince Ivan, succeeds in marrying his three sisters to three brave knights, each of whom flies into his castle's window in avian form—falcon, eagle and raven, respectively—as they seek his three sisters' hands. Each has his wish granted and each carries his betrothed into his own land. Russia's mythic fascination with the bird kingdom is strong, and instances of transmogrification into bird-like creatures abound in its tales and epics. The theme is also well represented in Russia's oldest stone cathedral decorations, in objects of folk handwork, and in traditional cross-stitch embroidery designs. This powerful symbolic significance may be traced even in Russia's choice of the Byzantine double-headed eagle as its national emblem. In this context it is perhaps natural that Russia's foremost prose writer, N. V. Gogol, chose his pen-name from the bird kingdom—*gogol'* in Russian is a goldeneye duck—and that one of Turgenev's major novels is titled *The Nest of Gentlefolk*. By Turgenev's time the word "nest" was mainly used as a metaphor for home comfort, but in *Marya Morevna* the nests inhabited by the Prince Ivan's sisters are far closer to their avian counterparts', and their raptor-husbands' ability to fly plays an important role later in the tale. In many ways, then, *Sputnik* and Russia's primacy in space exploration were the technological realization of a national folk dream.

The second utopian motif in *Marya Morevna*, a theme closely connected with the ability to fly to distant reaches, is the innate human desire to overcome death. As opposed to Christian teachings which promise eternal life-after-death

---

7. The horse is in general an extremely important symbol in Slavic folklore, both as a totemic animal and the symbolic incarnation of celestial and atmospheric forces. In other tales Baba Yaga is depicted as the keeper of a herd of horses with special powers, one of which the hero must steal in order to fulfill his quest.

somewhere outside of temporal reality, this folk tale and many others advance
the notion that the miracle of resurrection into temporal life can be achieved by
a proper application of certain magic agents, available to those who seek them.
This motif appears after Prince Ivan's bride Maria Morevna has been kidnapped by Koschey the Deathless—the villain in this tale. Setting out to find
her, the Prince leaves silver talismans (a spoon, a fork and a snuffbox) with each
of his three brothers-in-law, all of whom can assume bird form at will. Twice
the Prince rescues Maria Morevna but is overtaken—and spared—by Koschey,
who warns him that a third attempt will mean his death.

> Once again Koschey the Deathless left the castle where he kept her. Once again
> the Prince came riding, begged Maria to come with him. "But Prince Ivan, he
> will catch us, hew you into little pieces." "Let him do so-for I cannot live in
> happiness without you." They made ready, left the castle as Koschey was
> wending homewards. In pursuit The Deathless galloped, overtook the Prince's
> charger. Then he hewed the Prince in pieces, put them in a tar-daubed barrel,
> bound it well with hoops of iron, flung it in the deep blue ocean. At that very
> hour and moment, each small talisman of silver shone no more, grew black
> with tarnish. Eagle hurried to the ocean, seized the barrel, hove it shorewards.
> Falcon flew to fetch the *Water That Gives Life*. Likewise did Raven fetch the
> *Water That Gives Death*, and then the brothers broke the barrel, ranged the
> pieces all in order. Raven flecked them with the *Water That Brings Death*—
> they grew together. Falcon flecked the new-formed body with the *Water That
> Brings Life*—the Prince awakened. "Ah, how long have I been sleeping?" he
> inquired. "Longer had you slept without us," Eagle answered.

It must be noted that the hero in any tale may be revived only if he has
helpers who can obtain the *Water of Life* and the *Water of Death* and who
know how to use them. Above, had the brothers merely sprinkled the
pieces of Prince Ivan's body with the *Water of Life* each piece might have
become animated, but would have then remained separate from all the others in a surrealist or neo-Boschian way.

The final utopian aspect of *Marya Morevna* worth noting is found in
its projection of gender equality. Unlike *Vasilisa the Beautiful*, in which
most of the participants are female, *Marya Morevna* presents its characters
in an equilibrium of the sexes. Prince Ivan's three sisters get three male-bird
husbands, Ivan himself marries Marya Morevna, and even Baba Yaga, who
in this tale returns to her normal villainous ways, is paired with an evil
male counterpart, Koshchei the Deathless (apparently a Russian folk-tale
progenitor of the Skeletor character in TV cartoons). Marya Morevna is
introduced as a famed female warrior, and in both the evil and the good
agencies of the tale the female character is at least as strong as the male.
Even if it is Prince Ivan who rescues Marya Morevna from Koshchei the

Deathless and who finishes the villain off with his mace, it is noteworthy that at the tale's outset it was Marya Morevna who had captured Koschey and kept him chained in her dungeon. The Russian folk belief in the innate worth of both genders also finds expression in numerous iconic representation of twin male and female saints. It recurs repeatedly in written literature, for example in *The Life of the Archpriest Avvakum*. The fact that this ideal was not realized in Russia's developing industrial society is clearly expressed in Chernyshevsky's novel *What is to be Done*.

Russian folk epics, however, are nearly entirely dominated by male heroes and some folklore specialists find their genesis around the tenth century, during the creation of a Christian Russian statehood. The oldest of them center around the court of Prince Vladimir of the Riurik dynasty who christianized Russia in 988 AD. His court had its seat in Kiev, the capitol of modern-day Ukraine, which is regarded as the ancient locus of Russian culture. Kiev—a city situated on the edge of the northern forest zone and the southern *steppes*— enjoyed fame as early as the ninth century. Kievan princes controlled much of the territory all the way to the Black Sea, conquering individual nomadic tribes and threatening at times to conquer Constantinople. Kiev's day came to an end in 1237 when the city was sacked by the Mongol hordes. Heroic exploits of Kievan princes were recorded by the folk of these regions in the epic songs, called *byliny*.[8] Unlike the *Igor Song*, most of these *byliny* were not recorded before the 19th century. They interweave factual and mythical elements in fantastic ways, and their protagonists exhibit superhuman strength.[9] Some, such as *Volkh Vseslavyevich* (a child of a human mother and a serpent), adopt animal forms to achieve their ends (Volkh can, for instance, shift his shape to become a falcon when he needs to cover great distances, or an ant, when he needs to crawl under the gates), others rely on their gigantic size. Some *byliny* are not without irony relative to this attribute, as in the case of *Svyatogor*, one of Russia's oldest epic heroes or *bogatyrs*:

---

8. Byliny were originally called *stariny* (tales of the old) before I. P. Strakhov coined in the 1830s the term *bylina* (tale that was), which remains in use to this day for classifying its generic appurtenance.

9. In any discussion of *byliny*, a Western reader might be immediately tempted to draw an analogy between this relatively small body of surviving texts and "The Matter of Britain"—a term coined as early as the 13th century to describe the complex of narratives surrounding the semi-legendary King Arthur and his knights. In some aspects the analogy holds. The Kievan *bylina* cycle, containing what might be called "The Matter of Rus," also centers around a royal figure: Vladimir, Grand Duke of Kiev. But whereas the search for evidence of a historical King Arthur reaches back into the fifth century and is speculative at best, "Vladimir the Fair Sun" is clearly an imaginative composite of Old Russia's notable rulers-chiefly Vladimir I (d. 1015) and Vladimir II Monomakh (d. 1125). Like Arthur in his seat of Camelot, Vladimir *Krasnoe Solntse* (The Exquisite Sun) holds great feasts in his palace, and assigns various quests to his heroes. He too rewards success and punishes failure or bad faith. But unlike Arthur, whose tragic personal fate and messianic legend is integral to the Round Table stories, Vladimir himself is never the *bylina's*

High is the height under the heavens, deep is the depth of the ocean sea,
Wide is the plain across the whole earth,
    Swift must be the rider attempting to cross it.
Not far, not far away in the open field,
    A cloud of dust was swirling in a column,
As Svyatogor, the mighty Russian bogatyr appeared
    In the wide golden steppe:
His shoulders were wider than two yards,
    And his steed was like a fierce animal.
He was riding in the field and amused himself
    By throwing his steel mace into the skies:
Higher than the towering forest, yet lower than the moving clouds.
When the mace would come down, he would catch it with one hand.
Then he came across a tiny skomorokh's (minstrel's) bag in the open plains.
He didn't dismount his good steed
    And wanted to lift the purse with his whip,
But the little bag wouldn't be moved.
He now dismounted his good steed and wanted to lift it with his one hand,
But the little bag wouldn't be budged.
He then grabbed it with his both hands
    And strained with his all bogatyr's strength,
But the little bag wouldn't be lifted.
Instead he sank into Mother Damp Earth up to his knees
    And couldn't move.
Svyatogor then muttered to himself,
    "I have ridden much around the wide world,
    But I have never seen such a wonder:
    This tiny bag won't give way to all my bogatyr's strength;
    My death must be near."
He then implored his horse:
    "Hail to thee, my faithful bogatyr steed!
    Now come and save your master."
He took hold of the gilded girth and held fast by the silver stirrup.
His mighty steed then strained and pulled Svyatogor
    Out of the damp sinking earth.

---

focal point. Nor does the earthy Russian *bogatyr* much resemble a Lancelot or a Galahad. Bogatyrs like Ilyia of Murom and Aliosha Popovich protect Rus from foreign invaders and monsters, and occasionally from native enemies like robbers and brigands. In this they are motivated by a fierce innate love for Russia itself, and not by feudal ties to Vladimir—with whom they occasionally quarrel bitterly—nor by the desire to prove themselves worthy of a lady's affection. The complete absence of courtly love is perhaps what most clearly distinguishes the Kievan from the Arthurian legends. The knight's chaste worship of an inaccessible female to whom he dedicates his exploits reflects the form that Mariolatry typically assumed in the West, where youth and beauty were important attributes of the Virgin. In the Orthodox East it is above the maternal qualities of Mary which excite devotion. A bogatyr may have an occasional erotic adventure, but his heroic deeds are inspired by a devotion to Mother Russia and his strength is drawn from Mother Earth herself.

He then mounted his good steed
    And rode through the open fields toward the Ararat mountains.
But as he was tired from the skomorokh's little bag,
    He fell asleep on his good steed,
A bogatyr's deep sleep it was under the height of the open heavens.

Irony permeates the ultimate fate of *Svyatogor,* which is related to the metaphoric significance of his name, literally the *Sacred Mount.* Sviatogor is destined to die on a mount, as is recorded in the second major *bylina* about him, to which the passage quoted above serves as a preamble, and which introduces one of the most popular heroes of the Russian folk epos, Ilya of Murom. Ilya has many *byliny* composed solely about himself, but in this older tale, of which the following is a summary in prose, he is presented as not yet fully experienced, but as a worthy heir to Sviatogor's strength:

> Ilya comes from out of the wide plains and cannot stand seeing the giant Sviatogor, sleeping on his horse as if wanting to sneer at Ilya. Ilya attempts to wake Sviatogor by striking him with a mighty mace. This first and the second blow have no affect and the giant continues to sleep, as "size clearly matters" in this *bylina.* With the third blow Ilya wounds his own hand, whereupon Sviatogor wakes up and complains "how badly Russian flies can bite." When he sees Ilya he seizes the young warrior by the hair and pockets him. As he rides on toward Mount Ararat, his horse begins to stumble and to complain about having to carry two bogatyrs and another bogatyr's horse. Only then does Svyatogor notice Ilya as a potential peer and invite him to test his strength in an open combat. Ilya wisely declines, asking instead to become his sworn brother. Sviatogor agrees and the warriors exchange their gold baptismal crosses. Now as brothers, they journey on and reach the Mount of Olives, where they see an oaken coffin. Sensing this as an omen, Svyatogor asks Ilya to try it first. It is clearly too big for Ilya, and Svyatogor then tries it himself. The coffin is exactly to Svyatogor's measure and he asks Ilya to close its lid so that he can admire it from the inside. Ilya does so, but in a short while Svyatogor complains that he can no longer breathe. Ilya attempts but fails to raise the lid again. Svyatogor now understands that it is his destiny to remain in the coffin. Before he dies, he wants to breathe his spirit into Ilya and give him his horse. Ilya, however, declines, saying that if Svyatogor's strength were added to his, Mother Earth could not bear him. Thereafter they say farewell to each other, Svyatogor now lying forever in the damp earth with his horse by his side on the Mount of Olives, and Ilya riding back to Holy Rus, to the city of Kiev.

Annointed by Svyatogor as his successor, Ilya becomes the central hero of the Russian epic, whithin the tradition of which he has the most complete biography. Several versions exist of his becoming a *bogatyr,* but nearly all record the following miracle:

In the great city of Murom, in the village of Karacharovo,
There sat upon the stove-ledge a peasant lad, Ilya of Murom,
Up this ledge he sat and sat, paralyzed, for thirty long years.
One day his good father and mother set off to labor in the fields.
The while two pilgrims came to his window and begged admittance.
"I cannot throw open our wide gates dear elders," replied Ilya,
"These thirty years I have been unable to stand, I am not master of my
    arms and legs."
"Rise up, Ilya," repeated the pilgrims,
And lo—Ilya rose up at once on legs now swift and strong,
He flung open the wide gates, and let them in.
Making the sign of the cross and and bowing, as custom demanded,
They entered and offered what they had brought, a rare draught brewed
    with honey.
"Drink, Ilya,"—they said—"and you will become a great bogatyr'."
Ilya, downing the beaker, on the instant felt a great strength flowing through
    his veins.

The belief that a true Russian-born hero shall arise from slumber in time of need—struck a most responsive cord in Russia, as legends of King Arthur's return have in England. Indeed, in many *byliny* the tenth-century hero Ilya—now displaced in time—becomes the principal warrior challenging the invading Tartar hordes of the thirteenth century. His encounters with any heathens are handled in the following manner, with some topoi of the genre interchangeable with other *byliny*:

Ilya attended matins in Murom and resolved to see vespers in the great city of Kiev.
On the way he rode up to the famous city of Chernigov.
Near it a vast army had been assembled, as black as the blackest of ravens.
No man might pass there on foot, none could pass on a good steed,
No bird flew by and no grey beast scoured past.
But no bright falcon flew by, swooping down on small birds of passage—
Ilya of Murom rode up to this great black army,
Attacked it, trampled it with his steed, and crushed it with his mace.

A famous nineteenth-century Russian writer, I. A. Goncharov, devoted a whole novel, entitled *Oblomov*, to a very likable and gentle protagonist who spends nearly a third of the novel's narrative in one place—his bed, from which he is trying to get up. This work is generally understood as Goncharov's satire on the laziness of the Russian landed gentry and their inability to cope with the advent of western civilization and industrialization. Yet by naming his protagonist *Ilya* and giving him a disability virtually identical to that of Ilya of Murom, Goncharov might also have been implying that Oblomov's times were unworthy of miracles and heroic deeds.

It must be noted that while neither folk tales nor folk epics can ever be properly called travelogues, they nearly always involve—just as their written counterparts noted earlier—a great deal of travel. Here again is Ilya continuing on his ride to Kiev:

> *Having defeated the black army, he rode up to the famous city of Chernigov,*
> *The men of this city invited him to be their commander, hailing him as a*
>   *great bogatyr of Holy Russia.*
> *Ilya, declining, asked only to be shown the straightest path to Kiev.*
> *The men of Chernigov replied that the straight-traveled road to Kiev was*
>   *overgrown with grass*
> *And no man might pass it on foot, nor yet ride there on a good steed.*
> *By the Black Swamp and the crooked birch, by the Lingonberry stream,*
>   *near to the cross of Lebanon,*
> *Sits Nightingale the Robber—Odikhmanty's son—in a green oak tree,*
> *The villainous robber whistles and shrieks like a wild beast, and at that*
>   *whistle and shriek,*
> *All the grasslands and meadows become entangled, all the azure flowers*
>   *loose their petals,*
> *All the dark woods bend down to the earth, and all the good people lie dead.*
> *The straight-traveled road was five hundred versts, but the round-about*
>   *road was a whole thousand.*
> *Ilya urged on his good steed and rode along the straight road to Kiev.*
> *Deep are the pools of the Dnieper River, long are the reaches of the*
>   *Lingonberry Stream,*
> *Miraculous is the cross of Lebanon, dark are the forests, and black are the*
>   *swamps past Chernigov . . .*

Ilya's most memorable deed in this popular *bylina* is bagging the man-bird creature, Nightingale the Robber, whose whistling can conjure up storms, and finally bringing him to the court of Vladimir. But the narrative space devoted to his travel over the enchanted landscapes from Murom to Kiev is at least as memorable as his deeds on the way to his ultimate destination. This can be perhaps explained by what the famous Russian cultural historian and theorist Yuri Lotman (1922-1993) called the *semiosphere* (a concept that he developed especially in his essay "Symbolic Spaces"). Medieval Russian thought understood locality and travel to have a religious and moral significance unknown to modern geography. Travel was a way to prove oneself in heroic deeds, to attain Utopia or Paradise (almost exclusively to be found in the East, the South, or in the high mountains) or to set off on a path to sanctity usually found in a monastery. Since social ideals were imagined to exist in geographical space—the idea of the travel itself had, as he would term it, a *semiospheric* significance.

Russia had looked primarily South and East for seven centuries of organized statehood, Kiev being Russia's southernmost capital ever founded. After its utter devastation by the Mongol hordes in 1237, Russia was effectively sealed off from the West as well as from its former southern reaches. Kiev, the strategic center founded by the Riurik princes, continued to exist as a resplendent city only in the folk epos. A new center founded by the descendants of the Riurik line gradually arose within the northern forests, namely Moscow. It was nearly a century and a half before one of its princes, Dmitrii, could wage the first successful battle against the Golden Horde in 1380. This prince, unlike Ilya of Murom, was a real historical personage. But since his victory was just as vital for the Russian nation as any of Ilya's exploits, he received the appellation Dmitrii of the Don in the epic realm of Russian history. The Don was the same river on whose banks his ancestor, Prince Igor (see *The Lay* above), had waged his unsuccessful campaign against a different foe two centuries earlier. It would be two centuries before another Prince from the same dynasty could take control of those lands formerly subordinated to Vladimir. Ivan the Awe-wielding (or the Terrible, as he is known in English, due to a mistranslation) would even expand these territories, but now under Muscovy.

Three and a half centuries of incessant struggle to resurrect its independence from the power which had come from the East had exhausted the Riurik line. A new dynasty, the Romanov, was elected to face Poland—a western foe which nearly subjected Muscovy to its rule at the outset of the seventeenth century. Russia was able to secure its political independence from Poland under the Romanovs, but the first century of their reign was marked by religious strife, undermining Russia's unity and also inspiring such works as *The Life of Avvakum*. As that century was coming to a close, a new Romanov, Peter I, charted a fresh course for Russia, envisioning a social order based on modern science and technology. He was the first czar to leave his realm and to travel (*incognito*) to the West—or to Hell, for believers like Avvakum. The immediate post-Petrine period of Russian literature largely glorified Peter's course, and many of those who were on the side of his reforms also provided entirely new readings of the cosmos surrounding Man. Much of this new awareness was directly tied to the efforts of M. V. Lomonosov (1711-65)—the Russian Newton and a member of several western academies. Equally and uniquely famous for his literary craft and his science, Lomonosov was among the first to express in a newly devised syllabotonic system of prosody (akin to that of English and German) far grander visions of space than had been previously offered in Russia's oral tradition. His seminal work in this regard was the following sacred ode (1743), which he later appended to his treatise on the nature of electricity:

EVENING MEDITATION ON THE MAJESTY OF GOD
ON THE OCCASION OF THE GREAT NORTHERN LIGHTS

Its face concealed, now hides the Day;
As meads are cloaked in gloomy Night;
Tall hills are scaled by blackest shade;
That bends the beams from out our sight;
The depthless star-vault gapes ajar:
Unending vault, unnumbered stars!

A grain of sand caught in the wave,
A spark within an icy maze,
A speck of dust borne on the gale,
A feather in a raging blaze,
Thus I now drown in this dark vault
Adrift and lost in weary thought!

The mouths of wise men teach us thus:
One finds there countless worldly spheres;
Unnumbered there are burning suns,
There nations mark the circling years:
For Godhead's greater glory there
Does Nature reign as it reigns here.

Yet Nature, where is now thy Law?
The northlands see the dawn arise!
May Sol establish there his throne?
May frozen seas breed storms of fire?
Lo, we are rapt in icy flame!
Lo, night now ushers in the Day!

O you whose swift all-seeing minds
Descry the Book of ageless law,
To whom the smallest atom's signs
Show Nature's rule without a flaw,
To you the planets' course is known,
What is it then perturbs us so?

What strength the midnight's rays can jolt?
How may thin flame the welkin cleave?
How, absent clouds, may lightning bolt
Its rising path to Zenith weave?
Can steam pent in an icy frame
Mid Winter's snow engender flame?

There viscous fogs and seas contend;
Or Sol its darting rays does turn,
Through thickened air to us they bend;
Or peaks of pregnant mountains burn;
Or Ocean's zephyrs cease to blow,
And tranquil waves 'gainst ether flow.

Replete with doubt is your retort
About the near—much less the far.
Canst tell the measure of the world?
What lies beyond the smallest star?
How endless is Creation's chord?
Tell then: how great our Author-Lord?

The questions with which Lomonosov ends here embody the poet's wish to express the greatness of God. This will be picked up in the works of other poets, such as Derzhavin, as we shall see, but *Evening Meditation* exemplifies a curious hybrid: one might expect the scientist Lomonosov to frown on the reverent acceptance of such a natural event as the *aurora borealis*, yet Lomonosov the poet celebrates its paradox via the oxymoron—a favorite trope of the Baroque which negates rational resolution. By imagining his rhethorical persona to be immersed, adrift in space earlier in the poem, Lomonosov can be still seen as the first scientist who seeded the ideas from which the Russian space program ultimately sprang. Having no spaceships at his disposal, Lomonosov's poetic "eye" could transcend the necessity of their use and offer accurate visions of the physical processes occurring in space— concretely on the Sun—in the companion piece to his *Evening Meditation*, the *Morning Meditation on the Majesty of God*:

If we—the mortals—had the fortune
To soar beyond the Earth in flight,
And train our eye on Sol's orb scorching,
Enhancing thus our fleeting sight,
We would behold then from all sides
A burning Sea of timeless tides.

There fiery billows swell up, seeking
Repose on shores not to be found,
There flaming whirlwinds churn by, streaking,
Contend through ages' ceaseless round;
There rocks like water come to boil,
And rains blast down—in flames embroiled.

Two centuries later these grand visions would inspire sci-fi writers, like Ivan Efremov (author of our last selection) to imagine and advocate a space program which could actually impel Russia's first space-faring vessel to leap from the decks of Avvakum's dream-ships into the Cosmos itself.

A2. *From Myth & Poetry to the Shifted Realities in Prose*

Gavrila Romanovich Derzhavin
(1743-1816)

> *O Thou, in universe so boundless,*
> *Alive in planets as they swarm*
> *Within eternal flow, yet timeless*
> *Unseen, you reign in triune form!*
> *Embracing all, Thy single Spirit*
> *Knows no abode, no cause to stir it,*
> *Nor paths that Reason ever trod,*
> *Who fills, incarnate, all that's living,*
> *Embracing, keeping and fulfilling,*
> *To Whom we give the name of GOD!*[1]

AFTER ITS PUBLICATION in 1784, Derzhavin's *God* (Bog), initial stanza of which is quoted here in lieu of a proem to his works below, became the first Russian poem to gain worldwide acclaim. This ode has been recognized over the last two centuries as one of the greatest works of Russian literature. Even major literary protagonists (for instance, Dmitrii in *Brothers Karamazov*) are fond of quoting from it, and—just to feel the expanse of the poem's universal reach—let us quote four additional stanzas:

To put the ocean depths to measure,
To sum the sands, the planet's rays,
A lofty mind might want at leisure—
But knows no rule for Thee, nor scales!
Nor can the spirits brought to seeing,
Born from Thy light into their being,
Trace the enigmas of Thy ways:
Our thought, with daring, space traverses,
Approaching Thee, in Thee disperses,—
A blink in the Abyss—no trace.

Thou didst call forth great Chaos' presence
From out the timeless, formless deep,
And then didst found Eternal essence,
Before the Ages born in Thee:
Within Thyself didst Thou engender
Thy selfsame radiance's splendor,
Thou art that Light whence flows light's beam.
Thine ageless Word from the beginning
Unfolded all, for aye conceiving,
Thou wast, Thou art, and Thou shalt be!

The chain of Being Thou comprisest,
And dost sustain it, give it breath;
End and Beginning Thou combinest,
Dost Life bestow in Thee through death.
As sparks disperse, surge upward, flying,
So suns are born from Thee, undying;
As on those cold, clear winter's days
When specks of hoarfrost glisten, shimmer
Gyrate and whirl—from chasms' glimmer
So Stars cast at Thy feet bright rays.

Those billions of lumens flaming
Flow through the measureless expanse,
They govern laws, enforce Thy bidding,
They pour forth life in gleaming dance.
Yet all those lampions thus blazing,
Those scarlet heaps with crystal glazing,
Or rolling mounds of golden waves,
All ethers in their conflagration,
Each world aflame in its own station—
To Thee—they are as night to day.

---

1. All Derzhavin citations in this volume are taken from: *G. R. Derzhavin: Poetic Works. A Bilingual Album.* Brown Slavic Contributions v. XII, Ed. by A. Levitsky; Translated by A. Levitsky and M. T. Kitchen (Providence: Dept. of Slavic Languages, Brown U., 2001), xii + 590 pp.

What has not been recognized so widely is that the poem is not only a magnificent celebratory ode, clearly displaying the poet's penchant for the fantastic in his resplendent visions and images, but the presentation of an entire philosophical system. Going well beyond mere praise of the Deity, the poet imbues man's relationship to God with a multidimensional, spherical character, as exemplified in the words, "Thou formest in me Thine own likeness, as in a drop Sol finds its trace..." (7th stanza). It must be said that Derzhavin was the last poet in Russia in whose fantasy worlds God's omnipotence is not questioned. Yet, however successful in representing a seamless progress from the crevices of the poet's inner persona to the outer reaches of Universe, touching the very fabric of "God," when probing further about the meaning of the Maker's creation Derzhavin wisely refused to provide banal answers as to the purpose of either the divine plan or our own afterlife. His vast contemplative poetry shows instead that the paradoxes with which Life endlessly confronts us are manifested not so much in the decoding of their meaning, as in seizing those rare flashes of time when we feel whole and attuned to its pulse. If "this world's but dreams" and "the Dreamer—God," as he ends his *Magic Lantern* (1803), presented as our first full selection below, then it is surely futile for a man to do the dreaming himself. For this reason, the famous question "to be or not to be," posed by Hamlet and repeated *ad nauseum* in the cultural histories of mankind to this day, would have been *a priori* devoid of meaning to Derzhavin, since man cannot create his own being. A better question from his viewpoint would have been *how* to be? Holistic images of a well-lived life encoded in the vast canvas of his poetry vibrantly pierce the fabric of time and provide the modern reader with hope that there is eternal value to what God giveth to be appreciated not only at the time when He taketh away.

Derzhavin overcomes death's seeming omnipotence by capturing *life* as it fantastically manifests itself in varied colors, smells, sounds and moods. He covets life and easily assures us of its continuance in his art. Such is, for instance, the transformative tally of Nature's wealth as he experienced on his country estate, Zvanka:

> I see there, from the barns and hives, the cotes and ponds,
> Rich gold in butter and in honeycombs on tree limbs,
> In berries—royal purple, on mushrooms—velvet down,
>   And silver, in the bream atremble;

All phenomena of life were possible subjects for transformation in his poetry. He was one of the first Russian poets to sing of feasts, and the objects of his mature poetic vision are as richly vibrant as the most accomplished 17th-century Dutch still-lifes: their specificity is attained not only by descriptions of their visual and tactile texture, but by their origin as well. Hence his fish is from the river Sheksna or from Astrakhan, his beer Russian or English, his ham Westphalian, his seltzer water drunk from Viennese crystal glasses, his coffee sipped from Chinese faience. In depicting such native foods as *borscht* or *pirogi*, as tastier to his persona than the foods of French origin, Derzhavin raises Russian cuisine to the status of a self-sustained, rich tradition worthy of respect in world culture:

> The crimson ham, green sorrel soup with yolks of gold,
> The rose-gold pie, the cheese that's white, the crayfish scarlet,
> The caviar, deep amber, black, the pike's stripes bold,
> Its feather blue—delight the eyesight.
>
> Delight the eye, and joy to every sense impart;
> Though not with glut, or spices brought from foreign harbors,
> But with their pure and wholesome Russian heart:
> Provisions native, fresh and healthful.
>
> When downing good Crimean or Don-region wine,
> Or linden mead, blond beer from hops, or black beer spuming,
> Our crimson brows a little fuddlement avow,
> The talk is merry through the pudding.

Derzhavin's poetic celebrations of life on his estate anticipated the views that Tolstoy was to voice in prose much later, and his art—just as Tolstoy's—found true admirers in Europe. For instance, John Bowring, contemplating Russia's advances in his anthology of Russian poetry of 1821, and certain that in this land "the foundation is now laid, on which the proud edifice of civilization will be raised," found the following words to characterize the poet:

> But of all the poets of Russia, Derzhavin is in my opinion entitled to the very first place. His compositions breathe a high and sublime spirit; they are full of inspiration. His versification is sonorous, original, characteristic; his subjects generally such as allowed him to give full scope to his ardent imagination and lofty conceptions.[2]

In order to continue echoes of Shakespeare's voice in Dezhavin's fantasy space we quote—in lieu of an epigraph to *The Magic Lantern*—some celebrated lines from *The Tempest*. Across the space of a further two centuries both works speak to us as well, embodying one of the dominant

---

2. Bowring, J. *Specimens of the Russian Poets*. With Preliminary Remarks and Bibliographical Notices, 2nd edition with additions (London: 1821), xii-xiii.

threads uniting the writings chosen for this volume. There are other threads to be sure, yet rarely so eloquently expressed and so visually endowed. For this reason, it would be futile to interweave here the remaining threads in any kind of expository prose. In *The Magic Lantern*, with the cinematic richness of its visual montage, Derzhavin anticipates modernity in a way that very few poets of the period can rival. The poem briefly describes a traveling magic-lantern show as preface to eight *tableaux*—to continue the prescient cinematic metaphor, eight clips—each of which depicts a scene of earthly vitality or happiness, and each of which ends abruptly as disaster is about to strike. The poem concludes with a meditation on the absurd unreality of the "insubstantial pageant" of existence. Derzhavin makes no reference to immortality in the Christian sense, and the all-powerful Mage who orchestrates the universe appears to be a capricious and indifferent deity, a fact, which the poet accepts stoically. The abrupt alternation of longer and shorter iambic lines admirably conveys the changing of the lantern's slides and the sudden darkness that follows each *tableau*, demonstrating that the ultimate mage in the text is the poet himself.

The second work chosen to represent Derzhavin's reach into the fantastic realm is *Zlogor, Volkhv of Novgorod* (1813). In the late 18th and early 19th centuries a vogue for literary works in the folkloric style and on folkloric subjects swept Europe, Russia included. The Romantics turned to the native cultures somehow forgotten by Neo-classicim as a powerful source of creative inspiration. In Russia as elsewhere men of letters trolled dusty archives for gems of their people's earliest literature and, following the example of Germany's Grimm brothers, traveled about recording remnants of oral tradition as dictated to them by a bemused peasantry. Derzhavin had no need to travel far afield in search of such material. Indeed, his own estate, his beloved Zvanka, provided a rich source of such ancient lore, as is evidenced by *Zlogor*. According to legend, Zlogor was a *vokhv*—a sorcerer or pagan shaman—who held sway in the Novgorod region in the early Middle Ages, and a kurgan said to be his tomb was in fact located at Zvanka. For economy's sake, we have adapted this entry in such a way that it omits the repeated chorus lines and presents individual stanzas in paragraphs of rhythmic prose which can be scanned as an iambic pentameter.

[In lieu of an epigraph, A.L.]

And like the baseless fabric of this vision,
The cloud-capp'd tow'rs, the gorgeous palaces,
The solemn temples, the great globe itself,
Yea, all which it inherit, shall dissolve,
And, like this insubstantial pageant faded
Leave not a wrack behind. We are such stuff
As dreams are made on . . .

The Magic Lantern

The thunder of an organ's pipes
Cuts through the peace of darkened field:
A luminous, enchanting lamp
Paints on the wall a brilliant orb,
And motley shadows move therein.
The wise and wonder-working mage,
With gestures of his staff, his eyes,
Creates—and then destroys them all.
Apace the townsmen gather round
To see these marvels at his hands.

Appear!
And there came forth . . .
The wild cave's monstrous denizen,
Emerging from its horrid shade
          A Lion comes.
He stands and with his paw he grooms
His gleaming mane. His tail he lashes
          And his roar,
His gaze, like gales from murky depths,
Or like a livid lightning bolt
That flashes through the forest, rumbles.
He roots and pounces, seeking prey,
          And, through the trees,
He spies a peaceful grazing Lamb:
His leap is made—his jaws agape . . .
          No more! No more.

Appear!
And there came forth . . .
Along the smooth and glassy main,
The hour when dawn flings over all
          Her rosy light,
Bewhiskered monarch of the seas,
The silver Sturgeon, eyes aglow,
          Comes forth,
Emerging from the water's depths.
His wing-like fins around him ripple,
He sports about the ocean's portals.

But up from the abyss there glides
    A hideous Beast.
Which, spouting, pipes forth rushing streams
And gapes his horrid, toothy jaws . . .
    No more! No more.

    Appear!
    And there came forth . . .
Serene and verdant lie the dales
O'er which at noon a white Swan soars.
    Beneath the clouds
He lets resound his cheering song.
The far-off vale, the glade, the hill,
    The rushing stream
Give back a hundred-fold reply.
But then, as swift as thunderbolt,
Upon his silvery pinions gliding,
The Eagle with his grasping claws
    Stoops for his prey.
He rends and tears and beats his wings,
And snow-white swans-down falls to Earth . . .
    No more! No more.

    Appear!
    And there came forth . . .
The sun has set, the evening dark
Reveals a host of burning stars
    In heaven's arc.
And fiery, fleeting meteors
Hurl downwards, in a glistening clew,
    From realms
On high: they cheer the watcher's gaze
Like warm and welcome firelight:
One falls upon a darkened house,
Borne thither by the wind: it catches—
    The town's ablaze!
A smoky, soot-black column rears,
And flames, like scarlet waves, pour forth . . .
    No more! No more.

    Appear!
    And there came forth . . .
Beset by cares and lust for gold,

The merchant at his tally beads
    Makes up his sums:
He grudges all his partners' gain
As he apportions out the wares,
    And sleepless sits,
As hour by hour the voyage charts
He cons: surveys with greedy gaze
The ocean and its billowing waves,
Descrying there his distant ship.
    Through tears of joy he spies
Her sails and flags, her cannon's flare:
But near the wharf—a hidden shoal . . .
    No more! No more.

    Appear!
    And there came forth . . .
The worthy ploughman in his fields
Fears God and waits on Nature's will,
    Spares not his sweat;
In summer's heat the plough he follows,
Then supples well and stores the traces,
    And bides the season,
Awaiting increase from the seeds
That he with his own hand has sown.
The golden ears of wheat are full,
They bend and sway like ocean waves,
    And heaven's shade
Gives blessing to his honest toil;
A cloud then spills both hail and ruin . . .
    No more! No more.

    Appear!
    And there came forth . . .
Young man and maiden, newly wed,
All golden, shining, shadowless,
    Their nuptial chains—
In Love's pure blessedness they drown;
A conqueror and suer both,
    The worthy groom
Now melts in ecstasy of love,
And to her charms surrenders all,
Forgetting there his former cares,

Salutes his lover's lips, her hands,
        And, through the veil,
His hand, outstretched, has grasped the prize;
Dame Death rears up with gleaming scythe . . .
        No more! No more.

                Appear!
        And there came forth . . .
The Son of Fortune, proud and bold
In spirit fully arrogant
        And adamant,
Has scattered all opposing banners
And round his brow has gathered,
        Encircled,
Green laurels culled from many lands,
And, kingly rights annihilating,
Now drunk with heady fumes of power,
In every tribe the people's sway
        Usurps;
He harks not to good subjects' groans,
But reaches out to claim the crown . . .
        No more! No more.

Is not this world a magic play,
Wherein the lantern shadows change,
Enchanting and deceiving men?
Does not some lord or sorcerer
Or mighty mage divert himself
Thereby, his prowess vaunting,
As he with idle finger sets
The planets' course? Does he not call
All earthly creatures to behold
His dreams—and they but dreams themselves?

Why, Man, so arrogant though mortal,
So ignorant for all your lore,
Now soaring in your reason's pride,
Now crawling, bug-like, in the dust,
Why chase thus after fortune's phantoms
Which flicker into sight and, passing,
Entice us to the fatal feast?
Were it not best to scorn their gleam,

And laud instead the Master's hand
That made this world so fair of sight?

We may be—nay, we shall be—then,
Unmoved observers of His works
Whose will directs obedient Fate.
Let other eyes admire our course,
And let His hand direct our way
Who sets the suns and stars aspin:
He knows their end as He knows ours!
He orders it—and I ascend;
He speaks—and I descend once more.
This world's but dreams: the Dreamer—God.

(1803) Translated by A.L. & M. K.

Zlogór, Volkhv of Novgorod

Chorus
Boyán's disciple, grey-haired skald!
Arise o'er Vólkhov's sombrous river,
And let your harpstrings newly quiver
With ancient lays and lore recalled—
Freed from the dust of past resplendence—
Bemuse with wonders your descendants;
Bring on your harp old deeds to sight,
From darkness strike them with new light!

Skald
Hearken! From his dwelling in the southlands came Odin to the land of midnight sun. With him came Véles, and Zlogór the shaman, whose funeral libations flowed so free they formed a river, ever since hight Vólkhov; this river's currents lap his funeral mound, they writhe and twist like snake with scales of silver, they circle, like the raven or the owl.

Thus he, once spewed from out the bowels of Tophet, a creature fashioned of demonic guile, yet scion of the Slavic tribe, and mage within its fortress, by his arts did blind the people's eyes with conjurings and visions; from time to time would he transform himself, appear as thunder, lightning, wind or rainstorm. A crocodile—their volkhv, their prince, their priest.

By force and fear of him did he inspirit the ignorant to bow to black-horned god—to vile Perún—instead of unto Heaven, and with their prayers bring sacrifice in blood; but such as would refuse to make their off'rings he and his offspring, lurking 'neath the streams of swift Nevá, Ilmén' and deepest Mshága, Shelón or Ládoga, would drown, and thus destroy.

To shrive Zlogór's black soul came hell-born demons, but still so fearsome was his powers' fame, that when he died, good people of the northlands made sure to lay him face-down on his bier, and hide him there as well as they were able. So that the tyrant might not harm them more, they drove down through his heart a stake of aspen, then piled atop his grave a ponderous mound.

Yet even when his earthly life was ended, Zlogor did not cease making mischief here—as to this day you may hear tales related by goodwives and by aged crones alike. Deceits he wove, cabals he brewed and discord, and was the pet of many a worthy dame; full well he knew their cellars and their turrets, as birdlike he went flitting through the house.

Kikímora herself could never spy him; he took his ease curled up upon the stove, and oft would he the meal set by for evening devour, with great gnashing of his teeth. Or in the night, much to the master's wonder, he'd force a nag to gallop league on league; he'd weave and plait his favorite horse's forelock and bind its waving tail into a club.

Vadim and all the people were incited 'gainst Gostomysel by Zlogor himself, and thus between the Slav and the Varangian was strife ignited, in despite of sense; he also was it that forbade Dobrynia to baptize all the folk of Novgorod, to raise up holy altars on the hilltops, and then to drown their idols in the streams.

Next would he Yaroslav the Wise have hindered from setting forth the Code of Russian Law, then bade the folk to draw in heavy oxcart unto the veche, in good Marfa's stead, that spiteful crone Yagá, the crafty Bába—that evil witch—with iron pestle swift. And at Khutinsky Abbey he attempted to burn Iván the Dread with flames from hell.

So to this day he plays his pranks at Zvanka, weaves fantasies of shadows in the night: he creeps down to the Volkhov with the moonrise, in golden moonbeams paints there hills and trees; his visage, bending down, is limned in brightness with trailing dreadlocks, and with snow-white beard, he flickers in the current—or, reposing in darkness 'neath his mound, like thunder snores.

(1813) Translated by A.L. & M. K.

Alexander Sergeevich Pushkin
(1799-1837)

O UT OF SHEER RESPECT for tradition one ought to begin any selection from Pushkin's *oeuvre* by offering at least one of his lyrical poems simply because he is considered to this day Russia's foremost poet. Every Russian schoolchild knows that Pushkin's favorite season was autumn, hence our first choice—his most famous autumnal poem—*Autumn: a Fragment*. The trouble with received knowledge is that it often petrifies thinking, and the average Russian schoolchild rarely gets beyond the poem's first stanza (the only one published in school anthologies) to the entire text which embodies Pushkin's musings on the Romantics' notion of the "moment of inspiration," during which unseen forces guide the poet as he creates a new and fantastic world of verbal brilliance. Writing this work on his beloved estate Boldino in the early 1830's, Pushkin reveals later on in the poem that he is no longer enslaved by ordinary Romantic themes or satisfied by the tenets of Romantic discovery, which for him had already become cliches. To illustrate this he chooses one of the most characteristic Romantic genres—the fragment—and describes the process that normally induces the *inspired* state of mind for his persona, and which happens for him most naturally in the autumn months. Yet when he reaches this creative state the poet's persona is paradoxically left with no path to follow. A ship under way is the work's culminating metaphor for poetic inspiration, but the unanswered question "Where shall we sail?" ends the poem; these words are followed not by a complete stanza, but by a series of dotted lines which verbally express nothingness rather than a higher or revealed truth. A prescient note of modern absurdity is struck by Pushkin. Reaching this end-point, the reader is forced to reflect upon the beginning— the incomparable description of a Russian October with which the poem opens—and to recognize in this "fragment" an exquisite poetic artifact, grander than any obscure fantastic world.

As epigraph to "Autumn" Pushkin chose the line "What nimble thoughts do not them brim my sleep-drowned mind?" from Derzhavin's pastoral masterpiece *To Eugene. Life at Zvanka*: Just as Pushkin a generation later was to celebrate the Russian landscape at Boldino, Derzhavin in this 1807 work unscrolls before the reader an enchanting celebratory catalogue of Zvanka's virtues, describing the course of one idyllic early summer's day on the estate. The concluding stanzas of Derzhavin's poem were long considered "flawed," given their abrupt shift in tone from the idyllic to the fey as the poet imagines the estate's eventual decay and an indifferent Nature's obliteration of his own tomb. In choosing as "Autumn's" epigraph the very line that begins this final section of *Zvanka*, Pushkin signals his understanding that this "flaw" was in fact the poem's essence, just as the "unfinished" stanza of "Autumn" carries that text's ultimate—absurd and, hence, fantastic—meaning.

A similar level of absurdity is struck in *The Bronze Horseman*, also set in autumn, but with prodigiously different workings of its agency. Written roughly at the same time and subtitled "A Petersburg Tale" this work is hailed in Russia as Pushkin's greatest narrative poem. Moreover the story has a dimension—its locale: the city of St. Petersburg—which embodies a theme of considerable wealth. One of the city's most potent symbols is the famed equestrian statue of Peter by Falconet, which in *The Bronze Horseman* becomes the incarnation of the monarch's great achievement, or more precisely of Peter's implacable will. His presence so charges the atmosphere of the poem's opening lines that, like the God of the Old Testament, he is not at first named directly, but referred to by the pronoun *He*. Further on Peter is called "The Idol," a deity embodying the vastness and colossal power of the Russian Empire to be sure, but also associated with History—and with Eternity itself.

The plot establishes a contrastive parallelism with Falconet's Horseman on one side and the narrative's protagonist Eugene on the other. The resulting juxtaposition comes perilously close to parody. Peter the Great's god-like musings as he plans his city recall the first chapter of Genesis, and in fact Petersburg seems almost to spring into being at his word, created in his image. But Eugene is a man writ small, reduced to virtual non-entity. His family name is not given; he has lost any connection with his forbears and lineage, has no history himself and aspires to create none. He occupies a lowly position on any scale used to measure such things: he is poor, with no great ambitions or talents, his needs are modest and his dream of marital bliss and small comforts fulfills them all.

Eugene does have one quality that the Horseman lacks, and which is essential for our sympathy. He is human: the statue is literally and figuratively *inhuman*. Larger than life, Peter's image is a demi-god, the Idol, the master of Destiny who inspires adulation, awe and also terror. And here we must feel the great historical impact on Russia—for good or ill—of Peter's reforms, and of their steep price. Peter's dream city on the banks of the Neva is juxtaposed with the real city in which Eugene must live, and which is subject to devastating floods: the great monarch's conquest of Nature is not without its setbacks. The Horseman remains secure in his saddle, but the powerless Eugene, distractedly mounted backwards on a stone lion, sees all *his* dreams literally washed away. The particular form of Eugene's resulting madness with its echoes of *Don Juan* heightens this contrast to an absurd degree.

There are, however, not two but three personages occupying the narrative space of *The Bronze Horseman*, the last represented by the poet-narrator himself. Incidentally, the original is fully executed in verse. We have chosen to render only the prologue in its rhymed iambic tetrameter, rendering its narrative section in metered (iambic octameter) prose. The poet's paean to Peter's city (beginning with "I love thee, Peter's own creation . . .") comprises some of the most famous lines in all of Russian literature and establishes the poet as mediator between Peter and Eugene. He celebrates the former's indisputable accomplishment: this expression of St. Petersburg's uncanny beauty has never been equaled. Yet he also acknowledges the human tragedy that Peter's unwavering and merciless will made inevitable. The poet holds these two aspects in a delicate balance, with no attempt at resolution. And it is precisely the irreconcilability, the irreducible complexity of life, which is, if anything, the meaning of the poem. To insist on resolving the dilemma in *Bronze Horseman* is in fact to impoverish the poem—even to misread it, since its meaning in the profoundest sense is the dilemma it constructs.

Our third Pushkin selection, *The Queen of Spades*, is a fully representative sample of Pushkin's experimentation with the prose narrative, a form which he felt was produced by a creative process radically different from poetic inspiration. Elegant to the point of dryness, with a minimum use of descriptive modifiers (especially prevalent in Romantic poetry), the *Queen of Spades* succeeds in its kaleidoscopic density of narrative information, its unexpected twists of plot and meanings, shifts in the narrative time-line, and in the very meaning of concepts presented. The story, to which Petersburg again functions as an important backdrop, is a splendid victory of Pushkin's verbal narrative craft, involving a mock story of the supernatural (à la Hoffman), a mock romance, a mock murder with a mock weapon, a mock mystery—all framed by an elegantly symmetrical beginning and ending, both of which involve a depiction of a closed room in which different people play cards with very different outcomes. *The Queen of Spades* is also Pushkin's glorious achievement in the portraiture of the exceptional man (exceptional not in the term's superlative sense, but rather in the sense of an outsider) as the varied permutations of his persona appear to others and to himself. It is also one of the first major Russian prose works dealing with the subject of madness—a state of mind vibrantly explored in the volume by such varied writers as Gogol, Turgenev, Dostoevsky, Chekhov, et al—but also a state of mind elevated to the level of exceptionality by the Romantic movement itself. The focus of the plot revolves around the secret of three winning cards, a secret of unique interest to the protagonist of the story, Herman. A descendant of Germans (implicitly of those who helped Peter to found the city) who, instead of following reason and the disciplined work for which his forefathers were famous in Russia, goes insane due to his fixation on the three-card sequence and the idea of enriching himself with it. Petersburg functions as the midpoint as well as the final disposition of the protagonist's march towards insanity.

We thus have two narratives in which Pushkin's protagonists are driven to madness within (and perhaps by) this eerie locale. Such are, however, only the explicit degrees of madness Pushkin explores in these narratives. Switching our focus back to the first, we must note that this "Petersburg Tale" speaks to the motif so important in planning for any future, namely the irrational foundation of a utopian city built in the middle of nowhere and the historical consequences of this. Considering the fact that Peter chose the most inhospitable site—a place of swamps, shifting river banks, and floods—we must conclude it was *a priori* Peter's madness that forced future inhabitants of his creation to succumb to the same malady. Note that although we have preserved the poem's standard English title, Pushkin in fact does not use the word *bronze*. The poem's true title is *The Copper Horseman* and Peter's fame is thus rung not on sonorous bronze—a noble metal and a metaphor for lasting fame—but on tinny copper. Aware of its hollow sound, Pushkin may have intended Falconet's equestrian figure to morph in readers' minds into a tin soldier, or as Ecclesiastes would say: *vanitas vanitatum*. The city as a utopian and dystopian space for human habitation is richly represented in this volume—especially in the section devoted to Russian early modern utopian works, the writings of Gogol' and Dostoevsky, as well as in the fiction of the Symbolists—but *The Bronze Horseman* is the first major elaboration of such a theme in Russia.

Autumn
(fragment)

What nimble thoughts do not then brim my sleep-drowned mind?

Derzhavin

I

October's long been here—and the grove's already shaking
From off its naked boughs the leaves that cling there still;
The road grows harder as it feels the fall wind's raking.
The stream still runs its course and babbles past the mill,
But icebound lies the pond; my neighbor now is taking
His hunting pack in haste to fields far over hill,
The fall crop suffers from their wild and reckless playing,
And drowsing woods are startled by the hound's sharp baying.

II

The Autumn is my time: Spring's never to my taste;
The weary thaw, the slush, the reek—spring sets me sneezing;
My blood is roused, by sadness heart and mind oppressed.
Gruff Winter by my seasoned count is far more pleasing,

I love her snows; when by the moon your sleigh glides f⟨
And free and light—there is your sweetheart's ardor tea⟨
How fresh and warm she is, wrapped in that sable bed⟨
She grips your hand, she trembles, and her cheeks glow red.

III

How gay, our boots now shod with well-honed iron crescents,
To glide across the frozen rivers' mirror-glow!
And when the sparkling holidays demand our presence?...
But draw the line; full half a year of snow on snow—
When all is said and done, the very burrow's tenant,
The bear, grows bored with that. We can't forever go
A-sleighing with Armidas, however young and handsome,
Or sour at the stove, behind a double transom.

IV

O Summer fair! Alas, my love for you might grow,
Were not your heat and dust, your insects so assailing.
All higher sentiments of ours you soon bring low,
You harrow us, we wither like the meadows parched and failing.
How best to slake our thirst, how cool refreshment know,
No other thoughts have we—Dame Winter's end bewailing,
With wine and pancakes having sent her on her way,
We make her requiem with ice and with sorbet.

V

The days of waning Autumn almost none admires,
And yet, dear reader, I'll admit to you I'm drawn
To her calm beauty, to her softly glowing fires;
A slighted child, of whom her family's not fond,
She lures me to her side. If anyone inquires,
With Autumn's days alone I feel a joyous bond.
She offers much that's good; a not vainglorious lover,
I find my fancy really quite enamoured of her.

VI

How to explain this? She appeals to me, I think,
As might perhaps a delicate consumptive lass be
Appealing just to you. Condemned in death to sink,
Her days without revolt or rage serenely passing,
Her fading lips are smiling. And, on its very brink,
The chasm she sees not, her peril not yet grasping;
Life's crimson tincture on her visage yet may play.
Alive this moment, but tomorrow—lifeless clay.

VII

Enchantment of the eyes! O sweet yet mournful season,
Your splendors as they fade grow dear, and make me glad—
For in her waning days is Nature sumptuous, pleasing,
The forests all in crimson and in gold are clad;
Beneath their shade—the wind-rush, and a freshness breathing,
With coils of swirling haze are now the heavens spread,
A ray of sun is rare, the early frosts come searing,
And other still-faint signs disclose gray winter's nearing.

VIII

I bloom anew each time the leaves come whirling down;
Our frigid Russian air for me is healthy, bracing;
Anew I come to love my habits' daily round:
Sleep, wakefulness and hunger come in timely pacing;
With joy and lightness in my heart the humors bound,
I'm young again and blithe—desires through me are racing,
Again I brim with life—such is my organism.
(Kind reader, pardon this intrusive prosaism.)

IX

They bring my horse to me, and through the distant clearing
With flowing mane a-toss, he bears his rider on,
Beneath his gleaming hoof resounds with icy pealing
The valley floor, now frozen, and the crackling pond.
But then the brief day wanes, the hearthside embers yielding
A fiery glow—it brightly flares and then is gone,
But slowly gone—and here before it I sit reading,
The while with long-spun thoughts my fancy feeding.

X

And I forget the world—in sweet serenity
Then sweetly am I lulled by my imagination,
And thereupon does poetry awake in me:
My soul is stirred, opressed by lyric agitation,
It shivers and it chimes, and seeks, as in a dream,
To issue forth at last in streams of free creation.
And many guests then visit me in unseen swarm,
All old acquaintances, my musings gave them form.

XI

And through my slumbering mind do thoughts then boldly caper,
And nimble, flowing rhymes to meet them lightly course,
My eager fingers long for pen, my pen for paper,
An instant more—and forth comes freely flowing verse.

Thus sleep-drowned lies a ship becalmed in breathless vapor,
But look!—the boatswain calls, the crewmen stir, disperse,
Swarm up and down the masts, with sails at full wind's power
The giant now awakes, the cresting swell devours.

XII

It sails. Where shall we sail?..
....

The Bronze Horseman

A Petersburg Tale

(The event described in this tale is based on fact. Details of the flood have been borrowed from contemporary journals. The curious may have recourse to the acccount captured by V. N. Berkh)

FOREWORD

Upon a shore of trackless waves
Stood *HE*; immersed in thoughts, his gaze
Was fixed afar. The river's current
Rushed broadly by. A skiff made way
Along it on some lonely errand.
Along the mossy, marshy strand
Small blackened huts were wont to stand
In which the starveling Finn took cover,
And forest—midst this darkened land
Where mist-cloaked sun but dimly hovered—
Still murmured 'round.
            And thus HE thought:
From here the prideful Swede we menace,
Here shall a city-fort be wrought
To forge our haughty neighbor's penance.
Here Fate and Nature both ordain
We mount a westward window-pane,
Stand fast beside this ocean channel.
New flags, through once uncharted swells
To visit us now Fate compels,
And we shall keep our feast untrammeled.

A hundred years the city stood,
Once fledgling fort, now Northlands' wonder,
From marshy fen and shady wood
It rose in all its pride and splendor;

Where once, Creation's foster-child,
The Finn in humble skiff would wallow,
As he, alone on shorelines wild,
Cast wide upon the empty billow
His tattered nets—those shores along,
Now newly animate, there throng
Our comely mansions, lofty spires.
A horde of ships comes here to berth
From every corner of the Earth,
Each one rich mooring now requires.
In granite garments goes Neva;
Above it bridges arc, suspended;
With verdant gardens greenly splendid
Are nowadays her islands clad.
And now before this youthful city
Old Moscow dips her age-dimmed shield,
Thus to a new queen is befitting
That royal Dowager should yield.

      I love Thee, Peter's true creation,
I love Thy grave and graceful cast,
Neva's majestic undulation
Within its stone embankments clasped,
Thy iron railings' artful twining,
Thy midnights, pensive, dimly lit—
Transparent dusk and moonless shining—
When I within my chamber sit,
And write or turn to reading, lampless,
As clearly gleam the sleeping mansions
Along Thine empty streets, and bright
The Admiralty mast's alight,
When all nocturnal shade forbidding
Upon the golden skies to lour,
One dawn hies to another's bidding,
And bates to night but half an hour.
I love thy winters cruelly bracing,
Their frosts, that bite when no wind blows,
The sleighs that by Neva go racing,
Girls' cheeks more bright than any rose.
The flash, the stir of ballroom chatter,
The hiss as goblets foam and flow
When bachelors meet to feast and clatter,

The flaming punch, its pale blue glow.
I love the war-like animation
Where strife is play in Martial fields,
When Foot and Horse troops clash and wheel,
Their pleasing, ordered coloration
As in their serried ranks they sway,
Their flags, victorious though tattered,
The gleam upon their helms of copper,
Shot through and riddled in the fray.
I love Thee, Russia's bastion-city,
Thy ramparts' smoke and fearsome roar
When Northland's Queen—a gift most fitting—
A scion to the scepter bore,
When triumph o'er the foe once more
Rossiya hymns with joyful voices,
Or when Neva sheds Winter's vise,
And casts asea her dark blue ice.
And, sensing vernal days, rejoices.

Be splendid then, Great Peter's Port,
Unshakable, as is our nation.
The elements Thy favor court,
Untamed and wild from their creation,
The Finnish billows' will to thwart,
Their ancient quarrels, be forgotten.
Let not their fury ill-begotten
Disquiet Peter's timeless dream!

A time of terror it has been,
Still fresh in painful recollection . . .
Of it, my friends—for amity—
I now take up my retrospection.
My story will be full of woe.

PART I

Above a gloomy Petrograd November breathed the chill of autumn. Confined by handsome granite banks and splashing them with noisy billows, Neva was thrashing like a patient in a bed that gives no ease. It grew quite late and dark, the raindrops lashed the panes as if in anger. A doleful wind was blowing, howling. Young Evgeny by this time had left his friends and started home. I think we'll have our hero carry that name, it has a sound that's pleasing to the ear; and what is more, my pen has long been easy with its sound. His surname we won't need, though ages past it may perhaps have borne a luster, once resounding (thanks here to Karamzin) down through the annals of our native land. But nowadays it's quite forgotten by *le monde* and our young man lives in Kolomna, holds his place, avoids the swells and doesn't vex his head about his sleeping sires, or times forgotten long ago.

Thus, once at home, Evgeny shed his cloak, undressed, and went to bed. But it was long before he slept, as many troubling thoughts beset him. What were these thoughts? The fact that he was poor, and therefore through much labor would be constrained to win himself both independence and repute: that Heaven might have granted *him* more gold and wit— he had encountered God knows, his share of lucky clods, of muddle-headed layabouts who had an easy row to hoe, while *he'd* logged just two years in service. He noticed then the storm was not abating, and the river's crest had risen, was still rising, that some bridges must be down by now. Parasha and himself for two days, maybe three, must now be parted. Evgeny sighed a heartfelt sigh, sank deep in dreams, as poets do:

> "To marry? Well, why ever not? It is, of course, a solemn step, but what of that—I'm young and hale, I'll gladly toil from morn to evening. Somehow or other I'll procure a simple, quiet little nest and lodge Parasha snugly there. I'll put in one more year, perhaps, then get a better berth—and let Parasha manage family matters and raise our sons and daughters . . . With her hand in mine we'll start life's journey, and go our ways, until we die, a grandchild then may bury us . . ."

Such were his dreams. And all that night he felt oppressed, and willed—but vainly—the wind to howl less gloomily, the rain to beat upon the pane less angrily . . .

His weary eyes no sooner closed in sleep than the stormy mists of night dispersed, and pallid dawn announced the day... A frightful day!

All night Neva had battled seawards, fought the storm, yet failed to overcome its wild caprice . . . and lost the will to struggle . . . That dawn then found the river's banks aswarm with teeming crowds. They marveled at the spray, the towering waves, the waters' wrathful foam. But now Neva, its outlet to the gulf debarred by lashing northers, surged backwards in its course, enraged, aggrieved, and flooded all the isles; the weather rose from bad to worse, the swollen spate set up a roar, it seethed and steamed, a mighty cauldron—then suddenly in bestial frenzy, fell on the city. And before it all at once took flight, retreated, and all was empty—then the waters found their way into the vaults and rose to flood canals. Petropolis was whelmed like Triton, wading waist-deep in the main.

Assault! Attack! Malignant waves like thieves break through the window casements, as prows of empty boats now smash the glazing. Now hawker's trays with awnings sodden, with bits of shops, of beams and roofs, the goods attained through prudent trade, and destitution's faded trifles, and bridges borne off by the tempest, and coffins washed from flooded tombs—all swim the streets!

The people see God's wrath and bide His rod. Alas! All vanished, food and hearth, and shelter! What can we do?

In that same year of dread did Russia's Tsar, now gone. with all due glory reign. He stepped onto his balcony, cast down and grieved. He said "To countermand what God ordains no Tsar has warrant." He pensive sat, with mournful eye he gazed on this calamity. The city squares now stood like lakes, and streets into them broadly rushed like rivers, wild. The palace loomed, resembling then a gloomy island. From end to end, from streets nearby and far, the Tsar sent word: despite the peril of the rising spate, his generals set out to save the city folk, bemused by terror, and drowning at their very hearthsides.

Then—on the square that bore great Peter's name, just where a new built mansion had been raised up, and on its perron crouched, with paws up thrust, two Lion sentries keeping watch—astride now on a beast of marble, Evgeny sat, his arms crossed on his breast, immobile, hatless, pale. Poor man, his heart was overcome by deadly fear. Not for his own sake. He did not hear the now voracious wave that rose to lick his soles, nor heed the rain that lashed his features, nor yet the wildly howling wind that suddenly had filched his hat. His gaze, full of a bleak despairing, was fixed in one and only one direction, did not turn aside. Like mountains from the depths, bestirred and angered still, the waves reared up. Most fiercely then the wind was howling, wreckage churned . . . Great Heaven!

Alas—just on that very spot, right where those savage waves now break, just on the Gulf, had stood a fence in need of paint, a willow tree, the shabby cote where *they* had lived, the widow and her child, Parasha, his sweetest hope! Or but a dream? Is human life, perhaps, an empty vision, a thing of nothingness, a joke on Heaven's part that Earth must bear? And he, as if bewitched, as if enchained upon the marble Lion, cannot dismount. Around him now is nothing to be seen but waves! And with its back to him, uplifted on a height as yet unshaken, above Neva now sorely vexed, still looms with mighty arm outstretched the Idol on his steed of bronze.

PART II

But then, well sated with destruction, weary of this crude rebellion, Neva crept backwards, as she made her way surveyed with pride her doings; and heedlessly she let her booty drop. So might a highwayman, who with his savage band storms through a town: he breaks and enters, slashing, he crushes and despoils; then—shrieks and gnashing, rapine, fear and howls!... Yet burdened by his spoil, and fearing close pursuit, at last he falters. And now the bandits hurry homeward, dropping loot along the way.

The water ebbed, the pavement came to light once more, and our young man makes haste, his spirit quailing as he goes—with hope, with dread and longing—straight to the river, barely tamed. Yet prideful of their victory, the waters seethed in malice, just as if beneath them flames still burned, the foam still overspread them as before. Neva drew ragged breath, a charger returned from battle. My Evgeny looks, espies a skiff— thank God! He runs towards it, calls the boatman to his aid, who scorns the risk and for a mite agrees to ferry him across the fearsome billows.

Then long with practiced oar the boatman brooked the stormy combers. And every moment saw the little skiff and daring oarsmen seem to disappear in their troughs—at last they made safe landing on the distant beach-head.

The hapless youth flies down the well-known street to find familiar spots. He looks, there's naught to fix on. Horrid sight! Whatever meets his vision is heaped up, tumbled down, or simply gone. Some houses there were knocked askew, some quite destroyed, and others there the waves had overturned; and all about, as on a battlefield, the bodies lay. Evgeny, uncomprehending, rushes on. Now near to swooning with his fear, he flies to where—a folded missive tightly sealed, its news unknown and unforeseen—his Fate awaits. And now he races through the outskirts, and there's the bay, the nearby cote . . . But what is this?

He stops, returns, retraces every step and looks, in this spot should their dwelling stand. The willow's there... the gate beside it—gone, it seems. But where's the house gone? And, full of dark presentiment he walks the circuit, twice he walks it, debating loudly with himself— then strikes his forehead, starts to laugh.

The mists of night came down and cloaked the anxious byways; the city folk delayed their rest as all together they recalled the day just past.

                                    The rays of morning
gleamed from pale and weary cloudbanks upon the quiet capital, already
found no lasting trace of yesterday's despair. The royal glow of dawn dis-
guised the woe. All took up its accustomed course. Along the streets, now
unencumbered, the people went their ways with cool aplomb. The tribe of
penmen quit their nightly lodgings, set forth to their work. Tradesmen, hail
and brash, tenaciously uncovered all their stores Neva had drowned and
rifled. They schemed to make their losses good, and gouge their neighbors.
From the yards the boats are carried.

                        Count Khvostov,
a bard, beloved of the gods, already hymned in deathless verse the fate
Neva's embankments suffered.

But poor Evgeny, my poor youth . . . Alas, his mind was now unbal-
anced, could not prevail, prove master of this horrid shock. The stormy
roar Neva and all the winds had made still echoed in his ears. Black musings, but wordless, drove him on. He was beset by a tormenting dream. A
week went by, and then a month—he never sought his former lodgings. The
lease expired, the landlord let his corner out to some poor bard. Evgeny
never happened by to get his things. He soon became a stranger to the
world. He wandered throughout the day, slept on the dockside, and lived
on scraps from kitchen windows. The threadbare clothing that he wore
grew frayed, and moldered. Spiteful urchins threw their stones as he passed
by. Not seldom did the coachman's whiplash cut him, for he never seemed
to see them, or mark the roadway—simply failed to notice. He was made
deaf by inner tumult and its din. And thus his wretched life dragged on, not
beast, not man—no more at home with living men, not yet a specter . . .

                                         He slept
once down among the wharves. The summer days were winding downward
towards the fall. A chill wind blew. The murky rolling waves would splash
upon the wharf with restive foam, and tap the rain-slicked stairs, but feebly, as plaintiffs vainly tap the doors of judges who refuse to hear. The poor
tramp woke. How dreary: raindrops fell, a mournful wind was keening,
and through the dark of night, from far-off streets, the watchman gave
reply . . . Evgeny flinched: the memories of horrors past for *him* were real;
he rose to wander off, then halted suddenly, and fell to gazing quite slowly all around, a freakish terror on his face. He found himself before the
columns of a stately house. Its perron bore, with paws upthrust as though
alive, two Lion sentries keeping vigil. And opposite, against a darkened sky,
atop the warded cliff the Idol with his out-flung arm still sat upon his steed
of bronze.

Evgeny shuddered, then his reason cleared. In fear-struck recognition he knew the spot where once the flood had played, where predatory billows had surged around him, mutinous and cruel. The Lions and the square, and He who in the murk, unshaken, held his bronzen head uplifted, the One whose fatal will had built this city on the ocean verges...How fearsome was He in the circling mists! Upon his brow what thoughts are gathered, what power is in Him concealed! What fire animates his steed! Where do you gallop, prideful steed? Where will your hoof-beats land their mark? O mighty lord of Destiny—above the depthless void, did you not, with iron bit, make Rus to caracole on high and leap?

Around the idol's pedestal of stone the wretched madman paced, his wild eyes fixed upon the One whose gaze had once swayed half the planet. His breast contracted as he lent his head against the iron pale, his eyes were clouded over, a flame was coursing through his heart, the blood within him seethed. Morose before the haughty bronzen image, he clenched his teeth and made a fist, as if demonic force possessed him: "Take care, you wonder-builder," he then hissed, atremble in his spite, "I'll get you yet...!" Then suddenly he fled, in desperate haste retreating. It seemed to him the awesome Tsar, upon an instant flaming up in wrath, had slowly turned to face him... And Evgeny through the square, now emptied, ran headlong, hearing at his back—a sound like rolling thunder peals—the heavy, ringing hoof-beats clatter down the shaken cobble-stones. And by the pallid moon illumined, arm out-flung and pointing upwards, the Bronzen Horseman now pursues him on His thunder-gaited steed; and that whole night the wretched madman fled, at every turn he took the Bronzen Horseman followed him, pursued him with a heavy hoof-beat.

And from that day when, as might be, Evgeny came across that square, his face reflected inner consternation. Quickly to his heart he'd press his hand, as if to soothe the torment that he felt within. He'd doff his tattered forage cap, forbear to lift his flustered glances, and sidle off.

A tiny island can be seen offshore. At times a fisherman out trolling late will moor there with his net and tackle to cook his meager meal. Or else a civil servant comes to see this barren islet on his Sunday pleasure sail. No blade of grass now will grace this spot. The playful spate had driven there a shabby hut. It stood above the water, looking like a blackened hedge. Last Spring they hauled it off by barge. Inside the dwelling there was nothing but wreckage and decay. Stretched out upon the threshold of the hut they found my madman. Then and there they laid to rest his frozen corpse for kindness sake.

Translated by A.L. and M. K.

The Queen of Spades

The Queen of Spades signifies a secret misfortune.
FROM A RECENT BOOK ON FORTUNE-TELLING

CHAPTER ONE

> *And on rainy days*
> *They gathered*
> *Often;*
> *Their stakes—God help them!—*
> *Wavered from fifty*
> *To a hundred,*
> *And they won*
> *And marked up their winnings*
> *With chalk.*
> *Thus on rainy days*
> *Were they*
> *Busy.*

There was a card party one day in the rooms of Narumov, an officer of the Horse Guards. The long winter evening slipped by unnoticed; it was five o'clock in the morning before the assembly sat down to supper. Those who had won ate with a big appetite; the others sat distractedly before their empty plates. But champagne was brought in, the conversation became more lively, and everyone took a part in it.

"And how did you get on, Surin?" asked the host.

"As usual, I lost. I must confess, I have no luck: I never vary my stake, never get heated, never lose my head, and yet I always lose!"

"And weren't you tempted even once to back on a series . . . ? Your strength of mind astonishes me."

"What about Hermann then," said one of the guests, pointing at the young Engineer. "He's never held a card in his hand, never doubled a single stake in his life, and yet he sits up until five in the morning watching us play."

"The game fascinates me," said Hermann, "but I am not in the position to sacrifice the essentials of life in the hope of acquiring the luxuries."

"Hermann's a German: he's cautious—that's all," Tomskii observed. "But if there's one person I can't understand, it's my grandmother, the Countess Anna Fedotovna."

"How? Why?" the guests inquired noisily.

"I can't understand why it is," Tomskii continued, "that my grand-mother doesn't gamble."

"But what's so astonishing about an old lady of eighty not gambling?" asked Narumov.

"Then you don't know...?"

"No, indeed; I know nothing."

"Oh well, listen then:

"You must know that about sixty years ago my grandmother went to Paris, where she made something of a hit. People used to chase after her to catch a glimpse of *la vénus moscovite*; Richelieu paid court to her, and my grandmother vouches that he almost shot himself on account of her cruel-ty. At that time ladies used to play faro. On one occasion at the Court, my grandmother lost a very great deal of money on credit to the Duke of Orleans. Returning home, she removed the patches from her face, took off her hooped petticoat, announced her loss to my grandfather and ordered him to pay back the money. My late grandfather, as far as I can remember, was a sort of lackey to my grandmother. He feared her like fire; on hearing of such a disgraceful loss, however, he completely lost his temper; he pro-duced his accounts, showed her that she had spent half a million francs in six months, pointed out that neither their Moscow nor their Saratov estates were in Paris, and refused point-blank to pay the debt. My grandmother gave him a box on the ear and went off to sleep on her own as an indica-tion of her displeasure. In the hope that this domestic infliction would have had some effect on him, she sent for her husband the next day; she found him unshakeable. For the first time in her life she approached him with argument and explanation, thinking that she could bring him to reason by pointing out that there are debts and debts, that there is a big difference between a Prince and a coach-maker. But my grandfather remained adamant, and flatly refused to discuss the subject any further. My grand-mother did not know what to do. A little while before, she had become acquainted with a very remarkable man. You have heard of Count St-Germain, about whom so many marvelous stories are related. You know that he held himself out to be the Wandering Jew, and the inventor of the elixir of life, the philosopher's stone and so forth. Some ridiculed him as a charlatan and in his memoirs Casanova declares that he was a spy. However, St-Germain, in spite of the mystery which surrounded him, was a person of venerable appearance and much in demand in society. My grandmother is still quite infatuated with him and becomes quite angry if anyone speaks of him with disrespect. My grandmother knew that he had large sums of money at his disposal. She decided to have recourse to him, and wrote asking him to visit her without delay. The eccentric old man at once called on her and found her in a state of terrible grief. She depicted her husband's barbarity in the blackest light, and ended by saying that she pinned all her hopes on his friendship and kindness.

"St-Germain reflected. 'I could let you have this sum,' he said, 'but I know that you would not be at peace while in my debt, and I have no wish to bring fresh troubles upon your head. There is another solution — you can win back the money.'

"'But, my dear Count,' my grandmother replied, 'I tell you —we have no money at all.'

"'In this case money is not essential,' St-Germain replied. 'Be good enough to hear me out.'

"And at this point he revealed to her the secret for which any one of us here would give a very great deal..."

The young gamblers listened with still greater attention. Tomskii lit his pipe, drew on it and continued:

"That same evening my grandmother went to Versailles, *au jeu de la Reine*. The Duke of Orleans kept the bank; inventing some small tale, my grandmother lightly excused herself for not having brought her debt, and began to play against him. She chose three cards and played them one after the other: all three won and my grandmother recouped herself completely."

"Pure luck!" said one of the guests.

"A fairy-tale," observed Hermann.

"Perhaps the cards were marked!" said a third.

"I don't think so," Tomskii replied gravely.

"What!" cried Narumov. "You have a grandmother who can guess three cards in succession, and you haven't yet contrived to learn her secret."

"No, not much hope of that!" replied Tomskii. "She had four sons, including my father; all four were desperate gamblers, and yet she did not reveal her secret to a single one of them, although it would have been a good thing if she had told them—told me, even. But this is what I heard from my uncle, Count Ivan Il'ich, and he gave me his word for its truth. The late Chaplitskii—the same who died a pauper after squandering millions—in his youth once lost nearly 300,000 roubles—to Zorich, if I remember rightly. He was in despair. My grandmother, who was most strict in her attitude towards the extravagances of young men, for some reason took pity on Chaplitskii. She told him the three cards on condition that he played them in order; and at the same time she exacted his solemn promise that he would never play again as long as he lived. Chaplitskii appeared before his victor; they sat down to play. On the first card Chaplitskii staked 50,000 roubles and won straight off; he doubled his stake, redoubled—and won back more than he had lost. . . .

"But it's time to go to bed; it's already a quarter to six."

Indeed, the day was already beginning to break. The young men drained their glasses and dispersed.

CHAPTER TWO

"Il paraît que monsieur est décidément pour les suivantes."
"Que voulez-vous, madame? Elles sont plus fraîches."
FASHIONABLE CONVERSATION

The old Countess *** was seated before the looking-glass in her dressing-room. Three lady's maids stood by her. One held a jar of rouge, another a box of hairpins, and the third a tall bonnet with flame-coloured ribbons. The Countess no longer had the slightest pretensions to beauty, which had long since faded from her face, but she still preserved all the habits of her youth, paid strict regard to the fashions of the seventies, and devoted to her dress the same time and attention as she had done sixty years before. At an embroidery frame by the window sat a young lady, her ward.

"Good morning, *grand'maman*!" said a young officer as he entered the room. "*Bonjour, mademoiselle Lise. Grand'maman*, I have a request to make of you."

"What is it, Paul?"

"I want you to let me introduce one of my friends to you, and to allow me to bring him to the ball on Friday."

"Bring him straight to the ball and introduce him to me there. Were you at ***'s yesterday?"

"Of course. It was very gay; we danced until five in the morning. How charming Eletskaia was!"

"But, my dear, what's charming about her? Isn't she like her grandmother, the Princess Daria Petrovna . . . ? By the way, I dare say she's grown very old now, the Princess Daria Petrovna . . . ?"

"What do you mean, 'grown old'?" asked Tomskii thoughtlessly. "She's been dead for seven years."

The young lady raised her head and made a sign to the young man. He remembered then that the death of any of her contemporaries was kept secret from the old Countess, and he bit his lip. But the Countess heard the news, previously unknown to her, with the greatest indifference.

"Dead!" she said. "And I didn't know it. We were maids of honour together, and when we were presented, the Empress . . ."

And for the hundredth time the Countess related the anecdote to her grandson.

"Come, Paul," she said when she had finished her story, "help me to stand up. Lisanka, where's my snuff-box?"

And with her three maids the Countess went behind a screen to complete her dress. Tomskii was left alone with the young lady.

"Whom do you wish to introduce?" Lisaveta Ivanovna asked softly.

"Narumov. Do you know him? "

"No. Is he a soldier or a civilian?"

"A soldier."

"An Engineer?"

"No, he's in the Cavalry. What made you think he was an Engineer? "

The young lady smiled but made no reply.

"Paul!" cried the Countess from behind the screen. "Bring along a new novel with you some time, will you, only please not one of those modern ones."

"What do you mean, *grand'maman*?"

"I mean not the sort of novel in which the hero strangles either of his parents or in which someone is drowned. I have a great horror of drowned people."

"Such novels don't exist nowadays. Wouldn't you like a Russian one?"

"Are there such things? Send me one, my dear, please send me one."

"Will you excuse me now, *grand'maman*, I'm in a hurry. Good-bye, Lisaveta Ivanovna. What made you think that Narumov was in the Engineers?"

And Tomskii left the dressing-room.

Lisaveta Ivanovna was left on her own; she put aside her work and began to look out of the window. Presently a young officer appeared from behind the corner house on the other side of the street. A flush spread over her cheeks; she took up her work again and lowered her head over the frame. At this moment, the Countess returned, fully dressed.

"Order the carriage, Lisanka," she said, "and we'll go for a drive."

Lisanka got up from behind her frame and began to put away her work.

"What's the matter with you, my child? Are you deaf?" shouted the Countess. "Order the carriage this minute."

"I'll do so at once," the young lady replied softly and hastened into the ante-room.

A servant entered the room and handed the Countess some books from the Prince Pavel Alexandrovich.

"Good, thank him," said the Countess. "Lisanka, Lisanka, where are you running to?"

"To get dressed."

"Plenty of time for that, my dear. Sit down. Open the first volume and read to me."

The young lady took up the book and read a few lines.

"Louder!" said the Countess. "What's the matter with you, my child?

Have you lost your voice, or what . . . ? Wait . . . move that footstool up
to me . . . nearer . . . that's right!"

Lisaveta Ivanovna read a further two pages. The Countess yawned.

"Put the book down," she said; "what rubbish! Have it returned to
Prince Pavel with my thanks. . . . But where is the carriage?"

"The carriage is ready," said Lisaveta Ivanovna, looking out into the
street.

"Then why aren't you dressed?" asked the Countess. "I'm always having to wait for you—it's intolerable, my dear!" Lisa ran up to her room.
Not two minutes elapsed before the Countess began to ring with all her
might. The three lady's maids came running in through one door and the
valet through another.

"Why don't you come when you're called? " the Countess asked them.
"Tell Lisaveta Ivanovna that I'm waiting for her."

Lisaveta Ivanovna entered the room wearing her hat and cloak.

"At last, my child!" said the Countess. "But what clothes you're wearing . . . ! Whom are you hoping to catch? What's the weather like? It seems
windy."

"There's not a breath of wind, your Ladyship," replied the valet.

"You never know what you're talking about! Open that small window.
There; as I thought: windy and bitterly cold. Unharness the horses. Lisaveta,
we're not going out—there was no need to dress up like that."

"And this is my life," thought Lisaveta Ivanovna.

And indeed Lisaveta Ivanovna was a most unfortunate creature. As
Dante says: "You shall learn the salt taste of another's bread, and the hard
path up and down his stairs"; and who better to know the bitterness of
dependence than the poor ward of a well-born old lady? The Countess ***
was far from being wicked, but she had the capriciousness of a woman who
has been spoiled by the world, and the miserliness and cold-hearted ego-
tism of all old people who have done with loving and whose thoughts lie
with the past. She took part in all the vanities of the *haut-monde*; she
dragged herself to balls, where she sat in a corner, rouged and dressed in
old-fashioned style, like some misshapen but essential ornament of the ball-
room; on arrival, the guests would approach her with low bows, as if in
accordance with an established rite, but after that, they would pay no further attention to her. She received the whole town at her house, and
although no longer able to recognise the faces of her guests, she observed
the strictest etiquette. Her numerous servants, grown fat and grey in her
hall and servants' room, did exactly as they pleased, vying with one another in stealing from the dying old lady. Lisaveta Ivanovna was the household
martyr. She poured out the tea, and was reprimanded for putting in too
much sugar; she read novels aloud, and was held guilty of all the faults of

the authors; she accompanied the Countess on her walks, and was made responsible for the state of the weather and the pavement. There was a salary attached to her position, but it was never paid; meanwhile, it was demanded of her to be dressed like everybody else—that is, like the very few who could afford to dress well. In society she played the most pitiable role. Everybody knew her, but nobody took any notice of her; at balls she danced only when there was a partner short, and ladies only took her arm when they needed to go to the dressing-room to make some adjustment to their dress. She was proud and felt her position keenly, and looked around her in impatient expectation of a deliverer; but the young men, calculating in their flightiness, did not honour her with their attention, despite the fact that Lisaveta Ivanovna was a hundred times prettier than the cold, arrogant but more eligible young ladies on whom they danced attendance. Many a time did she creep softly away from the bright but wearisome drawing-room to go and cry in her own poor room, where stood a papered screen, a chest of drawers, a small looking-glass and a painted bedstead, and where a tallow candle burned dimly in its copper candle-stick.

One day—two days after the evening described at the beginning of this story, and about a week previous to the events just recorded—Lisaveta Ivanovna was sitting at her embroidery frame by the window, when, happening to glance out into the street, she saw a young Engineer, standing motionless with his eyes fixed upon her window. She lowered her head and continued with her work; five minutes later she looked out again—the young officer was still standing in the same place. Not being in the habit of flirting with passing officers, she ceased to look out of the window, and sewed for about two hours without raising her head. Dinner was announced. She got up and began to put away her frame, and, glancing casually out into the street, she saw the officer again. She was considerably puzzled by this. After dinner, she approached the window with a feeling of some disquiet, but the officer was no longer outside, and she thought no more of him.

Two days later, while preparing to enter the carriage with the Countess, she saw him again. He was standing just by the front-door, his face concealed by a beaver collar; his dark eyes shone from beneath his cap. Without knowing why, Lisaveta Ivanovna felt afraid, and an unaccountable trembling came over her as she sat down in the carriage.

On her return home, she hastened to the window—the officer was standing in the same place as before, his eyes fixed upon her; she drew back, tormented by curiosity and agitated by a feeling that was quite new to her.

Since then, not a day had passed without the young man appearing at the customary hour beneath the windows of their house. A sort of mute acquaintance grew up between them. At work in her seat, she used to feel him approaching, and would raise her head to look at him—for longer and longer each day.

The young man seemed to be grateful to her for this: she saw, with the sharp eye of youth, how a sudden flush would spread across his pale cheeks on each occasion that their glances met. After a week she smiled at him. . . . When Tomskii asked leave of the Countess to introduce one of his friends to her, the poor girl's heart beat fast. But on learning that Narumov was in the Horse Guards, and not in the Engineers, she was sorry that, by an indiscreet question, she had betrayed her secret to the light-hearted Tomskii.

Hermann was the son of a Russianised German, from whom he had inherited a small amount of money. Being firmly convinced of the necessity of ensuring his independence, Hermann did not draw on the income that this yielded, but lived on his pay, forbidding himself the slightest extravagance. Moreover, he was secretive and ambitious, and his companions rarely had occasion to laugh at his excessive thrift. He had strong passions and a fiery imagination, but his tenacity of spirit saved him from the usual errors of youth. Thus, for example, although at heart a gambler, he never took a card in his hand, for he reckoned that his position did not allow him (as he put it) "to sacrifice the essentials of life in the hope of acquiring the luxuries"—and meanwhile, he would sit up at the card table for whole nights at a time, and follow the different turns of the game with feverish anxiety.

The story of the three cards had made a strong impression on his imagination, and he could think of nothing else all night.

"What if the old Countess should reveal her secret to me?" he thought the following evening as he wandered through the streets of Petersburg. "What if she should tell me the names of those three winning cards? Why not try my luck . . . ? Become introduced to her, try to win her favour, perhaps become her lover . . . ? But all that demands time, and she's eighty-seven; she might die in a week, in two days . . . ! And the story itself . . . ? Can one really believe it . . . ? No! Economy, moderation and industry; these are my three winning cards, these will treble my capital, increase it sevenfold, and earn for me ease and independence!"

Reasoning thus, he found himself in one of the principal streets of Petersburg, before a house of old-fashioned architecture. The street was crowded with vehicles; one after another, carriages rolled up to the lighted entrance. From them there emerged, now the shapely little foot of some beautiful young woman, now a rattling jack-boot, now the striped stocking and elegant shoe of a diplomat. Furs and capes flitted past the majestic hall-porter. Hermann stopped.

"Whose house is this?" he asked the watchman at the corner.

"The Countess ***'s," the watchman replied.

Hermann started. His imagination was again fired by the amazing story of the three cards. He began to walk around near the house, thinking of its owner and her mysterious faculty. It was late when he returned to his humble rooms; for a long time he could not sleep, and when at last he did drop off, cards, a green table, heaps of banknotes and piles of golden coins appeared to him in his dreams. He played one card after the other, doubled his stake decisively, won unceasingly, and raked in the golden coins and stuffed his pockets with the banknotes. Waking up late, he sighed at the loss of his imaginary fortune, again went out to wander about the town and again found himself outside the house of the Countess ***. Some unknown power seemed to have attracted him to it. He stopped and began to look at the windows. At one he saw a head with long black hair, probably bent down over a book or a piece of work. The head was raised. Hermann saw a small, fresh face and a pair of dark eyes. That moment decided his fate.

CHAPTER THREE

Vous m'écrivez, mon ange, des lettres de quatre pages plus vite que je ne puis les lire.
CORRESPONDENCE

Scarcely had Lisaveta Ivanovna taken off her hat and cloak when the Countess sent for her and again ordered her to have the horses harnessed. They went out to take their seats in the carriage. At the same moment as the old lady was being helped through the carriage doors by two footmen, Lisaveta Ivanovna saw her Engineer standing close by the wheel; he seized her hand; before she could recover from her fright, the young man had disappeared—leaving a letter in her hand. She hid it in her glove and throughout the whole of the drive neither heard nor saw a thing. As was her custom when riding in her carriage, the Countess kept up a ceaseless flow of questions: "Who was it who met us just now? What's this bridge called? What's written on that signboard?" This time Lisaveta Ivanovna's answers were so vague and inappropriate that the Countess became angry.

"What's the matter with you, my child? Are you in a trance or something? Don't you hear me or understand what I'm saying . . . ? Heaven be thanked that I'm still sane enough to speak clearly."

Lisaveta Ivanovna did not listen to her. On returning home, she ran up to her room and drew the letter out of her glove; it was unsealed.

Lisaveta Ivanovna read it through. The letter contained a confession of love; it was tender, respectful and taken word for word from a German novel. But Lisaveta Ivanovna had no knowledge of German and was most pleased by it.

Nevertheless, the letter made her feel extremely uneasy. For the first time in her life she was entering into a secret and confidential relationship with a young man. His audacity shocked her. She reproached herself for her imprudent behaviour, and did not know what to do. Should she stop sitting at the window and by a show of indifference cool off the young man's desire for further acquaintance? Should she send the letter back to him? Or answer it with cold-hearted finality? There was nobody to whom she could turn for advice: she had no friend or preceptress. Lisaveta Ivanovna resolved to answer the letter.

She sat down at her small writing-table, took a pen and some paper, and lost herself in thought. Several times she began her letter—and then tore it up; her manner of expression seemed to her to be either too condescending or too heartless. At last she succeeded in writing a few lines that satisfied her:

> *I am sure that your intentions are honourable, and that you did not wish to offend me by your rash behaviour, but our acquaintance must not begin in this way. I return your letter to you and hope that in the future I shall have no cause to complain of undeserved disrespect.*

The next day, as soon as she saw Hermann approach, Lisaveta Ivanovna rose from behind her frame, went into the ante-room, opened a small window, and threw her letter into the street, trusting to the agility of the young officer to pick it up. Hermann ran forward, took hold of the letter and went into a confectioner's shop. Breaking the seal of the envelope, he found his own letter and Lisaveta Ivanovna's answer. It was as he had expected, and he returned home, deeply preoccupied with his intrigue.

Three days afterwards, a bright-eyed young girl brought Lisaveta Ivanovna a letter from a milliner's shop. Lisaveta Ivanovna opened it uneasily, envisaging a demand for money, but she suddenly recognised Hermann's handwriting.

"You have made a mistake, my dear," she said: "this letter is not for me."

"Oh, but it is!" the girl answered cheekily and without concealing a sly smile. "Read it."

Lisaveta Ivanovna ran her eyes over the note. Hermann demanded a meeting.

"It cannot be," said Lisaveta Ivanovna, frightened at the haste of his demand and the way in which it was made: "this is certainly not for me."

And she tore the letter up into tiny pieces.

"If the letter wasn't for you, why did you tear it up?" asked the girl. "I would have returned it to the person who sent it."

"Please, my dear," Lisaveta Ivanovna said, flushing at the remark, "don't bring me any more letters in future. And tell the person who sent you that he should be ashamed of . . ."

But Hermann was not put off. By some means or other, he sent a letter to Lisaveta Ivanovna every day. The letters were no longer translated from the German. Hermann wrote them inspired by passion, and used a language true to his character; these letters were the expression of his obsessive desires and the disorder of his unfettered imagination. Lisaveta Ivanovna no longer thought of returning them to him: she revelled in them, began to answer them, and with each day, her replies became longer and more tender. Finally, she threw out of the window the following letter:

> *This evening there is a ball at the *** Embassy. The Countess will be there. We will stay until about two o'clock. Here is your chance to see me alone. As soon as the Countess has left the house, the servants will probably go to their quarters—with the exception of the hall-porter, who normally goes out to his closet anyway. Come at half-past eleven. Walk straight upstairs. If you meet anybody in the ante-room, ask whether the Countess is at home. You will be told 'No'—and there will be nothing you can do but go away. But it is unlikely that you will meet anybody. The lady's maids sit by themselves, all in the one room. On leaving the hall, turn to the left and walk straight on until you come to the Countess' bedroom. In the bedroom, behind a screen, you will see two small doors: the one on the right leads into the study, which the Countess never goes into; the one on the left leads into a corridor and thence to a narrow winding staircase: this staircase leads to my bedroom.*

Hermann quivered like a tiger as he awaited the appointed hour. He was already outside the Countess' house at ten o'clock. The weather was terrible; the wind howled, and a wet snow fell in large flakes upon the deserted streets, where the lamps shone dimly. Occasionally a passing cab-driver leaned forward over his scrawny nag, on the look-out for a late passenger. Feeling neither wind nor snow, Hermann waited, dressed only in his frock-coat. At last the Countess' carriage was brought round. Hermann saw two footmen carry out in their arms the bent old lady, wrapped in a sable fur, and immediately following her, the figure of Lisaveta Ivanovna, clad in a light cloak, and with her head adorned with fresh flowers. The doors were slammed and the carriage rolled heavily away along the soft snow. The hall-porter closed the front door. The windows became dark. Hermann began to walk about near the deserted house; he went up to a lamp and looked at his watch; it was twenty minutes past eleven. He remained beneath the lamp, his eyes fixed upon the hands of his watch, waiting for the remaining minutes to pass. At exactly half-past eleven, Hermann ascended the steps of the Countess' house and reached the brightly-lit porch. The hall-porter was not there. Hermann ran up the stairs, opened the door into the ante-room and saw a servant asleep by the lamp in a soiled antique armchair. With a light, firm tread Hermann stepped past him. The drawing-room and reception-room were in darkness, but the lamp in the ante-room sent through a feeble light. Hermann passed through into the bedroom. Before an icon-case, filled with old-fashioned images, glowed a gold sanctuary lamp. Faded brocade armchairs and dull gilt divans with soft cushions were ranged in sad symmetry around the room, the walls of which were hung with Chinese silk. Two portraits, painted in Paris by Madame Lebrun, hung from one of the walls. One of these featured a plump, red-faced man of about forty, in a light-green uniform and with a star pinned to his breast; the other—a beautiful young woman with an aquiline nose and powdered hair, brushed back at the temples and adorned with a rose. In the corners of the room stood porcelain shepherdesses, table clocks from the workshop of the celebrated Leroy, little boxes, roulettes, fans and the various lady's playthings which had been popular at the end of the last century, when the Montgolfiers' balloon and Mesmer's magnetism were invented. Hermann went behind the screen, where stood a small iron bedstead; on the right was the door leading to the study; on the left the one which led to the corridor. Hermann opened the latter, and saw the narrow, winding staircase which led to the poor ward's room. . . . But he turned back and stepped into the dark study.

The time passed slowly. Everything was quiet. The clock in the drawing-room struck twelve; one by one the clocks in all the other rooms sounded the same hour, and then all was quiet again. Hermann stood leaning against the cold stove. He was calm; his heart beat evenly, like that of a man who has decided upon some dangerous but necessary action. One o'clock sounded; two o'clock; he heard the distant rattle of the carriage. He was seized by an involuntary agitation. The carriage drew near and stopped. He heard the sound of the carriage-steps being let down. The house suddenly came alive. Servants ran here and there, voices echoed through the house and the rooms were lit. Three old maid-servants hastened into the bedroom, followed by the Countess, who, tired to death, lowered herself into a Voltairean armchair. Hermann peeped through a crack. Lisaveta Ivanovna went past him. Hermann heard her hurried steps as she went up the narrow staircase. In his heart there echoed something like the voice of conscience, but it grew silent, and his heart once more turned to stone.

The Countess began to undress before the looking-glass. Her rose-bedecked cap was unfastened; her powdered wig was removed from her grey, closely-cropped hair. Pins fell in showers around her. Her yellow dress, embroidered with silver, fell at her swollen feet. Hermann witnessed all the loathsome mysteries of her dress; at last the Countess stood in her dressing-gown and night-cap; in this attire, more suitable to her age, she seemed less hideous and revolting.

Like most old people, the Countess suffered from insomnia. Having undressed; she sat down by the window in the Voltairean armchair and dismissed her maidservants. The candles were carried out; once again the room was lit by a single sanctuary lamp. Looking quite yellow, the Countess sat rocking to and fro in her chair, her flabby lips moving. Her dim eyes reflected a complete absence of thought and, looking at her, one would have thought that the awful old woman's rocking came not of her own volition, but by the action of some hidden galvanism.

Suddenly, an indescribable change came over her death-like face. Her lips ceased to move, her eyes came to life: before the Countess stood an unknown man.

"Don't be alarmed, for God's sake, don't be alarmed," he said in a clear, low voice. "I have no intention of harming you; I have come to beseech a favour of you."

The old woman looked at him in silence, as if she had not heard him. Hermann imagined that she was deaf, and bending right down over her ear, he repeated what he had said. The old woman kept silent as before.

"You can ensure the happiness of my life," Hermann continued, "and it will cost you nothing: I know that you can guess three cards in succession. . . ."

Hermann stopped. The Countess appeared to understand what was demanded of her; she seemed to be seeking words for her reply.

"It was a joke," she said at last. "I swear to you, it was a joke."

"There's no joking about it," Hermann retorted angrily. "Remember Chaplitskii whom you helped to win."

The Countess was visibly disconcerted, and her features expressed strong emotion; but she quickly resumed her former impassivity.

"Can you name these three winning cards?" Hermann continued.

The Countess was silent. Hermann went on:

"For whom do you keep your secret? For your grandsons? They are rich and they can do without it; they don't know the value of money. Your three cards will not help a spend-thrift. He who cannot keep his paternal inheritance will die in want, even if he has the devil at his side. I am not a spendthrift; I know the value of money. Your three cards will not be lost on me. Come . . . !"

He stopped and awaited her answer with trepidation. The Countess was silent. Hermann fell upon his knees.

If your heart has ever known the feeling of love," he said, "if you remember its ecstasies, if you ever smiled at the wailing of your new-born son, if ever any human feeling has run through your breast, I entreat you by the feelings of a wife, a lover, a mother, by everything that is sacred in life, not to deny my request! Reveal your secret to me! What is it to you . . . ? Perhaps it is bound up with some dreadful sin, with the loss of eternal bliss, with some contract made with the devil . . . Consider: you are old; you have not long to live—I am prepared to take your sins on my own soul. Only reveal to me your secret. Realise that the happiness of a man is in your hands, that not only I, but my children, my grandchildren, my great-grandchildren will bless your memory and will revere it as some-thing sacred. . . ."

The old woman answered not a word.

Hermann stood up.

"You old witch!" he said, clenching his teeth. "I'll force you to answer. . . ."

With these words he drew a pistol from his pocket. At the sight of the pistol, the Countess, for the second time, exhibited signs of strong emotion. She shook her head and raising her hand as though to shield herself from the shot, she rolled over on her back and remained motionless.

"Stop this childish behaviour now," Hermann said, taking her hand. "I ask you for the last time: will you name your three cards or won't you?"

The Countess made no reply. Hermann saw that she was dead.

CHAPTER FOUR

7 Mai 18**
Homme sans mœurs et sans religion!
CORRESPONDENCE

Still in her ball dress, Lisaveta Ivanovna sat in her room, lost in thought. On her arrival home, she had quickly dismissed the sleepy maid who had reluctantly offered her services, had said that she would undress herself, and with a tremulous heart had gone up to her room, expecting to find Hermann there and yet hoping not to find him. Her first glance assured her of his absence and she thanked her fate for the obstacle that had prevented their meeting. She sat down, without undressing, and began to recall all the circumstances which had lured her so far in so short a time. It was not three weeks since she had first seen the young man from the window—and yet she was already in correspondence with him, and already he had managed to persuade her to grant him a nocturnal meeting! She knew his name only because some of his letters had been signed; she had never spoken to him, nor heard his voice, nor heard anything about him...until that very evening. Strange thing! That very evening, Tomskii, vexed with the Princess Polina *** for not flirting with him as she usually did, had wished to revenge himself by a show of indifference: he had therefore summoned Lisaveta Ivanovna and together they had danced an endless mazurka. All the time they were dancing, he had teased her about her partiality to officers of the Engineers, had assured her that he knew far more than she would have supposed possible, and indeed, some of his jests were so successfully aimed that on several occasions Lisaveta Ivanovna had thought that her secret was known to him.

"From whom have you discovered all this?" she asked, laughing.

"From a friend of the person whom you know so well," Tomskii answered; "from a most remarkable man!"

"Who is this remarkable man?"

"He is called Hermann."

Lisaveta made no reply, but her hands and feet turned quite numb.

"This Hermann," Tomskii continued, "is a truly romantic figure: he has the profile of a Napoleon, and the soul of a Mephistopheles. I should think that he has at least three crimes on his conscience. . . . How pale you have turned. . . . !"

'I have a headache. . . . What did this Hermann—or whatever his name is—tell you?"

"Hermann is most displeased with his friend: he says that he would act quite differently in his place . . . I even think that Hermann himself has designs on you; at any rate he listens to the exclamations of his enamoured friend with anything but indifference."

"But where has he seen me?"

"At church, perhaps; on a walk—God only knows! Perhaps in your room, whilst you were asleep: he's quite capable of it . . ."

Three ladies approaching him with the question: "*oublie ou regret?*" interrupted the conversation which had become so agonisingly interesting to Lisaveta Ivanovna.

The lady chosen by Tomskii was the Princess Polina *** herself. She succeeded in clearing up the misunderstanding between them during the many turns and movements of the dance, after which he conducted her to her chair. Tomskii returned to his own place. He no longer had any thoughts for Hermann or Lisaveta Ivanovna, who desperately wanted to renew her interrupted conversation; but the mazurka came to an end and shortly afterwards the old Countess left.

Tomskii's words were nothing but ball-room chatter, but they made a deep impression upon the mind of the young dreamer. The portrait, sketched by Tomskii, resembled the image she herself had formed of Hermann, and thanks to the latest romantic novels, Hermann's quite commonplace face took on attributes that both frightened and captivated her imagination. Now she sat, her uncovered arms crossed, her head, still adorned with flowers, bent over her bare shoulders. . . . Suddenly the door opened, and Hermann entered. She shuddered.

"Where have you been?" she asked in a frightened whisper.

"In the old Countess' bedroom," Hermann answered: "I have just left it. The Countess is dead."

"Good God! What are you saying?"

"And it seems," Hermann continued, "that I am the cause of her death."

Lisaveta Ivanovna looked at him, and the words of Tomskii echoed in her mind: "he has at least three crimes on his conscience"! Hermann sat down beside her on the window sill and told her everything.

Lisaveta Ivanovna listened to him with horror. So those passionate letters, those ardent demands, the whole impertinent and obstinate pursuit— all that was not love! Money—that was what his soul craved for! It was not she who could satisfy his desire and make him happy! The poor ward had been nothing but the unknowing assistant of a brigand, of the murderer of her aged benefactress! . . . She wept bitterly, in an agony of belated repentance. Hermann looked at her in silence; his heart was also tormented; but neither the tears of the poor girl nor the astounding charm of her grief disturbed his hardened soul. He felt no remorse at the thought of the dead old lady. He felt dismay for only one thing: the irretrievable loss of the secret upon which he had relied for enrichment.

"You are a monster!" Lisaveta Ivanovna said at last.

"I did not wish for her death," Hermann answered. "My pistol wasn't loaded."

They were silent.

The day began to break. Lisaveta Ivanovna extinguished the flickering candle. A pale light lit up her room. She wiped her tear-stained eyes and raised them to Hermann: he sat by the window, his arms folded and with a grim frown on his face. In this position he bore an astonishing resemblance to a portrait of Napoleon. Even Lisaveta Ivanovna was struck by the likeness.

"How am I going to get you out of the house? " Lisaveta Ivanovna said at last. "I had thought of leading you along the secret staircase, but that would mean going past the Countess' bedroom, and I am afraid."

"Tell me how to find this secret staircase; I'll go on my own."

Lisaveta Ivanovna stood up, took a key from her chest of drawers, handed it to Hermann, and gave him detailed instructions. Hermann pressed her cold, unresponsive hand, kissed her bowed head and left.

He descended the winding staircase and once more entered the Countess' bedroom. The dead old lady sat as if turned to stone; her face expressed a deep calm. Hermann stopped before her and gazed at her for a long time, as if wishing to assure himself of the dreadful truth; finally, he went into the study, felt for the door behind the silk wall hangings, and, agitated by strange feelings, he began to descend the dark staircase.

"Along this very staircase," he thought, "perhaps at this same hour sixty years ago, in an embroidered coat, his hair dressed *à l'oiseau royal*, his three-cornered hat pressed to his heart, there may have crept into this very bedroom a young and happy man now long since turned to dust in his grave—and today the aged heart of his mistress ceased to beat."

At the bottom of the staircase Hermann found a door, which he opened with the key Lisaveta Ivanovna had given him, and he found himself in a corridor which led into the street.

CHAPTER FIVE

That evening there appeared before me the figure of the late Baroness von V**. She was all in white and she said to me: "How are you, Mr. Councillor!"
SWEDENBORG

Three days after the fateful night, at nine o'clock in the morning, Hermann set out for the *** monastery, where a funeral service for the dead Countess was going to be held. Although unrepentant, he could not altogether silence the voice of conscience, which kept on repeating: "You are the murderer of the old woman!" Having little true religious belief, he was extremely superstitious. He believed that the dead Countess could exercise a harmful influence on his life, and he had therefore resolved to be present at the funeral, in order to ask her forgiveness.

The church was full. Hermann could scarcely make his way through the crowd of people. The coffin stood on a rich catafalque beneath a velvet canopy. Within it lay the dead woman, her arms folded upon her chest, and dressed in a white satin robe, with a lace cap on her head. Around her stood the members of her household: servants in black coats, with armorial ribbons upon their shoulders and candles in their hands; the relatives—children, grandchildren, great-grandchildren—in deep mourning. Nobody cried; tears would have been *une affectation*. The Countess was so old that her death could have surprised nobody, and her relatives had long considered her as having outlived herself. A young bishop pronounced the funeral sermon. In simple, moving words, he described the peaceful end of the righteous woman, who for many years had been in quiet and touching preparation for a Christian end. "The angel of death found her," the speaker said, "waiting for the midnight bridegroom, vigilant in godly meditation." The service was completed with sad decorum. The relatives were the first to take leave of the body. Then the numerous guests went up to pay final homage to her who had so long participated in their frivolous amusements. They were followed by all the members of the Countess' household, the last of whom was an old housekeeper of the same age as the Countess. She was supported by two young girls who led her up to the coffin. She had not the strength to bow down to the ground—and merely shed a few tears as she kissed the cold hand of her mistress. After her, Hermann decided to approach the coffin. He knelt down and for several minutes lay on the cold floor, which was strewn with fir branches; at last he got up, as pale as the dead woman herself; he went up the steps of the catafalque and bent his head over the body of the Countess. . . . At that very moment it seemed to him that the dead woman gave him a mocking glance, and winked at him. Hermann, hurriedly stepping back, missed his footing, and crashed on his back against the ground. He was helped to his feet. At the same moment, Lisaveta Ivanovna was carried out in a faint to the porch of the church. These events disturbed the solemnity of the gloomy ceremony for a few moments. A subdued murmur rose among the congregation, and a tall, thin chamberlain, a near relative of the dead woman, whispered in the ear of an Englishman standing by him that the young officer was the Countess' illegitimate son, to which the Englishman replied coldly: "Oh?"

For the whole of that day Hermann was exceedingly troubled. He went to a secluded inn for dinner and, contrary to his usual custom and in the hope of silencing his inward agitation, he drank heavily. But the wine fired his imagination still more. Returning home, he threw himself on to his bed without undressing, and fell into a heavy sleep.

It was already night when he awoke: the moon lit up his room. He glanced at his watch; it was a quarter to three. He found he could not go back to sleep; he sat down on his bed and thought about the funeral of the old Countess.

At that moment somebody in the street glanced in at his window, and immediately went away again. Hermann paid no attention to the incident. A minute or so later, he heard the door into the front room being opened. Hermann imagined that it was his orderly, drunk as usual, returning from some nocturnal outing. But he heard unfamiliar footsteps and the soft shuffling of slippers. The door opened: a woman in a white dress entered. Hermann mistook her for his old wet-nurse and wondered what could have brought her out at that time of the night. But the woman in white glided across the room and suddenly appeared before him—and Hermann recognised the Countess!

"I have come to you against my will," she said in a firm voice, "but I have been ordered to fulfil your request. Three, seven, ace, played in that order, will win for you, but only on condition that you play not more than one card in twenty-four hours, and that you never play again for the rest of your life. I'll forgive you my death if you marry my ward, Lisaveta Ivanovna. . . ."

With these words, she turned round quietly, walked towards the door and disappeared, her slippers shuffling. Hermann heard the door in the hall bang, and again saw somebody look in at him through the window.

For a long time Hermann could not collect his senses. He went out into the next room. His orderly was lying asleep on the floor; Hermann could scarcely wake him. The orderly was, as usual, drunk, and it was impossible to get any sense out of him. The door into the hall was locked. Hermann returned to his room, lit a candle, and recorded the details of his vision.

CHAPTER SIX

"Attendez!"
"How dare you say to me: 'Attendez'?"
"Your Excellency, I said: 'Attendez, sir'!"

Two fixed ideas can no more exist in one mind than, in the physical sense, two bodies can occupy one and the same place. "Three, seven, ace" soon eclipsed from Hermann's mind the form of the dead old lady. "Three, seven, ace" never left his thoughts, were constantly on his lips. At the sight of a young girl, he would say: "How shapely she is! Just like the three of hearts." When asked the time, he would reply: "About seven." Every pot-bellied man he saw reminded him of an ace. "Three, seven, ace," assuming all possible shapes, persecuted him in his sleep: the three bloomed before him in the shape of some luxuriant flower, the seven took on the appearance of a Gothic gateway, the ace—of an enormous spider. To the exclusion of all others, one thought alone occupied his mind—making use of the secret which had cost him so much. He began to think of retirement and of travel. He wanted to try his luck in the public gaming-houses of Paris. Chance spared him the trouble.

There was in Moscow a society of rich gamblers, presided over by the celebrated Chekalinskii, a man whose whole life had been spent at the card-table, and who had amassed millions long ago, accepting his winnings in the form of promissory notes and paying his losses with ready money. His long experience had earned him the confidence of his companions, and his open house, his famous cook and his friendliness and gaiety had won him great public respect. He arrived in Petersburg. The younger generation flocked to his house, forgetting balls for cards, and preferring the enticements of faro to the fascinations of courtship. Narumov took Hermann to meet him.

They passed through a succession of magnificent rooms, full of polite and attentive waiters. Several generals and privy councillors were playing whist; young men, sprawled out on brocade divans, were eating ices and smoking their pipes. In the drawing-room, seated at the head of a long table, around which were crowded about twenty players, the host kept bank. He was a most respectable-looking man of about sixty; his head was covered with silvery grey hair, and his full, fresh face expressed good nature; his eyes, enlivened by a perpetual smile, shone brightly. Narumov introduced Hermann to him. Chekalinskii shook his hand warmly, requested him not to stand on ceremony, and went on dealing.

The game lasted a long time. More than thirty cards lay on the table. Chekalinskii paused after each round in order to give the players time to arrange their cards, wrote down their losses, listened politely to their demands, and more politely still allowed them to retract any stake accidentally left on the table. At last the game finished. Chekalinskii shuffled the cards and prepared to deal again.

"Allow me to place a stake," Hermann said, stretching out his hand from behind a fat gentleman who was punting there.

Chekalinskii smiled and nodded silently, as a sign of his consent. Narumov laughingly congratulated Hermann on forswearing a longstanding principle and wished him a lucky beginning. "I've staked," Hermann said, as he chalked up the amount, which was very considerable, on the back of his card.

"How much is it?" asked the banker, screwing up his eyes. "Forgive me, but I can't make it out."

"47,000 roubles," Hermann replied.

At these words every head in the room turned, and all eyes were fixed on Hermann.

"He's gone out of his mind!" Narumov thought.

"Allow me to observe to you," Chekalinskii said with his invariable smile, "that your stake is extremely high: nobody here has ever put more than 275 roubles on any single card."

"What of it?" retorted Hermann. "Do you take me or not?"

Chekalinskii, bowing, humbly accepted the stake.

"However, I would like to say," he said, "that, being judged worthy of the confidence of my friends, I can only bank against ready money. For my own part, of course, I am sure that your word is enough, but for the sake of the order of the game and of the accounts, I must ask you to place your money on the card."

Hermann drew a banknote from his pocket and handed it to Chekalinskii who, giving it a cursory glance, put it on Hermann's card.

He began to deal. On the right a nine turned up, on the left a three.

"The three wins," said Hermann, showing his card.

A murmur arose among the players. Chekalinskii frowned, but instantly the smile returned to his face.

"Do you wish to take the money now?" he asked Hermann.

"If you would be so kind."

Chekalinskii drew a number of banknotes from his pocket and settled up immediately. Hermann took up his money and left the table. Narumov was too astounded even to think. Hermann drank a glass of lemonade and went home.

The next evening he again appeared at Chekalinskii's. The host was dealing. Hermann walked up to the table; the players already there immediately gave way to him. Chekalinskii bowed graciously.

Hermann waited for the next deal, took a card and placed on it his 47,000 roubles together with the winnings of the previous evening.

Chekalinskii began to deal. A knave turned up on the right, a seven on the left.

Hermann showed his seven.

There was a general cry of surprise, and Chekalinskii was clearly disconcerted. He counted out 94,000 roubles and handed them to Hermann, who pocketed them coolly and immediately withdrew.

The following evening Hermann again appeared at the table. Everyone was expecting him; the generals and privy councillors abandoned their whist in order to watch such unusual play. The young officers jumped up from their divans; all the waiters gathered in the drawing-room. Hermann was surrounded by a crowd of people. The other players held back their cards, impatient to see how Hermann would get on. Hermann stood at the table and prepared to play alone against the pale but still smiling Chekalinskii. Each unsealed a pack of cards. Chekalinskii shuffled. Hermann drew and placed his card, covering it with a heap of banknotes. It was like a duel. A deep silence reigned all around.

His hands shaking, Chekalinskii began to deal. On the right lay a queen, on the left an ace.

"The ace wins," said Hermann and showed his card. "Your queen has lost," Chekalinskii said kindly.

Hermann started: indeed, instead of an ace, before him lay the queen of spades. He could not believe his eyes, could not understand how he could have slipped up.

At that moment it seemed to him that the queen of spades winked at him and smiled. He was struck by an unusual likeness . . .

"That old hag!" he shouted in terror.

Chekalinskii gathered up his winnings. Hermann stood motionless. When he left the table, people began to converse noisily.

"Famously punted!" the players said.

Chekalinskii shuffled the cards afresh; play went on as usual.

CONCLUSION

Hermann went mad. He is now installed in Room 17 at the Obukhov Hospital; he answers no questions, but merely mutters with unusual rapidity: "Three, seven, ace! Three, seven, queen!"

Lisaveta Ivanovna has married a very agreeable young man, who has a good position in the service somewhere; he is the son of the former steward of the old Countess. Lisaveta Ivanovna is bringing up a poor relative.

Tomskii has been promoted to the rank of Captain, and is going to marry Princess Polina.

Translated by Gillon R. Aitken; Edited by A. L.

Mikhail Iurievich Lermontov (1814-1841)

The soul-sick Demon, exile's Spirit,
Soared high above the guilty Earth,
And memories of better seasons
Swarmed by—of these he'd known no dearth,
Of days when, safe in pure Light's keeping
He shone—a brightest Cherubim,
When on her way the Comet, fleeting,
A smile of welcome and of greeting
Was pleased to interchange with him,
When through the drift of ageless ether
Athirst for knowledge, he had traced
Star caravans—whose cartwheels teetered
Above the emptiness of space;
Where he had known both Love and Faith,
The firstborn Son of all creation
Had felt no anger, vacillation,
His mind had still withstood Time's threat—
The empty eons aimless rolling . . .
So much, so much to recollect . . .
The will now failed him in recalling!

Long banished, he had wandered on,
Creation's wasteland gave no shelter,
The ages coursed by, one by one,
As minutes upon minutes pelter—
Each one monotonously drear.
Above this trifling earthly sphere
He ruled, sowed evil with no pleasure,
Nowhere opposed for his dark art,
His actions met no countermeasure,
Yet Evil came to dull his heart.

Above the grand Caucasian summits,
Now Heaven's exile, soaring, raced;
Kazbek—a diamantine facet
Below—in timeless snow-banks blazed.
And lower yet, an ebon crevice,
A fissure for a serpent's clevis,
Daryal unwound its ice-black lace.
And Terek, like a lion leaping—
A shaggy mane upon its spine—
Roamed wild. The beasts, the eagles
       sweeping
Their course along the azure height,
All hearkened to his thunderous calling;
In serried ranks the snow-white clouds
From southern climes, in gilded shrouds,
Accompanied its northward falling;
And closely packed massifs of stone
In deep dark slumber, full of dreaming,
Inclined their heads to Terek's moan
Above the river's billows gleaming;
The lofty castles on the steeps
Peered through the clouds like haughty
       sentries,
Who stand their post before the keep,
To Georgia's foe forbidding entry;
Untamed was God's world all around,
Estranged. And yet the Demon proud
Viewed all about him with derision,
Creation of his Maker's will
His lofty forehead scorned this vision,
Expressed no thought—precisely nil.

A proem to *Demon*, transl. by A.L. and M.K.

THIS SECTION CONTINUES with but a small sample of the creative craft of another superb Russian 19th-century poet who gradually switched his creative focus from poetry to prose: M. Iu. Lermontov. Of all Russia's nineteenth-century poets, it is Lermontov who at first glance seems to embody the Romantic image of the *poète-maudit*. Like Pushkin, Lermontov was both a superb poet and a rising master of the story and the novel. Lermontov, commisioned a cornet in the Life Guard Hussars at twenty, was only twenty-three when Pushkin's death in a duel inspired him to pen the elegy *On the Death of a Poet* (Na smert' poeta, 1837), which made him instantly famous. His bitter indictment of the Petersburg Imperial court—responsible, in his view, for Pushkin's demise—earned him exile to the Caucasus. These magnificent untamed mountains provide the setting for the highly Romantic verse narrative *The Demon* (Demon, 1839), the initial stanzas of which are quoted above in a new translation. This accomplished narrative poem—with dazzling highland imagery set against a truly cosmic panorama—is imbued with Miltonic pathos and Byronic loneliness, both embraced by the poet in his own life and art with grim earnestness. Also set in the Caucasus is the work of Lermontov best known in the west: the novel *A Hero of Our Time* (Geroi nashego vremeni, 1840) which is considered by many to be a pioneering work of psychological realism in Russian literature; in its period it stands on a par with Pushkin's earlier verse novel *Eugene Onegin* (Evgeny Onegin). While relishing *A Hero of our Time* as one of the greatest works of nineteenth-century fiction, what most Russians remember about the novel is that in one of its chapters Lermontov predicts with unsettling prescience the place and circumstances of his own death in the Caucasus. At the age of twenty-seven Lermontov, like his idol Pushkin at thirty-seven, was to be killed in a duel.

Only two complete short works representative of Lermontov's art are in this volume, one of poetry and the other of prose, though such a selection is doubtless an injustice to the scope of Lermontov's true accomplishments. First is the disquietingly prophetic poem *The Dream* (Son—in some translations called *The Triple Dream*), in which—a year before the event—the poet again foretells with eerie exactitude the locus of his own tragic death. The poem also represents Lermontov's uncanny ability to fold space and time in upon themselves, forming successive dream-layers of perception within a text.

The short story *Shtoss* (untitled in the manuscript) is another example of this sort of folding. Abandoning for once his beloved Caucasus, Lermontov sets the tale in the surreal urban labyrinth of St. Petersburg through which the protagonist, a painter named Lugin, must feel his way in his quest to transubstantiate ideal beauty—an ethereal female—both in art and life. Parenthetically it should be noted that Lermontov was a serious painter himself and some of the narrator's comments on the nature of the exceptional in art reflect his own views. Moreover, like Lugin, he apparently considered himself quite ugly. Nonetheless, romantic irony with respect to the protagonist's artistic quest and his fate permeates this text. For instance, in the mention of how Lugin's disturbed and excited mind produces the optical illusion that all other people are surrounded with and permeated by a yellow hue, yet by the story's end the narrator makes Lugin a part and part of that disturbed vision when he mentions that Lugin himself turned yellow. Also connected with the narrator's irony is the story's strange syllable "shtoss" (habitually used in lieu of a title, as the extant manuscript version bears none). *Shtoss* has more than one meaning in Russian: it is a card game (faro) which Lugin plays, but which also stands here for a surname. In addition the word mimics the phrase *Shto-s?* a colloquial elision of *Shto, sudar'?* or roughly "What did you say, sir?" At various stages of the story the narrator lets Lugin mistake one of these meanings for another.

Such irony with respect to his protagonist suggests that Lermontov directed his readers to grasp something that lay beyond Lugin's search— something encompassing narrativity itself and the story's enigmatic ending. This deliberate aspect is made clear by the story of Lermontov's single public reading of *Shtoss* in 1841: according to an account by E. P. Rostopchina, the author promised to read a just-completed *novel* during a mesmeric seance at her salon, and requested four hours for the presentation. He arrived bearing a huge tome and insisted that all doors to the room be locked and lights dimmed, creating in his audience a mood fraught with tension, an expectation of something monumental and mysterious about to happen. Whereupon Lermontov read through the brief manuscript in less than an hour, leaving an impression that he had planned the evening as an anti-climatic joke.

Lermontov died several months later and the event, as well as the manuscript, were forgotten for many years. When the story resurfaced, it was discussed as an unfinished piece precisely due to its abrupt ending. Nonetheless some scholars (Eikhenbaum, Mersereau) paid close attention to the fact that *Shtoss* is a story with a multilayered set of subtexts. They noted that Lugin, like Herman in the *Queen of Spades,* plays faro, and they surmised that Lermontov might have planned for him the same fate suffered by Pushkin's protagonist. References to Gogol's fiction were found to be especially abundant and evident, with many allusions to *Nevsky Prospect*, in which one of the protagonists, Piskarev, shares Lugin's notion of ideal female beauty (and commits suicide at the end of his story) and to *The Portrait*, in which a personage depicted in a mysterious painting seems to step out from its frame as a ghost. Some even wondered whether Gogol himself might have contributed to Lermontov's tale.

Be that as it may, it is clear that this accomplished story was considered unfinished for far too long and surely erroneously (as Vatsuro has also suggested recently). *Stoss* is closed in upon itself in various formal ways, and we know that it was read by the author himself as a finished work. A reader familiar with Petersburg's streets who attempted to retrace Lugin's steps would—in Petersburg's real topography—arrive at the very place from which the artist set out on his journey. Moreover the story's last sentence must be read as a pun (one of many Lermontov encoded into this text) on two Russian meanings of the verb *reshit'sia*, "to come to a decision" or "to go out of one's mind." Lermontov thus confronts us here with a *double denouement*, and his ending must be considered both *closed* and *open* at the same time. This does not mean that the author intended to resolve this duality: his end-focused "joke" enhances the enigma of the plot in a pre-modernist way and represents a clear advance over the host of concurrent works with the same subject matter—indeed, over the device of romantic irony itself.

The Dream

At blazing noon, in Dagestan's deep valley,
A bullet in my chest, dead still I lay,
As steam yet rose above my wound, I tallied
Each drop of blood, as life now seeped away.

Alone I lay within a sandy hollow,
As jagged ledges teemed there, rising steep,
With sun-scorched peaks above me, burning yellow,
I too was scorched, yet slept a lifeless sleep.

I dreamt of lights upon an evening hour,
A lavish feast held in my native land,
And fair young maidens garlanded with flowers:
Their talk—of me—was merry and off-hand.

But one of them, not joining their free chatter,
Sat timidly apart, bemused, alone
Sunk in a dream, her soul with sadness shattered:
God only knows what made her feel forlorn;

She dreamed of sand in Dagestan's deep valley,
That gorge in which a man she knew lay dead,
Black steam still rose above the wound's scorched hollow,
As blood streamed down and cooled like molten lead.

Translated by A. L.

< Shtoss >

1.

The Countess V . . . was hosting a musical evening. The finest artists of the capital were paying with their artistry for the honor of attending an aristocratic reception. Among the guests appeared several *literati* and scholars, two or three fashionable beauties, several society misses and elderly ladies, and one guards officer. A clutch of home-grown social lions struck poses around the doors of the second drawing room and by the fire. All was as usual; it was neither dull nor lively.

Just as a newly arrived singer was approaching the piano and unfolding her sheets of music . . . one of the young ladies yawned, rose, and went into the next room, which then was all but deserted. She was wearing a black gown, likely due to the Court's being in mourning. A diamond insignia fastened to a pale blue sash sparkled on her shoulder; she was of average height, graceful, slow and languid in her movements. Long, black, marvelous tresses set off her still young and regular but pale features, and on those features shone the stamp of thought.

"Good evening, Monsieur Lugin," said Minskaia, "I'm tired. Say something." She sank onto a broad divan by the fireplace. The gentleman to whom she had spoken took a seat opposite her and made no reply. They were the only two people in the room, and Lugin's cold silence showed clearly that he was not one of Minskaia's admirers.

"I'm bored," said Minskaia, and yawned again. "You see I don't play games with you," she added.

"And I'm having a fit of spleen!" answered Lugin.

"You feel like going to Italy again," she said after a short silence, "Isn't that so?"

Lugin for his part had not heard the question; he crossed his legs, unconsciously fixing his gaze on the marble-white shoulders of his interlocutor, and continued. "Imagine the misfortune that has befallen me! What could be worse for one such as myself, who has dedicated himself to painting? For two weeks now people have seemed yellow to me—and only people! It would be fine if it were everything—then there would be harmony in the general palette. But no! Everything else is just as it used to be; only faces have changed. At times it seems to me that people have lemons instead of heads."

Minskaia smiled. "Call a doctor," she said.

"Doctors can't help—it's spleen!"

"Fall in love!" (The look which accompanied this statement expressed something like the following: "I feel like tormenting him a bit!")

"With whom?"

"What about me!"

"No! You would be bored even flirting with me, and besides—to be frank—no woman could love me."

"What about that Italian countess, the one who followed you from Naples to Milan?"

"Well, you see," replied Lugin thoughtfully, "I judge others by my own feelings, and I'm certain that I don't err in doing so. I have in fact had occasion to awaken all the signs of passion in certain women. But since I know very well it is only thanks to artistry and skill that I am able to play on particular strings of the human heart, I derive no enjoyment from my success. I have asked myself if I could fall in love with an ugly woman—and it has turned out I cannot. I am ugly—consequently a woman could not love me, that is clear; artistic sensibility is more strongly developed in women than in us men; they are more frequently—and remain for much longer—under the sway of first impressions. If I have been able to arouse in a few women that which is called a *tendre*, it has cost me incredible effort and sacrifice. But since I always knew the artificiality of the feelings I inspired, and that I had only myself to thank for them—I have been unable to lose myself in a full, disinterested love; a little malice has always been mixed with my passions. This is all sad, but true!"

"What nonsense!" said Minskaia, but, glancing briefly at Lugin, she involuntarily agreed with him.

Lugin's features were in fact not the least bit attractive. In spite of the fact that there was much fire and intelligence in the strange expression of the eyes, you would not find in his overall appearance a single one of those traits which render a gentleman appealing in society. He was awkwardly and crudely built; he spoke abruptly and jerkily; the sickly and sparse hairs on his temples, the uneven color of his face (symptoms of a permanent mysterious ailment) all make him appear older than he really was. He had spent three years in Italy taking cure for morbid hypochondria; and although he had not been cured, had at least discovered a useful diversion. He had taken to painting; a natural talent, hitherto inhibited by the demands of work, developed broadly and freely under the influence of a vivifying southern sky and the marvelous works of the old masters. He returned a true artist, although only his friends were granted the right to enjoy his superb talent. His pictures were always suffused with a certain vague but oppressive feeling: they bore the stamp of that bitter poetry which our poor age has sometimes wrung from the hearts of its finest proponents.

It had already been two months since Lugin had returned to

Petersburg. He had independent means, few relatives, and several long-standing acquaintances in the highest social circle of the capital, where he intended to pass the winter. Lugin often called on Minskaia: her beauty, rare wit, and original views could not fail to make an impression on a man of intelligence and imagination. There was, however, no hint of love between them.

Their conversation ceased for a time, and they both seemed to be absorbed in the music. The singer engaged for the evening was performing "The Forest King," a ballad by Schubert set to the lyrics of Goethe. When she had finished, Lugin rose.

"Where are you going?" asked Minskaia.

"Good-bye."

"It's still early."

He sat down again.

"Do you know," he observed with some gravity, "that I am beginning to lose my mind?"

"Really?"

"All joking aside. I can tell you about this; you won't laugh at me. I have been hearing a voice for several days. From morning till night someone keeps repeating something to me. And what do you think it is?— An address. There—I hear it now: 'Stoliarnyi Lane, near the Kokukshin Bridge, the home of Titular Councilor Shtoss, apartment 27.' And it's repeated so rapidly, rapidly, as if the speaker were pressed for time . . . it's unbearable . . ."

He had turned pale. But Minskaia didn't notice.

"You don't see the person who is speaking, though, do you?" she asked absently.

"No. But the voice is a clear, sharp tenor."

"When did this begin?"

"Should I confess? I can't tell you for certain . . . I don't know . . . this is really most amusing!" he said with a forced smile.

"The blood is rushing to your head, and it's making your ears ring."

"No, no. Tell me—how can I be rid of this?"

"The best way" replied Minskaia after some thought, "would be for you to go to the Kokukshin Bridge and look for the apartment. And since some cobbler or watchmaker probably lives there, you could order something from him just for propriety's sake, and then when you return home, go to bed, because . . . you really are unwell!" she added, having glanced at Lugin's troubled face with concern.

"You're right," answered Lugin gloomily. "I will go without fail."

He rose, took up his hat, and went out.

She looked after him with surprise.

2.

A damp November morning lay over Petersburg. Wet snow was falling; the houses appeared dirty and dark and the faces of passers-by were green; coachmen, wrapped in red sleigh-rugs, dozed at their stands; their poor nags' long wet coats were curling like sheep's wool. The mist gave a sort of grayish-lilac color to distant objects. Along the pavement only rarely was heard the slap of clerks' galoshes— and from time to time noise and laughter rang out from an ale-cellar as a drunk in a green frieze coat and oilcloth cap was thrown out. Of course you would encounter such scenes only in the out-of-the-way parts of the city, for instance . . . near the Kokukshin Bridge. Across this bridge there now came a man of medium height, neither thin nor stout, not strongly built but with broad shoulders, wearing a greatcoat and in general dressed with taste. It was a pity to see his lacquered boots soaked through with snow and mud, but he, it seemed, did not care about this in the least. With hands thrust into his pockets and head lowered he walked along at an uneven pace, as though he were afraid to reach his goal or as if he had no goal at all. On the bridge he stopped, raised his head, and looked around. It was Lugin. His face showed the traces of mental exhaustion; in his eyes burned a secret anxiety.

"Where is Stoliarnyi Lane?" in an uncertain voice he addressed an idle cab driver with a shag rug pulled up to his neck who was whistling the "Kamarinskaia" as he drove past at a walk.

The driver glanced at Lugin, flicked his horse with the tip of his whip, and drove on.

This seemed very strange. Enough of this, is there really a Stoliarnyi Lane? Lugin stepped from the bridge and asked the same question of a boy who was running across the street with a half-liter of ale.

"Stoliarnyi?" said the boy. "Go straight along the Little Meshchanskaia and the first lane on the right will be Stolyarny."

Lugin was reassured. Coming to the corner, he turned right and saw a small, dirty lane along which there were no more than ten houses of any great size. He knocked at the door of the first small shop; when the shopkeeper appeared, Lugin inquired, "Where is Stoss's?

"Shtoss's? I don't know, sir. There is no such person here. But right next door is the house of the merchant Blinnikov, and further down . . ."

"But I need Shtoss's!"

"Well, I don't know . . . Shtoss!" said the shopkeeper, scratching the back of his neck, and then adding, "No, never heard of him, sir!"

Lugin set off to take a look at the nameplates on the houses himself; something told him that he would recognize the house at first sight, even though he had never seen it. He had almost reached the end of the lane, and not a single nameplate had coincided in any way with the one he had imagined, when suddenly he glanced casually across the street and saw over one of the gates a tin nameplate with no inscription whatsoever.

Lugin ran up to the gate, but no matter how he peered at it, he could make out nothing resembling a trace of an inscription erased by time. The nameplate was brand-new.

A yard-keeper in a discolored, long-skirted caftan was sweeping away the snow near the gate; he had a gray beard which had long gone untrimmed, wore no cap and had a dirty apron belted around his waist.

"Hey, yard-keeper!" cried Lugin.

The yard keeper grumbled something through his teeth.

"Whose house is this?"

"It's been sold," the yard keeper answered rudely.

"But whose was it?"

"Whose? Kifeinik's—the merchant."

"It can't be—this has to be Shtoss's!" Lugin cried involuntarily.

"No, it *was* Kifeinik's—it's only *now* that it's Stoss's.

Lugin faltered.

His heart began to pound, as if in presentiment of misfortune. Should he continue his search? Wouldn't it be better to stop it in time? Anyone who has never been in a similar situation will have difficulty understanding it: curiosity, they say, has ruined the human race; even today it is our cardinal, primary passion, such that all our other passions can be attributed to it. But there are times when the mysterious nature of an object gives curiosity an unusual power: obedient to it, like a rock cast off a mountain by a powerful arm, we cannot stop ourselves, even though we see an abyss awaiting us.

Lugin stood in front of the gate a long time. Finally he addressed a question to the yard-keeper.

"Does the new owner live here?"

"No."

"Well, then, where does he live?"

"The Devil only knows."

"Have you been yard keeper here a long time?"

"A long time."

"And are there people living in the house?"

"There are."

After a brief silence Lugin slipped the yard-keeper a ruble and said, "Tell me, please, who lives in apartment 27?"

The yard-keeper set the broom up against the gate, took the ruble, and stared at Lugin.

"Apartment 27? Who'd be living there? It's been empty God knows how long."

"Haven't they let it?"

"How do you mean, sir—not let it? They *have* let it.'

"Then how can you say that nobody lives there?"

"God knows! They don't live there, is all! They take it for a year, and then they don't move in."

"Well, who was the last to take it?"

"A colonel of the Injuneer Corps, or something like that."

"Why didn't he live there?"

"Well, he was about to move in, but then they say he was sent to Viatka—so the apartment's been empty ever since."

"And before the colonel?"

"Before him a baron—a German one—took it; but that one didn't move in either; I heard he died."

"And before the baron?"

"A merchant took it for his . . . ahem! But he went bankrupt, so he left us with just the deposit! . . ."

"Strange," thought Lugin.

"May I see the apartment?"

The yard-keeper again stared at him.

"Why not? of course you can," he answered and waddled off after his keys.

He soon returned and led Lugin up a wide, but rather dirty stairway to the first floor. The key grated in the rusty lock, and the door opened; an odor of damp struck them in the face. They went in. The apartment consisted of four rooms and a kitchen. Old dusty furniture which had once been gilt was stiffly arranged along walls covered in wallpaper depicting red parrots and golden lyres against a green background; the tile stoves were cracked here and there; the pine floor, painted to imitate parquet, squeaked rather suspiciously in certain places; oval mirrors with rococo frames hung in the spaces between the windows; in general, the rooms had a sort of strange, outmoded air.

For some reason—I don't know why—the rooms appealed to Lugin.

"I will take the apartment," he said. "Have the windows washed and the furniture dusted . . . just look how many spider webs there are! And you must heat the place well . . ." At that moment he noticed on the wall of the last room a half-length portrait depicting a man of about forty in a *Bohara* dressing-gown, with regular features and large gray eyes. In his right hand he held a gold snuffbox of extraordinary size. On his fingers a multitude of rings glittered. The portrait seemed to have been painted by a timid student's brush: everything—the clothes, hair, hand, rings—was very poorly done; yet, there breathed such a tremendous feeling of life in the facial expression—especially the lips—that it was impossible to look away.

In the line of the mouth there was a subtle, imperceptible curve of a sort which is inaccessible to art—unconsciously inscribed here, of course—which gave the face an expression by turns sarcastic, sad, evil, and tender. Have you never happened, on a frosty windowpane or in a jagged shadow accidentally cast by some object or other, to notice a human face, a profile sometimes unimaginably beautiful, and at other times unfathomably repulsive? Just try to get those features down on paper! You won't be able to do it. Take a pencil and try to trace on the wall the silhouette which has so struck you, and its charm will disappear; the human hand cannot intentionally produce such lines: a single, minute deviation, and the former expression is irrevocably destroyed. On the portrait's face was precisely that *inexpressible* quality which only genius or accident can produce.

"Strange that I only noticed the portrait at the moment I said I would take the apartment!" thought Lugin.

He sat down in an armchair, rested his head on his hand, and lost himself in thought.

The yard-keeper stood opposite Lugin for a long time, swinging his keys.

"Well then, sir?" he finally said.

"Ah!"

"Well then, if you're taking it—a deposit, please."

They agreed on a sum; Lugin gave him the deposit, then sent an order to his place to have his things brought over, while he himself sat opposite the portrait until evening; by nine o'clock the most essential things had been brought from the hotel in which Lugin had been staying.

"It's nonsense to think it impossible to live in this apartment," mused Lugin. "My predecessors obviously were not destined to move into it— that's strange, of course! But I took my own measures—I moved in immediately! And so?—nothing has happened!"

He and his old valet Nikita were arranging things in the apartment until twelve o'clock.

One ought to add that Lugin chose as his bedchamber the room where the portrait hung. Before going to bed he approached the portrait with candle in hand, wanting to take another good look at it. And in place of the artist's name, he found a word written in red letters: *Wednesday*.

"What day is today?" he asked Nikita.

"It's Monday, sir . . ."

"The day after tomorrow is Wednesday," said Lugin indifferently.

"Just so, sir!"

For God knows what reason Lugin became angry with him.

"Get out of here!" he shouted, stamping his foot.

Old Nikita shook his head and went out.

After this Lugin went to bed and fell asleep.

The next morning the rest of his things and a few unfinished pictures were brought over.

3.

Among the unfinished pictures, most of which were small, was one of rather significant size: in the middle of a canvas covered with charcoal, chalk, and greenish-brown primer was a sketch of a woman's head worth the attention of a connoisseur. Yet despite the charm of the drawing and the liveliness of the colors, the head struck one unpleasantly thanks to something indefinable in the expression of the eyes and the smile; it was obvious that Lugin had redrawn the head several times from different aspects, but had been unable to satisfy himself, because the same little head, blotted out with brown paint, appeared in several places on the canvas. It was not a real portrait; perhaps like some of our young poets, pining for beautiful women who have never existed, he was trying to embody on canvas his ideal angel-woman, a whim understandable in early youth, but rare in a person who has had any experience of life. However, there are people with whom experiences of the mind do not affect the heart, and Lugin was one of these unfortunate poetic creatures. The most cunning rogue or the most experienced coquette would have had difficulty duping Lugin, but he deceived himself daily with the naiveté of a child. For some time he had been haunted by a fixed idea—one which was torturous and unbearable, all the more so because his pride suffered as a result of it: he was far from handsome, it is true, but there was nothing repellent about him. Those acquainted with his intelligence, talent, and kindness even found his facial expression pleasant; but he was firmly convinced that the his degree of ugliness precluded the possibility of love, and he began to view women as his natural enemies, suspecting ulterior motives in their occasional caresses and explaining in a coarse, suggestive manner their most obvious good will.

I shall not examine the degree to which he was correct, but the fact is that such a state of mind excuses his rather fantastic love for an ethereal ideal—a love that is most innocent, but at the same time most harmful for a man of imagination.

That day, Tuesday, nothing special happened to Lugin: he sat at home until evening, although he needed to go out. An incomprehensible lassitude overwhelmed all his feelings: he wanted to paint, but the brushes fell from his hands; he tried to read, but his eyes flitted over the lines, and he read something quite different from what was actually printed; he had bouts of fever and chills, his head ached, and there was a ringing in his ears. When dusk came he did not order a candle brought to him: he sat by a window

which looked out on the courtyard; it was dark outside; his poorer neighbors' windows were dimly lit. He sat for a long time. Outside, a barrel
organ suddenly began to play; it played some sort of old German waltz;
Lugin listened and listened—and he became terribly sad. He began to pace
around the room; an unprecedented anxiety took hold of him: he felt like
weeping, like laughing... he threw himself on the bed and burst into tears.
He reviewed the whole of his past: he remembered how often he had been
deceived, how often he had hurt the very people he had loved, what a wild
joy had at times flooded his heart at the sight of tears which he had brought
to their eyes, now closed forever. And with horror he saw and admitted to
himself that he was unworthy of a disinterested and genuine love—and this
was so painful for him, so oppressive!

Around midnight he grew calmer, sat down at the table, lit a candle,
and took a sheet of paper and began a drawing—all was quiet. The candle
burned brightly and tranquilly; he was sketching the head of an old man,
and when he finished he was struck by the similarity between that head and
the head of someone he knew. He raised his eyes to the portrait hanging
opposite him; the resemblance was striking; he involuntarily shuddered and
turned around; it seemed to him that the doors leading into the empty parlor had squeaked; he could not tear his eyes from the door.

"Who's there?" he cried out.

He heard a rustle, like the shuffling of slippers, behind the door; plaster dust from the stove sprinkled down onto the floor. "Who is that?" he
repeated in a faint voice.

At that moment both leaves of the door began to open quietly, noise-
lessly; a chill breath wafted into room; the door was opening by itself—the
room beyond was as dark as a cellar.

When the doors had opened a figure in a striped dressing gown and
slippers appeared: it was a gray, hunched little old man; he moved slowly
in a cringing stoop. His face—long and pale——was motionless; his lips
were compressed; his gray, dull eyes, rimmed in red, looked straight ahead,
blankly. He sat down at the table, across from Lugin, pulled from his dressing gown two decks of cards, placed one of them opposite Lugin, the other
in front of himself, and smiled . . .

"What do you want?" said Lugin with the courage that comes from
despair. His fists clenched convulsively, and he was ready to throw the large
candleholder at the uninvited guest.

From the dressing gown came a sigh.

"This is unbearable," gasped Lugin. His thoughts were confused.

The little old man began to fidget on his chair; his whole figure was
changing constantly: he became now taller, now stouter, then almost
shrank away completely; at last he assumed his original form.

"All right," thought Lugin, "if this is an apparition, I won't yield to it."

"Wouldn't you like me to deal a hand of *shtoss*?" asked the little old man.

Lugin took the deck of cards lying in front of him and answered mockingly, "But what shall we play for? I want to warn you that I will not stake my soul on a card!" (He thought he would perplex the apparition with this.)". . . but if you want," he continued, "I'll stake a *klyunger* [a gold piece]. I doubt that you have those in your ethereal bank."

This joke did not confuse the little old man at all.

"I have this in the bank," he said, extending his hand.

"That?" said Lugin, taking fright and averting his gaze to the left. "What is it?" Something white, vague, and transparent fluttered near him. He turned away in repugnance. "Deal," he said, recovering a little. He took a *klyunger* from his pocket and placed it on a card. "We'll go on blind luck." The little old man bowed, shuffled the cards, cut the deck and began to deal. Lugin played the seven of clubs; it was beaten immediately. The little old man extended his hand and took the gold coin.

"Another round!" said Lugin with vexation.

The apparition shook his head.

"What does that mean?"

"On Wednesday," said the little old man.

"Oh! Wednesday!" cried Lugin in a rage. "No! I don't want to on Wednesday! Tomorrow or never! Do you hear me?"

The strange guest's eyes glittered piercingly, and he again squirmed uneasily in his seat.

"All right," he said at last. He rose, bowed, and walked out with his cringing gait. The door again quietly closed after him; from the next room again came the sound of shuffling slippers . . . and little by little everything became quiet. The blood was pounding inside Lugin's head like a mallet; a strange feeling agitated him and gnawed at his soul. He was vexed and offended that he had lost . . .

"But I didn't yield to him!" he said, trying to console himself. "I forced him to agree to my terms. On Wednesday?—But of course! I must be mad! But that's good, very good! He won't rid himself of me!

And he looks so much like that portrait! . . . Terribly, terribly like it! Aha! Now I understand!"

At this he fell asleep in his chair. The next morning he told no one what had occurred, spent the entire day at home, awaited the evening with feverish impatience.

"But I didn't get a look at what he had in the bank! . . ." he thought. "It must be something unusual."

When midnight had come, he rose from his chair, went out into the next room, locked the door leading into the vestibule, and returned to his seat. He did not have to wait long; again he heard a rustling sound, the shuffling of slippers, the old man's cough, and again his cadaverous figure appeared at the door. Another figure followed him, but it was indistinct and Lugin could not make out its shape.

Just as he had done the evening before, the little old man sat down, placed two decks of cards on the table, cut one, and prepared to deal: he obviously expected no resistance from Lugin; his eyes shone with an unusual confidence, as if they were reading the future. Lugin, completely under the magnetic spell of those gray eyes, was about to throw two half-imperials on the table, when suddenly he came to his senses.

"Just a moment," said Lugin, covering his deck with his hand.

The little old man sat motionless.

"There was something I wanted to say to you! Just a moment . . . yes!" Lugin had become confused.

Finally, with an effort, he slowly said, "All right—I will play with you—I accept the challenge—I am not afraid—but there is one condition: I must know with whom I am playing! What is your surname?"

The little old man smiled.

"I won't play otherwise," said Lugin, while at the same time his shaking hand was pulling the next card from the deck.

"*Chto-s?* [What, sir]," said the unknown one, smiling mockingly.

"Shtoss?—Who?" Lugin faltered; he was frightened.

At that instant he sensed a fresh, aromatic breath nearby; and a faint, rustling sound, and an involuntary sigh, and a light fiery touch. A strange, sweet, but at the same time morbid tremor ran through his veins. He turned his head for an instant, and immediately returned his gaze to the cards; but that momentary glance was sufficient to compel him to gamble away his soul. It was a marvelous divine vision: leaning at his shoulder there gleamed the head of a woman; her lips entreated him; and in her eyes there was an inexpressible melancholy . . . she stood out against the dark walls of the room as the morning star stands out in the misty east. Life had never produced anything so ethereal-heavenly; death had never taken from earth anything so full of ardent life; the vision was not an earthly being: it was made up of color and light rather than form and body, a warm breath in place of blood, and thought rather than feeling; nor was it an empty and deceitful vision . . . because these indistinct features were infused with a turbulent and avid passion, with desire, grief, love, fear, and hope. This was one of those marvelously beautiful women youthful imagination depicts for us—before which we fall to our knees in the high emotion accompanying ardent visions, and we cry, pray, and celebrate for God knows what reason—one of those divine creations of a soul in its youth, when with its surplus of power it creates for itself a new nature—better and more complete than the one to which it is chained.

At that moment Lugin could not have explained what had happened to him, but from that instant he decided to play until he won; that goal became the goal of his life; he was very happy about it.

The little old man began to deal. Lugin's card was beaten. A pale hand again drew the two half-imperials across the table.

"Tomorrow," said Lugin.

The little old man sighed gravely, but nodded his head in assent, and went out as he had the previous evening.

The scene repeated itself every night for a month: every night Lugin lost, but he didn't regret the money; he was certain that at least one winning card would ultimately be dealt to him, and for that reason he doubled his already large wagers. He suffered terrible losses, but nevertheless every night for a second he met the gaze and smile for which he was ready to give up everything on earth. He grew terribly thin and yellow. He spent entire days at home, locked in his room; he rarely ate. He awaited evening as a lover awaits a rendezvous: and every evening he was rewarded with an ever more tender gaze, a friendlier smile. *She*—I don't know her name—she seemed to take an anxious interest in the play of the cards; she seemed to be awaiting impatiently the moment when she would be released from the yoke of the old man; and each time Lugin's card was beaten, each time he turned to her with a sad look, he would find fixed upon him her passionate, deep gaze, which seemed to say, "Take courage, don't lose heart. Wait, I will be yours no matter what happens! I love you . . ." and a bitter, wordless sorrow would cast its shadow over her changeable features. And every evening, as they parted, Lugin's heart painfully contracted in despair and frenzy. He had already sold many of his belongings in order to sustain the game; he saw that in the not too distant future the moment would come when he would have nothing left to stake on the cards. It was necessary to make some sort of decision, or go mad. He did.—

Translated by David Lowe; edited by A. L. and M.K.

Ivan Sergeevich Turgenev
(1818-1883)

I am a writer of a transitional period,
and I am fit only for people
who are in a transitional state . . .

OF THE WRITERS CITED so far I. S. Turgenev was the first to travel exten-
sively abroad, though Gogol (introduced in the next section) had
done so at length before him; Turgenev was also the first major Russian
writer to die in emigration. In this regard he is the melancholy herald of a
tragic aspect of twentieth-century Russian cultural history—a period in
which a good half of Russia's brightest talents, men and women of extraordinary merits and accomplishments in many fields, would be forced to live
their lives abroad and die there as well. Gogol died in Moscow in 1852,
and shortly thereafter Turgenev was arrested, imprisoned for a month, then
forcibly confined for an additional sixteen-months exile to his own estate.
His offense had been writing an innocuous eulogy commemorating Gogol,
who was in official disfavor at the time. This draconian treatment was certainly a factor in Turgenev's eventual self-imposed exile. Finally—while in
no sense ever seriously affected by Gogol's style—there is yet a third aspect
which connects these two writers, namely that Turgenev, like Gogol, began
his immersion in literature as a poet, but gave it up early to become an
unquestioned master of prose. His achievements were so high in the latter
that popular consensus bestows on him a seat, along with Dostoevsky and
Tolstoy, in what some have called the "Holy Trinity of Russian Realism."
Yet, unlike Gogol, Turgenev never really gave up his fascination with the
succinct richness of poetic diction and, at the end of his life felt like uniting his very real achievements in prose with poetry again.

Turgenev was one of the first Russian writers to feel that the power of
his pen might affect the unfolding of actual history. For students of social
history, especially those who relish the petrified thought that Russia has
always lagged behind the West in social developments (a view which, incidentally, Turgenev himself was inclined to hold), it might be irksome to
recall that in the United States—the so-called bastion of democracy at the
time, and certainly very much admired by Turgenev—the loathsome institution of slavery was abolished a full three years *after* Tsar Alexander II
abolished serfdom in Russia. The young Alexander is known to have been
profoundly influenced in this connection by Turgenev's first famous collec-

tion of short prose, *A Sportsman's Sketches* (Zapiski okhotnika, 1852). Thematically devoted to a sympathetic portrayal of Russian peasants and exposure of the evils of serfdom, the work was undeniably instrumental in preparing the ground for Alexander's 1861 *Emancipation Proclamation*. By 1861 Turgenev was not only viewed as an active contributor to the great reform, but also as a first-rate novelist who had articulated contemporary life in three major works—the novels *Rudin* (1856), *A Nest of the Gentry* (Dvorianskoe gnezdo, 1859), and *On the Eve* (Nakanune, 1860). Now that Russia finally had a writer whose fiction could capture the aspirations of the times, it is ironic that Turgenev's best-wrought novel, *Fathers and Children* (Ottsy i deti, 1862), caused his prestige as a conduit of such aspirations to fall. Both radicals and conservatives saw in the personages of this work a lampoon of themselves and mercilessly attacked it, often for issues that lay outside its fictional universe. Pained by such a reception, Turgenev left his homeland and took up residence in Europe where he continued to write and to win a wide audience of admirers. Henry James, for instance, regarded Turgenev as his master and coined the appellation of "beautiful genius" to express this admiration.

Our volume attempts to provide a corrective to the notion that Turgenev's merits lay principally in the role of a writer occupied with social change. In fact, it would be surprising to expect of a writer whose prose was often said to read like poetry to be occupied with anything less than the *craft* of fiction itself. Indeed, it is precisely for the way his *Fathers and Children* was written and for the depiction of the trasformative drama within the soul of its protagonist, Bazarov, that Dostoevsky—Turgenev's otherwise lifelong nemesis—provided an isolated note of lavish praise within the heat of Russian polemics surrounding the novel's publication. It is then on Turgenev's art—and its collateral need for fantasy weaving—that the discussion of even his most socially influential works, such as the *A Sportsman's Sketche*s should be focused. If one takes up, for instance, his most memorable story *Bezhin Meadow* (Bezhin lug, 1851), available in nearly every collection of Russian short stories, one will encounter its traditional interpretation along the following lines: it is essentially a tale written by a budding realist foregrounding for the reader the mythopoetic world of the Russian folk: As peasant boys sit around their campfire artlessly narrating horror-stories and anecdotes of the supernatural, the reader should be supposedly aware that these are merely superstitions, even though such complacency is challenged at the end of the tale by the surprising fate of one of the boys. Rarely, however, it is noted that this story exists within a context of the wider meaning provided by the Russian title of the original collection, *Zapiski okhotnika*. None of this title's various English translations (*A Sportsman's Sketches*, *Diary of a Hunter*, etc.) has ever captured a crucial alternate sense of the word *okhotnik*. As Turgenev was well aware, the word—which commonly does mean "hunter"—also serves as a calque of the eighteenth-century French term *amateur*, signifying *connoisseur* or expert admirer, an enthusiast or devotee, and the title *Notes of a Connoisseur Enthusiast* would be truer to Turgenev's intentions than the traditional one, which focuses almost exclusively on the subject matter. The author is after far more elusive game here than snipe or grouse. Perhaps for this reason alone Turgenev never seems to have considered the collection as a whole, finished opus. It grew bulkier and bulkier as years went by as Turgenev added more and more stories, each representing varied degrees of immersion of the narrative space into the fantastic. *Bezhin Meadow*, one of the first to be composed for this collection, was an actual meadow on Turgenev's former estates. One of the last tales to be added was *A Living Relic* (Zhivye moshchi, 1874) a sympathetic depiction of a paralyzed Russian woman spending her entire adult life immobile in a village barn, who was considered by local folk as a living saint. One of the final works added by Turgenev was *Father Alexei's Story* (Rasskaz Otsa Alekseia, 1877). Here the principal narrator is a country priest. His story is framed by comments from the narrator—an aristocratic landowner—whose restraint foregrounds the intensity of Father Alexis' tale: the priest is grieving for the tragic fate of his son, Yakov. The boy's experiences with the supernatural, which intensify and become more harrowing as he grows older, are in his father's world explicable as satanic attacks on a Christian soul. The reader, however, is left with a more nuanced and ambivalent understanding which accommodates the pathological as well as the paranormal. Thematically, in *Father Alexis* Turgenev engages with the supernatural and the fantastic as they are experienced in the everyday world surrounding us.

Since we are fully cognizant of the fact that *A Sportsman's Sketches* are generally available to western readers, we chose to omit these wonderful tales from our volume. We offer instead his less well known *Phantoms* (Prizraki, 1864) and two selections from his last opus *Senilia: Poems in Prose* (Stikhotvorenia v proze, 1878-82). *Phantoms* can be read as autobiographical work, given its depictions of *ennui* (*toska*) and the author's complex, unsettling relationship with the French operatic singer, Pauline Viardot. An image that might have provided the genesis for the story is a painting at Baden-Baden, a spa frequented by Turgenev. The work is a fresco of a knight kneeling in front of a phantom female who drifts low above ground in front of him. Above both figures is a depiction of a circling bird and the backdrop is a forest with an old oak tree in the foreground. Whatever its origins the tale's fantastic elements are striking—indeed it is one of Russia's first works to be subtitled by the author as *Fantasy* in its generic sense, and we have chosen to abridge the work to give this greater prominence. The vampiric allusions of the narrator's encounters with the ghostly Ellis and the fantastic flight through space and time is the story's frame, within which the author expresses his distain for the barbarism of the past (especially focused on the Roman Empire) and the philistinism of the present. The latter is particularly found in Paris and in Petersburg, which Turgenev clearly sees as urban dystopias.

The two "poems in prose" we have added at the end represent the two oxymoronic poles of human existence, a dichotomy Turgenev starkly tackles at the end of his long creative life. The collection of *Senilia* from which they are taken attempts to combine prose with poetry, life and death, reality and dreams, beauty and ugliness. Alternating lyrical evocations of the beauty of life and putrid images of death which enter the proso-poetic narrator's space in the form of toothless hags, giant insectoid forms, etc., the collection as a whole is virtually unknown to both Russian and western readers, and cannot be thus considered Turgenev's lasting accomplishment. Yet for the purposes of this volume the chosen works clearly illustrate Turgenev's tragic realization at the end of his own life that no matter how satisfying the idyllic image of Russian village life he paints for us in the first "poem" might be, no matter how evocative this edenic utopia of emotional plenitude (recalling, in its painterly power, *The Orison on the Downfall of the Russian Land*) might be desirable, in the end—as the second "poem-in-prose" illustrates—it serves as a proof that Life itself is a self-perpetuating Fantasy, over which no poet's eye has any control whatsoever.

The Phantoms

(A Fantasy)

[ABRIDGED]

> *An instant—and the magic yarn is o'er—*
> *And again the soul is filled with hope.* . . .
> AFANASII FET

I

I could not sleep for a long time, constantly tossing and turning. "Damn that stupidity with the séance tables!—All it's done is irritate my nerves," I thought. Drowsiness overcame me gradually . . .

Suddenly it seemed to me that somewhere in the room a string had been plucked, softly and plaintively.

I raised my head. The full moon was low in the sky and shone directly into my eyes. Its light lay on the floor as white as chalk. The strange sound was distinctly repeated.

I lifted myself up on one elbow. A faint fear pricked at my heart. A minute passed, another . . . a cock crowed somewhere far off: from farther still another answered.

I lowered my head to the pillow. "Just see what you can do to yourself," again I thought. "Next you'll have ringing in the ears."

A bit later I fell asleep—seemed to fall asleep. I had an extraordinary dream. In this dream I was lying in my bedroom, on my bed—I wasn't sleeping and couldn't so much as close my eyes. Again the sound was heard . . . I turned . . . the moonlight on the floor quietly began to rise, straighten itself, round out at the top . . . before me, transparent as mist, unmoving, stood a pallid woman.

"Who are you?" with an effort I asked her.

A voice like the rustling of leaves answered: *It is I . . . I . . . . . . I come for you.*

"For me? But who are you?"

Come tonight to the foot of the wood, to the old oak. I will be there.

I tried to look more closely at the features of the mysterious woman— and suddenly shivered in spite of myself: a chill had come over me. And then I was no longer lying down, but sitting up in bed and there—where I thought the phantom had stood—the moonlight lay white upon the floor.

II

The day passed somehow or other. I recollect that I would sit down to read or to work . . . nothing held me. Night came on. My heart was pounding in anticipation. I went to bed and turned my face to the wall.

Why haven't you come?—the whisper was clear.

I quickly turned to look.

Again she was there . . . again this mysterious phantom. Motionless eyes in a motionless face—and a gaze full of sorrow.

Come!—the whisper was heard again.

"I'll come" I replied, helpless with dread. The phantom swung slowly forward, grew indistinct, rippling lightly, like smoke—and once more the moonlight serenely lay upon the floor.

III

I spent the next day in agitation. At supper I drank nearly a full bottle of wine, started for the porch, but turned back and threw myself onto my bed. My blood pulsed sluggishly through my body.

Once more the sound . . . I flinched, but did not look around. Suddenly I felt that someone behind me was tightly clasping me and babbling in my ear—*Come on then, come on, come on* . . . Trembling with fear, I moaned —"I'll come!"—and got up.

The woman stood bending over the headboard of my bed. She smiled faintly and disappeared. I had, however, managed to get a look at her face. I thought I'd seen her somewhere before; but where, when? I slept late and spent the whole day wandering over the fields. I came upon the old oak at the edge of the forest and looked attentively around.

As evening drew on I sat down by an open window in my study. My elderly housekeeper placed a cup of tea before me, but I didn't touch it . . . I was beset by doubt and asked myself: "Can it be that I'm losing my mind?" The sun had only just set, and not only the sky was dyed red, the very atmosphere was suddenly permeated with an almost unnatural crimson hue: the leaves and blades of grass, as if freshly lacquered, were motionless. In their petrified immobility, in their sharp brilliance of outline, in that combination of fierce radiance and deathly silence there was something strange and enigmatic. A rather large gray bird suddenly—with no sound whatsoever—flew up and lit on the very window sash. I looked at it—and it looked back at me askance with one round, dark eye. "Can *they* have sent you to remind me?" I wondered.

The bird immediately fluttered its soft wings and flew off as silently as before. I stayed by the window for a long time, but was no longer given over to doubt: It was as if I'd stepped into a magic circle—and an irresistible yet gentle force was drawing me on, just as a boat is carried on by the current long before nearing the waterfall. At last I roused myself. The crimson of the atmosphere had long since vanished, its hues had darkened, and the enchanted silence was broken. A breeze was rustling, the moon was rising more brilliant than ever in the dark-blue sky—and soon the leaves on the trees began their black and silver play in its cold light. My housekeeper entered the study with a candle, but a draft from the window caught it, and the flame died. I couldn't hold back any longer, leapt up, jammed my hat on my head and set off for the foot of the wood and the old oak.

IV

Many years ago the oak had been struck by lightning. Its crest was broken and withered, but it had continued alive for several centuries. As I approached it a cloud overtook the moon: it was very dark beneath the tree's broad limbs. At first I noticed nothing out of the ordinary; but I glanced to one side—and my heart sank. A white figure was standing near a tall hedge between the oak and the wood. My hair stood on end; but I gathered up my courage, and approached the trees.

Yes, it was she, my nocturnal visitor. As I drew near her the moon shone forth again. She seemed to be all woven of semi-transparent, milk-white mist—through her features I made out a branch softly swaying in the wind—only her hair and her eyes seemed slightly darker, and on one of the fingers of her folded hands shone a thin band of pale gold. I halted in front of her and attempted to speak, but my voice died in my chest, although I no longer felt any fear for myself. Her eyes turned to me: their gaze expressed neither sorrow nor joy, but some sort of lifeless concentration. I waited for her to speak a word, but she remained motionless and speechless and continued to gaze at me with her dead-fixed gaze. I grew terrified once more.

"I'm here!" I exclaimed at last, with an effort. My voice sounded hollow and strange.

I love you—came a whisper.

"You love me!" I repeated in amazement.

Trust yourself to me—again came a whisper in reply.

"Trust myself to you! But you're a phantom—you have no substance at all." A strange courage overcame me. "What are you made of? Smoke, air, mist? Trust myself to you! Answer me first, who are you? Did you once live on the earth? Where have you come from?"

Trust yourself to me. I'll do you no harm. Just say two words: 'Take me.'

I looked at her. "What is she saying?" I wondered. "What does it all mean? And how will she *take* me? Or attempt to?"

"All right then," I said aloud, and in an unexpectedly loud tone, exactly as if someone standing behind me had given me a push. "Take me!"

The words had not left my lips before the mysterious figure, some sort of suppressed smile causing her features to tremble, threw herself forward. She opened her arms and stretched them out to me. . . . I tried to jump aside; but I was already in her power. She seized me, my body rose a foot or two off the ground —and both of us set off smoothly and not too rapidly above the damp, still grass.

V

At first my head was spinning, and I involuntarily closed my eyes. . . . A minute later I opened them again. We were sailing along as before, but the wood was no longer visible: unfolding beneath us was a plain dotted with dark patches. With horror I concluded that we had risen to a fearsome height.

"I'm lost, I'm in Satan's power." This thought struck me like lightning. Until that instant the thought of diabolic possession, of the possibility of damnation, had not entered my head. We continued to speed along and, it seemed, were climbing higher and higher.

"Where are you taking me?" I moaned at last.

Wherever you like—my companion answered. She was pressed closely against me, her face nearly touching mine. Nonetheless I barely felt her touch.

"Take me back down to earth; I feel sick this high up."

Very well; but you must close your eyes and hold your breath.

I obeyed—and instantly felt myself falling like a stone . . . the wind whistled through my hair. When I came to myself we were once again smoothly sailing above the ground, low enough for our feet to brush the tops of the tall grass.

"Put me back on my feet" I began. "Where's the pleasure in flying? I'm not a bird."

I thought you would enjoy it. We have no other diversion.

"We? Who are you?"—There was no answer.

"You don't dare to tell me?"

A plaintive sound, like the one that had awakened me on the first night, trembled in my ears. Meanwhile we continued to move almost imperceptibly through the damp night air.

"Release me then!" I said. My companion slowly moved off and I found myself standing on my own feet. She halted in front of me and once more folded her hands. I became calmer and gazed into her face: as before it expressed a resigned grief.

"Where are we?" I asked. I didn't recognize my surroundings.

Far from your home, but you may be there in a single instant.

"How? Trusting myself to you again?"

I have done you no harm, and I will do you none. You and I may fly together until dawn, nothing more. I may carry you to any place you can imagine—to the ends of the earth. Trust yourself to me! Say it again: 'Take me!'

"Well then . . . take me!"

She embraced me once again, my feet left the ground—and off we flew.

VI

Where?—she asked me.

"Straight ahead, always straight ahead."

But the wood is in our way.

"Rise above the wood — but more slowly."

We shot upwards like a wood snipe alighting on a birch and sped onwards. Instead of grass, treetops now shimmered beneath our feet. It was marvelous to see the wood from above, with its bristly spine illuminated by the moon. It resembled some sort of immense, sleeping beast, and its resonant, ceaseless rustling accompanied us, like an incoherent muttering. Occasionally small glades could be seen, each with a handsome band of jagged black shadows along one side. . . . Now and then a hare would give its plaintive cry down below; above us an owl whistled, also plaintively. The air smelled of mushrooms and tree-buds, of meadow-sweet; the moonlight seemed to flow all around—cold and severe—the Pleiades shone just above our heads.

The forest was left behind; through the field stretched bands of mist: this was a river. We sped along one of its banks above bushes that were weighed down and motionless with dew. The swells of that river at moments glistened blue, at others they rolled darkly and almost malevolently. In places a delicate steam curled strangely above the surface—and the chalices of the water lilies glowed chastely and richly white with all of their full-blown petals, as if they were aware that they were out of reach. I took it into my head to pick one—and suddenly I found myself just above the surface of the river. . . . The damp struck me vindictively in the face as soon as I had broken the taut stem of the sturdy flower. We began to fly from bank to bank, like the sandpipers we occasionally roused and chased after. More than once we came upon families of wild ducks circled in open spots among the reeds. At most, one would dart its head out from under its wing, look about and anxiously thrust its beak back among the downy feathers, as another of the group would quack faintly, which made its entire body shiver. We startled a solitary heron: it bolted up from a willow clump, trailing its legs and with an clumsy effort flapping its wings. The fish were not rising—they too were asleep. I was beginning to get used to flying and even to find it pleasant; anyone who's flown in a dream will understand me. I began to concentrate my observations on that strange being under whose auspices I was having such an implausible experience.

VII-XVIII

She was a smallish woman with un-Russian features. Grayish-white, semi-transparent with barely perceptible shadings, she recalled a figure on an alabaster vase lit from within—and yet once more she seemed familiar.

"May I speak with you?" I inquired.

Speak then.

"I see you wear a ring on your finger: so you must have lived on earth —were you married?"

I paused . . . There was no answer.

"What is you name? Or at least, what was it?"

Call me Ellis.

"Ellis! An English name! Are you English? Did you know me in the past?"

No, I didn't.

"Then why do you come for *me*?"

I love you.

"And this is all that you want?"

Yes, when we're together, rushing along and circling through the pure air.

"Ellis!" I interjected. "Are you perhaps . . . a criminal, or a damned soul?"

My companion's head drooped.—*I cannot understand you*—she whispered.

"I abjure you in the name of God . . ." I began.

What are you saying?—she murmured uncomprehendingly. And then it seemed to me that her arm, which lay like a chill band about my waist, shifted slightly . . .

Don't be afraid—Ellis implored—*Don't be afraid, my dear one!*

Her face turned and moved closer to mine . . . I felt on my lips a strange sensation, like the touch of a delicate, soft sting . . . harmless leeches feel like that. < . . . >

A sudden daring flared up within me. "Take me to South America!"

To America I cannot. It is day there now.

"And you and I are birds of the night . . . Well, wherever you can then, but as far away as possible."

Close your eyes and hold your breath—replied Ellis—and we set off at a dizzying speed. The wind burst into my ears with a deafening noise. Then we halted, but the noise did not cease. Instead it became some sort of ominous roar, a thunderous din . . . *You may open your eyes now*—said Ellis.

IX

I obeyed. My God, where was I?

Above our heads clouds hung like heavy smoke; they bunched together and moved about like a flock of malignant monsters . . . and there, below us, was another monster: an enraged, yes truly enraged sea. A white foam spasmodically flashed atop the swells—raising shaggy crests, with a rough thunder it beat against an immense pitch-black cliff. The roiling storm, the icy breath from the rolling deep, the heavy crashing of the surf in which from time to time I seemed to hear something like howling, or like distant cannon fire, or alarm bells, the heart-rending shriek and grinding of the boulders, or the sudden cry of an unseen gull, the bobbing wreckage of stove boats on the murky horizon—everywhere death, death and horror. . . . My head began to spin, and near fainting I once again closed my eyes . . . "What is this? Where are we?"

On the south shore of the Isle of Wight, before the Blackgang Chine—the cliff where ships are so often wrecked—Ellis replied, for once in particular detail and, I felt, with some gloating relish.

"Take me away, away from here . . . Home! Home!"

I hunched over and buried my face in my hands. . . . I felt us rushing along at even greater speed than before; the wind now was not just whistling, but shrieking through my hair and clothing, my breath caught in my throat. . . .

You can stand on your feet, now—came Ellis's voice.

I tried to get hold of myself, of my thoughts . . . I felt the earth move under my feet and heard nothing, just as if everything had died . . . but my blood still surged through my temples with a faint internal sound, and my head continued to whirl. I straightened up and opened my eyes.

X

We were standing on the dam that spanned my own pond. Just before me, through the sharp leaves of a willow, I could see its wide smooth surface with wisps of downy mist arising here and there. To the right a field of rye gleamed dimly; to the left rose the trees of the orchard, elongated, motionless and drenched . . . morning had already breathed on them. In the clear gray sky, like ribbons of smoke, hung two or three sloping clouds; they seemed to have a yellowish tinge—an early, faint reflection of sunrise was falling on them from God knows where: the eye could not yet distinguish on the paling horizon the spot where dawn would break. The stars were disappearing: nothing moved as yet, although everything was awake in the enchanted quiet of early half-dawn.

Morning! It's morning!—exclaimed Ellis just above my ear . . . *Until tomorrow!*

I turned. . . . Lightly hovering, she floated past me, and suddenly lifted both arms above her head. For an instant her head, arms and shoulders flared up with warm, living hues; in her dark eyes trembled living sparks; a smile of secret bliss passed over her reddened lips—a beautiful woman suddenly appeared before me—but she fell backwards at once as if fainting, and melted like mist.

I was left rooted to the spot.

When I came to myself and looked about me, it seemed to me that the living, rosy hue that had come over my phantom had not yet disappeared, it was suffusing the air and washing over me . . . Dawn was breaking. Suddenly I felt extremely tired and set off for home. As I passed the barnyard I heard the first murmurs of the goslings (no birds awaken earlier than they do); along the roof-line a dawn perched on every bracepole—each was carefully and silently preening its feathers, sharply outlined against the milky sky. From time to time they would all take flight—and having flown about for a moment, would alight again in a row, without a sound . . . Twice from the nearby wood carried the hoarse cry of a black grouse settling into the dewy, dripping grass . . . My body was trembling slightly as I made my way to my bed and soon fell deeply asleep.

XI

The following night as I approached the old oak Ellis rushed out to greet me as you would greet a friend. I didn't fear her now as I had before, and was almost glad to see her; I no longer attempted to understand what was happening; I simply wanted to fly farther, to strange places.< . . . >

XIV

Look around you, and calm yourself—Ellis said to me. I did and, as I recall, my first impression was so pleasurable that I could do nothing but sigh. A smoky-blue, silvery-soft something that was neither light nor shadow inundated me from all sides. At first I could make out nothing, blinded by that azure shimmer, but little by little there emerged the outlines of beautiful mountains, forests—a lake spread out before me, starlight twinkling in its depths as it broke on the shore with a quiet murmur. The scent of orange blossoms overwhelmed me like a wave—at the same instant, also like a breaking wave, came the intense, pure tone of a young woman's voice. That scent and those tones seemed to entice me, and I began to descend . . . towards a sumptuous marble villa. Its whiteness gleamed hospitably in the midst of a cypress grove. The singing poured out from its wide-open windows; the waves of the lake, covered with orange blossom pollen, broke against its walls—and directly opposite, clad in a radiant haze, all adorned with statues, delicate colonnades and porticoes, arose from the lake a lofty, rounded island. . . .

Isola Bella . . . Lago Maggiore—Ellis announced.

"Ah!" was my only response as I continued to descend. The woman's voice rang through the villa with increasing strength and brightness: it drew me irresistibly. . . . I wished to see the face of the singer who was filling such a night with such music. We halted before a window.

In the center of a chamber decorated in the Pompean taste and resembling more an ancient shrine than a modern drawing room, amid Greek figurines, Etruscan vases, exotic plants and rare carpets, illumined from above by the soft rays of two spherical crystal lamps—a young woman sat at the fortepiano. With her head bowed and her eyes half-closed she was singing an Italian aria; she sang and smiled, and at the same time her features expressed assurance, even sternness . . . a sign of pure pleasure! She smiled . . . and Praxilites' faun—indolent, young as she was young, delicate, passionate—seemed to return her smile from a corner, through a curtain of oleander blossoms and the light smoke arising from a bronze brazier on an antique tripod. The stunning woman was alone. Enchanted by her singing and beauty, by the brilliance and fragrance of the night, shaken to the depths of my soul by her youthful, serene radiance, I had completely forgotten my companion, the strange way I had come to witness a life so far-removed from and alien to my own—I wished to go through the window and say. . . .

My body shuddered from a harsh shock—exactly as if I'd touched a

Leyden jar. I glanced back . . . Ellis' face, for all its transparency, was dark and threatening; anger flared in her suddenly wide-open eyes . . .

Away!—she whispered irately, and once again the whirlwind, and darkness, and my head aspin . . . But the singer's voice, cut off as she reached a high note, still lingered in my ears . . . < . . . >

XVII-XVIII

Next morning I had a headache, and my legs would barely carry me; but I paid no attention to my physical disarray, remorse was gnawing at me and anger at myself was suffocating me. < . . . >

I summoned my housekeeper: "Marfa, what time did I go to bed last night, do you remember?"

"Hard to say with you, Master . . . It was late, seems like. You went out at dusk, and your boot-heels were knocking about in there after midnight. Near daybreak—yes. For the third night in a row. You must have some trouble or other on your mind."

"Ah-ha!" I thought. So the flying is real and no doubt. "Well, and how do I look to you today?" I asked aloud.

"How do you look? Let me have a peek . . . You've gone a little hollow-cheeked. And you're pale, Master: it's as if you'd got no blood in your face."

I felt myself sag a bit . . . and dismissed Marfa.

"Keep on like this and you'll die, or go out of your mind—I concluded as I sat pensively by the window. "You have to give it up. It's dangerous. Feel how strangely your heart is beating. And when I'm flying I feel as if something is sucking away at my heart, or as if something is leaking from it, just like sap from a birch tree in the spring, if you sink an ax into it. I'll be sorry to give it up, though. Yes, and Ellis . . . She's playing cat and mouse with me . . . But she can't really wish me any harm. I'll trust myself to her one last time—I'll look my fill—and then . . . But what if she's drinking my blood? That's horrible. What's more, moving that fast can't help but be bad for you: they say that even in England the trains are forbidden to travel more than one hundred and twenty versts an hour . . ."

In this way I reasoned with myself — but at ten o'clock that evening I was already standing at the old oak. < . . . > Ellis came, threw over my head the end of her long, flowing sleeve. Immediately I was enveloped in a sort of white mist, soporific with the scent of poppies. Everything disappeared instantaneously; all light, all sound—and almost consciousness itself. Only the sensation of life remained—and this wasn't unpleasant. Suddenly the mist vanished; Ellis had removed her sleeve, and I saw before me a huge mass of buildings crowded together, brilliance, movement, din . . . I saw Paris.

XIX

I'd been in Paris before and therefore immediately recognized the spot to which Ellis had shaped her course. It was the garden of the Tuileries, with its old chestnut-trees, wrought-iron fences, fortress-moat, and beast-like Zouaves on guard. Passing the palace, passing the Church of St. Roch, on whose steps the first Napoleon shed French blood for the first time, we halted high above the *Boulevard des Italiens*, where the third Napoleon did the same thing, and with equal success. Crowds of people—young and old dandies, workmen, women in sumptuous attire—were thronging the side-walks; the gilded restaurants and cafes were blazing with lights, carriages of all sorts and kinds drove up and down the boulevard; everything was fairly seething and glittering, in every direction, wherever the eye fell. . . . But, strange to say, I didn't feel like leaving my pure, dark, airy height; I didn't want to approach that human ant-hill. It seemed as though a burn-ing, oppressive, red-hot exhalation arose from it, not precisely fragrant, yet not precisely foul either; a lot of life, of living things were jumbled together there in a heap. I wavered. . . . But then the voice of a street-walker, sharp as the screech of iron rails, abruptly assaulted my ear; like a naked blade it thrust itself upward, that voice; it stung me like the fangs of a viper. I imme-diately pictured to myself a stony, greedy, flat Parisian face with high cheek-bones, and the eyes of a pawn-broker, the rouge, powder, and curled hair, and the bouquet of garish artificial flowers on the high-peaked hat, the nails filed in the shape of claws, the monstrous crinoline. . . . I also pictured a brother steppe-dweller pursuing this venal doll with a detestable tripping gait. . . . I pictured to myself how, confused to the point of rudeness, and lisping with the effort, he tries to imitate the manners of the waiters at Véfour's, how he squeals, fawns, wheedles—and a feeling of loathing took possession of me. . . . "No,"—I thought,—"Ellis will have no need to feel jealous here. . . . "

In the meantime I noticed that we were gradually beginning to descend. . . . Paris rose to meet us with all its din and reek. . . .

"Stop!"—I turned to Ellis.—"Don't you find it stifling here, oppres-sive? < . . . > Carry me away, Ellis, I'm begging you. It's just as I thought: there goes Prince Kulmamétov, hobbling along the boulevard; and his friend Baráksin is beckoning him and calling: 'Iván Stepánitch, *allons souper*, as quickly as possible, and engage Rigolbosch itself!' Take me away from these *Mabilles* and *Maisons Dorés*, away from fops, male and female, from the Jockey Club and Figaro, from the soldiers with their shaved heads and the fancied-up barracks, from the *sergeants de ville* with their goatees and the glasses of cloudy absinthe, from the domino players in the cafés and the gamblers on the 'Change, from the bits of red ribbon in the but-tonhole of the coat and the buttonhole of the overcoat, from Monsieur de

Foi, the inventor of 'the specialty of weddings,' and from the free consultations of Dr. Charles Albert, from liberal lectures and governmental pamphlets, from Parisian comedies and Parisian operas and Parisian ignorance.
. . . Away! Away! Away!"

Look down—Ellis answered me:—*you're no longer over Paris.*

I glanced down. . . . It was a fact. A dark plain, here and there intersected
by the pale lines of roads, was swiftly passing beneath us and only on the
horizon far behind us did the reflection of the innumerable lights of the world's
capital throb upward like the glow of a huge conflagration. < . . . >

We're now flying towards Russia—said Ellis. This wasn't the first time
I'd noticed that she almost always knew what I was thinking.—*Do you
want to go home?*

"Yes, home. . . . or, no! I've been in Paris; take me to Petersburg."

Now?

"This instant . . . Only cover my head with your veil or I'll be dizzy."

Ellis raised her arm . . . but before the mist enveloped me I felt on my
lips the touch of that soft, dull sting . . .

XXII

"AT-TE-E-E-ENTION!"—a prolonged cry resounded in my ears.
"At-te-e-e-ention!" came the response, as though in despair, from the dis-
tance. "At-te-e-e-ention!" died away somewhere at the end of the world.
I started. A lofty golden spire met my eye: I recognized the Peter-and-Paul
Fortress.

It was one of the north's "white nights"! Yes, but was it night? Wasn't
it more of a pale, sickly day? I've never liked the Petersburg nights; but this
time I was actually terrified: Ellis' form disappeared entirely, melted like
morning mist in the July sun, and I clearly saw my own body as it hung
heavily and alone on a level with the Alexander column. So this was Petersburg! Yes, it really was. Those broad, empty, gray streets; those grayish-
white, yellowish-gray, grayish-lilac, stuccoed and peeling buildings with
their sunken windows, brilliant sign-boards, and iron pavilions over their
porches; the nasty little vegetable shops; those facades; those inscriptions,
sentry-boxes, watering-troughs; the golden cap of St. Isaac's Cathedral; the
useless, piebald Exchange; the granite walls of the fortress and the broken
wooden pavement; those barges laden with hay and firewood; that odor of
dust, cabbage, bast-matting and stables; those petrified yard-porters in
sheepskin coats at the gates. Those cab-drivers curled up in death-like sleep
on rickety carriages. Indeed it was our Northern Palmyra. Everything was
visible and clear, painfully clear and distinct; everything was sadly asleep,
strangely heaped up and outlined in the dimly-transparent air. The glow of
sunset—a consumptive glow—had not yet departed, and would not depart

until morning from the white, starless sky. It lay on the silky surface of Neva, and the river barely murmured, undulating as it hurried its cold, blue waters along . . .

Let's fly away—pleaded Ellis.

And without waiting for an answer she carried me over the Neva, across Palace Square to Liteinaia Street. Footsteps and voices were audible below: along the street walked a cluster of young men with drink-sodden faces, discussing their dancing-classes. "Sub-lieutenant Stolpakov seventh!" a soldier dozing on guard by a pyramid of rusty cannon balls at the artillery barracks, suddenly cried out in his sleep. A little further on, at the open window of a tall house I caught sight of a young girl in a sleeveless crumpled silk gown, with a pearl snood on her hair and a cigarette in her mouth. She was avidly perusing a book: it was the work of one of the newest Juvenals.

"Let's fly away from here, "I said to Ellis.

A minute more, and the mangy forests of decaying spruce-trees and mossy swamps surrounding Petersburg were flitting past us. We headed southwards; both sky and earth gradually grew darker and darker. The diseased night, the diseased day, the diseased city—all were left behind.

XXIII

We flew more slowly than usual, and I was able to watch the broad expanse of my native land unrolling before me in a series of endless panoramas. Forests, copses, fields, ravines, rivers—now and then villages and churches—and then again fields, and forests, and copses, and ravines. . . . I began to feel melancholy and bored in an indifferent sort of way, somehow. And it wasn't because we were flying over Russian in particular that I felt melancholy and bored. No! The earth itself, that flat surface unfolding beneath me; the entire globe with its inhabitants, transitory, impotent, crushed by want, by sorrow, by diseases, fettered to a clod of contemptible earth; that rough, brittle crust, that excrescence on the fiery grain of sand that was our planet—our planet where a mold has sprung up that we celebrate as the organic, vegetable kingdom; and those man-flies, a thousand times more insignificant than actual flies; their huts stuck together with mud, the tiny traces of their petty, monotonous pother, their amusing struggles with the unchangeable and the inevitable,—how disgusting all this suddenly seemed! My heart slowly sickened, and I no longer wanted to look at those insignificant pictures, at that stale exhibition. . . . Yes, I was bored—worse than bored. I didn't even feel compassion for my fellow men: all my emotions were sunk in one which I hardly dare to name: in a feeling of revulsion; and that revulsion was strongest of all and most of all toward myself.

Stop—whispered Ellis—*Stop, or I won't be able to carry you. You're getting heavy.*

"Head home."—I replied in the very voice I used when addressing the same words to my coachman—as I emerged, at four in the morning, from the houses of my Moscow friends with whom I had been discussing the future of Russia and the significance of the peasant commune ever since dinner.—"Head home," I repeated, and closed my eyes.

XXIV

But I soon opened them again. Ellis was pressing against me in a strange sort of way; she was almost pushing me. I looked at her, and the blood curdled in my veins. Anyone who has happened to see on someone else's face a sudden expression of profound terror, without understanding what's causing it, will understand me. Terror, harassing terror, contorted, distorted the pale, almost obliterated features of Ellis. I had never seen anything like it even on a living human face. This was a lifeless, shadowy phantom, a shadow . . . and that swooning terror. . . .

"Ellis, what's wrong?"—I said at last.

She . . . she . . . the shadow replied with an effort—*She!*

"She? Who's she?"

Don't say it, don't—hurriedly stammered Ellis—*We must get away, or it will all will be over. . . . Look: there!*

I turned my head in the direction of her trembling hand and saw something . . . something truly horrifying. It was all the more horrifying because it had no definite shape. Something heavy, gloomy, yellowish-black in hue, mottled like the belly of a lizard—not a storm-cloud, and not smoke—was moving over the earth with a slow, serpentine motion. A measured, wide-reaching undulation downward and upward—an undulation which brought to mind the ominous wing-sweep of a bird of prey in search of its quarry. Then the inexpressibly revolting swoop earthwards—just the way a spider swoops down to the captured fly. . . . Under the influence of this threatening mass—I saw this, I felt it— everything was annihilated, everything was silenced. . . . A rotten, pestilential odor emanated from it and a chill that sickened the heart, darkened the sight, made the hair stand on end. A power was advancing; the irresistible power to which all are subject, a power which—without sight, form, thought—sees everything, knows everything, and, like a bird of prey selects its victims and crushes them like a serpent, licking them with its chilly sting. . . .

"Ellis! Ellis!"—I shrieked like a madman.—"Is that Death?—Death itself?"

The wailing sound I had heard earlier burst from Ellis's mouth. This time it was more like a despairing, human scream—and we dashed away. But our flight was strange and frighteningly uneven; Ellis turned somersaults in the air; she fell downward, she threw herself from side to side like a partridge when mortally wounded, or when she wants to lure the hound away from her brood. Even so, long, waving tentacles separating themselves from the inexpressibly dreadful mass rolled after us like outstretched arms, like claws. The huge form of a muffled figure on a pale horse rose up for one moment, and soared up to the very sky. . . . Still more agitated, still more despairing Ellis threw herself about.

It saw me! It's all over! I'm lost!—her broken whispers could now be heard—*What a horrid fate! I could have enjoyed—I could have come to—life . . . but now. . . . annihilation, annihilation!*

This was too unbearable. . . . I fainted.

XXV

When I came to myself I was lying stretched out on the grass, with a dull pain all through my body, as though I'd been severely hurt. Dawn was breaking in the sky: I could make out objects clearly. Not far away, along the edge of a birch-coppice ran a road fringed with willows; the surroundings seemed familiar to me. I began to recall what had happened to me, and shuddered all over when the last, monstrous vision recurred to my mind . . .

"But what was Ellis afraid of?" I thought. "Is it possible that even *she* isn't immortal? That *she* is doomed to annihilation, to destruction? How can that be?"

A soft moan sounded close at hand. I turned my head. Two paces off lay, outstretched and motionless, a young woman in a white gown, with disheveled hair and bared shoulders. One arm was thrown up over her head, the other fell across her chest. Her eyes were closed, and a light scarlet froth foamed from between her compressed lips. Could that be Ellis? But Ellis was a phantom, and I saw before me a living woman. I approached her, bent down. . . .

"Ellis? Is it you?" I exclaimed. Suddenly, with a slow quiver, the broad eyelids were lifted; dark, piercing eyes bored into me—and at that same moment her lips also clung to me, warm, moist, scented with blood . . . the soft arms wound themselves tightly around my neck, the full, burning breast was pressed convulsively to mine. *Farewell! Farewell forever!*—a fading voice said distinctly—and everything vanished.

I rose to my feet staggering like a drunken man, and passing my hands several times across my face, looked attentively about me. I was close to the highway, a couple of miles from my manor. The sun had already risen when I reached home.

All the following nights I waited—and not without terror, I admit—for the appearance of my phantom; but it didn't visit me again. I even—once—

went at twilight to the old oak; but nothing unusual happened there either. I didn't grieve much, however, at the end of my strange friendship. I thought long and hard about this incomprehensible, almost inexplicable business and concluded that not only would science be unable to explain it, but that in folk-tales and legends there was nothing like it. What was Ellis, really? A vision, a wandering soul, an evil spirit, a sylph, a vampire? At times it seemed to me once more that Ellis was a woman whom I had formerly known, and I made strenuous efforts to recall where I had seen her. . . . There now—it sometimes seemed to me—I'm just about to remember it, in another moment. . . . In vain! Again everything would melt like a dream. Yes, I pondered a great deal, and as might be expected, I arrived at no conclusion. I couldn't make up my mind to ask the advice or opinion of other people, because I was afraid of gaining the reputation of a madman. In the end I have cast aside all my speculations: to tell the truth, I'm in no mood for them. The Emancipation has taken place, with its division of crop land, and so forth, and so on, whereas my health has failed and my chest gives me pain, I am subject to insomnia, and have a cough. My body is withering away. My face is as yellow as the face of a corpse. The doctor declares that I have very little blood, and calls my malady by a Greek name—*anaemia*—and has ordered me to Gastein. But the Justice of the Peace tells me that he won't be able to make the peasants "toe the line" without me. . . .

So you see how things are with me now!

But what of those keen, piercingly-clear sounds—the sounds of a *harmonium*—which I hear as soon as anyone begins to speak to me about death? They grow ever louder and more piercing. . . . And why do I shudder at the mere thought of annihilation?

Translated by Isabel F. Hapgood; revised by A.L. and M.K.

Senilia: Poems in Prose

1. COUNTRYSIDE VILLAGE.

Last day of June; Russia all around for a thousand versts—my native land.

The seamless blue of the entire sky; a single cloudlet neither floating nor melting. Absolute stillness and gentle warmth, air like fresh milk! Larks peal from on high; curved-neck doves coo; swallows hover in silence; horses quietly snort and chew; dogs do not bark and stand still, wagging their tails.

It smells of smoke and grass—a bit of tar—and a bit of leather. Hemp-fields are in full growth and give off their strong but pleasant smell.

A deep, but gently sloping ravine. Down its sides are several rows of top-heavy broom, splintered at their base. Through ravine runs a stream; small pebbles on its bed are atremble through the shimmer. Far away, at the vanishing point of the earth and the sky, lies the bluish thread of a great river.

Along one side of the ravine—neat barns, grain cribs with close-fitting doors, on the other—half a dozen pine huts with shake roofs. Atop each roof the tall stave of a starling-roost, on every porch roof a short-maned horse in cast iron. The wavy window glass gives off rainbow colors. Baskets with bouquets of painted daisys on the shutters. In front of each hut proudly stands a well-made bench. On the earthworks the cats have curled up, pricking up their transparent ears; behind the tall thresholds the dark storerooms beckon.

I am lying at the very edge of the ravine on an outspread horse blanket; all around are great heaps of new mown hay whose fragrance is overwhelming. The shrewd owners have strewn the hay in front of their huts: let it bake out a little, and then into the barn! That'll make it good to sleep on!

The curly heads of children poke out of each heap: cockaded chickens search the hay for moths and bugs; a white-muzzled pup rolls around in the tangled stalks.

Tow-headed lads, in clean tunics belted low, in heavy top boots, exchange spirited remarks while leaning on an unharnessed cart—and scoff.

A moon-faced girl looks out of a window; she's laughing partly at their words, partly at the antics of the youngsters playing in the piles of hay.

Another girl, with strong arms, is hauling a large wet bucket from the well . . . The bucket trembles and sways on its rope, spilling out long fiery drops.

Before me stands the old farm-wife in a new checkered apron and new slippers.

A strand of large blown-glass beads are wound around her thin swarthy neck; her grey head is covered with a yellow scarf with red dots; it has slipped down over her dim eyes.

But those old eyes smile cordially; her wrinkled face smiles. After all the old lady is in her seventh decade . . . one can see even now: she was a beauty in her day! On the outspread weatherbeaten fingers of her right hand she balances a jug of unskimmed milk, fresh from the cool cellar; the sides of the jug are covered with beads of dew, like jewels. On the palm of her left hand the old lady brings me a large piece of still-warm bread, as if saying: "Here, eat in good health, dear visiting traveller!"

Suddenly the cock crows, restlessly flapping his wings: unhurrriedly, the stalled calf lows in answer.

"O what a rich yield of oats it'll be!" I hear the voice of my coachman.

O the bliss, peace and plenitude of a free Russian village! So still, yet so abundant!

And the thought comes to me: what need do we have for the cross on the cupola of St. Sophia in the City of Kings—Constantinople, and everything else we strive for—we city folk?

February, 1878

2. NESSUN MAGGIOR DOLORE.

(There is no greater grief)

The azure of skies, the weightless down of clouds, aroma of flowers, sweet sounds of a young voice, translucent splendor of great works of art, the smile of happiness on a lovely woman's face and those magic eyes . . . what for, what is all this for?

A spoon of a horrid, useless medication every two hours—that's what is really needed.

June, 1882

Translated by A.L. and M. K.

Nikolai Vasilievich Gogol
(1809-1852)

"Take the winter scene. It's only fifteen rubles!
The frame alone is worth more than that."
From the final version of *The Portrait*

N. V. Gogol, established as a writer well before Lermontov was out of his teens, is regarded in Russia as second in literary importance only to Pushkin. If the latter's writings are marked by conciseness, economy, and clarity, Gogol's style is noted for expansiveness, ambiguity, and verbal play amounting to true virtuosity. Selections from Gogol's *oeuvre* are placed here after Lermontov's because they mark a transition in the Russian aesthetic awareness which began to favor prose over poetry as an *exclusive* vehicle for all literary needs. The most prominent of these was the utilitarian aspect of literature, as a national art form serving the masses—a notion to which Gogol himself contributed greatly. Within this context poetry fared quite poorly, as its multiple intricacies and nuances could be only understood by an exclusive club of like-minded, well educated individuals. But Gogol might have inaugurated the reign of the dominance of prose over poetry for personal reasons, as his first published work, a super-romantic narrative poem, was an utter fiasco which he decided to burn. Thereafter Gogol did not publish a single poem.

Gogol's fame began with his very first collection of stories, *Evenings on a Farm near Dikanka* (1831-2) which, together with its sequel *Mirgorod* (1835), constituted a series of tales united by a Ukrainian setting, descriptions of local color and nature. The stories expressed both the pathos of heroism and supernatural terror stemming from native beliefs and myths, and the bathos of folksy humor, banality, silliness and sheer stupidity permeating provincial life. Cossacks, Gypsies, seminarians and local folk are described selling and buying pretzels, kerchiefs, bushels of wheat and all kinds of wares at country fairs and relishing their food to the point of choking on their dumplings. But drowned maidens, witches, devils and other "colossal creations of the popular imagination," as Gogol put it, also make their appearance. Comprising a grotesque gallery of creatures and characters with radish-shaped heads, overgrown bellies, magnetic eyes—all inextricably bound to the countryside, at once coarsely prosaic, enchanted and mystical, and strung together by the narration of the bee-keeper Pan'ko—*Evenings* and *Mirgorod* tales were more a product of Gogol's oxymoronic mind with its taste for the carnavalesque than the "slice-of-life" episodes many contemporary critics saw in them. Yet the series was received in the capital as a picture-postcard-perfect reflection of Ukrainian folk life and assured for Gogol instant recognition. Since *Evenings* marked Gogol's first leap into the fantastic realm, we have chosen to excerpt one of its stories, *Vji*, to represent this period. *Vyi* provides all the ingredients that would normally startle a city-dweller: the local color and customs of the provinces, the flight of an unsuspecting protagonist mounted on a witch's back over this enchanted countryside (an image used to great effect a century later by M. A. Bulgakov in his exquisite fantasy-novel, *Master and Margarita*), the horror of witnessing an old hag turn into that witch, and also of meeting a truly horrific ruler of the netherworld—Vyi—to whose magnetic powers the protagonist succumbs. The fact that Petersburg dwellers of Gogol's time (and, regrettably, subsequent commentators on Gogol) failed to notice that Vyi—despite the author's claim to the contrary in his footnote—did *not* have a Ukrainian folk genesis, but German, never became an issue: Gogol's rise to a leading place in Russian prose was assured.

The surprise which affected Russian readers of Gogol's early fiction only increased when the author changed the locale of his stories to St. Petersburg in *Arabesques* (1835).[1] A word must be said about a fantasy-making device found in *Arabesques* which made possible Gogol's absurd fusion of the Real and the Other. The term *arabesque* has been used in diverse fields, but Gogol paid special attention to its function in art and framing. In the book's first essay, "Sculpture, Painting, and Music," the art of painting, when personified, "reaches out from behind the multitude of antique gilded frames," and is caught in the whirlwind of "long galleries, flashing by, as if in a fog." It is important to note that in European art, arabesque frames allowed parts of the represented world (usually some form of vegetation like branches of trees or curling vines) to protrude or "grow beyond" the confines of the painting. This function of *protruding beyond the ordinary frame of things* is at the core of Gogol's poetics in *Arabesques*. Images of grapevines reaching into the heavens, together with other vegetation, breaking the simple geometry of buildings, the sense of boundlessness in his depictions of genius (all found in his essays), moonlight unable to be contained by the frame of the window in *The Portrait*,

---

1. During his life and for a century after his death, Gogol's *Arabesques* were erroneously seen as a shapeless miscellany of essays (cf. N. V. Gogol', *Polnoe sobranie sochinenii* 14 vols. Moscow: AN SSSR, 1937-52, which is typical in this regard). Gogol's title in fact alludes to an aesthetic function which underlies the design of the whole volume.

as well as the notion of the portrait stepping out of its frame, fogs causing the narrative to take abrupt shifts in a related story, *The Nose*—all these were but a fraction of the imaging with which the author bombarded his readers, as if afraid of stasis or a moment's calm contemplation.

The frames unable to contain the pictures they hold unite Gogol's fictional and non-fictional prose into a whole which may properly be called nothing else but *Arabesques*. From these we offer *Nevsky Prospect* and the *Diary of a Madman*. The former was especially valued by Pushkin for its remarkable symmetry and perhaps better than any other tale shows Gogol to be the true progenitor of the Petersburg myth. At first depicted in the daylight, the city when night falls is veiled with disorienting mists and fogs, which confuse perceptions and cause the protagonists to make mistakes with fatal consequences. Nothing is to be trusted on Nevsky Prospect for it "deceives at all hours < ... > especially when night descends on it < ... > and when the Devil himself ignites the street lamps for the purpose of showing everything not in its true guise." It is this central Petersburg avenue which is frequented by the protagonist of the *Diary of a Madman*, Poprishchin. Quite apart from its general relevance for the insanity theme in Russian literature, this work had a unique meaning within *Arabesques*, relative to the issue primarily concerning Gogol at the time—the ability to touch the Sublime. Gogol created a persona one might call the "lofty narrator," who alternately appears in the book as a historian or an expert on architecture, but who in the first essay (mentioned above) poses as an art-loving *friar*, raising successive toasts to Sculpture, Painting, and Music "in his peaceful cell." This detail has a bearing on the overall symmetry of *Arabesques*, thematically relating to the final tale, *The Diary of a Madman*, in one episode of which Poprishchin's head is shaved in prison—an act he mistakenly believes to signify a consecration into a monastic order by force, something he really dreads.

It is also noteworthy that Poprishchin (whose name derives its meaning in Russian from a furuncle or boil) is the only protagonist in *Arabesques* who is a narrator in his own right, thus implicitly serving as an alter-ego to the lofty monk-narrator. The parallel is further reinforced by the fact that the monk-narrator proper ends his essay by choosing music as the supreme form of art—in his early drafts Gogol planned to make Poprishchin a musician. Some references to music still remain in the *Diary*. The daughter of Poprishchin's superior sings like a canary, a friend of Prprishchin's plays the trombone beautifully, and in the tale's final passage there is "a chord resounding in the mist". But there are no clues available as to what made Gogol to switch the narrator from a musician to a clerk. Given Gogol's facetious alter-ego motif in the *Diary of the Madman* however, there is reason to suspect that the author wished to hide the true source of his inspiration, namely E.T.A. Hoffmann's novel, *Lebensansichten des Katers Murr nebst fragmentarischer Biographie des Kapellmeisters Johannes Kreisler in zufaelligen Makulaturblaettern.* (The Life and Opinions of Tomcat Murr, along with A Fragmentary Biography of the Conductor Johannes Kreisler as recorded on Random Galley-proofs). Hoffman's protagonist, the tomcat Murr, has supposedly written his wild autobiography on the backs of the pages of a manuscript which he has clawed to shreds. Interspersed with Murr's horrid poetry and musings on the superiority of cats to humans is the biography of Johannes Kreisler, Murr's owner. Kreisler is a composer who, although suffering bouts of paranoia, is a true musical genius. His story proceeds in reverse order to Murr's, creating a fragmentary, schizophrenic text, with the resultant effect not unlike Gogol's. *The Diary of a Madman*, which Gogol originally titled *The Diary of the Mad Musician* and then *Tatters from the Diary of the Madman*, features a correspondence between two pampered lapdogs. Finally, it must be noted that Gogol, just as Hoffmann, felt unappreciated as a child, admitted to hearing the Devil's and other voices in his head, and it is no accident that he was under the influence of Hoffmann's amazing creative output.

Gogol's adaptation of nightmarish themes from *The Tales* of E.T.A. Hoffmann has been noted by a host of commentators. The reason that the threads to Hoffman's lesser-known novel were not heretofore noted might lie in the care Gogol took to separate his persona from the protagonist of *The Diary of the Madman* as well as from the likely source of its inspiration. After all, Kreisler was the actual pseudonym under which Hoffmann himself published his brilliant essays on music, and Murr was the real name of his own cat. Gogol's dogs in the *Diary* had, of course, no relation to reality, nor did their "writings." Regardless of its initial designs, the *Diary of a Madman* is clearly a masterpiece in its own right, perfectly reflecting not only Gogol's own crisis, but also convincingly tracing the humorous, yet tragic, progress of a perfectly average Petersburg clerk to the point when he can imagine himself to be the King of Spain and hear dogs talking. Firmly anchored in the world of the 1830s, there is nonetheless a touch of modernity in the tale's focus on the absurdity of human existence.

The same sense can be gained in a story related to the *Arabesques* cycle, *The Nose*, which concludes our sampling of Gogol's fiction. In it the Nose—magically separated from its normal place—independently achieves a rank higher than its owner, the protagonist Kovalev. The story's modernity can be demonstrated by comparing the beginning of Kafka's *Metamorphosis*—"As Gregor Samsa awoke one morning from uneasy dreams he found himself transformed in his bed into a gigantic insect"—with the way Gogol anticipated an equally absurd state eight decades earlier, as he has Kovalev wake up early one morning and "to his great astonishment find a completely flat space where his nose should have been." Kafka's explicit verbal modeling expresses the static and exitless existence of an insectoid human with an apple (symbol of original sin) embedded in its carapace. Gogol's noseless protagonist shows a remarkable agility in his endless and humorous search for his just as remarkably mobile nose; the sins of Gogol's story—if there are any indeed—exist only on the implicit level (such as the sexual connotations of the subject matter, or the sacrilegious overtones of finding a "nose" instead of the "body of Christ" in the daily bread). It must be also said that the real and quite typical horrors of twentieth-century Soviet Russia, such as a wife "going to the police herself to report" on her husband, or the dictum that a writer must only write "useful literature for his country," and if he does not, he just might become a candidate for physical extermination in a concentration camp, all these true horrors are anticipated by the power of Gogol's prophetic writing. Indeed, there is a dreadful accuracy in the economy with which Gogol can paint when he is at his best, and that he most definitely is in *The Nose*. For instance, the scene of the barber waking up at his home and seeing his portly wife who didn't like any caprices is used on a number of occasions in Russian literature. In our volume this uneven family situation is exploited by Fyodor K. Sologub in his short story *A Little Man*, but for an altered purpose and with a prodigiously different outcome. Even one gesture, such as the one expressing Praskovia Osipovna's demeaning attitude to her husband when she "tossed a loaf of bread on the table"— in lieu of a cup of coffee—to appease his modest wishes, would be developed as a leitmotif for a matriarch's attitude to her sons in an entire novel, *The Golovlev Family*, by Satykov-Shchedrin. In that social satire of the 1870s a just-as-portly mother would occasionally "fling a bone" to her children whom for reasons of economy she kept half starved—just as Gogol's Praskovia Osipovna did to her husband.

But if we can find in this *Petersburg Tale* genesis for all kinds of transformations in future works, nothing should prevent us from enjoying the story's own metamorphoses. There are plenty, starting from the history of its making. Originally planned as a dream from which the protagonist awakes at the end of the story, its final format shapes an estranged and mixed-up reality—a series of waking dreams—in which Petersburg barbers may just find noses in their daily bread, noses themselves may stroll as civil councilors, ride in carriages, or piously pray in churches, and runaway house serfs may in fact be runaway poodles. In Gogol's imagination the nose must be understood as precisely that arabesque protrusion from the plane of the human face, which allows not only for his best characterization, but also for contact between the inner self and its surroundings. The central enigma of the story is paraded for the reader right from the beginning at the mention of the barbershop's signboard, "where a gentleman is depicted with his cheeks covered with soapsuds," to which a naturally arising question—

as to whether his nose is or is not seen from the midst of the soapsuds—is never answered. Instead the author quotes an inscription on the signboard "also lets blood," but again the reader never discovers to his full satisfaction why this is mentioned. Does it stand for the then common practice of applying leeches to reduce blood-pressure, or does it threaten the true horror of cutting a nose from human face, or does it—as the bread-flinging reference—function as yet another sacrilegious symbol? We may never know, yet it is clear that Gogol, who began with horror stories against a rural backdrop, found Petersburg to be just as viable a setting for weaving estranged fantastic scapes. Due to his technique of *arabesque modeling*, these new works could easily transcend both the bathos and pathos of his earlier creations and achieve universal significance in their fantasy-making.

Gogol holds a unique place in Russian fiction—indeed, the period from about 1835 to his death in 1852 is commonly referred to as the age of Gogol—and it is for this reason that we devote a full section of this volume to his works.

Vyi

[ABRIDGED]

Vyi is a collosal creation of the popular imagination. It is the name among the Little Russians for the chief of the gnomes, whose eylids droop down to the earth. The whole story is folklore. I was unwilling to change it, and tell it in the simple words in which I heard it. (N. GOGOL)

As soon as the rather musical seminary bell which hung at the gate of the Bratskii Monastery rang out every morning in Kiev, schoolboys and students hurried thither in crowds from all parts of the town. Students of grammar, rhetoric, philosophy and theology trudged to their class-rooms with exercise-books under their arms. The grammarians were quite small boys; they shoved each other as they went along and quarrelled in shrill altos; almost all wore muddy or tattered clothes, and their pockets were full of all manner of rubbish, such as knucklebones, whistles made of feathers, or a half-eaten pie, sometimes even little sparrows, one of whom suddenly chirruping at an exceptionally quiet moment in the class-room would cost its owner some resounding whacks on both hands and sometimes a thrashing. The rhetoricians walked with more dignity; their clothes were often quite free from holes; on the other hand, their countenances almost all bore some decoration, after the style of a figure of rhetoric: either one eye had sunk right under the forehead, or there was a monstrous swelling in place of a lip, or some other disfigurement. They talked and swore among themselves in tenor voices. The philosophers conversed an octave lower in the scale; they had nothing in their pockets but strong, cheap tobacco. They laid in no stores of any sort, but ate on the spot anything they came across; they smelt of pipes and horilka to such a distance that a passing workman would sometimes stop a long way off and sniff the air like a setter dog.

As a rule the market was just beginning to stir at that hour, and the workmen with bread-rings, rolls, melon seeds, and poppy cakes would tug at the skirts of those whose coats were of fine cloth or some cotton material.

"This way, young gentleman, this way!" they kept saying from all sides, "here are bread-rings, poppy cakes, twists, tasty white roles; they are really good! Made with honey! I baked them myself."

Another woman, lifting up a sort of long twist made of dough, would cry, "Here's a bread stick! Buy my bread stick, young gentleman!"—"Don't buy anything off her; see what a horrid woman she is, her nose is nasty and her hands are dirty . . ."

But the women were afraid to worry the philosophers and the theologians, for they were fond of taking things to taste and always a good handful.

On reaching the seminary, the crowd dispersed to their various classes, which were held in low-pitched but fairly large rooms, with little windows, wide doorways, and dirty benches. The class-room was at once filled with all sorts of buzzing sounds: the "auditors" heard their pupils repeat their lessons; the shrill alto of a grammarian rang out, and the window-panes responded with almost the same note; in a corner a rhetorician, whose stature and thick lips should have belonged at least to a student of philosophy, was droning something in a bass voice, and all that could be heard at a distance was, "Boo, boo, boo . . ." The "auditors," as they heard the lesson, kept glancing with one eye under the bench, where a roll or a cheese cake of some pumpkin seed were peeping out of a scholar's pocket.

When the learned crowd managed to arrive a little too early, or when they knew that the professors would be later than usual, then by general consent they got up a fight, and everyone had to take part in it, even the monitors whose duty it was to maintain discipline and look after the morals of all the students. Two theologians usually settled the arrangements for the battle: whether each class was to defend itself individually, or whether all were to be divided into two parties, the bursars and the seminarists. In any case the grammarians launched the attack, and as soon as the rhetoricians entered the fray, they ran away and stood at points of vantage to watch the contest. Then the devotees of philosophy, with long black moustaches, joined in, and finally those of theology, very thick in the neck and attired in enormous trousers, took part. It commonly ended in theology beating all the rest, and the philosophers, rubbing their ribs, were forced into the classroom and sat down on the benches to rest. The professor, who had himself at one time taken part in such battles, could, on entering the class, see in a minute from the flushed faces of his audience that the battle had been a good one, and while he was caning rhetorics on the fingers, in another classroom another professor would be smacking philosophy's hands with a wooden bat. The theologians were dealt with in quite a different way: they received, to use the expression of a professor of theology, "a peck of peas a piece," in other words, a liberal drubbing with short leather thongs.

On holidays and ceremonial occasions the bursars and seminarists went from house to house as mummers. Sometimes they acted a play, and then the most distinguished figure was always some theologian, almost as tall as the belfry of Kiev, who took the part of Herodias of Potiphar's wife. They received in payment a piece of linen, or a sack of millet, of half a boiled goose, or something of the sort. All this crowd of students—the seminarists as well as the bursars, with whom they maintain an hereditary feud—were exceedingly badly off for means of subsistence, and at the same time had extraordinary appetites, so that to reckon how many dumplings each of them tucked away at supper would be utterly impossible, and therefore the voluntary offerings of prosperous citizens could not be sufficient for them. Then the "senate" of the philosophers and theologians dispatched the grammarians and rhetoricians, under the supervision of a philosopher (and sometimes took part in the raid themselves), with sacks on their shoulders to plunder the kitchen gardens—and pumpkin porridge was made in the bursars' quarters. The members of the "senate" ate such masses of melons that next day their "auditors" heard two lessons from them instead of one, one coming from their lips, another muttering in their stomachs. Both the bursars and the seminarists wore long garmets resembling frock-coats, "prolonged to the utmost limit," a technical expression signifying below their heels.

The most important event for the seminarists was the coming of the vacation; it began in June, when they usually dispersed to their homes. Then the whole highroad was dotted with philosophers, grammarians and theologians. Those who had nowhere to go went to stay with some comrade. The philosophers and theologians took a situation, that is, undertook the tuition of the children of prosperous families, and received in payment a pair of new boots or sometimes even a coat. The whole crowd trailed along together like a gipsy encampment, boiled their porridge, and slept in the fields. Everyone hauled along a sack in which he had a shirt and a pair of leg-wrappers. The theologians were particular thrifty and precise: to avoid wearing out their boots, they took them off, hung them on sticks and carried them on their shoulders, especially if the road was muddy; then, tucking their trousers up above their knees, they splashed fearlessly through the puddles. When they saw a village they turned off the high road and going up to any house which seemed a little better looking than the rest, stood in a row before the windows and began singing a chant at the top of their voices. The master of the house, some old Cossack villager, would listen to them for a long time, his head propped on his hands, then he would sob bitterly and say, turning to his wife: "Wife! What the scholars are singing must be very deep; bring them fat bacon and anything else that we have." And a whole bowl of dumplings was emptied into the sack, a good-sized piece of bacon, several flat loaves, and sometimes of trussed hen would go into it too. Fortified with such stores, the grammarians, rhetoricians, philosophers and theologians went on their way again. Their numbers lessened, however, the farther they went. Almost all wandered off towards their homes, and only those were left whose parental abodes were farther away.

Once, at the time of such a migration, three students turned off the high road in order to replenish their store of provisions at the first homestead they could find, for their sacks had long been empty. They were the theologian, Khaliava; the philosopher, Khoma Brut; and the rhetorician, Tiberii Gorobets.

The theologian was a well-grown, broad-shouldered fellow; he had an extremely odd habit—anything that lay within his reach he invariably stole. In other circumstances, he was of an excessively gloomy temper, and when he was drunk he used to hide in the tall weeds, and the seminarists had a lot of trouble to find him there.

The philosopher, Khoma Brut, was of a cheerful disposition, he was very fond of lying on his back and smoking a pipe; when he was drinking he always engaged musicians and danced the *trepak*. He often had a taste of the "peck of peas," but took it with perfect philosophical indifference, saying that there is no escaping from the inevitable. The rhetorician, Tiberii Gorobets, had not yet the right to wear a moustache, to drink *horilka*, and to smoke a pipe. He only wore a forelock round his ear, and so his character was as yet hardly formed; but, judging from the big bumps on the forehead, with which he often appeared in class, it might be presumed that he would make a good fighter. The theologian, Khaliava, and the philosopher, Khoma, often pulled him by the forelock as a sign of their favour, and employed him as their messenger.

It was evening when they turned off the high road; the sun had only just set and the warmth of the day still lingered in the air. The theologian and the philosopher walked along in silence smoking their pipes; the rhetorician, Tiberii Gorobets, kept knocking off the heads of the wayside thistles with his stick. The road weaved in between the scattered groups of oak- and nut-trees standing here and there in the meadows. Sloping uplands and little hills, green and round as cupolas, were interspersed here and there about the plain. The cornfields of ripening wheat, which came into view in two places, were the evidence that they were nearing some village. More than an hour passed, however, since they had seen the cornfields, yet there were no dwellings in sight. The sky was now completely wrapped in darkness, and only in the west there was a pale streak left of the glow of sunset.

"What the devil does it mean?" said the philosopher, Khoma Brut. "It looked as though there must be a village in a minute."

The theologian did not speak, he gazed at the surrounding country, then put his pipe back in his mouth, and they continued on their way.

"Upon my soul!" the philosopher said, stopping again, "not a devil's fist to be seen."

"Maybe some village will turn up farther on," said the theologian, not removing his pipe.

But meantime night had come on, and a rather dark night. Small clouds increased the gloom, and by every token they could expect neither stars nor moon. The students noticed that they had lost their way and for a long time had been walking off the road.

The philosopher, after feeling the ground about him with his feet in all directions, said at last, abruptly, "I say, where's the road?"

The theologian did not speak for a while, then, after pondering, he brought out, "Yes, it is a dark night."

The rhetorician walked off to one side and tried on his hands and knees to grope for the road, but his hands came upon nothing but foxes' holes. On all sides of them there was the steppe, which, it seemed, no one had ever crossed.

The travellers made another effort to press on a little, but there was the same wilderness in all direction. The philosopher tried shouting, but his voice seemed completely lost on the steppe, and met with no reply. All they heard was, a little afterwards, a faint moaning like the howl of a wolf.

"I say, what's to be done?" said the philosopher.

"Why, halt and sleep in the open!" said the theologian, and he felt in his pocket for flint and tinder to light his pipe again. But the philosopher could not agree to this: it was always his habit at night to put away a quarter-loaf of bread and four pounds of fat bacon, and he was conscious on this occasion of an insufferable sense of loneliness in his stomach. Besides, in spite of his cheerful temper, the philosopher was rather afraid of wolves.

"No, Khaliava, we can't," he said. "What, stretch out and lie down like a dog, without a bite or a sup of anything? Let's make another try for it; maybe we shall stumble on some dwelling-place and get at least a drink of *horilka* for supper."

At the word "horilka" the theologian spat to one side and brought out, "Well, of course, it's no use staying in the open."

The students pushed on, and to their intense delight soon caught the sound of barking in the distance. After listening which direction it came from, they walked on more boldly and a little later saw a light.

"A farm! It really is a farm!" said the philosopher.

He was not mistaken in his supposition; in a little while they actually saw a little homestead consisting of only two cottages looking into the same farmyard. There was a light in the windows; a dozen plum-trees stood up by the fence. Looking through the cracks in the paling-gate the students saw a yard filled with carriers' waggons. Here and there the stars peeped out in the sky.

"Look, mates, don't let's be put off! We must get a night's lodging somehow!"

The three learned gentleman banged on the gates with one accord and shouted, "Open up!"

The door of one of the cottages creaked, and a minute later they saw before them an old woman in a sheepskin.

"Who is there?" she cried, with a hollow cough.

"Give us a night's lodging, Granny; we have lost our way; a night in the open is as bad as a hungry belly."

"What manner of folks may you be?"

"We're harmless folks: Khaliava, a theologian; Brut, a philosopher; and Gorobets, a rhetorician."

"I can't," grumbled the old woman. "The yard is crowded with folk and every corner in the cottage is full. Where am I to put you? And such great hulking fellows, too! Why, my cottage will fall to pieces if I put such fellows in it. I know these philosophers and theologians; if one began taking in these drunken fellows, there'd soon be no home left. Be off, be off! There's no place for you here!"

"Have pity on us, Granny! How can you let Christian souls perish for no rhyme or reason? Put us where you please; and if we do aught amiss of anything else, may our arms be withered, and God only knows what befall us—so there!"

The old woman seemed somewhat softened. "Very well." she said as though reconsidering, "I'll ley you in, but I'll put you up all in different places, for my mind won't be at rest if you are all together."

"That's as you please; we'll make no objection," answered the students.

The gate creaked and they went into the yard.

"Well, Granny," said the philosopher, following the old woman, "how would it be, as they say . . . upon my soul, I feel as though somebody were driving a cart in my stomach: not a morsel has passed my lips all day."

"What next will he want!" said the old woman. "No, I've nothing for you, and the oven's not been heated today."

"But we'd pay for it all," the philosopher went on, "tomorrow morning, in hard cash. Yes!" he added in an undertone. "The devil a bit you'll get!"

"Go in, go in! and be satisfied with what you're given. Fine young gentlemen the devil has brought us!"

Khoma the philosopher was thrown into utter dejection by these words; but his nose suddenly aware of the odour of dried fish, he glanced at the trousers of the theologian who was walking at his side, and saw a huge fish-tail sticking out of his pocket. The theologian had already succeeding in filching a whole crucian from a waggon. And as he had done this simply from habit, and, quite forgetting his crucian, was already looking about for anything else he could carry off, having no mind to miss even a broken wheel, the philosopher slipped his hand into his friend's pocket, as though it were his own, and pulled out the crucian.

The old woman put the students in their separate places: the rhetorician she kept in the cottage, the theologian she locked in an empty closet, the philosopher she assigned a sheep-pen, also empty.

The latter, on finding himself alone, instantly devoured the crucian, examined the hurdle walls of the pen, kicked an inquisitive pig that woke up and thrust its snout in from the next pen, and turned over on his right side to fall into a sound sleep. All of a sudden the low door opened, and the old woman bending down stepped into the pen.

"What is it, Granny, what do you want?" said the philosopher.

But the old woman came towards him with outstretched arms.

"Aha, ha!" thought the philosopher. "No, my dear, you are too old!"

He moved a little aside, but the old woman unceremoniously approached him again.

"Listen, Granny!" said the philosopher. "It's a fast time now; and I am a man who wouldn't sin in a fast for a thousand gold pieces."

But the old woman spread her arms and tried to catch him without saying a word.

The philosopher was frightened, especially when he noticed a strange glint in her eyes. "Granny, what is it? Go—go away—God bless you!" he cried.

The old woman tried to clutch him in her arms without uttering a word.

He leapt to his feet, intending to escape; but the old woman stood in the doorway, fixing her glittering eyes on him and again began approaching him.

The philosopher tried to push her back with his hands, but to his surprise found that his arms would not rise, his legs would not move, and he perceived with horror that even his voice would not obey him; words hovered on his lips without a sound. He heard nothing but the beating of his heart. He saw the old woman approach him. She folded his arms, bent his head down, leapt with the swiftness of a cat upon his back, and struck him with a broom on the side; and he, prancing like a horse, carried her on his shoulders. All this happened so quickly that the philosopher scarcely knew what he was doing. He clutched his knees in both hands, trying to stop his legs from moving, but to his extreme amazement they were lifted against his will and executed capers more swiftly than a Circassian racer. Only when they had left the farm, and the wide plain lay stretched before them with a forest black as coal on one side, he said to himself, "Aha! she's a witch!"

The waning crescent of the moon was shining in the sky. The timid radiance of midnight lay mistily over the earth, light as transparent veil. The forests, the meadows, the sky, the dales, all seemed as though slumbering with open eyes; not a breeze fluttered anywhere; there was a damp warmth in the freshness of the night; the shadows of the trees and bushes fell on the sloping plain in pointed wedge shapes like comets. Such was the night when Khoma Brut, the philosopher, set off galloping with a mysterious rider on his back. He was aware of an exhausting, unpleasant, yet voluptuous sensation assailing his heart. He bent his head and saw that the grass which had been almost under his feet seemed growing at a depth far away, and that above it lay water, transparent as a mountain stream, and the grass seemed to be at the bottom of a clear sea, limpid to its very depths; anyway, he clearly saw in it his own reflection with the old woman sitting on his back. He saw shining there a sun instead of a moon; he heard the bluebells ringing as the bent their little heads; he saw a water-nymph float out from behind the reeds, there was the gleam of her leg and back, rounded and supple, all brightness and shimmering. She turned towards him and now her face came nearer, with eyes clear, sparkling, keen, with singing that pierced to the heart; now it was on the surface, and shaking with sparkling laughter it moved away; and now she turned on her back, and her cloudlike breasts, milk-white like faience, gleamed in the sun at the edges of their white, soft and supple roundness. Little bubbles of water like beads bedewed them. She was all quivering and laughing in the water . . .

Did he see this or did he not? Was he awake or dreaming? But what was that? The wind of music? It is ringing and ringing and eddying and coming closer and piercing his heart with an insufferable thrill . . .

"What does it mean?" the philosopher wondered, looking down as he flew along full speed. He was bathed in sweat, and aware of a fiendishly voluptuous feeling, he felt a stabbing, exhaustingly terrible delight. It often seemed to him as though his heart had melted away, and with terror he clutched at it. Worn out, desperate, he began trying to recall all the prayers he knew. He went through all the exorcisms against evil spirits, and all at once felt somewhat refreshed; he felt that his step was growing slower, the witch's hold upon his back seemed feebler, thick grass brushed him, and now he saw nothing extraordinary in it. The clear crescent moon was shining in the sky.

"Good!" the philosopher Khoma thought to himself, and he began repeating the exorcisms almost aloud. At last, quick as lightning, he sprang from under the old woman and in his turn leapt on her back. The old woman, with a tiny tripping step, ran so fast that her rider could scarcely breathe. The earth flashed by under him; everything was clear in the moonlight, though the moon was not full; the ground was smooth, but everything flashed by so rapidly that it was confused and indistinct. He snatched up a piece of wood that lay on the road and began whacking the old woman with all his might. She uttered wild howls; at first they were angry and menacing, then they grew fainter, sweeter, clearer, then rang out gently like delicate silver bells that stabbed him to the heart; and the thought flashed through his mind: was it really an old woman?

"Oh, I'm done in!" she murmured, and sank exhausted to the ground.

He stood up and looked into her face (there was the glow of sunrise and the golden domes of the Kiev churches were gleaming in the distance): before him lay a lovely creature with luxuriant tresses all in disorder and eyelashes as long as arrows. Senseless she tossed her bare white arms and moaned, looking upwards with eyes full of tears.

Khoma trembled like a leaf on a tree; he was overcome by pity and a strange emotion and timidity, feelings he could not himself explain. He set off running full speed. His heart throbbed uneasily, and he could not account for the strange new feeling that had taken possession of him. He did not want to go back to the farm; he hastened to Kiev, pondering all the way on this incomprehensible adventure.

There was scarcely a student left in the town. All had scattered about the countryside, either to situations or simply without them, because in the villages of the Ukraine they could get cheese cakes, cheese, sour cream, and dumplings as big as a hat without paying a kopek for them. The big rambling house in which the students were lodged was absolutely empty, and although the philosopher rummaged in every corner and even felt in all the holes and cracks in the roof, he could not find a bit of bacon or even a stale roll such as were commonly hidden there by the students.

The philosopher, however, soon found means to improve his lot: he walked whistling three times through the market, finally winked at a young widow in a yellow bonnet who was selling ribbons, buckshot and assorted wheels, and was that very day regaled with wheat dumplings, a chicken . . . in short, there is no telling what was on the table laid before him in a little hut in the middle of a cherry orchard.

That same evening the philosopher was seen in a pot-house; he was lying on the bench, smoking a pipe as his habit was, and in the sight of all he flung the Jew who kept the house a gold coin. A mug stood before him. He looked at the people that came in and went out with eyes full of quiet satisfaction, and thought no more of his extraordinary adventure.

Meanwhile rumours were circulating everywhere that the daughter of one of the richest Cossack *sotniks* [an officer of a company of a hundred Cossacks], who lived nearly fifty versts from Kiev, had returned one day from a walk terribly injured, hardly able to crawl home to her father's house, was on the verge of death, and had expressed a wish that one of the Kiev seminarists, Khoma Brut, should read the prayers over her and the psalms for three days after her death. The philosopher heard of this from the rector himself, who summoned him to his room and informed him that he was to set off on the journey without any delay, that the noble *sotnik* had sent servants and a carriage to fetch him.

The philosopher shuddered from an unaccountable feeling which he could not have explained to himself. A dark presentiment told him that something evil was awaiting him. Without knowing why, he bluntly declared that he would not go.

"Listen, Domine Khoma!" said the rector. (on some occasions he expressed himself very courteously with those under his authority.) "Who the devil is asking you whether you want to go or not? All I have to tell you is that if you go on jibing and making difficulties, I'll order you a good flogging on your back and the rest of you."

The philosopher, scratching behind his ear, went out without uttering a word, proposing at the first suitable opportunity to put his trust in his heels.

[*However Khoma was unable to avoid the* sotnik's *request and was compelled to present himself at the* sotnik's *residence and pray for three succesive nights over the young woman's corpse. Following is Gogol's depiction of the final night*]:

Everything was the same, everything wore the same sinister familiar aspect. He stood still for a minute. The horrible witch's coffin was still standing motionless in the middle of the church.

"I won't be afraid; by God, I will not!" he said and, drawing a circle around himself as before, he began recalling all his spells and exorcisms. There was an awful stillnes; the candles spluttered and flooded the whole church with light. The philosopher turned one page, then turned another and noticed that he was not reading what was written in the book. With horror he crossed himself and began chanting. This gave him a little more courage; the reading made progress, and the pages turned rapidly one after the other.

All of a sudden . . . in the midst of the stillness . . . the iron lid of the coffin burst with a crash and the corpse rose up. It was more terrible than the first time. Its teeth clacked horribly against each other, its lips twitched convulsively, and incantations came from them in wild shrieks. A whirlwind swept through the church, the icons fell to the ground, broken glass came flying down from the windows. The doors were burst from their hinges and a countless multitude of monstrous beings trooped into the church of God. A terrible noise of wings and scratching claws filled the church. Everything flew and raced about looking for the philosopher.

All trace of drink had disappeared, and Khoma's head was quite clear now. He kept crossing himself and repeating prayers at random. And all the while he heard the fiends whirring round him, almost touching him with their loathsome tails and the tips of their wings. He had not the courage to look at them; he only saw a huge monster, the whole width of the wall, standing in the shade of its matted locks as of a forest; through the tangle of hair two eyes glared horribly with eyebrows slightly lifted. Above it something was hanging in the air like an immense bubble with a thousand claws and scorpion-stings protruding from the centre; black earth hung in clods on them. They were all looking at him, seeking him, but could not see him, surrounded by his mysterious circle. "Bring Viy! Fetch Viy!" he heard the corpse cry.

And suddenly, a stillness fell upon the church; the wolves' howling was heard in the distance, and soon there was the thud of heavy footsteps resounding through the church. With a sidelong glance he saw they were bringing a squat, thickset, bandy-legged figure. He was covered all over with black earth. His arms and legs grew out like strong sinewy roots. He trod heavily, stumbling at every step. His long eyelids hung down to the very ground. Khoma saw with horror that his face was of iron. He was supported under the arms and led straight to the spot where Khoma was standing.

"Lift up my eyelids. I do not see!" said Viy in a voice that seemed to come from underground—and all the company flew to raise his eyelids.

"Don't look!" an inner voice whispered to the philosopher. He could not restrain himself and he looked.

"There he is!" shouted Viy, and thrust an iron finger at him. And the whole horde pounced upon the philosopher. He fell expiring to the ground, and his soul fled from his body in terror.

There was the sound of a cock crowing. It was the second cock-crow; the first had been missed by the gnomes. In panic they rushed to the doors and windows to fly out in utmost haste; but they stuck in the doors and windows and remained there.

When the priest went in, he stopped short at the sight of this defama-
tion of God's holy place, and dared not serve the requiem on such a spot.
And so the church was left for ever, with monsters stuck in the doors and
windows, was overgrown with trees, roots, rough grass and wild thorns,
and no one can now find the way to it.

[. . . *A brief epilogue follows. A.L*]

Nevsky Prospekt

There is no finer sight than Nevsky Prospect, at least not in St.
Petersburg; it epitomizes the whole city. No aspect of this thoroughfare
fails to dazzle—the fairest of our capital! I know not a single one of the
pale officials who live there would exchange Nevsky Prospect for anything
on earth. Not only those who are twenty-five years old, with fine moustaches and surprisingly well-made frock coats, but even those with white
hairs sprouting on their chins and with heads as smooth as silver dishes,
they too find Nevsky Prospect a source of great delight. And women! Oh,
for women Nevsky Prospect is an even greater attraction! And who could
resist it! As soon as you set foot on Nevsky Prospect you're aware of the
fairground atmosphere. Even if you have some important, pressing business to attend to, once there you'll most likely forget about business of any
kind. This is the only place where people put in an appearance for reasons
other than expediency, where they have not been driven to by necessity and
the business interests which motivate all St. Petersburg. It seems that a man
encountered on Nevsky Prospect is less greedy than on Morskaia (Marine),
Gorokhovaia (Pease), Liteinaia (Foundry) or Meshchanskaia (Bourgeois)
or any other street, where acquisitiveness, profits and necessity are written
all over the faces of the people walking along or flying past in their carriages. Nevsky Prospect is St. Petersburg's main artery of communication.
An inhabitant of the Petersburg or Vyborg district who has not visited his
friend from Peski (The Sands) or the Moscow Gate neighborhood for years
can be sure of meeting him here. No street-guide or information bureau
could provide you with such trustworthy information as Nevsky Prospect.
Almighty Nevsky Prospect! The only entertainment for the poor people of
Petersburg out for a stroll! How cleanly the pavements are swept and,
Lord! how many feet have left their mark there! The clumsy, muddy boots
of the retired soldier, under whose weight the very granite seems to crack,
and the dainty, ethereal shoes of the young lady who turns her pretty head
towards the shining shop windows like a sunflower turning towards the

sun, and the jingling saber of the hopeful ensign, which leaves a deep scratch in it—both the power of strength and the power of weakness batter it. The fleeting phantasmagoria that is enacted there in the course of a single day! How many changes it undergoes between one day and the next!

Let's begin with early morning, when all of Petersburg smells of hot, freshly-baked loaves and is packed with old women in tattered dresses and coats making their forays on the churches and sympathetic passersby. Then Nevsky Prospect is empty: thickset shop owners and their salesmen are still asleep in their Dutch shirts or are soaping their noble cheeks and drinking coffee; beggars are gathering around the cafe doors, where a sleepy shop boy, who the day before had flown like a gadfly, carrying cups of chocolate, now creeps with broom in hand and tieless, and tosses the beggars stale pies and leftovers. The needy people trudge through the streets; sometimes Russian peasants, dashing to work in lime-covered boots which even the Yekaterinsky (Catherine's) canal, so renowned for its purity, could never wash clean. It's usually not done for Russian ladies to walk there at this time because Russians love to express themselves in such spicy terms as they would likely never hear even in the theater. Sometimes a sleepy official trudges along with a brief-case under his arm if the way to his office takes him across Nevsky Prospect. One can say definitely that at this time of day, that is up to twelve noon, Nevsky Prospect constitutes a means rather than an end for people: it gradually fills up with people preoccupied with their jobs, their worries and anxieties, who are totally oblivious of it. A Russian peasant speaks about ten kopeks or seven copper farthings, old men and women gesticulate with their hands or converse with each other, sometimes with rather uninhibited gestures, but nobody listens to them or laughs at them, except perhaps for the little boys in cotton smocks, carrying empty bottles or newly-made boots in their hands, running along Nevsky Prospect like lightning. At this time of day, no matter what you're wearing, even if you have a cap on your head instead of a hat, or if your collar comes up too high above your tie—nobody will notice.

At twelve o'clock tutors of all nationalities invade Nevsky Prospect with their pupils in cambric collars. English Joneses and French Coqs walk arm in arm with the pupils entrusted to their parental supervision and with proper decorum explain to them how the signboards over the shops are intended as a means of informing people of what is to be found in the shops themselves. The governesses, these pale misses and pink-skinned Slavs, walk majestically along behind their dainty, fidgety little girls, ordering them to lift their shoulders a little higher and to hold themselves more erect; to sum up, at this time of day Nevsky Prospect is educational Nevsky Prospect. But the closer it gets to two o'clock the more the number of tutors, teachers and children decreases: finally they are replaced by their genteel sires, walking arm-in-arm with their gaudy, multi-colored excitable ladies. Little by little they are joined by those who have concluded important private errands—that is, those who have spoken to their doctors about the weather and the insignificant pimple which has erupted on their nose, those who have made inquiries about the health of their horses and their children, who have, by the way, shown great talent, those who have read a billboard or an important newspaper article about people arriving and departing, and finally those who have been drinking coffee or tea; these are joined by those whose enviable fate has endowed them with the revered profession of official-with-special-responsibilities. And these are joined by people who serve in the Department of Foreign Affairs and who are distinguished by the exalted nature of their occupations and habits. Lord! What splendid posts and jobs there are! How they ennoble and delight the soul! But alas! I am not a civil servant and am deprived of the pleasure of observing the bosses' refined treatment of me! Everything you are likely to come across on Nevsky Prospect, everything, is permeated with good taste: men in long frock coats, with their hands thrust into their pockets, ladies in pink, white and pale blue satin redingotes and hats. Here you'll see unique side-whiskers tucked into collars with rare and surprising artistry; velvety, satiny side-whiskers as black as sable or coal, but, alas, belonging only to members of the Department of Foreign Affairs. Providence has not endowed members of other departments with black side-whiskers and they must wear ginger ones, to their great displeasure. Here you'll encounter wonderful mustaches no pen could describe and no paintbrush depict; mustaches to which the better half of a life has been devoted; the objects of long vigils by day and night, mustaches which have been doused in the most seductive perfumes and scents and colored by all the most expensive and rarest of pomades; mustaches which are wrapped in gossamer vellum paper for the night; mustaches for which their owners demonstrate a most touching affection and which become the envy of passersby. Thousands of kinds of hats, dresses, scarves—particolored ones, gauzy ones which sometimes retain the affection of their owners for two whole days, dazzle anyone who happens to be on Nevsky Prospect. It seems that a whole sea of butterflies has suddenly taken flight from its flower stems and surges like a glimmering cloud about the men, who resemble black beetles. Here you'll see such waistlines as you've never even dreamed of: slender, narrow waists, no thicker than the neck of a bottle, for which you chivalrously step aside so as not to carelessly brush against them with a disrespectful elbow; your heart is overcome by timidity and fear, lest with just a careless breath you cause this most delightful product of nature and art to disintegrate. And what ladies' sleeves you'll see on Nevsky Prospect. Oh, what sheer delight! They look rather like two air balloons, which make you think that the lady would float up into the air if the gentleman did not have tight hold of her: because it's as easy and as pleasant to lift a lady into the air as it is to raise a glass of champagne to your lips. Nowhere do people bow as gallantly or unaffectedly when they meet one another as they do on Nevsky Prospect. Here you'll see that singular smile, that smile which is beyond art and which will sometimes make you melt away with pleasure, and will sometimes make you feel smaller than a blade of grass and lower your head, and also one which will sometimes make you feel taller than the Admiralty Tower and capable of lifting it up. Here you'll meet people talking of a concert or the weather with such unusual refinement and feelings of personal dignity. Here you'll meet a thousand inscrutable characters and types. Lord! What strange characters one meets on Nevsky Prospect! There are a great many people who, when they meet you, unfailingly stare at your boots, and, if you walk past they turn round to scrutinize your coattails. I've never been able to understand why this is so. At first I thought they were cobblers, but this is not the case: for the most part they work in various departments, and many of them are capable of writing a memorandum from one government department to another in excellent fashion; or they are people out for a walk, or reading the newspapers in the cafes—in a word, they are, for the most part, respectable people. And during that hallowed hour, from two to three in the afternoon, which may be termed the high spot of the afternoon on Nevsky Prospect, the supreme exhibition of Man's finest products takes place. One person displays a dandyish tail-coat, edged with the finest beaver, another—a fine Greek nose, a third has excellent side-whiskers, a fourth—a pair of pretty eyes and a breathtaking hat, a fifth—a talisman ring on a foppish little finger, a sixth—a foot in an enchanting little shoe, a seventh—a remarkable tie, and an eighth— a mustache to amaze anyone. But the clock strikes three and the exhibition comes to an end, the crowd thins out At three o'clock—another change. It's suddenly Spring on Nevsky Prospect, the street is covered with officials in green uniforms. Hungry titular, court, and other councilors try to make their way as fast as they possibly can. Young collegiate registrars, provincial and collegiate secretaries, hurry to seize their opportunity of walking along Nevsky Prospect with a bearing that shows *they* certainly haven't spent the last six hours sitting in an office. But the old collegiate secretaries, the titular and court councilors, they walk along quickly and with bowed heads: they have no interest in scrutinizing the passersby; they still haven't torn themselves completely away from their work; inside their heads there's a jumble and veritable archive of matters begun and as yet unfinished; instead of signboards for a long while they see a box of documents or their office manager's full face.

From four o'clock on Nevsky Prospect is deserted, and not a single official is to be seen there. The odd seamstress from a dressmaker's might dash across Nevsky Prospect, carrying a small bandbox; some pitiful victim of a philanthropic attorney thrust into the world in a frieze coat; some passing eccentric for whom time is meaningless; some long, tall Englishwoman carrying a purse and small book in her hands; a cooperative worker, a Russian wearing a high-waisted calico frock coat and sporting a slender beard, who's lived all his life in a hurry and whose every part, as he makes his way deferentially along the sidewalk, is in constant motion: back, arms, legs and head, and sometimes a low-class artisan . . . you won't meet anyone else on Nevsky Prospect at this time.

But as soon as dusk descends on the houses and streets and the watchman, wrapped in matting, clambers up the ladder to light the lamp, and the notice cards which dare not be shown in broad daylight appear in the shops' lower windows, then Nevsky Prospect takes on new life and begins to stir. Then arrives that mysterious hour when the lamps bathe everything in a beckoning, wondrous light. You will see a great many young men, mostly unmarried, in warm frock coats or greatcoats. At this time a certain sense of purpose can be detected, or rather something resembling a sense of purpose, something completely inexplicable; everybody's footsteps quicken and, generally speaking, become very erratic; elongated shadows, their heads reaching almost as far as the Politseisky (Police) Bridge, flash across the walls and pavements. Young collegiate registrars, provincial and collegiate secretaries stroll about for hours on end; but the old collegiate registrars, titular and court advisers usually stay indoors, either because such people are married or because the German cooks living in their houses cook such excellent dishes for them. Here you'll find the respectable old men who at two o'clock were strolling along Nevsky Prospect with such an air of importance and unbelievable sophistication. You'll see them on the run, just like the young collegiate registrars, to have a sly look at a lady they've spotted in the distance, and whose full lips and cheeks, caked with rouge, are such a delight to many passersby, and particularly to the tradesmen, cooperative workers and merchants who can always be seen walking along in a group, all wearing German frock coats and usually arm-in-arm.

"Stop!"—shouted Lieutenant Pirogov (Pie) just at that moment. holding back the young man who was walking along with him in a frock coat and cape. "Did you see?"

"Yes, I did. An enchanting girl; a real Perugino's *Bianca*."

"Whom are you talking about?"

"About her, that one with the dark hair. And what eyes! Lord, what eyes! The way she holds herself, and her figure! And the shape of her face—all wonderful!"

"I'm talking about the blonde who passed her on the other side. Why don't you follow the brunette, since you seem to fancy her so much ?"

"How could I?" exclaimed the young man in the dress coat, blushing. "That would be like saying she was one of those ladies who walk to and fro along Nevsky Prospect of an evening," he continued, sighing. "She must be very well-to-do, why, her cape alone must be worth about eighty rubles."

"Fool!" shouted Pirogov, forcibly pushing him in the direction of the lady's brightly colored cape. "Go on, you numbskull, you're missing your chance! And I'll go after that blonde!"

The two friends parted company.

"We know you, all of you," Pirogov thought to himself, smiling in a self-satisfied, conceited way, totally convinced that no beauty existed who could resist him.

The young man in the frock coat and cape set off with a shy and hesitant gait, in the direction of the many-hued cape, which was now was bathed in a bright light as it approached the light of the street lamp, and now momentarily concealed in darkness as it moved away. His heart pounded and he increased his speed without realizing it. He didn't even dare to think he might have some right to the attention of the beautiful girl who had flown away into the distance, let alone admit to any shady thoughts of the kind hinted at by Lieutenant Pirogov; but he did want just to see the house and make a note of where this delightful creature lived, this creature who, it seemed, had flown down from Heaven straight onto Nevsky Prospect, and, doubtless would fly away again Heaven knows where. He was flying along so quickly that he kept on knocking middle-aged, gray-whiskered gentlemen off the sidewalk. This young man belonged to that class of people who seem such a strange phenomenon to us and who belong to the citizens of Petersburg about as much as a face appearing to us in a dream belongs to the material world. This exclusive class is very unusual in a city where everybody is officials, merchants or German craftsmen. He was an artist. They *are* a strange phenomenon, aren't they? A Petersburg artist! An artist in the land of snows, an artist in the land of the Finns, where everything is damp, slippery, flat, pale, gray or misty. These artists are totally unlike Italian artists, who are proud and passionate like Italy and her sky; on the contrary, these are for the most part kind, timid, shy, easy-come-easy-go people, quietly in love with their art, who drink, tea with a couple of friends in their small rooms and unaffectedly talk about their favorite subject, heedless of all else. They are always inviting some old beggar-woman back to their rooms and making her sit for six whole hours so that they can transpose her pitiful, lifeless face onto canvas. They draw the perspective of their own rooms, in which there's all sort of artists' rubbish: plaster hands and feet, coffee-colored with time and dust, broken artists' work benches, an overturned palette, a friend playing a guitar, paint-spattered walls and an open window, through which are glimpsed the pale Neva and fishermen in red shirts. Almost everything they own has a murky gray cast to it—the indelible stamp of the North. But with all this they labor over their work with genuine enjoyment. They often nurture real talent within them, and if only the fresh breeze of Italy could blow on them this talent doubtless would blossom as freely, expansively and brilliantly as a plant which is taken at last out of doors and into the fresh air. They're generally very shy: the star and broad epaulette throw them into such confusion that they automatically lower the prices of any of their works. Occasionally they like to play the dandy, but their dandyism always seems too abrasive and has a slap-dash look. You'll sometimes see them wearing an excellent tailcoat with a soiled cape, an expensive velvet waistcoat and a paint-stained frock coat. Just as, on one of their unfinished landscapes you'll sometimes see sketched at the bottom the head of a nymph which the artist, unable to another spot for it, had dashed off in outline on the filthy primer coat of a previous work he'd once painted for pleasure. They never look you straight in the eye; or if they do, then they do so in a somewhat hazy, indecisive way, theirs is not the penetrating hawk-like stare of an examiner or the falcon glance of a cavalry officer. This stems from the fact that they see at the same time both your features and those of some plaster Hercules standing in their room, or they're imagining a picture of their own, one which they're still *thinking* of doing. For this reason they often answer incoherently, sometimes off the point, and the jumbled-up subjects in their mind only increase their timidity. And to such a breed belongs the young man we've just described, the artist Piskarev, shy and timid, but concealing feelings in his soul which, at the right moment, were ready to burst into flame. With secret trembling he hurried along after the subject who had made such a strong impression on him, and he himself seemed surprised at his own audacity. The unknown creature on whom his eyes, thoughts and feelings were fixed suddenly turned her head and looked at him. Lord! What heavenly features! The dazzling whiteness of her delightful forehead was framed in beautiful jet-black hair. They curled, those wonderful locks, and some of them, cascading down from beneath her hat, caressed her cheeks, which were touched with a delicate fresh pinkies due to the evening chill. Her lips were sealed by a host of the most delightful dreams. All those things which recall memories of our childhood and which provide dreams and quiet inspiration in the light of a glowing lamp—all these, it seemed, gathered, merged and were expressed in her harmonious lips. She looked at Piskarev, and that look made his heart flutter; she looked sternly at him, a sense of the vexation evoked by such impudent pursuit overspread her features; but on this beautiful face even anger was captivating. Overcome with shame and timidity, Piskarev (Squeak) simply stood there with his eyes lowered; but how could he let such a divine being out of his sight without even discovering the sacred place in which she condescended to abide? Such were the thoughts which entered the young dreamer's head, and he decided to continue the chase. But to avoid being noticed, he moved further back, casually looked in both directions and examined the signboards, but all the while he didn't allow a single step the girl took to escape his notice. Pedestrians began to flash past less often, the street was becoming quieter; the beautiful girl turned around, and it seemed to him that a slight smile flashed across her lips. He was all a-quiver and could not believe his own eyes. No, it was the lamp with its deceptive light drawing on her face something like a smile; no, it was his own dreams laughing at him. But his breath faltered within his breast and was converted there into an undefined trembling, all his senses were on fire and everything in front of him was swallowed up by a kind of mist. The sidewalk swam beneath him, carriages with galloping horses seemed stock still, the bridge stretched and snapped at its arch, a house was standing upside down, a sentry box stooped to meet him, and the watchman's halberd together with the golden lettering of a signboard and the pair of scissors pictured on it shone as if they hung on his very eyelashes. And all this was the effect of a single glance, a single turn of a beautiful little head. Hearing nothing, seeing nothing, noticing nothing, he scurried along in the traces of those beautiful little feet, trying to regulate the speed of his steps, which were keeping time with his heartbeats. At times he was overcome by doubts: was the expression on her face really so favorable—and then he would stop for a moment, but his heart-beats, the invincible force and turmoil of all his feelings urged him on. He didn't even notice how a four-story building suddenly appeared in front of him, with four rows of windows, all lit up and all looking at him at once, and the balustrade by the entryway barred his way with an iron jolt. He saw the unknown lady fly up the stairs, look around, put her finger to her lips and signal him to follow her. His knees trembled; his emotions and thoughts were on fire; a lightning flash of joy, unbearably sharp, pierced his heart. No, this was no longer a dream! Lord, how much happiness in a single moment! A lifetime's ecstasy in two minutes!

But was this not all a dream? Was it possible that this woman, in exchange for whose single heavenly glance he was prepared to surrender his whole life, and to approach whose house he considered the most inexpressible of pleasures, was it possible that she was really favorably inclined towards him and attentive of him just now? He flew up that staircase. He was experiencing no earthly thoughts; he was consumed by no earthly passion; no, at that moment he was pure and chaste, like a virginal youth, still breathing an undefined spiritual craving for love. And what would in a licentious man have roused daring thoughts was the very thing which, on the contrary, sanctified them to him. This trust which the weak, beautiful creature displayed to him, this trust placed him under a vow of chivalrous self-restraint, a vow to carry out her every command as if he were her slave. He only wished that these commands be as demanding and difficult to execute as possible so that he could fly to overcome them with a greater exertion of strength. He did not doubt that some secret and at the same time important occurrence had obliged this unknown girl to confide in him; and that without doubt, great favors would be demanded of him, and he could already feel inside himself a strength and decisiveness equal to anything.

The staircase swirled upwards, and his rapid dreams swirled with it. "Go carefully!" a voice resounded like a harp, infusing his veins with renewed trembling. At the dark top of the third floor the unknown girl knocked at a door—it opened and they walked in together. A rather pleasant-looking woman met them with a candle in her hand, but she looked at Piskarev in such a strange, insolent manner that he involuntarily lowered his eyes. They entered the room. There, feminine shapes in different corners met his eyes. One of the women was laying out cards, another was sitting at the piano, making a pitiful, two-fingered attempt at an old Polonaise; the third was sitting in front of a mirror combing her long hair, with no intention whatever of interrupting her toilette for a stranger's entry. A certain unpleasant disorder, such as one only sees in the room of a carefree bachelor, reigned supreme. The furnishings, of fairly high quality, were covered in dust; a spider had veiled the molded cornice with its web; through the partly open door into the other room the spurs of a pair of boots and the red braid of a uniform could be seen; a loud male's voice and a woman's laughter resounded unrestrainedly.

Lord! Where had he come to! At first he didn't want to believe it and began to stare harder at the objects filling the room; but the bare walls and undraped windows didn't bespeak the presence of a conscientious landlady; the haggard faces of these pitiful creatures, one of whom was sitting right under his nose, surveying him as calmly as she would a stain on someone else's gown—all this convinced him he had come upon one of those dens of iniquity in which pitiful vice, born of tawdry education and the fearful overcrowding of the capital, had made its abode. It was one of those dens where men sacrilegiously trample on and mock all that is pure and holy and makes life beautiful, where Woman, the jewel of the world, the crown of creation, is transformed into some strange, ambiguous being, where she and the purity of her soul are stripped of everything feminine and repulsively acquires the tricks and shamelessness of men, and ceases to be that weak, beautiful creature so different from us. Piskarev scanned her from head to foot with astonished eyes, as if still trying to assure himself this was the same girl who had charmed and captivated him on Nevsky Prospect. But she stood before him, looking just as beautiful as before, her hair was just as beautiful, and her eyes seemed every bit as heavenly. She was fresh-complected, not a day more than seventeen years old, and it was obvious that she had only recently been caught up in horrifying depravity; it still had not dared to touch her cheeks, they were so fresh and slightly tinged with alight blush—she was beautiful.

He stood motionless before her, ready to be swept off his feet by her again, as he had been earlier. But the beautiful girl grew impatient with such a long silence and smiled insinuatingly, looking him straight in the eye. But that smile was full of a somehow pitiful insolence; it looked so strange and unsuited to her face, as a pious expression is to a bribe-taker's mug, or an accountant's ledger to a poet. He shuddered. She opened her pretty little mouth and began to say something, but it was all so stupid, so banal . . . as if intelligence had disappeared with chastity! He didn't want to hear anything else. He was extraordinarily abashed and as artless as a child. Instead of using such favor, instead of rejoicing at such an opportunity, which without doubt would have rejoiced any other man in his position, he took to his heels like a wild goat and ran out into the street.

Head hung low and limbs drooping, he sat in his room like a poor man who has found a priceless pearl and then immediately dropped it into the sea. "Such a beauty; such a divine creature—what's she doing in a place like that?" They were the only words he could utter.

Indeed, remorse never overcomes us so powerfully as when we see beauty touched by the rotten breath of debauchery. We can accept ugliness as vice's companion, but beauty, such tender beauty . . . in our minds it can only be associated with chastity and purity. The beautiful girl who had so charmed poor Piskarev was a truly wonderful, unusual creature, and her living in the despicable milieu seemed more and more unbelievable. Her features were all so finely traced and the expression on her beautiful face bore the stamp of such nobility it was impossible to think that debauchery had clasped her in its terrible claws. She could have been the priceless pearl, the whole world, the whole of paradise, or all the wealth of a passionate husband, she could have been the beautiful, gentle star of an ordinary family circle and with just a movement of her beautiful mouth she could have uttered her sweet instructions. She could have been a goddess in a crowded room, on the bright parquet floor in the gleam of the candles, surrounded by the silent reverence of a multitude of faithful admirers at her feet. But alas! By the horrid will of the denizen of Hell, athirst to destroy the harmony of life, she had been cast, sped on by laughter, into his abyss.

Overcome with heartrending pity, Piskarev sat before a guttering candle. It was already long past midnight, the bell in the tower struck half-past while he sat motionless, not yet asleep yet at the same time not fully awake. Drowsiness, taking advantage of his inertia, was about to steal up on him; already the room was beginning to disappear, only the glow of the single candle was shining through the dreams overpowering him, when suddenly a knock at the door made him start and brought him around. The door opened, and in came a servant in a fine livery. No fine livery had ever entered into his isolated room, especially at such a late hour He was amazed, and with impatient curiosity he stared at the servant who had just arrived.

"The lady," the servant said with a polite bow, "at whose house you deigned to spend some time, has ordered me to invite you to call on her and has sent a carriage for you."

Piskarev stood in silent amazement: A carriage, a servant in livery! No, surely there must be some mistake. . . .

"Listen, my good man," he said timidly, "perhaps you've called at the wrong house. The lady must have sent you to fetch someone else, not me."

"No sir, I'm not mistaken. Was it not you who were so good as to walk the lady home to her room on the third floor, on Liteinaia Street?"

"It was."

"Well, then, please hurry. The lady wishes to see you without fail and asks you to come straight to her house. "

Piskarev ran downstairs. Outside there really was a carriage. He got into it, the doors slammed shut, the cobblestones of the road-way clattered under the wheels and hooves—and the illuminated perspective of the houses with bright signboards flashed past the carriage windows. Piskarev pondered for the entire journey and didn't know what to conclude about this adventure. Her own house, a carriage, a servant in fine livery—he couldn't reconcile all this with the room on the third floor, the dusty windows and the out-of-tune piano. The carriage drew up outside a brightly-lit entrance gate and Piskarev was immediately stunned: a line of carriages, the chatter of coachmen, brightly-lit windows and the sound of music. The servant in the fine livery helped him down from the carriage and respectfully led him into a hall with marble columns, a doorman bedecked in gold, scattered capes and furs and a bright lamp. An airy staircase suffused with perfumes and with a gleaming balustrade led upwards. He was already on it and had already gone up to the first room, stunned and frightened into taking a step backwards from the terrifying crowd of people. The extraordinarily variegated mass of people confused him utterly; it seemed to him that some devil had crumbled up the world into thousands of different pieces and was now, with no significance or meaning, mixing them together. The gleaming shoulders of the ladies and the black tail-coats, the chandeliers, the sconces, the incorporeal, flickering gas lamps, the ethereal ribbons and the fat bassoon, staring out from behind the railings of the great choirs—all this was dazzling to him. He saw at a glance so many dignified old and middle-aged men with stars on their frock coats, ladies, so lightly, proudly and graciously stepping out onto the parquet floor or sitting in rows, he heard so many French and English words, and, moreover, the young men in black frock coats were infused with such an air of nobility, they spoke and kept silent with such propriety, as they had learned not to say anything superfluous, and they joked so magnificently and smiled so respectfully, wore such wonderful whiskers, had such a talent for displaying their wonderful hands while arranging their neckties, and the ladies were so incorporeal and so steeped in complete self-conceit and ecstasy, they lowered their eyes so enchantingly that . . . but the mere sight of Piskarev's benumbed expression, pressed timidly as he was against a column, illustrated how completely his nerves had been shattered. At that moment the crowd clustered around a group of dancers. They surged on, draped in their transparent Parisian creations, in their dresses woven out of the air itself; they stepped carelessly over the parquet with their dainty gleaming feet and they could not have appeared more ethereal if they had been walking on air. But one was more lovely and dressed so much more sumptuously and strikingly than all the rest. An inexplicable, subtle combination of taste was evident in her garb and for all that it seemed that *she* had not troubled herself about it; it just happened by itself, spontaneously. She was both looking and not looking at the surrounding crowd, she lowered her beautiful long eyelashes indifferently, and the gleaming whiteness of her face dazzled the eye most blindingly when her enchanting brow lightly shaded it as she inclined her head.

Piskarev used all his strength to force away through the crowd to have a look at her; but, to his great annoyance, some huge head with dark curly hair kept getting in the way; moreover, the crowd hemmed him in to such an extent that he did not dare edge forward, nor move backwards, so afraid was he of unintentionally nudging into some privy councilor. But then he managed to edge forward and glance down at his coat, thinking to adjust it. God in Heaven, what was this! He was wearing a frock coat stained all over with paint; hurrying off, he had forgotten all about changing into a decent coat. He blushed to the ears and, head down, wanted to sink through the floor but there was no room to sink: the gentlemen-of-the-bedchamber in their gleaming suits moved into position behind him like a veritable wall. He wanted to get as far away as possible from the beautiful girl with the beautiful forehead and eyelashes. In terror he raised his eyes to see if she was looking at him—Lord! She was standing right in front of him But what's this? What's this? "It's she"—he shouted almost at the top of his voice. Indeed, it was she, that very same girl whom he had met on Nevsky Prospect and whom he had taken home.

Meanwhile, she raised her eyelashes and was looking at everyone with her clear eyes. "Oh, oh, oh how beautiful she is! . . ." was all he could say, with halting breath. She cast her eyes over the circle of people vying with each other to attract her attention, but with a certain aloofness and inattention she quickly put them off, and then her eyes met Piskarev's. Oh! What Heaven! What Paradise! God give me strength to bear all this! It's more than life can stand, it will destroy and carry off my soul! She signaled to him, not with her hand but with a nod of her head—no, in her ravish-ing eyes this sign was expressed in such a slight, unnoticeable expression, that nobody could have seen it, but he did see, did understand her. The dance went on a long time; the weary music seemed to die down and fade away completely, then again swell up, shriek and thunder: at last—it was over! She sat down, her breast was heaving in the faint smoke from the gaslight, her hand (Lord, what a wonderful hand!) fell onto her lap, pressed her incorporeal dress down and beneath it the dress seemed to breathe the music, and its faint lilac color outlined more vividly the whiteness of this beautiful hand. If only he could touch it—nothing more! No other desires—they would only be an impertinence. He was standing behind her chair, not daring to speak, not daring to breathe.

"You were bored," she said. "So was I. I see you despise me . . ." she added, lowering her long eyelashes.

"Despise you? Me? . . . I" The completely nonplussed Piskarev was about to speak, and he would have surely uttered a mass of incoherent words but at this moment a gentleman-in-waiting with a beautiful tuft of hair gathered up on top of his head approached them, making witty and pleasant remarks. He rather good naturedly displayed a row of reasonably good teeth and with each of his witticisms banged a sharp nail through Piskarev's heart. At last somebody standing to the side, fortunately, turned to the gentleman-in-waiting with a question.

"I can't stand any more!" she said, raising her heavenly eyes toward him. "I'm going to sit down at the other end of the hall: you must come there!"

She slipped through the crowd and disappeared. He shot through the crowd as one demented and got there before her.

Yes, this was she! She was sitting, like a *tsaritsa*, more lovely and more beautiful than the rest, searching for him with her eyes.

"You've come," she said quietly. "I'll be frank with you: I'm sure the circumstances of our meeting seem strange to you. But surely you can't believe that I belong to that despicable class of creatures among whom you found me. My behavior must seem strange to you, but I'm going to reveal my secret to you. Will you be able," she said, riveting her eyes on him, not to betray it?"

"Oh, I will! I will! I will!"

But at that moment a rather elderly man approached and began talking to her in a language which Piskarev could not understand, and offered her his arm. She looked at Piskarev imploringly and signaled to him to stay where he was and wait till she returned, but a fit of impatience made him unable to hear a single command even from her lips. He set off after her, but the crowd separated them. He could no longer see her lilac dress; he walked from room to room in a state of agitation and mercilessly jolted people who got in his way, but in all the rooms there were only aces seated at their whist, steeped in deathly silence. In one corner of the room some elderly people were arguing about the advantages of military service over civilian; in another, people dressed in magnificent frock coats were making flippant remarks about the voluminous works of a poet-worker. Piskarev became aware of an elderly gentleman, of respectable appearance, who seized hold of his coat button and asked his opinion on a very justifiable remark, but he rudely pushed him away, without even noticing that the man was wearing a rather prestigious order around his neck. He ran through to another room— she was not there either. Nor was she in the third room. "Where is she? Give her to me! Oh, I cannot live without seeing her! I want to hear what she was going to tell me!" But all his searchings were in vain. Agitated, exhausted, he huddled in a corner and simply gazed at the crowd; but his strained eyes began to make him see things unclearly. Finally, the walls of his room became plainly visible to him. He raised his eyes; in front of him stood a candlestick with the flame burned almost right down into the socket; the candle had all melted away; the wax had spilled onto his table.

He had been asleep! Lord, what a beautiful dream! And why did he wake up ? Why could it not have gone on for just a moment longer? She surely would have appeared again! The irritating daylight looked in through the window with its unpleasant, dingy brilliance. The room was in such gray, murky disorder . . . Oh, how loathsome reality is! How can it compare with a dream ? He quickly undressed and lay down on his bed, wrapped in a blanket, wishing to recapture the retreating dream if only for a moment. Sleep, in fact, was not long returning, but it presented him with a dream that was not at all what he desired: now Lieutenant Pirogov appeared smoking a pipe, now an Academy guard, now a real state councilor, now the head of the Finnish woman whose portrait he had once drawn, and other such nonsense.

He lay in bed as late as midday, trying to get to sleep; but she never returned. If only for a fleeting moment she would show her beautiful features, if only for a fleeting moment he could hear her gentle footsteps, if only her bare arm, as white as heavenly snow, would flash before his eyes!

Oblivious of everything, abandoning everything, he sat with a distraught, hopeless look on his face, completely engrossed in the dream. He didn't think of taking up anything; his eyes stared lifelessly and distractedly through the window overlooking the yard where a filthy water-carrier was pouring out water which froze in mid-air and the goatish voice of some peddler rattled "Old clothes for sale. " Anything connected with daily life or reality had a strangely grating effect on his ears. So he sat till evening and then threw himself eagerly onto his bed. He wrestled for a long time with insomnia and finally conquered it. Again a dream, a common, vulgar dream. "God have mercy on me; show her to me, just for a minute, just for a single minute! " He again waited for evening again fell asleep, again dreamed of some official who was both an official and a bassoon at the same time. Oh! It was unbearable! Finally she appeared! Her head and ringlets . . . She looked at him . . . but how briefly! Then again a mist, again some stupid dream.

Eventually dreaming became his life, and from then on his entire life took a strange turn: he, one might say, slept while awake and was only awake in his sleep. If someone were to see him sitting quietly at a bare table or walking along a street, they doubtless would take him for a sleepwalker or for someone the worse for drink; the look in his eyes was totally absent of any meaning, and his natural absentmindedness eventually increased and peremptorily banished all sensations and movement from his face. He revived only with the onset of night.

This situation sapped his strength, but the most awful torture for him was that finally the dream began to leave him completely. Wishing to save this, his only remaining treasure, he used all his efforts to bring it back. It came to his ears that there was a means of recalling his dream—all one needed to do was take opium. But where was he to get opium? He remembered about a certain Persian who kept a gown shop and who, when they met, nearly always asked Piskarev to draw him a portrait of a beautiful woman. He decided to approach him, supposing that he would be bound to have this opium. The Persian received him seated on a couch with his feet folded under him.

"What do you want opium for?" he asked him.

Piskarev told him about his insomnia. "Very well, then, I'll let you have some opium, but you must draw me a beautiful woman. And I mean beautiful! With black eyebrows and eyes as big as olives; with me lying beside her smoking a pipe! You hear! She's got to be good looking! A real beauty!" Piskarev promised everything. The Persian went out for a moment and returned with a small jar filled with a dark liquid, carefully poured part of it into another jar and gave it to Piskarev with instructions to use no more than seven drops in a little water. Piskarev avidly seized this precious jar, which he would not have sold for a pile of gold, and dashed off home.

When he got home he poured a few drops into a glass of water and, drinking it down, collapsed on the bed to sleep.

Lord! What joy! She! She was back! But in a completely different form. Oh, how pretty she was as she sat by the window of a bright little country cottage! Her clothes breathed such simplicity as only poets' thoughts are clothed in. Her coiffure Lord, how simple that coiffure was and how it suited her! A pretty little scarf was lightly flowing about her pretty neck; everything about her was modest, everything about her displayed a mysterious, inexplicable sense of taste. How delightfully and gracefully she walked! How musical was the sound of her footsteps and the swish of her simple dress! How beautiful her arm was, encircled by a bracelet with locks of dear ones' hair! She spoke to him with tears in her eyes: "Don't despise me: I am not at all the kind of girl you took me for. Look at me, look me in the eye and tell me: surely I'm not capable of what you thought." "Oh, no, no! Just let anyone dare think, just let . . ." But he wakened, agitated, unnerved, with tears in his eyes. "It would have been better had you never existed, had never been born and had remained no more than the creation of some inspired artist. I would never have left the canvas, I would have gazed at you and kissed you for eternity. I would have lived and breathed you as the most beautiful of dreams, and I would have been happy. That would have been all I desired. I would have invoked you, as my guardian angel, on going to sleep and on awakening, and I would have waited for you when I had to create something divine and holy. But now . . . what a terrible life! What purpose does she serve by living? Surely a madman's life brings no joy to his relatives and friends who were once so fond of him. Lord, what kind of life is ours! An eternal conflict between dreams and reality!" Such thoughts occupied him almost constantly. He could think of nothing, he ate practically nothing and awaited the night and his desired dream with the impatience and passion of a lover. This constant concentration of his thoughts on one thing finally assumed such control over his whole being and imagination that the desired vision appeared to him almost every day, always in a way which was opposite to reality, because his thoughts were always pure like those of a child. Through these dreams their subject became more pure and was completely transformed.

The doses of opium inflamed his thoughts even more and if ever there was a man driven by love to the greatest degree of insanity, so relentlessly, terribly, destructively and ruinously—then this was that unfortunate soul.

Of all his dreams there was one which was more joyous for him than all the rest: in it he had a vision of his studio, in which he was so happy, sitting so contentedly with a palette in his hands. And she was there too, now his wife, sitting by his side, her beautiful elbow resting on the back of his chair, and she was surveying his work. In her eyes, weary and tired, the burden of joy was evident; everything in the room breathed paradise; everything was so bright, so tidy. Lord! She lowered her delightful head onto his chest. This was the most enthralling dream he had ever known. He got up after it feeling somehow refreshed and less distraught than before. Strange thoughts came to him. "Perhaps," he thought, "she was drawn into vice by some terrible event over which she had no control; perhaps the workings of her soul incline towards repentance; perhaps she would like to get herself out of this terrible situation. And surely I can't stand by, indifferent, and watch her destroy herself when all I have to do is hold out my hand to save her from going under." And his thoughts went further. "Nobody knows me," he said to himself, "and I am no more concerned about what others do than they are about me. If she displays genuine repentance and changes her life, then I'll marry her. I must marry her, and surely I would be doing something far better than many who marry their housekeepers or sometimes even the most despicable of creatures. Mine, however, will be an entirely altruistic act, perhaps even great: I'll be returning something of rare beauty to the world."

When he had devised his simple plan, he felt the color rush to his cheeks; he walked over to the mirror and was himself shocked by his sunken cheeks and the pallor of his face. He began to smarten himself up, taking great care; he washed, smoothed down his hair; put on a few frock coat, a smart waistcoat, threw on a cape and went out of the house. He breathed in the fresh air and his heart responded to the feeling of freshness, like a convalescent who has decided to venture out of doors for the first time after a prolonged illness. His heart was pounding as he drew near to that street which he had not set foot on since that fateful meeting.

He searched for the house for a long time; it was as if his memory was playing tricks on him. Twice he walked up and down the street, not knowing which house to stop in front of. Finally one seemed likely. He ran quickly up the steps and knocked on the door: the door opened and who came out to meet him? His ideal, his mysterious image, the model for the pictures in his dreams—the girl who had become life itself for him in such a terrible, agonizing, blissful way. She stood in front of him: he trembled, his legs could scarcely support him for weakness, he was seized by a sudden fit of joy. She stood before him, so beautiful, though her eyes were sleepy and a certain pallor had crept over her face, which had lost some of its freshness. But she was still beautiful.

"Ah," she exclaimed, seeing Piskarev and rubbing her eyes (it was already two o'clock): "why did you run away from us back then?"

Exhausted, he sat down on a chair and looked at her.

"I've only just awakened. I was brought home this morning at seven o'clock. I was quite drunk," she continued, smiling.

Oh, better you were mute and missing your tongue than to say such things! She had suddenly revealed the whole panorama of her life to him. However, despite this, and wrestling with his emotions, he decided on trying to see if his exhortations would have any effect on her. Mustering his courage, he began in a quivering, but at the same time passionate, voice to describe her dreadful predicament to her. She listened to him with an attentive look and that feeling of surprise which we display at the sight of something strange and unexpected. Faintly smiling, she glanced at her friend sitting in the corner who, breaking off from cleaning her comb, also listened attentively to the new preacher.

"It's true that I'm a poor man," said Piskarev at last, after lengthy and persuasive exhortations. "But we'll work, we'll each try to out do the other, to make a better life for ourselves. There's nothing sweeter than to owe everything to one's own labors. I will sit over at my paintings, you'll sit at my side and give me the inspiration for my work while you're busy sewing or doing some other handiwork, and we'll lack for nothing."

"Not likely" she interrupted what he was saying with an expression of scorn. "I'm nobody's washerwoman or seamstress to be made to work."

Lord! All the despicable and degraded aspects of her life were revealed in these words—a life full of emptiness and idleness, the faithful companions of vice.

"Marry me!" said her friend, who had hitherto been sitting in silence in the corner, with a cheeky look in her eyes. "If you make me your wife, I'll sit like this! "And with that her pitiful face assumed a witless expression which threw the beautiful girl into fits of laughter.

Oh, that was too much! That was more than he could stand! He turned and ran, his feelings and thoughts out of control. His mind clouded over: he wandered about all day in a stupor, aimlessly, seeing and hearing nothing. It is impossible to say if he found anywhere to spend the night or not; but the next day, kept going by some blind instinct, he found his way back to his own room, pallid, with a terrified aspect, his hair disheveled and signs of insanity on his face. He locked himself in his room, admitted nobody and asked for nothing. Four days passed, during which time the locked door was not opened even once; at last a week had passed and the door still remained locked. People hurled themselves against the door and began to call out to him, but there was no reply; finally they smashed the door in and found his lifeless body with the throat cut. A razor, dripping blood, was lying on the floor. From the convulsively outstretched arms and terrifyingly distorted look on his face one could tell that his hand had faltered and he had suffered for a long time before his sinful soul had departed from his body.

Thus perished poor Piskarev, the victim of a mindless passion; the quiet, timid, humble, childishly simple-hearted artist, carrying within him that spark of genius which in time might have flared up expansively and glowingly. No one shed a tear for him ; there was no one to be seen watching by his lifeless body, except for the usual presence of the constable and the indifferent face of the town doctor. His coffin was conveyed to the Okhta in silence; there were no religious rites, even. A solitary soldier-guard walked behind it, crying, and that was really only because he had drunk a drop too much vodka. Even Lieutenant Pirogov did not come to view the corpse of the poor, wretched man to whom he had extended his high patronage when he was alive. Moreover, Pirogov had other things on his mind: he was preoccupied with a very unusual event. But let's return to him. I don't like corpses and the deceased, and it always upsets me when a long funeral procession passes and an invalid soldier, dressed like some sort of Capuchin monk, takes a pinch of snuff with his left hand because he is holding the torch in his right. It always vexes me deep down to see a resplendent catafalque and velvet coffin; but my vexation is tinged with sorrow when I see a drayman pulling along a pauper's completely unadorned pine coffin, behind which a solitary beggar woman, having met the procession at a cross-roads, trudges for want of something to do.

We, left Lieutenant Pirogov, I believe, at the point where he parted from poor Piskarev and shot off after the blonde. This blonde was a dainty, rather attractive creature. She stopped in front of every shop and gazed at the sashes, scarves, earrings, gloves and other knick-knacks, while she swirled around ceaselessly, looking all around her and behind her. "You, my little darling, belong to me!" said Pirogov, confidently, continuing his pursuit with his face thrust into his coat collar in case he met someone he knew. But it won't do any harm to tell the reader what sort of person Pirogov was.

But before we say what sort of person Lieutenant Pirogov was, it won't do any harm to say a few words about the society to which Pirogov belonged. There are officers in Petersburg who constitute a sort of middle class in society. You'll always find them at soirees or dinners at the home of a state councilor or an acting councilor who has earned his rank by forty years of hard work. Daughters, pale and completely colorless, like Petersburg itself, some of whom are past their prime, a tea-table, a piano, house parties—all these are inextricably associated with the gleaming epaulette which shines in the lamplight between a virtuous little blonde and the black coat of her brother or of some friend of the family. It is extremely difficult to rouse these cold-hearted young ladies and make them laugh: to do this one needs great skill or, rather, no skill at all. It is essential not to say anything either too intelligent or too amusing, but to talk in terms of the trivialities which women love to hear. In this respect, credit must be given to the above-mentioned gentlemen. They are particularly gifted when it comes to making these colorless beauties laugh and listen. Exclamations, smothered in laughter, such as: "Oh stop it! You ought to be ashamed of yourself, saying such ridiculous things," are often their greatest reward. Such gentlemen are seldom, or rather never, encountered in high society. They are completely shouldered out by those society calls aristocrats; they are, however considered learned and well-bred. They love to discuss literature; they praise Bulgarin, Pushkin and Grech, and talk disparagingly, and with sarcastic wit, of A. A. Orlov. They never miss a single public lecture, whether it concerns accountancy or even forestry. At the theater, whatever play is on, you'll always find one of them, except perhaps if it's a Filatka farce, which is so offensive to their discerning taste. In the theater they're permanent fixtures. These are the theater manager's most profitable customers. They're particularly fond of good poetry in a play, and also enjoy bellowing their "encores"; many of them, by teaching in government establishments or by coaching pupils for them, eventually acquire a carriage and pair. Then their circle becomes wider and they finally succeed in marrying a piano-playing merchant's daughter who has a hundred thousand, more or less, in ready cash and many, many bearded kinfolk. However, they cannot attain this honor before working their way up to the rank of at least colonel. For this reason the bearded Russian merchants, despite the fact that they still reek of cabbage, have no desire whatever to see their daughters marry anything less than a general, or at the very least, a colonel. Such are the principal characteristics of young men of this class. But Lieutenant Pirogov had a great many unique talents. He could give an excellent recital of verse from *Dmitry Donskoi* and *Woe from Wit,* and had mastered the exacting art of blowing smoke rings from his pipe so skillfully he could string nearly a dozen of them together one on top of the other. He could relate an anecdote very well, showing that a cannon is one thing and a unicorn another. But its rather difficult to list all the talents with which nature had endowed Pirogov. He loved to talk about actresses and dancers, but not so coarsely as a young ensign would normally express himself on such a matter. He was very satisfied with his rank to which he had recently been promoted and although at times, lying on his couch, he would say "Oh! Oh! Vanity of vanities! What does it matter that I'm a lieutenant?" in secret he was extremely proud of his new rank; in conversations he often tried to hint at it in a roundabout way, and once in the street, when he came across some petty clerk who failed to show him sufficient respect, he immediately stopped the man and in a few sharp words let him know that before him stood not just any officer, but a lieutenant. He tried to be particularly eloquent in his remarks, since at the time a couple of attractive ladies were passing by. Pirogov, generally speaking, demonstrated a passion for everything elegant, and encouraged the artist Piskarev; however, this was probably because of a consuming urge to see his own virile face on canvas. But that's enough about Pirogov's qualities. The man is such a wonderful creature that it would not be possible to enumerate fully all his qualities just off the cuff, and the more one examines him the more new characteristics become apparent, and a description of them would be endless. And so, Pirogov continued in his pursuit of the unknown girl, from time to time putting questions to her which she would answer tersely, abruptly and with incomprehensible utterances. They walked through the dark Kazan Gate, onto Meshchanskaia Street, a street full of tobacconists and dingy little shops, of German craftsmen and Finnish nymphets. The blonde was running quickly and flitted in through the gate of a rather grubby-looking house. Pirogov went after her. She ran up a narrow, dark stair-case and in at a door through which Pirogov also boldly went. He found himself in a large room with black walls and a soot-covered ceiling. On the table lay a heap of iron screws, locksmith's tools, gleaming coffee pots and candlesticks; the floor was littered with copper and iron filings. Pirogov immediately grasped that this was a craftsman's apartment. The unknown girl dashed through into a side-room. He hesitated for a second, then obey-ing the Russian rule, continued ahead decisively. He entered a room which, totally unlike the first, was tidy and neat, indicating that the tenant was a German. He was struck by an unusually strange sight.

Before him sat Schiller, not the Schiller who wrote *William Tell* and *A History of the Thirty Years' War*, but the famous Schiller, the master tin-smith of Meshchanskaia Street. Near Schiller stood Hoffmann, not the writer Hoffmann, but the better-than-average cobbler from Offitserskaia (Officer) Street, the staunch friend of Schiller. Schiller was sitting on a chair, drunk, tapping his foot and saying something animatedly. All this would not have been particularly surprising to Pirogov, but he *was* surprised at the strange positions the two were in. Schiller was seated, his rather fat nose and head pointing upwards, and Hoffmann was holding his nose with two fingers and was twirling the blade of his cobblers' knife just above it. Both of them were speaking in German and so Lieutenant Pirogov, who only knew the German "*Gut morgen*," could understand nothing of this drama. However, Schiller's words amounted to this:

"I don't want it, I don't need my nose!" he said, waving his arms about. "My nose alone uses up to three pounds of snuff a month. And I put my money into some filthy Russian shop, because the German shop doesn't stock Russian snuff, I put forty kopeks per month into the filthy shop for every pound; that makes it one ruble twenty kopeks; and twelve times a ruble twenty kopeks makes fourteen rubles forty kopeks. Do you hear, Hoffmann, my friend? Fourteen rubles forty kopeks on my nose alone! And on holidays I take rappee, because I don't want to sniff filthy Russian snuff on holidays. In a year I sniff two pounds of rappee, at two rubles a pound. Six and fourteen make twenty rubles forty kopeks on snuff alone. That's daylight robbery! I ask you, my friend, is that not so?"

Hoffmann, who was also drunk, answered in the affirmative.

"Twenty rubles forty kopeks! I'm a Schwabian German; I have a king in Germany. I don't want my nose! Cut off my nose! There's my nose!"

And had it not been for Pirogov's sudden appearance, Hoffmann, no doubt, would have cut off Schiller's nose without more ado, for he was already holding the knife as if he were about to cut out a shoe-leather.

Schiller seemed very annoyed at this unknown, uninvited person, who had interrupted him at such an inopportune moment. And, despite the fact that he was in such a drunken daze from wine and beer, he felt it was rather indecent to be seen by an onlooker in such a state and performing such a deed. Meanwhile Pirogov made a slight bow and in his characteristically pleasant way said:

"If you will excuse me . . ."

"Clear off!" answered Schiller in a drawling voice.

This perplexed Lieutenant Pirogov. Nobody had ever addressed him like this before. The faint smile which was just beginning to appear on his face suddenly vanished. With a feeling of offended dignity, he said,

"I find it rather strange, my dear sir . . . you must not have noticed . . . I'm an officer. . . ."

"What's an officer to me? I'm a Schwabian German." "I too (and with that Schiller thumped the table with his fist) am able to be officer; eighteen months a *junker*, two years a lieutenant and next day I'm already an officer. But I don't want to enlist. This is what I think of officers: Pfooey!" said Schiller, extending his palm and snorting into it.

Lieutenant Pirogov saw that the only thing left for him to do was to withdraw; such a course of action, totally unbecoming in one of his rank, was disagreeable to him. Several times on the stairs he stopped short, trying to muster his courage and think of a way of making Schiller realize how impertinent he had been. Finally he came to the conclusion that it was possible to excuse Schiller on the grounds that the latter's head was saturated with beer; and in addition the image of the pretty blonde appeared to him and he decided to consign all this to oblivion. The next morning, very early, Lieutenant Pirogov went to the tinsmith's workshop. In the hallway he was met by the pretty blonde who asked him in a rather stern voice, which suited her little face very well:

"What do you want?"

"Oh, good day, my dear! Don't you recognize me? You little rogue, what beautiful eyes you've got!"

As he said that, Liuetenant Pirogov tried to give her a gentle pat under her chin. But the blonde let out a startled cry and with the same severity asked:

"What do you want?"

"To see you, that's all," said Lieutenant Pirogov, smiling quite pleasantly and moving in closer; but, noticing that the timid blonde was trying to slip out the door, he added; "I need to order some spurs, my dear. You can make spurs, can't you ? Although as far as loving you is concerned, it's a halter I need, not spurs. What beautiful little hands you've got!" Lieutenant Pirogov was always very charming in declarations of this sort.

"I'll tell my husband this minute," exclaimed the German girl and went out, and in a few minutes Pirogov saw Schiller emerging with sleep-blurred eyes, not yet fully recovered from the previous day's binge. Looking at the officer, he remembered, as though in a dream, the events of the previous day. He couldn't remember now what state he'd been in, but he sensed that he'd done something stupid, and so he received the officer with a very sullen face.

"I can't make a pair of spurs for less than fifteen rubles," he said, wishing to get rid of Pirogov because he, as an honorable German, felt very embarrassed coming face to face with someone who had seen him in such a disgraceful condition. Schiller liked to drink completely unobserved, with two or three friends, and at such times even locked himself in, away from his own workmen.

"Why so expensive?" asked Pirogov in a pleasant tone. "German work," said Schiller nonchalantly, stroking his chin. "A Russian would take the job on for two rubles."

"With your permission, and in order to prove that I like you and would like to make your acquaintance, I'll pay the fifteen rubles."

Schiller thought it over for a moment; he, an honorable German, felt somewhat guilty. And wishing to make Pirogov withdraw his order, he explained that it would take a minimum of two weeks. But Pirogov agreed to this completely and without making any protests.

The German thought for a while and pondered about how best to do the job so that it really would be worth fifteen rubles. At that moment the blonde came into the workshop and began to rummage about on the table, which was cluttered with coffee mugs. The lieutenant took advantage of Schiller's preoccupation, went up to her and squeezed her arm, which was bare right up to the shoulder. Schiller took great exception to this.

"*Meine Frau*," he shouted.

"*Was wollen Sie doch*?" answered the blonde.

"*Gehen Sie* to the kitchen." The blonde went out.

"So then, in two weeks?" said Pirogov.

"Yes, in two weeks," answered Schiller, deep in thought. "Just at the moment I've got a lot of work to do."

"Goodbye. I'll call in again."

"Goodbye," answered Schiller, closing the door behind him.

Lieutenant Pirogov decided not to abandon his quest, having been so cursorily rejected by the German woman. He could not understand how anyone could resist him, particularly as his charming manner and impressive rank gave him every right to her attention. It is, however, necessary to point out that Schiller's wife, for all her attractiveness, was extremely stupid. But in a pretty wife stupidity is a charming characteristic. At least I have known many husbands who were simply thrilled with their wives' stupidity and took it as a sign of childlike innocence. Beauty can work absolute wonders. All the spiritual shortcomings in a beautiful girl, instead of evoking revulsion, somehow become unusually attractive; even vice can exude charm in them; but when beauty fades, then a woman needs to be twenty times more intelligent than a man if she is to elicit affection, or at least respect. But Schiller's wife, for all her stupidity, was always faithful to her obligations and hence it was rather difficult for Pirogov to succeed in his daring undertaking; but satisfaction always accompanies the overcoming of obstacles, and the blonde became a greater source of interest for him with the passing of each day. He took to inquiring about the spurs at regular intervals so that, eventually, Schiller got sick and tired of it. He worked full out to get the spurs finished; finally they were ready.

"Oh what a beautiful job you've made of them!—Lieutenant Pirogov exclaimed, when he saw the spurs. "Lord, how splendid! Not even our general has a pair of spurs like these!"

Feelings of self-satisfaction penetrated right into Schiller's heart. His eyes shone with delight and he became quite friendly towards Pirogov. "This Russian officer is an intelligent man," he thought to himself.

"So I suppose you could make a sheath for a dagger or something?"

"Of course I could," said Schiller, smiling.

"Well, make me a sheath for my dagger. I'll bring it to you; I've got a beautiful Turkish one, but I'd like to get another sheath made for it."

This hit Schiller like a bomb. His brows knitted. "So that's your game?" he thought, inwardly cursing himself for having brought the work on himself. To refuse now would be dishonorable and the Russian officer had praised his work. Nodding his head slightly, he expressed his consent; but the kiss which Pirogov cheekily planted on the pretty blonde's lips as he went out completely confounded him.

I consider it necessary here to briefly acquaint the reader with Schiller. Schiller was a typical German in the fullest sense of the word. From the age of twenty, from that happy time during which Russians live foot-loose and fancy free, Schiller had already planned out his life and he made no changes whatever in those plans. He made it a rule to get up at seven o'clock, to dine at two, to be exacting in everything and to get drunk on Sundays. He gave himself ten years to amass capital to the tune of fifty thousand, and all this was as certain and inevitable as fate, because an official will forget to curry favor with his chief's porter before a German will decide to go back on his word. Under no circumstances would he increase his expenditure, and if the price of potatoes rose more than usual, then he would not fork out an extra kopek, but would reduce the amount consumed, and although he sometimes went a little hungry, he soon became accustomed to it. His punctiliousness went so far as to include his kissing his wife no more than twice a day, and to be sure of not kissing her an extra time he never put more than one teaspoon of hot pepper in his soup; but on Sundays Schiller relaxed this rule a little because he would drink two bottles of beer that day and a bottle of Kummel, which, however, he always cursed. He didn't drink at all like an Englishman who locks the door immediately after dinner and hits the bottle all alone. On the contrary, he, like a German, was an inspired drinker, and would drink either with Hoffmann the cobbler or the locksmith Kuntz, who was also a German and a heavy drinker. Such was the character of the noble Schiller, who now found himself in an extremely difficult position. Although he was an easygoing German, Pirogov's behavior roused in him something akin to jealousy. He racked his brains, but could come up with no ideas on how to get rid of this Russian officer. Meanwhile, Pirogov, smoking his pipe with a group of friends—for Providence has decreed that where you find officers you also find pipes—smoking his pipe with a group of friends, he hinted meaningfully and with a pleasant smile on his lips at this intrigue with the pretty little German girl, with whom, to use his words, he was already on familiar terms, but in actual fact he had already lost almost all hope of making a conquest of her.

One day he was out for a stroll along Meshchanskaia Street, and he glanced at the house adorned by Schiller's signboard with its coffee pots and samovars; to his great joy he saw a blonde head leaning out of a window and staring at the passersby. He stopped, waved to her and said, "*Gut morgen.*" The blonde nodded to him as to an acquaintance.

"Tell me, is your husband at home?"

"He is," she answered.

"When is he not at home?"

"He's always out on Sundays," the silly little German girl said.

"That's not bad," thought Pirogov to himself, "I must take advantage of that." And the following Sunday, out of the blue, he turned up at the blonde's house. Schiller really was out. The pretty landlady took fright, but Pirogov conducted himself with more caution this time, behaving respectfully and, bowing, displayed his tightly-belted figure in all its beauty. He joked in a pleasant and agreeable way but the slow-witted little German girl only responded in monosyllables. Finally, having attempted his attack from all angles, and realizing that he was not making any headway, he invited her to dance. The German girl agreed to this in a flash, as all German women are very keen on dancing. All Pirogov's hopes rested on this: in the first place, it gave her great pleasure, in the second place it would give him a chance to display his suppleness and agility, and in the third place, while dancing he could get closer to and embrace the pretty little German girl and lay the foundations for what was to follow; in short, his scheme worked beautifully. He began to hum some sort of gavotte, knowing that German women prefer something sedate. The pretty little German girl moved out into the middle of the room and lifted her beautiful little foot. This stance enraptured Pirogov to such an extent that he hastened to kiss her. The German girl began to cry out, but this only made her all the more charming in Pirogov's eyes, and he smothered her with kisses. All of a sudden the door opened and in came Schiller, Hoffmann and the locksmith Kuntz. All these worthy artisans were as drunk as cobblers.

But I'll leave it to the readers to form their own judgements regarding Schiller's rage and indignation.

"You scoundrel!" he bawled with consummate indignation, "How dare you kiss my wife?! You're no Russian officer, you're a rogue. Devil take him, eh Hoffmann, my friend? I'm a German and no Russian pig!" Hoffmann answered affirmatively. "Nobody's going to make a cuckold out of me! Grab him by the collar, Hoffmann my friend. Nobody's going . . ." he continued, furiously waving his fists about, which made his face go as red as the material his waistcoat was made of. "I've been living in Petersburg for eight years, I have a Schwabian mother and an uncle living in Nuremburg; I'm a German and nobody is going to plant cuckold's horns on me! Let's kick him out, Hoffmann, my friend! Grab him by his arms and legs, Kamerad Kuntz! "And the Germans grabbed Pirogov by his arms and legs.

His efforts to break away were futile; these three artisans were the heftiest of Petersburg Germans. If Pirogov had been in full uniform, then, most likely, respect for his rank and position would have stopped the unruly Teutons. But he had come as a private, civilian person, in a suit-coat and without his epaulettes.

I am sure that Schiller the next day was in a terrible fever, that he was shaking like a leaf, expecting the arrival of the police at any moment, and that he would have given God knows what for all that had happened to have been just a dream. But what's done is done. There was nothing to equal Pirogov's rage and indignation. The mere thought of such a terrible insult was enough to make him furious. He considered Siberia and the lash too light a punishment for Schiller. He flew home to dress and go straight to the general and describe in the most vivid colors the German artisans' violent conduct. At the same time he wanted to make a complaint in writing to Headquarters. And if Headquarters would not prescribe adequate punishment then he would go to the State council, if not to the Monarch himself.

But all this ended in a rather strange way: on his way he called in at a cafe, ate a couple of puff-pastries and read something from the *Northern Bee*, and when he emerged from there his rage had somewhat subsided. Moreover, the rather pleasant, cool evening induced him to take a stroll along Nevsky Prospect, and by nine o 'clock he had calmed down completely and he decided that it was just not done to disturb the General on a Sunday, and moreover that doubtless he had probably been called away somewhere, and for this reason Pirogov set off to spend the evening with one of the directors of the control board, where there would be an agreeable company of officers

and officials. There he spent a pleasurable evening and so outdid himself in
the mazurka that the gentlemen, as well as the ladies, were entranced.

"How amazingly our world is arranged!" I thought, walking along
Nevsky Prospect the day before yesterday and recalling these two events.
"How strangely, how inscrutably Fate plays with us! Do we ever get what
we desire? Do we achieve what our abilities seem especially suited for?
Everything turns out contrary to expectations. Those who have been given
fine horses by Fate ride about on them unaware of their beauty, while another,
whose heart burns with a passion for horses, goes about on foot and has to
be content with merely clicking his tongue when a fine trotter is led past
him. One has a marvelous cook, but unfortunately, such a small mouth that
he can't eat more than two morsels; another has a mouth the size of the
Headquarters arch, but alas! He must be content with some German dinner
made from potatoes. How strangely our Fate plays with us!"

But strangest of all are the things which happen on Nevsky Prospect!
Oh, never believe Nevsky Prospect! I always wrap my cloak around me
more tightly when walking along it, and I try not to look at the things I see
there. It's all an illusion, it's all a dream, nothing is what it seems! You think
that a man walking along in a beautifully cut coat is rich? Not at all: his
coat is all he possesses. You imagine that those two fat men stopped in
front of a church under construction are discussing its architecture? Not at
all: they're talking about the two crows who alit opposite each other in
such a strange manner. You think that that enthusiast, waving his arms
about, is talking about how his wife threw a ball out of the window to an
officer whom he did not know? Not at all. he's talking about Lafayette.
You think that these ladies . . . but you must believe the ladies least of all.
Look even less at the shop windows: knick-knacks, beautifully displayed
but smacking of vast amounts of money! But God preserve you from peek-
ing under ladies' hats. However much a beautiful lady's cape may flutter
in the distance, nothing would induce me to take a peek out of curiosity.
Keep away, for God's sake, keep away from the street lamp. Walk past as
fast as you possibly can. Consider yourself lucky if you escape with only a
few drops of its foul-smelling oil on your foppish coat! But not it's only the
street lamps, everything else breathes deception as well. It deceives at all
hours, does Nevsky Prospect, but especially when night descends on it in a
thick mass, throwing into relief the white and pastel walls of the houses,
when the whole town is transformed into noise and brilliance, when hoards
of carriages roll over bridges, the postillions shout and bounce about on
their saddles and when the Devil himself ignites the street lamps for the sole
purpose of showing everything not in its true guise.

(1835) Translated by A. Tulloch, revised by A.L.

Diary of a Madman

October 3

　　Something extremely odd happened today. I got up rather late, and when Mavra brought me my cleaned boots I asked her the time. Hearing that ten had struck long ago, I hurried to get dressed as quickly as possible. I confess that I wouldn't have gone to the office at all, had I known earlier what a sour face the chief of our department would pull. For ages now he's been saying to me: "Tell me, my man, why's your head always in such a muddle? Sometimes you dash about like one possessed, and you get your work so mixed up that Satan himself couldn't sort it out, putting small letters in the title and not noting the date or number." The damned heron! He's obviously just jealous of my sitting in the director's office sharpening quills for His Excellency. In a word, I wouldn't have gone to the office had it not been for the hope of seeing the pay clerk and seeing what the chances were of getting, however small, an advance on my salary from that yid. Now there's a creature for you! My God, Last Judgment will arrive before he'll give anyone their month's pay in advance. You can ask till you're blue in the face, he won't give you anything even if you're dead broke, the gray-haired devil. But at home even his own cook slaps his face all the time. Everybody knows this. I can't see any advantage in working in an office. Absolutely no future in it. But in provincial government, in civil and treasury offices it's a completely different matter: there you'll see someone huddled up in the corner, doing a bit of writing from time to time. His coat may be filthy and his mug may make you want to spit, but just have a look at the *dacha* he can rent! And don't take him a gilt porcelain cup: "That's a doctor's present," he'll say; but do give him a pair of trotting horses, or a carriage or a three-hundred-ruble beaver-pelt. He's such a quiet man to look at, and he says so politely, "Do just lend me your penknife to sharpen this one little quill," and then he'll fleece a petitioner, right down to the shirt on his back. On the other hand, it is true our office is very refined, and the standard of cleanliness there is such as you would never see in provincial government: the tables are mahogany, and the chiefs all address each other very formally. Yes, I confess, were it not for the dignified nature of the position, I'd have left the office long ago.

　　I put on my old greatcoat and picked up my umbrella, as the rain was lashing down. Outside there was nobody about; the only people whom I saw were a few women who had covered themselves with their skirt flaps, Russian merchants beneath their umbrellas, and messengers. Of quality folk only one of my fellow officials, shuffling along. I spotted him at the corner. As soon as I spotted him I said to myself: "Oh, no, my dear chap, you're not on your way to the office, you're after that blonde who is racing along in front of you, and you're staring at her ankles." What sly beasts we officials are! Lord! We're a match for any officer: if a lady in a hat walks by we never fail to latch on. While this was running through my mind, I noticed a carriage which had drawn up at the shop I was passing. Immediately I recognized it; it was our director's carriage. "But he has no cause to be going into the shop," I thought. "It must be his daughter." I stood close against the wall. A footman opened the door, and she suddenly fluttered from the carriage like a little bird. How she glanced from right to left, how her eyebrows and eyes flashed . . . Great God Almighty! I was devastated, utterly devastated. And why would she need to venture out in the rain like this? Tell me now that women have no great passion for all these frills. She didn't recognize me, and for my part I deliberately tried to wrap myself up as much as possible, because my greatcoat was filthy and, moreover, old-fashioned. Nowadays people wear capes with long collars, but mine were short, one on top of the other; and the material was not at all rainproof. Her little dog, who had not been quick enough to get through the shop door, remained outside. I know this little dog. It's called Madgie. I hadn't spent a minute there when suddenly I heard a weak little voice: "Hello, Madgie!" Well I never! Who said that? I looked all around me and saw two ladies walking along under an umbrella: one was old, the other young; but they had already walked past and again I heard, close by me: "You should be ashamed of yourself, Madgie." What the Devil! I saw Madgie sniffing at a lapdog which was walking along behind the ladies. "Oh!"—I said to myself,—that's enough; am I drunk? But that very rarely is the case with me." "No, Fidele, you've got the wrong idea." I myself saw Madgie say that. "I've been, bow-wow, very ill." So then, little dog, it's you! I confess I was very surprised when I heard her speak in human language. But later, when I had had time to think about it, I ceased being surprised. In fact the world knows of many such examples already. They say that in England a fish came to the surface and uttered a couple of words in such a strange language that for the past three years scientists have been trying to identify it, but so far they've discovered nothing. I also read in the newspapers about two cows who went into a shop and asked for a pound of tea. But, I confess, I was far more surprised when Madgie said, "I wrote you, Fidele; obviously, Polkan (Rover) didn't deliver my letter." May I never draw my salary again if I'm lying! Never in my life have I heard of a dog who could write. Only noblemen can write correctly. Some merchant-clerks can do it, of course, and even some serfs occasionally write a little; but their writing is mostly mechanical; no commas, full stops, or style.

This puzzled me. I confess that I have recently begun to hear and see such things from time to time as nobody else has ever seen or heard. "I'll follow that little dog," I said to myself, "to find out what she is about and what sort of things she's thinking." I unfurled my umbrella and set off after the two ladies. They crossed into Gorokhovaia (Pease) Street, turned into Meshchanskaia (Bourgeois) Street, then into Stolyarnaia (Carpenter's) Lane and, finally, made for Kokushkin Bridge, where they stopped in front of a large house. "I know this house," I said to myself. "This is Zverkov's (Mr. Beast's) house." What a bustling hive! All sorts of people live there: so many cooks, so many Polacks! And so many of my fellow officials, like dogs, all piled one on top of another. One of my friends lives in there, he's very good at playing the horn. The ladies went up to the fourth floor. "Fine" I thought, "I won't go in just now, but I'll make a note of the place and I won't fail to take advantage of it at my first chance."

October 4

Today is Wednesday and so I've been in the chief's office. I came a little early on purpose and, sitting myself down, began to re-sharpen quills. Our director must be a very intelligent man. His room is all lined with bookshelves. I read the titles of some of them: so much erudition, such erudition that it's all beyond the likes of me: everything is either in French or German. And if you glance at his face: whew! What importance there is in his eyes! I have never yet heard him say a superfluous word. It's only when you hand him papers that he may ask, "What's it like outside?"—"Damp, Your Excellency!" Yes, people like me are no match for him! He's a statesman. But I notice that he's particularly fond of me. If only his daughter also . . . oh, you rogue! . . . Never mind, never mind, silence! I read *The Bee*. What a stupid lot the French are! What do they want, eh? I'd like to give them all a damn good thrashing with the birch! I read there a very pleasant description of a ball which was written by some landowner from Kursk. Those landowners from Kursk write well. After this I noticed that it was already half past twelve and that our chief was still not out of his bedroom. But, at about half past one an event occurred which no pen could describe. The door opened. I thought it was our director and I jumped up from my chair with the papers; but it was she, she herself! Holy Saints, how she was dressed! The dress she wore was as white as a swan: whew! How sumptuous! And how she looked: a veritable ray of sunshine. She bowed and said: "Has father not been in?" Oh! Oh! Oh! What a voice! A canary, a veritable canary! "Your Excellency" I was about to say, "don't condemn me to death, but if you wish to condemn me, then carry out the sentence with your own high-ranking hand." But, Devil take it, I became tongue-tied and could only say: "No, ma'am." She looked at me, at the books, and dropped her handkerchief. I rushed forward as fast as I could, slipped on the damned parquet floor and almost broke my nose, but I managed to regain my balance and picked up the handkerchief. Holy Saints, what a handkerchief! the finest cambric—ambergris, perfect ambergris! It simply reeked "general's daughter". She thanked me and smiled almost imperceptibly, so that her sweet lips barely moved and then she went away. I remained seated for another hour when suddenly a servant came in and said, "You can go home, Axenty Ivanovich, the master's already left." I cannot stand these servants: they're always lounging about in the hall and they can't even be bothered to nod give you a nod. And that's not all: once, one of these curs had the nerve to offer me some snuff without getting up from his seat. Don't you know I'm an official of noble birth, you stupid lackey? However, I took my hat and put on my greatcoat by myself, as these gentlemen will never assist you, and went out. At home I spent most of the time lying on my bed. Then I copied out some excellent little verses: *Sweet Psyche for an hour I did not see,/A year this little hour seemed to me./I came to quite despise this life of mine:/ "Poor me, should I live?" I did opine.* This must be Pushkin's work. In the evening, wrapped in my greatcoat, I walked as far as the entrance to Her Excellency's house and waited for a long time to see if she would come out and get into her carriage, so that I could get a brief glimpse at her—but no, she never appeared.

November 6

The chief got into a mean temper today. When I arrived at the office he called me in to him and began to talk to me like this : "Well, tell me, please, just what you're doing?"—What do you mean? I'm not doing anything," I answered. "Well, just use your loaf! You're past forty now, y'know—time you had some sense. What're you thinking of? Do you think I don't know your little game? You've got your eye on the director's daughter! Well, just look at you; just think; you're a nobody, that's all. And you don't have a penny to your name. Just have a look at your face in the mirror; how could you even think of such a thing?" Damn it all, just because his face is like a chemist's jar and he has a lock of hair on his head tied up in a Tatar tuft and he keeps it in its rosette shape by plastering it with pomade, he thinks he's the only one allowed to do anything. I understand, I understand why he's so mean to me. He's jealous; maybe he's noticed signs of preferential treatment being afforded to me. Well, I spit on him! A court councilor's not so important as all that! He's hung a gold chain on his watch, he orders boots at thirty rubles the pair—well, he can go to the Devil! Am I some low-class intellectual son of a tailor or non-commissioned officer? I'm a nobleman. And I may even get promoted. I'm still only forty-two years old—the age when one's service career is really only just beginning. Wait, friend! We'll make the rank of colonel yet, and perhaps, God willing, even something higher. We'll acquire a reputation, too, and a better one than yours. What gives you the idea that you're the only respectable gentleman? Give me a Ruchevsky dress coat, fashionably cut, and let me tie a cravat like yours around my neck—then you won't hold a candle to me. I don't have the wherewithal—that's the trouble.

November 8

Went to the theater. They put on a performance of the Russian fool Filatka. Had a good laugh. There was also some vaudeville with amusing lines about lawyers, particularly about one college registrar, so freely written that I was amazed that it got past the censor, and they're right when they talk about how merchants swindle the people and how their debauched sons are worming their way into the nobility. There was also a very amusing couplet about journalists: how they love to abuse everything and how the author begs the public for support. Writers nowadays write very amusing plays. I adore going to the theater. As soon as a penny lands in my pocket I can't resist going. But some of my fellow officials are real swine: they definitely refuse to go to the theater, the peasants! Except perhaps if you give them a free ticket. A certain actress sang very well. I remembered about her . . . Oh, you rogue! . . . Never mind, never mind . . . Silence.

November 9

Set off to the office at eight o'clock. The departmental chief pretended not to notice my arrival. For my part, I, too, acted as if nothing had passed between us. I looked over and checked some papers. Left at four o'clock; walked past the director's flat, but didn't see anyone. After dinner spent most of the time lying on the bed.

November 11

Today I sat in the director's office and repaired twenty-three quills for him and for her—aie! aie! . . . for Her Excellency, four pens. He always likes to have plenty of quills. Oh! He must be a real brain-box! He never says anything, but I think he's always turning things over in his head. I'd like to know what he thinks of most; what goes on in that head of his. I'd like to get a closer look at the lives these gentlemen lead, the subtleties and court affairs—what they're like, what they do in their own circle—that's what I'd like to know! Several times I've thought of striking up a conversation with His Excellency, but, Devil take it, my tongue won't obey me: I can only say that it's cold or warm outside, and that's absolutely all I can utter. I'd like a peek at whose open door you occasionally get a glimpse of, and through the drawing room into the next room. Oh! What sumptuous furniture! Such mirrors and porcelain! I'd love to get a peek in there, into the wing where Her Excellency lives—that's the place for me! Into her boudoir: there are so many little jars standing there, and little bottles, such flowers that one is afraid to breathe on them; see how her dress lies thrown onto the floor, and looks more like air than a dress. I'd like to get a glimpse inside her bedroom . . . what wonders, I feel, must be in there, such paradise, I feel, as doesn't even exist in heaven. I'd like a glimpse at the footstool on which she places her. foot when she gets out of bed, and watch her putting stockings on her snow white legs . . . Aie, aie, aie! Never mind, never mind . . . Silence puts a little snow-white stocking on that little foot . . . Aie, aie, aie! never mind, never mind . . . silence!

Today, however, it's as if the light has suddenly dawned on me: I remember the conversation I heard on Nevsky Prospect between the two little dogs. "Fine," I thought to myself, "now I'll find out everything. I must intercept the correspondence these scraggy little dogs have been carrying on. Then I'll be sure to learn a thing or two." I confess, I was even on the point of calling Madgie to me once and saying, "Listen, Madgie, now we're alone, I'll close the door if you wish so that nobody will see us—tell me. every thing you know about the young lady, tell me what she's like, and I swear to you I won't tell anyone." But the sly little dog put her tail between her legs, doubled herself up and went out through the door as quietly as if she hadn't heard a thing. A long time ago I used to suspect that dogs were more intelligent than human beings; I was even sure they could speak, if it weren't for a certain stubbornness inside them. They're extremely tactful: they notice everything, every step a human being takes. No, whatever happens, tomorrow I'm off to Zverkov's house, I'll ask to see Fidele and, if possible, I'll seize all the letters Madgie has written to her .

November 12
Set off at two o'clock in the afternoon to be sure of seeing Fidele and questioning her. I can't stand the smell of cabbage which pours from all the little shops on Meshchanskaia Street; and moreover the hellish stench wafts out from under the doors of every house, so holding my nose, I ran past as fast as I could. And the grubby little artisans release so much smoke and soot from their workshops that it's absolutely impossible for a gentleman to stroll along here. When I had made my way to the fifth floor and rung the bell, a young girl came out, not bad-looking and with tiny freckles on her face. I recognized her. This was the very same girl who had been walking along with the old woman. She blushed slightly and I immediately realized: you, my dear, are after a husband. "What do you want?" she said. "I want a word with your dog." What a stupid girl she was! I could tell at once she was stupid! Just then the little dog came running up, barking; I tried to catch hold of it but the disgusting creature almost got its teeth into my nose. But I caught sight of its basket in the corner. That was just what I was after! I went over, rummaged about a bit in the little straw-filled wooden box and, to my great

delight, pulled out a small bundle of paper. When the filthy little doggie saw this, she first of all bit me on the calf, then, when she sensed that I had taken her bits of paper, she began to whine and make up to me, but I said, "No, my dear, goodbye!"—and took to my heels. I think the young girl took me for a madman, because she was extremely frightened. As soon as I got home I wanted to get down to work sorting out these letters because my eyes are not too good in candlelight, but Mavra had taken it into her head to wash the floor. These stupid Finnish women always become house-proud at the wrong times. So I went for a stroll to give some thought to what had happened. Now, at last I'll find out about their affairs, their thoughts and what makes them tick and I'll get to the bottom of the matter. These letters will reveal all to me. Dogs are intelligent beings, they know all the political considerations and so everything is bound to be there: a portrait of a man and all his affairs. And there'll be something there about her . . . never mind, silence! Towards evening I returned home. Most of the time I lay on my bed.

November 13

Well, we shall see! The writing is fairly distinct; at the same time there is something doggy about the handwriting. Let us read:

> *Dear Fidele,*
> *I still can't get used to your bourgeois name. Surely they could have given you a better one? Fidele, Rose—how common they sound! But that's all by the way. I'm very glad that we thought of writing to each other.*

The letter was written very correctly: the punctuation and even the "i" before "e" spelling were all correct. Even our department chief couldn't write like this, though he talks of having been to some university. Let's see what else there is:

> *It seems to me that sharing one's thoughts, feelings, and impressions with another is one of the greatest blessings on earth.*

Hm! That idea was taken from a work translated from German. I don't remember the title.

> *I say this from experience, though I've been no further than the door of our house. Is my life not passing in a pleasurable way? My mistress, whom Papa calls Sophie, loves me to distraction.*

Aie, aie! never mind, never mind! Silence!

> *Papa is also very affectionate. I drink tea and coffee with cream. Oh, ma chère, I must tell you that I get no pleasure at all from the big chewed bones which our Polkan devours in the kitchen. The bones of game are the only*

tasty ones, and then only when nobody has sucked all the marrow out of them. It's very nice to mix several sauces together, but only if there are no capers or greens mixed in; but I know of nothing worse than the usual habit of giving dogs rolled-up balls of bread. A gentleman sits at a table and begins to crush up the bread with his hands, which have been in contact with all sorts of garbage, calls you over and thrusts the little ball into your teeth. It's improper to refuse, so you eat it, it's nauseating, but you eat it . . .

What the Devil's all this! What rubbish! As though there was nothing better to write about. Let's have a look at another page. There may be something a bit more sensible.

I should be delighted to keep you informed about what happens here. I've already told you something about the most important man here, the one Sophie calls Papa. He's a very strange man.

Ah! At last! Yes, I knew: they look at everything from a political angle. Let's see what Papa is like:

. . . a very strange man. He doesn't say very much. He very rarely speaks; but a week ago he was talking to himself constantly, saying: "Will I get it or won't I?" He would take a slip of paper in one hand, then clench the empty one and say to me, "Will I get it or won't I?" Once he put the question to me, "What do you think, Madgie? Will I get it or won't I?" I couldn't understand a single thing; I just sniffed his boots, then walked away. Then, ma chère, Papa came in a week later feeling on top of the world. All that morning uniformed gentlemen called on him and congratulated him about something. At the table he was more exuberant than I had ever seen him, cracking jokes, and after dinner he lifted me up to his neck and said: "See, Madgie, what's this?" I could see some sort of ribbon. I sniffed at it, but I couldn't detect any aroma; finally I gave it a sly lick: a bit salty.

Hm, I think this little cur is too . . . so she won't get whipped! So, he's ambitious! I'll make a note of that.

Goodbye, ma chère, I must be off . . . etc. . . . . etc. I'll finish the letter tomorrow. Well, hello! Now I'm back with you. Today my mistress Sophie . . .

Ah! well, let's see what Sophie's like. Oh! Canaille . . . All right, all right . . . we'll continue.

. . . my mistress Sophie was in terrible confusion. She was getting ready to go to a ball, and I was glad because I would be able to write to you while she was away. My Sophie greatly enjoys going to a ball, although she always gets angry while she's getting dressed. I just cannot understand, ma chère, how anyone can derive pleasure from going to a ball. Sophie always

gets back home from a ball at six o'clock in the morning, and I can nearly always tell by her pale, drawn look if she wasn't given anything to eat there, the poor thing. I must admit that I could never live like that. If I didn't get my grouse and gravy or roast chicken wings . . . well, I don't know what would happen to me. That gravy goes well with porridge, too, but carrots or turnips, or artichokes will never taste good . . .

Extraordinary unevenness of style. It's immediately obvious that it wasn't written by a human being. It starts off all right but finishes in a canine style. Let's have a look at another little note. A longish one. Hm! And there's no date on it.

Oh, my dear, one can feel the approach of spring now. My heart is thumping as if in expectation of something. There's a constant noise in my ears so that I frequently stand with one paw in the air, listening at the door for several minutes. I'll confess to you that I have a number of suitors. I often watch them from the window. Oh! If only you knew what monsters some of them are. One is a very unprepossessing common mongrel, frightfully stupid, there's even stupidity written all over his face, and he walks along the street with such an air of importance and he imagines he's a very upper-class individual, and that everybody else is looking at him. Not a bit of it, I paid no attention to him at all; just as if I didn't see him. But there's such a terrifying Great Dane who comes and stops in front of my window! If it were to stand on its hind legs—which I don't think the lout could do—then he'd be a head taller than my Sophie's papa, who is fairly tall and of ample proportions. That numbskull must be frightfully cheeky. I growled at him but it didn't bother him one bit. He hardly frowned! He thrust out his tongue, dangled his huge ears and stared in through the window—a real clod! But surely you don't think, ma chère, *that my heart is indifferent to all requests —ah, no . . . If only you had seen a certain cavalier, named Trésor, climbing over my neighbor's wall. Ah!* Ma chère, *what a nice little snout he has!*

Hell! What rubbish! How can anyone fill letters with such . . . nonsense? Give me the man! I want to see the man; I demand food of the sort which will feed and delight my soul; but instead, such nonsense . . . let's turn over the page to see if it's any better:

Sophie was sitting at the little table sewing something. I was looking out of the window, as I like to watch the people walking past. Suddenly, in came the servant and said "Teplov!"—"Ask him in," said Sophie, as she rushed to embrace me. "Ah, Madgie, Madgie! If only you knew who this is: he's a dark-haired gentleman-of-the-bedchamber, and what eyes he's got! They're dark and bright, like fire." And Sophie ran off to her room. A minute later a young gentleman-of-the-bedchamber with dark side-

whiskers came in, walked over to the mirror, tidied his hair and surveyed the room. I began to growl and sat in my usual place. Sophie soon appeared and curtseyed gaily to his shuffling; and I continued to look out of the window, pretending not to notice anything; however, I did incline my head slightly to one side in an attempt to hear what they were talking about. Oh, ma chère! What nonsense they were talking. They were discussing how a certain lady had made a wrong step at a dance; also how a certain Bobov in his jabots looked like a stork and had almost fallen over, and how a certain Lidina thought her eyes were light blue, when all the time they were green—things like that. "How could one possibly compare the gentleman-of-the-bedchamber with Tresor?" I thought to myself. Heavens! What a difference! In the first place, the gentleman-of-the-bedchamber has a completely smooth, broad face encircled by side-whiskers as if he had tied a black kerchief around it; but Tresor has such a slender snout and a bald patch right on his forehead. You couldn't compare Tresor's waist with the gentleman-of-the-bedchamber's. And his eyes, his ways and his manners are all wrong. Oh, what a difference! I don't know, ma chère, what she sees in her Teplov. Why does she admire him so much?

I think myself that there's something wrong here. It's not possible for her to be so fascinated by this gentleman-of-the-bedchamber. Let's see what's next:

I think if she finds that gentleman-of-the-bedchamber attractive then she'll soon be attracted to that official who sits in Papa's office. Oh, ma chère, if only you knew what a monster he is. A real tortoise in a sack . . .

Who could this official be ?

He has a really strange surname. He's always sitting repairing quills. The hair on his head looks very much like hay. Papa always sends him in place of a servant.

I think the filthy little cur means me. How have I got hair like straw?

Sophie simply cannot restrain herself from laughing when she looks at him.

You lie, you damned little cur! What a nasty tongue! As though I didn't know this is the result of jealousy. As though I didn't know whose jokes these are. These are the departmental director's jokes. The man, you know, has vowed implacable hatred and so he keeps on hurting me at every step. But let's look at just one more letter. There, perhaps, the matter will be explained.

Ma chère Fidele, excuse me for not writing for so long. I have been in absolute ecstasy. A certain writer was quite justified in saying that love is a second life. Moreover, there have been a great many changes in our house. The gentleman-of-the-bedchamber comes around every day now. Sophie loves him to distraction. Papa is very happy. I've even heard from Gregory, who sweeps the floor and nearly always talks to himself, that the marriage will take place soon; because Papa definitely wants to see Sophie marry either a general or a gentleman-of-the-bedchamber or an army colonel . . .

Damn and blast! I can't read any further . . . It's all about gentlemen-of-the-bedchamber or generals. It's always the gentlemen-of-the-bedchamber or the generals who get the best things in this world. If you come across some meager treasure and you think it's within your grasp—some gentleman-of-the-bedchamber or general will seize it from you. Damn it all! I wish I could become a general: not just to win her hand and everything, no, I'd like to see them grovel and perform all these different court pranks and subtleties, and then tell them: I spit on you both. Damn it all. It's annoying! I tore the stupid cur's letters into tiny shreds.

December 3

It cannot be. Nonsense! There can't be a marriage! What if he is a gentleman-of the-bedchamber? It's nothing but a rank, you know: it's not a visible object you can take hold of. Just because he 's a gentleman-of-the-bedchamber doesn't mean he's got a third eye in his forehead. His nose isn't made of gold, you know, it's just the same as mine or anybody else's; he sniffs with it but he doesn't eat with it, he sneezes but he doesn't cough with it. Several times now I've tried to fathom how all these differences arise. Why am I a titular councilor, and for what reason am I a titular councilor? Perhaps I'm some count or general and only think I'm a titular councilor? Perhaps I don't know what I am. How many examples have there been in history: some ordinary man, not even a nobleman, but just some petty bourgeois or even a peasant, and suddenly it's discovered that he's a grandee and sometimes even the monarch. If a peasant can sometimes turn out to be something like that, then what could a nobleman turn out to be? Suddenly, let's suppose, I walk in wearing a general's uniform: on my right shoulder there is an epaulette and on my left shoulder there's an epaulette, across my shoulder there's a light blue ribbon—what then? What song would my beauty sing then? And what would Papa himself, our director, say? Oh, there's an ambitious man! He's a Mason, he's a Mason through and through; although he pretends to be this that and the other I noticed at once, he was a Mason: if he shakes hands with anyone he only offers two fingers. So why should I not this very minute be promoted to governor-general or a quartermaster or something like that? I should like to know why I'm a titular councilor? Why exactly a titular councilor?

December 5

I spent all this morning reading the newspapers. Strange things are going on in Spain. Even I can't understand them. They write that the throne is vacant and that the nobles are in a difficult position about choosing an heir and because of this riots have broken out. It seems extremely strange to me. How can you have a vacant throne? They say some *donna* or other must ascend to the throne. You can't have a *donna* ascending to the throne. It's not possible. You have to have a king on the throne. Yes, they say, there's no king, it's impossible to be without a king. A state cannot be without a king. The king exists, but he's just lying low somewhere. It's quite possible that he's staying away for family or other reasons, or because the threat of neighboring powers like France and other lands forces him to stay in hiding, or there may be other reasons.

December 8

I had every intention of going to the office, but various reasons and reflections kept me from doing so. I still can't get the Spanish affairs out of my mind. How could a *donna* possibly become a queen? It would never be allowed. And, in the first place, England wouldn't allow it. Then there are the political affairs of all Europe: the Austrian emperor, our monarch . . . I confess that these events have mortified and shaken me to such an extent that I haven't been able to settle down to do anything all day. Mavra passed the remark that I was extremely distracted at dinner. And certainly I did, I think, throw two plates onto the floor, absent-mindedly, and they smashed there and then. After dinner I went down the hills. I gained nothing instructive out of that. I spent most of the time lying on my bed and pondered the affairs of Spain.

Year 2000, April 43rd

Today is the day of greatest celebration. There's a king in Spain. He has been found. I am this king. And I only found out about it this very day. I confess it struck me like lightning. I don't understand how I could think or imagine that I was a titular councilor. How could that ridiculous idea have got into my head? It's a good thing nobody thought of putting me in a lunatic asylum. Now everything is revealed to me. Now I see it all as if spread out on the palm of my hand. But I couldn't understand it till now; everything till now has been in a sort of haze. And I think that it all stems from people imagining that the human brain is in the head; not at all: it's borne on the wind from the direction of the Caspian Sea. First of all I explained to Mavra who I am. When she heard that the King of Spain was standing in front of her, she threw up her hands and almost died of horror. She, the stupid woman, had never even seen the King of Spain. I, however, tried to calm her and with kind words tried to assure her of my benevolence, and that I was not at all angry

at her for having sometimes cleaned my boots so badly. But these are ignorant folk. One should not talk to them about such elevated matters. She took
fright because she is convinced that all the kings of Spain are like Philip II.
But I was able to convince her that there was no similarity between me and
Philip and that I don't possess a single Capuchin monk . . . I did not go to
the office . . . To the Devil with that! No, friends, don't lure me there; I'm not
going to start copying out your filthy papers.

Martober 86th.
Between day and night.
Today our executor came round to get me to go to the office, as I have
not been to work for over three weeks. I did go to the office for a joke. The
department head thought I would bow to him and start apologizing, but I
looked at him indifferently, not too angrily and not too favorably, and I sat
down in my place, as if I hadn't noticed anybody. I glanced at all the office
scum and thought: "If only you knew who is sitting among you . . . Heavens
above! What a commotion you would cause, and the department head
himself would start bowing from the waist as he now bows to the director
. . ." They placed some papers in front of me so that I could make a pré-
cise of them. But I didn't lift a finger. A few minutes later things started to
get busy. Someone said the director was coming. Many of the officials hurried to outdo each other and show off in front of him. But I stayed put.
When he was walking past our department, everyone buttoned up their
coats; but I did absolutely nothing! So he's the director! Am I supposed to
stand in his presence—never! What sort of a director is he? He's a cork, not
a director. An ordinary cork, a simple cork, nothing more. The sort you
cork up bottles with. But for me the funniest thing was when they shoved
papers at me to copy out. They thought I would write on the very bottom
of the page: "such-and-such" or "head clerk". How could it be otherwise?
But in the most important place, where the department head signs, I scribbled "FERDINAND VIII." You should have seen the respectful silence
which reigned; but I just waved my hand, saying: "Such signs of allegiance
are not necessary!"—and went out. I went straight from there to the director's flat. He was not at home. The servant didn't want to let me in, but I
said such things to him that he just threw up his hands. I made straight for
the dressing room. She was sitting in front of the mirror, she jumped up and
backed away from me. I did not, however, tell her that I was the King of
Spain. I merely told her that happiness awaited her of a kind she could
never imagine, and that, despite my enemies' machinations, we would be
together. That was all I wished to say and went out. Oh, they're cunning
creatures, women! I have only just grasped what a woman is. Until now
nobody had found out who she was in love with. I'm the first to discover

it: womankind is in love with the Devil. Yes, no joking, scientists write nonsense saying a woman is this or that—but she loves nobody but the Devil. You can see her in a first-tier box adjusting her lorgnette. You think she is looking at that fat man wearing a star? Not at all, she's looking at the Devil standing behind him. Now he's concealed himself in the fat man's star. Now he's beckoning to her with his finger! And she'll marry him. She will. And they're all alike, their fathers the officials, all alike; they play up to anyone and everyone and grovel at court, calling themselves patriots: but it's dividends, dividends that these patriots are after. They'd sell their own mother, father and God for money, ambitious men they are! Traitors! It's all because of ambition, ambition which comes from having a tiny pimple under the tongue and in it a little worm no bigger than a pinhead, and the person behind all this is a certain barber who lives on Gorokhovaia Street. I don't remember his name; but it's a well-known fact that he and a certain midwife want to spread Mohammedanism throughout the world, and that's why, they say, most people in France profess the Mohammedan faith.

No date.
The day had no number.
Walked incognito along Nevsky Prospect. His Majesty the Tsar drove past. Everyone took off his cap, and I also; but I gave no sign that I was the King of Spain. I considered it improper to reveal myself suddenly in the presence of all the others, because my esteemed peer would surely ask me why the King of Spain had not yet presented himself in court. And indeed one should first present oneself to the court. The only thing stopping me was that I still don't possess any clothing suitable for a king. If only I could lay my hands on some regalia. I'd like to order it from a tailor, but they're such asses, and moreover, they're so careless with their work, and they've gone in for speculating and most of them are now laying paving stones for a living. I decided to make regalia out of a new uniform which I had worn only twice. But to avoid having it ruined by those rogues I decided to make it myself, with the door locked, so nobody would see. I cut the whole thing up with scissors, because the cut has to be completely different and the fabric had to give a look of ermine tails.

I don't remember the date. Nor was there any month.
Devil only knows when it was.
My regalia is all ready and made up. Mavra cried out when I put it on. However, I still have no intention of making an appearance at court. There have not yet been any deputations from Spain. It's not done to go without any deputies. No importance would be attached to my rank. I await them by the hour.

The 1 st.

I am surprised at the exceptional tardiness of the deputies. What could be the reason for the hold-up? Surely it's not France? Yes, that's the most malicious of Powers. I went to the post office to check if the Spanish deputies had arrived. But the postmaster is extremely stupid; he doesn't know anything: no, he says there are no Spanish deputies here, but if you would care to write any letters then we'll follow the established procedures. Devil take them all! What good would a letter do? Letters are rubbish. Apothecaries write letters . . .

Madrid. February thirtieth.

So, I'm in Spain, and it happened so quickly that it's hardly dawned on me yet. The Spanish deputies came to me this morning and I got into a carriage with them. The unusual speed seemed strange to me. We traveled so fast that we reached the Spanish border in half an hour. But of course there are railroads everywhere in Europe now and the locomotives move with such extraordinary speed. Spain is a strange land: when we entered the first room I saw a lot of people with their heads shaved. But I guessed that these must have been either the Dominicans or Capuchins, because they shave their heads. The State Chancellor's behavior seemed very strange to me as he led me by the hand; he pushed me into a small room and said: "Sit here, and if you refer to yourself as King Ferdinand again then I'll beat the notion out of you." But I, realizing that this was only a test, answered negatively —for which the Chancellor thumped me across the back a couple of times with a stick so hard that I almost cried out, but I restrained myself, remembering that this was a custom of chivalry on elevation to a high rank, because in Spain the customs of chivalry are preserved even today. When I was left alone I decided to get down to the affairs of State. I discovered that China and Spain are one and the same country and it is only through ignorance that they are considered separate states. I advise everyone to deliberately write the word "Spain" on a piece of paper, and it will always come out as "China." But I was particularly grieved by an event which takes place tomorrow. Tomorrow at seven o'clock a strange event will occur: the earth will land on the moon. The famous English chemist Wellington has written about this. I confess that I felt my heart tremble when I thought about the unusual softness and fragility of the moon. The moon, you know, is usually made in Hamburg; and very badly made as well. I find it surprising that England has paid any attention to all this. A lame cooper makes it and its obvious that the fool doesn't know a thing about the moon. He mixed in a tarred rope and one part of lamp-oil; and that's why there's such an awful smell over the whole earth that it's necessary to hold one's nose. And because of this the moon itself is such a tender ball that people could never live on it, and now only a few noses live there. And it's for that same reason that we cannot see our own noses, because they're all on the moon. And when I thought of how heavy an article the world is and how it would grind our noses into flour, then I was overcome with such anxiety that, putting on my socks and shoes, I dashed into the hall of the state council with the intention of ordering the police not to let the earth land on the moon. The Capuchins, whom I encountered in great number in the State council hall, were very intelligent people and when I said, "Gentlemen, let us save the moon, because the earth is going to land on it," they all rushed to carry out my royal wishes, and many of them began to climb up the wall in an attempt to catch the moon; but at that moment in came the High Chancellor. Seeing him, they all dispersed in great haste. I, as King, was the only one who stayed. But the Chancellor, to my surprise, hit me with a stick and chased me back to my room. Such is the power of national customs in Spain!

January of the Same Year, coming after February

So far I have not been able to understand what sort of a country Spain is. The national traditions and the customs of the court are quite extraordinary. I can't understand it, I can't understand it, I absolutely can't understand it. Today they shaved my head, although I shouted at the top of my voice that I didn't want to become a monk. But I can't even remember what happened afterward when they poured cold water on my head. I have never endured such hell. I was almost going frantic, so that they had difficulty in holding me. I cannot understand the meaning of this strange custom. It's a stupid, senseless practice! The lack of good sense in the kings who have not abolished it to this day is beyond my comprehension. Judging from all the circumstances, I wonder whether I have not fallen into the hands of the Inquisition, and whether the man I took to be the Grand Chancellor isn't the Grand Inquisitor. But I cannot understand how a king can be subject to the Inquisition. It can only be through the influence of France, especially of Polignac. Oh, that beast of a Polignac! He has sworn to harm me to the death. And he pursues me and pursues me; but I know, my friend, that you are the tool of England. The English are great politicians. They poke their noses into everything. All the world knows that when England takes a pinch of snuff, France sneezes.

The twenty-fifth

Today the Grand Inquisitor came to my room, but I heard his footsteps in the distance and hid under the chair. When he saw that I was not there be began to shout. At first he shouted, "Poprishchin"—I didn't say a word. Then: "Axenty Ivanov! Titular Councillor! Nobleman!" I still kept silent. "Ferdinand VIII, King of Spain! " I was about to thrust out my head, but then thought: "No, brother, you don't fool me! We know you: you'll be pouring water on my head again." But he saw me and chased me from behind the chair with his stick. That blasted stick hurts a great deal. But I was repaid for all this by a discovery I made yesterday: I found out that every cock has its Spain and it's situated under its feathers. The Grand Inquisitor, however, went away fuming and threatening me with all sorts of punishment. But I scorned his impotent malice, knowing that he was acting like a machine, like a tool of the Englishman.

34 yraurbeF Yrae 349

No, I don't have the strength to take any more. Lord! What are they doing to me! They pour cold water on my head! They won't listen to me, they don't see me, won't hear me. What have I done to them? What are they torturing me for? What do they want from me, wretch that I am? What can I give them? I have nothing. I have no strength, I can't take their tortures, my head is burning, and everything is swimming before my eyes. Save me! take me! Give me three horses as swift as a whirlwind! Get in, coachman; ring, my little bell; dash on, horses, and take me from this world. Further, further till I can see nothing, nothing. The sky whirls before me; a little star twinkles in the distance; the forest rushes past with its dark trees and the moon; a gray mist stretches out beneath my feet; a chord resounds in the mist; on one side the sea, on the other Italy; over there you can see the cottages of Russia. Is that my home in the blue distance? Is my mother sitting by the window? Mother, save your wretched son! Shed a tear on his aching head! See how they are torturing him! Take your wretched orphan to your breast! There's nowhere for him on earth! They're persecuting him! Mother! Take pity on your sick child! . . . And do you know that the Dey of Algiers has a pimple right under his nose?

(1835) Translated by A. Tulloch, revised by A.L. and M.T.K.

The Nose

I

On the 25th of March an extraordinarily strange event took place in St. Petersburg. Ivan Yakovlevich the barber, residing on Voznesensky [Ascension] Prospect (his surname has been lost, and even on his sign—which depicts a gentleman with his cheek well-soaped and an inscription: *Blood let as well*—there is nothing more) the barber Ivan Yakovlevich awoke rather early and smelled the aroma of baking bread. Raising himself up a little in bed, he saw that his wife, a rather imposing woman very fond of her coffee, was removing from the oven some freshly-baked loaves.

"Today, Praskovia Osipovna, I will not have coffee," said Ivan Yakovlevich. "But instead I would like to have some hot bread with some onions." (That is to say, Ivan Yakovlevich would have liked to have both one and the other, but he knew it was quite impossible to request two things at once: Praskovia Osipovna had a great dislike for such caprices.) "Let the fool eat bread: all the better for me," his spouse thought. "There'll be an extra cup of coffee." And she tossed a loaf onto the table.

For propriety's sake Ivan Yakovlevich donned his tail-coat over his shirt and, sitting down at the table, he poured out the salt, peeled the two small globelets of onion, took up the knife and, assuming a deliberate air, cut into the load. Having cut it in two, he glanced inside and, to his surprise, saw something whitish. Ivan Yakovlevich gave a careful prod with the knife and poked the inside with a finger: "Something solid!—he said to himself—what would that be now?"

He thrust his fingers into the bread and pulled out—a nose! . . . Ivan Yakovlevich's heart sank; he rubbed his eyes and felt the object: it was a nose, a nose and nothing else! And what's more, he felt it was somehow familiar. Horror etched itself on Ivan Yakovlevich's face. But that horror was nothing compared to the indignation that seized his spouse.

—You beast, where ever did you cut off that nose?—she cried out angrily. —Crook! Drunkard! I'll report you to the police myself. You bandit! I've heard from three different people that when you shave them you pull on their noses so hard they barely stay put.

But Ivan Yakovlevich was more dead than alive. He had recognized that this nose belonged to none other than the collegiate assessor Kovalev, whom he shaved on Wednesdays and Sundays.

—Wait, Praskovia Osipovna! Once I've wrapped it up in a rag I'll put it here, in the corner: let it lie there for a bit; later on I'll take it outside.

—I won't hear of it! Am I to have a cut-off nose lying about in my room? . . . You over-baked crust! All you can just about manage nowadays is to strop your razor, but soon you won't be up to doing your duties, you strumpet, scoundrel! Why should I have to answer for you to the police? . . . Ah you bungler, stupid log! Get it out of here! Out! Take it wherever you want! Just so I don't get a whiff of it again!

Ivan Yakovlevich stood like one struck dumb. He thought and thought— and couldn't decide what to think. "Devil only knows how it happened,—he said finally, scratching behind his ear. Drunk or not drunk, how I came home last night I can't tell for sure. But by all the signs something incredible has happened: because bread is a baked good, but a nose is something else entirely. I can't make it out! . . ." Ivan Yakovlevich fell silent. The thought that the police would discover the nose in his possession and would accuse him frightened into a complete stupor. He could already picture the scarlet collar with its handsome silver embroidery, the saber . . . and he trembled from head to foot. Finally he found his smock and his boots, put on all this tattered get-up and, to the accompanying severe admonitions of Praskovia Osipovna, wrapped up the nose in a rag and went out unto the street.

He tried to hide it somewhere; in a bin or by a gate, or, just as if by accident, to drop it and duck down a side street. But unfortunately he kept meeting up with this acquaintance or that, who'd set right in with questions: "Where are you off to?" or "Who're you going to shave this early in the day?" So that Ivan Yakovlevich could not seize his moment. Once he did actually manage to drop it, but from down the street the constable pointed at him with his halberd and said: "Pick that up! You dropped something over there!" And Ivan Yakovlevich had to pick up the nose and hide it in his pocket. Despair seized him, all the more so since the crowd was increasing as stores and shops began to open.

He decided to go to St. Isaac's Bridge: mightn't it be possible to hurl it into the Neva? . . . But I'm to a certain degree at fault here, in that up to this point I've told you nothing of Ivan Yakovlevich, in many respects an estimable man.

Ivan Yakovlevich, like any proper Russian artisan, was a terrible drunkard. And although he shaved others' chins every day, his own remained eternally unshaven. Ivan Yakovlevich's tail-coat (Ivan Yakovlevich never wore a frock coat) was piebald; that is, it had been once black, but had come out all over in brownish-yellow and gray splotches; the collar was shiny with grease; and instead of three buttons there was only one hanging by a thread. Ivan Yakovlevich was a great cynic and when collegiate assessor Kovalev would say, as he usually did when being shaved: "Ivan Yakovlevich, your hands always stink!" then Ivan Yakovlevich would respond with a question: "Why should they stink?" —I don't know, my good fellow, but stink they do," the collegiate assessor would reply,— and Ivan Yakovlevich, taking a pinch of snuff, would retaliate for this by lathering not only Kovalev's cheeks but under his nose and behind his ear and under his beard, in a word wherever he took a fancy to.

This estimable citizen had reached St. Isaac's Bridge. First he looked all around; then he leant on the balustrade as if looking under the bridge: perhaps to see if many schools of fish were running, and he quietly tossed in the rag with the nose. He felt was if a hundred-weight had fallen from his shoulders: Ivan Yakovlevich even laughed. Instead of setting off to shave clerkly chins, he headed for an establishment with the designation "Comestibles and Tea" to demand a glass of punch, when suddenly he noticed at the end of the bridge a constable of noble appearance, with sweeping side-whiskers, in a tricorne hat, with a saber. He froze; meanwhile the constable pointed to him and said:

—You come here, my good fellow!

Ivan Yakovlevich, knowing the proper forms, took off his hat when he was still at a distance and approaching smartly, said:

—Good health to your honor!

—No, no, sunshine, I'm not your honor: tell us, what were you doing out there on the bridge?

—God is my witness, sir, I was on my way to give a shave and just looked over to see if the river was flowing fast.

—That's a lie, a lie! You're not going to wiggle out with that one. Be so good as to answer!

—I'm ready to shave your grace twice a week, or even three times, no strings attached,—answered Ivan Yakovlevich.

—No, chum, that's nothing to me. I've got three barbers who come to shave me and what's more they take it for a great honor. But you just be so good as to tell me what you were doing out there?

Ivan Yakovlevich grew pale . . . But here events become completely enveloped in mist and what happened further is absolutely unknown.

2.

Collegiate assessor Kovalev awoke rather early and made the sound "brrr . . ." with his lips, which he always did when he woke up, although he himself couldn't explain why. Kovalev stretched, asked for the small mirror which stood on the table. He wanted to look at a pimple which had surfaced on his nose the evening before; but with the very greatest astonishment he saw that in place of his nose there was a completely smooth expanse! Frightened, Kovalev asked for water and wiped his eyes: just so, no nose! He began to feel about with his fingers in order to find out: wasn't he asleep? It seemed he was not. Collegiate Assessor Kovalev leapt out of bed and shook himself: no nose! He immediately ordered that he be dressed and off he flew to the police chief's.

But in the meanwhile I must a tell bit about Kovalev so that the reader might see what sort of collegiate assessor this was. Collegiate assessors who attain that rank with the help of academic certificates are in no way comparable with those collegiate assessors who've come up in the Caucasus. These are two completely different species. The erudite collegiate assessors . . . But Russia is such a bizarre land that whatever you say of one collegiate assessor will inevitably be taken personally by every collegiate assessor from Riga to the Kamchatka. You can count on the same from all callings and ranks.—Kovalev was a Caucasus collegiate assessor. He had only attained the rank two years ago and was therefore unable to forget it for a moment; and in order to give himself more nobility and weight he never called himself a collegiate assessor, but always a major. "Listen, dearie,—he would often say when he met a woman selling shirt-fronts on the street—you come to my house: my rooms are on Sadovaia [Garden Street]; just ask: is this Major Kovalev's—anyone will show you." Yet if he met with a pretty one he would give her additional, secret, instructions, adding: "You just ask, darling, for Major Kovalev's place."—For this reason we too will in the future call this collegiate assessor the major.

Major Kovalev had the daily habit of strolling along Nevsky Prospect. The collar of his shirtfront was always extraordinarily white and well-starched. His side whiskers were of the type one can still observe on provincial land surveyors, architects, and regimental surgeons, also on those fulfilling certain constabulary duties and, in general, on men who boast plump, ruddy cheeks and are very good at playing the game of boston: these whiskers grow right up to the midpoint of the cheek and go straight across to the nose. Major Kovalev customarily wore numerous cornelian fobs, both the kind with heraldic crests and the kind with incised inscriptions: *Wednesday, Thursday, Monday*, and so forth. Major Kovalev had come to Petersburg out of need, namely the need to find a position suitable to his rank: if possible, a vice-governorship, failing that, the executor of some important department or other. Major Kovalev was also not averse to marriage; but only under such circumstances as would bring him a bride with two hundred thousand in capital. And therefore now the reader can judge for himself the position in which this Major found himself when he saw, in place of his rather handsome and well-proportioned nose, a most idiotic, flat, and smooth spot.

To make things worse, not a single cab appeared on the street, and he was forced to go on foot, wrapping himself up in his cloak and swathing his face in his handkerchief, as if he had a nosebleed. "But perhaps it was just my imagination: a nose just can't vanish in some stupid accident." He stepped into a pastry-shop to look in a mirror. Fortunately, there was no one in the shop; boys were sweeping up the rooms and moving the chairs about; others with sleep eyes were carrying out trays of hot *pirozhki*; on the table and chairs were scattered yesterday's papers, stained with coffee. "Well thank heavens there's no one here,—he said,—now I can have a look." Timidly he approached the mirror and looked: "Damn it, what rubbish is this!—he spat . . . —If there were now something there in place of the nose, but for there just to be nothing at all! . . ."

He bit his lips in irritation, left the pastry-shop and decided that, contrary to his usual habit, he would not look at anyone and not smile at anyone either. He came to a sudden halt, as if rooted to the ground, at the doors of a certain house: before his very eyes and event took place which was totally inexplicable: a carriage pulled up to the portico; its doors opened; a gentleman in uniform, bent over, jumped out and ran up the

stairs. Imagine the horror and with it the amazement of Kovalev as he recognized that this was his own nose! With this extraordinary sight it seemed
to Kovalev that everything went topsy-turvy; he felt himself barely able to
stand but, trembling all over as if in delirium, decided that come what may
he would want for the gentleman to return to his carriage. In two minutes
the nose in fact did come out. He was in a uniform embroidered in gold
thread with a tall standing collar; he wore suede breeches; there was a
sword at his side. From his plumed hat one deduced that he held the rank
of state councilor. All in all it was clear that he had been paying a visit. He
looked both ways, called to the coachman "Drive on!" took his seat and
drove off.

Poor Kovalev nearly lost his mind. He had no notion what to think
about such a strange event. How was it even possible that his nose which
only yesterday had been on his face and could not ride in a carriage or
walk,—be wearing a uniform? He ran after the carriage which, fortunately,
had not driven far but had stopped in front of Kazan Cathedral.

Kovalev rushed into the Cathedral, making his way past the ranks of
beggar women with their faces swathed in rags and two holes for the eyes,
at which he used to laugh heartily, and entered the church. There were few
worshippers inside; they all stood near the entry doors. Kovalev felt himself in such a state of consternation that he was utterly unable to pray, and
he darted his gaze about looking for the gentleman in every corner. Finally
he saw him, off to one side. The nose had completely concealed his face in
his tall standing collar and with an air of the very greatest piety was saying
his prayers.

"How can I approach him?—thought Kovalev—All the signs, his uniform, his hat, make it clear that he's a state councilor. Devil only known
how it's to be done!"

He began to cough in the gentleman's vicinity: but the nose did not for
a moment abandon his pious demeanor, and made deep bows.

—Gracious sir . . .—said Kovalev, mentally forcing himself to take
courage,—gracious sir . . .

—What is it you want?—replied the nose, turning.

—I find it strange, gracious sir . . . I feel . . . you must know your place.
And then I come upon you, and where?—in church. You must agree . . .

—Excuse me but I can make nothing of what you say . . . Explain
yourself

"How am I to explain things to him?" thought Kovalev, and, with a
deep breath, he began:

—Of course I . . . in fact, I am a major. For me to go about with no nose,
you must agree, this is inappropriate. Some sort of market-woman selling
sliced oranges on Vosnesensky bridge, she can do without a nose; but given

my expectations . . . and moreover being acquainted with ladies in many respectable homes: Chekhtyreva the state counselor's wife, and others . . . Judge for yourself . . . I don't know, gracious sir . . . (at this point Major Kovalev shrugged his shoulders) . . . Excuse me . . . if you look at this in the light of the laws of duty and honor.. you yourself can understand . . .

—I understand absolutely nothing at all,—replied the nose.—Explain yourself in a more satisfactory way.

—Gracious sir . . .—said Kovalev with a sense of his own dignity,—I don't know how to take your words . . . Everything about this affair is, I think perfectly obvious . . . Or do you mean to say . . . After all, you're my personal nose!

The nose looked at the major and slightly knit his brows.

—You are mistaken, gracious sir. I am a person in my own right. There can be no close relationship between us. Judging by the buttons on your uniform, you must serve in the Senate or, at least, somewhere in the judiciary. I am in the academic service.—With these words the nose turned away and continued his devotions.

Kovalev was completely confounded, with no idea what to do or even what to think. At that moment he heard the pleasant rustle of a lady's gown: an elderly lady approached, all decked out in lace, and with her was a slender miss, in a white dress that delineated her slender figure very prettily, wearing a straw hat light as a cream-puff. Behind them waited a tall footman with immense sideburns and fully a dozen capes to his coat, who flicked open his snuff-box.

Kovalev edged nearer, tugged at the batiste collar of his shirt-front, put the seals on his gold watch chain in good order and, looking about him with a smile, turned his attention to the delicate young lady who, like a spring blossom, had slightly bowed her head and raised to her brow her small white hand with its semi-translucent fingers. The smile on Kovalev's face broadened even more when beneath her hat-brim he caught a glimpse of her small, round, snow-white chin and a bit of her cheek, flushed with the tint of the first rose of spring. But suddenly he leapt back as if scorched. He had remembered that where his nose should be he had nothing at all, and tears started from his eyes. He turned, intending to tell the uniformed gentleman straight out the her was only pretending to be a state counselor, that he was a buffoon and a scoundrel and that he was nothing more than Kovalev's own nose . . . But the nose was gone: he had managed to dash off, very likely to pay someone else a call.

This sent Kovalev into despair. He retraced his steps and stood for a minute beneath the colonnade looking carefully in all directions for a glimpse of the nose. He remembered very clearly that the nose's hat had had a plume and his uniform gold embroidery; but he hadn't noticed the greatcoat, nor the color of his carriage or horses, or even if there had been any sort of footman, and in what sort of livery. And then there were so many carriages rushing to and fro with such speed that it was difficult to pick one out; but if he did manage to pick it out he had no means of stopping it. It was a lovely sunny day, There was a swarm of people on Nevsky; an absolute floral waterfall of ladies flowed along every inch of sidewalk from the Politseisky [Police] Bridge to the Anichkin. And just there was a court counselor of his acquaintance, whom Kovalev would address as "lieutenant" especially if they happened to be in the presence of others. And there was Yaryzhkin, head clerk of the senate, a great friend of his, who at boston always got into difficulties when he played the eight. And there another major who had received his assessorship in the Caucasus was waving at Kovalev, beckoning him over . . .

—O damn it all!—said Kovalev.—Hey, driver, take me straight to the chief of police!

Kovalev got into the droshky and to the coachman shouted only: "Go hell for leather!"

—Is the police chief in?—he cried, entering the reception.

—No,—responded the private secretary,—he's just left.

—A fine thing!

—Yes,—added the secretary,—not so long ago either, but he did leave. If you'd come a minute earlier maybe you would have caught him in.

Kovalev, without lowering his handkerchief from his face, got into his droshky and cried in a despairing voice: "Drive on!"

—Where?— said the driver.

—Straight ahead!

—How do you mean, straight ahead? The road turns: left or right?

The question gave Kovalev pause and forced him to think once more. It his position it was better to set off directly for the police station, not because it was directly connected to the police but because its actions could be much swifter than others: to look for satisfaction in the offices of the department in which the nose claimed to work would be senseless because from the nose's own words it was plain that he was a person who held nothing sacred and could just as easily have lied about that as he had lied when he swore he had never seen Kovalev before. And so Kovalev was just about to order the driver to take him to the police station when he had another thought, namely that this buffoon and charlatan, who in their first meeting had behaved in such an unscrupulous manner, might again easily, seizing the moment, slip out of town,—and then all searches might be in vain or might drag on, God forbid, for an entire month. Finally, it seemed, Providence itself enlightened him. He decided to set off straight for the newspaper office, and immediately post an advertisement with a detailed description of the nose's every particular, such that anyone meeting him could bring him to Kovalev instantly or at least let the latter know of his whereabouts. And so, Kovalev, having made this decision, ordered the driver to the newspaper office and along the way did not leave off pounding the man's back with his fist and repeating "Faster, scum! Faster, crook!" "Eh now, barin!"—said the driver, shaking his head and slapping the reins of his horse, which had a long coat like a lapdog's. The droshky finally halted and Kovalev, panting, ran into the small reception room where a grey-haired clerk in an ancient frock coat and spectacles sat at a desk and, his pen between his teeth, was counting the coins he had received.

—Who is it here accepts the advertisements?— cried Kovalev.—Ah, hello!

—At your service,—said the grey-haired clerk. raising his eyes for an instant and lowering them again to the serried heaps of coins.

—I should like to print . . .

—To be sure. If you would be so good as to wait,—said the grey-haired clerk, with his right hand noting a figure on the paper and moving two beads of his abacus over with the fingers of his left. A footman in braided livery and an air which showed his familiarity with the aristocratic home stood next to the table holding a note, and considered appropriate to make a show of his wide experience: "Believe me, sir, when I say the dog isn't worth eight pounds, that is, I wouldn't give eight pence for it; but the countess loves it, by God she does,—so him that kidnapped it gets one hundred roubles! To put it proper, just as we're talking now, people's tastes are incompatible: well if you're a hunter, you want to keep a hound or a poodle; then don't blink at giving five hundred or a thousand for it, just so long as it's a fine dog."

The respectable clerk was listening to all this with an air of importance and was at the same time making up his estimate; how many letters were in the proposed announcement? Along the walls were standing many old ladies, merchants' shop-men and lackeys, all with announcements. One noted that a coachman of sober deportment was seeking employment; another—a slightly used carriage, brought from Paris in 1814; there a servant girl of nineteen, experienced in laundry matters but good for other types of work, was on offer, a sturdy droshky, lacking only springs; a young spirited horse, dapple grey, seventeen years old; new seeds, received from England, for turnips and radishes; a dacha with all the conveniences; two horse-stalls and a plot on which an excellent birch or fir grove could be established; also there was a call for any interested in the purchase of old shoe-leather together with an invitation to present themselves at the exchange any day between the hours of eight and three. The room in which this company milled about was small and the air was extraordinarily close;

but collegiate assessor Kovalev was not able to sense the smells because he had his kerchief to his face and his nose itself was God knows where.

—Gracious sir, if I may be so bold as to request . . . I am in great need, —Kovalev uttered finally, with impatience.

—Directly, directly! Two roubles forty three kopeks! This instant! One rouble sixty-four kopeks—said the grey-haired gentleman, tossing the old ladies' and lackeys' notices back in their faces.

—What may I do for you?—he finally said, turning to Kovalev.

I request . . .—said Kovalev,—there's been a crime or a prank, as yet I have no way of knowing which. I merely wish to advertise the fact that any person who will bring the scoundrel to me will receive an appropriate reward.

—May I ask your surname?

—No, what do you need my surname for? I must not reveal it. I have such a large acquaintance: Chetyrekheva, the state counselor's wife, Palegeya Grigorevna Podtochina, [Mrs. Undercut] the staff-officer's wife. If they were suddenly to find out, God forbid! You may simply put: a collegiate assessor or, even better, one who holds the rank of major.

—And the runaway was your lackey?

—What lackey? That wouldn't be such a great crime! The one who's run away is . . . my nose . . .

—Hmmm what a strange surname! And has this Mr. Mynose robbed you of a good sum?

—My nose, that is . . . You're mistaken! My nose, my very own nose has disappeared to who knows where. The Devil's played a trick on me!

—How do you mean, it's disappeared? There's something here that I can't quite grasp.

—I can't tell you how it happened; the main thing is that it's now riding around town and calling itself a state counselor. And therefore I ask you to announce that whoever catches it should come to me immediately, losing as little time as possible. Judge for yourself, really, how can I go on without such a prominent part of the body? It's not anything like a little toe, where I stick the foot into my boot—and no one will see it's not there. On Thursdays I visit Chekhtyreva the state counselor's wife: Palageya Grigorievna Podtochina, the staff-officer's wife, her daughter is very pretty, and has pretty friends, and judge for yourself, how could I now . . . I can't appear there now.

The clerk became pensive, as signaled by his firmly compressed lips.

—No, I can't place such an announcement in the papers,—he said at last, after a long silence.

—What? Why?

—Because. The paper might loose its reputation. If everyone were to start writing in that his nose had run off . . . As it is, they say we publish lots of absurdities and false rumors.

—Just how is this an absurdity? There is, I think, nothing like that in it at all.

—It seems to you there isn't. But just last week there was a case of the same kind. An official like yourself came in here, the same as you just did, he brought in a notice, it came to two roubles 73 kopeks, and the whole of the announcement was that a poodle with a black coat had run away. You'd think—what of that? But it turned out to be a lampoon: the poodle was a bursar, can't recall what department.

But I'm not making an announcement about a poodle, but about my own nose: so it's almost as if it were about myself.

—No, I can't put in an announcement like that.

—Even if my nose really has disappeared!

—If it's disappeared, that's a case for a doctor. They say there are people who can put on any sort of nose you want. But I have to say, by the way, that you must be a person with a merry disposition who likes to have his joke in public.

—I swear to you, as God is my witness! Well if it comes to that, I'll show you.

—Why trouble yourself!—continued the clerk, taking a pinch of snuff. —However, if it's no trouble,—he added with a gesture of curiosity,—then I'd like to have a look.

The collegiate assessor lowered the kerchief from his face.

—In point of fact it's extraordinarily strange! —said the clerk,—the spot is perfectly smooth, like a pancake right out of the pan. Yes, it's unbelievably flat!

—So are you going to argue with me any more? you can see for yourself that you can't not print it. I'll be especially grateful and very glad that this occurrence has given me the opportunity of making your acquaintance . . .—the major, as is clear from the forgoing, had decided to resort to a bit of low flattery.

—To print it, of course, is no great thing,—said the clerk, it's just that I don't foresee any profit for you in doing so. If you like give it to someone with a clever pen who can describe it as a rare phenomenon of nature and print the piece in *The Northern Bee* (at this juncture he took another pinch of snuff) for the edification of youth (here he wiped his nose) or just as is, for general interest.

The collegiate assessor was left utterly hopeless. He ran his eye down the news sheet to the theatrical notices; his face was preparing to smile when he encountered the name of an actress who was quite pretty, and his hand moved towards his pocket: did he have a blue bank-note? Because staff-officers, in Kovalev's opinion, must sit in the stalls,—but the thought of his nose spoiled everything!

Even the clerk, it seemed, was touched by the difficult position Kovalev was in. Wanting to relieve his sorrow in some way he thought it would be appropriate to express his sympathy in a few words: "I am, truly, very distressed that you've experienced this sort of anecdote. Wouldn't you like a pinch of snuff? It dispels headaches and gloomy moods: even in connection with hemorrhoids it's helpful. Saying this the clerk offered Kovalev his snuff-box, rather cleverly flipping back the lid with its portrait of a lady wearing a hat.

This thoughtless action put an end to Kovalev's patience. "I fail to understand how you can make jokes," he said heatedly:—Can't you see I don't have the very thing I could take a pinch with? Devil take your snuff! I can't even look at it now, and not just at your nasty Berezin, but even if you offered me real rappee. With this, deeply agitated, he left the newspaper offices and set off for the home of the constable, who was extraordinarily fond of sugar. In his home the foyer, and the dining room as well, were well-furnished with the sugar-loaves that merchants had brought to him as tokens of friendship. His cook was at that moment pulling off his official boots; the sword and all his professional armor had already been hung peaceably in the corners, his intimidating tricorne hat was in the hands of his three-year old son, and he himself, after his fierce martial service, was preparing to taste life's pleasures.

Kovalev came upon him just as he had stretched, (wheezed/quacked) and said: "Eh, I could use a good two hour's sleep!" One might therefore foresee that the collegiate assessor's arrival would not be very well-timed. And I don't know whether even if Kovalev had brought him several pounds of tea or a length of cloth he would have been received too joyfully. The constable was a great admirer of all the arts and manufactures; but he preferred a bank-note to anything. "That's a thing,—he customarily said;— than which there is no thing better: it doesn't get hungry, doesn't take up much room, always fits in your pocket, and if you drop it—it won't break."

The constable received Kovalev rather coldly and said that after dinner was no time to pursue an investigation, that nature itself decreed that, having eaten, one should take a rest (from this the collegiate assessor could see that the constable was not unacquainted with the pronouncements of the ancient sages), that proper gentlemen didn't get their noses torn off and that there are all kinds of majors in the world whose linen isn't even in a respectable condition and who gad about to all sorts of indecent places.

That is to say, no glancing blow, but a facer! It must be noted that Kovalev was an extraordinarily thin-skinned person. He could forgive anything said about himself, but could never excuse anything relating to his rank or title. He even proposed that in theatrical productions one might allow anything at all concerning chief officers, but that field-rank officers must not be impugned in any way. The reception given him by the constable flustered him to such a degree that he shook his head to clear it and said with a sense of dignity: "I confess that after such insulting remarks on your part, I have nothing to add . . ."—and he left.

He came to his door barely able to feel his legs beneath him. It was already dusk. After all these fruitless searches his rooms seemed gloomy or even extraordinarily nasty to him. Entering the foyer he saw on the stained leather divan his servant Ivan who, lying on his back was spitting at the ceiling and hitting the same spot with considerable accuracy. Such indifference in a human being infuriated Kovalev; he struck Ivan on the forehead with his hat, saying: "You, you swine, you're always doing something stupid.!"

Ivan hastily jumped from his position and threw himself with all his might into helping Kovalev off with coat.

Entering his bed-chamber the major, tired and gloomy, threw himself into an armchair and at last, after heaving several sighs, said:

"My God! My God! What kind of rotten luck is this? If I were missing a hand or a foot—it would still be better; if I were missing my ear—that would be vile, but still more tolerable; but a man missing his nose is—Devil knows what; neither fish nor fowl nor good red herring; just take him and throw him out the window! And let's say it was cut off in battle or in a duel, or it was my own fault; but it just disappeared for no reason, for nothing! . . . But no, it can't be,—he added after a moment's thought.—It's unbelievable that a nose should disappear, unbelievable in every way. This is probably either a dream or a hallucination; maybe somehow, by accident, instead of water I drank down the vodka I wipe down my bead with after I shave. That fool Ivan didn't take it away and I got hold of it somehow." To really convince himself that he wasn't drunk the major gave himself such a painful pinch that he yelped. The pain absolutely convinced him that he was acting and living in the waking world. He cautiously approached the mirror and at first screwed up his eyes with the notion that maybe the nose would appear in its rightful place. But that instant he jumped back saying "What a travesty!"

This was, really, incomprehensible. If some button had been lost, a silver spoon, a watch, or some other similar thing—but to have lost this, and in his own apartment to boot! . . . Thinking over all the circumstances, Major Kovalev concluded that the nearest thing to the truth must be that the guilty person was none other than Madame Podtochina, who had wanted him to marry her daughter. He himself had liked flirting with the girl, had but avoided a definite engagement. When the mother told him to his face that she wanted to give him her daughter's hand, he had slyly put her off with his compliments, saying that he was still young, that he must serve for five years so as to be exactly forty-two. And for this reason Madame Podtochina had made up her mind, probably for revenge, to ruin him, and had hired for the purpose some peasant witches, because it was impossible to suppose that the nose had been cut off in any way; no one had come into his room; the barber Ivan Yakovlevich had shaved him on Wednesday, and all Wednesday and even all Thursday his nose had been all right—that he remembered and was quite certain about; besides, he would have felt pain, and there was no doubt that the wound could not have healed so soon and been as flat as a pancake. He formed various plans in his mind: either to summon Madame Podtochina formally before the court or to go to her himself and confront her with it These reflections were interrupted by a light which gleamed through all the cracks of the door and informed him that a Ivan had lit a candle in the hall. Soon Ivan himself appeared, holding the candle before him and lighting up the whole room. Kovalev's first movement was to snatch up his handkerchief and cover the place where yesterday his nose had been, so that his really stupid servant might not gape at the sight of anything so peculiar in his master.

Ivan had hardly time to retreat to his lair when there was the sound of an unfamiliar voice in the hall, pronouncing the words: "Does the collegiate assessor Kovalev live here?"

"Come in, Major Kovalev is here," said Kovalev, jumping up hurriedly and opening the door.

A police officer walked in. He was of handsome appearance, with whiskers neither too fair nor too dark, and rather fat cheeks, the same officer who at the beginning of our story was standing at the end of St. Isaac's Bridge.

"Did you lose your nose, sir?"

"That is so."

"It is now found."

"What are you saying?" cried Major Kovalev. He could not speak for joy. He stared at the police officer standing before him, on whose full lips and cheeks the flickering light of the candle was brightly reflected. "How?"

"By extraordinary luck: he was caught almost on the road. He had already taken his seat in the stagecoach and was intending to go to Riga, and had already taken a passport in the name of a government clerk. And the strange thing is that I myself took him for a gentleman at first, but fortunately I had my spectacles with me and I soon saw that it was a nose. I *am* a bit shortsighted. And if you're standing right in front of me I only see that you have a face, but I don't notice your nose or your beard or anything. My mother-in-law, that is my wife's mother, doesn't see anything either."

Kovalev was beside himself with joy. "Where? Where? I'll go at once."

"Don't disturb yourself. Knowing that you were in need of it I brought it along with me. And the strange thing is that the man who has had the most to do with the affair is a rascal of a barber on Voznesensky Avenue, who is now in our custody. For a long time I've suspected him of drunkenness and thieving, and only the day before yesterday he carried off a strip of buttons from a shop. Your nose is exactly as it was." With this the police officer put his hand in his pocket and drew out the nose just as it was.

"That's it!" Kovalev cried. "That's certainly it You must have a cup of tea with me this evening."

"I'd consider it a great pleasure, but I can't possibly manage it: I have to go from here to the penitentiary. . . . How the price of food is going up! . . . At home I have my mother-in-law, that is my wife's mother, and my children, the eldest particularly gives signs of great promise, he is a very intelligent child; but we have absolutely no means for his education . . ."

Kovalev took the hint and, taking from the table a red bank-note he thrust it into hand of the officer who, clicking his heels, took his leave. The next instant Kovalev heard his voice on the street, raking over the coals a stupid peasant who had driven his cart right out onto the boulevard.

For some time after the policeman's departure the collegiate assessor remained in a state of bewilderment, and it was only a few minutes later that he was capable of feeling and understanding again: so reduced was he to stupefaction by this unexpected good fortune. He took the recovered nose carefully in his two hands, holding them together like a cup, and once more examined it attentively.

"Yes, that's it, it's certainly it," said Major Kovalev. "There's the pimple that came out on the left side yesterday." The major almost laughed aloud with joy.

But nothing in this world is of long duration, and so his joy was not so great the next moment; and the moment after it was still less, and in the end he passed imperceptibly into his ordinary frame of mind, just as a circle on the water caused by a falling stone gradually passes away into the unbroken smoothness of the surface. Kovalev began to think, and reflected that the business was not finished yet; the nose was found, but it had to be put on, fixed in its proper place.

"And what if it won't stick?"

Asking himself this question, the major turned pale.

With a feeling of irrepressible terror he rushed to the table and moved the mirror forward so as m not to put the nose on crooked. His hands trembled. Cautiously and gently he replaced it in its former position. Oh horror, the nose wouldn't stick! . . .

He put it to his lips, slightly warmed it with his breath, and again applied it to the flat space between his two cheeks; but nothing would make the nose stick.

"Come on, come on, *stick*, you fool!" he said to it; but the nose felt wooden and fell on the table with a strange sound like a bottle-cork. The major's face twisted convulsively.

"It's not possible it won't go back, is it?" But however often he applied it to the proper place, each attempt was as unsuccessful as the first.

He called for Ivan and sent him for the doctor who lived in the best apartment on the first floor of the same house. The doctor was a handsome man; he had magnificent pitch-black whiskers, a fresh-faced and healthy wife, he ate fresh apples in the morning, and kept his mouth extraordinarily clean, rinsing it out for nearly three-quarters of an hour every morning and cleaning his teeth with five different sorts of brushes. The doctor appeared immediately. Asking Major Kovalev how long ago the trouble had occurred, he took him by the chin and with his thumb gave him a flip on the spot where the nose had been, making the major jerk back his head so abruptly that he knocked the back of it against the wall. The doctor said that was nothing to worry about, and, advising Kovalev to move a little away from the wall, he told him to tilt his head: first to the right, and feeling the place where the nose had been, the doctor said, "Hmm!" Then he told Kovalev to tilt his head to the left side and again said "Hmm!" And in conclusion he gave him another flip with his thumb, so that Major Kovalev threw up his head like a horse when his teeth are being looked at. After making this experiment the doctor shook his head and said:

"No, it's impossible. You'd better stay as you are, or it might get much worse. Of course, it *could* be stuck on; I could stick it on for you at once, if you like; but I assure you it would be worse for you."

"That's a nice thing to say! How can I stay without my nose?" said Kovalev. "Things can't possibly be worse than they are now. This whole affair is Devil knows what! Where can I show myself with this caricature of a face? I have a good circle of acquaintances. Today, for instance, I ought to be at two evening parties. I know a great many people; Chekhtyreva, the wife of the state councilor, Podtochina, the staff-officer's wife . . . though after the way she's behaved, I won't have anything more to do with her except through the police. Do me a favor," Kovalev went on in a pleading voice; "isn't there any way? . . . Even if it's not perfect, just as long as it would stay on; I could even hold it steady with my hand at risky moments. I wouldn't dance in any case, because I might hurt it without meaning to. As for remuneration for your services, you may be assured that as far as my means allow . . ."

"Believe me," said the doctor, in a voice neither loud nor low but persuasive and magnetic, "that I never work from mercenary motives. That is opposed to my principles and my calling. It's true I do accept a fee for my visits, but that's simply to avoid wounding my patients by refusing it. Of course I could replace your nose; but I assure you on my honor, since you do not believe my word, that it will be much worse for you. You'd better wait for the action of nature itself. Wash the spot frequently with cold water, and I assure you that even without a nose you'll be just as healthy as with one. And I advise you to put the nose in a bottle, in spirits or, better still, put two tablespoonfuls of strong vodka on it, and distilled vinegar—and then you might get quite a sum of money for it. I'd even take it myself, if you don't ask too much for."

"No, no, I wouldn't sell it for anything," Major Kovalev cried in despair; "I'd rather lose it altogether!"

"Excuse me!" said the doctor, bowing himself out, "I was trying to be of use to you. . . . Well, there's nothing I can do! Anyway, you see that I've done my best."

Saying this the doctor walked out of the room with a majestic air. Kovalev had not noticed his face, and, almost unconscious, had seen nothing but the cuffs of his immaculate white shirt peeping out from the sleeves of his black tail coat.

Next day he decided, before lodging a complaint with the police, to write to Madame Podtochina to see whether she would consent, without argument, to compensate him appropriately. The letter was as follows:

> *Most gracious Madam,*
> *ALEXANDRA GRIGORIEVNA!*
>
> *I cannot understand this strange conduct on your part. You may rest assured that you will gain nothing by what you have done, and you will in no way force me to marry your daughter. Believe me that the business with my nose is perfectly clear to me, as is the fact that you and only you are the person chiefly responsible. The sudden parting of the same from its natural position, its flight and its masquerading at one time as a government clerk and finally in its own shape, is nothing else than the consequence of the sorceries engaged in by you or by those who are versed in the same honorable arts as you are. For my part I consider it my duty to warn you that if the above-mentioned nose is not in its proper place today, I shall be obliged to resort to the assistance and protection of the law.*
>
> *I have, however, with complete respect to you, the honor to be*
> *Your respectful servant,*
> *PLATON KOVALEV*

> *Most gracious Sir,*
> *PLATON KUZMICH!*
>
> *Your letter greatly astonished me. I must frankly confess that I did not expect it, especially in regard to your unjust reproaches. I assure you I have never received the government clerk of whom you speak in my house, neither*

*in masquerade nor in his own attire. It is true that Filipp Ivanovich
Potanchikov has been to see me, and although, indeed, he is asking me for my
daughter's hand and is a well-conducted, sober man of great learning, I have
never encouraged his hopes. You also make some reference to your nose. If you
wish me to understand by that that you imagine that I've been thumbing my
nose at you, that is, giving you a formal refusal, I am surprised that you should
speak of such a thing when, as you know perfectly well, I was quite of the
opposite way of thinking, and if you are courting my daughter with a view to
lawful matrimony I am ready to satisfy you immediately, seeing that has
always been the object of my keenest desires, in the hopes of which I remain
always ready to be of service to you.*
        ALEXANDRA PODTOCHINA

"No," said Kovalev to himself after reading the letter, "she's really not
guilty. It's impossible. This letter is written in a way that no one guilty of a
crime could write." The collegiate assessor was an expert on this subject,
as he had been sent several times to the Caucasus to conduct investigations.
"In what way, by what fate, has this happened? Only the devil could understand it!" he said at last, throwing up his hands.

Meanwhile the rumors of this strange occurrence were spreading all
over the town, and of course, not without special additions. At just that time
everyone was particularly interested in the marvelous: experiments in the
influence of magnetism had been attracting public attention only recently.
Moreover the story of the dancing chair in Koniushennaia [Horse] Street
was still fresh, and so it's not surprising that people were soon beginning to
say that the nose of a collegiate assessor called Kovalev went walking along
Nevsky Prospect at exactly three in the afternoon. Numbers of inquisitive
people flocked there every day. Somebody said that the nose was in Yunker's
shop—and near Yunker's there was such a crowd and such a crush that the
police were actually obliged to intervene. One speculator, a man of dignified
appearance with whiskers, who used to sell all sorts of cakes and tarts at the
doors of the theaters, purposely constructed some very strong wooden
benches which he offered to the curious to stand on for eighty kopeks each.
One very worthy colonel left home earlier on account of it, and with a great
deal of trouble made his way through the crowd; but to his great indignation, instead of the nose, he saw in the shop windows the usual woolen
undershirt and lithograph depicting a girl pulling up her stocking while a
foppish young man, with a cutaway waistcoat and a small beard, peeps at
her from behind a tree; a picture which had been hanging in the same place
for more than ten years. As he walked away he said with vexation: "How
can people be led astray by such stupid and incredible stories!" Then the
rumor spread that it was not on Nevsky Prospect but in Tavrichersky Park

that Major Kovalev's nose took its walks; that it had been there for a long time; that even when Khozrev-Mirza had lived there he had been greatly surprised at this strange freak of nature. Several students from the Academy of Surgery made their way to the park. One worthy lady of high rank wrote a letter to the superintendent of the park asking him to show her children this rare phenomenon with, if possible, an explanation that would be edifying and instructive for the young.

All the gentlemen who invariably attend social gatherings and like to amuse the ladies were extremely thankful for all these events, since their stock of anecdotes had been completely exhausted. A small group of worthy and well-intentioned persons were greatly displeased. One gentleman said with indignation that he could not understand how in the present enlightened age people could spread abroad these absurd stories, and that he was surprised that the government took no notice of it. This gentleman, as may be seen, belonged to the number of those who would like the government to meddle in everything, even in their daily quarrels with their wives.

After this . . . but here again the whole adventure is lost in fog, and what happened afterward is absolutely unknown.

3.

Perfect absurdities do happen in the world. Sometimes there's not the slightest verisimilitude to it: all at once the very nose which had been driving about the place in the shape of a civil councilor and had made such a stir in the town, turned up again as though nothing had happened, in its proper place, that is, right between the two cheeks of Major Kovalev. This happened on the seventh of April. Waking up and casually glancing into the mirror, he saw—his nose! He puts up his hand—actually his nose! "Aha!" said Kovalev, and in his joy he almost danced a jig barefoot about his room; but the entrance of Ivan stopped him. He ordered Ivan to bring him water at once, and as he washed he glanced once more into the mirror—the nose! As he wiped himself with the towel he glanced into the mirror—the nose!

"Look, Ivan, I think I have a pimple on my nose," he said, while he thought: "How horrible it will be if Ivan says, 'No, indeed, sir, there's no pimple and, indeed, there is no nose either!'"

But Ivan said: "There's nothing, there's no pimple: your nose is quite clear!"

"Damn it, that's wonderful!" the major said to himself, and he snapped his fingers. At that moment Ivan Yakovlevich the barber peeped in at the door, but as timidly as a cat who's just been beaten for stealing the bacon.

"Tell me first: are your hands clean?" Kovalev shouted to him while he was still some way off.

"Yes."

"You're lying!"

"My right hand to God, they're clean, sir."

"Well, be careful."

Kovalev sat down. Ivan Yakovlevich covered him up with a towel, and in one instant with the aid of his brushes had smothered the whole of his beard and part of his cheek in the kind of crème they serve at merchants' name-day parties. "Would you look at that!" Ivan Yakovlevich said to himself, glancing at the nose and then turning his customer's head to the other side and looking at it from that angle. "Really makes you wonder." He went on pondering, and for a long while he gazed at the nose. At last, delicately, with a quite understandable caution, he raised two fingers to take it by the tip. This was Ivan Yakovlevich's system.

"Now, now, now, careful!" cried Kovalev. Ivan Yakovlevich let his hands drop, and was flustered and confused as he had never been confused before. At last he began gently tickling him with the razor under his beard, and, although it was awkward and not at all easy for him to shave without holding on to the olfactory portion of the face, at last he did somehow, pressing his rough thumb into Kovalev's cheek and lower jaw, overcome all difficulties, and finish shaving him.

When it was all over, Kovalev dressed hurriedly, hailed a cab, and drove to a cafe. Before he was inside the door he shouted: "Waiter, a cup of chocolate!" and at the same instant peeped at himself in the mirror. The nose was there. He turned around gaily and, with a satirical air, slightly screwing up his eyes, looked at two military men, one of whom had a nose hardly bigger than a vest button. After that he started off for the office of the department in which he was urging his claims to a post as vice-governor or, failing that, the post of an executive clerk. Crossing the reception room he glanced at the mirror; the nose was there. Then he drove to see another collegiate assessor or major, who was very fond of making fun of people, and to whom he often said in reply to various biting observations: "Ah, you! I know you, you're as sharp as a pin!" On the way he thought: "If the major doesn't split with laughter when he sees me, then it's a sure sign that everything is in its place." But the sarcastic collegiate assessor said nothing. "Good, good, damn it all!" Kovalev thought to himself. On the way he met Podtochina, the officer's wife, and her daughter; he was profuse in his bows to them and was greeted with exclamations of delight—so there could be nothing wrong with him, he thought. He conversed with them for a long time and, taking out his snuffbox, purposely put a pinch to each nostril while he said to himself: "So much for you, you silly petticoats, you biddies! but I'm not going to marry your daughter anyway. This is only *par amour*!"

And from that time forth Major Kovalev promenaded about as though nothing had happened, on Nevsky Prospect, and at the theaters, and everywhere. And the nose, too, as though nothing had happened, sat on his face without even a sign of coming off at the sides. And after this Major Kovalev was always seen in a good humor, smiling, resolutely pursuing all the pretty ladies, and even on one occasion stopping before a shop in Gostiny Court and buying the ribbon of some order, I cannot say for what purpose, since he was not himself a cavalier of any order.

And this kind of thing took place in the northern capital of our vast land! Only now, taking everything under consideration, we can see that much of it is implausible. Saying nothing of the fact that the supernatural separation of the nose and its appearance in various locales in the guise of a state councilor is truly odd,—how was it that Kovalev failed to realize one can't advertise for a nose in the newspaper? I don't mean to say here that I feel an announcement is too expensive: that's nonsense, and I'm not the mercenary sort. But it's inappropriate, clumsy, bad form! And then again—how did the nose end up in a fresh-baked roll, and how did Ivan Yakovlevich himself? . . . *that* I can in no way understand, I positively cannot. But what's stranger and more incomprehensible than anything else is how authors can choose such subjects. I concede that it's absolutely incomprehensible, it's truly . . . no, no, I absolutely don't understand. In the first place it's decidedly no use whatever to the fatherland; in the second place . . . but in the second place there's no use either. I simply don't know what to make of it . . .

But all the same, taking everything into account, although, of course, one might assume both one thing and another, and even another, perhaps even . . . well and then where *don't* absurdities occur? But still and all the same, when you stop and think, there's something to all this. No matter what anyone says, such things do happen in the world: rarely, but they *do* happen.

(1835-6) Translated by A.L. and M.T.K.

Section B
Early-modern Utopias and Dostoevsky's responses
to Utopian Thought

A N ALTERNATIVE TO individual escape from present-day realities was found in Russian utopian visions with their genesis in the epoch of Enlightenment. The period's rationalist definition of Man was appropriated by social theorists, who began to chart a new destiny for Russia in the Masonic lodges in St. Petersburg and Moscow, out of which most of Russia's early-modern literary discourse grew. For instance, Lomonosov's literary rival and a Mason, A. P. Sumarokov, who began his first *Epistle on Poetry* in 1747, by postulating that "Man has an advantage over cattle, because he can reason better," published his first utopian Russian work, *The Happy Society: A Dream* (Son: Schastlivoe obshchestvo) in his journal *The Industrious Bee* (Trudoliubivaia pchela) as early as 1759.

In the century and a half that followed the publication of this early utopian document a number of works envisioning societies made happy by reason were published in Russia, but they were more often than not of questionable literary merit. The notable exceptions are curious in that nearly all of them—despite their embrace of western rationalism as a precondition to technological progress—generally exhibit an animus towards western social constructs. Most portray the future world as desirable only if controlled by Russia. Sumarokov's younger Mason-compatriot, M. M. Kheraskov (1733-1807), gives us a Cadmus (in one of his three Masonic allegorical novels, *Cadmus and Harmonia*, 1789) who forgets about any further search for his sister Europa once he reaches the promised land of the Slavs. F. V. Bulgarin (1789-1859), generally regarded as a true progenitor of modern Russian sci-fi with his triad of utopias *Plausible Fantasies, or Travels around the World in the 29th Century* (Pravdopodobnye nebylitsy, ili stranstvovania po svetu v 29-m veke, 1824), *Incredible Implausibles, or a Journey to the Center of the Earth* (Neveroiatnye nebylitsy, ili Puteshestvie k sredotochiiu zemli), and *A Scene from a Private Life in 2028* (Stsena iz chastnoi zhizni v 2028-m godu, 1828), envisions a credibly different technological future, but one in which the social order is a replica of the Russian society of his own day. To convey the flavor of this early utopian patriotism we offer an abridged sampling of Bulgarin's work without much additional commentary, as its predictions of technological advances speak for themselves.

Indeed, exhaustive commentary on individual works will no longer be possible for the rest of the volume which is subdivided into sections highlighting a particular theme or school, and each writer will be introduced within the confines of the section's preface. Yet, a longer aside must be devoted to another work from this period, titled *The Year 4338. Letters from Petersburg* (4338-j god. Peterburgskija pis'ma).[1] Its author, prince V. F. Odoevsky (1803-69), was arguably as important a personage in the nineteenth century as Lomonosov had been in the eighteenth. On the surface, it might be hard to imagine what prompted this sober-minded writer and literary critic (who was also a foremost musicologist, inventor, collector of archival materials, and walking encyclopedia) to turn to the subject of utopia in the work *The Year 4338*. But from another point of view it is perhaps not so strange. As one of the principal founders of the society *Lovers of Wisdom*, Odoevsky was interested in the creation of a national school of philosophy which would allow Russia to objectify its cultural heritage and project Russia's destiny as a civilization uniquely equipped to surpass all European accomplishments.[2] In this sense, Odoevsky's work functions as an extended polemic with P. Ia. Chaadaev's famous denunciations of the Russian cultural heritage (published, also in letter format, in the mid-1830s)[3] and as a reflex on Lomonosov's struggle a century earlier to open the professorial ranks at the Russian Academy to native Russians. In a fictional fulfillment of Lomonosov's dreams, Odoevsky promises Russia a glorious future, governed solely by Russian scientists and philoso-

---

1. First published in the *Utrennjaja zarja* almanac (St. Petersburg, 1840), 307-52. Relevant material to this story (as discussed below) was published earlier in excerpts under the title "Peterburgskija pis'ma" and signed by the pseudonym V. Bezglasnyj in *Moskovskij nabljudatel'*, part 1 (1835), 55-69.

2. Indeed, *4338* was most often considered as just such an extension of his dreams for Russia, since Odoevsky portrays the world 2,500 years in the future as divided into only two hemispheres, the technologically advanced Russian and the more backward Chinese. Significantly, both are cultures of the East, while the West has simply ceased to exist. The meaning of the word "Germans," for instance, is the subject of some controversial debates among scholars in the future with the obvious implications that the Germans disappeared as a nationality shortly after the time of Goethe.

3. P. Ia. Chaadaev's first and only *Philosophical Letter* (of eight) that was allowed to be published during his lifetime in *Teleskop* in 1836 produced such a negative reaction from the government that the authorities felt compelled to proclaim him insane and put him under house arrest. They reacted so forcefully on account of what they considered to be an outright slander on the Russian cultural tradition and the sheer provocation of an author who denigrated everything held sacrosanct by the Russian nation. To be sure, such statements as "we have something in our blood that drives off all true progress, or "we have nothing that is ours, on which to base our thinking," or "we have turned to miserable, despised Byzantium for a moral code," or the author's repeated allusions to the "barbarism" of Russia's past and the present, are statements in the extreme and can hardly be used in building any nationalistic utopia. But if Chaadaev's letters were allowed to be published in full, they would have shown their author full of compassion for Russia, and resorting to statements like these in order to jolt his country from stagnation on a path to true reform for the well-being of its citizens.

phers, a future—in refutation of Chaadaev's claims—based on the innate Russian character which he depicts as cultured, pleasant and hospitable.[4]

Some of these visions may provoke a condescending smile from the modern reader, but others are quite interesting. Among the latter are predictions for the future use of air transportation as essentially the sole means of travel, buildings transparent when viewed from the skies, telegraph and general communication accomplished solely by means of electricity, a huge water-pump system that relieves Petersburg from the danger of floods, artificial lighting for greenhouses, exclusive use of plastics in clothing with electrical ornaments, artificial scents for freshening rooms, and a magnetic memory system—perhaps an early imaginative conception of a computer—centralized in a huge, multi-story building of the Academy with cables leading to all the reaches of the civilized hemisphere. Based on the approbative nature of these visions some Soviet scholars have argued that *The Year 4338* is an allusion to G. F. W. Hegel's three-phase dialectic of cultural history, was planned as part of a trilogy concerned with alternate visions of Russia in the past (Petrine Russia), the present (Odoevsky's Russia), and the future, in the last phase according of which, two formerly antagonistic societies, those of Moscow and Petersburg respectively, were to merge into one *metropolis* and thus form a Hegelian "synthesis." In this way, Russia was to represent the only civilization capable of *synthesizing* the desirable attributes of the native Muscovy character with the best Western features of Petersburg.[5]

---

4. While Odoevsky's opposition to Chaadaev's perception of the Russian cultural heritage is generally known, Odoevsky might have had at least three other Russian writers in mind when writing *4338*. In its subtitle, *Letters from Petersburg*, Odoevsky's work echoes Vil'gel'm Kjukhel'beker's *Letters from Europe* (Evropejskija pis'ma), published in *Nevskij zritel'* (February & April, 1820). Kjukhel'beker's work is set only 700 years in the future and depicts the visit to a now backward Europe by an American traveler. Odoevsky did not share Kjukhel'beker's rhapsodic perception of Americans, and instead had his Chinese visitor in futuristic Russia refer to them as "savage" in the very first letter of *4338*. Moreover, Odoevsky's work exhibits multiple similarities with the already cited Faddej Bulgarin's *Plausible Fantasies, or Travels around the World in the 29th Century* (first published in the September, October and December issues of *Literaturnyja listki*, 1824), particularly in the description of aerostats and other machinery of the future. In addition, like Bulgarin, Odoevsky feels compelled to portray the limited knowledge that future historians and archeologists would profess when discussing artifacts well known in the nineteenth century. Finally, *4338* represents a curious transposition of Aleksandr Vel'tman's title *The Year MMM-CDXLVIII [3448] or the Manuscript of Martyn Zadeka* (3448 god ili rukopis' Martyna Zadeki, Moscow, 1833), and its relation to Vel'tman's deserves further study.

5. P. N. Sakulin in his most impressive, detailed, and yet to be surpassed study, *Iz istorii russkago idealizma. Knjaz' V. F. Odoevsky, myslitel' - pisatel'*, vol. 1, part 2 (Moscow, 1913), 170-202, was the first to recognize *4338* as part of such a trilogy and describe its component parts in minutest particulars. Unfortunately, the former two parts do not substantially contribute to a fuller understanding of *4338*, except in very general ways as discussed here. Incidentally, Sakulin lists several other possible sources for Odoevsky's writing *4338*, including L. Marcier's *L'an 2440, reve s'il en fut jamais* and others.

But Hegel's notion of human history unfolding independent of divine will—a vision central to the ideology which ultimately fueled the Bolshevik Revolution of 1917—was at odds with Odoevsky's. In this connection it is thus significant to emphasize that the title date projects the *destruction* of Russia (along with the rest of the world) due to a collision with a comet predicted to occur 2,500 years from 1838.[6] It is also noteworthy that any elucidation of Russia's technological response to this coming event is poignantly absent. Instead, the work exists in the form of a *fragment*, in which the promise of Russia's golden future and the threat of its demise from the comet were left in a delicate balance. In order to comprehend such an equivocal ending, one must understand that Odoevsky never understood history in Hegelian terms, but rather in terms of the brothers Schlegel and F. W. J. von Schelling. If Odoevsky planned his trilogy with reference to Hegel's dialectics, he must have proceeded on an assumption which would reject rather than confirm Hegel's theory, as he does in his seminal work, *The Russian Nights* (Russkie nochi), first published four years later.[7] This novel reasserts the Schellingean view of philosophy as a poetic form of cognition; in it any true meaning would be revealed through the "inner feelings"[8] of the select few younger philosopher-poets, destined to lead Russia to an ultimate union with the Absolute—God. *The Year 4338* seems to be modeled along similar assumptions and offers two possibilities for the future of Russia: it may elect to develop on a path predicated by Hegelian concepts of human "progress" and thus ascend to world supremacy through the ever-present dialectic of History. However desirable such a path might appear, it is doomed in a *relativist* universe to a *nonrelative physical* collision and to destruction by Halley's Comet. However, if Russia were to strive for an absolute, *nonrelative knowledge* of itself, it would become a non-materialist society on a path leading Man to the absolute union of Spirit and Matter. Seeking the ultimate unity with the Absolute on Schelling's terms, Russia

---

6. This prediction was made in the journal *The Russian Disabled Veteran* (Russkij invalid), *Literaturnyja pribavlenija k Russkomu Invalidu*, 23 (June 10, 1839), 499. Indeed, it could have been a perfect touch of irony first to describe a triumphant culture in all of its attainments and then have it replaced, not by a higher form evoked by the former, as Hegel's postulates would suggest, but by the vacuum which would surely result after impact with the comet. However, Odoevsky did not employ such a scenario, ending the work on an ambiguous note.

7. Cf. *Sochineniia Kniazia V. F. Odoevskago*, I, (St. Petersburg: 1844).

8. *Systemes des Transcendentalen Idealismus* (Tübingen, 1804), §4. Schelling, whom he knew personally and to whom the novel is particularly indebted, held that Nature and Mind cannot be separated and that their Unity is found only in the *Absolute*; God, for him, takes part in that unfolding of the Absolute which we call History, the ultimate goal of which is reunification with the Absolute. This is, of course, a far cry from the Hegelian view of the Universe as a self-perpetuating creation in which Nature gains ascendancy from the lower into the more complex forms by the ever present process of cosmic dialectic, and where Mind is an independent faculty contemplating and registering such changes.

could then perhaps transform the comet into an *anagogic* harbinger of the union with God. Just such a thing happens in another *fragment* devoted to a collision with a comet, written by Odoevsky some years prior to *4338*. In the story, *Two days in the Life of Earth* ("Dva dni v zhizni zemnogo shara"),[9] Earth inexplicably avoids the physical impact of the comet at the last moment only to be drawn, just as oddly, into a *union* with the "non-burning" Sun the very next day. The survival of Earth is predicted within the narrative by an old sage, no doubt representing Schelling's (and Odoevsky's) concept of the philosopher-poet, whose inner feeling (vnutrennee chuvstvo) dictates such an outcome, while his very own son and the rest of the people are overwhelmed by the frenzy of an impending catastrophe.[10]

Now, admittedly, this is a very Romantic and certainly a non-empirical solution to the problem of a comet impacting the Earth. But since the idea of dealing with such cosmic impact is gaining greater currency in these days, Odoevsky's alertness to the issue might be said to be prescient in and of itself. Parenthetically it must be said that despite the fact that literally thousands of asteroids and comets are mapped and closely tracked by modern-day astronomers in hopes that such an impact might be predicted in time and somehow averted—and despite a most impressive display of multiple imagined advances in technology which could possibly prevent such a collision (rockets, A-bombs, laser or particle beams) with an oncoming "chunk" of inter-planetary matter—nearly all late 20th-century movies and fiction on the theme represent mankind facing such a scenario in terms no less *Romantic* than Odoevsky's. Nearly all their plots show mankind utopically united in the face of such danger and led by either an extraordinary scientist, president, secret agent, pilot, computer wizard, etc., or any combination of these. All mankind thus entrusts its fate to a select few agents of the materialistic universe just as Odoevsky does with his philosopher-poets in *4338*. But somehow such modern scenarios are hardly more reassuring to those who remember mankind's *non-poet* leaders' casual use of technology in wiping out human lives on an incredible scale in the past cen-

---

9. *Moskovskij vestnik* IX, 14 (1828), 120-8.

10. This particular story has an obvious bearing on the decoding of *4338* because it provides a concrete solution to virtually the same set of circumstances envisioned by the author. The fact that Odoevsky must have thought along the same lines in the 1830's as in the 1820's is evident in the first letter from the Chinese visitor which Odoevsky did not, for some reason, utilize in 1840, but which has become part of the canonic text in modern Soviet editions of *4338*. (Cf. the second Cekhnovitser edition of *4338* in *V. F. Odoevskij. Romanticheskie povesti* [Priboj, Leningrad 1929], p. 352). The letter ends with the following passage: "The thing is, my dear friend, that the fall of Halley's Comet onto the Earth, *or*, if you wish, *its union with Earth*, is an inevitable matter . . ." Manifestly, Odoevsky envisions here two alternate solutions to end the society in *4338*: either its ultimate destruction from the physical collision with the Comet, or precisely the scenario of *Two Days* which paradoxically ends in a union not with the Comet but with the Sun.

tury. Nor is the response of humanity—which is now aware that a meteorite collision likely caused the extinction of the dinosaurs and countless other species—more united or constructive at present than in Odoevsky's story.

Be that as it may, Odoevsky's implicit rejection of neo-Hegelian philosophy as the sole guiding principle for attaining a glorious future was one of the first notes of caution to sound in nineteenth-century Russia. It is then ironic that the future-fictions of both Odoevsky and Bulgarin (whose writings are alluded to by Odoevsky in 4338) were mainly remembered by those interested in the varied possibilities that technological advances might bring to the future. Indeed, a rich catalogue of such predictions—predating Jules Verne's by decades—can be compiled from their writings, and excerpts from them are chosen for this reason for this anthology. It must be reasserted, however, that neither author posited his visions of an improved world solely in materialistic terms.

Utopian constructs based on notions of natural advantage began to appear only after the 1850s and the import of neo-Hegelian, Marxist views: in these the belief in the betterment of mankind rested on satisfying material needs. Chernyshevsky's novel, mentioned earlier, was the most influential example. From it we offer in this section "Vera Pavlovna's Fourth Dream," perhaps the most influential passage in this extremely popular and influential work. Our brevity cannot do the justice to the power that this work as a whole exercised on the imagination of the Russian intelligentsia. *What is to be Done* was one of the principal texts used to justify the Russian Revolution. Some of the novel's idealism carried into early post-revolutionary thinking: there was to be an Edenic society in which the Lion and the Lamb would lie together in the tranquility of social justice and in a world with no further need of a divine presence.

Dostoevsky found such blatantly idealistic designs for the future of human society annoyingly delusional, as already discussed with particular regard to the *Notes from Underground*. The latter is an early example of Dostoevsky's well-known mastery of the novel. In contrast, we offer here three examples of Dostoevsky's prowess as a writer of short stories. All come from the *Diary of the Writer*, (Dnevnik Pisatelia) which appeared in a serialized form between 1873-1881, but was difficult to obtain in Russia in its entirety for nearly a century.[11] The *Diary* contains elements crucial to our understanding of Dostoevsky's philosophy and his reactions to the *cityscape* human culture which Peter had compelled Russia to embrace as a utopian dream, calling it a *paradise*. In the earliest of our three stories Dostoevsky transports us into the final underground—the netherworld of the city cemetery. This work might easily be renamed *Dialogues of the*

---

11. Cf. F. M. Dostoevsky, *Polnoe sobranie sochinenij v tridcati tomax*, vols. XXI-XXVII. (Leningrad: Nauka. 1980-84).

Dead, as it indeed is Dostoevsky's shrewd and incredibly acidic variation on this ancient theme. The city's literal *underground* and its attendant real, non-philosophical suffering are also richly evoked in another masterpiece from *The Diary*, *The Little Boy and the Savior's Christmas Tree* (Mal'chik u Khrista na Elke). They, and our third selection, *Dream of A Ridiculous Man* (Son Smeshnogo Cheloveka) were chosen as superb examples of the author's continuing experimentation with the fantastic realm, which began with *The Double* (1846), one of Dostoevsky's earliest published works. In it the protagonist clearly suffers from morbid delusions, but Dostoevsky's narrative forces the reader to guess where reality ends and madness begins. Similarly, but in a much more intense fashion, in both *Bobok* and *The Boy* the narrative "reality" transgresses the boundaries between the living and the dead. Teetering on the same boundary is the protagonist of the *Dream of A Ridiculous Man*, whose persona provides a shrewd commentary on the impossibility of materialistic utopian dreams as advocated in Chernyshevsky's work. Embracing such tangible yet fragile concepts as the value of individual freedom and dignity, Dostoevsky's fiction as a whole negates Petersburg as a setting in which humanity can flourish.

The metaphysical intersects with the physical in Dostoevsky's entire oeuvre, but most poignantly in his last novel, *The Brothers Karamazov*, in which a devil, dressed as a gentleman, makes an entirely casual appearance to Ivan. But the reader is especially encouraged to revisit *The Grand Inquisitor* section of the novel, which offers one of the most famous appearances by Christ in world literature and Dostoevsky's most comprehensive rejection of benevolent tyranny in the human search for utopia. Ivan's monologue exploring the nature of human freedom proved integral to the philosophical core of the most famous Russian *dystopia* of the twentieth century, Zamiatin's *We*.

Faddei Venedikovich Bulgarin
(1789–1859

[Im-]Plausible Fantasies, or
A Journey in the 29th Century

[ABRIDGED]

[From a Dialogue in Bulgarin's Present]

I: *I believe that the gradual process of education, from the Australian savage to the enlightened European, has its limits and cannot extend beyond a point drawn by Nature.* < . . . > *Enlightened ancient peoples devoted all their intellectual efforts to the perfecting of philosophy, morality, politics, the fine arts and the social arts. It must be admitted that they reached the highest level in all these spheres of human understanding. From the time of Socrates and Plato there has been hardly anything new in social morality and philosophy.*

My friend: *But on the other hand, we have far surpassed them in the physical sciences! More discoveries have been made in the last century than in the thousand years of ancient history. In our times chemistry, physiology, physics, mechanics, medicine, have been established; electricity and magnetism have been discovered; gases studied, etc. This will all advance us far in the field of discoveries and improvements . . .*

[An Awakening in the Future]

When I came to consciousness, the darkness of night made it impossible for me to see where I was, but I could feel that I lay in a soft bed wrapped in blankets. Shortly afterwards light began to penetrate through the shutters—I opened them and was speechless with astonishment. The walls of my rooms, made out of precious porcelain, were decorated with gold filigree and bas-reliefs out of the same metal. The shutters were of ivory and all the furniture of pure silver. To assure myself that I was not asleep I pinched myself, bit my lip, and ran about the room, and finally assured that I was indeed awake, I thought my reason was affected and that in some strange fashion my imagination was supplying me with these objects. I opened the window and saw a splendid square surrounded by beautiful painted houses of various colors. Around the square and along the sides of the broad street which intersected the city were covered walkways for

pedestrians, while the streets were equipped with iron ways for the carriages'
wheels. As yet the streets were still empty; I saw only one guard who stood at
the fountain in the midst of the square. He was wearing a red velvet cape; on
his head was a round straw hat with marabou feathers; in his hand he held a
long staff on which about a dozen small pistols were attached on rings, while
at the center of the staff was a long musket. Apparently this weapon was very
light, because the guard turned it as easily as a feather. Finally, doors and windows were opened in the houses one by one. Imagine my astonishment when I
saw gentlemen and ladies dressed in brocade and velvet who swept the streets
or hurried with baskets to the market in little single-place two-wheeled carts,
like easy chairs: with astonishing speed they rolled along the iron channels in
the street without any visible source of power. Then large wagons with various
cargoes appeared which also moved without any horses drawing them. Under
the wagons were mounted iron boxes, from which rose pipes: the smoke which
issued from them led me to surmise they were steam engines. The peasant men
and women who rode on the wagons were dressed in the same splendid bro-
cades and velvet; this sight more than ever convinced me that I had lost my
mind and I began to weep bitterly for the loss of a not inconsiderable share of
my reason. A half an hour later, a door opened in my chamber and a gentleman
in a brocade coat and silk stockings and curling hair down to his shoulders
entered. With a low bow he declared in good Russian that his master had sent
him to inquire about my health and to ask if there was anything I desired.

"Tell me, for God's sake, where am I and what is happening to me?" I
said in a trembling voice.

The servant, it seemed, did not understand my question and therefore
he did not answer.

"What's the name of this city?" I asked.

"Hope City," the servant answered.

"What country is it in?"

"In Siberia, on Cape Shelagski."

At his words I burst into laughter. "How could this be Siberia!" I
exclaimed.

"But it is," the servant answered. "Permit me to report to my master
that you are awake; he will come to see you and it would be better if you
talked to him."

The servant helped me dress in somewhat Asiatic clothing made out of
a very delicate light blue fabric.

"And who is your master?" I asked. "Probably some kind of a prince,
judging by his opulent home."

"He is a professor of history and archaeology at our university," said
the servant as he left the room.

"Oh my poor reason," I cried, "are you now to suffer from madness in the midst of wealth, perhaps because it has never concerned you? But let's see what the professor will say, since he has collected in his home the wealth of all the learned men of all the world. Perhaps he will remove the veil which is covering my mind and eyes."

At that moment he entered my room dressed in the same simple and light clothing as I wore, and bowing politely he asked me to sit next to him on the divan. Not allowing him to say a word, I repeated my question—where was I?—and I heard the previous answer and then I asked how had I come to be where I was?

"Yesterday," the professor said, "men working on the seashore found you in a chalk cavern wrapped in a rare herb. *Radix Vitalis* (Root of Life), which we employ to revive drowning victims and others whose life forces have ebbed thanks to loss of breath but without vital damage to their organs. But tell me, how did you come to be in the cavern?"

"I don't know how to answer you," I said. "Yesterday, that is, September 15, 1824, I fell into the sea between Kronshtat and Peterhof not far from St. Petersburg, but today I'm in Siberia on Cape Shelagski in a magnificent city! I must admit," I continued, "that I have doubts about my health and I think my powers of imagination are disturbed. Everything I see and hear astonishes me and leads me into perplexity."

"There's nothing in this world which is astonishing, except that people can find new things to be astonished of," answered the professor. "The most astonishing thing is the creation of the universe, and there's nothing astonishing about anything else. You should know that today is September 15, 2824 and that you slept a thousand years in that cave!" < . . . > but let us go to breakfast now; I will present you to my family."

We descended to the lower floor of the house on a circular ivory staircase and entered a room magnificent beyond description. As we awaited the arrival of the ladies I spoke with the professor.

I: Who would have thought that Cape Shelagski which had only recently been described in our time and which consisted only of blocks of snow and ice would someday be inhabited? That the harsh regions of Northern Siberia would be transformed into a luxuriant tropical country, into an Eldorado; and that a professor would have more gold than all the pawn-brokers, money-changers, and usurers in our times?—incredible!

The Professor: And who in ancient Greece or Rome at the time of Herodotus or Tacitus would have thought that the Northern Wastes, covered with eternal mists, as the former described them; that the North, as I say, in a thousand years would be adorned with rich cities, inhabited by enlightened peoples and in their glory comparable to Greece and Rome? Compare Tacitus' Germany or Julius Caesar's Gaul with the situation of those countries in the 19th century: the climate and the people, all have changed. The same thing occurred in Siberia: it is all very natural and not at all astonishing. Clearing the forests, draining the marshes, the transfer of the Earth's internal heat towards the North, have altered our climate; now cold reigns in India and Africa and the Polar Lands have become the richest and most fertile on Earth." < . . . >

I: But tell me, how did you acquire such a mass of gold and silver? In our times one wouldn't dare speak of such wealth even in a fairy tale.

Professor: In your times gold and silver were wealth, but now these metals are quite ordinary, low in cost and used only by poor people. The desire for richness led to such mining of the earth that finally men discovered veins of pure metals in extraordinary abundance, and everyone acquired more than enough gold with its vacuous gleam. Because of the great abundance of gold and silver their price fell and human fancy identified these metals as symbols of poverty according to the ancient rule: only that is attractive which is rare and high in cost.

I: Then from what do you mint your money and make articles of value?

Professor: From oak, pine, and birch wood.

I: Do you mean from wood that we used to heat our stoves, and from which we made barges and peasant huts, and paved our roads! . . .

Professor: Yes. because without any foresight our ancestors destroyed the forests and took no concern for growing or preserving trees: finally they became rarities and objects of great value. < . . . >

I: It's true that wealth is a relative thing.

At this point the Professor's wife entered with two charming daughters and a little son. The women were dressed in tunics made of felt very skillfully woven, and colored the tints of the rainbow. The ten-year-old boy wore a simple robe. All of the women wore a heavily varnished leather shield on their left arms to protect themselves from immodest eyes; they were equipped with telescopic spectacles, which were very fashionable. The mistress of the house said several words to me in a language which I did not understand, but seeing my incomprehension, said in Russian:

"Then you don't speak Arabic?"

"No," I answered. "In my day only a very few scholars studied that language."

"It's our language of fashion and diplomacy," said the professor. "Just as in your time it was French."

The women could not conceal their smiles as he spoke and the eldest daughter asked me:

"Could it have been that your ladies spoke French, a monotonous tongue, with almost only one-syllable words and so poor in means of expression compared with all other languages?"

"In my day," I answered, "ladies spoke Russian only to footmen, coachmen and servants; and their major concern was the acquisition of a proper French accent. Whoever did not speak French," I continued, "was considered an ignoramus in high society, although it happened that sometimes those Russians who always spoke French were also fools."

"The same thing is true with us," said the professor. "The only difference being that French today is like Finnish in your time, and the rich, resonant, and supple Arabian language has taken the place of French."

At that moment a servant brought a tray with unpainted wooden cups, placed it on a golden table, and then shortly afterwards brought in two wooden bowls, one with Russian cabbage soup, the other with buckwheat groats, and a bottle with pickles. I firmly declined the meal, which greatly surprised the whole family.

"My wife," said the professor, "wanted to treat you to a meal of the most precious imported foods; understand that she doesn't know history and therefore she failed to please your taste. I will have coffee, tea and chocolate brought from the kitchen: these delicacies from your day are now drunk only by the commonest people."

"It's true," I said, "that in our time the common people had begun to drink tea and coffee in excess; I foresaw that wealthy people would decline to drink them in order to be different. But I don't understand how it came to be that you have replaced tea and coffee with the commonest sorts of vegetables: cabbage, buckwheat, and cucumbers."

"Because they are so rare," the professor answered. "When the climate was altered, the vegetable kingdom was affected too and those foods common and coarse in your time are now brought by ship from India in exchange for bananas, pineapples, coconuts, cinnamon, pepper, and cloves which we send there. May I add that as the result of their research our physicians report that cabbage, buckwheat and cucumbers are healthy and nutritious, worthy of the high place we have given them. One can also say with confidence that these vegetables are much more worthwhile than the spicy foods which were eaten in such abundance in your day which caused gout, weakened the nerves, and induced premature aging."

After I had drunk my tea, I asked the professor to accompany me for a walk through the city to inspect some of its institutions; he agreed, and donning large straw hats, we went onto the street.

As I observed his house from the street I could not help but admire the beautifully executed friezes, capitals, columns and other decorations on its exterior. The fruit, flowers, and various figures depicted on the spaces between the windows exceeded in beauty anything of this sort I had ever seen.

"What superb carvings!" I said.

"You are wrong," answered the professor. "All our buildings with their decorations are made out of iron."

"Are these buildings made of iron?" I exclaimed. "That is very extraordinary. Although we had begun to employ iron for railroads, bridges, columns, stairways, machinery, floors, and even in the arts, and fashionable objects, it had never occurred to me that it might be possible to construct buildings out of iron."

"Nothing is easier," said the professor. "The architect designs the building with its facade at a foundry and then the necessary number of units, columns, the floor, ceilings, and roof are cast for him and screwed together. The units, which are fully enclosed, each have a small opening into which dry sand can be poured; and then to strengthen the walls and to protect them from the atmosphere's influence, the units are welded together into one mass by a special kind of adhesive. Such buildings can easily be moved from place to place, and a few large wagons with steam engines can shift a building in a few hours."

"Now, I can understand that it wouldn't be difficult if you have a wealth of iron ore," I said. "But the demand for fuel must be very high, especially since you have no wood, and no doubt it is very expensive for those who are not rich, and, too, your factories must consume an enormous quantity of coal, peat, or other materials."

"You are wrong again," said the professor. "A new method for isolating the elements of the atmosphere which was discovered in 1946 by the famous member of the Samoyed tribe, Shamuromai, a member of the Obdorsk Academy, produces an illuminating gas which provides heat and lights for us and maintains our factories. Every section of the city has a central laboratory from which pipes lead to all the homes. If the owner wishes, he can open a valve and the rooms will be lighted; another valve will heat the stoves in a few seconds, while a third delivers a flame to the kitchen." < . . . > But let's go in this self-propelled vehicle to see the arrival of an air coach. Today is mail day and I'm expecting letters from my sister in Australia." < . . .>

"At the present time all these inventions are employed only by air travelers and they aren't needed in the fleet," said the professor. "First of all, we don't have shipwrecks any more because our vessels are made of bronze and iron, and during storms they descend to the bottom of the sea; secondly, because sea water can be transformed into fresh water in a few minutes with the help of aquatic purifiers; thirdly, the ocean floor provides our sailors and undersea divers with an abundance of plants and animals to be utilized as food; and fourthly and lastly, at the present time there aren't any uninhabited lands: the whole earth is populated, fertilized and adorned by the hands of men who have multiplied to an unbelievable extent." < . . . >

[After a full day in the city a dinner was served at the professor's home, attended by the city's mayor, the president of the Kamchatka Academy of Sciences, and the Eskimo Prince, and other men and women]. We entered the dining room and sat at a round table in no special order, each as he wished—

with the exception of the women who sat in a row together. The table was set with various foods in wooden dishes; they stood on gold trays and tripods which were heated by lamps burning hydrogen. Most of the dishes, which were very tasty, consisted of vegetables and meats unknown to me: only the fish seemed familiar. The mayor who had noted my bewilderment, said: "Everything you see on the table, with the exception of bread and fruit, comes from the sea. Because of the immense human population on land and because of the destruction of forests, nearly all the birds and animals, which were once so common, have now become extinct; horses we protect as our faithful comrades; camels, cows and sheep we preserve for their milk and fleece, and elephants for war. But on the other hand the sea provides an inexhaustible store of food. Once underwater craft had been invented and the technique of deep water diving perfected, the sea's floor became a rich pasture, offering a limitless abundance of edible plants while the water supplies us with a profusion of fish, amphibians and mollusks. In regions far from the sea, men work in factories, at handicrafts, cultivate fruits, grains, and the vine; air communications makes it possible to transport various products from place to place very rapidly."

"And here's to the vine!" I said, pouring myself a goblet and drinking to the health of the company. The wine seemed to have a remarkable taste: it had the sparkle and mildness of Champagne with the body of Burgundy, and an enchanting bouquet.

"Tell me. Gentlemen," I inquired, "does man's improved condition still permit the use of wine?"

"In *vino veritas*!" said the president of the Kamchatka Academy of Sciences with dignity. At these words, all the goblets were filled and then emptied to my health.

"That is in our manner," I thought.

Finally, the attendants cleared the table, leaving only fruit, hors-d'oeuvres, and wine. Then the professor rose from his chair, stepped to the wall, pressed a spring, and charming music like the sound of several harps captured my ears. < . . . > I was especially taken by the geographic maps which the president of the Kamchatka Academy of Sciences interpreted for me. All the areas in Asia, Africa, America, and Australia which in our time had been indicated as empty and uninhabited were now dotted with the names of cities and canals. Near the Poles were large islands as heavily populated as France in our time. In addition, I was surprised to see that all the rivers had straight courses, like canals. The president told me that now all rivers are navigable: the banks were excavated and made into straight lines to protect improved areas from floods and to provide large expanses of land for agriculture; the canals had drained all marshes and provided a new means of transportation over the entire globe. In the meantime the sun had descended and in a moment all the buildings and streets were lighted by gas. < . . . >

[The Eskimo prince whom I met at the reception invited me to travel with him the next morning to his native land on the admiral's ship, which] was built of bronze plates welded together and stretched with screws. Air cannons, aquatic purifiers, a chemical kitchen heated with gas, and the ship's ability to obtain food supplies on the sea floor were the reason that the ship was not weighted down by a heavy cargo. < . . . > The wind was following and we flew like an arrow over the open sea. The next day we were at the latitude of Icy Cape. In our day this was the limit of human discovery beyond Bering Strait and only a few Russian navigators had dared to advance beyond Cook's route into these seas which were bordered with ice on the north. In our day, nature, sunk here in its chill sleep, produced nothing to enhance human life, and was as stern as its eternal ice and cliffs. Now fruit trees and grape vines were green on the hillsides; golden towers and steeples, splendid buildings and ships' masts in the port gave evidence of this country's flourishing state. The city on Icy Cape was called Cook's Discovery. We had no time to stop here; but the prince, who noticed my curiosity, said with a smile that if I wanted to see the city then he would bring it to me aboard the ship in one minute, in spite of the fact that it was twenty miles away. Immediately a camera equipped with an enormous telescope was hoisted onto a mast: several convex and concave mirrors set at various angles which reflected objects with astonishing precision presented us with a view of the entire city through a dark tube as though it was on a table before us (exactly like a model) with its inhabitants, carriages and all the city's activities. < . . . > I [also] looked at the moon through the telescope and saw cities, fortresses, mountains, woods, just like the regions of Strasbourg with its cathedral. Animals moved like ants over the moon, but it was impossible to distinguish their forms and species. Distant stars seemed like Suns in their glory, like ours; an astonishing multitude of Planets of extraordinary size were visible in space. In transport I fell on my knees before the grandeur of Creation. The prince turned the telescope to the open sea and a space of thousands of miles disappeared, the goal of our journey, the Polar Country, seemed so close that involuntarily I started, thinking that we were about to crash onto its shore. < . . . >

Finally, we entered the polar archipelago. Just as we approached its shores the barometer indicated the coming of a storm. The prince immediately ordered the fleet to descend to the sea's floor. In a moment the masts were folded, the wheels covered, portholes sealed, with the exception of several openings with valves to allow water to enter a special container in the hold, and the ship began to descend to the ocean floor. When it had reached a certain depth, the valves were closed, engines were started, and the ship quickly moved forward. Inside the ship it was light enough and I felt no difficulty breathing; the air reserves and purifiers were operated incessantly. I never left the window and I delighted in the novel sights before me. Fish and other sea life swirled in schools next to the ship and all one had to do was cast a net to capture enough food for a year. In the meantime the sea's motion had become palpable under the water, and the prince gave the command to fire a signal from the air cannon to drop anchor. All the other ships repeated their signals and dropped anchor. Our ship had stopped next to an underwater plantation belonging to a rich inhabitant of the polar countries. I wanted very much to inspect this new type of sea floor estate which in our day had belonged to seals, crabs and oysters. The prince told me to dress myself in an air suit equipped with two air bags and placed me on an underwater bench which he taught me to operate. He did not forget to send an experienced diver with me as an escort. When I was ready for my journey, I was placed next to a door, which was then unlocked. I and my guide were expelled into the water, and the door was quickly locked behind us. As I settled to the bottom of the sea, I saw that it was divided by stone walls, and in places by columns with inscriptions which marked property lines, while here and there were pyramidal structures. The guide informed me that these were underwater houses, like our farms, where workers and proprietors lived after their labors or excursions. All around me were fields of sea plants and huge square structures with iron grills in the place of roofs. I looked into some of them to see they were underwater cages filled with various fish, underwater animals, oysters, etc. Suddenly I heard the sound of a bell emanating from one of the pyramids. The guide told me that this was a form of invitation and we hurried toward the door at its base; it opened and we entered. There were several feet of water in the lower floor which a mechanical pump was removing. We dismounted our benches and climbed a stairway to the second floor where the workers lived; there was no water here, nor was there any on the magnificently decorated third floor, where lived the owner and a few of his friends. When he learned who I was, the host conducted me through the rooms, showing me all the operation of the underwater home and explaining how it was built. The pyramid rested on the firmest foundation made of stone blocks reinforced by iron bands and lead; the windows were made of thick glass with iron grills. When the structure had been completed, the water was pumped out of its interior and pipes were extended to introduce air. Near the shore these pipes emerged on the surface of the water, while in the open sea a special pyramid projecting from the water had been erected to which were sent all the pipes from the underwater structures. Air pumps aided the circulation of the atmosphere and from my experiences I discovered that the air was much purer in the underwater houses than it was on the surface. After conversing for some time with the master of the house and his friends, I returned to the ship. In the meantime the storm had passed and the prince ordered his fleet to rise to the surface. Mechanical pumps were immediately put into action; as water was removed from the hold the ship rose and soon it floated on the surface of the sea. Everything was put into its previous order and a half an hour later we dropped anchor at Parry City, the capital of the Polar Empire.

The prince took me with him into town and I was even more astonished than I had been with Hope City. Here all the houses were built of thick masses of the purest glass. The walls were covered with bas-reliefs of different colors, and reflecting the sun they seemed to be enveloped in flame. At every step charming porticoes, temples, and noble buildings with colored columns attracted and delighted my eyes. The roadway was made of some gleaming metal like zinc. The Prince, although he was occupied with greeting the happy people who came to meet him, noticed my surprise:

"It seems strange to you that you don't see iron buildings here as in Hope City. We have little iron, and therefore, rather than employing imported products, we turn to our own industry. Our mountains abound in materials to make glass, and since it is simple to extract it from the earth with the help of fire, we have transformed mountains into glass by means of the powerful action of burning hydrogen gas, and with minimal labor we have the strongest possible building material. Glass houses are sturdy, handsome, fireproof, resistant to mildew, and easily heated by small gas fires."
< . . . > Self-propelled vehicles were as common here as in Hope City; in addition many people were dashing through the streets in running boots. These were nothing other than iron boots with springs and wheels under the surface; when they were wound up, they moved by themselves, and pedestrians were transported on them from place to place as easily as on skates, accelerating and decelerating at will. < . . . >

[After being shown many more wonders at Parry City, I was invited to to the prince's residence, where I met the king of the polar countries, who asked me if I wishes to remain there or return to St. Petersburg, my native city. Upon learning of my preference for the latter, the king appointed me to become his literary correspondent in that Capital of Enlightenment, and provided me with ample resources to live in the future of my own native land. An air coach was leaving the Parry City that very evening and I chose to go with it.]

We were underway forty eight hours. The land lay below me like a map with shading for forests, water, and cities. On the third morning we saw the Gulf of Finland, Kronshtat and St. Petersburg, and then dropped somewhat lower. My heart beat with joy to see the golden roofs, the buildings, cupolas, and towers of my native city. Its extent astounded me; broad streets and great buildings extended as far as Pulkovo Hill, to the sea, and far inland. On the hill rose a monument resembling an Egyptian pyramid. I was told that it was a monument to the great memories of the 19th century. Finally, the air coach landed, and I, after kissing my native soil, set off for the city to find an apartment. < . . . >

(1824) Translated by Leland Fetzer, ed. by A.L.

Vladimir Fyodorovich Odoevsky
(1803–1869)

The Year 4338
Letters from St. Petersburg

[ABRIDGED]

FOREWORD

Note. These letters were delivered to the individual whose name appears below by a man remarkable in many respects (he chooses not to make his name known). Engaged many years in experiments with mesmerism, he finally achieved such skill in this art that he can at will place himself in a somnambulistic trance; most curious of all he can in advance select the subject of his mesmeric vision.

In this manner he can transport himself to any country and period of time or transform himself into any individual he wishes without any effort at all; his native skill, refined by lengthy exercise, allows him to narrate or transcribe what his magnetic fantasy perceives; when he awakes he has forgotten it all and he himself, to say the least, reads with curiosity what he has written. Astronomers' calculations, which indicate that in the year 4339, that is 2500 years from now, Biela's Comet must certainly collide with the Earth, strongly agitated our somnambulist; he wanted to know the condition of the human race one year before that terrible minute; what will people be saying about the Comet, what kind of impression will it make upon mankind, in general, what will be the customs and manner of life; what form will man's strongest emotions take: ambition, curiosity, love; with this purpose he plunged into a somnambulistic state which continued for a lengthy period; when he emerged from it he saw before him pages covered with his own handwriting from which he discovered that during his trance he was a Chinese in the 44th century traveling through Russia and corresponding very assiduously with a friend who remained in Peking. < . . .>

Current accomplishments in chemistry have made the invention of an elastic glass, such as once was offered to Nero, which is a fact accepted by all historians, a real possibility—it would meet a great need in contemporary industry. The medical use of gasses must also someday become a daily occurrence, just as pepper, vanilla, alcohol, coffee, and tobacco were employed only as medicines at one time. The future of air ships is beyond doubt; in our age we have seen the use of steam, discovered as the result of a weight laid on a tea kettle, extended to industry and there is little reason to doubt that perhaps before the 19th century ends, air ships will be common and will alter social life a thousand times more than the steam engine and railroads. In a word, my friend continued, in the story of my Chinese I find nothing which cannot be deduced in a natural fashion from the general laws of the development of man's powers in nature and art. Therefore, my fantasy should not be accused of excessive exaggeration.

We have found it essential to append these lines as a foreword to the letters which follow.

Prince V. Odoevsky, [1839]

From: Hypolite Tsungiev, student of the Central Peking University,
To: Lingin, student of the same university.

FIRST LETTER

St. Petersburg, January 4, 4338

Finally I am at the capital of the Russian hemisphere and world Enlightenment. I'm writing to you in a beautiful building on whose rounded dome the words "Hotel for Air Travelers" is written in great crystal letters. Such is the custom here: the larger houses are roofed with glass or covered with clear tiles, while the name of the owner is shown in colored glass. At night when the houses are lighted within, these gleaming ranks of roofs are enchanting; besides, it's very useful—not like with us in Peking, where at night you can't find the home of your friend and have to drop down to earth. We had a quiet air journey; although the local air ships are well built, we were frequently detained by head winds. Imagine, it required eight days to reach here from Peking! What a city, my dear friend, what splendor, what immensity! As I flew over it I could believe the legendary account that once there were two cities, one called Moscow, and the other St. Petersburg, and they were separated from each other by a great open plain. It's true that there is something distinctive about the architecture in that part of the city called the Moscow District, where the stately ruins of the ancient Kremlin still stand. By the way, don't expect a great deal of news from me; I hardly had time to look closely at anything because my uncle constantly pushed me on. I had time to note only one thing: that the air lanes are maintained here in excellent order, and I nearly forgot, we flew to the equator, but only for a brief time to inspect the heating system which extends from there into nearly all of the northern hemisphere. Indeed a remarkable project, the work of centuries of scientists! Imagine, huge machines constantly drive hot air through pipes which are connected with major reservoirs, heat storage depots constructed in every city of this expansive state are connected with the reservoirs, and from the city depots the warm air is conducted either into buildings or covered gardens or in part into the open air so that at no time, in spite of the severe climate, we were hardly aware of the cold. In this way the Russians have even conquered their inhospitable climate! I heard that, on the other hand, an association of Russian industrialists offered to deliver cold Russian air to our government to cool the streets of Peking. But enough of that now; everyone here is concerned about the Comet which must destroy our Earth a year from now. You know that my uncle was sent here to St. Petersburg by our Emperor to negotiate precisely on this subject. Several meetings of diplomats have already taken place. Our primary concern is to inspect the measures which have been taken to prevent that disaster, and secondly to take China into the alliance of states which has been formed for mutual assistance in the case of such an event. By the way, scientists here remain calm and state firmly that if only the workers do not lose heart when operating the equipment, it will be possible to prevent the Comet's collision with the Earth; we must only know in advance the exact point of collision, and astronomers have promised to calculate that precisely as soon as the Comet is visible in a telescope. In one of my next letters, I will describe for you all the measures taken here by the government in such a case. What knowledge! What perception! The learning, and even more the ingenuity of these people is amazing! It's obvious at every step; on the basis of the manner alone in which they have prepared for the Comet's fall you can judge them. < . . . >

SECOND LETTER

One of the local scientists, Mr. Khartin, yesterday conducted me to the local Museum, which occupies a huge building which resembles a whole city on an island in the river Neva. Numerous bridges link the river's banks; from my windows I can see the huge water barrier which protects the low-lying part of St. Petersburg from floods. The nearest island, which in ancient times was called Vasilevski Island, also belongs to the Museum. It is now a huge covered garden where trees and shrubbery grow, and various wild animals roam unrestrained in enclosures. The garden is a masterpiece of art! It is built on arches which are slowly heated, so that only a few paces separate a tropical climate from a temperate one. In a word, the garden is a sample of the entire planet; to walk through it is to make a journey around the world. The products of all countries are collected here in the order in which they exist on the Earth. In addition, a huge heated pool which contains many rare fish and amphibians has been constructed in the center building belonging to the Museum, right on the Neva. On both sides of it are mounted exhibits from the natural world shown in chronological order, from the antediluvian period to our own times. As I examined them, in even cursory fashion, I understood how Russian scientists had acquired such remarkable knowledge. All that is necessary is to visit the Museum and without resorting to books you can become an informed naturalist. There is a remarkable collection of animals here too . . . how many species have disappeared from the face of the Earth or changed their forms! I was especially struck by a rare exhibit of a giant horse which even had its hair. It quite resembled the horses which ladies today keep along with their lap dogs, but these horses were of an enormous size: I could barely reach its head. < . . . >

THIRD LETTER

I neglected to say that we arrived in St. Petersburg at the worst possible time for a foreigner's visit, the so-called Vacation Month. There are two of them among the Russians, one early in the year and the other at its mid-point. During these months all business ceases, government offices are closed, and no one makes calls. This custom pleases me very much: a time has been found when everyone can find solitude, and abandoning his daily tasks, occupy himself with a search for inner perfection, or if it is desired, with his personal concerns. At first it was feared that it would cause a breakdown in daily life, but the opposite occurred: when everyone has a certain time for his personal life, then he dedicates the rest of his time exclusively to public life without distractions and therefore all occupations proceed at a double pace. In addition, this practice has the beneficial effect of reducing the number of law suits: everyone has time to consider his actions and the closure of law offices prevents the injured from taking legal action in a moment of passion. Only a very extraordinary event, such as the expectation of the Comet could to a certain extent disrupt such an admirable custom, but nonetheless, there have been no entertainments or social functions. But finally today we received a home newspaper from the Prime Minister, which contained, among other things, an invitation to a party at his home. < . . . >

FOURTH LETTER

The Prime Minister's house is located in the best part of the city, not far from Pulkovo Hill near the famous ancient observatory, which they say was built 2500 years ago. When we approached the house there was already a host of air ships above its roof: some were in the air while yet others were moored to columns specially designed for this purpose. We stepped onto a

platform which lowered itself under us and we found ourselves in a beautiful enclosed garden which served as the minister's reception room. Planted
with rare vegetation, the entire garden was illuminated by a beautifully
made electric device in the likeness of the Sun. I was told that it not only
illuminates the garden, but acts chemically on the shrubbery and trees. In a
word, I have never before seen such luxurious vegetation.

I wish that our Chinese traditionalists could see the Russian assemblies
and manners. There is nothing like the Chinese courtliness from which we
have not yet been able to free ourselves. The Russian simplicity of manner
at first seems chill, but then you become accustomed to it and it seems very
natural and you become convinced that this apparent coolness is combined
with a natural conviviality. When we entered the reception room it was full
of guests. In various places among the trees small groups were strolling
about; some spoke with fervor while others listened silently. I should tell
you that no one is obligated to speak. One can enter a room without saying a word, and one need not even answer questions—this doesn't seem
strange to anyone. Popular individuals often say nothing during the course
of entire parties. This is considered very fashionable at the present time. To
ask anyone about his health, his business, the weather, or in general to put
a vacuous question is considered very impolite; but on the other hand, when
a conversation begins it is lively and heated. There were many women present, beautiful and particularly fresh in appearance. Emaciation and pallor
are considered marks of ignorance because principles of health, and in part
medicine, are included in the course of education here and so anyone who
does not guard his health is considered to be poorly educated and this is
particularly true of women.

The women were splendidly attired, for the most part in dresses made
of flexible crystalline facets of various colors. They flashed with all the
colors of the rainbow. Others wore fabrics which were decorated with
metallic crystals, rare plants, butterflies and gleaming beetles. One of the
most fashionable women wore living fireflies in the folds of her dress which
produced a blinding light when she walked through the dark ways of the
garden. Such dresses, they say, are very expensive and can be worn only
once because the insects do not survive long. To my great surprise I noted
that the fateful Comet attracted much less attention in high society than I
expected. It was mentioned only in passing. Some spoke learnedly about the
possibility of successful counter-measures, calculated the weight of the
Comet, and rapidity of its fall, and the degree of resistance required from
the equipment now under construction. Others recalled all the triumphs
achieved by man over nature, and their faith in the powers of mind was so
great that they spoke with amusement about the coming catastrophe.
Others found another reasons for complacency: they remarked that life had

had its day and everything had to end. But most talked about their daily interests and their future plans as though nothing could change. Some of the women wore coiffures à la comère; this was a little electrical device which constantly emitted sparks. I noticed that these women, for the purposes of coquetry, often stood in the shadows to display the beautiful electrical fountain in the shape of a Comet's tail which touched their hair as though by a brilliant pen and gave a distinctive cast to their complexions.

At various places in the garden from time to time concealed music could be heard, but at a very low volume so as not to hinder conversation. Music lovers were seated on a resonating structure built directly over an invisible orchestra. I was also invited to sit, but thanks to the fact that it was a novelty to me my nerves were so irritated by the pleasant, but to my mind, violent vibration, that unable to sit more than two minutes, I leaped from my seat onto the ground, which greatly amused the ladies. In general, the guests at the party devoted much attention to my uncle and me since we were foreigners, seeking, in accordance with the ancient Russian custom, to show us in every way their generous hospitality, and especially the ladies, who, to speak without vanity, were very fond of me, as you will shortly see. As we walked along a path spread with a velvet carpet, we paused at a small murmuring pool which cast off drops of scented water. One of the ladies, beautiful and beautifully dressed, whom I had come to know earlier, approached the pool and in a moment the murmuring was transmuted into beautiful soft music; I have never heard such sounds before. I came closer to my lady and to my astonishment saw she was playing on a keyboard near the pool. It was connected with openings from which water emerged from time to time to fall onto crystal bells, producing a wondrous harmony. Sometimes the water flowed swiftly and unevenly and then the sounds were reminiscent of the roar of raging waters in a wild but regular harmony; sometimes the water flowed serenely and then as though from great distance came stately rich accords; sometimes the water fell in tiny drops onto the resounding glass and then I could hear a soft melodic murmur. This instrument is called a hydrophone. It was invented here and is still not common. My beautiful lady had never seemed so charming: violet sparks from her coiffure fell in a fiery rain onto her white and splendid shoulders and were reflected in the swiftly flowing water and their passing gleam illuminated her beautiful mobile face and luxuriant curling hair; through the iridescent folds of her dress flashed streams of light and from time to time they momentarily outlined its beautiful patterns, which almost seemed transparent. Soon her pure expressive voice joined the sounds of the hydrophone and merged with the harmonious waves of music from the instrument. As the result of the music, which seemed to come from the water's immeasurable depths, the marvelous and magic light, the scented air, and finally the beautiful woman, who, it seemed, floated in that marvelous merging of sounds, water and light, I became so transported that the beautiful woman stopped singing and for long I was unable to come to my senses, which she, if I am not wrong, took note of.

She had nearly the same effect on others as well, but they neither applauded nor passed her compliments—this is not done. Everyone knows the level of his art. A bad musician does not torture the ears of his listeners, and a good musician does not ask to be heard. I should add that music is part of the general plan of education here as one of its essential subjects and it is as customary as reading and writing. Sometimes they play music written by others, but most often people, and especially women such as my beautiful friend, improvise without demand whenever they feel on inclination towards it.

At various places in the garden stood trees heavy with fruit for the guests. Some of these fruits were the marvelous products of horticulture which is so well developed here. As I looked at them I could not help but think what an expenditure of mind and effort it had cost to combine the various varieties of fruit by grafts to produce new unheard of varieties. For example, I noticed a fruit which was something between a pineapple and a peach—nothing could be compared to its taste. I noticed figs growing on a cherry tree and bananas growing on pear trees. It is impossible to count all the new varieties invented, so to speak, by Russian gardeners. In the midst of these trees stood small urns with golden spigots. The guests seized the urns, opened the spigots, and without more ado drank what I assumed to be the beverage they contained. I followed the general example. The urns contained an aromatic mixture of stimulating gasses. It was like the bouquet of wine, and immediately it spread throughout the whole organism an astonishing vivacity and cheerfulness, which at times reached such a point that it was impossible to abandon a constant smile. These gasses are absolutely harmless and their use is strongly approved by physicians. In high society these gaseous beverages have completely replaced alcohol, which is used only by simple workmen who cannot surrender their common drink.

A short time later the host invited us to a special structure which houses the magnetic bath. I must tell you that this device is a favorite occupation in drawing rooms and has completely replaced the ancient cards, dice, dances and other games. This is the way it is done: one of those present stands by the bath—usually someone who is more accustomed to magnetic force—and all the others hold a cord which extends from the bath, and the flow begins. Some fall into a simple magnetic sleep beneficial to the health; on others it has no effect at all; others fall into a trance and this is the purpose of the diversion. Thanks to my inexperience I was among those on whom electricity had no effect and therefore I remained a spectator of the entire incident.

Soon very interesting talk began. Those in a trance poured out their most hidden thoughts and feelings. "I admit," said one, "that although I try to show that I am not afraid of the Comet, I am in fact very concerned about its approach." "Today I intentionally angered my husband," said one beautiful woman, "because when he is angry he is so very handsome." "Your iridescent dress," said one fashion-plate to her neighbor, "is so beautiful that I would very much like to copy it, although I'm very ashamed to ask you for it."

I came up to a circle of women where the lady that I admired so much was sitting. I no sooner spoke to them, than she said, "You can't imagine how I like you; when I saw you I was on the point of kissing you!" "And I too," "And I too," cried several women's voices. Others laughed and congratulated me on my brilliant success with the ladies of Petersburg.

The diversion continued for about an hour. Those who emerged from their trances had forgotten everything they had said, but what they had spoken in candor provided a thousand amusements which served to enliven social life. Marriages began here, romances, and also friendships. Often people who are hardly acquainted discover their attraction to each other and even old ties are strengthened by these sincere expressions of one's inner feelings. Sometimes the men alone are subjected to it while the ladies serve as witnesses; in turn, the ladies sometimes sit at the magnetic bath and tell their secrets to the men. In addition, the spread of magnetic baths has completely driven hypocrisy and sham from the society—obviously they are impossible. However, diplomats, as the result of their calling avoid this diversion and thus they play an insignificant role in drawing rooms here. In general, those who decline to participate in the trances are not well liked; it is assumed that they harbor inimical ideas or perverse inclinations.

Fatigued by the diverse impressions I had received during the course of the day. I didn't wait for dinner. I sought out my air ship. A blizzard was raging, and in spite of the fact that enormous quantities of warm air were being released into the atmosphere from the heating system, I had to wrap myself in my glass mantle, but the image of the beautiful lady warmed my heart—as the ancients say. As I discovered, she was the only daughter of the Russian Minister of Medicine, but in spite of her interest in me, how could I hope to earn her favor, so long as I had not distinguished myself by some scientific discovery and therefore would no longer be considered less than an adult!

FIFTH LETTER

In my last letter, which was so long, I still did not have time to tell you about several remarkable individuals I met at the home of the Prime Minister. Here, as I have already written, had assembled all of high society:

the Minister of Philosophy, the Minister of Fine Arts, the Minister of the Air Forces, poets and philosophers, and historians of the first and second rank. To my good fortune there I also met Mr. Khartin with whom I had become acquainted at my uncle's home. He told me various curious details about these gentlemen, which I shall leave for another time. In general, the training and education of the highest officials is most remarkable. They are all educated in a special institution which is called the School for State Officials. The best students from all other institutions are sent there, those who have attracted attention at the earliest age. After they have passed a very demanding examination they attend the sessions of the State Council for several years to obtain necessary experience in such matters; from this training ground they proceed to the highest state positions. Hence it is not unusual to meet young men among the highest officials. This seems to be essential, for only youth's vigor and energy is competent to fulfill the difficult assignments which are given to them. They age prematurely, and this harmful effect on their health is expected, but this is the price which is required to maintain the well-being of the entire society.< . . . >

SIXTH LETTER

This morning Mr. Khartin came to invite me to visit the general meeting of the Academy. "I don't know," he said, "whether we will be permitted to remain at the meeting, but before it opens you will have the opportunity to meet some of the scholars."

As I have already noted, the Congress Hall is located in the Museum building. Here scholars assemble nearly every day in addition to the regular weekly meetings. Most of them also live here in order to utilize the Museum's huge libraries and laboratories. Physicists and historians, poets, musicians and painters assemble here. They generously share their ideas and experiments (even those which are not successful) and their earliest conceptions, concealing nothing, without false modesty and vanity. Here they consult on the methods for coordinating their work to give it a single direction. The organization of the Congress, which I will describe in a subsequent letter, also contributes importantly to this purpose. We entered a large hall decorated with statues and portraits of great men; several tables were covered with books while equipment ready for experiments rested on others. To one of the tables extended wires from the largest galvanic-magnetic circuit in the world, which occupies a special multi-storied building.

It was still early and as yet few visitors had appeared. A small circle was arguing heatedly about a recently published book. It was submitted to the Congress by a certain young archeologist and had as its purpose the elucidation of a very debatable and curious question, namely the ancient name

of St. Petersburg. You may know that there are many contradictory opinions on this question. Historical evidence maintains that the city was
founded by the great ruler whose name it bears. No one contests this point,
but the discovery of several ancient manuscripts has led to the theory that,
for unexplained reasons, this famous city during the millenia changed its
name several times. These discoveries have excited all the local archeologists. One of them contends that the most ancient name of St. Petersburg was
Petropolis, and he submits as proof the line from the ancient poet
[Derzhavin]:

> Now sunk in slumber was < . . . >Petropolis amidst its spires . . .

Others assert, and not without foundation, that there is a misprint in
that line. One individual asserts, also arguing on the basis of ancient evidence, that the antcient name of St. Petersburg was Petrograd. I will not list
all the remaining theories on this subject. The young archeologist has overthrown them all without exception. Digging through half-decayed piles of
ancient books, he found a bundle of manuscripts which had been spared by
the touch of time more than most. Several lines which had been preserved
gave him occasion to write a volume of commentary in which he asserts
that the ancient name of St. Petersburg was Peter. As proof he presented to
the Congress the manuscript he had found. I saw that ancient text; it was
written on the material which the ancients called paper whose secret of
manufacture has been lost, but this is no cause for mourning because its
fragility was the reason that all the ancient written records have disappeared. < . . . > While we were examining this ancient text, the members of
the Academy assembled in the hall, but since it was not a public meeting we
were forced to leave. Today the Congress is to take up the question of various projects which are planned to meet the Comet's fall, therefore a closed
meeting was held. On ordinary days the hall can barely hold all the visitors,
such is the love for scholarly endeavor!

As we left for our airship we saw a crowd on one of the nearby platforms who were shouting, waving their arms and, it seemed, cursing.—
"What is that?" I asked Khartin.

"It would be better if you didn't ask," answered Khartin. "That crowd
is one of the strangest phenomena of our century. In our hemisphere Enlightenment has reached the lowest levels of society. As a consequence many
people, who are hardly competent to be even simple workmen, make claim
to learning and literary gifts. Nearly every day these people gather at the
entrance to the Academy where the door is locked to them, and with their
shouting they try to attract the attention of passersby. They can't understand why our scholars abhor their company, and in their frustration they

mimic them, producing something resembling learning and literature. But since they are alien to the noble inspiration of the genuine scholar, they have turned to one or another occupations: some assemble absurdities, some deal out praise, some sell—and he who sells the most is a great man. They quarrel constantly over money, or as they say, they form parties: one deceives the others—that's two parties, and they almost come to blows. All of them want monopolies, and most of all they want control over real scholars and writers. In this cause they forget their squabbles and act in unison. Those who avoid their slander they call aristocrats, and they make friends with their servants, try to discover their domestic secrets and then spread false rumors about their imaginary enemies. But these dealings are not successful and they only increase every day that contempt which others feel towards them."

"But tell me," I asked, "where did such people come from in the blessed Russian Empire?"

"For the most part they are immigrants from other countries. Unacquainted with the Russian spirit, they cannot love Russian enlightenment. They only wish to prosper—and Russia is wealthy. In ancient times such people did not exist, or at least there are not traditions about them. One of my friends, a comparative anthropologist, believes that these people are descended in a direct line from pugilists who once lived in Europe. What can be done! These people represent the dark side of our century. One can hope that with increased education these spots also will disappear from the Russian Sun."

And so we came to our home.

(1838-9)
Translated by Leland Fetzer, edited by A.L.

Nikolai Gavrilovich Chernyshevsky
(1828–1889)

Vera Pavlovna's Fourth Dream

(From the Novel *What Can Be Done?*)

Once more Vera Pavlovna has a dream, seemingly: She hears a voice—a voice oh so familiar to her now!—a voice from far away which comes yet nearer, yet nearer:

> How grandly Nature
> Shines over me!
> How gleams the Sun!
> How laughs the Field!

And Vera Pavlovna sees that it is so, that it is all so . . .

A cultivated field shines with a golden light; a plain is covered with flowers, hundreds, thousands of flowers are unfolded on the shrubbery which encompasses it, the woods which rise behind the shrubbery glow green and murmur, and they too are bright with flowers; fragrances waft from the field, from the meadow, from the shrubs, from the flowers abounding in the woods; birds flutter through the boughs and thousands of their voices come from the branches with their fragrance; and beyond the field, beyond the meadow, beyond the shrubs and woods can be seen more cultivated fields which glow in gold, and meadows covered with flowers, shrubs covered with flowers as far as the distant mountains covered with woods bright in the sun, and over their summits here and there, there and here, light, silver, gold, purple, transparent clouds shadow lightly the bright blue of the horizon with their iridescence; the sun has risen, nature is joyous and celebrant, sending light and warmth, fragrance and song, love and bliss into one's breast, and a song of joy and bliss, love and goodness swells out of one's breast—"Oh Earth, oh bliss! oh love! oh love, golden, beautiful, like morning clouds over the summits of those mountains!"

> Oh Earth! Oh Sun!
> Oh bliss! Oh joy!
> Oh love, oh love.
> So golden bright
> As morning clouds
> On distant heights!

"Do you know me now? Do you know I am good? But you do not know; none of you have yet seen me in all my beauty. See what was, what is, and what will be. Listen and see:

> Gleams the glass of crimson wine,
> Gleam the eyes of all the guests . . .

At the foot of the mountain on the edge of the forest among the blossoming shrubs of high thick hedges rises a castle.

"Let us go there."—They walked on, as though flying. A magnificent banquet. Wine foams; the eyes of the guests shine. Noise, and whispers under the noise, laughter, and secretly, pressing of hands and at times a stealthy silent kiss. "A song! A song! There cannot be joy unconfined without a song!" The poet rises to his feet. His brow and his thought are touched by inspiration, and nature tells to him her secrets, history reveals to him its intent, and the centuries are heard in his song in a succession of scenes.

1.

(The first scene described by the poet is in the Middle East where flocks graze against a background of olives, palms, and snowcapped mountains. A Beautiful Woman speaks to the poet and says that she does not exist here; this is the time of Astarte, a goddess who is the slave of her master and whose task in life is to please him.)

2.

(The poet describes the beautiful city of Athens, and its magnificent goddess, Aphrodite. But the Athenians do not respect women and she too is half a slave, and so in spite of her beauty the Beautiful Woman says she is not in Athens.)

3.

(The European Middle Ages and the time of the Cult of the Fair Lady. Here the knights either worship women at a distance or abuse the peasant girls who are their vassals. The ideal woman of the time is modest, gentle, delicate, and beautiful, more beautiful than Astarte or Aphrodite, but her beauty is cast over with melancholy and pain. "The earth," she says "is a vale of tears." The Beautiful Woman says she has no place here.)

4.

(The poet summarizes the status of women in these ages: when women were prized for beauty alone, then Astarte ruled. When Aphrodite ruled men women were admired as beautiful objects, but men still refused to accept them as human beings. When woman was pure, but untouchable on one hand, and the object for men's lust on the other, then it was the time of the melancholy kingdom of the Virgin. The first man to recognize that woman was also a human being was Jean Jacques Rousseau (1712-78) as he described her in his book, *La Nouvelle Héloise*. Now the world has begun to understand the nature of woman and to sense what she might mean in the future.)

5.

(Vera Pavlovna sees that she is identical with the Beautiful Woman when she is loved, more beautiful than any of the goddesses of the past).

6.

(Women can come into their own only when men see them as equals, not as property. Then a woman loves a man as he loves her; then he has no rights over her and she none over him. This is the source of women's greatest charm. Without equality, the love of women as objects of beauty is evil. But as yet, her kingdom is small, and it will reach its fullness only in the future.)

7.

- -

8.

"Oh, my love, now I know all your Freedom; I know that it will come; but what will it be like? How will men live then?"

"I alone cannot tell you that, to do so I need the help of my older sister—she who long ago appeared to you. She is my mistress and my servant. I can be only what she makes me; but she also serves me. Sister, come to our aid." Then the sister and the bride of her bride-grooms appeared: "Greetings, my sister," she says to the empress. "And are you here too, my sister?" she says to Vera Pavlovna, "Do you want to see how people will live when the empress, my ward, reigns over all? Look then."

A building, an enormous, enormous building, such as exists now in few of the largest capitals—or no, there is now not one like it! It stands in the midst of cultivated fields and meadows, orchards and groves. There are fields of grain, but not such as we have now, but dense, dense, rich, rich. Is it really wheat? Who has ever seen such ears? Who has ever seen such grain? Only in a hothouse could one grow such ears with such grain. Those fields, those are our fields; but such flowers grow now only in our hothouses. Orchards, lemon and orange, peach and apricot—how could they grow in an open field? Ah, but those columns which surround them, open for the summer; yes, this is a hothouse open for the summer. Those woods—they are ours: oak and linden, maple and elm—yes, the woods are as they are now; but they have very solicitous care, there is not one tree among them that is diseased, but the woods are the same—only they have remained as they are now. But that building—what is its architecture? There is nothing like it now; no, there is one which is reminiscent of it—the palace which stands on the hill at Sydenham; iron and glass, iron and glass—and nothing more. No, this is not all: this is only the framework of the building; its external walls; there within is the actual building, an immense building: it is enclosed by this iron and crystal building, as though in a shell; it forms broad galleries around it at all levels. How airy is the architecture in the interior, what slender pillars between the windows—and the windows are huge, wide, the whole height of the story! Its stone walls are like a row of pilasters forming a frame for the windows which look onto the galleries. But what kind of floors and ceilings are these? Of what are the doors and window frames made? What is this? Silver? Platinum? And the furniture is made of the same substance—wooden furniture is only a caprice, for the sake of novelty—but out of what are made the rest of the furniture, the ceilings and floors?

"Try to move this chair," says the elder empress. This metal furniture is lighter than ours made of walnut. But what kind of metal is it? Ah, now I know. Sasha had shown me a sheet of it, it was light like glass, and earrings and brooches are made of it, yet, Sasha said that sooner or later aluminum would take the place of wood, and also stone. And how richly everything is adorned here! Aluminum can be seen everywhere and all the intervals between the windows are hung with great mirrors. And what rugs on the floor! In this hall half of the floor is uncovered, and it too is made of aluminum.

"You can see it is unpolished, so that it would not be slippery—that is where the children play with their elders; and in the other hall the floor is also without rugs—for dancing."

And everywhere there are tropical trees and flowers; the entire building is a great greenhouse.

But who lives in this great building which is more splendid than palaces?

"Many people live here; walk on and we will see them."

They go onto a balcony which projects from the upper floor of one of the galleries. How could it have been that Vera Pavlovna had not seen them earlier?

"In the fields are groups of people; everywhere are men and women, the elderly, the young, and children together. But most of them are young; there are few old men and yet fewer old women, more children than old

people, but still they are not numerous. More than half of the children are
at home where they maintain the quarters: they do almost all such work,
for they love it; with them are a few old women. And there are few old men
and women because they age only late in life, here life is healthy and tranquil; this maintains their youth."

The groups working in the fields are almost all singing; what kind of
work are they doing? Ah, they are harvesting grain. How quickly their
work goes! And of course their work goes quickly and why should they
not sing! Machines do almost everything for them—cutting and binding
the sheaves and carrying them away—people only walk about, ride, and
operate the machines. And how conveniently they have arranged their
work; the day is sultry, but this means nothing to them: over that part of
the meadow where they are working a great cloth has been spread; as their
work advances so does it—how they have arranged a cool place for themselves! Why should they not work joyfully and quickly and sing at their
work! I would like to join them in the harvest! And songs, always songs—
unknown songs, new songs; but now they have remembered one of ours; I
recognize it:

> We will live together nobly,
> These people are our friends,
> Whatever your heart desires,
> With them it will be yours . . .

But now the work is done and everyone is proceeding toward the
building.

"Let us enter the hall once more to see how they will dine,"
says the elder sister. They enter the largest of the great halls. Half
of it is full of tables—the tables are set—how numerous they are!

"How many will come to eat?"

"A thousand people or more: Not everyone is here; he who
desires so may eat alone."

Those old women and men and children who did not go into
the fields have prepared all of this.

"Cooking, domestic work, cleaning—this is too light work for
the others to do it," says the elder sister. "It can be done by those
who are too young or cannot do anything else."

The table service is excellent. Everything is made of aluminum
and crystal; along the center of the broad tables are vases with
flowers, the dishes are on the table, the workers enter and sit down
to eat, both they and those who prepared the dinner.

"And who will wait on the tables?"

"When? During the meal? And why? After all, there are only

five or six dishes: those which must be hot are placed on areas which do not cool; you see in those sunken areas containers with boiling water," said the elder sister.

"You live well, you enjoy good food, do you have such dinners as this often?"

"A few times each year."

"But this is their usual meal; he who wishes may have yet better food, but this is at an extra cost; but he who demands nothing other than what is given to all, pays nothing. And thus it is everywhere: those who want only what is common to all receive without cost, but for every special thing or whim there is a cost."

"Is this really us? Is this our land? I heard one of our songs and they are speaking Russian."

"Yes, you can see a river not far away—that is the Oka; these people, like you and I, are Russian!"

"And have you done all this?"

"It has been done for me, and I inspired its doing. I inspired its perfection, but it was done by her, my elder sister, she is a laborer, while I live for pleasure."

"And will everyone live like this?"

"Everyone," said the elder sister, "for everyone will have eternal spring and summer, eternal joy for all. But we have showed you only the end of my half of the day, labor, and the beginning of her half; we will look upon these people once more in the evening two months from now."

9.

The flowers have begun to fade; the leaves have begun to fall from the trees; the picture has become doleful.

"You see, it is such a dreary scene and it would be dreary to live here," says the younger sister. "I would not want to do that."

"The halls are empty and no one is in the fields and orchards," says the elder sister. "This I have done at the request of your sister, the empress."

"Is the palace in fact now vacant?"

"Yes, it is cold and damp, why remain here? Out of the 2,000 who were here, only ten or twenty independent people have felt that it would lend pleasant variety to their lives to linger here in the country to observe the northern autumn in solitude. In a short time new people will come, small parties of those who love winter walks to spend a few days with winter diversions."

"But where are they now?"

"Any place where it is warm and pleasant," says the elder sister. "When there was much work and it was pleasant here many guests came from the south to spend the summer; we were in a building where all the residents were of your kind; but many buildings have been built for guests, in others live foreign visitors and their hosts together, those who like and have chosen such company. But although you have received multitudes of guests and workers for the summer, you yourselves for seven or eight of the bad months of the year go to the south—wherever one desires. But there is a special country which most of your people visit. This district is called New Russia."

"Is this where Odessa and Kherson are located?"

"In your time yes, but now see where you will find New Russia."

Mountains adorned with orchards; among the mountains are narrow valleys and broad plains.

"These mountains were formerly barren cliffs," says the elder sister. "Now they are covered with a thick layer of soil, and on them in the midst of the orchards are groves of the tallest trees; further below in the humid defiles are coffee plantations; higher there are date and fig groves; vineyards are interspersed with sugar cane plantations; in the fields also grows wheat, but rice is more common."

"What land is this?"

"Let us climb a minute more and you will see its boundaries."

In the distant northeast are two rivers which merge directly to the east from where Vera Pavlovna stands in contemplation; further south but still in a southeast direction is a long and broad gulf; the land extends far to the south, expanding still more between the gulf and a long narrow bay which forms its western boundary. Between the narrow western gulf and the sea which is far to the northwest is a narrow isthmus.

"But are we in the center of a desert?" says Vera Pavlovna in astonishment.

"Yes, in the midst of a former desert; but now as you see all of the space from the north from that great river on the northeast has been transformed into such a land as that strip of land along the sea to the north of us which was said to be in olden days and is once more 'a land of milk and honey.' We are not far, as you can see, from the southern boundary of the cultivated territory, the mountain district of the peninsula is still sand, a barren steppe, which all the peninsula was in your time; every year people, you Russians, are pushing back the edge of the desert to the south. Others work in different countries: there is much room for all and work enough, and life is spacious and rich. Indeed, from the great northeastern river all the territory to the south including half of the peninsula is green and flowering, great buildings, as in the north, stand two or three miles apart, like innumerable great chessmen on an enormous board."

"Let us visit one of them," says the elder sister.

The same enormous crystal building, but its columns are white.

"They are made of aluminum," says the elder sister, "because it is very hot here and the white metal becomes less heated in the sun, and thus although it is more expensive it is more convenient."

See what else they have devised here: at some distance around the crystal palace are rows of slender, very tall columns, and from them extends a white cloth high above the palace, covering it completely and stretching for a third of a mile beyond it.

"It is constantly sprinkled with water," says the elder sister. "You can see a little fountain rising out of every column above the cloth which sprinkles water in its vicinity so that it is cool here; you can see that they alter the temperature as they wish."

"But what of those who like the heat and the bright local sun?"

"You can see pavilions and tents in the distance. Everyone can live as he desires; I am leading them to that and it is for this alone that I work."

"Does this mean that there are cities for those who like them?"

"There are not many such people; there are fewer cities than formerly —they exist almost entirely as centers of communication and transportation, at the best harbors, and other central points, but they are larger, more splendid than those of old; everyone visits them for the sake of variety; the greater part of their inhabitants are constantly changing and visit them to work for short periods of time."

"But what of those who want to live in them permanently?"

"They live as you live in your Petersburgs, Parises, or Londons—why not? Who would hinder them? Everyone lives as he wishes; but the great majority, 99 people out of 100, live as your sister and I have shown you, because it is more pleasant and advantageous. But go into the palace, it is already rather late and it is time to observe the inhabitants."

"But first I want to know, how was this done?"

"What was done?"

"The manner in which this barren desert was transformed into a fertile land where almost all of us now spend two-thirds of our time."

"How was it done? Is it so difficult to understand? It was not done in one year, not in ten years. I advanced the work but slowly over a long period of time. From the northeast from the banks of the great river, from the northwest from the great sea—they have many powerful machines— they brought clay to bind the sands, dug canals, introduced irrigation, and vegetation appeared and the air became more humid; they took one step after another, a few miles at a time, sometimes only a mile a year, and now they are advancing to the south, and what is so unusual about this? They have only become intelligent and begun to employ their great strength and resources which were formerly wasted and indeed were harmfully turned inward. It is not in vain that I work and teach. It was only difficult for people to understand what was useful, for in your time they were still savages, so coarse, cruel, and thoughtless but I taught and taught them; and when they began to understand it was not difficult for them to work. I make no great demands, as you know. You are doing something in my fashion, for me—is that really bad?"

"No."

"Of course it is not. Remember your workshop, did you have many resources to build it? More than others?"

"No, and what were our resources?"

"But your seamstresses had ten times more conveniences, twenty times more pleasures in life, and only one hundredth of the pains than those who had the same resources as you. You have proved that in your time people can live very freely. One must only be judicious and be able to manage and discover how most advantageously to employ one's resources."

"Yes, yes. I know that."

"Go to see the way that people will live some time after they began to understand what you understood long ago."

10.

They entered the building. The same enormous and splendid hall. It was evening and there were great diversion and merriment, for the sun had set three hours earlier: it was the time for merriment. How brilliantly the hall was lighted, but how was it done? Neither candelabras nor chandeliers were visible—ah there it was!—in the dome was a large flat area made of opaque glass from which streamed light—as it should be: precisely like sunshine, white, bright, and soft—it was electrical lighting. There were about one thousand people in the hall, but it could easily hold three times as many.

"And it sometimes happens that guests come," said the radiant and beautiful woman, "sometimes there are more."

"Then what is the occasion? Isn't this a grand ball? Is this simply an ordinary evening?"

"Certainly."

"But by our standards this would be a royal ball, the women's attire is so magnificent, but this is a different time as can be seen from the fashions. Several of the women are wearing our styles, but this is obviously for novelty, in jest; yes, they mock their own costumes; others are wearing the most varied apparel, of different eastern and southern styles, all of them more graceful than ours; but the most common dress resembled that worn by Greek women during the refined Athenian period—light and free, and the men are also wearing full, long robes free at the waist, something like robes: it is apparent that this is their usual domestic dress and how modest and beautiful it is! How softly and delicately it outlines the body, how it enhances the movement of the body! And what an orchestra is playing, more than one hundred men and women performing, but particularly, what a choir!"

"Yes, in all of Europe you did not have ten voices to compare with a hundred which are in this hall alone, and there are as many in every hall: they live differently, both in good health and with refinement, and therefore their chests are better and their voices too," said the radiant empress.

But the orchestra members and the singers change constantly: some leave while others take their place; they leave to dance, or the dancers take their place.

This is their evening, their common, ordinary evening; every evening they amuse themselves and dance; but when else have I seen such energetic merriment? But why should their merriment not be so energetic, so unknown to us? Their work was completed in the morning. He who has not worked to his satisfaction is not ready to feel the fullness of merriment. And now the merriment of simple people, when they find time to divert themselves is more joyous, lively, and unconstrained than ours; but our simple people do not have the means to amuse themselves, but here the resources are richer than with us; and the merriment of our simple people is shadowed by the recollection of inconveniences and deprivations, of poverty and suffering, shadowed by the premonition of what is to come— it is a passing moment to forget need and misery—and can need and misery be completely forgotten? Will not the sands of the desert be overwhelming? Will the *miasmas* of the marsh not infect the little strip of good land with its good air lying between the desert and the marsh? But here there are no recollections, no fears of need or misery; here there are only recollections of free labor granted willingly, with satisfaction, good will, and pleasure, and the anticipation of more to come in the future. What a comparison! And besides: our working people have strong nerves and therefore they are prepared for much merriment, but their nerves are crude and insensitive. But here their nerves are strong, as with our working people, and they are well developed, impressionable, as are ours; and readiness for merriment, a healthy, strong thirst for it, which we do not have, and which comes only from great health and physical labor, is united in these people with a delicacy of feelings which we possess too; they have all our moral development as well as the physical development of our working people; it is understandable that their merriment, their pleasures, their passions—are more lively, more vigorous, more expansive, more voluptuous than ours. Happy people!

No, now people do not know what authentic merriment is, because such a life is not yet possible which is essential for it, and there are not yet such people. Only such people could amuse themselves and know all the ecstasy of pleasure! How they glow with health and strength, how handsome and graceful they are, how energetic and expressive are their features! They are all happy, beautiful people leading free lives of labor and pleasure— happy people!

Half of the people are amusing themselves in the enormous hall, and where are the others?

"Where are the others?" says the radiant empress. "They are everywhere; some are in the theater, they are actors, others are musicians, others are spectators, as each wishes; some are dispersed in auditoriums, museums, and libraries; some stroll in the gardens, some are in their rooms to rest alone or with their children, but most of them, most of them—that is my secret. You saw in the hall how checks were blushing, eyes shining; you saw how some left and others arrived—it is I who drew them away, here the room of every man and woman is my refuge, in them my mysteries are inviolable, curtains on the doors, luxuriant carpets which swallow sounds, there it is quiet, there it is secret; they have returned—it is I who have recalled them from the kingdom of my mysteries to light merriment. Here rule I."

"Here rule I. Here everything is for me! Labor prepares freshness of feeling and strength for me, merriment is to prepare for me, and rest after me. Here I am the goal of life, here I am all of life."

11.

"My sister holds the greatest happiness in life," said the elder sister, "but you see here any kind of happiness that anyone could need. Everyone lives here in a manner that would be impossible to better, here everyone has complete freedom, boundless freedom."

"What we have shown you will not soon come into being as you saw it. Many generations will pass away before what you have sensed will be realized. No, not many generations: my work goes rapidly, every year more rapidly, but still you will not enter my sister's completed kingdom; but at least you have seen it, you know the future. It is radiant, it is beautiful. Tell everyone: this is what will be in the future, the future is radiant and beautiful. Love it, strive for it, work for it, bring it nearer, bring from it what you can into the present: your life will be as radiant and good, full of happiness and pleasure, depending how much of the future you can bring into it. Strive toward it, work for it, bring it nearer, bring from it into the present all that you can."

(1862) Translated by Leland Fetzer, edited by A.L.

B2. *Three Responses to Utopian Thought by*

Fyodor Mikhailovich Dostoevsky
(1821–1881)

Bobok

This time I'm giving space to "The Notes of a Certain Individual." It's not myself; it's a completely different individual. I think that no other preface is necessary.

THE NOTES OF A CERTAIN INDIVIDUAL

Semion Ardalionovich said to me all of a sudden the day before yesterday: "Will you, Ivan Ivanych, ever be sober? Be so good as to tell me that."

A strange demand. I take no offense, I am a timid man; but all the same, here they have actually made me out to be mad. By chance an artist once painted a portrait of me: "After all, you are a literary man," he said. I submitted, he exhibited it. Then I read: "Go and observe that pathological, almost insane, face."

Allow for the truth of it, but all the same how can you put it so bluntly into print? In print everything ought to be put decently; there ought to be ideals, but here . . .

Say it indirectly, at least; that's what you have style for. But no, he doesn't care to do it indirectly. Nowadays humor and fine style are disappearing, and abuse is mistaken for wit. I take no offense: God knows I'm not enough of a literary man to go out of my mind. I wrote a short novel—they didn't publish it. I wrote a *feuilleton*—they rejected it. I took those *feuilletons* about from one publisher to another; they were rejected everywhere: "You," they said, "have no salt."

"What sort of salt do you want?" I asked with a sneer. "Attic salt?"

That they did not even understand. More often I translate from the French for the booksellers. I write advertisements for shopkeepers too: "A rarity! The very finest tea, from our own plantations . . ." I made quite a tidy sum for a eulogy on his deceased excellency, Piotr Matveevich. "The Art of Pleasing the Ladies" I compiled as a commission for a bookseller. I've brought out some six little works of this kind in the course of my life. I'd like to do a collection of Voltaire's *bon mots*, but fear it might seem a little flat to our public. What good is Voltaire now? Nowadays we want a cudgel, not Voltaire. We've already knocked each other's teeth out—to the last tooth. Well, so that's the extent of my literary activity. Though indeed I do send letters around to the editors, gratis and fully signed. I give them all sorts of admonitions and advice, I critique their work and point out the true path. The letter I dispatched last week to an editor's office was the fortieth in the last two years. Four roubles wasted on stamps alone. I've got a nasty disposition, that's the thing.

I think that the artist painted me not for the sake of literature, but for the sake of the two symmetrical warts on my forehead, a natural phenomenon, he would say. They have no ideas, so now they're out for phenomena. And he certainly managed to get my warts down in his portrait—to the life! That's what they call realism.

And as to madness, a great number of people were written up as mad among us last year. And in what language! "With such an original talent . . . and yet in the end it appeared . . . however, one ought to have foreseen it long ago." That is rather clever; so that from the point of view of pure art one might even commend it. Well but then these so-called madmen turn out to be more intelligent than ever. So, we can drive people mad all right, but we can't produce anyone more intelligent.

The most intelligent man of all, in my opinion, is the one who, if only once a month, can admit himself to be a fool—an ability unheard of nowadays. It used to be that, once a year at any rate, a fool would recognize that he was a fool, but nowadays no such thing. And they've tangled everything up so that there's no telling a fool from a wise man. This they did on purpose.

I remember a Spanish wit who, two hundred and fifty years ago when the French built their first madhouses, observed: "They have shut up all their fools in a house apart, to make sure that they are wise men themselves." Indeed: you don't show your own wisdom by shutting someone else in a madhouse. "K. has gone out of his mind, which means that we are now the sane ones." No that's not what it means.

But what the devil . . . why have I taken leave of my own senses? I grumble on and on. Even the maid is sick of me. Yesterday a friend stopped by. "Your style is changing," he said; "it's choppy: you chop and chop—and then a parenthesis, then a parenthesis in the parenthesis, then you stick in something else in brackets, then you begin chopping and chopping all over again . . ."

My friend is right. Something strange is happening to me. My disposition is changing and my head aches. I am beginning to see and hear strange things. Not voices exactly, but it's as though someone beside me were muttering, "Bobok, bobok, bobok!"

What's the meaning of this *bobok*? I must divert my mind.

I went out in search of diversion, I hit upon a funeral. A distant relation—but he *was* a collegiate counselor. A widow, five daughters—all pure as a driven snow. What must it come to, even to keep them in slippers?

Their father managed it, but now there is only a pittance for a pension. They'll have to beg like dogs. They have always received me ungraciously. And indeed I should not have gone to the funeral now had it not been for a peculiar circumstance. I followed the procession to the cemetery with the rest; they were proud and held aloof from me. My uniform was certainly rather shabby. It must be some twenty-five years, I believe, since I was at the cemetery; what a wretched place!

To begin with, there's the smell. About fifteen corpses had been brought there already. Palls of varying prices; there were even two catafalques: one for a general and one for some fine lady or other. Many mourners, a great deal of feigned mourning and a great deal of open buoyancy. The clergy have nothing to complain of; it brings them a good income. But the smell, the smell. I wouldn't care to serve with the clergy here, even allowing for the odor of sanctity.

I kept stealing cautious glances at the faces of the dead, distrusting my impressions. Some had a mild expression, some looked unpleasant. As a rule the smiles were disagreeable, and in some cases very much so. I don't like them; they haunt one's dreams.

During the service I went out of the church into the air: it was a gray day, but dry. It was cold too, but then it was October. I walked about among the tombs. They are of different grades. The third grade costs thirty roubles; decent yet inexpensive. The first two grades are tombs inside the church and under the porch; they cost a pretty penny. On this occasion they were burying six persons in tombs of the third grade, among them the general and the lady.

I glanced into the graves—it was horrible: water everywhere, and such water! Absolutely green, and . . . but why go on about that! The gravedigger kept bailing it out by the bucketful every few moments. I went out while the service was going on and strolled about beyond the gates. Close by was an almshouse, and a little further off there was a restaurant. It was not a bad little restaurant: you could lunch and be done with it. It was crowded, even a good number of the mourners had shown up. I noticed a great deal of gaiety and genuine animation. I had something to eat and drink.

Then I took a part in bearing the coffin from the church to the graveside. Why is it that corpses in their coffins are so heavy? They say it's due to some sort of inertia, that the body is no longer controlled by its owner . . . or some nonsense of that sort, contradictory to the laws of mechanics and common sense. I don't like to hear people who have nothing but a general education put themselves forward to settle matters that require a specialist; and with us that's done continually. Civilians love to give opinions about subjects that are the province of the soldier and even of the field-marshal, while men who have been educated as engineers prefer discussing philosophy and political economy.

I didn't go to the requiem service. I have some pride, and if I'm only received owing to extraneous circumstances, why drag myself to their dinners, even after a funeral. The only thing I don't understand is why I stayed on at the cemetery; I sat down on a tombstone and sank into appropriate reflections.

I began with the Moscow exhibition and ended with reflecting upon surprise in the abstract. My conclusions about *surprise* were these:

"To be surprised at everything is stupid of course, while to be surprised at nothing is a great deal more becoming and for some reason accepted as good form. But that's not really the case. As I see it, to be surprised at nothing is much more stupid than to be surprised at everything. Moreover to be surprised at nothing is very nearly the same as having respect for nothing. And indeed, a stupid man is incapable of feeling respect."

"But what I desire most of all is to respect something. I thirst to respect something," one of my acquaintances said to me the other day.

He thirsts to respect something! Heavens, I thought, what would happen to you if you dared to print that nowadays?

At that point my mind went blank. I don't like reading grave inscriptions: they are everlastingly the same. An unfinished sandwich was lying on the headstone near me; a stupid thing, and out of place. I threw it on the ground, since it was not bread but only a sandwich. Though I believe it's not a sin to throw bread on the ground, but only on the floor. I must look it up in Suvorin's calendar.

I suppose I sat there a long time—too long a time, in fact; that is, I even stretched out on a long stone in the shape of a marble coffin. But how did it happen that I then began to hear all sorts of things? At first I paid no attention to this, but treated it with contempt. Still the conversation went on. What I heard was muffled, as though the speakers' mouths were covered with a pillow, and at the same time the voices were distinct and very near. I came to myself, sat up and began listening attentively.

"Your Excellency, it's utterly impossible. You led hearts, I return your lead, and here you play the seven of diamonds. You ought to have given me a hint about diamonds."

"What, play by hard and fast rules? Where's the charm of that?"

"You must, your Excellency. One can't do anything without something to go on. We must play with a dummy, keep one hand face-down."

"Well, you won't find a dummy here."

But what conceited words! And how queer and unexpected. One voice was so ponderous, dignified, the other softly suave; I wouln't have believed it if I hadn't heard it myself. I had not been to the requiem dinner, I believe. And yet how could they be playing preference here, and what general was this? That the sounds came from under the tombstones—of that there could be no doubt. I bent down and read on the tomb:

"Here lie the remains of Major-General Pervoedov . . . a cavalier of such and such orders." Hm! "Passed away in August of this year . . . fifty-seven . . . Rest, beloved ashes, till the joyful dawn!"

Hm, the devil, it really is a general! There was no monument yet over the grave from which the obsequious voice came, only a marker. He must have been a fresh arrival. From his voice he was a Court Councilor.

"Uh-uh-uh-uh!" I heard a new voice a dozen yards off from the general's place, coming from quite a fresh grave—a man's voice, and a plebeian one, but enfeebled by an ingratiatingly pious manner.

"Uh-uh-uh-uh!"

"Oh, here he is hiccuping again!" cried the haughty and disdainful voice of an irritated lady, apparently of the highest society. "It's an affliction to be by this shopkeeper!"

"I didn't hiccup; why, I've had nothing to eat. It's simply my nature. And really, madam, it's your own crotchets that give you no peace here"

"Then why did you come and lie down here?"

"They put me here, my wife and little children put me here, I didn't lay myself down. The Sacrament of Death! And I wouldn't lay myself down beside you, not for any money; I lie here because I had the capital, judging by the price. For we can always do that—spring for a tomb of the third grade."

"You made piles of money, I suppose? You fleeced people?"

"How could we be fleecing you, we haven't seen the color of your money since January. There's a little bill against you at the shop."

"Well, that's really stupid; to try and recover debts here is too stupid, to my thinking! Go to the surface. Ask my niece—she inherited."

"There's no asking anyone now, and no going anywhere. We've both reached the limit, and before the judgment-seat of God we are equal in our transgrissions."

"In transgrissions," the lady mimicked him contemptuously. "Don't you presume to speak to me!"

"Uh-uh-uh-uh!"

"All the same, the shopkeeper obeys the lady, your Excellency."

"Why shouldn't he?"

"Well, your Excellency, because, as we all know, there's a new order of things here."

"What is this new order then ?"

"Well—but we have, in a manner of speaking, died, your Excellency."

"Oh, yes! But the order of things is still . . ."

Well, much obliged to them; nothing to say but that it's quite a consolation! If it's come to this down here, why even bother looking into things upstairs? But all the same, these are strange doings! I went on listening all the same, though with extreme indignation.

"No, I'd have liked to see a little more of life! No . . . you know, a little more of life . . . that is, to live for a time," a new voice suddenly sounded from somewhere in the space between the general and the irritable lady.

"Do you hear, your Excellency, our friend is at the same game again. For three days at a time he says nothing, and then he bursts out with 'I'd like to see a little more of life, yes, a little more of life!' And with such relish, hee-hee!"

"And such frivolity."

"It gets hold of him, your Excellency, and do you know, he's growing sleepy, quite sleepy—he's been here since April; and then all of a sudden 'A little more of life!'"

"It is rather dull, though," observed his Excellency.

"It is, your Excellency. Shall we tease Avdotia Ignatyevna again, hee-hee?"

"No, spare me, please. I can't endure that quarrelsome virago."

"And I can't endure either of you," cried the virago disdainfully. "You are both of you bores and can't tell me anything that has ideals in it. I know certain little story about you, your Excellency—don't turn up your nose, please—how a manservant swept you out from under a married couple's bed one morning."

"Nasty woman," the general muttered through his teeth.

"Avdotia Ignatyevna, ma'am," the shopkeeper wailed suddenly again, "my dear lady, don't hold a grudge, but tell me, is this what I'm going through the ordeal by torment now, or is it something else?"

"Ah, he's started up again, and I knew he was going to because there's a smell from him that means he's turning over!"

"I'm not turning over, ma'am, and there's no particular smell from me, for I've kept my body whole as it should be, while you, my fine lady, have gone right off—the smell is really more than a body can stand, even for a place like this. It's just from politeness that I keep quite about it."

"Ah, you horrid, insulting wretch. He positively stinks and then he talks about me."

"Uh-uh-uh-uh! If only the day for my requiem would come : I'd hear their tearful voices over my head, my wife's lament and my children's soft crying! . . ."

"Well, that's a thing to fret for! They'll stuff themselves with funeral rice and go home. . . . Oh, I wish somebody would wake up!"

"Avdotia Ignatyevna," said the insinuating government clerk, "wait a bit, the new arrivals will speak."

"And are there any young people among them?"

"Yes, there are, Avdotia Ignatyevna. There are some that are not more than lads."

"Oh, how welcome that would be!"

"Haven't they begun yet?" inquired his Excellency.

"Even those who came the day before yesterday haven't awakened yet, your Excellency. As you know, they sometimes don't speak for a week. It's a good job that today and yesterday and the day before they brought in a whole lot. As it stands, they're all last year's for seventy feet round."

"Yes, it will be interesting."

"Yes, your Excellency, they buried Tarasevich, the Privy Councilor, to-day. I knew it from the voices. I know his nephew, he helped to lower the coffin just now."

"Hm, where is he, then?"

"Five steps from you, your Excellency, on the left. . . . Almost at your feet. You should make his acquaintance, your Excellency."

"Hm, no—I shouldn't go first"

"Oh, he'll start things off himself, your Excellency. He'll be flattered. Leave it to me, your Excellency, and I . . ."

"Oh, oh! . . . What is happening to me?" croaked the frightened voice of a new arrival.

"A new arrival, your Excellency, a new arrival, thank God! And how quick he's been! Sometimes they don't say a word for a week."

"Oh, I believe it's a young man!" Avdotia Ignatyevna cried shrilly.

"I . . . I . . . it was a complication, and so sudden!" faltered the young man again. "Only the evening before, Schultz said to me, 'There's a compli-cation,' and I died suddenly before morning. Oh! oh!"

"Well, there's no help for it, young man," the general observed gra-ciously, evidently pleased at a new arrival. "You've got to be resigned. You are kindly welcome to our Vale of Jehoshaphat, as you might call it. We're kind-hearted people, you'll come to know us and appreciate us. Major-General Vassily Vassilich Pervoedov, at your service."

"Oh, no, no! I simply can't be! I was at Schultz's; I had a complication, you know, at first it was my chest and a cough, and then I caught a cold: my lungs, and influenza . . . and all of a sudden, quite unexpectedly . . . the worst thing was its being so unexpected."

"You say it began with the chest," the government clerk put in suavely, as though he wished to reassure the new arrival.

"Yes, my chest and catarrh, and then no catarrh but still the chest, and I couldn't breathe . . . and you know . . ."

"I know, I know. But if it was the chest you ought to have gone to Ecke and not to Schultz."

"You know, I kept meaning to go to Botkin's, but then . . ."

"Botkin takes quite a bite," observed the general.

"Oh, no, he doesn't bite at all; I've heard he's so attentive and tells you everything that's going to happen before it does."

"His Excellency was referring to the fees," the government clerk corrected him.

"Oh, not at all, he only charges three roubles, and then he examines you so thoroughly, and gives you a prescription . . . and I was very anxious to see him, because people said . . . Well, gentlemen, should I go to Ecke or to Botkin?"

"What? Where?" The general's corpse shook with agreeable laughter. The government clerk echoed it in falsetto.

"Dear boy, dear, delightful boy, how I love you!" Avdotia Ignatyevna squealed ecstatically. "I wish they had put someone like you next to me."

No, I simply could not accept this! And these, these were the dead of our times! Still, I should listen some more and not jump to conclusions. That sniveling new arrival—I remember him just now in his coffin—had the expression of a frightened baby chick, the most repellent expression in the world! However, we'll wait and see.

———————————

But then such a cacophony started up that I haven't been able to remember it all. Because a great many woke up at once; an official, a Civil Councilor, awoke, and right then and there began to discuss with the general the project of a new sub-committee in a government department, and the probable transfer of various functionaries in connection with the sub-committee—thereby amusing the general very, very much. I admit I learned a great deal that was new to me, such that I was amazed by the channels through which one may sometimes learn government news in our capital. Then an engineer half woke up, but for a long time he muttered absolute nonsense, so that our friends stopped worrying him and let him lie till he was ready. At last signs of sepulchral re-animation were evinced by the distinguished lady who had been buried that morning under the catafalque. Lebeziatnikov (for the obsequious Lower Court Councilor whom I detested and who lay beside General Pervoedov was, it appears, named Lebeziatnikov) became much excited, and surprised that they were all waking up so soon this time. I admit I was surprised too; but then some of those who awoke had been buried for three days, for instance, one very young girl, just sixteen, who kept giggling . . . giggling in a horrible and predatory way.

"Your Excellency, Privy Councilor Tarasevich is waking!" Lebeziatnikov announced with extreme urgency.

"Eh? What's that?" mumbled the Privy Councilor in a tone of distaste as he suddenly awoke. There was a note of willful peremptoriness in the sound of his voice. I listened with curiosity—for during the last few days I had heard something about Tarasevich, something suggestive and alarming to the highest degree.

"It's I, your Excellency, so far only I."

"What is your petition? What do you want?"

"Merely to inquire after your Excellency's health; in these unaccustomed surroundings everyone feels at first, as it were, oppressed. General Pervoedov wishes to have the honor of making your Excellency's acquaintance, and hopes . . ."

"I've never heard of him."

"Surely, your Excellency! General Pervoedov, Vassily Vassilich . . ."

"Are you General Pervoedov?"

"No, your Excellency, I am only Lower Court Councilor Lebeziatnikov, at your service, but General Pervoedov . . ."

"Nonsense! And I must ask you to leave me alone."

"Let him be." In a dignified manner General Pervoedov himself, finally, checked the disgusting officiousness of his sycophant in the grave.

"He's not fully awake, your Excellency, you must consider that; it's the novelty of it all. When he is fully awake he'll take it differently."

"Let him be," repeated the general.

———————

"Vassily Vassilich! Ahoy, your Excellency!" an entirely new voice shouted loudly and aggressively from close beside Avdotia Ignatyevna. It was a voice of gentlemanly insolence, with the languid pronunciation now fashionable and an arrogant drawl. "I've been watching you all for the last two hours; been lying here for three days. Do you remember me, Vassily Vassilich? My name is Klinevich, we met at the Volokonskys' where they'd let you in too, I don't know why."

"What, Count Piotr Petrovich? . . . Can you really be . . . and at such an early age? How sorry I am to hear it."

"And I'm very sorry myself, though I really don't mind, and I want to get what I can out of wherever I am . And I'm not a count but a baron, only a baron. We 're just set of mangy barons, shot up from being lackeys, but why I don't know and damned if I care. I'm only a scoundrel of pseudo-aristocratic society, and I'm regarded as 'a charming *polisson*'. My father's a wretched little general, and my mother was at one time received *en haut lieu*. With the help of the Jew Zifel I forged fifty thousand-rouble notes last year and then I informed against him, while Julie *Charpentier de Lusignan* carried off the money to Bordeaux. And just think, I was engaged to be married—Shchevalevskaia, three months shy of sixteen, still in school, with a dowry of ninety thousand. Avdotia Ignatyevna, do you remember how you seduced me fifteen years ago when I was a boy of fourteen in the *Corps des Pages*?"

"Ah, that's you, you rascal! Well, you're a godsend, anyway, for here . . ."

"You were mistaken in suspecting your neighbor, the business gentleman, of an unpleasant fragrance . . . I kept quiet, but I laughed. The stench came from me: they had to bury me in a nailed-up coffin."

"Ugh, you horrid creature! Still, I am glad you're here; you can't imagine the lack of life and wit here."

"Quite so, quite so, and I intend to start here something original. Your Excellency—I don't mean you, Pervoedov—the other Your Excellency, Tarasevich, the Privy Councilor! Speak up! Klinevich here, the one who took you to *Mlle*. Furie in Lent, do you hear?"

"I do, Klinevich, and I am delighted, and, trust me . . ."

"I wouldn't trust you with a halfpenny, and damned if I care. I simply want to kiss you, dear old man, but luckily I can't. Do you know, gentlemen, what this *grand-pere*'s little game was? He died three or four days ago, and would you believe it, he left a deficit of four hundred thousand in government money. It was from the fund for widows and orphans, and for some reason he was the only person in charge of it, so his accounts hadn't been audited for the last eight years. I can just imagine what long faces they all have now, and what names they're calling him. It's a delectable thought, isn't it? I've been wondering for the last year how a wretched old codger of seventy, with gout and rheumatism, came by the physical energy for his debaucheries—and now the riddle is solved! Those widows and orphans—the very thought of them must have fired him up! I knew about it long ago, I was the only one who did know; it was Julie told me, and as soon as I discovered it, I immediately, at Easter it was, attacked him in a friendly way week: 'Give me twenty-five thousand, if you don't they'll be auditing you to-morrow.' And just think, he only had thirteen thousand left then, so it seems he died very conveniently. *Grand-pere, grand-pere*; do you hear?"

"*Chèr* Klinevich, I quite agree with you, and there was no need for you to . . . to go into such details. Life is so full of suffering and torment and so little to make up for it . . . that I wanted finally to be at rest, and so far as I can see I hope to get all I can from here too."

"I'll bet he's already sniffed Katiche Berestov!"

"Who? What Katiche?" There was a rapacious quiver in the old man's voice.

"A-ah, what Katiche? Why, here on the left, five paces from me and ten from you. She's been here for five days, and if you only knew, *grand-pere*, what nasty little piece she is! Comes from a good family, well brought up, and a monster, a regular monster! I haven't introduced her to anyone there, I was the only one who knew her . . . Katiche, speak up!"

"Hee-hee-hee!" the response came in an unmusical girlish treble, in which there was a note sharp as the prick of a needle. "Hee-hee-hee!"

"And is she a lit-tle blo-onde?" the *grand-pere* faltered, drawling out the syllables.

"Hee-hee-hee!"

"I've . . . for a long time I've," the old man faltered breathlessly, "dreamed of a little blonde, about fifteen or so, and a situation just like this."

"Ah, what a monster!" cried Avdotia Ignatyevna.

"Enough!" Klinevich decided. "I see there's excellent material here. We'll soon arrange things better. The main thing is to enjoy the rest of our time; but how much time? Hey, you, government clerk, Lebeziatnikov or whatever it is, I think that's what they called you!"

"Semion Yevseich Lebeziatnikov, Lower Court Councilor, at your service and very, very, very delighted to meet you."

"Delighted or not, damned if I care; but you seem to know everything here. Tell me first of all how it is we can talk? I've been wondering ever since yesterday. We're dead but all the same we 're talking and we seem to be moving-and yet we're not talking and not moving. What kind of *hocus-pocus* is this?"

"If you want, Baron, Platon Nikolaevich could explain it better than I could."

"What Platon Nikolaevich is that? Get to the point, don't beat about the bush."

"Platon Nikolaevich is our home-grown philosopher, a scientist and Master of Arts. He brought out several philosophical works, but for the last three months he's been getting quite drowsy, and there's no stirring him up now. Once a week he'll mutter a few words, completely irrelevant."

"To the point, to the point!"

"He explains all this by the simplest fact, namely, that when we were living on the surface we mistakenly thought that death there was death. The body revives, as it were, here, the remains of life are concentrated, but only in the consciousness. I don't know how to express it, but life goes on, as it were, by inertia. In his opinion everything is concentrated somewhere in the consciousness and goes on for two or three months . . . sometimes even for half a year. . . . There's someone here, for instance, who is almost completely decomposed, but once every six weeks he'll suddenly utter one word, quite senseless of course, about some bobok: 'Bobok, bobok.' Which means that even in him life is still warm, an imperceptible spark . . ."

"It's rather stupid. Well, and how is it I have no sense of smell and yet I feel there's a stench?"

"That . . . hee-hee . . . Well, on that point our philosopher is a bit foggy. Apropos of smell, he remarked that the stench one perceives here is, so to speak, a moral one—hee-hee! It's the stench of the soul, he says, which has these two or three months to recover itself . . . and this is, so to speak, the last mercy. . . . Only I think, Baron, that these are mystical ravings, very excusable in his position . . .

"Enough; all the rest of it, I'm sure, is nonsense. The great thing is that we have two or three months more of life and then—bobok! I propose to spend these two months as agreeably as possible, and so to arrange every- thing on a new basis. Gentlemen! I propose to be ashamed of nothing."

"Ah, let's, let's not be ashamed of anything!" many voices could be heard saying; and strange to say several new voices were audible, these must have belonged to others newly awakened. The engineer, now fully awake, boomed out his agreement with peculiar delight. The girl Katiche giggled gleefully.

"Oh, how I long to be ashamed of nothing!" Avdotia Ignatyevna exclaimed rapturously.

"You hear that? If even Avdotia Ignatyevna wants to be ashamed of nothing . . ."

"No, no, no, Klinevich, I was ashamed, up there I was, anyway, but here I terribly, terribly want to be ashamed of nothing."

"I understand, Klinevich," boomed the engineer, "you propose to rearrange life here on new and rational principles."

"Damned if I care about that! For that we'll wait for Kudeiarov, who was brought here yesterday. When he wakes he'll tell you all about it. He's such a personality, such a titanic personality! To-morrow they'll bring along another natural scientist, I believe, an officer for certain, and three or four days later a journalist, and, I believe, his editor with him. But the devil can take them all so long as we have our own little group, and things arrange themselves. Though meanwhile I don't want us to be telling lies. That's all I care about, since that's one thing that does matter. You can't exist on the surface without lying, because living and lying are synonymous, but here we won't lie, for the fun of it. Devil take it, the grave has some value after all! We'll all tell our stories aloud, and we won't be ashamed of anything. First of all I'll tell you about myself. I'm one of the predatory kind, you know. Up on the surface all that was held in check by rotten cords. Away with the cords and let's spend these two months in shameless truthfulness! Let's strip and be naked!"

"Let's be naked, let's be naked!" cried all the voices.

"I long to be naked, I long to be," Avdotia Ignatyevna shrilled.

"Ah . . . ah, I see we'll have fun here; I don't want Ecke after all."

" No, I'd like to see a little more of life . . . you know, a little more of life!"

"Hee-hee-hee!" giggled Katiche.

"The great thing is that no one can interfere with us, and though I see Pervoedov is in a temper, he can't reach me with his hand. *Grand-pere*, do you agree?"

"I fully agree, fully, and with the utmost satisfaction, but on condition that Katiche is the first to give us her biography."

"I protest! I protest with all my heart!" General Pervoedov brought out firmly.

"Your Excellency!" in hurried excitement and lowering his voice the scoundrel Lebeziatnikov murmured persuasively, "your Excellency, it will be to our advantage to agree. Here, you see, there's this girl . . . and all their little affairs."

"There's the girl, it's true, but . . ."

"It's to our advantage, your Excellency, upon my word it is! If only as an experiment, let's try it. . ."

"Even in the grave they won't let us rest in peace."

"In the first place, General, you were playing preference in the grave, and in the second you . . . be . . . damned." drawled Klinevich.

"Sir, I beg you not to forget yourself."

"What? You know you can't get me, and I can tease you from here as though you were Julie's lapdog. And another thing, gentlemen, how is he a general here? He was a general there, but here he's zero."

"No, not zero. . . . Even here . . ."

"Here you 'll rot in the grave and six brass buttons will be all that's left of you."

"Bravo, Klinevich, ha-ha-ha!" roared voices.

"I have served my sovereign . . . I have the sword . . ."

"Your sword is only fit to prick mice, and you never drew it even for that."

"That makes no difference; I formed a part of the whole."

"There are all sorts of parts in a whole."

"Bravo, Klinevich, bravo! Ha-ha-ha!"

"I don't understand what the sword stands for," boomed the engineer.

"We shall run away from the Prussians like mice, they'll crush us to powder!" cried a voice in the distance that was unfamiliar to me, that was positively spluttering with glee.

"The sword, sir, is an honor," the general cried, but only I heard him. There arose a prolonged and furious roar, clamor, and hubbub, and only the hysterically impatient squeals of Avdotia were audible.

"But hurry up, hurry up! Ah, when do we start being ashamed of nothing!"

"Uh-uh-uh! . . . The soul does in truth pass through torments!" exclaimed the plebeian voice, and . . .

And at that moment I suddenly sneezed. It happened unexpectedly and unintentionally, but the effect was striking: everything became as silent as one expects it to be in a churchyard, it all vanished like a dream. The real silence of the grave set in. I don't believe they were embarrassed by my presence: they had made up their minds to be ashamed of nothing! I waited five minutes or so—not a word, not a sound. It also can't be supposed that they were afraid of my informing the police; because what could the police do to them? I reluctantly conclude that they must have some secret, unknown to the living, which they carefully conceal from every mortal.

"Well, my dears," I thought, "I'll be visiting you again." And with those words, I left the cemetery.

No, that I cannot accept; no, I truly cannot! Bobok doesn't trouble me (there, so that's what "bobok" turned out to mean!)

Depravity in such a place, depravity of the last aspirations, depravity of sodden and rotten corpses —and not even sparing the last moments of consciousness! Those moments have been granted, vouchsafed to them, and . . . and, worst of all, in such a place! No, that I cannot accept.

I'll go to tombs of other grades, I'll listen in everywhere. To be sure I should listen everywhere, and not merely in one spot, in order to form an idea. I just might stumble on something reassuring.

But I'll certainly return there. They promised their biographies and anecdotes of all sorts. Phew! But I'll go, I'll certainly go; it's a question of conscience!

I'll take it to the *Citizen*; there's an editor there who's had his portrait exhibited too. He just might print it.

Translated by Jessie Coulson; ed. by A. L. and M. K.

The Little Boy at the Savior's Christmas Tree

But I'm a novelist, and there's a certain "tale" that, I suppose, I've made up. Why do I write "I suppose?" Of course I know for a fact that I've made it up, but still I keep imagining that it must have occurred, that precisely this did occur on Christmas Eve in *a certain* great city, on Christmas Eve, in a time of terrible frost.

I imagine that in a cellar there was a boy, but still very young, about six or even younger. This boy woke up that morning in the damp and cold cellar. He was dressed in a sort of tiny thin dressing-gown and was shivering with cold. His breath floated out in a cloud of white steam, and, sitting on a trunk in the corner, in his boredom he was voluntarily blowing the steam out of his mouth, entertaining himself as he watched it float away. But he was very hungry. Several times that morning he had approached up to the pallet where his sick mother lay on a mattress thin as a pancake, some sort of bundle under her head for a pillow. How had she come here? She must have come with her boy from some other town and suddenly fallen ill. The landlady who rented these "corners" had been taken, two days before, to the police station. The lodgers had dispersed for the holiday, and the one remaining layabout had for the whole last twenty-four hours been sprawled out dead drunk, not even waiting for the holiday. In another corner of the room, moaning with her rheumatism, lay a wretched old woman of eighty who had once been a children's nurse somewhere, but was now left to die alone, groaning, scolding and grumbling at the boy so that he was afraid to go near her corner. He'd gotten a drink of water in the outer room, but couldn't find a little piece of crust anywhere, and had been on the point of waking his mother a dozen times. He got frightened, at last, in the darkness: evening had fallen long since, but no fire had been lit. Touching his mother's face, he was surprised that she didn't move at all, and that she was as cold as the wall. "But it's very cold in here," he thought. He stood for a while, unconsciously forgetting that his hand still rested on the dead woman's shoulder, then he blew on his small fingers to warm them, and suddenly, having fumbled for his cap on the bed, haltingly, feeling his way, he left the cellar. He would have gone earlier, but was afraid of the big dog which had been howling all day by the neighbor's door at the top of the stairs. However the dog was not there now, and the boy went out into the street.

Heavens, what a city! He'd never seen anything like it before. Where he'd come from there was such black darkness at night, with one lamp for a whole street. The little, low-pitched, wooden houses were closed up with shutters; dusk fell—there was no one about, everyone shut themselves up in their homes and there was nothing but the howling packs of dogs, hundreds and thousands of them barking and howling all night. But it had been so warm there and they gave him food, while here—oh dear, if only he had something to eat! And what a noise and rattle here, what light and what people, horses and carriages, and what a frost—what a frost! The frozen steam hangs in clouds over the hard-driven horses, over their warmly breathing muzzles; their hoofs clink against the stones through the powdery snow, and everyone pushes so, and—oh, dear, he wants so much to eat something, even just a little piece of something—and *how* his fingers suddenly began hurting him. A policeman walked by and turned away to avoid seeing the boy.

There was another street—oh, what a wide one, here he'd be run over for certain; how everyone was shouting, racing and driving along, and the light, the light! And what was this? A huge glass window, and through the window a tree reaching up to the ceiling; it was a fir tree, and on it were ever so many lights, so many gold paper ornaments and apples, and around the tree little dolls and horses; and running about the room there were children, dressed up and clean, laughing and playing and eating and drinking something. And then a little girl began dancing with one of the boys, what a pretty little girl! And he could hear the music through the window. The boy looked and wondered and laughed, though his toes were aching with the cold and his fingers were red and stiff so that it hurt him to move them. And all at once the boy remembered how his toes and fingers hurt him, and began crying, and ran on; and again through another window-pane he saw another Christmas tree, and on a table cakes of all sorts—almond cakes, red cakes and yellow cakes, and three grand ladies were sitting there, and they gave the cakes to anyone who came up to them, and the door kept opening, lots of gentlemen and ladies went in from the street. The boy crept up, suddenly opened the door and went in. Oh, how they shouted at him and waved him back! One lady went up to him hurriedly and slipped a kopeck into his hand, and with her own hands opened the door into the street for him! How frightened he was. And the kopeck rolled away and clinked upon the steps; he couldn't bend his red fingers to hold it right. The boy ran away and went on, where he did not know. He was ready to cry again but he was afraid, and ran on and on and blew on his fingers. And he was miserable because he felt suddenly so lonely and terrified, and all at once, mercy on us! What was this again? People were standing in a crowd admiring something. Behind a glass window there were three little dolls, dressed in red and green dresses, and exactly, exactly as though they were alive. One was a little old man sitting and playing a big violin, the two others were standing close by and playing little violins, and nodding in time, and looking at one another, and their lips moved, just as if they were really talking only you couldn't hear through the glass. And at first the boy thought they were alive, and when he grasped that they were dolls he laughed. He had never seen such dolls before, and had no idea there were such dolls! And he wanted to cry, but he the dolls were funny, so funny. All at once he fancied that some one behind him caught at his smock: a wicked big boy was standing beside him and suddenly hit him on the head, snatched off his cap and tripped him up. The boy fell down on the ground, at once there was a shout, he was numb with fright, he jumped up and ran away. He ran, and not knowing where he was going, ran in at the gate of some one's courtyard, and sat down behind a wood-stack: "They won't find me here, besides it's dark!"

He sat huddled up and was breathless from fright, and all at once, quite suddenly, he felt so happy: his hands and feet suddenly left off aching and grew so warm, as warm as though he were on a stove; then he shivered all over, then he gave a start, why, he must have been asleep. How nice to have a sleep here! "I'll sit here a little and go and look at the dolls again," said the boy, and smiled thinking of them. "Just as though they were alive! . . ." And suddenly he heard his mother singing over him. "Mama, I'm sleeping; how nice it is to sleep here!"

"Come to my Christmas tree, little one," a soft voice suddenly whispered over his head.

He thought that this was his mother again, but no, it was not she. Who it was calling him, he could not see, but someone bent over and embraced him in the darkness; and he stretched out his hands to him, and . . . and all at once—oh, what a bright light! Oh, what a Christmas tree! And yet it was not a fir tree, he had never seen a tree like that! Where was he now? Everything was bright and shining, and all round him were dolls; but no, they weren't dolls, they were little boys and girls, only so bright and shining. They all came flying round him, they all kissed him, took him and carried him along with them, and he was flying himself, and he saw that his mother was looking at him and laughing joyfully. "Mama; oh, how nice it is here, Mama!" And again he kissed the children and wanted to tell them at once about those dolls in the shop window.

"Who are you, boys? Who are you, girls?" he asked, laughing and admiring them.

"This is Jesus' Christmas tree," they answered. "Jesus always has a Christmas tree party on this day, for the little children who have no tree of their own . . ." And he found out that all these little boys and girls were children just like himself; that some had frozen to death still in the baskets in which as babies they had been laid on the doorsteps of well-to-do Petersburg people, others had been boarded out with Finnish women by the Foundling Hospital and had been suffocated, others had died at their starved mother's breasts (in the Samara famine), others had died in third-class railway carriages from the foul air; and yet they were all here, they were all like angels about Christ, and He was in the midst of them and held out His hands to them and blessed them and their sinful mothers . . . And the mothers of these children stood on one side weeping; each one knew her boy or girl, and the children flew up to them and kissed them and wiped away their tears with their little hands, and begged them not to weep because they were so happy.

And down below in the morning the porter found the little dead body of a frozen child behind the wood stack; they sought out his mother too . . . She'd died before him. They met before the Lord God in Heaven.

Why have I made up such a story, so out of keeping with an ordinary diary, and a writer's diary at that? And I had promised two more stories dealing primarily with real events! But that's just it, I keep thinking and imagining that all this may have happened really—that is, what took place in the cellar and on the wood stack; but as for Christ's Christmas tree party—I don't even know what to say to you, could that have happened, or not? That's why I'm a novelist, to think things up.

Translated by Jessie Coulson; edited by A. L. and M.K.

The Dream of a Ridiculous Man

I

I am a ridiculous person. Now they call me a madman. That would be a promotion if it were not that I remain as ridiculous in their eyes as before. But now I do not resent it, they are all dear to me now, even when they laugh at me—and, indeed, it is just then that they are particularly dear to me. I could join in their laughter—not exactly at myself, but through affection for them, if I did not feel so sad as I look at them. Sad because they do not know the truth and I do know it. Oh, how hard it is to be the only one who knows the truth! But they won't understand that. No, they won't understand it.

In old days I used to be miserable at seeming ridiculous. Not seeming, but being. I have always been ridiculous, and I have known it, perhaps, from the hour I was born. Perhaps from the time I was seven years old I knew I was ridiculous. Afterwards I went to school, studied at the university, and, do you know, the more I learned, the more thoroughly I understood that I was ridiculous. So that it seemed in the end as though all the sciences I studied at the university existed only to prove and make evident to me as I went more deeply into them that I was ridiculous. It was the same with life as it was with science. With every year the same consciousness of the ridiculous figure I cut in every relation grew and strengthened. Every one always laughed at me. But not one of them knew or guessed that if there were one man on earth who knew better than anybody else that I was absurd, it was myself, and what I resented most of all was that they did not know that. But that was my own fault; I was so proud that nothing would have ever induced me to tell it to any one. This pride grew in me with the years; and if it had happened that I allowed myself to confess to any one that I was ridiculous, I believe that I should have blown out my brains with a revolver the same evening. Oh, how I suffered in my early youth from the fear that I might gave way and confess it to my school-fellows. But since I grew to manhood, I have for some unknown reason become calmer, though I realized my awful characteristic more fully every year. I say "unknown," for to this day I cannot tell why it was. Perhaps it was owing to the terrible misery that was growing in my soul through something which was of more consequence than anything else about me: that something was the conviction that had come upon me that nothing in the world mattered. I had long had an inkling of it, but the full realization came last year almost suddenly. I suddenly felt that it was all the same to me whether the world existed or whether there had never been anything at all: I began to feel with all my being that there was nothing existing. At first I fancied that many things had existed in the past, but afterwards I guessed that there never had been anything in the past either, but that it had only seemed so for some reason. Little by little I guessed that there would be nothing in the future either. Then I left off being angry with people and almost ceased to notice them. Indeed this showed itself even in the pettiest trifles: I used, for instance, to knock against people in the street. And not so much from being lost in thought: what had I to think about? I had almost given up thinking by that time; nothing mattered to me. If at least I had solved my problems! Oh, I had not settled one of them, and how many they were! But I gave up caring about anything, and all the problems disappeared.

And it was after that that I found out the truth. I learnt the truth last November—on the third of November, to be precise—and I remember every instant since. It was a gloomy evening, one of the gloomiest possible evenings. I was going home at about eleven o'clock, and I remember that I thought that the evening could not be gloomier. Even physically. Rain had been falling all day, and it had been the coldest, gloomiest, almost menacing rain, with, I remember, an unmistakable grudge against mankind. Suddenly between ten and eleven it had stopped, and was followed by a horrible dampness, colder and damper than the rain, and a sort of steam was rising from everything, from every stone in the street, and from every by-lane if one looked down it as far as one could. A thought suddenly occurred to me, that if all the street lamps had been put out it would have been less cheerless, that the gas made one's heart sadder because it lighted it all up. I had had scarcely any dinner that day, and had been spending the evening with an engineer, and two other friends had been there also. I sat silent—I fancy I bored them. They talked of something rousing and suddenly they got excited over it. But they did not really care, I could see that, and only made a show of being excited. I suddenly said as much to them. "My friends," I said, "you really do not care one way or the other." They were not offended, but they all laughed at me. That was because I spoke without any note of reproach, simply because it did not matter to me. They saw it did not, and it amused them.

As I was thinking about the gas lamps in the street I looked up at the sky. The sky was horribly dark, but one could distinctly see tattered clouds, and between them fathomless black patches. Suddenly I noticed in one of these patches a star, and began watching it intently. That was because that star had gaven me an idea: I decided to kill myself that night. I had firmly determined to do so two months before, and poor as I was, I bought a splendid revolver that very day, and loaded it. But two months had passed and it was still lying in my drawer; I was so utterly indifferent that I wanted to seize a moment when I would not be so indifferent—why, I don't know. And so for two months every night that I came home I thought I would shoot myself. I kept waiting for the right moment. And so now this star gave me a thought. I made up my mind that it should certainly be that night. And why the star gave me the thought I don't know.

And just as I was looking at the sky, this little girl took me by the elbow. The street was empty, and there was scarcely any one to be seen. A cabman was sleeping in the distance in his cab. It was a child of eight with a kerchief on her head, wearing nothing but a wretched little dress all soaked with rain, but I noticed her wet broken shoes and I recall them now. They caught my eye particularly. She suddenly pulled me by the elbow and called me. She was not weeping, but was spasmodically crying out some words which she could not utter properly, because she was shivering and shuddering all over. She was in terror about something, and kept crying, "Mammy, mammy!" I turned facing her, I did not say a word and went on; but she ran pulling at me, and there was that note in her voice which in frightened children means despair. I know that sound. Though she did not articulate the words, I understood that her mother was dying, or that something of the sort was happening to them, and that she had run out to call some one, to find something to help her mother. I did not go with her; on the contrary, I had an impulse to drive her away. I told her first to go to a policeman. But clasping her hands, she ran beside me sobbing and gasping, and would not leave me. Then I stamped my foot, and shouted at her. She called out "Sir! sir! . . ." but suddenly abandoned me and rushed headlong across the road. Some other passerby appeared there, and she evidently flew from me to him.

I mounted up to my fifth story. I have a room in a flat where there are other lodgers. My room is small, poor, with a garret window in the shape of a semicircle. I have a sofa covered with American leather, a table with books on it, two chairs and a comfortable arm-chair, as old as old can be, but of the good old-fashioned shape. I sat down, lighted the candle, and began thinking. In the room next to mine, through the partition wall, a perfect Bedlam was going on. It had been going on for the last three days. A retired captain lived there, and he had half a dozen visitors, gentlemen of doubtful reputation, drinking vodka and playing *Stoss* with old cards. The night before there had been a fight, and I know that two of them had been for a long time engaged in dragging each other about by the hair. The land-lady wanted to complain, but she was in abject terror of the captain. There was only one other lodger in the flat, a thin little regimental lady, on a visit to Petersburg, with three little children who had been taken ill since they came into the lodgings. Both she and her children were in mortal fear of the captain, and lay trembling and crossing themselves all night, and the youngest child had a sort of fit from fright. That captain, I know for a fact, sometimes stops people on the Nevskii Prospect and begs. They won't take him into the service, but strange to say (that's why I am telling this), all months that the captain has been here his behavior has caused me no annoyance. I have, of course, tried to avoid his acquaintance from the very beginning, and he, too, was bored with me from the first; but I never care how much they shout the other side of the partition nor how many of them there are in there—I never care: I sit up all night and forget them so completely that I do not even hear them. I stay awake till daybreak, and have been going on like that for the last year. I sit up all night in my arm-chair at the table, doing nothing. I only read by day. I sit—don't even think; ideas of a sort wander through my mind and I let them come and go as they will. A whole candle is burnt every night. I sat down quietly at the table, took out the revolver and put it down before me. When I'd done so I asked myself, I remember, "Is that so?" and answered with complete conviction, "It is." That is, I'll shoot myself. I knew that I should shoot myself that night for certain, but how much longer I should go on sitting at the table I did not know. And no doubt I should have shot myself if it had not been for that little girl.

II

You see, though nothing mattered to me, I could feel pain, for instance. If any one had struck me it would have hurt me. It was the same morally: if anything very pathetic happened, I should have felt pity just as I used to do in old days when there were things in life that did matter to me. I had felt pity that evening. I should have certainly helped a child. Why, then, had I not helped the little girl? Because of an idea that occurred to me at the time: when she was calling and pulling at me, a question suddenly arose before me and I could not settle it. The question was an idle one, but I was vexed. I was vexed at the reflection that if I were going to make an end of myself that night, nothing in life ought to have mattered to me. Why was it that all at once I did not feel that nothing mattered and was sorry for the little girl? I remember that I was very sorry for her, so much so that I felt a strange pang, quite incongruous in my position. Really I do not know better how to convey my fleeting sensation at the moment, but the sensation persisted at home when I was sitting at the table, and I was very much irritated as I had not been for a long time past. One reflection followed another. I saw clearly that so long as I was still a human being and not nothingness, I was alive and so could suffer, be angry and feel shame at my actions. So be it. But if I am going to kill myself, in two hours, say, what is the little girl to me and what have I to do with shame or with anything else in the world? I shall turn into nothing, absolutely nothing. And can it really be true that the consciousness that I shall completely cease to exist immediately and so everything else will cease to exist, does not in the least affect my feeling of pity for the child nor the feeling of shame after a contemptible action? I stamped and shouted at the unhappy child as though to say—not only I feel no pity, but even if I behave inhumanly and contemptibly, I am free to, for in another two hours everything will be extinguished. Do you believe that that was why I shouted that? I am almost convinced of it now. It seemed clear to me that life and the world somehow depended upon me now. I may almost say that the world now seemed created for me alone: if I shot myself the world would cease to be at least for me. I say nothing of its being likely that nothing will exist for any one when I am gone, and that as soon as my consciousness is extinguished the whole world will vanish too and become void like a phantom, as a mere appurtenance of my consciousness, for possibly all this world and all these people are only me myself. I remember that as I sat and reflected, I turned all these new questions that swarmed one after another quite the other way, and thought of something quite new. For instance, a strange reflection suddenly occurred to me, that if I had lived before on the moon or on Mars and there had committed the most disgraceful and dishonorable action and had there been put to such shame and ignominy as one can only conceive and realize in dreams, in nightmares, and if, finding myself afterwards on earth, I were able to retain the memory of what I had done on the other planet and at the same time knew that I should never, under any circumstances, return there, then looking from the earth to the moon—should I care or not? Should I feel shame for that action or not? These were idle and superfluous questions for the revolver was already lying before me, and I knew in every fiber of my being that it would happen for certain, but they excited me and I raged. I could not die now without having first settled something. In short, the child had saved me, for I put off my pistol shot for the sake of these questions. Meanwhile the clamor had begun to subside in the captain's room: they had finished their game, were settling down to sleep, and meanwhile were grumbling and languidly winding up their quarrels. At that point I suddenly fell asleep in my chair at the table—a thing which had never happened to me before. I dropped asleep quite unawares.

Dreams, as we all know, are very queer things: some parts are presented with appalling vividness, with details worked up with the elaborate finish of jewelry, while others one gallops through, as it were, without noticing them at all, as, for instance, through space and time. Dreams seem to be spurred on not by reason but by desire, not by the head but by the heart, and yet what complicated tricks my reason has played sometimes in dreams, what utterly incomprehensible things happen to it! My brother died five years ago, for instance. I sometimes dream of him; he takes part in my affairs, we are very much interested, and yet all through my dream I quite know and remember that my brother is dead and buried. How is it that I am not surprised that, though he is dead, he is here beside me and working with me? Why is it that my reason fully accepts it? But enough. I will begin about my dream. Yes, I dreamed a dream, my dream of the third of November. They tease me now, telling me it was only a dream. But does it matter whether it was a dream or reality, if the dream made known to me the truth? If once one has recognized the truth and seen it, you know that it is the truth and that there is no other and there cannot be, whether you are asleep or awake. Let it be a dream, so be it, but that real life of which you make so much I had meant to extinguish by suicide, and my dream, my dream—oh, it revealed to me a different life, renewed, grand and full of power! Listen.

III

I have mentioned that I dropped asleep unawares and even seemed to be still reflecting on the same subjects. I suddenly dreamt that I picked up the revolver and aimed it straight at my heart—my heart, and not my head; and I had determined beforehand to fire at my head, at my right temple. After aiming at my chest I waited a second or two, and suddenly my candle, my table, and the wall in front of me began moving and heaving. I made haste to pull the trigger.

In dreams you sometimes fall from a height, or are stabbed, or beaten, but you never feel pain unless, perhaps, you really bruise yourself against the bedstead, then you feel pain and almost always wake up from it. It was the same in my dream. I did not feel any pain, but it seemed as though with my shot everything within me was shaken and everything was suddenly dimmed, and it grew horribly black around me. I seemed to be blinded and benumbed, and I was lying on something hard, stretched on my back; I saw nothing, and could not make the slightest movement. People were walking and shouting around me, the captain bawled, the landlady shrieked—and suddenly another break and I was being carried in a closed coffin. And I felt how the coffin was shaking and reflected upon it, and for the first time the idea struck me that I was dead, utterly dead, I knew it and had no doubt of it, I could neither see nor move and yet I was feeling and reflecting. But I was soon reconciled to the position, and as one usually does in a dream, accepted the facts without disputing them.

Now I was buried in the earth. They all went away, I was left alone, utterly alone. I didn't move. Whenever before I had imagined being buried the one sensation I associated with the grave was that of damp and cold. So now I felt that I was very cold, especially the tips of my toes, but I felt nothing else.

I lay still, strange to say I expected nothing, accepting without dispute that a dead man had nothing to expect. But it was damp. I don't know how long a time passed—whether an hour, or several days, or many days. But all at once a drop of water fell on my closed left eye, making its way through the coffin lid; it was followed a minute later by a second, then a minute later by a third—and so on, regularly every minute. There was a sudden glow of profound indignation in my heart, and I suddenly felt in it a pang of physical pain. "That's my wound," I thought; "that's the bullet . . ." And drop after drop every minute kept falling on my closed eyelid. And all at once, not with my voice, but with my entire being, I called upon the power that was responsible for all that was happening to me:

"Whoever you may be, if you exist, and if anything more rational than what's happening here is possible, suffer it to be here now. But if you're revenging yourself upon me for my senseless suicide by the hideousness and absurdity of this subsequent existence, then let me tell you that no torture could ever equal the contempt which I'll go on dumbly feeling, though my martyrdom may last a million years!"

I made this appeal and held my peace. There was a full minute of unbroken silence and again another drop fell, but I knew with infinite unshakable certainty that everything would change immediately. And behold my grave suddenly was rent asunder, that is, I don't know whether it was opened or dug up, but I was caught up by some dark and unknown being and we found ourselves in space. I suddenly regained my sight. It was the dead of night, and never, never had there been such darkness. We were flying through space far away from the earth. I did not question the being who was taking me; I was proud and waited. I assured myself that I was not afraid, and was thrilled with ecstasy at the thought that I was not afraid. I do not know how long we were flying, I cannot imagine; it happened as it always does in dreams when you skip over space and time, and the laws of thought and existence, and only pause upon the points for which the heart yearns. I remember that I suddenly saw in the darkness a star. "Is that Sirius?" I asked impulsively, though I had not meant to ask any questions.

"No, that is the star you saw between the clouds when you were coming home," the being who was carrying me replied.

I knew that it had something like a human face. Strange to say, I did not like that being, in fact I felt an intense aversion for it. I had expected complete non-existence, and that was why I had put a bullet through my heart. And here I was in the hands of a creature not human, of course, but yet living, existing. "And so there is life beyond the grave," I thought with the strange frivolity one has in dreams. But in its inmost depth my heart remained unchanged. "And if I have got to exist again," I thought, "and live once more under the control of some irresistible power, I won't be vanquished and humiliated."

"You know that I am afraid of you and despise me for that," I said suddenly to my companion, unable to refrain from the humiliating question which implied a confession, and feeling my humiliation stab my heart as with a pin. He did not answer my question, but all at once I felt that he was not even despising me, but was laughing at me and had no compassion for me, and that our journey had an unknown and mysterious object that concerned me only. Fear was growing in my heart. Something was mutely and painfully communicated to me from my silent companion, and permeated my whole being. We were flying through dark, unknown space. I had for some time lost sight of the constellations familiar to my eyes. I knew that there were stars in the heavenly spaces the light of which took thousands or millions of years to reach the earth. Perhaps we were already flying through those spaces. I expected something with a terrible anguish that tortured my heart. And suddenly I was thrilled by a familiar feeling that stirred me to the depths: I suddenly caught sight of our sun! I knew that it could not be our sun, that gave life to our earth, and that we were an infinite distance from our sun, but for some reason I knew in my whole being that it was a sun exactly like ours, a duplicate of it. A sweet, thrilling feeling resounded with ecstasy in my heart: the kindred power of the same light which had given me light stirred an echo in my heart and awakened it, and I had a sensation of life, the old life of the past for the first time since I had been in the grave.

"But if that is the sun, if that is exactly the same as our sun," I cried, "where is the earth?"

And my companion pointed to a star twinkling in the distance with an emerald light. We were flying straight towards it.

"And are such repetitions possible in the universe? Can that be the law of Nature? . . . And if that is an earth there, can it be just the same earth as ours . . . just the same, as poor, as unhappy, but precious and beloved for ever, arousing in the most ungrateful of her children the same poignant love for her that we feel for our earth?" I cried out, shaken by irresistible, ecstatic love for the old familiar earth which I had left. The image of the poor child whom I had repulsed flashed through my mind.

"You shall see it all," answered my companion, and there was a note of sorrow in his voice.

But we were rapidly approaching the planet. It was growing before my eyes; I could already distinguish the ocean, the outline of Europe; and suddenly a feeling of a great and holy jealousy glowed in my heart.

"How can it be repeated and what for? I love and can love only that earth which I have left, stained with my blood, when, in my ingratitude, I quenched my life with a bullet in my heart. But I have never, never ceased to love that earth, and perhaps on the very night I parted from it I loved it more than ever. Is there suffering upon this new earth? On our earth we can only love with suffering and through suffering. We cannot love otherwise, and we know of no other sort of love. I want suffering in order to love. I long, I thirst, this very instant, to kiss with tears the earth that I have left, and I don't want, I won't accept life on any other!"

But my companion had already left me. I suddenly, quite without noticing how, found myself on this other earth, in the bright light of a sunny day, fair as paradise. I believe I was standing on one of the islands that make up on our globe the Greek archipelago, or on the coast of the mainland facing that archipelago. Oh, everything was exactly as it is with us, only everything seemed to have a festive radiance, the splendor of some great, holy triumph attained at last. The caressing sea, green as emerald, splashed softly upon the shore and kissed it with manifest, almost conscious love. The tall, lovely trees stood in all the glory of their blossom, and their innumerable leaves greeted me, I am certain, with their soft, caressing rustle and seemed to articulate words of love. The grass glowed with bright and fragrant flowers. Birds were flying in flocks in the air, and perched fearlessly on my shoulders and arms and joyfully struck me with their darling, fluttering wings. And at last I saw and knew the people of this happy land. They came to me of themselves, they surrounded me, kissed me. The children of the sun, the children of their sun—oh, how beautiful they were! Never had I seen on our own earth such beauty in mankind. Only perhaps in our children, in their earliest years, one might find some remote, faint reflection of this beauty. The eyes of these happy people shone with a clear brightness. Their faces were radiant with the light of reason and fullness of a serenity that comes of perfect understanding, but those faces were gay; in their words and voices there was a note of childlike joy. Oh, from the first moment, from the first glance at them, I understood it all! It was the earth untarnished by the Fall; on it lived people who had not sinned. They lived just in such a paradise as that in which, according to all the legends of mankind, our first parents lived before they sinned; the only difference was that all this earth was the same paradise. These people, laughing joyfully, thronged round me and caressed me; they took me home with them, and each of them tried to reassure me. Oh, they asked me no questions, but they seemed, I fancied, to know everything without asking, and they wanted to make haste and smooth away the signs of suffering from my face.

IV

And do you know what? Well, granted that it was only a dream, yet the sensation of the love of those innocent and beautiful people has remained with me for ever, and I feel as though their love is still flowing out to me from over there. I have seen them myself, have known them and been convinced; I loved them, I suffered for them afterwards. Oh, I understood at once even at the time that in many things I could not understand them at all; as an up-to-date Russian progressive and contemptible Petersburger, it struck me as inexplicable that, knowing so much, they had, for instance, no science like ours. But I soon realized that their knowledge was gained and fostered by intuitions different from those of us on earth, and that their aspirations, too, were quite different. They desired nothing and were at peace; they did not aspire to knowledge of life as we aspire to understand it, because their lives were full. But their knowledge was higher. and deeper than ours; for our science seeks to explain what life is, aspires to understand it in order to teach others how to live, while they without science knew how to live; and that I understood, but I could not understand their knowledge. They showed me their trees, and I could not understand the intense love with which they looked at them; it was as though they were talking with creatures like themselves. And perhaps I shall not be mistaken if I say that they conversed with them. Yes, they had found their language, and I am convinced that the trees understood them. They looked at all Nature like that—at the animals who lived in peace with them and did not attack them, but loved them, conquered by their love. They pointed to the stars and told me something about them which I could not understand, but I am convinced that they were somehow in touch with the starts, not only in thought, but by some living channel. Oh, these people did not persist in trying to make me understand them, they loved me without that, but I knew that they would never understand me, and so I hardly spoke to them about our earth. I only kissed in their presence the earth on which they lived and mutely worshipped them themselves. And they saw that and let me worship them without being abashed at my adoration, for they themselves loved much. They were not unhappy on my account when at times I kissed their feet with tears, joyfully conscious of the love with which they would respond to mine. At times I asked myself with wonder how it was they were able never to offend a creature like me, and never once to arouse a feeling of jealousy or envy in me? Often I wondered how it could be that, boastful and untruthful as I was, I never talked to them of what I knew—of which, of course, they had no notion—that I was never tempted to do so by a desire to astonish or even to benefit them.

They were as gay and sportive as children. They wandered about their lovely woods and copses, they sang their lovely songs; their fare was light—the fruits of their trees, the honey from their woods, and the milk of the animals who loved them. The work they did for food and raiment was brief and not laborious. They loved and begot children, but I never noticed in them the impulse of that cruel sensuality which overcomes almost every man on this earth, all and each, and is the source of almost every sin of mankind on earth. They rejoiced at the arrival of children as new beings to share their happiness. There was no quarreling, no jealousy among them, and they did not even know what the words meant. Their children were the children of all, for they all made up one family. There was scarcely any illness among them, though there was death; but their old people died peacefully, as though falling asleep, giving blessings and smiles to those who surrounded them to take their last farewell with bright and loving smiles. I never saw grief or tears on those occasions, but only love, which reached the point of ecstasy, but a calm ecstasy, made perfect and contemplative. One might think that they were still in contact with the departed after death, and that their earthly union was not cut short by death. They scarcely understood me when I questioned them about immortality, but evidently they were so convinced of it without reasoning that it was not for them a question at all. They had no temples, but they had a real living and uninterrupted sense of oneness with the whole of the universe; they had no creed, but they had a certain knowledge that when their earthly joy had reached the limits of earthly nature, then there would come for them, for the living and for the dead, a still greater fullness of contact with the whole of the universe. They looked forward to that moment with joy, but without haste, not pining for it, but seeming to have a foretaste of it in their hearts, of which they talked to one another.

In the evening before going to sleep they liked singing in musical and harmonious chorus. In those songs they expressed all the sensations that the parting day had given them, sang its glories and took leave of it. They sang the praises of nature, of the sea, of the woods. They liked making songs about one another, and praised each other like children; they were the simplest songs, but they sprang from their hearts and went to one's heart. And not only in their songs but in all their lives they seemed to do nothing but admire one another. It was like being in love with each other but an all-embracing, universal feeling.

Some of their songs, solemn and rapturous, I scarcely understood at all. Though I understood the words I could never fathom their full significance. It remained, as it were, beyond the grasp of my mind, yet my heart unconsciously absorbed it more and more. I often told them that I had had a presentiment of it long before, that this joy and glory had come to me on our earth in the form of a yearning melancholy that at times approached insufferable sorrow; that I had had a foreknowledge of them all and of their glory in the dreams of my heart and the visions of my mind; that often on our earth I could not look at the setting sun without tears . . . that in my hatred for the men of our earth there was always a yearning anguish: why could I not hate them without loving them? Why could I not help forgiving them? And in my love for them there was a yearning grief: why could I not love them without hating them? They listened to me, and I saw they could not conceive what I was saying, but I did not regret that I had spoken to them of it: I knew that they understood the intensity of my yearning anguish over those whom I had left. But when they looked at me with their sweet eyes full of love, when I felt that in their presence my heart, too, became as innocent and just as theirs, the feeling of the fullness of life took my breath away, and I worshipped them in silence.

Oh, every one laughs in my face now, and assures me that one cannot dream of such details as I am telling now, that I only dreamed or felt one sensation that arose in my heart in delirium and made up the details myself when I woke up. And when I told them that perhaps it really was so, my God, how they shouted with laughter in my face, and what mirth I caused!

Oh, yes, of course I was overcome by the mere sensation of my dream, and that was all that was preserved in my cruelly wounded heart; but the actual forms and images of my dreams, that is, the very ones I really saw at the very time of my dream, were filled with such harmony, were so lovely, enchanting and so actual, that on awakening I was, of course, incapable of clothing them in our poor language, so that they were bound to become blurred in my mind; and so perhaps I really was forced afterwards to make up the details, and so of course to distort them in my passionate desire to convey some at least of them as quickly as I could. But on the other hand, how can I help believing that it was all true? It was perhaps a thousand times brighter, happier and more joyful than I describe it. Granted that I dreamed it, yet it must have been real. You know, I will tell you a secret: perhaps it was not a dream at all! For then something happened so awful, something so horribly true that it could not have been imagined in a dream. My heart may have originated the dream, but would my heart alone have been capable of originating the awful event which happened to me after-wards? How could I alone have invented it or imagined it in my dream? Could my petty heart and my fickle, trivial mind have risen to such a reve-lation of truth? Oh, judge for yourselves: hitherto I have concealed it, but now I will tell the truth. The fact is that I . . . corrupted them all!

V

Yes, yes it ended in my corrupting them all! How it could come to pass I do not know, but I remember it clearly. The dream embraced thousands of years and left in me only a sense of the whole. I only know that I was the cause of their sin and downfall. Like a vile trichina, like a germ of the plague infect-ing whole kingdoms, so I contaminated all this earth, so happy and sinless before my coming. They learnt to lie, grew fond of lying, and discovered the charm of falsehood. Oh, at first perhaps it began innocently, with a jest, coquetry, with amorous play, perhaps indeed with a germ, but that germ of fal-sity made its way into their hearts and pleased them. Then sensuality was soon begotten, sensuality begot jealousy, jealousy—cruelty . . . Oh, I don't know, I don't remember; but soon, very soon the first blood was shed. They marveled and were horrified, and began to be split up and divided. They formed into unions, but it was against one another. Reproaches, upbraidings followed They came to know shame, and shame brought them to virtue. The concep-tion of honor sprang up, and every union began waving its flags. They began torturing animals, and the animals withdrew from them into the forests and became hostile to them. They began to struggle for separation, for isolation, for individuality, for mine and thin. They began to talk in different languages. They became acquainted with sorrow and loved sorrow; they thirsted for suffering, and said that truth could only be attained through suffering. Then science appeared. As they became wicked they began talking of brotherhood and humanitarianism, and understood those ideas. As they became criminal, they invented justice and drew up whole legal codes in order to observe it, and to ensure their being kept, set up a guillotine. They hardly remembered what they had lost, in fact refused to believe that they had ever been happy and innocent. They even laughed at the possibility of this happiness in the past, and called it a dream. They could not even imagine it in definite form and shape, but, strange and wonderful to relate, though they lost all faith in their past happiness and called it a legend, they so longed to be happy and innocent once more that they succumbed to this desire like children, made an idol of it, set up temples and worshipped their own idea, their own desire; though at the same time they fully believed that it was unattainable and could not be realized, yet they bowed down to it and adored it with tears! Nevertheless, if it could have happened that they had returned to the innocent and happy condition which they had lost, and if some one had shown it to them again and had asked them whether they wanted to go back to it, they would certainly have refused. They answered me:

"We may be deceitful, wicked and unjust, we know it and weep over it, we grieve over it; we torment and punish ourselves more perhaps than that merciful Judge Who will judge us and whose Name we know not. But we have science, and by means of it we shall find the truth and we shall arrive at it consciously. Knowledge is higher than feeling, the consciousness of life is higher than life. Science will give us wisdom, wisdom will reveal the laws, and the knowledge of the laws of happiness is higher than happiness."

That is what they said, and after saying such things every one began to love himself better than any one else, and indeed they could not do otherwise. All became so jealous of the rights of their own personality that they did their very utmost to curtail and destroy them in others, and made that the chief thing in their lives. Slavery followed, even voluntary slavery; the weak eagerly submitted to the strong, on condition that the latter aided them to subdue the still weaker. Then there were saints who came to these people, weeping, and talked to them of their pride, of their loss of harmony and due proportion, of their loss of shame. They were laughed at or pelted with stones. Holy blood was shed on the threshold of the temples. Then there arose men who began to think how to bring all people together again, so that everybody, while still loving himself best of all, might not interfere with others, and all might live together in something like a harmonious society. Regular wars sprang up over this idea. All the combatants at the same time firmly believed that science, wisdom and the instinct of self-preservation would force men at last to unite into a harmonious and rational society; and so, meanwhile, to hasten matters, "the wise" endeavored to exterminate as rapidly as possible all who were "not wise" and did not understand their idea, that the latter might not hinder its triumph. But the instinct of self-preservation grew rapidly weaker; there arose men, haughty and sensual, who demanded all or nothing. In order to obtain everything they resorted to crime, and if they did not succeed—to suicide. There arose religions with a cult of non-existence and self-destruction for the sake of the everlasting peace of annihilation. At last these people grew weary of their meaningless toil, and signs of suffering came into their faces, and then they proclaimed that suffering was a beauty, for in suffering alone was there meaning. They glorified suffering in their songs. I moved about among them, wringing my hands and weeping over them, but I loved them perhaps more than in old days when there was no suffering in their faces and when they were innocent and so lovely. I loved the earth they had polluted even more than when it had been a paradise, if only because sorrow had come to it. Alas! I always loved sorrow and tribulation, but only for myself, for myself; but I wept over them, pitying them. I stretched out my hands to them in despair, blaming, cursing and despising myself. I told them that all this was my doing, mine alone; that it was I had brought them corruption, contamination and falsity. I besought them to crucify me, I taught them how to make a cross. I could not kill myself, I had not the strength, but I wanted to suffer at their hands. I yearned for suffering, I longed that my blood should be drained to the last drop in these agonies. But they only laughed at me, and began at last to look upon me as crazy. They justified me, they declared that they had only got what they wanted themselves, and that all that now was could not have been otherwise. At last they declared to me that I was becoming dangerous and that they should lock me up in a madhouse if I did not hold my tongue. Then such grief took possession of my soul that my heart was wrung, and I felt as though I were dying; and then . . . then I awoke.

It was morning, that is, it was not yet daylight, but about six o'clock. I woke up in the same arm-chair; my candle had burnt out; every one was asleep in the captain's room, and there was a stillness all round, rare in our flat. First of all I leapt up in great amazement: nothing like this had ever happened to me before, not even in the most trivial detail; I had never, for instance, fallen asleep like this in my arm-chair. While I was standing and coming to myself I suddenly caught sight of my revolver lying loaded, ready—but instantly I thrust it away! Oh, now, life, life! I lifted up my hands and called upon eternal truth, not with words but with tears; ecstasy, immeasurable ecstasy flooded my soul. Yes, life and spreading the good tidings! Oh, I at that moment resolved to spread the tidings, and resolved it, of course, for my whole life. I go to spread the tidings, I want to spread the tidings—of what? Of the truth, for I have seen it, have seen it with my own eyes, have seen it in all its glory.

And since then I have been preaching! Moreover I love all those who laugh at me more than any of the rest. Why that is so I do not know and cannot explain, but so be it. I am told that I am vague and confused, and if I am vague and confused now, what shall I be later on? It is true indeed: I am vague and confused, and perhaps as time goes on I shall be more so. And of course I shall make many blunders before I find out how to preach, that is, find out what words to say, what things to do, for it is a very difficult task. I see all that as clear as daylight, but, listen, who does not make mistakes? And yet, you know, all are making for the same goal, all are striving in the same direction anyway, from the sage to the lowest robber, only by different roads. It is an old truth, but this is what is new: I cannot go far wrong. For I have seen the truth; I have seen and I know that people can be beautiful and happy without losing the power of living on earth. I will not and cannot believe that evil is the normal condition of mankind. And it is just this faith of mine that they laugh at. But how can I help believing it? I have seen the truth—it is not as though I had invented it with my mind, I have seen it, seen it, and the living image of it has filled my soul for ever. I have seen it in such full perfection that I cannot believe that it is impossible for people to have it. And so how can I go wrong? I shall make some slips no doubt, and shall perhaps talk in second-hand language, but not for long: the living image of what I saw will always be with me and will always correct and guide me. Oh, I am full of courage and freshness, and I will go on and on if it were for a thousand years! Do you know, at first I meant to conceal the fact that I corrupted them, but that was a mistake—that was my first mistake! But truth whispered to me that I was lying, and preserved me and corrected me. But how establish paradise—I don't know, because I do not know how to put it into words. After my dream I lost command of words. All the chief words, anyway, the most necessary ones. But never mind, I shall go and I shall keep talking, I won't leave off, for anyway I have seen it with my own eyes, though I cannot describe what I saw. But the scoffers do not understand that. It was a dream, they say, delirium, hallucination. Oh! As though that meant so much! And they are so proud! A dream! What is a dream? And is not our life a dream? I will say more. Suppose that this paradise will never come to pass (that I understand), yet I shall go on preaching it. And yet how simple it is: in one day, in one hour everything could be arranged at once! The chief thing is to love others like yourself, that's the great thing, and that's everything; nothing else is wanted—you will find out at once how to arrange it all. And yet it's an old truth which has been told and retold a billion times—but it has not formed part of our lives! The consciousness of life is higher than life, the knowledge of the laws of happiness is higher than happiness—that is what one must contend against. And I shall. If only every one wants it, it can all be arranged at once.

And I tracked down that little girl . . . and I shall go on and on!

Translated by C. Garnett, ed. by A.L. and M.K.

PART II
Modern Russian Fantasy, Utopia, and Science Fiction

S LOWING DOWN THE PACE of the volume from its "warp-drive" across Russia's first millennium, Part II retraces the country's fictional leaps into the unknown within the mere half century culminating with the launch of Sputnik, when one no longer needed a writer or a composer to imagine the sound of the celestial spheres, but could *hear* it on radio. Another difference resides in the fact that every writer represented below died in the 20th century, and thus lived to see the epoch when technology began to fulfill humanity's primordial dreams.

Yet even a half-century turns out to be an insufficiently short yardstick to measure a country's literary heritage in a sensible way, most particularly the heritage of a country as vast as Russia. This is especially true given the tumultuous social changes of these years: the two World Wars, a revolution, and the Civil War—events which destroyed a good half of Russia's population, leaving virtually no family untouched and a vast number of families exterminated altogether. If the current universally accepted memory of human suffering in the 20th century is repeatedly reinforced by remembering or revisiting such sites as Auschwitz or the beaches of Normandy, this repository of remembrance seems reluctant to acknowledge the fact that Russians were subject to the same genocidal practices as Hitler's victims, and that Russia's losses in combat during WWII are measured not in thousands or millions, but in tens of millions. However, Russia's greatest losses in the pre-Sputnik years of the 20th century, challenging in their scope any cataclysm or plague surviving in mankind's cultural memory, resulted from a peculiar merger of utopian beliefs, advanced through works literature, with the political aims of the power elite that governed Russia from 1917— the Bolsheviks. Using utopian idealism posited in literature to excuse the ruthless extermination of all who threatened their authority, they imposed a new social order which was to be the culmination of all mankind's dreams. By most accounts over 50 million Russians died (the noted Russian historian, Medvedev, has estimated the losses to have been closer to 80 million) in the gulags—those weird, real-life permutations of classic utopian designs—in which their subjects faced not the green wall of Zamiatin's *We*, but barbed wire, torture and execution.

While fully aware that dividing literary history by socially relevant dates rarely reflects strictly literary concerns—indeed, noting that all writers entered here lived and created equally prolifically before and after 1917—we nonetheless find it serviceable to split the material below into three sections. Section C-1 contains those literary works which were mostly written prior to 1917 and in an atmosphere relatively free from political coercion. We offer a sampling of the poetry and prose by the Russian poet-Symbolists, Alexander Blok, Valery Briusov, Fyodor Sologub and Andrei Bely. We continue in Section C-2 with the post-symbolist prose by Alexander Kuprin, newly translated writings of Alexei Remizov, important selections from Evgeny Zamiatin, and end with new translations of the haunting writings of Boris Pilniak. Section C-3 introduces works—some for the first time in English—by Nikolai Zabolotsky, Daniel Kharms, Yuri Olesha, and Mikhail Bulgakov, written after the first decade of Soviet rule. Utopian idealism, when present, is viewed in nearly all works of Section C with suspicion or outright rejection. Conversely, our Section D represents authors who saw in space a fruitful frontier for reaching Utopia; selections chosen here are abridged from longer writings by these authors, as our aim was to familiarize the reader solely with their unique representations of outer space itself.

Section C
Russia's Silver Age and the Fantastic of the Twenties and Thirties

C1. *Sampling Russian Symbolist Enigmas*

I T IS A HISTORICAL fact that the term *fin de siècle*—and, some would argue, the very notion of modernity accompanying it—arose in France. But it is just as true that Russia, originally influenced by the French visual arts and literature of the 1880s and 1890s, contributed to the international sense of modernity in its own ebullient and inimitable way. After the celebrated Paris exhibitions of Russian paintings in the first decade of the new century and the premiere of Diaghilev's *Ballets Russe* in the teens, the Russian sense of the The Modern effectively eclipsed the movement's French origins, shaping international understanding for years to come. In many spheres of art and science Russia was at last regarded as an equal partner, paving the way for a new future of mankind. So of course were the western empires of England, Germany and Austria—and other, smaller countries overtaken by the international sense of modernity. In the eighteenth century Russia had been still barely known to Europeans, and Peter I and his successors, notably Catherine The Great, were mostly importing European art—amassing in the process the largest extant collection of Rembrandts and other masters in the world's richest museum, The Hermitage. Now, however, at the turn of the twentieth century, Russia was no longer merely assimilating and absorbing European culture, she was for the first time in European memory transforming and creating it as well—in music with Rachmaninov, Scriabin, and Stravinsky, and later with Prokofiev and Shostakovich; in painting with Kandinsky, Chagall, and Bakst, or later the Constructivists; in cinema, ballet, costume design, and so on.

Modernism was as much about seeing the old in new ways as exploring new worlds, formerly hidden by established artistic conventions. Its early phase—Symbolist literature—originated indeed in France, spawned by the works of its first poet-practitioners Rimbaud, Verlaine, Baudelaire and Mallarmé. The movement was a reaction against positivism and the working assumptions of the realist artists. The dominance of socially conscious, "engaged" art had been particularly strong in Russia for more than half a century. The Symbolist challenge to realism and social utilitarianism was correspondingly strong. Symbolist writers held that empirical reality was a *chimera*, a mysterious veil through which—as in Baroque poetry—the artist could discern hidden meaning or fragments of higher truth, indeed of Truth itself. Like the earlier Romanticism which Symbolism in many ways recapitulated, the movement rediscovered the Orient and the exotic as an escape from the everyday and exercised a pervasive cultural influence in Europe, expressing itself in aspects of literature, music, and the fine arts. In fact, a distinguishing feature of Symbolism and Modernism was the degree to which they creatively merged and combined previously distinct art forms: literature and music, music and painting, etc. Writers and painters wrote symphonies and sonatas, such as Bely's *Four Symphonies* or Chiurlionis' *Sonata to the Stars, Allegro*; composers rendered the essence of painting, poetry, or myth in music, as Rachmaninov did in his *Isle of the Dead*, Mussorgsky in *Pictures at an Exhibition*, and Scriabin in *Prometheus: The Poem of Fire*; Russian painters drew inspiration from motifs of written and oral literature, such as Vrubel's *The Demon* and Bilibin's famous illustrations of Russian folk tales. Most of the ideas connected to this synthesizing tendency were born within an association of artists called *The World of Art* (Mir Isskustva), which began publishing their trend-setting journal in 1898.

Since non-verbal arts are quite readily absorbed and shared across linguistic and cultural borders, many westerners of this period became familiar with a broad range of Russia's visual arts, its music, dance and graphic design. The same cannot be said of the art of poetry in which the Symbolist and consequent schools had their true flowering in Russia. Often called Russian literature's Silver Age, this period remains largely unknown in the west. Regrettably, our volume can in no way attempt to remedy this situation, but the reader should be aware that the three Russian Symbolists whose prose is given an entry or two in this section— Valery Briusov, Fyodor Sologub and Andrei Bely—like the Golden Age writers Derzhavin, Pushkin and Lermontov—were all first-rate poets. We supply a newly translated sampling of the poetry of Briusov and Sologub, and (in lieu of translating any poem by Bely) provide a major new translation of one of the best known poems of the period, *The Stranger* by Alexander Blok (1880-1921), arguably the Silver Age's greatest poet. This work best exemplifies how the Russian Symbolist school transformed the original French movement and gave it a new expression. The phrase "vernal and decaying breath" in the poem's first stanza signifies Blok's aesthetic choice to expand on the Decadent poetics of Baudelaire's *Les Fleurs du Mal*, but the eerily divine features of the *female* which Blok's poetic persona—in a drunken stupor—sees in a tavern window, has uniquely Russian origins. The image evokes the notion of Sofia, or Holy Wisdom, found in the writings of Vladimir Solovyov (1853-1900) Russia's most influential philosopher, who predated and greatly influenced the Russian Symbolist school. It is preeminently due to his writings that Russian Symbolism combined philosophical idealism and Orthodox mysticism with the French movement's interest in decadence and artistic experimentation. While the seeds of Russian Symbolist idealist poetry go back to such mystical poets as Tiutchev and Fet (not represented in our volume), Solovyov's teachings on the feminine aspect of God had a profound effect on Russian Symbolists, indeed on an entire school of Russian Orthodox philosophy—the Sophians—which sprang into being in the twentieth century. Solovyov's teachings anchored their rhetoric in three visions experienced by the philosopher in which he saw Sophia incarnated as a beautiful female, most fully described in his poem "Three Meetings" (Tri svidaniia). The first vision occurred in a church in Solovyov's youth, the second in the British Museum during his trip abroad in 1875, and the third in the Egyptian desert. Blok's image of the enigmatic female stranger is a reflex on Solovyov's visions, but the sacrilegious use of holy symbols and of the phrase *in vino veritas* is the poet's own, as is this poem's unique musicality and expression of the existential paradox by which one may sit in a city bar yet travel, motionless, to enchanted shores.

The use of sacrilegious motifs in poetry was not, of course, invented by Blok, but rather followed the general Symbolist wish to discard clichéd concepts of universal beauty, propriety, or objective art in favor of the subjective, elitist view of representation with limited disclosure. The previously held convention of the beautiful female representing beauty itself, for instance, was later replaced by the evocation of the masculine—in the poetry of Sologub and Kuzmin—or by the androgynous, in the works of far too many artists to list here. This trend can even be seen from the public reactions to the single-line poem by one of the founders of Symbolism in Russia, Valery Iakovlevich Briusov (1873-1924):

O, close your barren pale legs! (O zakroi svoi blednye nogi. [1894])

The poem's ambiguity is derived from Briusov's use of the Russian verb "zakroi" (in its imperative mood meaning either *cover* something naked, or *close* something which is open), and its possibly implicit androgyny: to whose *legs* (male of female) was the poet referring? A. Izmajlov, for example felt it necessary to ask Briusov if he might have meant the legs of Christ taken down from the cross, since the poem would then indeed carry a profound significance for Izmajlov. Briusov answered in the negative, claiming that the line was simply an attempt to write a poem modeled on the minimalist poetry of Roman poets, who considered a single line to be potentially a complete poem. If, on the other hand, the legs belonged to a female then the poem could read in a rather scandalous way (as it was read at the time), or even sacrilegious, if the female in question were imagined to be Sophia herself. Whatever Briusov might have meant, the principal point about the newly rising sensibility engulfing Russia at the time was that the ultimate key to the decoding of any poem could only be found within the persona of the poet himself, or as Blok would state in *The Stranger*: "There lies within my soul a treasure chest/its Key—a trust that's solely mine!" (cf. final stanza). Ambiguity—one of the mainsprings of artistic function—was thus elevated by the Symbolist school to the status of an aesthetic priority, indeed, its teleology. Briusov's prose is represented below by a far less ambiguous, clearly dystopian short story, *The Republic of the Southern Cross*, which reflects the period's general sense of doom. Yet the cause of the mental disease which overtakes the circumpolar society of the future—*Mania contradicens*—is in the typical Symbolist manner hidden and never explained.

The Symbolists' purposeful lack of disclosure led at times to unforeseen results. For instance, in 1899 Briusov—watching as the furniture in his room was dusted—composed what seemed to him an innocuous poem, *Demons the Dust-born* (Demony pyli); the poet attached little significance to the work, except for the pride he took in its metrical complexity. He was even a bit annoyed when, during a visit to Peterburg several months later, his audience requested that he declaim this poem; he simply felt there were more important works he wished to share with the listeners. Yet as Thomas Venclova has recently demonstrated, it was this poem that Briusov's Symbolist peer, Fyodor Kuzmich Sologub (1863-1927), productively utilized in the formation of his own celebrated novel, *Petty Demon* (Melkii bes). The novel, unlike the poem that inspired it, was a grand undertaking, deftly portraying the moral decay, silliness, and sheer banality of Russia's degenerate provincial society at the turn of the century. Sologub's works are represented here by more modestly sized selections: the poem *Asteroid*, expressing the poet's metaphysical loneliness, and a short story *A Little Man*, a masterpiece in its own right, blending fantasy and social satire. The work takes the celebrated (and by that time hackneyed) subject of Russian realism—the theme of the so-called "little man"—and literally makes it shrink into thin air. The ending might well represent the author's tongue-in-cheek hope that the subject had finally exhausted itself. But the greed of the corporate world surrounding the poor protagonist of *A Little Man*, as well as the plight of the authentic fairy-tale personages in other Sologub writings, show that the author had great misgivings about the survival of the fantastic in the unfolding twentieth century.

Indeed, it could be safely argued that the most prevalent form of envisioning the Russian future in Sologub's time was one heralding doom. The most influential apocalyptic vision of such a future was again to be found in the writings of Vladimir Soloviev. His principal work in this regard is the aforementioned *Three Conversations*, a text rarely cited by cultural historians. Its apocalyptic themes and prophecies of the Antichrist are productively explored in Andrei Bely's superb novel, *Petersburg*. Bely does not make clear the actual future he foresees as the outcome of the cataclysm about to engulf the St. Petersburg of 1905, but a Horseman of the Apocalypse does make an appearance. Within Bely's fictional world physical actions have metaphysical consequences and *vice versa*, as is patently evident in the selections we offer from the novel. Taken from the *Prologue* and *Chapter I*, they introduce the three major protagonists—Apollon Apollonovich Ableukhov, his son Nikolai, and Petersburg itself—as well as the novel's chief plot device, a terrorist bomb with which Nikolai hopes to assassinate his father. He fails, but the bomb's abortive explosion—a metaphor for the 1905 revolution—does have the tangible consequence of forever separating him from his family and propelling him on a quest for life's ultimate wisdom. The quest's Egyptian setting speaks to the influence of Solovyov's visions, especially since *St. Petersburg's* Sophia (Sophia Petrovna Likhutina), is in fact the true opposite of Solovyov's Holy Wisdom. At the same time our selections typify Bely's dialogue with Gogol's St. Petersburg tales and Pushkin's *Bronze Horseman*, texts embedded at the novel's core, but in Pushkin's poem Petersburg as an artifice survives the catastrophic flood, whereas Bely's vison for the city's future is far more enigmatic. Our selections form a prose companion to Blok's *The Stranger*, and showcase techniques which succeed in integrating Bely's poetry-in-prose into a victory of fantasy-making narrative. The brief example of Bely's actual poetry, *The Demon*, which we newly translate, simultaneously echoes the cited poems by Lermontov, Sologub and Briusov.

Modernism was not, of course, characterized by Symbolism alone but equally by those movements and schools which grew out of it or in reaction to it, such as Russian Acmeism, Imaginism, Futurism, etc. Anna Akhmatova, Osip Mandelstam, Sergei Esenin, Vladimir Mayakovsky, Marina Tsvetaeva, and Velemir Khlebnikov, to name but a few, are commonly understood in Russia to be the period's best poets. Much of the subject matter of their poetry is either pure fantasy or borders on the fantastic. The doomsday mentality of the early Russian Symbolists and other writers, reaffirmed by the traumatic experience of the 1905 Russo-Japanese War and the attendant revolution of the same year, came to a climax in the Bolshevik Revolution of 1917. Early on the regime was welcomed by some of the Symbolists and most certainly sung by Mayakovsky , as it seemed to promise a truly glorious and remarkable emancipation of mankind in blazingly radiant futuristic scapes. The pathos of these days was further affirmed by the ascendant art forms of the poster, to which Mayakovsky contributed in no small measure, and the cinema, with Eisenstein's films such as *Ten Days that Shook the World* being the most widely known. It is, however, ironic that Eisenstein's cinematic accomplishment is generally viewed as a documentary of revolution, and that indeed millions participated in the Bolshevik undertaking. In fact the storming of the Winter Palace involved fewer than one thousand individuals, thus making the film effectively a fantasy, and assigning to "airy nothing" a St. Petersburg address. Nonetheless once the overthrow was accomplished, the terror inflicted by the Bolshevik government on the people was massive and did involve millions. The terror also affected the lives of Russia's finest poets, writers and artists. Blok, after initially welcoming the Bolsheviks in an enigma-ridden poem, *The Twelve* (1918; cf. below)—in which he paradoxically saw the revolution led by Jesus Christ himself—died agonized by its consequences in 1921. The same year witnessed the suicide by drowning of Sologub's closest life-companion, his wife Anastasia, who simply could not bear the Bolshevik regime, thus leaving her husband utterly bereft till 1927, when he died just as utterly alone. Esenin committed suicide in 1924, and Mayakovsky in 1930; Bely died nearly insane in 1934; Mandelstam perished in a concentration camp in 1936-7; Tsvetaeva committed suicide in 1941. Such were the non-enigmatic endings of some of Russia's most talented explorers of unknown and alternate worlds.

Alexander Alexandrovich Blok
(1880–1921)

The Stranger

When dusk has come, above the restaurants
The burning air is wild and deaf,
The drunken cries consent to rest upon
Its vernal and decaying breath.

Afar, above the dust of alleyways—
The yawn of summer bungalows,
A gilt roll glints atop a bakery,
And there resound an infant's moans.

And every dusk, beyond the barriers,
A rakish angle to their hats,
Between the ditches with their lady-friends
Are strolling seasoned, witty lads.

Above the lake—the oarlocks' stridency;
And there resounds a woman's shriek,
As in the sky, inured to everything,
Inanely grins a silvery disk.

And every dusk, my sole associate
Is mirrored in my tumbler's sheen;
Through fumes—astringent and mysterious—
Like me, both tamed and deafened seems.

Around me, at the counters neighboring,
Are drowsy waiters standing by,
And drunks, their eyes blood-shot and rabbity:
In vino veritas they cry.

Each night—the hour never deviates,
(Or do I see this in my dreams?)
A slender form in silken mantelet
Beyond the misty pane appears.

And slowly, through the crude inebriates,
Alone, and every night the same,
Effusing vapors, mists and fragrances
She sits down by the window frame.

And wafted by the myths of ancientry
Her silken dress about her clings,
Her mourning hat with plumes of ebony,
Her narrow hand bares many rings.

And seized by fettering proximity,
I gaze beyond her dark-hued veils
And see a distant shore bewitching me,
To where bewitching distance pales.

In trust I hold deep-hidden mysteries,
Another's Sun in trust is mine,
And now are all my soul's interstices
Suffused by this astringent wine.

And ebon ostrich plumes sway languidly,
Cascading down within my brain,
And eyes, of deepest blue and fathomless,
Bloom in the distant shore's domain.

There lies within my soul a treasure chest,
Its Key—a trust that's solely mine!
You're right, you reeling-drunk monstrosity!
I know; the *Truth is in the wine.*

Translated by A.L. and M.K.

The Twelve

(An excerpt, 1918)

(1.)

Evening—pitch black.
Snow—pure white.
Blow winds, blow back!
"Standing up straight—man, it's a fight."
Blow winds, blow low—
Sweeping God's world—whole, in their tow!

< . . . >

(2.)

The wind runs riot, fans the snow.
There twelve men sally in a row.

Their guns' black slings, dark stocks and sights,
Around—dim lights, more lights and lights . . .

Cheap butts in teeth, and crumpled caps,
A diamond ace would suit those backs!

    "Red freedom, yah, freedom,
    Yah, yah—with no Cross!"

    Ra-tat-tah! [—It's a toss:
    Who gets killed, who gets lost]
              < . . . >

(11.)

. . .And they tramp—no holy name to utter,
    All twelve goons go on.
    Up for any slaughter,
    All their pity gone . . .
              < . . . >

12.

. . .On they go triumphant, marching . . .
"Who's there?—Out! Don't try no stunt!"
Just the wind—red banner's arching
As its plaything out in front . . .

"Out in front—the snowdrift quivers:
Who's that in the mound?— Stand clear!" . . .
Just a vagrant hound that shivers,
Hungry, limping in the rear . . .

"Beat it now you filthy bastard,
Else I'll scratch you with my gun:
With my bayonet I'll chop up
All you old-world, dog-gone scum!"

. . .Bares its teeth—a wolflike hunger—
Tail tucked in—yet so aware—
Follows frozen—that poor mongrel . . .
"Hey you—answer—who goes there?"

"Who's there waving that red banner?
—Pitch black—you can't see at all!
—Who's that there—he's done a runner,
Sliding down along the wall?"

"Wait and see, I'm gonna get you,
Better keep yourself alive!
Hey you, comrade, you'll regret it,
Come out now, or else you die!"

Ra-tat-tat—shots echo after
From the houses lifeless now . . .
Just the blizzard spills its laughter
Through the endless drifts of snow . . .

    Ra-tat-tat!
    Ra-tat-tat . . .

. . .On they go triumphant, marching,
    Rearwards lurks the hungry dog,
Forefront—bloodstained banner's arching,
    And unseen within the storm,
    'Mid the bullets safe from harm,
Gait above the tempest lifted,
As the pearls of snow roll drifted,
    In a thorny, white-rose crown—
    Forefront—Jesus Christ leads on.

(*1917-18) Translated by A.L. and M. K.*

Valery Iakovlevich Briusov
(1873–1924)

Demons the Dust-born

The dust has its demons,
Like demons of snow, of light's prism.
A dusting of demons!
Their attire, at all times deep crimson—
In fire ablaze—
They've sealed now in haze:
In grey they're cloaked, derisively hidden.

Demons, the dust-lit!
On the cupboards, in ambush, like omens
They've closed their eyelids.
But the moment the doors fly open,
They stir, amazed,
Wild is their gaze;
They swirl up and tumble—demons, the dust-lit.

Where they have been the victors,
There is peace, sleep—there are dreamings,
Spacious tombs hold such visions.
There they slumber and, motionless seeming,
Hide in a nook,
Disdaining to look
Through darkness; but in their dreams knowing they're victors.

O legion of demons!
You command this brightly-hued planet!
You dust-to-dust legion!
With each age, your realm grows the wider!
Your day shall come
When all is numb
Beneath the still fluttering of your grey pinions.

Translated by A.L. and M.K.

The Republic of the
Southern Cross

Recent times have seen the appearance of a whole series of descriptions of the terrible disaster which befell the Republic of the Southern Cross. They differ markedly and they recount a number of events which are patently imaginary and improbable. Apparently the authors of these descriptions have relied too faithfully on the accounts given by the survivors from Star City, who, as is well known, have all been affected by a psychic ailment. This is why we have found it both essential and timely to compile here a summary of reliable information concerning the tragedy in the South which we have so far been able to collect.

The Republic of the Southern Cross was founded forty years ago within the Antarctic Circle as a group of steel factories belonging to a certain Trust. In the note sent to all the countries of the world the new state claimed all the continent and islands within the Antarctic Circle, as well as any part of those lands extending beyond that limit. It declared itself ready to purchase lands belonging to other states with its claims. The Republic's pretensions found no resistance from Earth's fifteen great powers. Disputed questions concerning some isles lying outside the Antarctic Circle but adjacent to the southern regions were settled by special treaties. After certain formalities, the Republic of the Southern Cross was accepted by the family of great powers and its representatives accredited to those states.

The Republic's major city, which was named Star City, was established at the South Pole itself. At the imaginary point on the Earth's axis where all the meridians meet stood the city hall, and its steeple rising above the city's roofs was pointed at the heaven's nadir. From the city hall the city's streets radiated along the meridians, while they were crossed by other streets which formed concentric circles. All the buildings were of the same height and architecture. They had no windows because all buildings were lighted by electricity. Electricity also served to light the streets. Because of the harsh climate an opaque dome rose over the city which was supplied with a powerful ventilation system which constantly provided fresh air. These regions of the earth know only one day each year which persists six months, and one night also of six months duration, but the streets of Star City were always flooded with a bright and steady light. Similarly, at all seasons the temperature out of doors was held by artificial means at one and the same level.

According to the latest census Star City's population was 2,500,000 people. The remainder of the Republic's population, 50,000,000 inhabitants, was concentrated around the ports and factories. These locations also held millions of inhabitants and they too were of the same design as Star City. Thanks to the wise use of electrical power, the ports were ice-free the entire year. Elevated electric railroads over which passed tens of thousands of passengers and millions of tons of goods every day connected the inhabited regions of the Republic. However, the inland region of the country remained uninhabited. The traveler from his railroad car could see only monotonous waste lands uniformly white in winter and grown over with sparse grass during the three summer months. Wildlife had long ago been exterminated and nothing remained to support human life. By contrast, all the more remarkable was the vigorous life of the port cities and the manufacturing centers. One can grasp this fact by knowing that in recent years approximately seven-tenths of all the metals extracted on the Earth were processed in the Republic's state factories.

The Republic's constitution seemingly was an expression of extreme democracy. The only fully enfranchised citizens were the workers at the metallurgical factories who made up about 60 percent of the entire population. These factories were state property. The workers were provided not merely with all possible conveniences at the factories, one can even speak of luxury. In addition to splendid living quarters and excellent food, they had at their disposal various educational institutions and amusements: libraries, museums, theaters, concerts, gymnasiums, etc. The working day had been greatly reduced in length. The education of the young, medical and legal services, and religious observance of the various sects were matters of state concern. Broadly assured that all their needs and & even slightest wishes would be met, the workers at the state factories received no wages; but the families of citizens who had labored at the factories for twenty years or of those who had died or rendered incompetent to work during their years of service received a generous life pension on the condition that they not leave the Republic. From among the workers, representatives were chosen by means of a general election who were sent to the Republic's legislature which considered all the aspects of the country's political life, but which could not alter its fundamental laws.

However, this democratic shell concealed the pure despotism of the individuals who had founded the original Trust. Allowing others to serve as delegates to the legislature, they invariably placed their candidates as directors of the factories. The economic life of the country was in the hands of the Board of Directors. They accepted all orders and distributed them to the factories; they purchased materials and equipment; they managed all the factories. Through their hands passed enormous sums of money, calculated in the billions. The Legislature only confirmed their projections for expenditures and revenue for the operation of the factories although the total of these projections far exceeded the Republic's budget. In international relations the influence of the Board of Directors was enormous. Its decisions could bankrupt entire countries. The prices it established determined the earnings of millions of workers all over the world. At the same time, the influence of the Board, although not directly, was decisive in the Republic's internal affairs. The Legislature, in fact, was only the obedient servant of the Board's will.

Retaining power in its own hands, the Board was dedicated above all to the pitiless regimentation of the country's entire existence. Under conditions of apparent freedom, citizens' lives were regulated down to the smallest detail. The buildings in all the country's cities were built according to the same plan set by law. The decoration of the worker's quarters, in spite of its luxury, was severely standardized. Everyone ate the same food at the same time. Clothing issued from government warehouses was invariably of the same design for decades. After a certain hour, announced by a signal from City Hall, no one was allowed on the streets. All the Republic's press was under the watchful eye of a censor, and no articles critical of the Board's dictatorship were passed. It should be mentioned that the entire country was so convinced of the benevolence of the dictatorship that the compositors themselves refused to set lines critical of the Board. The factories were full of the Board's spies. At the slightest sign of discontent with the Board, these agents at hastily called meetings rushed to calm the disaffected with passionate speeches. Certainly one disarming argument which was employed was that the workers' way of life was envied by the entire world. It was also said that in the case of certain individuals who persistently conducted agitation, the Council was not above assassination. At any rate, in all the years of the Republic not a single director was elected to the Board who was unsympathetic to the founding members.

The population of Star City for the most part consisted of workers who were completing their time of service. They were, so to speak, owners of stock in the state. The support which they received from the state allowed them to live well. Therefore, it is not surprising that Star City was considered to be one of the gayest cities in the world. It was a gold mine for various entrepreneurs. The most talented people from all the world assembled here. Here were found the best operas, the best concerts, the finest art exhibits; here were published the best informed newspapers. The stores of Star City presented astounding wealth and selections; the restaurants were famed for their luxury and fine service; clubs offered all kinds of depravity devised by both the ancient and the modern world. However, government regulation of life was also preserved in Star City. It's true that the decoration of apartments and fashions were not controlled but no one was allowed to leave his home after a certain hour, censorship was strict, and the Board retained a large number of secret agents. Officially order was maintained by the state police, but parallel with it existed the secret agents of the all-knowing Board.

Such, in broadest outline, was the way of life in the Republic of the Southern Cross and in its capital. It will be the historian's task to determine in the future to what degree it caused the appearance and spread of the fateful epidemic which led to the destruction of Star City, and perhaps, that of the entire young state.

The first cases of Contradiction were noted in the Republic twenty years ago. At that time occurrences of the malady were sporadic and unpredictable. However, the local psychiatrists and neuropatholgists were intrigued by it, described it in detail, and several papers were devoted to it at an international medical congress held in Lhasa. Subsequently it was forgotten for some reason, although there was no lack of such cases in the mental hospitals in Star City. It received its name as the result of the fact that those who suffered from it constantly contradicted their own desires, wanted one thing, but said and did another (the scientific name of the disease is *Mania contradicens*). Customarily it begins with mild symptoms, particularly a kind of peculiar aphasia. A victim of the disease says "yes" instead of "no"; when he wishes to say affectionate words, he spews curses, etc. The majority of the victims also begin to perform contradictory acts; intending to turn to the left, he turns right; thinking to lift his hat to be able to see better, he pulls it down over his eyes, etc. As the disease progresses these contradictions seize the victim's entire physical and mental life and therefore, of course, it expresses itself in an infinite variety of forms in accordance with the particulars of his life. But in general, the victim's speech becomes incomprehensible and his actions absurd. Physiological functions also become disordered. Aware of the illogic of his actions, the victim becomes extremely agitated, sometimes to the point of hysteria. Many victims take their own lives, sometimes in an attack of madness, sometimes, on the other hand, in a lucid moment. Others die of brain hemorrhages. Almost always the disease terminates in death; cases of recovery are extremely rare.

Mania contradicens took on epidemic proportions in Star City at the middle of the year. Before that time the number of those suffering from Contradiction was never more than two percent of all those ill at the time. But in May (an autumn month in the Republic) the percentage of those stricken with this disease grew to twenty-five percent and then continued to increase, while at the same time the absolute numbers of the victims grew at the same rate. In the middle of June, two percent of the entire population that is, about 50,000 people, were officially recognized as suffering from Contradiction. We have no statistics for the later period, but the hospitals were over-flowing with patients. The number of physicians available was totally inadequate. And in addition, the physicians themselves and other medical personnel were subject to the same disease. Very soon the victims had no one to turn to for medical help and precise count of those suffering from the disease became impossible to maintain. It should be noted, that all witnesses agree that in July it was impossible to find a family which did not have someone suffering from the disease. In addition, the number of those who were not affected by the disease was in constant decline, thanks to mass emigration from the suffering city, and an increase in the number of the victims. One is nearly inclined to believe those who say that everyone who remained in Star City in August was stricken with this psychological disorder.

The first manifestations of the epidemic may be seen in the increasing occurrence of the headline MANIA CONTRADICENS in the local newspapers. Since the identification of the disease in its early stages is very difficult, the first days of the epidemic were full of comic incidents. Instead of taking money from passengers, the conductors on the city transportation system gave them money. Traffic policeman whose duty it was to regulate traffic spent their day misdirecting it. Museum visitors, as they made their way through the galleries, removed pictures and turned them to the wall. A newspaper corrected by a proofreader seized by the disease turned out to be full of the most amusing absurdities. At a concert a violinist suddenly produced the most horrible dissonances in the middle of an orchestral selection, etc. A long series of such events provided abundant material for local newspaper columnists. But several incidents of a different sort soon cut short the stream of witticisms. First of all, a physician suffering from the disease of Contradiction prescribed a deadly chemical for a girl under his care and his patient died. The newspapers were full of this case for three days. Then two nannies in the municipal gardens were seized by the disease and cut the throats of forty one children. The entire city was shaken by the news. And on the same day, two officers suffering from the disease rolled a machine gun up to the window of the city police station and fired on peaceful pedestrians as they walked by. Nearly 500 people were killed or wounded.

After this incident all the newspapers, all the population, demanded that measures be taken against the epidemic. An extraordinary combined meeting of the City Council and the Legislature decided to summon physicians from other cities and foreign countries, to enlarge the hospitals, to open new ones and construct special quarters to isolate the victims of Contradiction, to print and distribute 500,000 copies of a pamphlet describing the new disease and identifying its symptoms and treatment, to organize a special team of physicians and aides for all the sections of the city to visit private dwellings and render first aid, etc. It was also decreed that special trains reserved exclusively for victims of the disease would leave the city on every line every day because the physicians considered the best treatment for the disease to be a change in residence. Similar measures were taken at the same time by various private associations, unions, and clubs. A special Society to Combat the Epidemic was even organized, whose members displayed extraordinary self-sacrifice. But, in spite of the fact that all these and other measures were introduced with inexhaustible energy, the epidemic did not slacken, but grew worse every day, touching the old and the young, men and women, working men and those at leisure, the self-disciplined and the dissolute. And soon the entire community was seized by irresistible and primitive terror as a result of this incredible disaster.

Flight began from Star City. At first a few individuals, especially some high officials, directors, or members of the Legislature or the City Council hastened to send their families to Australia and Patagonia. They were followed by a transient population—visitors who had come voluntarily to "The gayest city of the Southern Hemisphere," artists of all sorts, various unscrupulous individuals, and women of unseemly behavior. They were followed by merchants who fled as the epidemic grew. They quickly sold out their goods or abandoned their shops to their fates. With them went bankers, theater and restaurant owners, and publishers. Finally, the masses of the city's residents were affected. According to the law, former workers were forbidden to leave the Republic without special permission under the threat of losing their pensions. But in the rush to save one's life, this threat was ignored. Mass flight began: municipal workers fled; the police fled; hospital workers, pharmacists, and physicians fled. The urge to flee, in turn, became a mania. Everyone who could, fled the city.

The electric train stations were besieged by enormous crowds. Train tickets were purchased for enormous sums and battles were fought over them. Entire fortunes were paid for places in the dirigibles which could hold only ten passengers. When trains were departing, individuals broke into the cars and would not give up their places. Mobs stopped the trains provided exclusively for the victims of the disease, threw them out of the cars, took their beds, and forced the engineers to proceed. Beginning at the end of May all the railroad crews of the Republic were recruited to work on the lines connecting the capital with the ports. Trains left Star City overloaded with passengers; passengers filled all the corridors and the more daring rode on the outside, although at the speeds attained by the electric trains this might result in death by suffocation. The Australian, South American, and South African steamship lines grew unbelievably rich transporting emigrants from the Republic to other countries. The two Southern Company dirigible lines profited no less, since they could make about ten trips a day and they brought the last belated millionaires out of Star City. . . . On the other hand, the trains arrived nearly empty in Star City; it was impossible to find anyone for any salary who was willing to work in the capital; only rarely an eccentric tourist in search of strong emotions would come to the city beset by the infection. It is calculated that from the beginning of the emigration until June 22 when regular train service ceased, one and a half million people left the city on all its six railroad lines, that is, almost two-thirds of the entire population.

In these days, Horace DeVille, the Chairman of the City Council acquired eternal fame, thanks to his enterprise, strength of will, and courage. At an extraordinary session on June 5 the City Council, the Legislature, and the Board of Directors gave him dictatorial powers over the city with the title Chief of the City, and the disposition of the city treasury, the police, and the city's institutions. Shortly afterwards, the state government and its records were removed form Star City to Northern Harbor. The name of Horace DeVille must be written in gold among the most illustrious names of humanity. For six weeks he fought against increasing anarchy in the city, collecting around him a group of like assistants. For a long period of time they maintained discipline among the police and city employees who were overcome by the horror of the general catastrophe and whose ranks had been decimated by the epidemic. Hundreds of thousands of citizens owe their lives to Horace DeVille, since thanks to his energy and skill they escaped the city. He lightened the last days for thousands of others, providing them the comfort of dying in hospitals with medical care and not under the blows of insane mobs. And finally, it is to DeVille that humanity owes the catastrophe's chronicle—there is no other name for the brief but expressive and precise telegrams which he dispatched several times each day from Star City to the Republic's Provisional Government located in Northern Harbor.

Upon taking office as Chief of the City, DeVille's first act was to attempt to calm the alarmed populace. Manifestoes were published which pointed out that the mental disease was most readily transmitted to individuals who were agitated and called upon healthy and balanced individuals to employ their influence on those who were weak and nervous. DeVille also turned to the Society to Combat the Epidemic, assigning to its members supervision over all public places, such as theaters, meeting halls, parks and streets. During this period there was hardly an hour when new outbreaks of the disease were not discovered. Now here, now there, individuals or groups of individuals could be seen who displayed obviously abnormal behavior. Most of the victims who understood their malady indicated a desire for help. But under the influence of their disturbed minds this desire was expressed as some kind of inimical acts directed against those around them. The victims wanted to hurry to their homes or to a hospital, but instead in their terror they rushed towards the city's limits. They wanted to ask for sympathy, but instead they seized passing strangers by the throat, choking them, beating them, sometimes even striking at them with knives or clubs. Therefore when the public saw a man who suffered from Contradiction they fled in every direction. It was at this time that the members of the Society came to his aid. Some of the members would seize the victim, calm him, and send him to the nearest hospital; others would try to talk to the public and explain to them that there was no danger, but that it was merely an additional misfortune with which they all must deal.

In theaters and meeting halls cases of sudden attacks of the disease very often led to tragic consequences. At the opera, several hundred members of the audience seized by mass insanity, rather than expressing their delight with the singers' performances, rushed onto the stage and beat them. At the Grand Theater an actor suddenly attacked by the disease, who was to feign suicide suddenly fired into the audience. The revolver, of course, was unloaded, but thanks to the nervous strain, a number of individuals who bore the incipient germs of the disease were also overcome. In the confusion which followed, the expected panic was intensified by the contradictory acts of the madmen and several score individuals were killed. But the most tragic occurrence was at a fireworks display where a squad of policemen assigned there in case of fire, in a fit of madness, ignited a backdrop and curtain behind which the fireworks were being arranged. Not less than two hundred people died in the subsequent fire and panic. After this event Horace DeVille took measures to close all dramatic and musical performances in the city.

Thieves and looters became a terrible threat to the inhabitants of the city, since they found ideal conditions for their deeds in the general collapse of society. It is said that some of them came to Star City from foreign countries. Some of them simulated madness in order to escape punishment. Other didn't even consider it necessary to conceal their looting. Gangs of thieves brazenly entered abandoned stores and carried away the more valuable goods, they broke into private apartments and demanded money and they halted pedestrians and robbed them of their valuables, watches, rings, bracelets. Violence was adding to looting and above all, violence against women. The Chief of the City sent whole squads of police against the criminals but they were so audacious they fought pitched battles with the police. There were horrible incidents when the disease of Contradiction appeared among the looters or the police and the affected turned their weapons against their comrades. At first the Chief of the City exiled the looters from the city, but the citizens freed them from the prison trains to take their place. Then the Chief of the City was compelled to sentence robbers and criminals to death. And so, after three hundred years, capital punishment returned to the earth.

In June a shortage of essential commodities became apparent. There was not enough food nor medicine. Shipments over the railroad lines were reduced and manufacturing within the city had nearly ceased. DeVille organized municipal bakeries and bread and meat distribution centers for the entire population. Public cafeterias were set up on the model of those which already existed in the factories. But it was impossible to find enough workers to staff them. Volunteers served to the point of exhaustion, but their number was on the decline. The municipal crematoria burned the day around, but the number of the corpses in the morgues was not reduced, but rather increased. Bodies now were found in private residences and on the streets. Fewer and fewer workers labored at the municipal telegraph, telephone, light, water, and sewer services. DeVille's activity was astonishing. He followed everything, managed everything. Judging from his reports he knew no rest, and all the survivors of the catastrophe were unanimous in their opinion that his actions were above praise.

In the middle of June the lack of workers on the railroads became palpable. There were not enough locomotive engineers and conductors to serve all the trains. On June 17, the first disaster occurred on the Southwestern Line, the result of an engineer falling victim to Contradiction. Seized by the disease the engineer took an entire train off its elevated tracks from a height of forty feet onto an ice-covered plain. Nearly all the passengers were killed or injured. The news of the catastrophe delivered by the next train hit the city like a peal of thunder and a medical rescue train was sent out. It brought back the dead and the mutilated survivors. But the evening of the same day brought the news that a similar disaster had befallen the First Line. The two major railroad routes connecting Star City with the outside world were now disabled. Teams were sent from both the city and Northern Harbor to repair the lines, but work was almost impossible during the winter months. Any hope of restoring the lines within a brief period of time had to be abandoned.

These two catastrophes were only the first of many. The more concern the engineers displayed for their occupation, the more likely they were to repeat the deeds of their predecessors. Just because they feared to wreck their trains, they brought them to disaster. In a five day period from June 18 through June 22, seven trains crowded with passengers left the rails. Thousands of people found their deaths from either injuries or starvation on the snow-swept plains. Very few of them had the strength to return to the city. Now all the six lines connecting Star City with the outside world were cut. Even earlier, travel by means of dirigible had ceased. One of them had been destroyed by an enraged mob infuriated by the fact that only the very rich could escape by air. All the remaining dirigibles, one after another, were lost, probably destroyed as the result of the same factors which caused the railroad disasters. The city's population, now reduced to

600,000, was isolated from the rest of humanity. For a time the only link
with the outer world was the telegraph line.

On June 24 all traffic on the city's transportation system halted as the
result of a lack of workers. On June 26 telephone service failed. On June 27
all pharmacies were closed, with the exception of the central one in the city.
On July 1 the Chief of the City ordered all the inhabitants to move to the
city's center, abandoning the periphery to facilitate the maintenance of
order and the supply of food and medical services. The citizens left their
apartments and transferred to those abandoned by their previous owners.
The idea of property disappeared. No one hesitated to abandon his belongings and no one hesitated to use those of others. It is true, there were still
robbers and looters, but now we would consider them insane. They continued their thefts and at the present time hoards of gold and valuables are still
being found in the abandoned houses, and near them the rotting corpses of
the thieves.

It is remarkable, however, that in spite of the general destruction, life
retained its usual pattern. Merchants still could be found who opened their
stores, selling—for some reason at incredible prices—various goods: gour-
met foods, flowers, books, weapons. . . . Customers without hesitation put
down their useless gold and the avaricious merchants hid it, no one knows
why. There were still underground dives—gambling, alcohol and women—
which unhappy individuals frequented to forget the awful present. There
the sick mingled with the healthy, and no one maintained a chronicle of the
terrible scenes which took place. Two or three newspapers were still published whose editors sought to preserve the meaning of the printed word in
the general panic. Copies of these newspapers are now being sold at prices
ten or twenty times higher than their original cost and they are destined to
become the greatest bibliographical rarities. In their columns written in the
midst of madness and set by half-demented compositors, one can see a vivid
and horrifying reflection of the unfortunate city's sufferings. There were still
reporters who wrote "City News," writers who heatedly commented on the
situation, and even humorists who tried to amuse their readers in those
tragic days. And those telegrams which arrived from other countries
describing a real and healthy life must have filled with despair the hearts of
the readers doomed to destruction.

Hopeless attempts were made to escape the city. Early in July a huge
mob of men, women and children, under the leadership of one John Dew
set out on foot for the nearest inhabited place, Londontown. DeVille realized the undertaking was insane, but he couldn't stop them and even provided warm clothing and food supplies. The entire group of about 2000
individuals became lost and perished in the snowy plains of the polar country during the night which is without light for six months. A certain

Whiting proposed another yet more heroic solution. He suggested that all the victims of the disease be destroyed after which the epidemic would cease. He found not a few followers, for in those dark days any insane or inhuman proposal which might promise relief would have found its adherents. Whiting and his friends ranged the entire city, breaking into buildings and killing the sick. They perpetrated massacres in the hospitals. In their frenzy they killed anyone they suspected of the disease. Those who murdered on principle were joined by the insane and looters. The entire city became a battlefield. In these difficult days, Horace DeVille collected his associates, inspired them, and personally led them against Whiting's forces. The pursuit continued for several days. Hundreds of individuals fell on both sides, but finally Whiting himself was captured. He was found to be in the last stages of Contradiction and he was therefore not executed but taken to a hospital where he soon died.

On June 8 one of the heaviest blows fell on the city. The men responsible for the central power plant destroyed all the generators in a fit of madness. The electric lights failed and the entire city, all its streets, all private homes, were plunged into total darkness. Because this was the only source of light and heat in the city, all the residents found themselves in an absolutely hopeless situation. DeVille, foreseeing such a danger, had prepared supplies of torches and fuel. Fires were lighted everywhere on the streets. Thousands of torches were distributed to the city's inhabitants. But these meager blazes could not illuminate Star City's enormous linear panoramas which extended for tens of miles and the threatening heights of its thirty-story buildings. With the darkness collapsed the last vestiges of discipline in the city. Horror and madness finally overwhelmed the city's residents and the healthy could not be distinguished from the diseased. Despairing men and women began a terrible orgy.

The moral collapse of all the city's inhabitants became apparent with remarkable speed. Civilization, like a thin layer of bark grown slowly for thousands of years, fell off these people, and there emerged the wild man, the animal man, as he had roamed the virginal earth long ago. Any conception of justice was lost—only force was recognized. For women the only law was the thirst for pleasure. The most seemly matrons behaved like prostitutes, going eagerly from man to man and speaking the obscene language of the bordellos. Girls ran through the streets offering their innocence to strangers, taking their favorites to the nearest door and giving themselves in unknown beds. Drunkards caroused in cellars, disregarding the corpses which lay forgotten around them. The situation of children abandoned to their fate by their parents was pitiful. Some were violated by disgusting libertines, others were tortured by sadists who now appeared in considerable numbers. Children died from hunger in their nurseries and from shame and injury after they were violated; they were slaughtered intentionally and accidentally. It was even said that human monsters hunted down children to eat their flesh to satisfy their awakening cannibalistic instincts.

In the last days of the tragedy Horace DeVille, of course, could not help all people. But he set up a refuge in the City Hall for those who were still sound in mind. The entrances to the building were barricaded and constantly guarded. Food and water for 3000 people for forty days was available. But DeVille was joined by only 1800 individuals, both men and women. Certainly there were others in the city who were still healthy, but they didn't know about DeVille's refuge and they remained hidden in their homes. Many individuals were afraid to go out onto the streets and even now the bodies of those who died of hunger alone in their rooms are still being found. It's remarkable that there were so few cases of Contradiction among those locked up in the City Hall. DeVille knew how to maintain discipline within his small group. Until his last day on earth, DeVille maintained a journal, and this journal, along with DeVille's telegrams is our best source of information concerning the catastrophe. The journal was found in a secret cabinet in the City Hall which was reserved for valuable papers. Its last entry is dated July 20. DeVille wrote that an enraged mob had begun to storm the City Hall, and that he had been forced to drive them away with revolver fire. "I don't know what hope there is," wrote DeVille. "We can't expect help until spring. But we'll never survive that long on the supplies which I have at my disposal. But I will do my duty to the end." Those were his last noble words!

We must assume that the City Hall was taken on July 21 and its defenders killed or scattered. DeVille's body has not yet been found. We have no reliable information about what happened in the city after July 21. From the evidence which has been found as the city is being cleaned up, we must assume that anarchy reached its final limits. You can imagine the gloomy streets dimly lighted by the glow from bonfires of burning furniture and books. The fires were ignited by striking flint against steel. Around the fires caroused crowds of drunken and insane people. A cup was passed from hand to hand, with both men and women drinking. Here too scenes of animal sensuality were enacted. Some kind of dark atavistic emotions stirred in the souls of these city people and half-naked, unwashed, unkempt, they danced the dances of their remote ancestors, the contemporaries of cave bears, and they sang the same wild songs as the hordes who fell onto mammoths with stone axes. With the songs, with incoherent speeches, with idiotic laughter could be heard the insane cries of the stricken who had even lost the ability to express their delirious dreams in words, and the groans of the dying who lay writhing in the midst of rotting corpses. Sometimes fighting took the place of the dances—for a barrel of wine, for a beautiful woman or simply for no reason at all, in a burst of madness which drove a man to absurd, contradictory acts. There was nowhere to flee: everywhere the same terrible scenes, everywhere orgies, fighting, animal joy and animal rage—or absolute darkness which seemed even more terrible, even more unbearable to the shattered imagination.

Star City became a huge, black box where a few thousand survivors in human form were imprisoned in the stench of hundreds of thousands of decaying corpses, where among the living there was not one individual who was aware of his situation. This was the city of the mad, a gigantic institution for the insane, the most gigantic and repulsive Bedlam the world had ever seen. And these madmen were destroying each other, striking with daggers, biting at each other's throats, dying from madness, dying from terror, dying from hunger and all the maladies which reigned in the infected air.

Of course the government of the Republic did not remain an indifferent spectator of the cruel misfortune which had struck the capital. But very soon it had to abandon any hope of providing assistance. Physicians, nurses, military units and government servants categorically refused to go to Star City. When the electric trains and dirigibles ceased to function, direct contact with the city was lost since the severe climate precluded any other means of communication. In addition, the government's attention was soon captured by the cases of Contradiction which appeared in other cities of the Republic. At times these occurrences also threatened to become epidemics and panic began in a manner similar to what had occurred in Star City. This led to a mass emigration from all the Republic's population centers. Work ceased at all factories and the country's industrial life declined. But, thanks to decisive and timely measures the epidemic was halted in other cities and nowhere did it reach the dimensions it had achieved in the capital.

The anxiety with which the entire world followed the misfortunes of the young Republic is well known. At first, when no one expected the disaster to grow to its monstrous proportions, the most common attitude was one of curiosity. The leading newspapers of all countries (and this includes our own Northern European Evening Herald) sent special correspondents to Star City to report on the epidemic's course. Many of these brave knights of the pen fell victims to their professional responsibilities. When news was received concerning the dangerous nature of the epidemic, various governments and private societies offered their services to the Republic's government. Some sent troops, others teams of doctors, yet others gave financial contributions, but events moved with such speed that the greater part of these measures could not be executed in full. When railroad communication with Star City was broken off, the only source of information about life in the city was the telegrams sent by the Chief of the City. These telegrams were immediately disseminated to all ends of the earth in millions of copies.

After the failure of the city's electrical system, the telegraph continued to function for a few more days on battery power. The exact reason why the telegraph service failed completely is not known: perhaps the equipment was sabotaged. Horace DeVille's final telegram was dated June 17. From that time for a period of nearly six weeks humanity had no word from the Republic's capital.

Several attempts were made to reach Star City by air during the month of July. Several new dirigibles and flying machines were sent to the Republic. However, for a long period of time these attempts ended in failure. Finally an aviator, Thomas Billy, succeeded in reaching the unfortunate city. He picked up two individuals from the city roof who had long since lost their reason and who were half dead from cold and hunger. Through the ventilators Billy could see that the streets were plunged in absolute darkness and he could hear wild cries which indicated that living beings were still in the city. Billy decided not to descend into the city itself. Late in August one of the electric railroad lines was opened as far as Lissis, sixty five miles from the city. A detachment of well-armed men equipped with food and emergency medical supplies entered the city through the Northwest Gates. This squad, however, could not penetrate beyond the first blocks of buildings as a consequence of the terrible stench. It was necessary to advance step by step, removing corpses from the streets and freshening the air by artificial means. All the people they met alive in the city were completely irresponsible. They were like frenzied animals and they had to be physically restrained. Finally, in the middle of September, regular communications were opened with the city and its systematic renovation was begun.

At the present time the greater part of the city has been cleared of the dead. Electric light and heat has been restored. Only the American quarter remains untouched, but it is assumed that no one remains alive there. Nearly 10,000 people survived, but most of them suffer from incurable mental afflictions. Those who have more or less recovered are very unwilling to talk about their experiences in those calamitous days. Moreover, their accounts are full of contradiction and very often they are not supported by documentary evidence. In some locations various copies of newspapers have been found which were published in the city before the end of July. The last of those which has been found, dated July 22, contains a description of the death of Horace DeVille and a call to restore the refuge in the City Hall. It is true that a sheet was found dated in August, but its contents are such that one must identify its author (who, probably, also set his raving into type) as totally irresponsible. Horace DeVille's journal, which provides a regular chronicle of events from June 28 to July 20, has been found in the City Hall. On the basis of the terrible discoveries on the streets and inside buildings it is possible to recreate a vivid picture of the frenzied events in those last days in the city. Terribly mutilated corpses have been found everywhere: people who died of starvation, people strangled and tortured, people murdered by madmen in a fit of fury, and finally—half eaten bodies. Corpses have been found in the most unexpected locations: in subways, sewers, storerooms, boilers: men who had lost their reason fled the terror around them everywhere. Almost all buildings had been pillaged and the goods which turned out to be useless to the looters had been hidden in secret rooms or in cellars.

There is no doubt that Star City will not be habitable for several more months. Now it is nearly abandoned. In the city which could house as many as 3,000,000 inhabitants there now live about 30,000 workers who are clearing the streets and buildings. One must add that some former habitants have returned to claim the bodies of their loved ones and to collect the remnants of their property. A few tourists have also arrived, attracted by the spectacle of the deserted city. Two businessmen have already opened two hotels which are doing rather well. Entertainers have already been hired for a night club which will be opening soon. *The Northern European Evening Herald*, for its part has sent a new correspondent, Mr. Andrew Ewald, to the city and it intends to acquaint its readers with any new discoveries which will be made in the unfortunate capital of the Republic of the Southern Cross.

(1905) Translated by Leland Fetzer

Fyodor Kuzmich Sologub
(1863–1921)

The Asteroid

Beyond the course of Mars, I race around the Sun,
Unknown to Earth am I—a dark-hued Asteroid.
A surge of molten metal is my living blood,
My living flesh—a quivering colloid.

My earthly twin, I cannot come to your embrace,
By Draco's breath I'm blown away to empty reaches.
And only from afar I view the Sun's bright face,
I'm cast to rest upon no Earthly beaches.

I envy you: you range at will, my weakling friend,
You change your wheeling course, yet cloaked in narrow vizard.
But my fate is—to trace my circle without end,
All in the selfsame, endless, weary, blizzard.

Translated by A.L & M.K.

A Little Man

I

Iakov Alexeevich Saranin was just short of average height. His wife, Aglaia Nikiforovna, from merchant stock, was tall and bulky. And now, in the first year of her married life, the twenty-year-old woman was already so hefty that beside her scrawny little husband she looked like an Amazon.

"And what if she fills out even more?" thought Iakov Alexeevich.

So he thought, even though he had married for love—love both for her and for her dowry.

The difference in the proportions of man and wife frequently provoked sarcastic remarks from their friends. These thoughtless gibes poisoned Saranin's peace of mind and made Aglaia laugh.

Once Saranin returned home thoroughly upset after an evening with some people from the office during which he'd had to put up with more than his share of barbed comments.

Lying in bed beside Aglaia, he kept muttering and nagging at his wife. Aglaia protested sluggishly and unenthusiastically, her voice sleepy.

"Well, what should I do? It's not my fault." She had a very calm and peaceful disposition.

Saranin grumbled: "Stop swilling down the meat, don't stuff your gut with so much starch; you're gobbling candy all day long."

"But look, you can't expect me to eat nothing if I have a healthy appetite," Aglaia replied. "When I was still single, my appetite was even better."

"I can imagine: I can just see you eating a whole bull at one sitting."

"You can't eat a bull at one sitting," Aglaia retorted calmly.

She soon fell asleep, but Saranin could not get to sleep on that strange autumn night.

He tossed and turned for a long time. When sleep denies itself to the Russian, he meditates. And Saranin gave himself up to that activity, which was so uncharacteristic of him at other times. For he was a civil servant: there was not much to think about, and no particular reason for doing so.

"There must be some way," Saranin ruminated. "Every day science makes amazing discoveries; in America they make noses of every imaginable shape for people. They grow new skin on your face. The kind of operations they do—they drill holes in your skull, they cut your guts or your heart open and then sew them back up again. Isn't there really any way either for me to grow or for Aglaia to take off a little flesh? What if there's some secret means? But how to find it? How? Well, just lying around you certainly won't find it. God helps them who help themselves. But as for looking . . . A secret remedy! Maybe he, the inventor, is just walking around in the streets looking for a customer. Sure, what else? After all, he can't advertise in the papers. But in the streets you can peddle anything you want when nobody's looking. That's very likely. So he walks around and offers it confidentially. Anyone who needs a secret remedy won't be lolling in bed."

After pondering things in this manner, Saranin quickly began to dress, purring to himself.

"'At twelve o'clock midnight . . .'"

He did not worry about waking his wife. He knew that Aglaia was a sound sleeper.

"Like a merchant," he said aloud; "like a clod," he thought to himself.

He finished dressing and went out into the street. He did not have the slightest desire to sleep. His heart felt light, and his mood was that of the inveterate seeker of adventures on the verge of a new and interesting experience.

The peaceful civil servant, who had lived a quiet and colorless life for a third of a century, suddenly felt stirring in him the heart of the hunter in the trackless deserts, enterprising and free—a hero of Cooper or Mayne Reid.

But after he had taken a few steps along the familiar route—toward his office—he stopped and began to reflect. Where exactly should he go? Everything was quiet and peaceful, so peaceful that the street seemed like the corridor of a vast building, quite ordinary, quite safe, and isolated from the unpredictable outside world. Janitors dozed by gates. At the intersection a policeman could be seen. The street lamps glowed. The paving stones of the sidewalks and the cobbles of the roadway gleamed faintly with the moisture of a recent rainfall.

Saranin thought a while, and then in quiet confusion he began to walk straight ahead, and then turned to the right.

II.

At the intersection of two streets he saw, in the light of the lamps, a man coming toward him. His heart lay heavy in joyful anticipation.

It was a strange figure.

A robe of bright colors, with a wide belt. A tall hat, sharp-pointed, with black designs. A thin beard dyed saffron, long and narrow. Gleaming white teeth. Burning black eyes. Feet in slippers.

"An Armenian!" Saranin suddenly thought for some reason or other.

The Armenian came up to him and said: "Dear heart, what is it you spend your nights looking for? Why do you not go to bed or else to beautiful maidens? Want me to take you there?"

"No, I have more than enough of my own beautiful maiden," said Saranin.

And he trustingly revealed his misfortune to the Armenian.

The Armenian bared his teeth and neighed: "Big wife, little husband—to kiss, you need a ladder. Oi, no good!"

"What could possibly be good about it!"

"Follow me. I will help a good man."

They walked through the quiet corridor-like streets for a long time, the Armenian in front, Saranin behind. As they moved from street lamp to street lamp, the Armenian kept undergoing a strange transformation. In darkness he grew, and the further he moved away from the street lamp, the more enormous he became. Sometimes the sharp peak of his hat seemed to be rising above the houses into the cloudy sky. Then, as he approached the light, he became smaller and directly under the lamp he would resume his former dimensions and would look like a plain ordinary peddler in a robe. And, strangely enough, Saranm was not surprised at this phenomenon. He was in such a trusting mood that the most spectacular wonders of the Arabian fairy tales would have seemed just as ordinary to him as the insignificant doings of drab everyday life.

At the gates of a house, a most ordinary structure, five stories high and painted yellow, they stopped. The light markings on the lamp at the gate stood out clearly, Saranin noted: "No. 41."

They went into the courtyard; then up the staircase of a building in the rear. The staircase lay in semi-darkness. But the door the Armenian stopped in front of was dimly illuminated by a small lamp, and Saranin could make out numbers: "No. 43."

The Armenian reached into his pocket, took out a small bell—the kind used in country houses to call servants—and rang it. The bell gave out a pure, silvery tinkle.

At once the door opened. Behind the door stood a barefoot boy, handsome, swarthy, with very bright red lips. His white teeth gleamed, for he was smiling, either in delight or in mockery. And he seemed to be always smiling. The comely boy's eyes glowed with a greenish luster. His whole body was lithe, like a kitten's, and impalpable, like the phantom of a quiet nightmare. He looked at Saranin, smiling. Saranin became terrified.

They went in. With a lithe and sinuous bend of his body the boy closed the door, and walked before them along a corridor, carrying a lantern in his hand. He opened a door, and again—another impalpable movement, then laughter.

A dreadful dark narrow room, the walls lined with cabinets holding some kind of flasks and small bottles. There was a strange odor, an irritating and mysterious odor.

The Armenian lit a lamp, opened a cabinet, rummaged around in it and brought out a flask containing a greenish liquid.

"Good drops," he said. "You will put one drop in a glass of water, she will just fall asleep without a sound and will not wake up."

"No, I don't want that," Saranin said irritably. "Did you think that was really what I came for?"

"Dear heart," the Armenian said persuasively. "You will take another wife, your own size—the simplest thing in the world."

"I don't want to!" cried Saranin.

"Now do not shout," the Armenian stopped him. "Why are you angry, dear heart, why are you upsetting yourself for nothing? You do not want them, do not take them, I will give you another kind. But the other ones are so expensive—oi, oi, so expensive!"

The Armenian squatted—which made his long figure look ludicrous—and brought out a square-shaped bottle. In it gleamed a transparent liquid. The Armenian said quietly, with a mysterious air: "You drink a drop—a pound will come off; you drink forty drops—forty pounds come off. A drop—a pound. A drop—a rouble. Count the drops, give the roubles."

Joy flamed in Saranin's heart.

"How much is it I need?" Saranin began to reckon. "There must be about two hundred pounds of her. Take off a hundred and twenty or so, and then there'll be a nice petite little wife. That'll be fine."

"Give me a hundred and twenty drops."

The Armenian shook his head. "You want much—no good will come of it."

Saranin flared up. "That's nobody's business but mine."

The Armenian looked at him searchingly. "Count the money."

Saranin took out his wallet. "All tonight's winnings, and I have to add some of my own," he thought.

In the meantime the Armenian had brought out a flask of cut glass, and he began to drip the liquid into it.

Sudden doubt quickened in Saranin's mind. "A hundred and twenty roubles is no little cash. And what if he should cheat me?" He asked hesitantly, "Are you sure they work?"

"The goods speak for themselves," said the proprietor. "I will show you right now how they work. Caspar!" he shouted.

The same barefoot boy entered. He was wearing a red jacket and short dark-blue trousers. His swarthy legs were exposed above the knees. They were shapely and beautiful, and they moved gracefully and nimbly.

The Armenian gave a wave of his hand. Caspar deftly shed his clothes. He approached the table.

The candles cast a dim light on his yellow body, lithe, strong, and beautiful. And on his obedient depraved smile. On his black eyes and the blue rings under them.

The Armenian said: "If you drink these drops straight, it will work at once. If you mix them in water or wine, it will work slowly—you will not see it happening before your eyes. If you do not mix them thoroughly, it will work in leaps, and that will not be pretty."

He took a narrow graduated cylinder, poured some liquid into it, and handed it to Caspar. Caspar simpered like a spoiled child who is given something sweet, drank the liquid to the bottom, threw his head back, licked the last sweet drops with his long sharp tongue, which was like that of a poisonous snake— and at once, before Saranin's very eyes, he began to shrink. He stood erect, looked at Saranin, laughed, and began to change, like the doll you buy at the Carnival fair which collapses when the air is let out.

The Armenian took him by the elbow and placed him on the table. The boy was the size of a candle. He danced and made faces.

"But what will become of him now?" asked Saranin.

"Dear heart, we will grow him again," replied the Armenian.

He opened the cabinet, and from the top shelf he took down another vessel of an equally strange shape. The liquid in it was green. The Armenian poured a bit of the liquid into a tiny goblet the size of a thimble. He handed it to Caspar.

Once again Caspar drank, as he had the first time. Slowly and surely, like water rising in a bathtub, the naked boy grew bigger and bigger. Finally he returned to his former dimensions.

The Armenian said: "Drink it with wine, or with water, or with milk, drink it with anything you want—only do not drink it with Russian kvas or your hair will start to fall out all over the place."

III.

A few days passed.

Saranin radiated happiness. He kept smiling enigmatically. He was awaiting an opportunity. The opportunity came. Aglaia was complaining of a headache.

"I have a remedy," Saranin said. "It really helps."

"No remedies will help," Aglaia said, making a sour face.

"No, this one will help. I got it from a certain Armenian."

He said this with such assurance that Aglaia was convinced of the effectiveness of the remedy he had got from the Armenian.

"Oh, all right, have it your way, I'll take it."

He brought the little flask.

"Does it have a nasty taste?" Aglaia asked.

"It tastes just fine and it really does help. Only it'll give you a touch of the runs."

Aglaia made a face.

"Drink it, drink it."

"Can I put it in some Madeira?"

"All right."

"And you have some Madeira with me too," Aglaia said in the tone of a spoiled child.

Saranin poured two glasses of Madeira, and emptied the potion into his wife's glass.

"I feel sort of chilly," Aglaia said softly and listlessly. "A shawl would be nice."

Saranin ran to get a shawl. When he came back the glasses were standing as before. Aglaia was sitting and smiling.

He wrapped the shawl around her.

"I seem to feel a bit more comfortable," she said. "Should I drink?"

"Drink, drink," Saranin exclaimed. "To your health."

He took up his glass. They drank. She roared with laughter. "What's the matter?" Saranin asked. "I switched the glasses. You're the one who'll have the runs, not me."

He shuddered. He turned pale. "What have you done?" he cried in despair.

Aglaia laughed and laughed. Her laughter seemed repulsive and cruel to Saranin.

Suddenly he remembered that the Armenian had a restorant. He ran to the Armenian.

"He'll really scalp me," he fretted. "But who cares about money? Let him take everything, as long as I can save myself from the horrible effects of this potion."

IV.

But ill fate had evidently fallen upon Saranin.

On the door of the apartment where the Armenian had lived hung a padlock. Saranin tugged at the bell in despair. A mad hope gave him strength. He rang the bell furiously.

On the other side of the door the bell rang loudly, distinctly, clearly—with that relentless clarity bells have only in empty apartments. Saranin ran to the janitor. He was pale. Tiny, fine beads of sweat, like dew on a cold rock, broke out on his face and especially on his nose.

He rushed into the janitor's room and shouted: "Where's Khalatyants?"

A phlegmatic black-bearded individual, the head janitor, was drinking tea from a saucer. He turned a disapproving gaze on Saranin. He asked imperturbably: "And what is it you want of him?"

Saranin stared blankly at the janitor, and did not know what to say.

"If you got some sort of business with him, mister," the janitor said, eying Saranin suspiciously, "then you better go away. On account of he's an Armenian we'd better look out or we'll get in trouble with the cops."

"Oh, where is that damned Armenian!" Saranin exclaimed in despair. "The one from No. 43."

"There ain't no Armenian," replied the janitor. "There was one, there sure was, I ain't saying there wasn't, except now there ain't no more."

"Well, where is he then?"

"Gone."

"Where?" Saranin shouted.

"Who knows?" the janitor answered with complete unconcern. "He fixed himself up a foreign passport and left the country."

Saranin turned pale.

"Look, try to understand," he said with a trembling voice, "I really need him desperately."

He began to weep.

The janitor looked at him sympathetically and said: "Don't break your heart over it, sir. If you really need the damned Armenian so, then you leave the country too, go to the address bureau there and you'll find him where the address is."

Saranin did not grasp the absurdity of what the janitor was saying. He took heart.

He ran home at once, whirled like a hurricane into the head janitor's office, and demanded that the head janitor arrange for a foreign passport without delay. But suddenly he remembered: "But where am I to go?

V.

The damned potion was doing its evil work as slowly and relentlessly as fate. With every passing day Saranin grew smaller and smaller. His clothes hung on him like a sack.

The people who knew him wondered. They said:

"Aren't you sort of smaller? Have you stopped wearing heels?" "You've gotten thinner too." "You're working too hard." "What's the point of killing yourself?"

Finally whenever they met him they would gasp: "What is the matter with you?"

Saranin's acquaintances began jeering at him behind his back: "He's growing down." "He's striving toward the minimum."

His wife finally noticed it a little later. He had been diminishing before her very eyes, gradually—and she had paid no attention. She noticed it from the baggy appearance of his clothing.

At first she roared with laughter at the peculiar decrease in her husband's dimensions. Then she began to get angry.

"This is very, very strange and indecent," she said. "Could I really have married such a Lilliputian!"

Soon it became necessary to alter all his clothing. All his old things were falling off him, his trousers came up to his ears, and his top hat fell down to his shoulders.

One day the head janitor of the building came into the kitchen.

"What's going on around here?" he asked the cook sternly.

"Ain't none of my affair," fat red-faced Matryona was just about to burst out angrily, but she caught herself in time and said: "Ain't nothing special going on. Everything's just like always."

"But look, your master's started manifesting certain actions— now, is this permitted? What we really should do is hand him over to the law," the head janitor said very sternly.

The chain on his belly bounced angrily.

Matryona suddenly sat down on a trunk and began to cry.

"You don't have to tell me, Sidor Pavlovich," she said. "The mistress and I can't get over it, we can't figure out what's the matter with him."

"For what reason? And on what grounds?" the head janitor exclaimed angrily. "Now is this really permitted?"

"Only one comfort," said the cook, sniffling, "he don't eat so much grub."

The longer—the smaller.

Domestics, tailors, and everyone Saranin happened to come in contact with began to treat him with un-concealed contempt. He would for instance be running to work—a little man, barely able to drag an enormous brief-case with both his hands—and he would hear behind him the gloating laughter of a doorman, a janitor, of cabbies, of kids.

"Our nice little gentleman!" said the head janitor.

Saranin tasted much gall. He lost his wedding ring. His wife made a scene. She wrote to her parents in Moscow.

"The damned Armenian!" Saranin thought.

He often recalled how the Armenian, in counting out the drops, had poured too much in.

"Oh!" Saranin had exclaimed.

"Do not worry, dear heart, that is my mistake; I will charge you nothing for it."

Saranin even went to a doctor. As he examined him he made playful comments. He found everything in order.

Or Saranin would be paying a visit to someone. At first the doorman would not let him in.

"Now, who would you be?" Saranin would tell him.

"I don't know," the doorman would say; "our folks don't receive this kind."

VI.

At work, in the office, people at first cast glances at him and laughed. Especially the young men. Still alive were the traditions of the colleagues of Akakii Akakievich Bashmachkin.

Then they began to grumble and speak what was on their minds.

The doorman now began to remove his overcoat with obvious reluctance.

"Look at the kind of officials we have nowadays," he grumbled; "such small fry. What can you expect to get from a type like this at Christmas?"

And to keep up his prestige Saranin was forced to tip more lavishly and more frequently than before. But this did very little good. The doorman accepted the money, but looked at Saranin suspiciously.

Saranin blurted out to one of his colleagues that it was an Armenian who had done him dirt. The rumor about an Armenian intrigue quickly spread through the office. It even reached other offices . . .

The head of the office on one occasion came upon the little official in the hall. He looked him over in surprise. He said nothing. He returned to his office.

Then it was deemed necessary to report the matter. The head of the office asked: "Has this been going on long?"

The deputy head began to stammer.

"It's a pity you didn't notice it in good time," the director said acidly, without waiting for an answer. "It's strange that I didn't know about it. I regret it very much."

He had Saranin summoned. While Saranin was on his way to the director's office, all the clerks looked at him with stern disapproval.

His heart trembling, Saranin went in to the boss's office. A faint hope still remained with him—the hope that His Excellency intended to entrust him with a very flattering mission, one that would take advantage of his small stature, such as sending him to an international exhibition, or on some secret mission. But with the first sounds of the acid, directorially departmental voice this hope vanished like smoke.

"Sit down here," said His Excellency, pointing at a chair.

Saranin managed to climb up. The director took one angry look at the official's legs dangling in the air. He asked: "Mr. Saranin, are you familiar with the laws of civil service by government appointment?"

"Your Excellency," Saranin began to babble, and folded his little hands on his chest in an imploring gesture.

"How did you have the audacity to go against government procedures so brazenly?"

"Believe me, Your Excellency . . ."

"Why have you done this?" asked the director.

And Saranin could no longer say anything. He began to cry. Of late he was very easily moved to tears.

The director looked at him. He shook his head. He began to speak very sternly: "Mr. Saranin, I have invited you here to inform you that your inexplicable behavior is becoming completely intolerable."

"But Your Excellency, it would seem that I . . . everything efficiently . . ." Saranin babbled, "as for my stature . . ."

"Yes, precisely."

"But this misfortune is beyond my control."

"I am in no position to judge to what extent this strange and improper occurrence is a misfortune for you, and to what extent it is beyond your control, but I must tell you that for the office which has been entrusted to me your strange diminution is becoming positively scandalous. Many insinuating rumors are already circulating in the town. I cannot judge how well founded they are, but I do know that these rumors link your behavior with propaganda for Armenian separatism. You must agree that the department cannot be a place for hatching an Armenian intrigue directed at the dismemberment of the Russian sovereign power. We cannot keep officials who behave so strangely."

Saranin jumped off the chair, trembled, squealed:

"A trick of nature, Your Excellency."

"Strange, but the service . . ." And again he repeated the same question: "But why have you done it?"

"Your Excellency, I myself don't know how this has happened."

"Such instincts! By taking advantage of your smallness you can easily conceal yourself under any lady's—excuse the expression— skirt. This cannot be tolerated."

"I have never done that," Saranin screamed.

But the director was not listening. He continued:

"I have even heard that you are doing this out of sympathy for the Japanese. But one must recognize a limit in everything."

"But how could I be doing this, Your Excellency?"

"I do not know. But I ask you to put a stop to it. You could be retained in the service, but only in the provinces, and on the condition that this be stopped at once, and that you resume your usual dimensions. To restore your health you are given a four-month leave of absence. I request that you no longer come to the department. All the necessary papers will be sent to your home. My respects."

"Your Excellency, I am capable of working. Why the leave of absence?"

"You will take it for reasons of health."

"But I am well, Your Excellency."

"Now, now, please."

Saranin was given a leave of absence for four months.

VII.

Before long, Aglaia's parents arrived for a visit. This was after dinner. At dinner Aglaia spent a long time ridiculing her husband. She had gone to her room.

He timidly went into his study, which was now so enormous for him, clambered up onto the couch, huddled in one corner, and began to cry. An oppressive feeling of bewilderment gnawed at him.

Why had such a misfortune fallen on him and nobody else? A ghastly, unparalleled misfortune.

What carelessness!

He sobbed and whimpered despairingly.

"Why, oh, why did I do it?"

Suddenly he heard familiar voices in the hallway. He began to tremble with fear. He tiptoed over to the washstand, so people would not notice his red and swollen eyes. But even washing was a chore—a chair had to be put in front of the stand.

The guests were already coming into the parlor. Saranin greeted them. He bowed to all of them and squeaked something unintelligible. Aglaia's father gaped at him oafishly. He was big, fat, with a bull's neck and a red face. Aglaia took after him.

Planting himself in front of his son-in-law with his legs wide apart he looked around warily, carefully took Saranin's hand, bent over slightly, and, lowering his voice, said: "Son-in-law, we've come for a little get-together."

It was evident that he intended to act circumspectly. He was feeling things out.

From behind his back emerged Aglaia's mother, a scrawny and spiteful type. She began to shrill: "Where is he? Where? Aglaia, show me this Pygmalion."

She was looking over Saranin's head. She deliberately did not notice him. The flowers on her head swayed strangely. She was coming straight for Saranin. He gave a squeak and jumped aside.

Aglaia began to cry and said: "Here he is, Mamma."

"I'm here, Mamma," Saranin squealed and clicked his heels in a bow.

"You rat, what have you done to yourself? Why have you lopped so much off yourself?"

The maid snorted.

"You, dearie, don't go snorting at your betters."

Aglaia blushed.

"Mamma, let's go into the living room."

"Wait a minute. Speak up, you little rat. What are you making such a pygmy of yourself for?"

"Now hold on, just a minute. Mother," the father stopped her.

She jumped on her husband too. "Didn't I tell you not to marry her off to someone without a beard? Well, it turns out I was right."

The father kept glancing warily at Saranin and trying to switch the conversation to politics. "The Japanese," he was saying, "are approximately of a not very great stature, but to all appearances they're a real brainy nation, and even, incidentally, resourceful."

VIII.

And so Saranin grew small, very small. By now he could walk under a table very easily. And every day he grew slighter. He had not yet put his leave of absence to full use, except that he no longer went to the office. But they had not yet made plans to go anywhere.

Aglaia sometimes jeered at him, sometimes cried and said: "Where can I take you the way you are? It's a shame and a disgrace."

A walk from the study to the dining room became a trip of consider-able scope. And furthermore, to climb up on a chair . . .

On the other hand, fatigue as such was pleasant.

It stimulated the appetite and the hope of growing. Saranin positively attacked his food. He devoured it out of all proportion to his miniature measurements. But he was not growing. On the contrary. He was getting tinier and tinier. Worst of all, the shrinking sometimes went in leaps, at the most inconvenient times. As if he were doing tricks.

Aglaia got the notion of passing him off as a boy and enrolling him in the gymnasium. She went to the nearest one. But the conversation with the director disheartened her.

Papers were required. It turned out that the plan could not be realized.

With an air of extreme bewilderment the director told Aglaia: "We can-not admit a senior civil servant. What would we do with him? The teacher might tell him to stand in the comer, and he would say: 'I wear the Anna Cross.' This is very awkward."

Aglaia put on an imploring face and made an attempt to plead with him: "Couldn't it be arranged somehow? He won't dare to be naughty—I'll see to that.'

The director remained adamant. "No," he said stub-bornly, "a govern-ment official cannot be admitted to a gymnasium. Nowhere, in no directive, has provision been made. And it would be most awkward to go to higher authority with a representation of this kind. One never knows how they would look at it. It might create serious trouble. No, absolutely impossible. If you wish, you may appeal to the superintendent."

But Aglaia no longer had the courage to go to see authorities.

IX.

One day a young man, his hair slicked down until it gleamed, came to see Aglaia. He clicked his heels in a courtly bow. He introduced himself. "I represent the firm of Strigal and Co. A top-quality store in the busiest cen-ter of the capital's aristocratic traffic. We have a great many customers in the best and highest society."

Aglaia, just to be on the safe side, made eyes at the representative of the illustrious firm. With a languid movement of her plump hand she directed him to a chair. She sat down with her back to the light. She inclined her head to the side. She prepared herself to listen.

The dazzlingly coiffured young man continued: "We have learned that it was your spouse's pleasure to prefer a singularly miniature size. Therefore, our firm, facilitating the very latest vogues in the domain of ladies' and gentlemen's fashions, has the honor to propose to you, madam, with a view toward advertising, that we should, at no charge at all, tailor some suits for the gentleman according to the very best Paris fashion magazine."

"For free?" Aglaia asked languidly.

"Not only for free, madam, but even with an honorarium, for your own, so to speak, benefit, but on one small and easily fulfilled condition."

Meanwhile Saranin, overhearing that the conversation was about him, had made his way into the living room. He pattered around the young man with the dazzling coiffure. He kept clearing his throat and tapping his heels. He was very much annoyed that the representative of the firm Strigal and Co. paid not the slightest attention to him.

Finally he ran right up to the young man. He gave a thunderous squeak: "Haven't you been told that I'm at home?"

The representative of the illustrious firm arose. He made a courtly bow. He sat down. He turned to Aglaia: "Only one tiny condition."

Saranin snorted disdainfully. Aglaia began to laugh. She said, her curious eyes gleaming: "All right, tell me what the condition is."

"Our condition is that the gentleman be good enough to sit in the window of our store as a living advertisement."

Aglaia chortled with malicious glee.

"Splendid! Anything to get him out of my sight."

"I won't agree," Saranin began to squeak in a piercing voice. "I can never bring myself to that. I am a senior civil servant and the holder of a decoration. To sit in the window of a store for advertising—why, I think that's positively ridiculous."

"Be quiet!" Aglaia shouted. "Nobody's asking you."

"What do you mean, nobody's asking me?" Saranin screamed. "How long will I suffer from these minority groups?"

"Oh, the gentleman is mistaken," the young man objected politely. "Our firm has nothing in common with minority elements. All our employees are Russian Orthodox and Lutherans from Riga. And we do not employ any Jews."

"I don't want to sit in the window!" Saranin shouted.

He was stamping his feet. Aglaia grabbed him by the arm. She pulled him into the bedroom.

"Where are you dragging me?" cried Saranin. "I won't. Let me go!"

"I'll quiet you down," Aglaia shouted.

She shut the door tight.

"I'll give you a beating you'll remember," she said, her teeth clenched. She started pummeling him. He thrashed around helplessly in her powerful arms. "You pygmy, you're in my power. I can do whatever I want to you. I can stick you in my pocket. How dare you resist me! I don't care anything about your titles. I'll give you such a beating you won't be able to tell night from day."

"I'll lodge a complaint," Saranin squealed.

But he soon realized that resistance was useless. He was too small, and it was obvious that Aglaia had decided to bring all her strength to bear on the business at hand.

"Enough, enough," he howled. "I'll go into Strigal's window. I'll sit there—the disgrace will be yours. I'll put on all my decorations."

Aglaia roared with laughter.

"You'll put on whatever Strigal gives you," she shouted.

She dragged her husband out into the living room. She threw him to the salesman. She shouted: "Here he is! Take him away at once! And the money in advance! Every month!"

Her words were hysterical shrieks.

The young man took out his wallet. He counted out two hundred roubles.

"Not enough!" Aglaia screamed.

The young man gave a smile. He reached for another hundred-rouble note.

"I am not empowered to go any higher," he said politely. "In a month you will be receiving the next installment."

Saranin was running around the room.

"Into the window! Into the window!" he was screaming. "You damned Armenian! What have you done to me?"

And suddenly he settled by another three inches or so.

X.

Saranin's helpless tears, Saranin's anguish . . . What do Strigal and his partners care about that?

They paid. They are asserting their rights. The cruel rights of the capital.

Under the sway of Mammon, even a senior civil servant and the holder of a decoration occupies a position which fully corresponds to his exact dimensions, but which in no way accords with his pride. A Lilliputian dressed in the latest style runs around in the window of a fashionable store. Sometimes he is lost in contemplation of the pretty girls—so enormous!—sometimes he angrily shakes his little fists at boys who laugh at him.

At the windows of Strigal and Co. there is a crowd.

In the store of Strigal and Co. the clerks are knocked off their feet.

The workshop of Strigal and Co. is deluged with orders.

Strigal and Co. are basking in glory. Strigal and Co. are expanding their workshops.

Strigal and Co. are rich. Strigal and Co. are buying up houses.

Strigal and Co. are magnanimous: they feed Saranin royally, they spare no expense for his wife.

Aglaia is already getting a thousand a month.

Aglaia has also found other sources of income.

And acquaintanceships.

And lovers. And diamonds.

And carriages. And a house.

Aglaia feels cheerful and satisfied. She has filled out even more. She wears high-heeled shoes. She selects charming hats of gigantic dimensions.

When she visits her husband she pets him and feeds him from her finger, as if he were a bird. Saranin, in a dress suit with short tails, patters around on the table before her and squeaks something. His voice is piercing, like the whine of a mosquito. But the words are inaudible.

Puny little people may speak, but their peeping is inaudible to people of larger dimensions—Aglaia, Strigal, and his entire company. Aglaia, surrounded by clerks, listens to the squealing and peeping of this person. She chortles. She goes away.

Saranin is carried to the window where a full apartment has been set up for him in a nest of soft fabrics, its open side facing the public.

The tough street kids see a tiny little man sitting down at the table and starting to write petitions. Tiny, tiny petitions for the restoration of his rights that have been violated by Aglaia and by Strigal and Co. He writes. He sticks them into a tiny envelope. The kids die laughing.

Aglaia, meanwhile, takes her seat in a resplendent carriage. She is going for a drive before dinner.

XI.

Neither Aglaia nor Strigal and Co. gave any thought to how all this would end. They were content with the present. It seemed that there would be no end to the rain of gold that showered on them. But the end came. A most ordinary one. One that should have been anticipated.

Saranin kept getting tinier. Every day several new suits were made for him, each time smaller.

And suddenly, just after he had put on some tiny new trousers, he became altogether miniscule, before the eyes of the astonished clerks. He swam out of his tiny trousers. And he had already become as small as the head of a pin.

There blew a light draft of air. Saranin, as tiny as a dust speck, rose into the air. He whirled around. He merged with a cloud of dust specks dancing in a sunbeam.

He disappeared.

All searches were in vain. Nowhere could Saranin be found.

Aglaia, Strigal and Company, the police, the clergy, the authorities—all were at a complete loss.

How was Saranin's disappearance to be officially formulated?

Finally, after consultation with the Academy of Sciences, it was decided to consider him as having been sent on a mission with a scientific purpose.

Then they forgot about him.

Saranin came to an end.

(1905) Translated by Maurice Friedberg

Andrei Bely
[Boris Nicholaievich]
(1880–1934)

Demon

But why does He, you whisper dreaming,
Disturb the muse of pallid days?
Pale porphyry—a pallid Demon—
I make my foray from the Shades.

You see how Space, my pitch-black raiment,
Slips down my form in dark cascade,
My hand—my endless arm extended—
Has raised on high a Comet's blade.

Let not your blushing gazes teeter:
From racing rains, the Meteor
Cuts clean across the cosmic Ether.
See now—such is my boundless World.

Moscow, 1907
Translated by A.L. and M.K.

Petersburg

[from] *The Prologue*

< . . . > Nevsky Prospect possesses a striking attribute: it consists of a space for the circulation of the public. It is delimited by numbered houses. The numeration proceeds house by house, which considerably facilitates the finding of the house one needs. Nevsky Prospect, like any prospect, is a public prospect, that is: a prospect for the circulation of the public (not of air, for instance). The houses that form its lateral limits are-hmmm . . . yes: . . . for the public. Nevsky Prospect in the evening is illuminated by electricity. But during the day Nevsky Prospect requires no illumination.

Nevsky Prospect is rectilineal (just between us), because it is a European prospect; and any European prospect is not merely a prospect, but (as I have already said) a prospect that is European, because . . . yes . . .

For this very reason, Nevsky Prospect is a rectilineal prospect. Nevsky

Prospect is a prospect of no small importance in this un-Russian-but nonetheless-capital city. Other Russian cities are a wooden heap of hovels.

And strikingly different from them all is Petersburg.

But if you continue to insist on the utterly preposterous legend about the existence of a Moscow population of a million-and-a-half, then you will have to admit that the capital is Moscow, for only capitals have a population of a million-and-a-half; but as for provincial cities, they do not, never have had, and never will have a population of a million-and-a-half. And in conformance with this preposterous legend, it will be apparent that the capital is not Petersburg.

But if Petersburg is not the capital, then there is no Petersburg. It only appears to exist.

However that may be, Petersburg not only appears to us, but actually does appear—on maps: in the form of two small circles, one set inside the other, with a black dot in the center; and from precisely this mathematical point, which has no dimension, it proclaims forcefully that it exists: from here, from this very point surges and swarms the printed book; from this invisible point speeds the official circular.

[from] *Chapter the First*
in which an account is given of a certain worthy person, his mental games,
and the ephemerality of being

> A time of terror it has been,
> Still fresh in painful recollection . . .
> Of it, my friends-for amity-
> I now take up my retrospection.
> My story will be full of woe . . .
>
> Pushkin, *The Bronze Horseman*
> *Translated by by A.L. and M.L.*

APOLLON APOLLONOVICH ABLEUKHOV

Apollon Apollonovich Ableukhov was of venerable stock: he had Adam as his ancestor. But that is not the main thing: it is more important that one member of this venerable stock was Shem, progenitor of the Semitic, Hessitic, and red-skinned peoples.

Here let us make a transition to ancestors of an age not so remote.

Their place of residence was the Kirghiz-Kaisak Horde, whence, in the reign of the Empress Anna Ioannovna, Mirza Ab-Lai, the great-great-grand-father of the senator, valiantly entered the Russian service, having received, upon Christian baptism, the name Andrei and the sobriquet Ukhov. For brevi-ty's sake, Ab-Lai-Ukhov was later changed to Ableukhov, plain and simple.

This was the great-great-grandfather who was the source of the stock.

< . . . >

The Carriage Flew into the Fog

An icy drizzle sprayed streets and prospects, sidewalks and roofs. It sprayed pedestrians and rewarded them with the grippe. Along with the fine dust of rain, influenza and grippe crawled under the raised collars of a school-boy, a student, a clerk, an officer, a shady type. The shady type cast a dismal eye about him. He looked at the prospect. He circulated, without the slight-est murmur, into an infinity of prospects—in a stream of others exactly like him—amidst the flight and din, listening to the voice of automobile roulades.

And—he stumbled on the embankment, where everything came to an end: the voice of the roulades and the shady type himself. From far, far away, as though farther off than they should have been, the islands sank and cowered in fright; and the buildings cowered; it seemed that the waters would sink and that at that instant the depths, the greenish murk would surge over them. And over this greenish murk the Nikolaevsky Bridge thun-dered and trembled in the fog.

On this sullen morning the doors of a yellow house flew open. The win-dows of the house gave onto the Neva. And a gold-braided lackey rushed to beckon the coachman. Gray horses bounded forward and drew up a car-riage on which was depicted a coat of arms: a unicorn goring a knight.

A jaunty police officer passing by the carriage porch gave a stupid look and snapped to attention when Apollon Apollonovich Ableukhov, in a gray coat and a tall black top hat, with a stony face resembling a paperweight, ran rapidly out of the entryway and still more rapidly ran onto the foot-board of the carriage, drawing on a black suede glove as he ran.

Apollon Apollonovich Ableukhov cast a momentary, perplexed glance at the police officer, the carriage, the coachman, the great black bridge, the expanse of the Neva, where the foggy, many-chimneyed distances were so wanly etched, and whence Vasilievsky Island looked back at him in fright.

The lackey in gray hastily slammed the carriage door. The carriage flew headlong into the fog; and the police officer who had happened by glanced over his shoulder into the dingy fog, where the carriage had flown head-long. He sighed and moved on. The lackey looked there too: at the expanse of the Neva, where the foggy, many-chimneyed distances were so wanly etched, and whence Vasilievsky Island looked back at him in fright.

Here, at the very beginning, I must break the thread of my narrative, in order to introduce the reader to the scene of action of a certain drama.

Squares, Parallelepipeds, Cubes

There, where nothing but a foggy damp hung suspended, at first appeared the dull outline, then descended from heaven to earth the dingy, blackish gray St. Isaac's Cathedral: at first appeared the outline and then the full shape of the equestrian monument of Emperor Nicholas I. At its base the shaggy hat of a Nicholas grenadier thrust out of the fog.

The carriage was flying toward Nevsky Prospect.

Apollon Apollonovich Ableukhov was gently rocking on the satin seat cushions. He was cut off from the scum of the streets by four perpendicular walls. Thus he was isolated from people and from the red covers of the damp trashy rags on sale right there at this intersection.

Proportionality and symmetry soothed the senator's nerves, which had been irritated both by the irregularity of his domestic life and by the futile rotation of our wheel of state.

His tastes were distinguished by their harmonious simplicity.

Most of all he loved the rectilineal prospect; this prospect reminded him of the flow of time between the two points of life.

There the houses merged cubelike into a regular, five-story row. This row differed from the line of life: for many a wearer of diamond-studded decorations, as for so many other dignitaries, the middle of life's road had proven to be the termination of life's journey.

Inspiration took possession of the senator's soul whenever the lacquered cube cut along the line of the Nevsky: there the numeration of the houses was visible. And the circulation went on. There, from there, on clear days, from far, far away, came the blinding blaze of the gold needle, the clouds, the crimson ray of the sunset. There, from there, on foggy days—nothing, no one.

And what was there were lines: the Neva and the islands. Probably in those distant days, when out of the mossy marshes rose high roofs and masts and spires, piercing the dank greenish fog in jags—

—on his shadowy sails the Flying Dutchman winged his way toward Petersburg from there, from the leaden expanses of the Baltic and German Seas, in order here to erect, by delusion his misty lands and to give the name of islands to the wave of onrushing clouds.

Apollon Apollonovich did not like the islands: the population there was industrial and coarse. There the many-thousand human swarm shuffled in the morning to the many-chimneyed factories. The inhabitants of the islands are reckoned among the population of the Empire; the general census has been introduced among them as well.

Apollon Apollonovich did not wish to think further. The islands must be crushed! Riveted with the iron of the enormous bridge, skewered by the arrows of the prospects . . .

While gazing dreamily into that illimitability of mists, the statesman suddenly expanded out of the black cube of the carriage in all directions and soared above it. And he wanted the carriage to fly forward, the prospects to fly to meet him—prospect after prospect, so that the entire spherical surface of the planet should be embraced, as in serpent coils, by blackish gray cubes of houses; so that all the earth, crushed by prospects, in its lineal cosmic flight should intersect, with its rectilineal principle, unembraceable infinity; so that the network of parallel prospects, intersected by a network of prospects, should expand into the abysses of the universe in planes of squares and cubes: one square per "solid citizen," so that. . . .

After the line, the figure which soothed him more than all other symmetries was the square.

At times, for hours on end, he would lapse into an unthinking contemplation of pyramids, triangles, parallelepipeds, cubes, and trapezoids.

While dwelling in the center of the black, perfect, satin-lined cube, Apollon Apollonovich revelled at length in the quadrangular walls. Apollon Apollonovich was born for solitary confinement. Only his love for the plane geometry of the state had invested him in the polyhedrality of a responsible position.

* * *

The wet, slippery prospect was intersected by another wet prospect at a ninety-degree right angle. At the point of intersection stood a policeman.

And exactly the same kind of houses rose up, and the same kind of gray human streams passed by there, and the same kind of yellow-green fog hung there.

But parallel with the rushing prospect was another rushing prospect with the same row of boxes, with the same numeration, with the same clouds.

There is an infinity of rushing prospects with an infinity of rushing, intersecting shadows. All of Petersburg is an infinity of the prospect raised to the nth degree.

Beyond Petersburg, there is nothing.

THE INHABITANTS OF THE ISLANDS STARTLE YOU

It was the last day of September.

On Vasilievsky Island, in the depths of the Seventeenth Line, a house enormous and gray looked out of the fog. A dingy staircase led to the floors. There were doors and more doors. One opened.

And a stranger with the blackest of small mustaches appeared on its threshold.

Rhythmically swinging in his hand was a not exactly small and yet not very large bundle tied up in a dirty napkin with a red border design of faded pheasants.

The staircase was black, strewn with cucumber peels and a cabbage leaf crushed under foot. The stranger slipped on it.

He then grasped the railing with one hand; the other hand (with the bundle) described a zigzag. The stranger wished to protect the bundle from a distressing accident, from falling onto the stone step, because the movement of his elbow mimicked a tightrope walker's turn.

Then, meeting the porter, who was climbing the stairs with a load of aspen wood over his shoulder, the stranger began to show increased concern about the fate of the bundle, which might catch against a log.

When the stranger reached the bottom, a black cat underfoot hitched up its tail and cut across his path, dropping chicken innards at the stranger's feet. And a spasm contorted his face.

Such movements are peculiar to young ladies.

And movements of precisely this same kind sometimes mark those of our contemporaries who are exhausted by insomnia. The stranger suffered from insomnia: his smoke-redolent habitation hinted at that. And the bluish tinge of the delicate skin of his face also bore witness.

The stranger remained standing in the courtyard, a quadrangle completely paved with asphalt and pressed in from all sides by the five stories of the many-windowed colossus. Stacked in the middle of the courtyard were damp cords of aspen wood. And visible through the gate was a section of the windswept Seventeenth Line.

Oh, you lines!

In you has remained the memory of Petrine Petersburg.

The parallel lines were once laid out by Peter. And some of them came to be enclosed with granite, others with low fences of stone, still others with fences of wood. Peter's line turned into the line of a later age: the rounded one of Catherine, the regular ranks of colonnades.

Left among the colossi were small Petrine houses: here a timbered one, there a green one, there a blue, single-storied one, with the bright red sign "Dinners Served:" Sundry odors hit you right in the nose: the smell of sea salt, of herring, of hawsers, of leather jacket and of pipe, and of nautical tarpaulin.

Oh, lines!

How they have changed: how grim days have changed them!

The stranger recalled: on a summer evening, in the window of that gleaming little house, an old woman was chewing her lips. Since August the window had been shut. In September a brocade-lined coffin was brought.

He was thinking it was getting more and more expensive to live. Life was hard for working folk. From over there pierced Petersburg, both with the arrows of prospects and with a gang of stone giants.

From over there rose Petersburg: there buildings blazed out of a wave of clouds. There, it seemed, hovered someone spiteful, cold. From over there, out of the howling chaos someone stared with stony gaze, skull and ears protruding into the fog.

All of that was in the mind of the stranger. He clenched his fist in his pocket. And he remembered that the leaves were falling.

He knew it all by heart. These fallen leaves were the last leaves for many. He became a bluish shadow.

* * *

And as for us, here's what we'll say: oh, Russian people, oh, Russian people! Don't let the crowd of shadows in from the islands! Black and damp bridges are already thrown across the waters of Lethe. If only they could be dismantled . . .

Too late. . . .

And the shadows thronged across the bridge. And the dark shadow of the stranger.

Rhythmically swinging in his hand was a not exactly small, yet not very large bundle.

AND, CATCHING SIGHT, THEY DILATED, LIT UP, AND FLASHED . . .

The aged senator communicated with the crowd that flowed in front of him by means of wires (telegraph and telephone). The shadowy stream seemed to him like the calmly current news of the world. Apollon Apollonovich was thinking: about the stars. Rocking on the black cushions, he was calculating the power of the light perceived from Saturn.

Suddenly—

—his face grimaced and began to twitch. His bluerimmed eyes rolled back convulsively. His hands flew up to his chest. And his torso reeled back, while the top hat struck the wall and fell on his lap.

The involuntary nature of his movement was not subject to explanation. The senator's code of rules had not foreseen . . . Contemplating the flowing silhouettes, Apollon Apollonovich likened them to shining dots. One of these dots broke loose from its orbit and hurtled at him with dizzying speed, taking the form of an immense crimson sphere—

—among the bowlers on the corner, he caught sight of a pair of eyes. And the eyes expressed the inadmissible. They recognized the senator, and, having recognized him, they grew rabid, dilated, lit up, and flashed.

Subsequently, on delving into the details of the matter, Apollon Apollonovich understood, rather than remembered, that the upstart intellectual was holding a bundle in his hand.

Hemmed in by a stream of vehicles, the carriage had stopped at an intersection. A stream of upstart intellectuals had pressed against the senator's carriage, destroying the illusion that he, Apollon Apollonovich, in flying along the Nevsky, was flying billions of miles away from the human myriapod. Perturbed, Apollon Apollonovich had moved closer to the window. At that point he had caught sight of the upstart intellectual. Later he had remembered that face, and was perplexed by the difficulty of assigning it to any of the existing categories.

It was at just that moment that the stranger's eyes had dilated, lit up, and flashed.

In the swarms of dingy smoke, leaning back against the wall of the carriage, he was still seeing the same thing in his eyes. His heart pounded and expanded, while in his breast arose the sensation of a crimson sphere about to burst into pieces. < . . . >

THUS IT IS ALWAYS

A phosphorescent blot raced across the sky, misty and deathlike. The Heavens gradually misted over in a phosphorescent glow, making iron roofs and chimneys flicker. Here flowed the waters of the Moika. On one side loomed that same three-storied building, with projections on top.

Wrapped in furs, Nikolai Apollonovich was making his way along the Moika, his head sunk in his overcoat. Nameless tremors arose in his heart. Something awful, something sweet . . .

He thought: could *this* too be love? He recalled. He shuddered.

A shaft of light flew by: a black court carriage flew by. Past window recesses it bore blood red, lamps that seemed drenched in blood. They played and shimmered on the black waters of the Moika. The spectral outline of a footman's tricorne and the outline of the wings of his greatcoat flew, with the light, out of the fog and into the fog.

Nikolai Apollonovich stood for a while in front of the house. He kept standing and then suddenly disappeared in the entryway.

The entryway door flew open before him; and the sound struck him in the back. Darkness enveloped him, as though all had fallen away (this is most likely how it is the first instant after death). Nikolai Apollonovich was not thinking about death now; he was thinking about his own gestures. And in the darkness his actions took on a fantastic stamp. He seated himself on the cold step by the door, his face buried in fur, listening to the beating of his heart.

Nikolai Apollonovich sat in the darkness.

* * *

The stone curve of the Winter Canal showed its plangent expanse. The Neva was buffeted by the onslaught of a damp wind. The soundlessly flying surfaces glimmered, the walls that formed the side of the four-storied palace gleamed in the moonlight.

No one, nothing.

Only the Canal streaming its waters. Was that shadow of a woman darting onto the little bridge to throw itself off? Was it Liza? No, just the shadow of a woman of Petersburg. And having traversed the Canal, it was still running away from the yellow house on the Gagarin Embankment, beneath which it stood every evening and looked long at the window.

Ahead the Square was now widening out. Greenish bronze statues emerged one after another from everywhere. Hercules and Poseidon looked on as always. Beyond the Neva rose an immense mass-the outlines of islands and houses. And it cast its amber eyes into the fog, and it seemed to be weeping.

Higher up, ragged arms mournfully stretched vague outlines across the sky. Swarm upon swarm they rose above the Neva's waves, coursing off toward the zenith. And when they touched the zenith, the phosphorescent blot would precipitously attack them, flinging itself upon them from the heavens.

The shadow of a woman, face buried in a muff, darted along the Moika to that same entryway from which it would dart out every evening, and where now, on the cold step, below the door, sat Nikolai Apollonovich. The entryway door closed in front of it; the entryway door slammed shut in front of it. Darkness enveloped the shadow, as though all had fallen away behind it. In the entryway, the black little lady thought about simple and earthly things. She had already reached her hand toward the bell, and it was then that she saw an outline, apparently masked, rise up before her from the step.

And when the door opened and a shaft of light illuminated the darkness of the entryway for an instant, the exclamation of a terrified maid confirmed it all for her, because first there appeared in the open door an apron and an overstarched cap; then the apron and cap recoiled from the door. In the sudden flash a picture of indescribable strangeness was revealed. The black outline of the little lady flung itself through the open door.

Behind her back, out of the gloom, rose a rustling clown in a bearded, trembling half-mask.

One could see how, out of the gloom, the fur of the caped greatcoat soundlessly and slowly slid from the shoulders, and two red arms reached toward the door. The door closed, cutting off the shaft of light and plunging the entryway stairs once more into utter darkness.

* * *

In a second Nikolai Apollonovich sprang out into the street. From beneath the skirts of his greatcoat dangled a piece of red silk. His nose, buried-in-the greatcoat, he raced in the direction of the bridge.

* * *

On the iron bridge he turned. And saw nothing. Above the damp railing, above the greenish waters teeming with germs, bowler, cane, coat, ears, nose, and mustache rushed by into the gusts of Neva wind.

You Will Never Ever Forget Him!

In this chapter we have seen Senator Ableukhov. We have also seen the idle—thoughts of the senator in the form of the senator's house and in the form of the senator's son, who also carries his own idle thoughts in his head. Finally, we have seen another idle shadow—the stranger.

This shadow arose by chance in the consciousness of Senator Ableukhov and acquired its ephemeral being there. But the consciousness of Apollon Apollonovich is a shadowy consciousness because he too is the possessor of an ephemeral being and the fruit of the author's fantasy: unnecessary, idle cerebral play.

The author, having hung pictures of illusions all over, really should take them down as quickly as possible, breaking the thread of the narrative, if only with this very sentence. But the author will not do so: he has sufficient right not to.

Cerebral play is only a mask. Under way beneath this mask is the invasion of the brain by forces unknown to us. And granting that Apollon Apollonovich is spun from our brain, nonetheless he will manage to inspire fear with another, a stupendous state of being which attacks in the night. Apollon Apollonovich is endowed with the attributes of this state of being. All his cerebral play is endowed with the attributes of this state of being.

Once his brain has playfully engendered the mysterious stranger, that stranger exists, really exists. He will not vanish from the Petersburg prospects as long as the senator with such thoughts exists, because thought exists too.

So let our stranger be a real stranger! And let the two shadows of my stranger be real shadows!

Those dark shadows will, oh yes, they will follow on the heels of the stranger, just as the stranger himself is closely following the senator. The aged senator will, oh yes, he will, pursue you too, dear reader, in his black carriage. And henceforth you will never ever forget him!

End of the First Chapter

Translated by A. Maguire and J. Malmstad

C2. *Russia's Modernist and Post-Symbolist Prose*

THIS BRIEF SUBSECTION, just as the previous one, devoted principally to the poets, cannot even pretend to convey the period's true thematic richness. Yet even those who initially shared neither apocalyptic apprehensions nor Symbolist sensibilities eventually came around to the conviction that the future unfolding of the century heralded doom for their homeland. Perhaps the best example of this kind of transmogrification is represented in the writings of Alexander Ivanovich Kuprin (1870-1938). Kuprin, then a rising star in literature and an associate of the politically conscious *Knowledge* (Znanie) group, was a writer whose best-known works exposed and dissected social ills. In the heat of events surrounding Russia's 1905 revolution he illustrated the hopes of contemporary Russians in a brief magazine piece, *The Toast* (1906), in which technology, social engineering and enlightened anarchy are shown to have made the Earth a paradise, thriving even in the harshest conditions for life—at the Earth's poles. The piece is saved from outright propaganda on the benefits of social engineering by the emotional tribute, voiced at the end of the story, to the visions and sacrifices of early 20th-century revolutionaries. Yet, Kuprin was prescient in one regard: the reader should be struck by his description of global festivities, eerily reminiscent of the round-the-clock, satellite-assisted celebrations of Y2K.

But such festivities were hardly in view in the years immediately following the aborted success of the 1905 revolution, and Briusov's *The Republic of the Southern Cross*, offered in the previous subsection and describing the fall of another circumpolar society, might have been written in response to this work by Kuprin. Kuprin's own disillusionment with futuristic dreaming is reflected in the story *Liquid Sunshine* (1913), generally regarded to be the first Wellsean work of science fiction produced in Russia. The protagonists of writers like Chernyshevsky, Bulgarin and Odoevsky had been usually no more than devices allowing the author to describe future political or scientific transformations. In contrast, Kuprin strikes a more human note. His characters (just as those crafted by Wells) are individuals, and the narration is much more concerned with their particular personal response to events as they unfold. The Wellsean theme of global cooling and its attendant catastrophes also makes its appearance in *Liquid Sunshine*, and once again Kuprin seems prescient—this time in describing the destructive power of a tsunami, which we have witnessed quite recently indeed. The story recalls Dostoevsky as well: the most enlightened, altruistic man of science will in the end find himself at the mercy of his own self-destructive emotions. Human nature at its irreducible core is the true enemy of any utopia.

But the "tsunami" produced by the arrival of Bolshevik rule in 1917 was unlike any natural catastrophe Russia had witnessed earlier, and Remizov, Zamiatin and Pilniak, the last three writers chosen to represent the Modernist period—just as all those listed in the previous subsection—suffered from its mindless terror: Remizov and Zamiatin were forced into emigration and Pilniak died in a concentration camp. None of them was a Symbolist but each represented the very best the Symbolist school spawned. Of these three Evgeny I. Zamiatin (1884-1937) is best known in the west, and his dystopian novel *We*, together with *Notes from Underground* by Dostoevsky and *Petersburg* by Bely, forms a trio of requisite readings in Russian fantasy. Zamiatin is represented here by the initial chapters of *We* (which project an embodiment of the Grand Inquisitor's society into the future), and by two shorter works. One is the prose-jewel *The Dragon* which testifies to Zamiatin's full control of a fantastic scape in a miniature, and the other, a powerful short story *The Cave*—with an embedded text from Plato—in which the once-proud capital Petersburg is engulfed by a true apocalypse. We may recall that Pushkin's *The Bronze Horseman* begins with Peter the Great standing on the shore of the Gulf of Finland, and takes the reader on a whirlwind time-journey forward, to the same spot a century later—site of the glorious city that Peter's imagination and will had called into being. Peter's creation survives a flood, just as Noah's Arc does in the biblical story: Pushkin may mourn the cost of his poor protagonist's life, but in a way that celebrates the city's magnificence nonetheless. Zamiatin takes his reader on the reverse journey—in which the formerly modern city exists only in memories—backwards in time, to the frozen wasteland of the ice age. No archangel sounds his horn here; the apocalypse is heralded by the trumpeting of a wooly mammoth, emblem of a society reduced to primeval savagery whose inhabitants see death as a longed-for privilege. Robert Frost's *Fire and Ice*, written two years before *The Cave*, was chosen by us to serve as a prescient summation of Zamiatin's apocalyptic vision.

Alexei M. Remizov (1877-1957), another giant of Russian fantasy predating Zamiatin, shows very convincingly the apocalypse about to engulf Russia in his superb early story *The Blaze*, in which the role of the mystical monk is just as enigmatic as that of any Symbolist protagonist. What is clear in the story is that Russian folk culture had degenerated by Remizov's time to a set of debased superstitions, richly challenging those represented in Sologub's far better known novel, *Petty Demon*. Remizov's art is in lifting his readers from the common perspectives of the everyday world, and even from the conventional representations of a fairy-tale world. In his exquisite story *The Bear Cub*, a child's power of fantasy-weaving is given free rein as a young girl associates a snowflake with the constellation Ursa Major. *Russia in a Whirlwind* (1927) clearly shows that the old Russian culture whose richness Remizov so keenly embraced is doomed to destruction under the new regime, and his *Orison* (1917) is a mournful reflex of its medieval prototype (cited in Section I). Finally, the "meaning" of Petersburg gets an interesting and profound alternate expression in Remizov's novel *In A Rosy Light* (1952) from which we give the Prologue just as we have done with an excerpt from Bely's novel.

Old Russia and its former customs are given a nuanced portrayal by Boris A. Pilniak (1897-1937?) from whose writing we choose one pre-revolutinary work, a realist-impressionist tale *A Year in their Life* (1915, an echo of the bear motif in Russian culture), and one post-revolutionary sample from his famous novel *The Naked Year* (1921). The latter serves as a mini-representation of Pilniak's newly found and unique telegraphic style in prose fiction (enabling him to create an entire chapter in three phrases, for instance); it also shows the disintegration of folk-culture. The author obviously holds the Russian countryside as dear as Remizov does; alas, he also clearly shows that its legendary hero, Ilia of Murom, no longer inhabits Rus' and that the Russian forest awaits in vain for his return.

Alexander Ivanovich Kuprin
(1870–19380

A Toast

The two hundredth year of the new era was drawing to its close. In fifteen minutes it would be the 200th anniversary, to the month, day, and hour, of the time when the last country with an organized state system, the most obstinate, conservative and obtuse of all nations—Germany—finally decided to abandon its ridiculous and outdated national identity and happily joined the worldwide anarchist union of free peoples, to the jubilation of all the Earth. According to the ancient Christian calendar it was early in the year 2906.

The new year 200 was greeted nowhere with greater festivities than at the North and South Poles in the main stations of the huge Electrogeomagnetic Association. During the last thirty years, thousands of technicians, engineers, astronomers, mathematicians, architects, and other specialists had worked selflessly to complete one of the most inspired and heroic ideas of the second century. They had decided to turn the globe into a gigantic electromagnetic inductance coil and to carry this out they had wound a spiral of insulated steel cable, approximately three billion miles long, around the Earth from north to south. At both poles they erected electroterminals of exceptional capacity and then ran countless connecting cables from both of the polar stations to all corners of the Earth. This astonishing project was not only closely observed on Earth but also on neighboring planets with which the inhabitants of the Earth maintained constant communications. Many looked upon the Association's undertaking with scepticism, others with misgivings, and some even with horror.

But in the year just ended the Association had secured a brilliant victory over the sceptics. The Earth's inexhaustible magnetic power had set into motions all factories, agricultural machinery, railroads and ships. It had lighted all the streets and homes and heated all residences. It had made unnecessary the further use of coal, the deposits of which had long been exhausted. It had wiped the ugly smokestacks which poisoned the air from the face of the Earth. It had rescued the flowers, grass, and trees— the Earth's true treasure—from impending death and obliteration. Lastly, it had made fantastic achievements possible in agriculture, multiplying the average yield of the soil by four fold.

One of the North Station engineers, chosen as chairman for the occasion, stood up and raised his glass. Everyone immediately fell silent. He began:

"Comrades! By your leave I shall now make contact with our cherished colleagues at the South Station. We have just now received their signal."

The huge hall was of enormous length. It was a magnificent structure of glass, marble, and steel, adorned with exotic flowers and luxuriant trees, more like a beautiful botanical garden than a public hall. Outside, the polar night prevailed, but thanks to the action of special condensers, bright sunlight flooded the green plants, the tables, the faces of a thousand participants, the slender columns supporting the ceiling, and beautiful paintings and statues decorating every available space. Three walls of the hall were transparent, but the fourth, to the rear of the chairman, consisted of a white rectangular screen of an unusually delicate, brilliant, and fine glass.

With the consent of the gathering the chairman touched his finger to the small control knob on his table. Immediately, a blinding inner light filled the screen and then promptly faded, replaced by a view of another lofty and beautiful glass palace stretching off into the distance, and just as at this pole, robust, handsome people with happy faces appeared, dressed in light, glittering clothing. Some, although separated by thirteen thousand miles recognized one another, exchanged smiles and raised their glasses in greeting. Due to the general excitement and laughter, they were as yet unable to hear the voices of their distant friends.

Again the chairman rose to his feet and began his speech. His friends and colleagues at both ends of the world immediately fell silent. He said:

"My dear sisters and brothers! And you, delightful women, present recipients of my passion! And you, my sisters, former loves to whom my heart overflows with gratitude! Give me your attention! Glory to the only god on Earth—Man. Let us praise all the delights of His body and render up solemn and exalted homage to His immortal mind!

"I look upon you—proud, brave, coequal, happy—and an ardent love fires my soul! There are no restraints on our minds and nothing bars the fulfillment of our desires. We know not subservience, arbitrary power, envy, hostility, violence, and deception. Every day thousands of the Earth's secrets open to us and with endless joy we sense the infiniteness and omnipotence of knowledge. Even death itself holds no fear, for we depart from life not disfigured by old age, with neither terror in our eyes, nor curses on our lips, but beautiful, godlike and smiling, for we do not cling convulsively to the wretched vestiges of life, but serenely close our eyes like tired wayfarers. Our work is our delight. And our love, liberated from the shackles of servitude and triviality, is like the love of flowers, free and beautiful. Our only master is human genius!

"My friends! Am I perhaps declaiming long-known platitudes? I find myself unable to do otherwise. This morning I read a remarkable and frightening book, unable to put it down. That book is *A History of the Twentieth Century Revolution.*

"At times I wondered whether it was some sort of a fairy tale I was reading. The life of our forefathers, separated from us by nine centuries, struck me as so improbable, so monstrous, and so absurd.

"Vicious, dirty, disease ridden, misshapen, cowardly—they were like loathsome creatures locked up in a cramped cage. One would steal a piece of bread from another, carry it off to a dark corner and lie on it, so that a third would not catch sight of it. They would deprive each other of living quarters, wood, water, land and air. Hordes of gluttons and libertines, escorted by bigots, cheats, thieves, and tyrants, would set one mob of drunken slaves against a second mob of quavering idiots and live parasitically on the festering abscesses of social corruption. The Earth, so vast and lovely, was for the people as small and confining as a dungeon and as oppressive as a crypt.

"But then, among these submissive beasts of burden, among these cowardly, cringing slaves, proud, no longer patient individuals, heroes with ardent souls, raised their heads high. How could they have been born in that corrupt and timorous century—this is completely beyond all understanding! They stood in the squares and crossroads and shouted 'Hail Freedom!' In that horrible and bloody time when not even one private home was a safe refuge, when coercion, torture and murder were royally rewarded, these men, in their divine madness, cried out: 'Down with tyrants!'

"With their righteous impassioned blood they stained the flagstones. They went mad in prisons. They died on the gallows and fell before firing squads. Voluntarily they renounced all the pleasures of life save one—dying for the future freedom of mankind. ·

"My friends! Do you not see that bridge of corpses which unites our glowing present with the fearful and dark past? Do you not sense the river of blood that bore all mankind to the resplendent sea of universal happiness?

"Oh you, the nameless, the mute sufferers, may your memory live forever! When you were dying, your farseeing eyes, fixed on future centuries, smiled. You perceived us, liberated, strong, triumphant, and in that great moment of death you sent us your blessing.

"My friends! Let each of us silently, without a single word, alone in our hearts, drink to the memory of those distant martyrs. Let each of us feel upon himself their peaceful and beneficent gaze."

All drank in silence. Suddenly a woman of extraordinary beauty sitting next to the orator pressed her head to his chest and silently began to weep. And when she was asked the reason for her tears, she answered in a barely audible voice:

"In spite of everything . . . how would I have loved to have lived in those days . . . with them . . . with them . . ."

(1906)

Translated by Leland Fetzer

Liquid Sunshine

I, Henry Dibble, turn to the truthful exposition of certain important and extraordinary events in my life with the greatest concern and absolutely understandable hesitation. Much of what I find essential to put to paper will, without doubt, arouse astonishment, doubt, and even disbelief in the future reader of my account. For this I have long been prepared, and I find such an attitude to my memoirs completely plausible and logical. I must myself admit that even to me those years spent in part in travel and in part on the six-thousand-foot summit of the volcano Cayambe in the South American Republic of Ecuador often seem not to have been actual events in my life, but only a strange and fantastic dream or the ravings of a transient cataclysmic madness.

But the absence of four fingers on my left hand, recurring headaches, and the eye ailment which goes by the common name of night blindness, these incontrovertible phenomena compel me to believe that I was in fact a witness to the most astonishing events in world history. And, finally, it is not madness, not a dream, not a delusion, that punctually three times a year from the firm E. Nideston and Son, 451 Regent Street, I receive 400 pounds sterling. This allowance was generously left to me by my teacher and patron, one of the greatest men in all of human history, who perished in the terrible wreck of the Mexican schooner *Gonzalez*.

I completed studies in the Mathematical Department with special studies in Physics and Chemistry at the Royal University in the year . . . That too, is yet another persistent reminder of my adventures. In addition to the fact that a pulley or a chain took the fingers of my left hand at the time of the catastrophe, in addition to the damage to my optic nerves, etc., as I fell into the sea I received, not knowing when nor how, a sharp blow on the right upper quarter of my skull. That blow left hardly any external sign but it is strangely reflected in my mind, specifically in my powers of recall. I can remember well words, faces, localities, sounds, and the sequence of events, but I have forgotten forever all numbers and personal names, addresses, telephone numbers, and historical dates; the years, months, and days which marked my personal life have disappeared without a trace, scientific formulae, although I am able to deal with them without difficulty in logical fashion, have fled, and both the names of those I have known and know now have disappeared, and this circumstance is very painful to me. Unfortunately, I did not then maintain a diary, but two or three notebooks which have survived, and a few old letters aid me to a certain degree to orient myself.

Briefly, I completed my studies and received the title Master of Physics two, three, four, or perhaps even five years before the beginning of the twentieth century. Precisely at that time the husband of my elder sister, Maude, a farmer of Norfolk who periodically had loaned me material support and even more important moral support, took ill and died. He firmly believed that I would continue my scientific career at one of the English universities and that in time I would shine as a luminary to cast a ray of glory on his modest family. He was healthy, sanguine, strong as a bull, could drink, write a verse, and box—a lad in the spirit of good old merry England. He died as the result of a stroke one night after consuming one-fourth of a Berkshire mutton roast, which he seasoned with a strong sauce: a bottle of whiskey and two gallons of Scotch light beer.

His predictions and expectations were not fulfilled. I did not join the scientific ranks. Even more, I was not fortunate enough to find the position of a teacher or a tutor in a private or public school; rather, I fell into the vicious, implacable, furious, cold, wearisome world of failure. Oh! who, besides the rare spoiled darlings, has not known and felt on his shoulders this stupid, ridiculous, blind blow of fate? But it abused me for too lengthy a time.

Neither at factories nor at scientific agencies—nowhere could I find a place for myself. Usually I arrived too late: the position was already taken.

In many cases I became convinced that I had fallen into some dark and suspicious conspiracy. Even more often I was paid nothing for two or three months of labor and thrown onto the street like a kitten. One cannot say that I was excessively indecisive, shy, unenterprising, or, on the other hand, sensitive, vain or refractory. No, it was simply that the circumstances of life were against me.

But I was above all an Englishman and I held myself as a gentleman and a representative of the greatest nation in the world. The thought of suicide in this terrible period of my life never came to mind. I fought against the injustice of fate with cold, sober persistence and with the unshakable faith that never, never would an Englishman be a slave. And fate, finally, surrendered in the face of my Anglo-Saxon courage.

I lived then in the most squalid of all the squalid lanes in Bethel Green, in the God-forsaken East End, dwelling behind a chintz curtain in the home of a dock worker, a coal hauler. I paid him four shillings a month for the place, and in addition I helped his wife with the cooking, taught his three oldest children to read and write, and also scrubbed the kitchen and the back stairs. My hosts always cordially invited me to eat with them, but I had decided not to burden their beggar's budget. I dined, rather, in the dark basement and God knows how many cats', dogs', and horses' lives lay on my black conscience. But my landlord, Mr. John Johnson, requited my natural tact with attentiveness: when there was much work on the East End docks and not enough workmen and the wages reached extraordinary heights, he always managed to find a place for me to load heavy cargoes where with no difficulty I could earn eight or ten shillings in a day. It was unfortunate that this handsome, kind, and religious man became intoxicated every Sunday without fail and when he did so he displayed a great inclination toward fisticuffs.

In addition to my duties as cook and occasional work on the docks, I essayed numerous other ridiculous, onerous, and peculiar professions. I helped clip poodles and cut the tails from fox terriers, clerked in a sausage store when its owner was absent, catalogued old libraries, counted the earnings at horse races, at times gave lessons in mathematics, psychology, fencing, theology, and even dancing, copied off the most tedious reports and infantile stories, watched coach horses when the drivers were eating ham and drinking beer; once, in uniform, I spread rugs and raked the sand between acts in a circus, worked as a sandwich man, and even fought as boxer, a middleweight, translated from German to English and vice versa, composed tombstone inscriptions, and what else did I not do! To be candid, thanks to my inexhaustible energy and temperate habits I was never in particular need. I had a stomach like a camel, I weighed 150 pounds without my clothes, had good hands, slept well and was cheerful in temperament. I had so adjusted to poverty and to its unavoidable deprivations, that occasionally I could not only send a little money to my younger sister, Esther, who had been abandoned in Dublin with her two children by her Irish husband, an actor, a drunkard, a liar, a tramp, and a rake—but I also followed the sciences and public life closely, read newspapers and scholarly journals, bought used books, and belonged to rental libraries. I even managed to make two minor inventions: a very cheap device which would warn a railroad engineer in fog or snow of a closed switch ahead, and an unusual, long-lasting welding flame which burned hydrogen. I must say that I did not enjoy the income from these inventions—others did. But I remained true to science, like a knight to his lady, and I never abandoned the belief that the time would come when my beloved would summon me to her chamber with her bright smile.

That smile shone upon me in the most unexpected and commonplace fashion. One foggy autumn morning my landlord, the good Mr. Johnson, went to a neighboring shop for hot water and milk for his children. He returned with a radiant face, the odor of whiskey on his breath, and a newspaper in his hand. He gave me the newspaper, still damp and smelling of ink, and, pointing out an entry marked with a line from the edge of his dirty nail, exclaimed:

"Look, old man. As easy as I can tell anthracite from coke, I know that these lines are for you, lad."

I read, not without interest, the following announcement:

"The solicitors 'E. Nideston and Son,' 451 Regent Street, seek an individual for an equatorial voyage to a location where he must remain for not less than three years engaged in scientific pursuits. Conditions: age, 22 to 30 years, English citizenship, faultless health, discrete, sober and forbearing, must know one, or yet better, two other European languages (French and German), must be a bachelor, and so far as it is possible, free of family and other ties to his native land. Beginning salary: 400 pounds sterling per year. A university education is desirable, and in particular a gentleman knowing theoretical and applied chemistry and physics has an advantage in obtaining the position. Applicants are to call between nine and ten in the morning." I am able to quote this advertisement with such assurance since it is still preserved among my few papers, although I copied it off in haste and has been subject to the action of sea water.

"Nature has given you long legs, son, and good lungs," Johnson said, approvingly pounding my back. "Start up the engine and full steam ahead. No doubt there will be many more young gentlemen there of irreproachable health and honorable character than at Derby. Anne, make him a sandwich with meat and preserves. Perhaps he will have to wait his turn in line for five hours. Well, I wish you luck, my friend. Onward, brave England!"

I arrived barely in time at Regent Street. Silently I thanked nature for my good legs. As he opened the door the porter with indifferent familiarity said: "Your luck, mister. You got the last chance," and promptly fixed on the outside doors the fateful announcement: "The advertised opening is now closed to applicants."

In the darkened, cramped, and rather dirty reception room—such are almost all the reception rooms belonging to the magicians of the City who deal in millions—were about ten men who had come before me. They sat about the walls on dark, time-polished, soiled wooden benches, above which, at the height of a sitting man's head, the ancient wallpaper displayed a wide, dirty, band. Good God, what a pitiful collection of hungry, ragged men, driven by need, sick and broken, had gathered here, like a parade of monsters! Involuntarily my heart contracted with pity and wounded self esteem. Sallow faces, averted, malicious, envious, suspicious glances from under lowered brows, trembling hands, tatters, the smell of poverty, cheap tobacco, and fumes of alcohol long since drunk. Some of these young gentlemen were not yet seventeen years of age while others were past fifty. One after another, like pale shades, they drifted into the office and returned from there looking like drowned men only lately removed from the water. I felt both sickened and ashamed to admit to myself that I was infinitely healthier and stronger than all of them taken together.

Finally my turn came. Someone invisible opened the door from the other side and shouted abruptly and disgustedly in an exasperated voice:

"Number eighteen, and Allah be praised, the last!"

I entered the office, nearly as neglected as the reception room, different only that it was papered in peeling checked paper; it had two side chairs, a couch, and two easy chairs on which sat two middle-aged gentlemen of apparently the same medium height, but the elder of the two, in a long coot was slim, swarthy, and seemingly stern, while the other, dressed in a new jacket with silken lapels, was fair, plump, blue-eyed and sat at his ease one leg placed upon the other.

I gave my name and bowed not deeply, but respectfully. Then, seeing that I was not to be offered a seat, I was at the point of taking a place on the couch.

"Wait," said the swarthy one, "First remove your coat and vest. There is a doctor here who will examine you."

I remembered the clause in the advertisement which referred to irreproachable health, and I silently removed my outer garments. The florid stout man lazily freed himself from his chair and placing his arms around me he pressed his ear to my chest.

"Well, at least we have one with clean linen." he said casually.

He listened to my lungs and heart, tapped my spine and chest with his fingers, sat me down and checked the reflexes of my knees, and finally said lazily:

"As fit as a fiddle. He hasn't eaten too well recently, however. But that is nothing and all that is required is two weeks of good food. To his good fortune, I find no traces of exhaustion from over-indulgences in athletics as is common among our young men. In a word, Mr. Nideston, I present you a gentleman, a fortunate, almost perfect example of the healthy Anglo-Saxon race. May I assume that I am no longer needed?"

"You are free, doctor," said the solicitor. "But can you, may I be assured, visit us tomorrow morning, if I require your professional advice?"

"Oh, Mr. Nideston, I am always at your service."

When we were alone, the solicitor sat opposite me and peered intently into my face. He had little sharp eyes the color of a coffee bean with quite yellow whites. Every now and then when he looked directly at you, it seemed as though diminutive sharp and bright needles issued from those tiny blue pupils.

"Let us talk," he said abruptly. "Your name, origins, and place of birth?"

I answered him in the same expressionless and laconic fashion.

"Education?"

"The Royal University."

"Subject of study?"

"Department of Mathematics, in particular, Physics."

"Foreign languages?"

"I know German comparatively well. I understand when French is not spoken too rapidly, I can put together a few score essential expressions, and I read it without difficulty."

"Relatives and their social position?"

"Is that of any importance to you, Mr. Nideston?"

"To me? Of supreme unimportance. But I act in the interests of a third party."

I described the situations of my two sisters. During my speech he attentively inspected his nails, and then threw two needles at me from his eyes, asking:

"Do you drink? And how much?"

"Sometimes at dinner I drink a half pint of beer."

"A bachelor?"

"Yes, sir."

"Do you have any intention of committing that blunder? Of marrying?"

"Oh, no."

"Any present love affairs?"

"No, sir."

"How do you support yourself?"

I answered that question briefly and fairly, omitting, for the sake of brevity five or six of my latest casual professions.

"So," he said, when I had finished, "do you need money?"

"No. My stomach is full and I am adequately clothed. I always find work. So far as it is possible I follow recent developments in science. I am convinced that sooner or later I will find my opportunity."

"Would you like money in advance? A loan?"

"No, that is not my practice. I don't take money from anyone . . . But we're not finished."

"Your principles are commendable. Perhaps we can come to an agreement. Give me your address and I will inform you, and probably very soon, of our decision. Good-bye."

"Excuse me. Mr. Nideston," I responded. "I have answered all your questions, even the most delicate, with complete candor. May I ask you one question?"

"Please."

"What is the purpose of the journey?"

"Oho! Are you concerned about that?"

"We may assume that I am."

"The purpose of the journey is purely scientific."

"That is not an adequate answer."

"Not adequate?" Mr. Nideston abruptly shouted at me, and his coffee eyes poured out sheaves of needles. "Not adequate? Do you have the insolence to assume that the firm of Nideston and Son now in existence for one hundred and fifty years and respected by all of England's commercial establishments would suggest anything dishonorable or which might compromise you? Or that we would undertake any enterprise without possessing reliable guarantees beforehand that it is unconditionally legal?"

"Oh, sir, I have no doubt of that," I responded in confusion.

"Very well, then," he interrupted me and immediately became tranquil, like a stormy sea spread with oil. "But you see, first of all I am bound by the proviso that you not be informed of any substantial details of the journey until you are aboard the steamship out of Southampton . . ."

"Bound where?" I asked suddenly.

"For the time being I cannot tell you. And secondly, the purpose of your journey (if indeed it comes to pass) is not completely clear even to me."

"Strange," said I.

"Passing strange." the solicitor willingly agreed. "But I may also inform you, if you so desire, that it will be fantastic, grandiose, unprecedented, splendid, and audacious to the point of madness!"

Now it was my turn to say "Hmmm," and this I did with a certain restraint.

"Wait," Mr. Nideston exclaimed with sudden fervor. "You are young. I am twenty-five or thirty years older than you. You are not at all astonished by many of the greatest accomplishments of the human mind, but if, when I was your age, someone had predicted that I would work in the evenings by the light of invisible electricity which flowed through wires or that I would converse with an acquaintance at a distance of eighty miles, that I would see moving, laughing human figures on a screen, that I would send telegraph messages without the benefit of wires, and so on, and so on, then I would have waged my honor, my freedom, my career against one pint of bad London beer that I was confronted with a madman."

"You mean the project involves some new invention or a great discovery?"

"If you wish, yes. But I ask you, do not view me with distrust or suspicion. What would you say, for example, if a great genius were to appeal to your young energy, strength, and knowledge, a genius who, we will assume, is engaged with a problem—to create a pleasing, nutritious, economical food out of the elements found in the air? If you were provided the opportunity to labor for the sake of the future organization and adornment of the earth? To dedicate your talents and spiritual energies to the happiness of future generations? What would you say? Here is an example at hand. Look out the window."

Involuntarily I arose under the spell of his compelling, swift gesture and looked through the clouded glass. There, over the streets hung a black-rust-gray fog, like dirty cotton from heaven to earth. In it only dimly could be perceived the wavering glow from the street lights. It was eleven o'clock in the morning.

"Yes, yes, look," said Mr. Nideston. "Look carefully. Now assume that a gifted, disinterested man is summoning you to a great project to ameliorate and beautify the earth. He tells you that everything that is on the earth depends on the mind, will, and hands of man. He tells you that if God in his righteous anger has turned his face away from man, then man's measureless mind will come to his own aid. This man will tell you that fogs, disease, climatic extremes, winds, volcanic eruptions—they are all subject to the influence and control of the human will—and that finally the earth could become a paradise and its existence extended by several hundred thousand years. What would you say to that man?"

"But what if he who presents me with this radiant dream is wrong? What if I find myself a dumb plaything in the hands of a monomaniac? A capricious madman?"

Mr. Nideston rose, and. presenting me his hand as a sign of farewell, said firmly:

"No. Aboard the steamship in two or three months from now (if we can come to an agreement) I will inform you of the name of that scientist and the meaning of his great task, and you will remove your hat as a mark of your great reverence for the man and his ideas. But I, unfortunately, Mr. Dibble, am a layman. I am only a solicitor—the guardian and representative of others' interests."

After this interview I had almost no doubt that fate, finally, had grown tired of my fixed inspection of her unbending spine and had decided to show me her mysterious face. Therefore, that same evening with the help of my small savings I produced a banquet of extraordinary luxury, which consisted of a roast, a punch, plum pudding and hot chocolate which was enjoyed in addition to myself by the worthy couple, the elder Johnsons, and, I do not remember exactly—six or seven of the younger Johnsons. My left shoulder was quite blue and out of joint from the friendly pounding of my good landlord who sat next to me on my left.

And I was not wrong. The next evening I received a telegram: "Call at noon tomorrow. 451 Regent Street, Nideston."

I arrived punctually at the appointed time. He was not in his office, but a servant who had been forewarned led me to a small room in a restaurant located around the corner at a distance of two hundred paces. Mr. Nideston was there alone. At first he was not that ebullient, and perhaps even poetic man, who had spoken with me so fervently about the future happiness of mankind two days earlier. No, once more he was that dry and laconic solicitor who on the occasion of our first meeting that morning had so commandingly instructed me to remove my outer clothing and had questioned me like a police inspector.

"Good day. Sit down," he said indicating a chair. "It is my lunch hour, a time I have at my disposal. Although my firm is called 'Nideston and Son' I am in fact a bachelor and a lonely man. And so—would you care to dine? To drink?"

I thanked him and asked for tea and toast. Mr. Nideston ate at leisure, sipped an old port and from time to time transfixed me with the bright needles of his eyes. Finally, he wiped his lips, threw down his napkin, and asked:

"Then, you are agreed?"

"To buy a pig in a poke?" I asked in turn.

"No," he said loudly and angrily. "The previous conditions remain in force. Before your departure to the tropics you will receive as much information as I am empowered to give you. If this is not satisfactory, you may, on your part, refuse to sign the contract and I will pay you a recompense for the time which you have employed in fruitless conversations with me."

I observed him carefully. At that moment he was engaged in an effort to crack two nuts, the right hand enveloping the knuckles of the left. The sharp needles of his eyes were concealed behind the curtain of his brows. And suddenly, as though in a moment of illumination, I perceived all the soul of that man—the strange soul of a formalist and a gambler, the narrow specialist and an extraordinarily expansive temperament, the slave of his counting house traditions and at the same time a secret searcher for adventures, a pettifogger, ready for two pennies to put his opponent in prison for a long sentence, and at the same time an eccentric capable of sacrificing the wealth acquired in dozens of years of unbroken labor for the sake of the shadow of a beautiful idea. This thought passed through me like lightning. And Nideston, suddenly, as though we had been united by some invisible current, opened his eyes, with a great effort crushed the nuts into tiny fragments and smiled at me with an open, childlike, almost mischievous smile.

"When all is said and done, you are risking little, my dear Mr. Dibble. Before you leave for the tropics I will give you several commissions on the continent. These commissions will not require from you any particular scientific knowledge, but they will demand great mechanical accuracy, precision, and foresight. You will need no more than about two months, perhaps a week more or less than that. You are to accept in various European locations certain expensive and very fragile optical glasses as well as several extremely delicate and sensitive physical instruments. I entrust to your care, agility, and skills their packing, delivery to the railroad, and sea and rail transport.

You must agree that it would mean nothing to a drunken sailor or porter to throw a crate into the hold and smash into fragments a doubly convex lens over which dozens of men have worked for dozens of years . . ."

"An observatory!" I thought joyfully. "Of course, it's an observatory! What happiness! At last I have my elusive fate by the forelock."

I could see that he had guessed my thoughts and his eyes became yet merrier.

"We will not discuss the remuneration for this, your first, task. We will come to agreement on details, of course, as I can see from your expression. But," and then he suddenly laughed heedlessly, like a child, "I want to turn your attention to a very curious fact. Look, through these fingers have passed ten or twenty thousand curious cases, some of them involving very large sums. Several times I have made a fool of myself, and that in spite of all our subtle casuistic precision and diligence. But, imagine, that every time that I have rejected all the tricks of my craft and looked a man straight in the eye, as I am now looking at you, I have never gone wrong and never had cause for repentance. And so?"

His eyes were clear, firm, trusting and affectionate. At that second this little swarthy, wrinkled, yellow-faced man indeed took my heart into his hands and conquered it.

"Good," I said. "I believe you. From this time I am at your disposal."

"Oh, why so fast?" Mr. Nideston said genially. "You have plenty of time. We still have time to drink a bottle of claret together." He pulled the cord for the waiter. "But please put your personal affairs in order, and this evening at eight o'clock you will leave with the tide on board the steamship *The Lion and the Magdalene* to which I will in time deliver your itinerary, drafts on various banks, and money for your personal expenses. My dear young man, I drink to your health and your successes. If only," he suddenly exclaimed with unexpected enthusiasm, "if only you knew how I envy you, my dear Mr. Dibble!"

In order to flatter him and in quite an innocent manner, I responded almost sincerely:

"What's detaining you, my dear Mr. Nideston? I swear that in spirit you are as young as I."

The swarthy solicitor lowered his long delicately modeled nose into his claret cup, was silent for a moment and suddenly said with a sigh of feeling:

"Oh, my dear Mr. Dibble! My office, which has existed nearly from the time of the Plantagenets, the honor of my firm, my ancestors, thousands of ties connecting me with my clients, associates, friends, and enemies . . . I couldn't name it all . . . This means you have no doubts?"

"No."

"Well, let us drink a toast and sing "Rule Britannia!"

And we drank a toast and sang—I almost a boy, yesterday a tramp, and that dry man of business, whose influence extended from the gloom of his dirty office to touch the fates of European powers and business magnates— we sang together in the most improbable and unsteady voices in all the world:

Rule, Britannia!
Britannia, rules the waves!
Britons never, never, never will be slaves!

A servant entered, and turning politely to Mr. Nideston, he said:

"Excuse me, sir. I listened to your singing with genuine pleasure. I have heard nothing more pleasing even in the Royal Opera, but next to you in the adjoining room is a meeting of lovers of French medieval music. Perhaps I should not refer them as gentlemen . . . but they all have very discriminating ears."

"You are no doubt correct," the solicitor answered gently. "And therefore I ask you to accept as a keepsake this round yellow object with the likeness of our good king."

Here is a brief list of the cities and the laboratories which I visited after I crossed the Channel. I copy them out in entirety from my notebook: The Pragemow concern in Paris; Repsold in Hamburg; Zeiss, Schott Brothers, and Schlattf in Jena; in Munich the Frauenhof concern and the Wittschneider Optical Institute and also the Mertz laboratory there; Schick in Berlin, and also Bennech and Basserman. And also, not distant in Potsdam, the superb branch of the Pragemow concern which operates in conjunction with the essential and enlightened support of Dr. E. Hartnack.

The itinerary composed by Mr. Nideston was extraordinarily precise and included train schedules and the addresses of inexpensive but comfortable English hotels. He had drawn it up in his own hand. And here, too, one was aware of his strange and unpredictable character. On the corner of one of the pages he had written in pencil in his angular, firm hand: "If Chance and Co. were real Englishmen they would have not abandoned their concern and it would not be necessary for us to obtain lenses and instruments from the French and Germans with names like Schnurbartbindhalter."

I will admit, not in a spirit of boasting, that everywhere I bore myself with the requisite weight and dignity, because many times in critical moments in my ears I heard Mr. Nideston's terrible goat's voice singing "Britons never, never, never will be slaves."

But, too, I must say that I cannot complain about any lack of attentiveness and courtesy on the part of the learned scientists and famous technicians whom I met. My letters of recom-mendation signed with large, black, completely illegible flourishes and reinforced below with Mr. Nideston's precise signature served as a magic wand in my hands which opened all doors and all hearts for me. With unremitting and deep-felt concern I watched the manufacture and polishing of convex and curving lenses and the production of the most delicate, complex and beautiful instruments which gleamed with brass and steel, shining with all their screws, tubing, and machined metal. When in one of the most famous workshops of the globe I was shown an almost complete fifty-inch mirror which had required at least two or three years of final polishing—my heart stood still and my breath caught, so overcome was I with delight and awe at the power of the human mind.

I was rendered very uneasy by the persistent curiosity of these serious, learned men who in turn attempted to ascertain the mysterious purpose of my patron whose name I did not know. Sometimes subtly and artfully, sometimes crudely and directly, they attempted to extract from me the details and goal of my journey, the addresses of the firms with which I had business, the type and function of our orders to other workshops, etc., etc. But, firstly, I remembered well Mr. Nideston's very serious warnings about indiscretions; secondly, what could I answer even if I wished to? I myself knew nothing and was feeling my way, as though at night in an unknown forest. I was accepting, after verifying drawings and calculations, some kind of strange optical glasses, metal tubing of various sizes, calculators, small-scale propellors, miniaturized cylinders, shutters, heavy glass retorts of a strange form, pressure gauges, hydraulic presses, a host of electrical devices which I had never seen before, several powerful microscopes, three chronometers and two underwater diving suits with helmets. One thing became obvious to me: the strange enterprise which I served had nothing to do with the construction of an observatory, and on the basis of the objects which I was accepting I found it absolutely impossible to guess the purpose which they were to serve. My only concern was to ensure that they were packed with great care and I constantly devised ingenious devices which protected them from vibrations, concussion, and deformation.

I freed myself from impertinent questions by suddenly falling silent, and not saying a word I would look with stony eyes directly at the face of my interrogator. But one time I was compelled to resort to very persuasive eloquence: a fat, insolent Prussian dared to offer me a bribe of two thousand Marks if I would reveal to him the secret of our enterprise. This happened in Berlin in my own room on the fourth floor of my hotel. I succinctly and sternly informed that stout insolent creature that he spoke with an English gentleman. He neighed like a Percheron, slapped me familiarly on the back and exclaimed:

"Oh, come now, my good man, let's forget these jokes. We both understand what they mean. Do you think that I have not offered you enough? But we, like intelligent men of the world, can come to an agreement, I am sure . . ."

His vulgar tone and crude gestures displeased me inordinately. I opened the great window of my room and pointing below at the pavement I said firmly:

"One word more, and you will not find it necessary to employ the elevator to leave this floor. One, two, three . . ."

Pale, cowed, and enraged, he cursed hoarsely in his harsh Berlin accent, and on his way out slammed the door so hard that the floor of my apartment trembled and objects leaped upon the table.

My last visit on the continent was to Amsterdam. There I was to transmit my letters of recommendation to the two owners of two world famous diamond cutting firms, Maas and Daniels, respectively. They were intelligent, polite, dignified, and sceptical Jews. When I visited them in turn, Daniels first of all said to me slyly: "Of course you have a commission also for Mr. Maas." And Maas, as soon as he read the letter addressed to him, said with a query in his voice, "You have no doubt spoken with Mr. Daniels?"

Both of them displayed the greatest reserve and suspicion in their relations with me; they consulted together, sent off simple and coded telegrams, put to me the most subtle and detailed questions about my personal life, and so on. They both visited me on the day of my departure. A kind of Biblical dignity could be perceived in their words and movements.

"Excuse us, young man, and do not consider it a sign of our distrust that we inform you," said the older and more imposing, Daniels, "that on the route Amsterdam—London all steamships are alive with international thieves of the highest skill. It is true that we hold in strictest confidence the execution of your worthy commission, but who can be assured that one or two of these enterprising, intelligent, at times almost brilliant international knights of commerce will not manage to discover our secret? Therefore, we have not considered it excessive to surround you with an invisible but faithful police guard. You, perhaps, will not even notice them. You know that caution is never unwanted. Will you not agree that we and your associates would be much relieved if that which you transport were under reliable, observant, and ceaseless observation during the entire voyage? This is not a matter of a leather cigarette case, but two objects which cost together approximately one million three hundred thousand francs and which are unique in all the world, and perhaps in all the universe."

I, in the most sincere and concerned tone hastened to assure the worthy diamond cutter of my complete agreement with his wise and farsighted words. Apparently, my trust inclined him even more in my favor, and he asked in a low voice, in which I detected a quaver, an expression of awe:

"Would you like to see them?"

"If that is convenient, then please," I said, barely able to conceal my curiosity and perplexity.

Both the Jews almost simultaneously, with the expression of priests performing a holy ritual, took out of the side pockets of their long frock coats two small boxes—Daniels' was of oak while that of Maas was of red morocco; they carefully unfastened the gold clasps and lifted the lids. Both boxes were lined in white velvet and at first to me they appeared to be empty. It was only when I had bent close over them and looked closely that I saw two round, convex, totally colorless lenses of extraordinary purity and transparency, which would have been almost invisible except for their delicate, round, precise outlines.

"Astonishing workmanship!" I exclaimed, ecstatically. "Undoubtedly the polishing of glass in this manner must have required much expenditure of time."

"Young man!" said Daniels in a startled whisper. "They are not glass, they are two diamonds. The one from my shop weighs thirty and one-half carats and the diamond of Mr. Maas in all weighs seventy-four carats."

I was so stunned that I lost my usual composure.

"Diamonds? Diamonds cut into spheres? But that's a miracle such as I have never seen or heard. Man has never succeeded in producing anything like them!"

"I have already told you that these objects are unique in all the world," the jeweler reminded me solemnly, "But, excuse me, I am somewhat puzzled by your surprise. Did you not know about them? Had you in fact never heard of them?"

"Never in my life. You know that the enterprise which I serve is a closely guarded secret. Not only I, but also Mr. Nideston, are unacquainted with it in detail. I know only that I am collecting parts and equipment in various locations in Europe for some kind of an enormous project, whose purpose and plan I—a scientist by training—as yet understand nothing."

Daniels looked intently at me with his calm capable eyes, light brown in color, and his Biblical face darkened.

"Yes, that is so," he said slowly and thoughtfully after a brief pause. "Apparently you know nothing more than we, but do I perceive, when I look into your eyes, that even if you were informed of the nature of the enterprise, you would not share your information with us?"

"I have given my word, Mr. Daniels," I said as softly as possible.

"Yes, that is so, that is so. Do not think, young man, that you have come to our city of canals and diamonds completely unknown."

The Jew smiled a thin smile.

"We are even aware of the manner in which you suggested an aerial journey out of your window to a certain individual with commercial connections."

"How could anyone have known of that incident except the two of us involved?" I said, astonished. "Apparently, that German swine could not keep his mouth closed."

The Jew's face became enigmatic. He slowly and significantly passed his hand down his long beard.

"You should know that the German said nothing about his humiliation. But we knew about it the next day. We must! We whose guarded fire-proof vaults contain our own and others' valuables sometimes worth hundreds of millions of francs, must maintain our own intelligence. Yes. And three days later Mr. Nideston also knew of your deed."

"That's going too far!" I exclaimed in confusion.

"You have lost nothing, my young Englishman. Rather you have gained. Do you know how Mr. Nideston responded when he heard of the Berlin incident? He said: 'I knew that Mr. Dibble, an excellent young man, would have done nothing else.' For my part I would like to congratulate Mr. Nideston and his patron on the fact that their interests have fallen into such faithful hands. Although . . . Although . . . Although this disrupts certain of our schemes, our plans, and our hopes."

"Yes," confirmed the taciturn Mr. Maas.

"Yes," repeated quietly the Biblical Mr. Daniels, and once more a sad expression passed over his face. "We were given these diamonds in almost the same form in which you now see them, but their surfaces, as they had only recently been removed from the matrix, were crude and rough. We ground them as patiently and lovingly as though they were a commission from an emperor. To express it more accurately; it was impossible to improve on them. But I, an old man, a craftsman and one of the great gem experts of the world, have long been tortured by one cursed question: who could give such a shape to a diamond? Moreover, look at the diamond— here is a lens—not a crack, not a blemish, not a bubble. This prince of diamonds must have been subjected to the greatest heat and pressure. And I," and here Daniels sighed sadly, "and I must admit that I had counted much on your arrival and your candor."

"Forgive me, but I am in no position . . ."

"That's enough, I understand. But we wish you a pleasant journey."

My ship left Amsterdam that evening. The agents who accompanied me were so skilled at their work that I did not know who among the passengers was my guard. But toward midnight when I wished to sleep and retired to my room, to my surprise I found there a bearded, broad shouldered stranger whom I had never seen on deck. He stretched out, not on the spare bunk, but on the floor near the door where he spread out a coat and an inflatable rubber pillow and covered himself with a robe. Not without repressed anger I informed him that the entire cabin to its full extent including its cubic content of air belonged to me. But he responded calmly and with a good English accent:

"Do not be disturbed, sir. It is my duty to spend this night near you in the position of a faithful watchdog. May I add that here is a letter and a package from Mr. Daniels."

The old Jew had written briefly and affectionately:

"Do not deny me a small pleasure: take as a souvenir of our meeting this ring I offer you. It is of no great value, but it will serve as an amulet to guard you from danger at sea. The inscription on it is ancient, and may indeed be in the language of the now extinct Incas.

Daniels"

In the packet was a ring with a small flat ruby on whose surface were engraved wondrous signs.

Then my "watchdog" locked the cabin, laid a revolver next to him on the floor and seemingly fell instantly asleep.

"Thank you, my dear Mr. Dibble," Mr. Nideston said to me the next day, shaking my hand firmly. "You have excellently fulfilled all your commissions, which were at times difficult enough, employed your time well, and in addition have borne yourself with dignity. Now you may rest for a week and divert yourself as you wish. Sunday morning we shall dine together and then leave for Southampton and on Monday morning you will be at sea aboard *The Southern Cross*, a splendid steamer. Do not forget, may I remind you, to visit my clerk to receive your two-months' salary and expenses, and during the next two days I will examine and re-pack all of your baggage. It is dangerous to trust another's hands, and I doubt if there is anyone in London as skilled as I in the packing of delicate objects."

On Sunday I bade farewell to kind Mr. John Johnson and his numerous family, leaving them to the sound of their best wishes for a happy journey. And on Monday morning Mr. Nideston and I were seated in the luxurious stateroom of the huge liner *The Southern Cross* where we drank coffee in expectation of my departure. A fresh breeze blew over the sea and green waves with white caps dashed against the thick glass of the portholes.

"I must inform you, my dear sir, that you will not be traveling alone," said Mr. Nideston. "A certain Mr. de Mon de Rique will be sailing with you. He is an electrician and mechanic with several years of irreproachable experience behind him and I have only the most favorable reports concerning his abilities. I feel no special affection for the lad, but it may well be in this case the voice of my own erroneous and baseless antipathy—an old man's eccentricity. His father was a Frenchman who took English citizenship and his mother was Irish but he himself has the blood of a Gaelic fighting cock in his veins. He is a dandy, handsome in a common sort of way, much taken with himself and his own appearance, and is fond of women's skirts. It was not I who selected him. I acted only in accordance with the instructions issued to me by Lord Charlesbury, your future director and mentor. De Mon de Rique will arrive in twenty or twenty-five minutes with the morning train from Cardiff and we shall speak with him. At any rate I advise you to establish good relations with him. Whether you like it or not you must live three or four years at his side on God-knows-what desert at the equator on the summit of the extinct volcano Cayambe, where you, white men, will be only five or six, while all the others will be Negroes, Mestizoes, Indians and others of their ilk. Are you perhaps frightened at such a prospect? Remember, the choice is yours to make. We could at any moment tear up the contract you signed and return together by the eleven o'clock train to London. And I may assure you that this would in nowise reduce the respect and affection I feel for you."

"No. my dear Mr. Nideston, I see myself already on Cayambe," I said with laughter. "I yearn for regular employment, particularly if it involves science, and when I think of it I lick my chops like a starveling in front of a White Chapel sausage shop. I hope that my work will be interesting enough that I will not become bored and involved in petty concerns and personal differences."

"Oh, my dear sir, you will have much beautiful and lofty labor before you complete your scheme. The time has come to be open with you and I will enlighten you on some matters of which I am informed. Lord Charlesbury has been laboring now nine years on a plan of unheard of dimensions. He has decided at any costs to accomplish the transformation of the sun's rays into a gas and what is more—to compress that gas to an extraordinary degree at terribly low temperatures under colossal pressures into liquid form. If God grants him the power of completing his plan, then his discovery will have enormous consequences . . ."

"Enormous!" I repeated softly, subdued and awed by Mr. Nideston's words.

"That is all I know," said the solicitor. "No, I also know from a personal letter from Lord Charlesbury that he is closer than ever to the successful completion of his work and less than ever has any doubts about the rapid solution of his problem. I must tell you, my dear friend, that Lord Charlesbury is one of the great men of science, one of few touched with genius. In addition, he is a genuine aristocrat both in birth and in spirit, an unselfish and self-denying friend of mankind, a patient and considerate teacher, a charming conversationalist and a faithful friend. He is, moreover, the possessor of such attractive spiritual beauty that all hearts are attracted to him . . . But here is your traveling companion coming up the gang plank now," Mr. Nideston said, breaking off his enthusiastic speech. "Take this envelope. You will find in it your steamship tickets, your exact itinerary and money. You will be at sea for sixteen or seventeen days. Tomorrow you will be overcome by depression. For such an occasion I have acquired and deposited in your cabin thirty or so books. And in addition, in your baggage you will find a suitcase with a supply of warm clothing and boots. You did not know that you will be required to live in a mountain region with eternal snows. I attempted to select clothing of your size, but I was so afraid of making an error, that I preferred the larger size to the smaller. Also you will find among your things a small box with seasickness remedies. I do not in fact believe in them, but at any rate . . . do you suffer from seasickness?"

"Yes, but not to a particularly painful degree. And anyway, 1 have a talisman against all dangers at sea."

I showed him the ruby, Daniels' gift. He examined it carefully, shook his head and said thoughtfully:

"Somewhere I have seen such a stone as that, and it seems with the same inscription. But now I see the Frenchman has noticed us and is coming our way. With all my heart, my dear Dibble, I wish you a happy voyage, good spirits and health . . . Greetings, Mr. de Mon de Rique. May I introduce you: Mr. Dibble, Mr. de Mon de Rique, future colleagues and collaborators."

I personally was not particularly impressed by the dandy. He was tall, slender, effete and sleek, with a kind of grace in his movements, an indolent and flexible strength, such as we see in the great cats. He reminded me first of all of a Levantine with his beautiful velvety dark eyes and small gleaming black mustache, which was carefully trimmed over his classic pink mouth. We exchanged a few insignificant and polite phrases. But at that moment a bell rang above us and a whistle sounded, shaking the deck with its full powerful voice—the ship's whistle.

"Well, now, good-bye, gentlemen," said Mr. Nideston. "With all my heart I hope you will become friends. My greetings to Lord Charlesbury. May you have good weather during your crossing. Until we meet again."

He walked briskly down the gang plank, entered a waiting cab, waved affectionately in our direction for the last time, and without looking back disappeared from our sight. I did not know why, but I felt a kind of sadness, as though when that man disappeared I had lost a true and faithful helper and a moral support.

I remember little that was remarkable in our journey. I will say only that those seventeen days seemed as long to me as 170 years, and they were so monotonous and dreary that now from a distance they seem to me to be one endlessly long day.

De Mon de Rique and I met several times a day at dinner in the salon. We had no other close meetings. He was coolly polite with me and I in turn re-paid him with restrained courtesy, but I constantly felt he was not interested in me personally nor indeed in anyone else in the world. But, on the other hand, when our conversation touched upon our special fields, I was overwhelmed by his knowledge, his audacity, and the originality of his hypotheses, and what was important, by his ability to express his ideas in precise and picturesque language.

I tried to read the books which Mr. Nideston had left for me. Most of them were narrowly scientific works which dealt with the theory of light and optic lenses, observations on high and low temperatures, and the description of experiments on the concentration and liquefaction of gases. There were also several books devoted to the description of remarkable expeditions and two or three books about the equatorial countries of South America. But it was difficult to read because a heavy wind blew constantly and the steamship oscillated in long sliding glides. All the passengers gave their due to seasickness except de Mon de Rique, who in spite of his great height and delicate build conducted himself as well as an old sailor.

Finally, we arrived at Colón in the northern part of the isthmus of Panama. When I disembarked my legs were leaden and would not obey my will. According to Mr. Nideston's instructions we were personally to oversee the trans-shipment of our baggage to the train station and its loading into baggage cars. The most delicate and sensitive instruments we took with ourselves into our compartment. The precious polished diamonds were, of course, in my possession, but—it is now painful to admit this—I not only did not even show them to my companion, I never said a word to him about them.

Our journey henceforth was fatiguing and consequently of little interest. We traveled by railroad from Colón to Panama, from Panama we hod two days' journey on the ancient quivering steamship *Gonzalez* to the Bay of Guayaquil, then on horseback and rail to Quito. In Quito, in accordance with Mr. Nideston's instruction we sought out the Equator Hotel where we found a party of guides and packers who were expecting us. We spent the night in the hotel and early in the morning, refreshed, we set off for the mountains. What intelligent, good, charming creatures—the mules. With their bells tinkling steadily, shaking their heads decorated with rings and plumes, carefully stepping on the uneven country roads with their long tumbler-shaped hooves, they calmly proceeded along the rim of the abyss over such defiles that involuntarily you closed your eyes and held to the horn of the high saddle.

We reached the snow about five that evening. The road widened and became level. It was obvious that people of a high civilization had labored over it. The sharp turns were always paralleled with a low stone barrier.

At six o'clock when we had passed through a short tunnel, we suddenly saw residences before us: several low white buildings over which proudly rose a white tower which resembled a Byzantine church spire or an observatory. Still higher into the sky rose iron and brick chimneys. A quarter of an hour later we arrived at our destination.

Out of a door belonging to a house larger and more spacious than the rest emerged to meet us a tall thin old man with a long, irreproachably white beard. He said he was Lord Charlesbury and greeted us with unfeigned kindness. It was hard to know his age from his appearance: fifty or seventy-five. His large, slightly protuberant blue eyes, the eyes of a pure Englishman were as clear as a lad's, shining and penetrating. The clasp of his hand was firm, warm, and open, and his high broad forehead was notable for its delicate and noble lines. And as I admired his slender beautiful face and responded to his handshake it clearly seemed to me that one time long ago I had seen his visage and many times I had heard his name.

"I am infinitely pleased at your arrival," said Lord Charlesbury, climbing up the stairs with us. "Was your journey a pleasant one? And how is the good Mr. Nideston? A remarkable man, is he not? But you can answer all my questions at dinner. Now go refresh yourselves and put yourselves in order. Here is our major-domo, the worthy Sambo," and he indicated a portly old Negro who met us in the foyer. "He will show you to your rooms. We dine punctually at seven, and Sambo will inform you of our remaining schedule."

The worthy Sambo very politely, but without a shadow of servile ingratiation, took us to a small house nearby. Each of us was given three rooms—simple, but at the same time somehow exceptionally comfortable, bright, and cheerful. Our quarters were separated from each other by a stone wall and each had a separate entrance. For some reason I was pleased by this arrangement.

With indescribable pleasure I sank into a huge marble bath (thanks to the rocking of the steamship I had been deprived of this satisfaction, and in the hotels at Colón, Panama and Quito the baths would not have aroused the trust even of my friend John Johnson). But when I luxuriated in the warm water, took a cold shower, shaved, and then dressed with the greatest care I was ridden by the question: why was Lord Charlesbury's face so familiar? And what was it, something almost fabulous, it seemed to me, that I had heard about him? At times in some corner of my consciousness I dimly felt that I could remember something, but then it would disappear, as a light breath disappears from a polished steel surface.

From the window of my study I could see all of this strange settlement with its five or six buildings, a stable, a greenhouse with low sooty equipment sheds, a mass of air hoses, with cars drawn over narrow rails by vigorous sleek mules, with high steam cranes which were smoothly carrying through the air steel containers to be filled with coal and oil shale out of a series of dumps. Here and there workers were active, the majority of them half-naked, although the thermometer attached to the outside of my window showed a temperature below freezing, and who were of all colors: white, yellow, bronze, coffee, and gleaming black.

I observed and thought how a flaming will and colossal wealth had been able to transform the barren summit of the extinct volcano into a veritable outpost of civilization with a manufactory, a workshop, and a laboratory, to transport stone, wood and iron to an altitude of eternal snows, to bring water, to construct buildings and machines, to set into motion precious physical instruments, among which the two lenses alone which I had brought cost 1,300,000 francs, to hire dozens of workers and summon highly paid assistants . . . Once more there arose clearly in my mind the figure of Lord Charlesbury and suddenly—but wait! enlightenment suddenly came to my memory. I recalled very precisely how fifteen years earlier when I was still a green student at my school all the newspapers for months trumpeted various rumors concerning the disappearance of Lord Charlesbury, the English peer, the only scion of an ancient family, a famous scientist and a millionaire. His photograph was printed everywhere as well as conjectures on the causes of this strange event. Some took it as murder, others asserted that he had fallen under the influence of some malevolent hypnotist who for his evil purposes had removed the nobleman from England, leaving no traces; a third opinion held that the nobleman was in the hands of criminals who were holding him in expectation of a great ransom, a fourth opinion, and the most prescient one, asserted that the scientist had secretly undertaken an expedition to the North Pole.

Shortly later it became known that before his disappearance Lord Charlesbury very advantageously had liquidated all his lands, forests, parks, farms, coal and clay pits, castles, pictures, and other collections for cash, guided by a very acute and farsighted financial sense. But no one knew what had happened to this immense sum of money. When he disappeared there also disappeared, no one knew where, the famous Charlesbury diamonds, which were rightly the pride of all of England. No police, no private investigators were able to illuminate this strange affair. Within two months the press and society had forgotton him, diverted by other earthshaking interests. Only the learned journals which had dedicated many pages to the memory of the lost nobleman long continued to recount in great detail and with respectful deference his major scientific accomplishments in the study of light and heat and in particular in the expansion and contraction of gases, thermostatics, thermometrics, and thermodynamics, light refraction, the theory of lenses, and phosphorescence.

Outside resounded the drawn-out doleful sound of a gong. And then almost immediately someone knocked on my door and then entered a little cheerful Negro lad, as active as a monkey, who, bowing to me with a friendly smile, reported:

"Mister, I have been appointed by Lord Charlesbury to be at your service. Would you, sir, please come to dinner?"

On the table in my sitting room was a small, delicate bouquet of flowers in a porcelain vase. I selected a gardenia and inserted it into the lapel of my dinner-jacket. But just at that moment Mr. de Mon de Rique emerged from his door wearing a modest daisy in the buttonhole of his frock coat. I felt a kind of uneasy displeasure sweep over me. And even at that distant time there must have been in me still much shallow juvenile peevishness, because I was very pleased to see that Lord Charlesbury who met us in the salon was not wearing a frock coat but a dinner-jacket as was I.

"Lady Charlesbury will be with us shortly," he said, looking at his watch. "I suggest, gentlemen, that you join me for dinner. During the dinner and afterwards there will be two or three hours of free time to converse about business or whatever. May I add that there is a library, skittles, a billiard room and a smoking room here at your disposal. I ask you to utilize them at your discretion as with everything I possess here. I leave you complete freedom as to breakfast and lunch. And this is true also of dinner. But I know how valuable and fruitful is women's- company for young Englishmen and therefore . . ."—he rose and indicated the door through which at that moment entered a slender, young, golden-haired woman escorted by another individual of the female sex. spare and sallow dressed all in black. "And therefore, Lady Charlesbury, I have the honor and the pleasure of introducing to you my future colleagues and, I hope, my friends, Mr. Dibble and Mr. de Mon de Rique."

"Miss Sutton," he said, addressing his wife's faded companion (later I discovered she was a distant relative and companion of Lady Charlesbury), "this is Mr. Dibble and Mr. de Mon de Rique. Please share with them your kindness and attention."

At dinner which was both simple and refined, Lord Charlesbury revealed himself as a cordial host and a superb conversationalist. He inquired animatedly of political affairs, the latest journalistic and scientific news and the health of one or another public figures. By the way, as strange as it may seem, he appeared to be better informed on these subjects than either of us. In addition, his wine cellar turned out to be above praise.

From time to time I secretly glanced at Lady Charlesbury. She took hardly any part in the conversation, only lifting her dark lashes occasionally in the direction of a speaker. She was much younger, even very much younger, than her husband. Her pale face, untouched by any equatorial tan and distinguished by an unhealthy kind of beauty, was framed by thick golden hair, and she had dark, deep, serious, almost melancholy eyes. And all of her appearance, her attractive, very slim figure in white gauze, and delicate white hands with long narrow fingers were reminiscent of some rare and beautiful, but also perhaps poisonous and exotic flower grown without light in a moist dark conservatory.

But I also noticed that de Mon de Rique, who sat opposite me during the meal, often turned an emotional and meaningful glance from his beautiful eyes on our hostess, a glance which persisted perhaps, a half a second longer than propriety permitted. I found myself disliking him more and more: his soft well-groomed face and hands, his languid sweet eyes, which seemed to conceal something, his confident posture, movements, and tone of voice. In my male opinion he seemed repugnant, but I did not doubt for a moment that he possessed all the marks and attributes of an authentic, life-long, cruel, and indifferent conquerer of women's hearts.

After dinner when everyone had left for the salon and Mr. de Mon de Rique had asked permission to retire to the smoking room, I gave the case with the diamonds to Lord Charlesbury, saying:

"These are from Maas and Daniels in Amsterdam."

"You carried them with you?"

"Yes, sir."

"And you did well. These two stones are more valuable to me than all my laboratory."

He went to his study and returned with an eight-power glass. For a long time he carefully examined the diamonds under an electric lamp, and finally, returning them to the case, he said in a satisfied voice, although not without agitation.

"The polishing is above reproach. They are ideally precise. This evening I will check their curved surfaces with instruments employed to measure lenses. Tomorrow morning. Mr. Dibble, we shall fix them into place. Until ten o'clock I shall be occupied with your comrade, Mr. de Mon de Rique, showing him his future laboratory but at ten I ask you to wait for me in your quarters. I shall come for you. Ah, my dear Mr. Dibble, I feel that together we shall advance our project, one of the greatest enterprises ever undertaken by that noble creature, Homo sapiens."

When he said this his eyes burned with a blue light and his hands stroked the lid of the case. And his wife continued to watch him with her deep, dark, fathomless eyes.

The next morning promptly at ten o'clock my doorbell rang and the smartly-dressed Negro boy, bowing deeply, admitted Lord Charlesbury.

"You are ready, I'm pleased to see," said my patron in greeting. "I examined the things you brought yesterday and they all seem to be in excellent order. I thank you for your concern and diligence."

"Three-quarters of that honor, if not more, is due to Mr. Nideston, sir."

"Yes, a fine human being and a true friend," the nobleman said with a gracious smile. "But, now, if there is nothing to hinder you, shall we go to the laboratory?"

The laboratory turned out to be a massive round white building, something like a tower, crowned with the dome which had been the first thing to strike my eye when we emerged from the tunnel.

Wearing our coats we passed through a small anteroom lighted by a single electric lamp and then found ourselves in total darkness. But Lord Charlesbury flipped a switch near me and bright light in a moment flooded a huge round room with a regular hemispherical ceiling some forty feet above the floor. In the midst of the room rose something like a small glass room, which resembled those medical isolation rooms which have lately appeared at university clinics in operating rooms which provide the exceptional cleanliness and disinfected air required during long and complicated operations. From that glass chamber which contained strange equipment such as I had never seen before rose three solid copper cylinders. At a height of about twelve feet both of the cylinders split into three pipes of yet larger diameter; those, in turn were divided into three and the upper ends of these final massive copper pipes touched the concave surface of the dome. A multitude of pressure gauges and levers, curved and straight steel shafts, valves, wiring, and hydraulic presses completed this extraordinary and for me, absolutely stunning laboratory. Steep circular staircases, iron columns and beams, narrow catwalks with slender hand rails which crossed high above me, hanging electric lamps, a host of thick pendant fiber hoses and long copper pipes—all of this was wound together, fatiguing the eye and giving the impression of a chaos.

Surmising my state of mind, Lord Charlesbury said calmly:

"When a person for the first time sees what is for him a strange mechanism, such as the workings of a watch or a sewing machine, he at first throws up his hands in despair at their complexity. When I, for the first time, saw the disassembled parts of a bicycle, it seemed to me that even the most ingenious mechanic in the world could not assemble them. But a week later I myself put them together and then disassembled them, astonished at the simplicity of its construction. Please, listen to my explanations patiently. If at first you do not understand, do not hesitate to ask me as many questions as you wish. This will give me only pleasure.

"Thus, there are twenty-seven closely placed openings in the roof. And in these openings are inserted cylinders which you see high above you which emerge into the open air through doubly-concave lenses of great power and exceptional clarity. Perhaps you now understand the scheme. We collect the sun's rays in foci and then, thanks to a whole series of mirrors and optic lenses made according to my plans and calculations, we conduct them, at times concentrating them and at other times dispersing them, through a whole system of pipes until the lowest pipes release concentrated sunlight here under the insulated cover into this very narrow and strong cylinder made of vanadium steel in which there is a whole system of pistons equipped with shutters, something like in a camera, which allow absolutely no light to enter when they are closed. Finally to the free end of this major cylinder with its internal closures I attach in a vacuum a vessel in the shape of a retort in the throat of which there are also several valves. When it is necessary I can open these closures and then insert a threaded stopper into the neck of the retort, unfasten the vessel from the end of the cylinder and then I have a superb means of storing compressed solar emanations."

"This means that Hook and Euler and Young . . . ?"

"Yes," Lord Charlesbury interrupted me. "They, and Fresnel, and Cauchy, and Malus, and Huygens and even the great Arago—they were all wrong when they perceived the phenomenon of light as one of the elements of the earth's atmosphere. I will prove this to you in ten minutes in the most striking fashion. Only the wise old Descartes and the genius of geniuses, the divine Newton, were right. The words of Biot and Brewster have only sustained and confirmed my experiments, but this was only much after I began them. Yes! Now it is clear to me and it will be shortly to you also that sunlight is a dense stream of very small resilient bodies, like tiny balls, which with terrible force and energy move through space, transfixing in their course the mass of the earth's atmosphere . . . But we will talk about theory later. Now, to be methodical, I will demonstrate the procedures which you must perform every day. Let us go outside."

We left the laboratory, climbed a circular staircase almost to the roof of the dome and found ourselves on a bright open gallery which circled the entire spherical roof in a spiral and a half.

"You need not struggle to open in turn all the covers which protect the delicate lenses from dust, snow, hail, and birds," said Lord Charlesbury. "All the more so that even a very strong man could not do that. Simply pull this lever toward yourself, and all twenty-seven shutters will turn their fiber rings in identical circular grooves in a counter-clockwise direction, as though they were all being unscrewed. Now the covers are free of pressure. You will now press that foot pedal. Watch!"

Click! And twenty-seven covers, metal surfaces resounding, instantly opened outward revealing glass sparkling in the sunlight.

"Every morning, Mr. Dibble," the scientist went on, "you are to uncover the lenses and carefully wipe them off with a clean chamois. Observe how this is done."

And he, like an experienced workman, rapidly, carefully, almost affectionately wiped all the glasses with a bit of chamois wrapped in cigarette paper which he brought out of his pocket.

"Now, let us go back down," he went on. "I will show you your other responsibilities."

Below in the laboratory he continued his explanations:

"Then you are 'to catch the sun.' To do this, every day at noon check these two chronometers against the sun. By the way, I checked them myself yesterday. The method is, of course, known to you. Note the time. Take the average time of the two chronometers: 10 hours, 31 minutes, 10 seconds. Here are three curving levers: the largest marks the hour, the middle one is for minutes, the smallest for seconds. Note: I turn the large circle until the hand of the indicator shows ten o'clock. Ready. I place the middle lever a little forward to 36 minutes. So. I move the little lever—that is my own favorite—forward to 50 seconds. Now place this plug in the socket. You can hear how the gears are whining and grinding below you. That is a clock device beginning to move which will rotate the entire laboratory and its dome, instruments, lenses and the two of us to follow the movement of the sun. Observe the chronometers and you will see that we are approaching 10:30. Five seconds more. Now. Can you hear how the clock mechanism has changed its sound? Those are the minute gears beginning to turn. A few seconds more . . . Watch! One minute more! Now there's a new sound, which neatly and precisely is marking off the seconds. That's all. The sun has now been captured. But it's not over yet. Because of its bulkiness and quite understandable crudity the clock mechanism cannot be especially accurate. Therefore as often as possible check this dial which indicates its movement. Here are the hours, minutes, and seconds; here is the regulator —forward, back. On the basis of the chronometers which are extraordinarily precise you will be able, as often as it is possible, to correct the revolution of the laboratory to a tenth of a second.

"Now we have caught the sun. But that is not all we must do. The light has to pass through a vacuum, otherwise it would become heated and melt all our equipment. And therefore when it is in our closed vessels from which all the air has been pumped the light is almost as cold as when it was passing through the endless regions of space outside the earth's atmosphere. When you look closely you can see a control button for an electromagnetic coil. In each of the cylinders is a stopper around which is a steel band circled by a wire. I press the control button and the current flows into the wire. All the bands are instantly affected and the stoppers leave their seats. Now I pull a bronze lever which starts a vacuum pump, one line of which is connected to each of the cylinders. The finest dust, microscopic flecks of matter, are removed with the air. Look at the gauge F on which is a red line indicating the pressure limit. Listen through an acoustic tube leading into the pump, the hissing has ceased. The gauge now crosses the red line. Disconnect the electricity by pressing the same control button a second time; the steel bands no longer are activated. The stoppers in response to the attraction of the vacuum close tightly in their conic seats. Now the light is passing through an almost absolute vacuum. But that is not adequate for the precision our work requires. We can transform all our laboratory into a giant vacuum chamber; in time we will be working in underwater diving equipment. Air will flow through the fiber pipes and the waste air systematically removed to the outside. In the meantime the air will be pulled out of the laboratory by powerful pumps. Do you understand? You will be in the position of a diver with the only difference being that you will have a container with compressed gas on your back: in case of an accident, the equipment's malfunction, a leak in the hoses, or anything else, open a small valve on your helmet and you will have enough air to breathe for a quarter of an hour. You must only keep your wits about you and you will leave the laboratory fresh and smiling, like a blooming rose.

"We still must check very carefully the installation of the piping. All of the pipes are firmly joined but at places some triple-unions allow an infinitesimal amount of play, two or three millimeters, and this might prove to be a problem. There are thirteen such points and you must check them about three times a day, working downward. Therefore, let us climb these stairs."

We mounted narrow staircases and unsteady platforms to the very top of the dome. The teacher went ahead with a youthful step while I followed, not without effort, because this was new to me. At the union of the first three pipes he showed me a small cover which he opened with one turn of the hand and lifted back so that it was held precisely vertical by springs. Its reverse side was a rigid, silver, finely polished mirror with various incisions and numbers on its edge. Three parallel gold bands, thin, like telescopic hairs, nearly touching each other, cut the smooth surface of the mirror.

"This is a small well through which we covertly follow the flow of the light. The three bands are reflections from three internal mirrors. Combine them into one. No, you do it yourself. Here you see three minute screws to adjust the positions of the lenses. Here is a very strong magnifying glass. Combine the three light bands into one but in such a manner that the total ray of light falls on zero. It is not difficult to do. You will shortly be able to carry it out in one minute."

In fact, the mechanism was very compliant and three minutes later, barely touching the sensitive screws I combined the light bands into one sharp line which was almost painful to look at, and then I introduced it into a narrow incision at zero. Then I closed the cover and screwed it down. I adjusted the remaining twelve control wells alone without Lord

Charlesbury's help. Every time I performed this operation it went more smoothly. But by the time we reached the second level of the laboratory my eyes so ached from the bright light that involuntarily the tears streamed down my face.

"Put on goggles. Here they are," said my chief, handing me a case.

But I could not approach the final cylinder which we were to adjust in its location inside the isolation chamber. My eyes would not accept the glare.

"Take some darker glasses," said Lord Charlesbury. "I have them in ten shades. Today we will attach the lenses which you brought yesterday to the main cylinder and then direct observation will be three times as difficult. Good. That's right. Now I am activating an internal piston. I'm opening the valve of a hydraulic pump. I'm also opening a valve with liquid carbon dioxide. Now the temperature inside the cylinder has reached 150 degrees centigrade and the pressure is equal to 20 atmospheres; the latter is indicated by a gauge, the former by a Witkowski thermometer which I have improved. The following is now underway in the cylinder: light is passing through it in a dense vertical stream of blinding brightness approximately the diameter of a pencil. The valve actuated by an electric current is opening and closing its shutter in one one-thousandth of a second. The valve sends the light on through a small, highly convex lens. From there the stream of light emerges yet denser, narrower, and brighter. There are five such valves and lenses in each cylinder. Under the compression of the last, smallest and most powerful piston, a needle-thin stream of light flows into the vessel, passing through three valves in series.

"That is the basis of my liquid sunlight collector," my teacher said triumphantly. "Now, in order that there can be no doubts at all, we will conduct an experiment. Press control button A. You have just stopped the movement of the valve. Lift that bronze lever. Now you have closed the interior covers of the collecting glasses in the building's dome. Turn the red valve as far as it will go, and lower handle C. The pressure is now released and the supply of carbon dioxide cut off. Now you must close the vessel, This is done by ten turns of that small rounded lever. Everything is now complete, my friend. Notice how I disconnect the receiver vessel from the cylinder. See, I have it in my hands now; it weighs no more than twenty pounds. Its internal shutters are controlled by minute screws on the exterior of the cylinder. I am now opening wide the first and largest shutter. Then the intermediate one. The final shutter I will open only one-half a micron. But, first, go and turn off the electric lights."

I obeyed and the room filled with impenetrable darkness.

"Now watch!" I heard Lord Charlesbury's voice from the other end of the laboratory. "I'm opening it!"

An extraordinary golden light, delicate, radiant, transparent, suddenly flooded the room, softly but clearly outlining its walls, gleaming equipment, and the figure of my teacher himself. And, at the same moment I felt on my face and hands something like a warm breath of air. This phenomenon lasted not more than a second or a second and a half. Then heavy darkness concealed everything from my eyes.

"Lights, please!" exclaimed Lord Charlesbury and once more I saw him emerging from the door of the glass chamber. His face was pale, but illuminated by joy and pride.

"Those were only the first steps, a schoolboy's trials, the first seeds," he said exultantly. "That was not sunlight condensed into a gas, but only a compressed weightless substance. For months I have compressed sunlight in my containers, but not one of them has become heavier by the weight of a human hair. You saw that marvelous, steady, caressing light. Now do you believe in my project?"

"Yes," I answered heatedly, with profound conviction. "I believe in it and I bow before an invention of great genius."

"But let's go on. Still further on! We will lower the temperature inside the cylinder to minus 275 degrees centigrade, to absolute zero. We will raise the hydraulic pressure to thousands, twenty, thirty thousand times the earth's atmosphere. We will replace our eight-inch light collectors with powerful fifty-inch models. We will melt pounds of diamonds by a technique I have developed and pour them into lenses to the specifications we require and place them in our instruments . . . ! Perhaps I will not live to see the time when men will compress the sun's rays into a liquid form, but I believe and I feel that I will compress them to the density of a gas. I only want to see the hand on an electric scales move even one millimeter to the left—and I will be boundlessly happy.

"But time is passing. Let us lunch and then before dinner we will concern ourselves with the installation of our new diamond lenses. Beginning tomorrow we will work together. For a week you will be with me as an ordinary worker, as a simple, obedient helper. A week from now we will exchange roles. The third week I will give you a helper, to whom in my presence you will teach all the procedures with the instruments. Then I will give you complete freedom. I trust you," he said briskly with a captivating. charming smile and reached out to shake my hand.

I remember very well that evening and dinner with Lord Charlesbury. Lady Charlesbury was in a red silk dress and her red mouth against her pale, slightly weary face glowed like a purple flower, like an incandescent ember. De Mon de Rique whom I saw at dinner for the first time that day, was alert, handsome, and elegant, as I had never seen him either before or afterwards, while I felt enervated and overwhelmed by the flood of impressions I had received during the day. At first I thought that he had spent the day at his customary, simple labors, mostly observations. But it was not I, but Lady Charlesbury who first drew our attention to the fact that the electrician's left hand was bandaged to above the knuckles. De Mon de Rique modestly recounted how he had scraped his hand as he was climbing down a wall with an insufficiently tightened safety belt. That evening he dominated the conversation, but gently and with tact. He told about his journeys to Abyssinia where he prospected for gold in the mountain valleys on the verge of the Sahara, about lion hunting, the races at Epsom, fox hunting in the north of England, and about Oscar Wilde, then becoming fashionable and with whom he was personally acquainted. He had a surprising and probably too rare conversational trait, which, I will add, I have never noticed in anyone else. When he told a story he was extremely abstracted: he never spoke of himself nor in his own voice. But by some mysterious means his personality, remaining in the background, was illuminated, now in mild, now in heroic half-tones.

Now he was looking at Lady Charlesbury much less frequently than she at him. Only from time to time his caressing and languid eyes passed over her from under his long, lowered lashes. But she hardly took her grave and mysterious eyes away from him. Her gaze followed the movements of his hands and head, his mouth and eyes. Strange! That evening she reminded me of a child's toy: a tin fish or a duck with a bit of iron in its mouth which involuntarily, obediently follows after a magnetized stick which compels it from a distance. Frequently in alarm I observed the expression on my host's face. But he was serenely high-spirited and composed.

After dinner when de Mon de Rique asked permission to smoke, Lady Charlesbury herself offered to play billiards with him. They left while the host and I made our way into his study.

"How about a game of chess," he said. "Do you play?"

"Indifferently, but always with pleasure."

"And do you know what else has happened? Let us have a glass of some lively wine."

He pressed a button.

"What is the occasion?" I asked.

"You already have guessed. Because, it seems to me I have found in you an assistant, and if fate wills it, someone to carry on my work."

"Oh, sir!"

"One minute. What drink would you prefer?"

"I'm ashamed to admit that I'm no expert in such matters."

"Very well, in such a case I will name four drinks which I love, and a fifth which I detest. Bordeaux wines, port, Scotch ale, and water. But I cannot bear champagne. And, therefore, let us drink Chateau-la-Rose. My dear

Sambo," he commanded the butler who stood near, waiting, "a bottle of Chateau-la-Rose."

Lord Charlesbury, to my surprise, played rather poorly. I quickly checkmated his king. After our first game we abandoned play and once more spoke of my morning's impressions.

"Listen, my dear Dibble," said Lord Charlesbury, laying his little, warm and energetic hand on my knuckles. "You have undoubtedly many times heard that one may obtain an authentic and accurate opinion of a man at first glance. I believe that to be a grave error. Many times I have seen men with the faces of convicts, cheats, or perjurers—and by the way, you will meet your assistant in a few days—and they turned out to be honest, faithful in friendship, and attentive, courteous gentlemen. On the other hand, very rarely, a generous, charming face, adorned with gray hair and the flush of age, and honorable speech conceals, as it becomes clear, such a villain that any London hooligan is by comparison an innocent lamb with a pink ribbon round his neck. Now may I ask you to help me to solve a problem? Mr. de Mon de Rique so far has not been involved in any way in the completion of my scientific work. On his mother's side he is distantly related to me. Mr. Nideston, who has known him from childhood informed me that de Mon de Rique was in a very difficult position (only not in the material sense). I immediately offered him a position which he accepted with a joy that testified to his precarious situation. I have heard tales about him, but I give no credence to rumors and gossip. He made absolutely no impression upon me when first we met. Perhaps this was because I have never met a person such as he. But for some reason it also seems to me that I have met millions of such men. Today I carefully observed him at work. I believe him to be clever, knowing, ingenious and industrious. In addition, he is cultured and can conduct himself well in any society, as it seems to me, and moreover, he is energetic and intelligent. But in one respect I have my doubts. Tell me frankly, dear Mr. Dibble, your opinion of him."

This unexpected and tactless question agitated and distressed me; to tell the truth I did not expect it at all.

"But, sir, I have none. Indeed, I don't know him as well as you and Mr. Nideston. I saw him for the first time on board the steamship *Southern Cross*, and during our journey we met and talked very rarely. And I must tell you that I suffered from seasickness the entire journey. But from our few meetings and conversations I have obtained approximately the same impression as you, sir: knowing, ingenious, energetic, eloquent, well-read and . . . a peculiar and perhaps very rare mixture, very cold-hearted but with a fervent imagination."

"You are right, Mr. Dibble, right. Beautifully said. My dear Mr. Sambo, bring another bottle of wine and then you may go. Thank you. I hardly expected any other evaluation from you. But I will return to my difficulty: should I inform him or not of what you witnessed today? Just imagine that a year or two will pass, perhaps less, and our dandy, our Adonis, our admirer of women, will suddenly become bored with his life on this God-forsaken volcano. I think that in such a case he would not come to me for my blessing and approval. Simply one beautiful morning he will pack his things and leave. The fact that I would be left without an assistant and a very valuable assistant at that is of secondary importance, but I cannot assure you that after he has arrived in the Old World he will not turn out to be loose-tongued, perhaps very innocently."

"Are you really concerned about this, sir?"

"I tell you frankly—I fear it very much! I am afraid of the notoriety, the publicity, and the invasion of reporters. I am afraid that some influential but talentless scientific reviewer who will base his attitude on a rejection of all new ideas and audacious conjectures will interpret my scheme to the public as a meaningless fantasy, the ravings of a madman. Finally, I am afraid most of all that some hungry upstart, a greedy failure, a talentless ignoramus will misunderstand my idea, and state, as has happened a thousand times, that it is his, thereby belittling, abusing and sullying something I have brought into the world in anguish and joy. Do you understand me, Mr. Dibble?"

"Completely, sir."

"If this happens, then I and my idea will perish. But what does this little 'I' mean when compared to my idea? I am deeply convinced that on the evening when in one of the huge London halls I order the lights extinguished and blind a selected audience of ten thousand with a stream of sunshine which will make flowers open and cause the birds to sing—that evening I will receive a million pounds for my cause. But, a trifle, an accident, an insignificant mistake, as I said, could destroy in a fateful manner the most selfless and grandiose idea. Therefore, I ask your opinion, should I trust Mr. de Mon de Rique or leave him in false and evasive ignorance? This is a dilemma which I cannot avoid without help. On one hand the possibility of a worldwide scandal and failure, and on the other a sure road for arousing a feeling of anger and revenge in a man thanks to my lack of trust in him. And so, Mr. Dibble?"

I wanted to give him the direct answer: "Tomorrow send this Narcissus with all honors back into the world and you can rest in peace." Now I regret deeply that a foolish sense of delicacy prevented me from giving that advice Instead of saying this, I took on an air of cool correctness and answered:

"I hope you will not be angry with me, sir, if I decline to pass judgment on such a difficult matter."

Lord Charlesbury looked directly at me, shook his head sadly and said with a mirthless smile:

"Let's finish our wine and visit the billiard room. I would like to smoke a cigar."

In the billiard room we saw the following picture. De Mon de Rique was bent over the billiard table telling some lively tale, while Lady Charlesbury, leaning against the mantelpiece, laughed loudly. This struck me more than if I had seen her weeping. Lord Charlesbury inquired into the cause of the merriment, and when de Mon de Rique repeated his story about a certain vain aristocrat who acquired a tame leopard in a desire to pass himself off as an original and then was compelled to sit three hours in his room with the animal because he was so afraid of it, my patron laughed loud and long, like a child . . .

Everything in the world is inter-related in the strangest manner.

That evening in some inscrutable fashion combined the beginnings, the engagement and the tragic denouement of our lives.

The first two days of my existence at Cayambe I remember very well, but as for the rest, the closer they come to the end, the hazier they become. And therefore, with more reason I turn for help to my notebook. The sea-water erased the first and last pages and in part the intervening pages also. But some of it, with difficulty, I can restore. Thus:

December 11. Today I rode on mule back with Lord Charlesbury into Quito to obtain copper wire. It happened that the subject of the material support of our project arose (it was not merely the result of my idle curiosity). Lord Charlesbury, who, it seemed to me, had long given me his full confidence, suddenly turned quickly in his saddle to face me and asked unexpectedly:

"You know Mr. Nideston?"

"Certainly, sir."

"A fine man, is he not so?"

"An excellent man."

"And is it not true, in the world, dry and something of a formalist?"

"Yes, sir. But he is also capable of great enthusiasm and even of high emotion."

"You are observant, Mr. Dibble," my mentor answered. "You should know that for fifteen years he has believed in me and my idea as stubbornly as a Mohammedan believes in his Kaaba. You know he is a London solicitor. He not only does not take any pay for my commissions, but long ago he offered to place his own private fortune at my disposal if I so wished. I am deeply convinced that he is the only eccentric left in old England. Therefore let us be of good cheer."

December 12. Today Lord Charlesbury for the first time showed me the force which drives the timing mechanism which turns the laboratory with the sun. It is obvious, simple, and ingenious. Down the slope of the extinct volcano a dressed basalt block weighing thirty five tons suspended by a steel cable almost as thick as a man's leg moves on almost vertical rails. This weight puts the mechanism into motion. It functions exactly for eight hours and early in the morning an old blind mule raises this counterweight with the help of another cable and a system of blocks without any great effort.

December 20. Today I sat with Lord Charlesbury after dinner in the hothouse sunk in the heady odor of narcissi, pomegranates and tuberoses. Recently my patron has been very withdrawn and his eyes seemingly have begun to lose their beautiful youthful brightness. I take this to be the result of fatigue because we are working very hard now. I am sure that he has guessed nothing about *it*. He suddenly changed the subject of the conversation, as is his wont:

"Our work is the most selfless and honorable on earth. To think about the happiness of one's children or grandchildren is both natural and egotistical. But you and I are thinking of the lives and happiness of humanity so far in the future that they will not know of us nor of our poets, kings, or conquerers, about our language and religion, about our national borders or even the names of our countries. 'Not for those who are near but those who come later!' Isn't that what our most popular philosopher has said? I am willing to give all my strength to this unselfish and pure service to the distant future."

January 3. I went to Quito today to accept a shipment from London. My relationship with Mr. de Mon de Rique has become cold, almost inimical.

February. Today we completed the work of connecting all our piping with the containers of chilling solutions. A combination of ice and salt gives minus 21 degrees centigrade, dry ice and ether—minus 80 degrees, hydrogen—minus 118 degrees, vaporized dry ice—minus 130 degrees, and it seems that we will be able to reduce the atmospheric pressure indefinitely.

April. My assistant continues to arouse my interest. He is some kind of a Slav. A Russian, or a Pole, and, so it seems, an anarchist. He is intelligent and speaks English well, but it seems he prefers not to speak any language at all, but to remain silent. Here is his appearance: he is tall, thin, slightly round-shouldered; his hair is straight and long and falls onto his face in such a manner that his forehead takes the shape of a trapezoid, the narrow end up; he has a tilted nose with great open hairy, but delicate nostrils. His eyes are clear, gray, and boundlessly impertinent. He hears and understands everything that we say about the happiness of future generations and often smiles with a benevolent but contemptuous smile, which reminds me of the expression on the face of a large old bulldog watching a pack of yelping toy terriers. But his attitude toward my mentor—and this I not only know, but feel to the marrow of my bones—is one of boundless adoration. My colleague's attitude, de Mon de Rique's attitude, is quite different. He often speaks to the teacher about the idea of liquid sunshine with such false enthusiasm that I blush for shame and I fear that the technician is mocking our patron. And he is not interested in him at all as a man, and in the most discourteous manner and in the presence of his wife disparages his position as husband and master of the house, although this is unwise and contrary to common sense, the result of his perverted temperament and. perhaps, out of jealousy.

May. Let us hail the names of three talented Poles—Wrublewski, Olszewski, and Witkowski and the man who completed their work, Dewar. Today we transformed helium into a liquid, and instantly reducing the pressure, reached a temperature of minus 272 degrees centigrade in our major cylinder and the dial on the electric scales for the first time moved, not one, but *five whole millimeters.* Silently, in solitude, I bow before you, my dear preceptor and teacher.

June 26. Apparently de Mon de Rique has come to believe in liquid sunshine—and now without sickening coyness and forced delight. At least today at dinner he made a remarkable statement. He said that in his opinion liquid sunshine would have a brilliant future as an explosive substance in mines or projectiles.

I objected, it is true, rather violently, in German: "You sound like a Prussian lieutenant."

But Lord Charlesbury responded succinctly and in a conciliatory tone:

"Our dreams are not of destruction, but of creation."

June 27. I am writing in great agitation, my hands trembling. I worked late this evening in the laboratory, until two o'clock. It was a matter of urgency to install a cooling unit. As I was returning to my quarters the moon shone brightly. I was wearing warm sealskin boots and my footsteps on the frozen path could not be heard. My route lay in shadow. Reaching my door I stopped when 1 heard voices.

"Come in, Mary dear, for God's sake, come in for only a minute. What are you always afraid of? And don't you always discover that there's no reason to be afraid?"

And then I saw them both in the bright light of the southern moon. He had his arm around her waist, and her head lay passively on his shoulder. Oh, how beautiful they were at that moment!

"But your friend . . ." Lady Charlesbury said timorously.

"What kind of a friend is he?" de Mon de Rique laughed heedlessly. "He's only a boring and sentimental drudge who goes to bed every night at ten o'clock in order to arise at six. Mary, please come in. I beg you."

And both of them, their arms around each other, went onto the porch illuminated by the blue light of the moon and disappeared in an open door.

June 28. Evening. This morning I went to see Mr. de Mon de Rique, refused his proferred hand, would not sit down on the chair he offered and said quietly:

"I must tell you what I think of you, sir. I believe that you, sir, in a situation where we should work together cheerfully and selflessly for the sake of humanity, are conducting yourself in a most unworthy and shameful manner. Last night at two o'oclock 1 saw you when you entered your quarters."

"Were you spying, you scoundrel?" shouted de Mon de Rique, and his eyes gleamed with a violet light, like a cat at night.

"No, I found myself in an impossible situation. I did not speak out, not because I did not want to cause you pain, but because I did not want to harm another person. But this gives me more reason than ever to tell you to your face that you, sir, are a villain and a sneak."

"You will pay for that with your blood with a weapon in your hands," shouted de Mon de Rique, leaping to his feet.

"No," I answered firmly. "First of all, we have no reason to fight except that I called you a villain, but not in the presence of witnesses, and secondly, because I am engaged in a great work of world-wide importance and I do not want to abandon it thanks to your ridiculous bullet until it is completed. Thirdly, would it not be easiest of all for you to pack your bags, mount the first mule available, leave for Quito, and then by your previous route return to hospitable England? Or did you dishonor someone or steal money there. Mr. Scoundrel?"

He leaped to the table and seized a leather whip which lay there.

"I'll kill you like a dog!" he roared.

But I remembered my old boxing skills. Acting quickly, I feinted with my left hand, and then hit him with my right below his chin. He cried out, spun like a top, and blood rushed out of his nose.

I walked out.

June 29. "Why is it that I haven't seen Mr. de Mon de Rique today?" Lord Charlesbury asked unexpectedly.

"It seems he isn't well," I answered, avoiding his eyes.

We were sitting together on the northern slope of the volcano. It was nine in the evening and the moon had not yet risen. Near us stood two porters and my mysterious helper, Peter. Against the quiet dark blue of the sky the slender electric lines, which we had installed that day, could hardly be seen. And on a great heap of stones rested receiver no. 6, firmly braced by basalt boulders, ready any second to open its shutters.

"Prepare the fuse," ordered Lord Charlesbury. "Roll the spool down the hill, I'm too tired and excited; give me your hand, help me down. This is good. And there is no risk of being blinded. Think on it, my dear Dibble, think on it, my dear boy, now the two of us in the name of glory and the happiness of future mankind, will light all the world with sunshine concentrated in gaseous form. Ready! Light the fuse."

The fiery snake of the lighted fuse ran up the hill and disappeared over the edge of the deep defile in which we sat. Listening carefully I could hear the instantaneous click of contacts closing and the penetrating roar of motors. According to our calculations gaseous sunshine should issue from the containers next to the explosion sites at a rate of approximately six thousand feet per second. At that moment above our heads there was a flash of blinding sunlight, at which the trees below rustled, clouds turned pink in the sky, distant roofs and the windows of houses in Quito gleamed brightly, and the cocks in the village nearby began crowing.

When the light faded as quickly as it had appeared, my teacher pressed the button on a stop watch, turned his flashlight on it, and said:

"It burned for one minute and eleven seconds. This is a genuine triumph, Mr. Dibble. I assure you that within a year we will be able to fill immense reservoirs with heavy liquid golden sunshine, like mercury, and compel it to provide light, heat and drive all our machinery."

When we returned home that night about midnight we discovered that in our absence Lady Charlesbury and Mr. de Mon de Rique in the daylight hours soon after our departure had seemingly gone for a walk but then on mules saddled beforehand had left for the city of Quito below.

Lord Charlesbury remained true to himself. He said without bitterness, but sadly and in pain:

"Why didn't they say anything to me, why this deceit? Didn't I see that they loved each other? I would not have hindered them."

At this point my notes end, and at that they were so damaged by water that I could restore them only with the greatest difficulty and I cannot guarantee their accuracy. Nor can I in the future guarantee the reliability of my memory. But this is always the case: the closer I draw to the final resolution the more confused my recollections become.

For about twenty five days we worked steadily in the laboratory filling more and more containers with solar gas. During this period we invented ingenious valves for our solar containers. We equipped each of them with a clock mechanism with a simple face, as on an alarm clock. Adjusting the dials of three cylinders we could obtain light over any given period of time, and lengthen the period of its combustion and its intensity from a dim half-hour of glimmer to an instantaneous explosion—depending on the time set. We worked without inspiration, almost unwillingly, but I must admit that this was the most productive time of my stay on Cayambe. But it all ended abruptly, fantastically, and horribly.

Once, early in August, Lord Charlesbury, even more tired and aged than usual, came to visit me in the laboratory; he said to me calmly and with distaste:

"My dear friend, I feel that my death is not far away, and old convictions are making themselves heard. I want to die and be buried in England. I will leave you some money, these buildings, the equipment, the land and this laboratory. The money, on the basis of what I have spent, should be ample for two or three years. You are younger and more active than I and perhaps you will obtain some results for your labors. Our dear Mr. Nideston would give his support at any time. Please think on it."

This man had become dearer to me than my father, mother, brother, wife or sister. And therefore I answered with deep assurance:

He embraced me and kissed me on my forehead.

"Dear sir, I would not leave you for one minute."

The next day he summoned all the workers and paying them two years in advance said that his work on Cayambe had come to an end and that day they were to leave Cayambe for the valley below.

They left carefree and ungrateful, anticipating the sweet proximity of drunkenness and dissipation in the innumerable taverns which swarmed in the city of Quito. Only my assistant, the silent Slav—an Albanian or a Siberian—tarried near the master. "I will stay with you as long as you or I am alive," he said. But Lord Charlesbury looked at him firmly, almost sternly and said:

"I am leaving for Europe, Mr. Peter."

"Then I will go with you."

"But you know what awaits you there, Mr. Peter."

"I know. A rope. But nonetheless I will not abandon you. I have always laughed in my heart at your sentimental concerns for men in the millions of years to come, but when I came to know you better I also learned that the more insignificant is mankind the more precious is man, and therefore I have stayed with you, like an old, homeless, embittered, hungry, and mangy dog turns to the first hand that sincerely caresses it. And therefore I will stay with you. That is all."

With astonishment and deep feeling I turned my eyes to this man whom I had always thought to be incapable of elevated feelings. But my teacher said to him softly and with authority:

"No, you must leave. Right now. I value your friendship and your tireless labors. But I'm leaving for my native land to die and the possibility that you might suffer would only darken my departure from this world. Be a man, Peter. Take this money, embrace me in farewell, and let us part."

I saw how they embraced and how blunt Peter kissed the hand of Lord Charlesbury several times and then left us, not turning back, almost at a run and disappeared around a nearby building.

I looked at my teacher: covering his face with his hands he was weeping . . .

Three days later we left on the old *Gonzalez* from Guayaquil for Panama. The sea was rough, but we had a following wind and to help out the small engine the captain had sails spread. Lord Charlesbury and I never left our cabins. I was seriously concerned about his condition and there were even times when I feared he was losing his mind. I observed him with helpless pity. I was especially troubled by the manner in which he invariably referred after every two or three phrases to container no. 216 which we had left behind on Cayambe, and every time he referred to it, he would say through tight lips: "Did I forget, how could I forget?" but then his speech would become melancholy and abstracted.

"Do not think," he said, "that a petty personal tragedy forced me to abandon my work and the persistent searches and inspirations which I have patiently worked out during the course of my conscious life. But circumstances jarred my thoughts. Recently I have much altered my ideas and judgments, but only on a different plane than before. If only you knew how difficult it has been to alter my view of life at the age of sixty-five. I have come to believe, or more correctly, to feel, that the future of mankind is not worth our concern or our selfless work. Mankind, growing more degenerate every day is becoming flabbier, more decadent, and hard-hearted. Society is falling under the power of the crudest despotism in the world— capital. Trusts, manipulating the supply of meat, kerosene, and sugar are creating a generation of fabulous millionnaires and next to them millions of hungry unemployed thieves and murderers. And so it will be forever. And my idea of prolonging the sun's life for the earth will become the property of a handful of villains who will control it or employ my liquid sunshine in shells or bombs of unheard of power . . . No, I do not want that . . . Ah, my God! that container! How could I forget! How could I!" and Lord Charlesbury clapped his hands to his head.

"What troubles you, my dear teacher?" I asked.

"You see, kind Henry. . . . I fear that I have made a small but fateful mistake . . ."

But I heard no more. Suddenly in the east flashed an enormous golden flame. In a moment the sky and the sea were all agleam. Then followed a deafening roar and a burning whirlwind threw me to the deck.

I lost consciousness and revived only when I heard my teacher's voice above me.

"What?" asked Lord Charlesbury. "Are you blind?"

"Yes. I can see nothing, except rainbow-colored circles before my eyes. Was it some kind of a catastrophe, Professor? Why did you do it or allow it to happen? Didn't you foresee it?"

But he softly laid his beautiful little white hand on my shoulder and said in a deep and gentle voice (and from that touch and his confident tone I immediately was calmed):

"Don't you believe me? Wait a moment, close your eyes tightly and cover them with the palm of your right hand, and hold it there until I stop talking or until you catch a glimpse of light; then, before you open your eyes, put on these glasses which I am placing in your left hand. They are very dark. Listen to me. It seems that you have come to know me better in a brief time than anyone else close to me. It was only for your sake, my dear friend, that I did not take on my conscience a cruel and pointless experiment which might have brought death to tens of thousands of people. But what difference would the existence of these dissolute blacks, drunken Indians, and degenerate Spaniards have made? If the Republic of Ecuador with its intrigues, mercenary attitudes and revolutions were instantly transformed into a great door to hell there would be no loss to science, the arts, or history. I am only a little sorry for my intelligent, patient, and affectionate mules. I will tell you candidly that I would have not hesitated for a second to sacrifice you and millions of lives to the triumph of my idea, if only I were convinced of its significance, but as I said only three minutes ago I have become totally disillusioned about the future generations' ability to love, to be happy and to sacrifice themselves. Do you think I could take revenge on a tiny part of humanity for my great philosophical error? But there is one tiling for which I cannot forgive myself: that was a purely technical mistake, a mistake which could have been made by any workman. I am like a craftsman who has worked for twenty years with a complicated machine, and on the next day falls into melancholy over his family affairs, forgets his work, ignores the rhythm of his machine so that a belt parts and kills several unthinking workmen. You see, I have been tormented by the idea that thanks to my forgetfulness for the first time in twenty years I neglected to shut down the controls on container no. 216 and left it set at full power. And that realization, like a nightmare, pursued me on board this ship. And I was right. The container exploded and as a result the other storage units also. Once more it was my mistake. Rather than storing such great amounts of liquid sunshine I should have conducted preliminary experiments, it is true at the risk of my life, on the explosive capabilities of compressed light. Now, look in this direction," and he gently but firmly turned my head toward the east, "Remove your hand and then slowly, slowly open your eyes."

At that moment with extraordinary clarity, the way, they say. that occurs in the seconds before death, I saw a smoking red glow to the east, now contracting, now expanding, the steamship's listing deck, waves lashing over the railings, an angry, bloody sea and dark purple clouds in the sky and a beautiful calm face with a gray, silken beard and eyes which shone like mournful stars. A stifling hot wind blew from the shore.

"A fire?" I asked, turning slowly, as though in a dream, to face the south. There, above Cayambe's summit stood a thick smoky column of fire cut by rapid flashes of lightning.

"No, that is the eruption of our good old volcano. The exploding liquid sunshine has stirred it into life. You must agree that it has enormous power! And to think it was all in vain."

I understood nothing . . . My head was spinning. And then I heard a strange voice near me, both gentle like a mother's voice and commanding like that of a dictator.

"Sit on this bale and do everything faithfully as I tell you. Here is a life belt, put it on and fasten it securely under your arms, but do not restrict your breathing; here is a flask of brandy which you are to place in your left chest pocket along with three bars of chocolate, and here is a waterproof envelope with money and letters. In a moment the *Gonzalez* will be swamped by a terrible wave, such as has rarely been seen since the time of the flood. Lay down on the ship's starboard side. That is so. Place your legs and arms around this railing. Very good. Your head should be behind this steel plate, which will prevent you from becoming deaf from the shock. When you feel the wave hitting the deck, hold your breath for twenty seconds and then throw yourself free, and may God help you! This is all I can wish and advise you. And if you are condemned to die so early and so stupidly . . . I would like to hear you forgive me. I would not say that to any other man, but I know you are an Englishman and a gentleman."

His words, said so calmly and with such dignity, aroused my own sense of self-control. I found enough strength to press his hand and answer calmly:

"You can believe, my dear teacher, that no pleasures in life could replace those happy hours which I spent working with you. I only want to know why you are taking no precautions for yourself?"

I can see him now, holding to a compass box, as the wind blew his clothes and his gray beard, so terrible against the red background of the erupting volcano. That second I noticed with surprise that the unbearably hot shore wind had ceased, but on the contrary a cold, gusty gale blew from the west and our craft nearly lay on its side.

"Oh!" exclaimed Lord Charlesbury indifferently, and waved his arm. "I have nothing to lose. I am alone in this world. I have only one tie, that is you, and you I have put into deadly peril from which you have only one chance in a million to escape. I have a fortune, but I do not know what to do with it," and here his voice expressed a melancholy and gentle irony, "except to disperse it to the poor of County Norfolk and thereby increase the number of parasites and supplicants. I have knowledge, but you can see that it too has failed. I have energy but I have no way to employ it now. Oh, no, I will not commit suicide; if I am not condemned to die this night, I will employ the rest of my life in some garden on a bit of land not far from London. But if death comes," he removed his hat and it was strange to see his blowing hair, tossing beard, and kind, melancholy eyes and to hear his voice resounding like an organ, "but if death comes I shall commit my body and my soul to God, may He forgive the errors of my weak human mind."

"Amen." I said.

He turned his back to the wind and lighted a cigar. His dark figure defined sharply against the purple sky was a fantastic, and magnificent sight. I could smell the odor of his fine Havana cigar.

"Make ready. There is yet only a minute or two. Are you afraid?"

"No . . . But the crew and the other passengers! . . ."

"While you were unconscious I warned them. Now there is not a sober man nor a lifebelt left on the ship. I have no fear for you. for you have the talisman on your finger. I had one, too, but I have lost it. Oh, hold on! Henry! . . ."

I turned to the east and froze in horror. Toward our eggshell craft from the east roared an enormous wave as high as the Eiffel tower, black, with a rosy-white, frothing crest. Something crashed, shook . . . and it was as though the whole world fell onto the deck.

I lost consciousness once more and revived only several hours later on a little boat belonging to a fisherman who had rescued me. My damaged left hand was tied in a crude bandage and my head wrapped in rags. A month later, having recovered from my wounds and emotional shock I was on my way back to England.

This history of my strange adventure is complete. I must only add that I live modestly in the quietest part of London, needing nothing, thanks to the generosity of the late Lord Charlesbury. I occupy myself with the sciences and tutoring. Every Sunday Mr. Nideston and I alternate as hosts for dinner. We are bound by close ties of friendship, and our first toast is always to the memory of the great Lord Charlesbury.

H. Dibble

P.S. All the personal names in my tale are not authentic but invented by me for my purposes.

(1913)

Translated by Leland Fetzer

Alexei Mikhailovich Remizov
(1877–1957)

The Bear Cub

1

Alionushka woke up in the middle of the night.

It was stuffy in the nursery. Nanny Vlasevna snored and wheezed. The icon candle had burned down: its red flame kept flaring up and sinking low.

And Alionushka simply could not sleep; she was frightened and hot.

"Papa came home last night," she remembered, "I was getting ready for bed and Papa said 'Look at the sky, Alionushka, the stars are falling!' And Mamma and I stood and looked out the window for a long time. Stars are so little, and there's so much runny gold in them, like in Mamma's brooch. It's cold by the window, you can't stay there long. When you go with Papa to morning mass, it's cold then too: the bell rings like it does when there's a funeral. Yesterday Nanny was telling how in her dream Ivan Stepanovich was trying to catch hold of her, and he's dead . . . And there are so many stars up in the sky, the stars talk to each other, but you can't hear. Uncle Fyodor Ivanovich says that he can fly up to the stars at night and listen to the stars singing, softly-softly. They aren't there in the daytime, in the daytime they sleep. I'll fly up there too, if I can only get some golden wings . . . But Papa came up and said 'Alionushka, there's a Star falling.' And this gold ribbon shone for a long time in the sky and then went away. The little Star must be cold, it's lying out there somewhere, it's crying—my little Star!"

Alionushka was so frightened and so sorry for the Star, Alionushka started to whimper.

"I need a drink, Nanny, a dri-i-ink!"

And when Nanny Vlasevna gave Alionushka her cup, Alionushka stretched out her lips and drank thirstily.

Now Alionushka has curled herself up like a bun and fallen asleep.

And it seems to her that she is flying off somewhere towards the stars, like Uncle Fyodor Ivanovich, that little stars are coming to meet her, stretching out their golden paws, setting her on their shoulders and whirling around with her, and that the Moon is stroking her hair and quietly whispering, right in her ear:

"Alionushka, Alionushka! Get up, the Sun is awake, get up!"

Alionushka opened her eyes a crack, but it still seemed to her that she was flying to the stars like Uncle Fyodor Ivanovich.

"Why can't anybody wake you, get up at once!"—It was Mamma, Mamma who had bent over the bed and was tickling Alionushka.

2.

Alionushka's little Star flew on for a long while and fell, finally. into a forest, into a thicket where old firs weave their mossy branches together and hum eerily.

A thick gray smoke awoke, slithered across the sky, and the winter night was over. The Sun, too, came out of his crystal palace, richly dressed, with a red fur coat, with a brocade cap.

Translucent, with blue sad eyes, Alionushka's little Star lies not far from a hare's burrow on the soft fir needles: it breathes in the frosty air.

And the Sun climbed up and up and over the forest, and went home to its crystal palace.

Snowy clouds rose up and covered the sky, and twilight began to fall.

In a tinkling voice the wind—old churl—took up his ancient winter song.

A wild snow-squall sprang up, raised a wild cry.

The snow began to dance.

The poor little Star lies dozing by the hare's burrow, a melting tear-drop runs down her starry cheek and freezes there.

And the little Star dreams that she is once again flying around in the dance with her golden friends, they are happy and they are laughing like Alionushka laughs. But the stern Night, like old Nanny Vlasevna, is watching them.

3.

They were taking out the windows.

The whole day Alionushka stands by the open casement.

Stangers are passing by the window, drays are rocking, over there a cart is staggering along with matresses, tables and armchairs.

"That's going to the dacha!" Alionushka decides.

And the sky, the blue, clear sky seemed to smile at Alionushka.

"Mamma, Mamma—when are we going to the dacha?" Alionushka keeps asking.

"We're going to tidy up, lambkin, pack everything, and set off for a long ride, farther than last summer!" said Mamma: Mamma was sewing a smock for Lev, and she was too busy.

"We should leave quicker!" Alionushka is fretting.

Alionuskha doesn't even want to glance at her toys, wooden toys like those—boring. The toys were tired of winter too.

They were a long time laying the table, clatttering the plates.

They were a long time at dinner. Alionushka didn't even feel like eating.

And Alionushka slouches from one corner of the room to another, keeps looking out the windows, fusses, her tummy even starts to hurt.

They didn't wait for Papa, they tucked her into bed.

And through her dream Alionushka heard Papa and Mamma and Uncle Fyodor Ivanovich. At tea, talking about leaving for the dacha, into the woods the deep woods, where the trees even grow inside the house, grow over the roof. That's the kind of country it is!

Alionushka's head is spinning.

A big green Christmas tree appears before her; brightly lit with rainbow candles, strung with beads, hung with gingerbread cookies, the Christmas tree comes towards her, and from dark corners creep black and white bears in gold collars with little bells, they have drums and all around the bears are falling and flying little golden stars.

"But where is it, mine, where's my little Star?"—Alionushka is remembering—Uncle said that it would grow up to be a little girl like me, or a little animal. And what kind of animal is that?"

"Well now, Alionushka, how's your tummy?" That was Papa, Papa was leaning quietly over Alionushka, he was making the sign of the cross.

"No-o-o!" Alionushka squeals in her sleep.

"Get better quick, lambkin, tomorrow we're going to the dacha, the mountains there are high, the woods are deep!"

Alionushka turned over onto her other side, hugged her pillow tightly-tightly, and began to snuffle.

4.

Somehow all at once the stormwinds died down, and the overflowing rivers fell back asleep.

The buds turned crimson, here and there the first silken leaflets peeped out.

The grey, stony bracts of reindeer moss were palely greening, softening; many-colored lichens crept along on their sticky, velvet-green paws; the bearberries were covered with waxy blossoms.

The birds had arrived, and in their nests the little nestlings had begun to cheep.

By the hare's burrow Alionushka's little Star had awakened too. Over the winter she had become all covered with fur, like a cublet. On her paws grew sharp bear claws, and the little Star became not a Star, but a chubby, roly-poly little he-Bear.

The Bear Cub likes to jump from stump to stump and tussock to tussock, likes to break off the branches, deck himself with flowers.

Soon he will learn how to roar like a bear and frighten the little nestlings.

"Stay in your nests, children," the mother bird instructs them, "the Bear Cub is prowling about. He won't bite you, but he'll give you an awful fright."

For whole days together the Bear Cub wanders through the wood, and if he tires—he'll lie down somewhere in the sunlight and watch: he'll watch how the ants and their kingdom swarm, how the flowers and grasses grow, and how the moths play—everything pleases and interests him.

The Bear Cub will lie there for a bit, have a rest, and start off again. And where doesn't he go? Once he almost got mired in a swamp, it was all he could do to fight off the gnats, and the forget-me-nots laughed at him, the mosses chortled and teased him. But then he met a monster . . . The birds said it was—a HUNTER.

"Watch out for Man, stupid!" Woodpecker drummed." Man will put you on a chain. Here they went and caught Starling, he's in a cage now, they don't let him go free. I flew over to see him. 'Well, I'm alive,' he squeaks, 'They feed me enough, but I'm bored.' That's how everything is with them."

But the Bear Cub isn't troubled, he jumps about and chases beetles, and only when the sky turns crimson and gray clouds come out on patrol and the Moon rises to admire the sleepy wood—then he falls asleep where he is and sleeps deeply until the morning.

Somehow or other the Bear Cub got himself lost.

And the night came on, dark and stifling. There was not a peep from the birds and the animals in their nests and burrows.

The Bear Cub walked on and on, and suddenly became so frightened that he set up a howl—but no voices answer. And he was about to lie down underneath a thicket, but Woodpecker came to mind.

"They'll catch me and put a chain on me—better keep going!"

Through the wood there ran a long, rumbling din, and the leaves began to shake, just as they would from fear. Little blue serpents leaped up from the cross-branches of the firs and something cracked, struck the ancient, horned roots.

The Bear Cub took off as if he'd been scalded, he ran and ran, no matter where to, he was all scratched, he couldn't catch his breath, and then— voices and a light. The Cub was overjoyed.

"A bird's nest," he thought.

But the light went out and voices rang.

The Cub parted the bushes and he sees: a huge lighted room, many hunter-monsters are there, the hunters are eating and gabbling something or other.

"You Alionushka," Mamma says, "are not to go into the wood alone, bears will eat you up in there. The other day Uncle Fyodor Ivanovich went out hunting, and a little Bear Cub comes to meet him, tiny, just your size!"

"Papa, oh Papa," Alionushka was overjoyed, "you catch me that Bear Cub, I'm going to play with him!"

And as soo as the Bear Cub heard this he started to roar, and came out of hiding.

"Look, look," cried Mamma, there's the Cub!"

Then everyone sprang up from the table, Papa spilled the soup.

"Little Bear Cub, come here, here to us, have supper with us, Bear Cub!" Alionushka was jumping up and down.

So the Bear Cub came up to her and sniffed—he had already taken a great liking to the little fair-haired girl.

And Alionushka had taken a liking to the Bear: she sat him down next to her, stroked his muzzle, poked a morsel of white bread under his nose. And he gazed affectionately into her bright eyes and panted: he was so tired and had had such a fright.

"Well then, you've got your Bear Cub, you may play with him. But now get off to bed, you've stayed up late as it is!"

"Can he come with me?" Alionushka asked timidly.

"Certainly not, you go on by yourself, Papa will tie him to the thicket!" Mamma had been angry with Papa about the soup, and Alionushka, just holding back her tears, went on to the nursery alone.

For a long time she couldn't get to sleep, she kept thinking about the Cub, about how they would walk in the wood together, gather berries— there'd be nothing to be afraid of, nobody would eat her up when she was with the Bear Cub.

"Little Bear Cub. my dear little Bear Cub, poor little thing!" whispered Alionushka and fell asleep.

5.

A soon as she awoke Alionushka would run straight to the Bear Cub, untie him from the thicket and play all sorts of games: she would squeeze him and dress him up in Papa's old hat and ride on his back or lead him about by the paw for a long while and talk to him.

The Cub understood everything, only he couldn't speak, he growled.

In this way the days passed unnoticed.

With Alionushka the Cub is happy, but tied up he pines, remembers the birds and the other animals.

Autumn arrived, the nights grew colder. They would even sometimes light the stove.

The Bear Cub heard Papa and Mamma speak about leaving for home, and then Alionushka took him by the paw, stroked him, kissed his muzzle.

"You'll be left all alone soon," she said to the Cub, "Papa and Mamma don't want to take you, you'll bite."

And today Mamma told Alionushka not to go about with the Bear so much.

"Uncle went to pet him, but your Cub scratched him on the nose!"

"I better make a run for the wood, or they'll kill me!" reasoned the

Bear, and he felt so lonesome and heartsick and sorry for Alionushka.

They were getting ready to go.

In the evening guests arrived and Mamma was playing the piano.

But when Uncle began to sing, the Bear Cub started to howl an accompaniment from the thicket. And suddenly he flared up, broke his collar and ran straight into the room.

Everyone was horribly frightened, as if there were a fire, sprang up to catch the Bear Cub, and when they did catch him he bit Mamma on the finger. Then everyone started to shout.

"It's my Cub, don't you touch him!" shrieked Alionushka. But they tied up the Cub and dragged him away.

"Where'd you hide my Cub?", Alionushka squealed, her little mouth open wide as it would go.

"There there, lambkin," Nanny Vlasevna consoled her, "They'll let him free in the wood, it will be better for him there. Shh, Alionushka, shhh: tomorrow we're going home, and how your toys have missed you!"

I don't need toys, the Cub is mi-i-ne, you're all horrid!"

Her little face is all crimson, her tears are falling fast.

6.

Thick as can be, the stars of Autumn—silver ones, gold ones—are quietly flying back and forth, pouring across the sky.

The Moon has disappeared somewhere. Branches crack. Leaves fly off, they buzz.

"The Bear Cub is coming, hide yourselves quick" the birds and the animals call out. Noisily parting the twigs, the Cub emerges—on his neck is the broken rope and his fur hangs in clumps.

He scowled.

So the Cub comes to his den, tears through the thicket, lowers himself into the cave, growls:

"I'm going to sleep, and get a little rested up!"

And snoring resounds throughout the whole wood: it's the Bear Cub, sucking his paw and sleeping.

Flocks of birds disperse and gather into flocks again, the birds are flying off to warm lands, leaving behind the cold, forsaking their old nests until a new Spring.

The icon candle began to flicker, flared up and went out.

The gray light of morning stealthily crept up to the double windowpane and slyly looked into the nursery, and the darkness of night took its way slowly across the ceiling and walls, while in the corners shadows arose, murky columns that were somehow drowsy.

Kotofey Kotofeyich, the velvety black cat, stood up on his white, cushiony-soft paws, stretched, and, having yawned luxuriously, leapt onto Alionushka's bed.

Alionushka rubbed her sleepy eyes: was it the Bear Cub coming to eat her?

And Nanny Vlasevna wasn't there . . .

There was a dull thumping and footsteps.

The cat tuckeed in his paws, stretched out his whiskery nose and began to purr.

Now she was no longer frightened.

"Lordy,"Alionushka muses, "if only Christmas would hurry up and come, and then there'd be Easter, I'll go to morning mass, Easter is so nice!"

Her sleep-swollen lips wore a serious expression, but her little face was shining and Alionushka smiles, just as if the Magi were already approaching with the Star, hauling a great big Christmas tree with gingerbread ornaments.

Translated by A.L. and M.K.

The Blaze

CHAPTER ONE

Somehow White Fiokla, a sorceress and a witch, had spawned on a fall morning a black-winged mouse—a newly born scion of the Devil, as everyone could plainly see. Her son Ermil, born mute and without legs, hanged himself after laying the filth to rest in the cesspit.

On the night of St. Catherine's Day—when, following the old lore, young girls gnaw twigs off the branch and sleep with them in their teeth to bring on a dream of their destined mate—amidst the cruel and raging blizzard, thunder clapped suddenly on high. And little saintly Alionka, the railway foreman's daughter, was found in the town garden at dawn, deflowered and dead, with a twig clenched in her teeth.

On St. Nicholas' Day, three rainbow suns showed up in smoky clouds, encircling the ferociously-cold Sun. And those three immanent suns lay like a silent yoke upon the town.

"Hey, a hell of a burning fever, that's what's waiting for poor folks like us."

"Quit croaking up the Devil, we all walk under one God—everybody's equal in His eyes."

"Did I come up with it? It's got nothing to do with me, the priest, no, the deacon brought it up at the *ectenia* prayers the other day."

The alarming news was whispered back and forth . . . People already had vague premonitions of misfortune; it stood at the door, biding its time.

"The Chinaman with an army of a thousand-million'll come down right on top of Russia, together with the Turk."

"Great God, what a horde!"

"So you think our boys will just roll over?"

"Everybody knows what they say: *Borr* is on their side."

"We're done for, that's for damn' sure!"

With great care the windows were marked for the night with the sign of the cross, and watch was kept staunchly so that the icon lamp would not burn out.

"Did you hear this, Makarikha—the other day Avdotya was saying that at merchant Podkhomutov's they were calling for the unclean one right from out of the table."

"Ee-ee! What are you talking about!?"

"By the cross and the Heavenly Queen! Avdotya's a sly old girl and Podkhomutov's wife doesn't say a peep against it: there he was, all blue, and had six paws."

"Holy Virgin save us! What else is coming!"

"We're done for, that's for damn' sure!"

Bad dreams were common. Some saw The Church of the New Savior as it was at Easter, but with no altar and no icons. And inside the church Ermil, Fiokla's mute, legless son—the one who hanged himself—was walking about giving people the triple Easter kiss. Others saw some kind of bloated little boy covered with splinters, somersaulting around the floor.

Semion the railway workshop watchman went around mumbling: "This little soldier, an *Old Tabeliever*, says to me, 'Gramps,' he says, 'woe's hitting Russia everywhere: in Moscow the Tsar Bell's shattered into smithereens and every bit turned into a snake and the snakes crawled off under Great Ivan's bell tower. The bell tower's rocking and when it comes crashing down peoples' hearts will fly to pieces and the end of all life will begin.'"

"What don't they say nowadays, you could die laughing! The primary cause of it all is in the production force, and all the rest is a side-show, an adstruction. Let's disavow the old world . . .

"Shut your trap, they won't treat the likes of you with kid gloves—off to the precinct, you rebels!"

"And in general," stated the police commissioner's circular, "if necessary, proper measures will be adopted, holding nothing back, to snuff out the suns that have just appeared, about which ill-intended parties are spreading rumors and disturbing the peaceful population."

But the rainbow suns did not disappear; now and again they would appear in the sky encircling the ferociously-cold Sun.

Life went on the same old way.

Never before was such an abundant yield seen in the district—no memory of a harvest like this year's. The mills were loaded to capacity and ground the choice grain unflaggingly. Along criss-crossing railway tracks boxcars overfilled with every kind of grain and flour were driven up and driven off to all four corners. The trading was fast and furious, and buyers were reasonable.

On Christmas Eve White Fiokla was butchered. And it felt like a millstone rolled off everyone's heart. The oldsters cleansed themselves for Epiphany by cutting holes in the ice and washing themselves with freezing epiphany water. Little crosses were painted in chalk in the corners and on the doors of their homes. And all went on swimmingly, as if cooked on a well-buttered pan.

Spring came in good time, early and warm. The gardens greened at Easter and the winter wheat came in strong and sturdy.

The first week after Easter wedding celebrations were getting into swing.

A few even remembered White Fiokla with a bit of kindness:

"If only the old woman could go on living—they killed the poor soul for nothing!"

New houses sprang up: solemnly blessed with holy water strong foundations were being laid, and ever higher, piling up, day after day, the scaffolding sped upwards against the siding, board crosses overshadowing the future dwellings.

At the Easter observance a fire at the Bishop's had caused quite a stir: they carried from the Bishop's flaming bathhouse the charred body of the Mother Superior of the Bogodukhovo Convent, and his worship couldn't appear at services for a long while due to his burns.

There was winking and smirking.

And dejection too.

"The Devil has stolen the Cross, it's with the Devil now," mumbled Semion, the railway workshop watchman.

And the little soldier, the *Old Tubeleiver*, seconded:

"The heelless one has taken over God's temple and His throne. The goblin is fouling the paten and spitting in the chalice. And people are receiving not Christ's blood in the eucharist, but the Devil's spittle, and are eating not Christ's body but the Devil's filth."

"We're done for, that's for damn' sure!" concluded the listeners.

On the heels of warm and flowery May the summer heat came hard. Drought took over and not a single sprinkle quenched the thirst of desiccating fields, dust-swathed meadows and worm-ridden gardens.

CHAPTER TWO.

On a fine St. John the Baptist's noon an urgent alarm rang from the Cathedral belfry: a blaze had broken out in town.

Fire took over whole streets of different corners of town, jam-packed with working people and every sort of beggar. Little wooden hovels and awkwardly cumbersome, clumsy flophouses went up like piles of rotten tinder. Flame broke through and disappeared in giant spindles of dust. Dusty spindles swept whirling through the town. And it was as if an unseen hand were spinning stifling, searing, smoke-gray yarn in a sky that was incandescent and unmarred by a single cloud. Taken by surprise, people now tongue-tied in awe rushed about in confusion and howled wildly like beasts.

Then, as the factory whistle began to whistle at its usual time, how alien it sounded amidst the fire's whistling and the lonely shrill cries, cries that begged for mercy, for children to be saved, for goods to be safeguarded . . .

Icons were carried out; it was believed that the icons would intercede and protect from disaster.

Yet the flame, creeping on, a-buzz as it went, tried out secret nooks and then took off, engulfing still intact houses in its embrace. Dusty spindles, dark-blue in the evening light, swept whirling through the town. And it was as if a dark-blue fiery bit was boring a hole through the heavy air. A puffed-up rosy glow poured shuddering over the town, above black chimneys jutting from the fire-ruins.

The railway workshops and petroleum were burning.

Burning locomotives, in a kind of scarlet rage, in a kind of terror, as if baited beyond endurance, leapt out of their iron stalls. They whistled all along the tracks with a stuttering, dry whistle. And something sighed and sizzled, uncanny and sinister, under their red-incandescent wheels.

Roasting grain elevators sputtered and overflowed like fountains. Someone, rabid and howling with laughter at the top of his lungs, was pouring the bloodied bits of amber grain from hand to hand.

On St. John the Baptist's enchanted midnight an urgent alarm began to peal in the Cathedral belfry once again: the jolly haunts in the narrow lanes had started going up in smoke.

Fire entered, a guest that gives no quarter, fire zealously sank its fangs into the walls and licked the ceiling with its delicate tongue.

Naked bodies—any which way, cut by glass and covered in burns, fell from the upper floors onto the pavement.

The kindled pupils of the choking crowd seemed to expand and explode in the heat, and a creaking, crazy laughter mixed with their beseeching wails.

A dark-clothed monk with an immobile stony face stood in the fire's hell. He alone was unperturbed, as he might have stood at midday, so stood

he now, awesome in his calm. The fire boiling in the depths of his eyes penetrated the tongues of flame.

A thousand hands seized his skirts, the black soaring wings of his
monastic cap, a thousand hands crawled toward his feet . . .

"You, our savior, preserve us!"

"You, our savior, save us!"

"You, our savior, pity and forgive us!"

And the frightful urgent alarm was struck in the Cathedral belfry a
third time, when the lazily ascending sun, panting in blood-gold rays,
dawned upon the earth: a horrific thick smoke came rolling from two opposite ends of town.

The prison was in flames. The hospital was in flames.

What a holiday for vengeful fire, willful fire, tearing asunder the living
coffins, the cursed prison!

The inmates broke out the iron doors, crushed the warder with a grating, and, beaten up and shot, crawled their way into town.

And in the hospital's suffocating wards, in yellow-green light amidst
dancing orange suns, heart-lacerating groans arose and the Gehenna laughter of lunatics spilled out.

The fire squeals and darts about like a squirrel. And now it has thrown
its burning meshes over the hospital walls, onto the abattoir.

The town shuddered all at once under the antediluvian yowling; the
animals yowled too, in human anguish.

Next to the prison, the cemetery went up in flames.

Fire with its glowing hot, heavy crow-bar pried open the silent tombs.
And the dead, it seemed, rose from their coffins and grew into black pillars
of stinking black smoke.

The dark-clad monk, lips tensely compressed, arms crossed, stood
among the mobs turned bestial and the sorrowing beasts.

Sparks flew, coiling upwards round his head like flights of golden birds.

The alarm beat unceasingly.

People ran—flayed, seared, despairing.

State liquor stores were burning.

How many hungry souls fell upon the gratis vodka! And the fire-water
ate into their hearts. And the miserable creatures writhed in the dark-blue,
unbearable flame.

The alarm beat unceasingly.

People went out of their minds from the terror. Mothers could not find
their children. Children were dragging about heavy loads. No one dared to
stay under any roof that still survived. They fled their homes, finding their
way into the street. They searched for the arsonists. It seemed they were
picking up the scent . . . Dark-robed women snooped about the undersides

of house gates. Old Semion the watchman, carelessly lighting up his pipe, was torn limb from limb. The little soldier, the *Old Tabeliever*, had his arm torn off. Someone was tossed into the fire. Someone else had his arm torn off as well. Another was rent apart.

"Who is it? Where should we search? Where's the arsonist?" they asked the monk. "You, our savior, preserve us! You, our savior, save us! You, our savior, pity and forgive us!"

And on the fences in black letters stood the inscription: *There Will Be No Fire Tomorrow.*

CHAPTER THREE.

A fine mesh of scarlet smoke hung above the town. The bloody-burning kernel of the sun, spreading taint, stench, and fuming cinders, swam behind the scarlet mesh.

The third morning was beginning, the third and last day.

Overnight the cathedral with its powerful relics had burned down. The bell tower came crashing down. And the loud, throaty voice of the alarm bell ceased to sound and call.

There was nothing left to burn. The town had reached the end of burning.

Mind-befogged crowds wandered about. They bludgeoned with charred logs any old enemies who came in their way. As night approached, drunk on terror, despair, and blood, they left the town behind.

At the dump behind the town those who were still in one piece, huddled tightly together, went to earth themselves that final night.

And the monk in his dark habit stood in the midst of the survivors.

But no voice called out to or beseeched the monk—only eyes, hundreds of eyes bent themselves on the heart concealed beneath his cassock, begging merciful forgiveness.

And look! For the first time there was a flicker in the monk's immobile face of stone.

The monk removed a vessel from his breast, and moistening the aspergillum, sprinkled the beseeching eyes.

And in a wink, like a single dry bonfire, the whole field burst into flame. A fiery cloud rent the heavens and split the night, and sparks flew from the heavens to earth and from earth to the heavens.

———————

In the distance a profound darkness lay above the fire-consumed town. And only the stars looked upon the earth, on the monk in dark tatters. He alone stood in the midst of the ashes of his native town, that he had incinerated and damned, and his offended heart burned worse than any blaze and harsher than any fire.

(1914) Translated by A.L. and M.K.

The Orison on the Downfall
of the Russian Land

(A fragment from *Russia in the Whilwind*)

Unbounded and wide—Thou art, Rus'!

I see Thy fine Kremlin bells, Thy gold-roofed Annunciation Cathedral —snow-white as the unblemished breast of a maiden. But no silvery tribute is promised to me, nor do Thy radiant bells ring. Or are they drowned by the whistle of countless and merciless bullets which have stripped the world's heart of compassion—the heart of all Earth?

All that I hear is the clamor of warfare—Thy moaning, ablaze: all Rus' has erupted in flames, and Thy timber—all charred—flies about. For time out of mind it was otherwise: all knew that Thou, standing erect, would go on standing wide and unbounded, and never be cast down—not even in all Thy travails and Thy passions. And were the plague to cover Thy body with scabs, the wind would remove the pestilence—blow it away, and Thou wouldst arise once again in Thy brightness and yet more bright—more joyful once more, yet again more sublime—above Thy green forests, Thy feather-grass steppe, the steppe bursting with joy.

O leaders so blind, what have you brought to pass? That blood that you've spilled on our brotherly fields has stripped now a man's heart of pity, uprooting the soul. And now it is warfare and moans that I hear—my Rus', Thou art on fire! My Rus', Thou hast fallen, and there is no raising Thee, Thou canst not rise! My Rus', my Russian land, my motherland: stripped of pity by the blood on brotherly fields—

Thou hast been set on fire and art on fire!

(1920 and 1928) Translated by A.L. and M.K.

Petersburg

(A prologue to the novel *In a Rosy Light*)

Petersburg—the city transparently nordic and lucent!

Only jealous Moscow has slandered you so far this way and that—the same Moscow where folk from its own quarters revel in bad-mouthing its other dwellers: those from Taganka sneer at Zemlianka, and from Zemlianka they jeer at Zamoskvorechie, Zamoskvorechie—Arbat, and Arbat—Pokrovka. *Their* common despair has seen in *you* only heavy fogs, laden with devils and apparitions; it's the hard-heatedness of the "Servants in Christ of Latter-day Russia" which—from Moscow's earthen dungeons and flaming log cabins—has noised about that damning curse: "Thou shalt lie waste!"

No, Neva is unique. Neva—like the Sea, and not only by Gogol's measure, but by that of its own Admiralty—is wide indeed. What a Sea of the Sun burns atop its deep blueness, tirelessly riding pillion!

And the pure ducat-gold of St. Isaac's dome has gathered such a sheaf of rays—above all your prospects, streets, and rows it burns—burns not like the roof of poured gilt on Moscow's Kremlin, or all of Moscow, but a like a flaming globe of pure, red gold.

And if sometimes fogs creep up in Autumn, or if in Winter one gets lost in the misty smoke and can't get down Nevsky on foot or by car, since the etched green spheres of the electric street lamps fail to pierce the mists . . . if *they* tease you about this—well, it is the same all over the Globe: in London, and in Paris, where from the cresting Seine such a milky horror creeps that grippe starts choking folk right and left, or in Berlin, where passers-by huff like horses in the poisonous wintry mists and, hunched over, run along the streets not knowing where to find comforting warmth.

Yes, there are fogs in Petersburg, and so there are in London, Paris and Berlin—impassable on foot or otherwise! But then that biting Muscovy frost will suddenly strike, and the evening will be swathed in a scarlet-blue northern veil, beyond which Night is forging a formidable Epiphany to the stars.

And bonfires will flare up on snowy squares and beside your white bridges—flaming up to the stars themselves.

(1912-17 and 1952), Translated by A.L. and M.K.

Evgeny Ivanovich Zamiatin
(1884–1937)

The Dragon

Sunk in acrid cold, Petersburg burned in its delirium. It was obvious: out there, unseen behind the veil of mist, creaking and shuffling, red and yellow columns, spires, and gray balustrades tiptoed by. A feverish, freakish, icy Sun hovered through the fog—to the left, the right, up, down—like a dove over a burning house. From the delirious misty world dragon-men were surfacing into the earthly world—belching fog which was heard in the misty world as words, but here transmuted into round white whiffs of smoke—they were surfacing and drowning in the mist. And the screeching street-cars careened into the unknown, out of the earth-world.

At the street-car stop a dragon with a rifle came into existence for a moment, careening into the unknown. Its cap slid down over the nose and of course it would have swallowed up the dragon's head, if it hadn't been for its ears: on these protruding ears the cap had settled. Its army coat dangled to the ground; the sleeves flapped; its boot-toes turned up, empty. And a hole in the mist—its mouth.

This was now happening in the leaping-off, rushing world; and here the bitter-cold fog belched out by the dragon was visible and audible: "So I'm taking this bastard along, a smart-ass intellectual mug—made you sick to look at. And it even talks, the sonofabitch! Wouldn't you know it? Talks!"

"And so—you brought him in?"

"I sure brought him—nonstop—to the Pearly Gates. With my little friend—the bayonet."

The hole in the mist closed. Now there was only empty cap, empty boots, and empty army coat. The screeching street-car careened out of the world.

And suddenly—out of the empty sleeves—from their depths—emerged red dragon paws. The empty army coat hunkered down on the floor: and in the paws there was a tiny, grayish, cold lump, materialized out of the acrid cold mist.

"Mama mia! A baby sparrow—you're frozen stiff, huh? Whattaya say!"

The dragon pushed the peak of its cap back—and in the mist two eyes—two narrow chinks from the feverish world into the human.

The dragon with all his might blew into his red paws, and these were clearly words addressed to the tiny sparrow—but they were inaudible in the feverish world. The street-car screeched.

"The sonofabitch: he gave a little flutter, didn't he? Not yet? He'll come to, by Go . . . Whattaya you say!"

With all his strength he blew. The rifle dropped to the floor. And at the instant ordained by fate, at a point ordained in space, the grayish baby sparrow gave a jerk, another—and fluttered off the dragon's red paws into the unknown.

The dragon gaped his fog-belching maw open, to the ears. Slowly the chinks into the human world were covered over by the cap which came to rest again on the protruding ears. The Guide to the Pearly Gates picked up his rifle.

The street-car gnashed its teeth and rushed into the unknown, out of the human world.

(1918)

Translated by A.L. and M.K.

In lieu of an epigraph (ed.)

SOME say the world will end in fire,
Some say in ice.
From what I've tasted of desire
I hold with those who favor fire.
But if it had to perish twice,
I think I know enough of hate
To know that for destruction ice
Is also great
And would suffice.

—ROBERT FROST, *Fire and Ice* (1920)

The Cave

Glaciers, mammoths, wastelands. Black rocks in the night that somehow resemble houses; in the rocks—caves. And no one knows who trumpets at night along the stony path among the rocks; and, sniffing out the path, blows about the white snow-dust. Perhaps it is a gray-trunked mammoth; perhaps the wind; but perhaps—the wind *is* the icy roar of some super-mammothish mammoth. One thing is clear: it is Winter. And you have to clench your teeth as tight as you can to keep them from chattering; and you have to split kindling with a stone axe; and each night you have to move your fire from cave to cave, deeper and deeper; and you have to bundle yourself with more and more shaggy animal hides. . . .

Among the rocks, where ages ago had stood Petersburg, a gray-trunked mammoth roamed at nights. And wrapped in hides, coats, blankets, rags, the cave dwellers retreated from cave to cave. On the Day of Intercession Martin Martinych and Masha boarded up the study; on the Day of the Kazan Mother of God they made their way out of the dining room and entrenched themselves in the bedroom. There was no further retreating: here they must withstand the siege—or die.

In the cavelike Petersburg bedroom everything was just as it recently had been in Noah's Ark: clean and unclean creatures—flood-confounded. Martin Martinych's mahogany desk; books; stone-age flat cakes resembling some pottery; Scriabin's *Opus 74*; a flat-iron; five potatoes lovingly washed white; nickel-plated bed frames; an axe; a chiffonier; firewood. And in the middle of this universe—its god: a short-legged, rusty-red, squat, greedy cave-god: a cast-iron stove.

God droned powerfully. In the dark cave—a great fiery wonder. The people—Martin Martinych and Masha—reverently, silently, thankfully, stretched forth their hands to him. For one hour—Spring was in the cave; for one hour—animal hides, claws and fangs were thrown off, and through the ice-covered brain crust broke green shoots—thoughts.

"Mart, you haven't forgotten that tomorrow—never mind, I see that you have!"

In October, when leaves have already yellowed, dulled and drooped, there come blue-eyed days; on such a day, throw back your head so you cannot see the earth, and you can believe there is still joy, it is still summer. And so it was with Masha, if you just close your eyes and only listen: you can believe that she is her former self, and that this very minute she will break into laughter, rise from the bed, embrace you; and an hour ago as a knife scraped on glass—it was not her voice, not her at all. . . .

"Oh Mart, Mart! How is everything . . . You never forgot before. The twenty-ninth: St. Mary's—my names-day. . . ."

The cast-iron god still droned. As always, there was no light: it would go on only at ten. The dark, shaggy vaults of the cave swayed. Martin Martinych, squatting with his head thrown back—the knot is tighter! ever tighter!—keeps on looking into the October sky—so as to not see the yellowed, drooping lips. But Masha—

"You understand, Mart. If the fire were started in the morning, so that all day long it would be as it is now! Eh? Well, how many have we? Well, is there still about half a cord in the study?"

For a long, long time now Masha had not been able to get to the arctic study, and she did not know that there was already . . . Tighter the knot, ever tighter!

"Half a cord? More! I think that there . . ."

Suddenly—the light: it is exactly ten. And not having finished, Martin Martinych squinted and turned away: in the light it is more difficult than in the dark. And in the light one can clearly see: his face is crumpled, clayey (nowadays many have faces of clay: back—to Adam). And Masha—

"And you know. Mart, I'd try—maybe I'll get up . . . if you'll start the fire in the morning."

"Why, Masha, of course . . . Such an occasion . . . Why of course, from morning."

The cave-god grew quieter, contracted, became still; now and then he crackles. Listen: downstairs, at the Obertyshevs' [the Shifters'], they are splitting logs of a barque with a stone axe—with that stone axe they are splitting Martin Martinych into pieces. A piece of Martin Martinych clayishly smiled at Masha and ground dried potato peels in the coffee grinder for flat cakes; and a piece of Martin Martinych, like a free bird which had flown into a room, aimlessly and blindly beat against the ceiling, the windows, the walls: "Where would I get some wood, where to get some wood, where to get wood?"

Martin Martinych put on his coat, girded himself with a leather belt (the cave dwellers have a myth that it is warmer this way), and banged a pail by the bureau in the corner.

"Where to, Mart?"

"I'll be right back. Downstairs for water."

On the dark stairway, icy with water splashes, Martin Martinych stood for a moment, rocked to and fro, took a deep breath, and then, with a fetter-like rattle of the pail, he went downstairs to the Obertyshevs': they still had running water. The door was opened by Obertyshev himself, dressed in a coat tied with rope, long unshaven, his face—a waste overgrown with some sort of reddish, dust-laden weed. Showing through the weeds—yellow stone teeth; and between the stones—the flick of a lizard's tail—a smile.

"Ah, Martin Martinych! What? You've come for some water? Come in, come in, come in."

In the narrow cage between the outer and inner doors you could not turn around with a pail in hand—in that cage was Obertyshev's firewood. Martin Martinych, made of clay, bumped his side painfully against the firewood: there was a deep indentation in the clay. And still deeper— against the corner of a chest of drawers in the dark corridor. Through the dining room— in the dining room was the she-Obertyshev and three Obertyshlings; the she-Obertyshev was hastily hiding a bowl under a napkin: a man has come from another cave and God knows, he might suddenly pounce and grab.

In the kitchen, having turned on the faucet, Obertyshev gave a stony-toothed smile:

"Well, how's your wife? How's your wife? How's your wife?"

"Oh well, still the same, Alexei Ivanych. Bad! Tomorrow is her names-day, but I have no . . ."

"It's the same, Martin Martinych, the same with everyone, the same, the same."

Listen: a bird has flown into the kitchen; it flutters, and rustles its wings; to the right, to the left—and suddenly in desperation it strikes the wall full with its breast:

"Alexey Ivanych, I wanted . . . Alexey Ivanych, couldn't you . . . just five or six logs . . ."

Yellow stone teeth showing through the weeds, yellow teeth—from his eyes, all of Obertyshev was being over-grown with teeth, teeth that grew longer and longer.

"Oh, come now, Martin Martinych, come now, come now. We our-selves have but . . . You know yourself how things are nowadays, you know, you know. . . ."

Tighter the knot! Tighter—ever tighter! Martin Martinych wound him-self up, lifted the pail, and—through the kitchen, through the dark corridor, through the dining room. At the dining room threshold Obertyshev stuck out his hand—a momentary lizardy whisk.

"Well, so long. . . . Only the door, Martin Martinych, don't forget to slam it shut, don't forget. Both doors, both, both—you just can't get enough heat!"

On the dark ice-encrusted landing Martin Martinych set down the pail, turned around, firmly pulled shut the first door. He listened: he heard only the dry shivering of his bones and his tremulous breathing, punctuated like a dotted line. In the narrow cage between the two doors he stretched forth a hand, felt around—a log, and another, and another. . . . No! Quickly he shoved himself out onto the landing, closed the door. Now only to slam it more tightly, so the lock would click. . . .

But—he had no strength. He had no strength to slam the door on Masha's tomorrow. And on a line delineated by his scarcely perceptible punctuated breathing, two Martin Martinyches grappled in a struggle to the death: the one, of old, of Scriabin, who knew: he must not—and the new one, of the cave, who knew: he must. He of the cave, with teeth grind-ing, trampled, strangled the other—and Martin Martinych, breaking his nails, opened the door, stuck his hand into the firewood—a log, a fourth, a fifth,—under his coat, in his belt, into the pail—slammed the door and up the stairs—with huge animal's bounds. In the middle of the stairs, on some icy step, he suddenly froze, and pressed into the wall: below, the door clicked again—and Obertyshev's dust-laden voice:

"Who's—there? Who's there? Who's there?"

"It's me, Alexey Ivanych. I . . . I forgot the door . . . I wanted to . . . I returned to close the door more tightly . . ."

"You? Hm . . . How could you do that? You must be more careful, more careful. Nowadays everybody steals, you know yourself, you know yourself. How could you do that?"

The twenty-ninth. From morning—a low, cottony sky full of holes, and through the holes—an icy breath. But the cave-god stuffed his belly from morning, graciously began to drone—and let there be holes, let Obertyshev, overgrown with teeth, count his logs—let him, it makes no difference: if only for today; tomorrow has no meaning in the cave; only after ages have passed will "tomorrow" and "the day after tomorrow" be known.

Masha got up and, rocked by an invisible wind, combed her hair as of old: over her ears with a parting in the middle. It was like the last, withered leaf fluttering on a bare tree. From the middle drawer of the desk Martin Martinych took papers, letters, a thermometer, some kind of blue phial (he hurriedly shoved it back, so Masha would not see) and, finally, from the furthest corner, a black lacquered box. In it, on the bottom, there still was some real—yes! yes! some most real tea! They drank real tea. Martin Martinych, having thrown back his head, listened to a voice so similar to that of the past:

"Mart, do you remember: my nice blue room, and the piano with its cover, and on the piano—a little wooden horse—an ashtray, and I was playing, and you came up from behind—"

Yes, that evening the universe was created, and the wonderful, wise old snout of the moon, and the nightingale-trill of bells in the hallway.

"And do you remember, Mart: the window open, the green sky—and below, from another world—the organ-grinder?"

Organ-grinder, marvelous organ-grinder—where are you?

"And on the embankment . . . remember? Branches—still bare, the water—reddish, and the last blue block of ice, resembling a coffin, floats by. And the coffin only made us laugh, for we—we'll never die. Remember?"

Downstairs they began splitting wood with a stone axe. Suddenly they ceased, some sort of scurrying, a shout. And split in two, Martin Martinych with one half saw the immortal organ-grinder, the immortal little wooden horse, the immortal block of ice, and with the other—his breath punctuated— he was re-counting with Obertyshev the logs of firewood. Now Obertyshev has already counted them, now he is putting on his coat; all overgrown with teeth he savagely slams the door, and—

"Wait, Masha, it seems—it seems that someone is knocking at our door."

No. No one. No one as yet. He can still breathe, he can still throw back his head and listen to the voice—so similar to the other, the former.

Dusk. The twenty-ninth of October has grown old. The staring, blurry eyes of an aged woman—and everything shrivels, wrinkles, hunches up under the fixed gaze. The vaulted ceiling is settling; the armchairs, the desk,

Martin Martinych, the beds were flattened, and on the bed—a completely flat, paper-thin Masha.

Selikhov, the house-chairman, came at dusk. At one time he had been well over two hundred pounds, but now half of that had gone; he knocked about in his jacket-husk like a nut in a rattle. But he rumbled with laughter as of old.

"W-e-ll, Martin Martinych, in the first place—secondly, I congratulate your wife on the great day of her saint. Ah, yes! Of course! Of course! Obertyshev told me. . . ."

Martin Martinych was shot from the armchair, he bolted, hurried to speak, to say something. . . .

"Some tea . . . I'll immediately—this very minute . . . Today we have real tea. Real tea! I only . . ."

"Some tea? You know, I'd prefer champagne. There ain't any? No kidding? Har-har-har! And you know, the day before yesterday me and my friend brewed our own from Hoffman drops. What fun! He got potted. 'I am Zinoviev;' he says, 'on your knees!' What fun! And I was going home from there when on Mars Field a man comes toward me in shirt sleeves, by God! 'What's with you?' I say. 'Oh, nothing,' he says, 'They just undressed me and I am running home to Vasilievsky.' What fun!"

Flattened, paper-thin, Masha laughed on the bed. Tying himself into a tight knot, Martin Martinych laughed louder and louder—in order to stoke Selikhov; so he would not stop, so he would say something more. . . .

Selikhov was stopping, snorting slightly; he became still. He swayed in his jacket-husk—to the right, to the left: he got up.

"W-e-ll, ma'am, your hand. Pam! What? You don't know? In their lingo, the pleasure's all mine—p.a.m. What fun!"

He thundered in the hallway, in the vestibule. The last second: he will leave now, or . . .

The floor swayed and spun slightly under the feet of Martin Martinych. Smiling a clay smile, Martin Martinych supported himself on the door-jamb. Selikhov puffed while pounding his feet into huge overshoes.

In his overshoes, in his fur coat, mammoth-like, he straightened up, caught his breath. Then silently he took Martin Martinych by the arm, silently he opened the door into the arctic study, silently he sat down on the sofa.

The floor in the study—a block of ice; scarcely audible, the block cracked, broke from the shore—and carried, carried, spun Martin Martinych, and from there—from the sofa, the distant shore—Selikhov can barely be heard.

"In the first place—secondly, my dear sir, I must tell you: I'd take that Obertyshev, like a louse, and by God . . . But you understand: since he has complained officially, since he says—'tomorrow I'll go to the criminal investigation office.' . . . What a louse! I can suggest only one thing: go to him, today, right now—and stuff those logs down his throat."

The block of ice—faster and faster. The minute, flattened, scarcely visible—a splinter—Martin Martinych answered to himself; and not about firewood, but about something else:

"Very well. Today. Right away."

"That's fine, that's fine! He's such a louse, such a louse, I'll tell you. . . ."

It is still dark in the cave. Cold, blind, made of clay—Martin Martinych dully stumbled against the flood-confounded objects in the cave. He started: a voice resembling Masha's, her former voice:

"What were you and Selikhov talking about? What? Ration cards? Mart, I was lying and thinking: if we'd gather our strength and go somewhere, where there is Sun . . . Oh! How noisy you are! As if on purpose. Don't you know!—I can't, I can't, I can't!"

A knife on glass. However—now it made no difference. Mechanical arms and legs. Some sort of chains, a winch, are needed to raise and lower them, like the sheers of a ship; and to turn the winch—one man is not enough: three are needed. Tightening the chains beyond his strength, Martin Martinych set a teakettle and saucepan to heat, threw on the last Obertyshev logs.

"Do you hear what I am telling you? Why are you silent? Do you hear?"

This, of course, is not Masha; no, it is not her voice. Martin Martinych moved slower and slower, his feet were swallowed by quicksand, the winch turned harder and harder. Suddenly a chain tore loose from some block, a sheer-arm crashed down, awkwardly bumped the tea-kettle and saucepan—they clattered to the floor, the cave-god hissed like a snake. And over there, from the distant shore, from the bed—a strange piercing voice:

"You did that on purpose! Go away! This very instant! I don't want to see anybody, I don't need anything, I don't need anything! Go away!"

The twenty-ninth of October died, and the immortal organ-grinder died, and the blocks of ice on the reddish water at sunset, and Masha. And this is good. There should be no fantastic tomorrow, no Obertyshev, no Selikhov, no him—no Martin Martinych; everything should die.

The mechanical, distant Martin Martinych was still doing something. Perhaps he again was lighting the stove, and was gathering the contents of the saucepan from the floor, and was setting the teakettle to boil; and perhaps Masha was saying something—he did not hear; there were only dully aching indentations in the clay from some sort of words, from the corners of the chiffonier, chairs, desk.

Martin Martinych was slowly extracting from the desk bundles of letters, a thermometer, sealing-wax, a little box of tea, and again—letters. And finally, somewhere from the very bottom, a small dark-blue phial.

Ten o'clock: the light was turned on. Bare, harsh, plain, cold (like cave life, and death) electric light. And beside the flat-iron, the 74th *Opus*, the flat cakes—such a plain, blue phial.

The cast-iron god droned kindly, devouring the parchment-yellow, bluish and white paper of the letters. The teakettle rattled its lid, quietly bringing itself to mind. Masha turned around:

"Has the tea boiled? Mart dear, give me—"

She saw it. One second, pierced through and through by the clear, bare, cruel electric light: huddled before the stove—Martin Martinych; on the letters—a reddish reflection, like the water at sunset; and there—the blue phial.

"Mart . . . You . . . you already want to . . ."

It is quiet. Indifferently devouring the immortal, bitter, tender, yellow, white, blue words—quietly purred the cast-iron god. And Masha—just as simply as when asking for tea:

"Mart, dear! Mart—give it to me."

Martin Martinych smiled from afar.

"But you do know, Masha: there's only enough for one."

"Mart, I'm gone anyway. This is not me—it makes no difference, I'll . . . Mart, you do understand—Mart, have a pity for me—Mart!"

Oh, that same—that same voice . . . And if you would throw back your head . . .

"Masha, I deceived you: there's not a single log in our study. And I went to Obertyshev, and there between the doors . . . I stole—do you understand? And Selikhov told me . . . I must take them back right away—but I've burned them all, I've burned them all—all of them!"

Indifferently, the cast-iron god drowses. Dying out, the cave vaults shudders slightly, and slightly shudder the houses, the rocks, the mammoths, Masha.

"Mart, if you still love me . . . Please, Mart. Remember! Mart, dear, give it to me!"

The immortal wooden little horse, the organ-grinder, the block of ice. And this voice . . . Martin Martinych slowly rose from his knees. Slowly, with difficulty turning the winch, he took the phial from the table and gave it to Masha.

She threw off the blanket, sat on the bed—rosy, quick, immortal, like the water had once been at sunset, grabbed the phial, laughed.

"So you see: not without cause have I lain and thought of leaving here. Turn on another lamp—that one, on the table. That's right. Now throw something else in the stove—I wish the the fire would . . ."

Martin Martinych, without looking, scooped some papers out of the desk, threw them in the stove.

"Now . . . Go take a short walk. It seems that the moon is out there—*my* moon: remember? Don't forget—take the key, otherwise you'll lock the door, and won't be able to . . ."

No, there was no moon there. Low, dark thick clouds—a vault, and everything—one huge, quiet cave. Narrow, endless passageways between walls; and resembling houses—dark, ice-encrusted rocks; and in the rocks—deep holes glowing crimson; there, in the holes by the fire—squatting people. A light, icy draught blows white dust from under their feet, and heard by no one—over the white dust, over the boulders, over the caves, over the squatting people—the huge, measured tread of some super-mammothish mammoth.

(1920-2)
Translated by Gleb Struve

[from] WE

Record 1
Synopsis: An Announcement / The Wisest of Lines / A Poem

I am simply transcribing—word for word—what was printed in the *State Gazette* today:

"In 120 days the construction of INTEGRAL will be completed. The mighty, historical hour is near when the first INTEGRAL will soar into universal space. One thousand years ago, your heroic ancestors subjugated the entire earthly sphere to the power of the United State. Awaiting you is an even more glorious feat: the integration of the infinite equation of the universe by means of the glass, electrical, fire-breathing INTEGRAL. Awaiting you is the subjugation of those unknown creatures inhabiting other planets to the beneficent yoke of reason—and perhaps still living in a wild state of freedom. If they will not comprehend that we bring them a mathematically infallible happiness, our duty is to force them to be happy. But before arms—we will attempt words.

In the name of the Benefactor it is hereby announced to all the numbers of the United State:

Everyone who feels capable is obliged to compose treatises, poems, manifestoes, odes or other works, on the beauty and grandeur of the United State.

This will be the first cargo which the INTEGRAL will carry.

All hail to the United State, all hail to the numbers, all hail to the Benefactor!"

I am writing this—and I feel: my cheeks are burning. Yes: the integration of the grandiose universal equation. Yes: to unbend the wild curve, to straighten it out along a tangent—an asymptote—to a straight line. Because the line of the United State—is a straight line. A great, divine, precise, wise, straight line—the wisest of lines . . .

I, D-503, the builder of the INTEGRAL,—I am only one of the mathematicians of the United State. My pen, accustomed to figures, is not capable of creating the music of assonances and rhythms. I am merely attempting to record what I see, what I think—more accurately, what we think (that is it precisely: we, and let this WE be the title of my records). Yet this will be a derivative of our life, of the mathematically perfect life of the United State, and if that is so, will it actually not be in itself, independently of my will, a poem? It will—that I believe and know.

I am writing this and I feel: my cheeks are burning. Probably, this is similar to what a woman experiences when for the first time she senses within herself the pulse of a new—still tiny, blind human being. It is I and simultaneously—not I. And for long months it will be necessary to nourish it with one's life fluid, with one's blood, and then—painfully tear it away from oneself and lay it at the feet of the United State.

But I am ready, just as everyone is,—or almost everyone of us. I am ready.

Record 2
Synopsis: **Ballet / Square Harmony / X**

Spring. From beyond the Green Wall, from the wild invisible plains, the wind carries the yellow pollen of some kind of flowers. Your lips grow dry from this sweet pollen—every minute you pass your tongue over them—and it must be that all the women you meet have sweet lips (and the men as well, of course). This somewhat hinders logical thinking.

But then, what a sky! Blue, unspoiled by a single cloud (what wild tastes the ancients had if their poets could be inspired by those ugly, disorderly, clumsily jostling clumps of vapor). I love—I am certain that I will not be mistaken if I say: we love—this same sterile, immaculate sky alone. On such days—the whole world is cast of that very same immutable eternal glass as the Green Wall, as all of our buildings. On such days you see into the bluest depths of things, you see certain of their amazing equations, hitherto unknown—in something most common, prosaic.

Why, just take this example. This morning I was at the launching site where the INTEGRAL is being built—and suddenly I caught sight of the machine benches: with eyes closed, in self-oblivion, the spheres of the regulators were spinning; flashing, the levers were bending to the right and to the left; the pendulum rod was proudly dipping its shoulders; to the rhythm of an inaudible music the blade of a tooling lathe bobbed up and down in a dance. I suddenly perceived all the beauty of this grandiose mechanical ballet suffused with the buoyant azure sun.

And further—in the same vein: why—beautiful? Why is the dance beautiful? Answer: because it was a *nonfree* motion, because the whole profound meaning of the dance is precisely in its absolute, aesthetic subordination, in its ideal nonfreedom. And if it is true that our ancestors would surrender themselves utterly to dance during—the most inspired moments of their life (religious mysteries, military parades), then this signified but one thing: from time immemorial, the instinct for nonfreedom has been organically inherent in man, and in our present-day life—are only consciously . . .

I shall have to finish later: the intercom has clicked. I looked up: 0-90, of course. In half a minute she herself would be here: to take me for the walk.

Dear O!—it always seemed to me—that she resembled her name: approximately 10 centimeters shorter than the Maternal Norm—and thus seemingly turned so roundly as though on a lathe,—and the pink O—her mouth—opened wide to greet every word of mine. And moreover: the round, plump little fold of skin on the wrist of her hand—the kind that children often have.

When she entered, the logical flywheel was still humming at full force in me and because of its momentum I began to talk about the formula I had just constructed which included all of us, as well as the machines and the dance.

"Marvelous. Isn't it?" I asked.

"Yes, marvelous. Spring," 0-90 gave me a pink smile.

Well, there, how do you like that: spring . . . She talks about spring. Women . . . I fell silent.

Downstairs. The avenue was full: the post-lunch private hour, in weather like this—we usually spend on a supplementary walk. As always, the music factory was playing the March of the United State with all its pipes. In even ranks, four abreast, solemnly keeping time to the rhythm, the numbers walked—hundreds, thousands of numbers, in pale-blue unifs (probably from the ancient *Uniforme*), with golden badges on their chests—a state number for every male and female. I too—we, the four of us,—were one of the countless waves in this mighty torrent. To the left of me was 0-90 (if one of my hairy ancestors had been writing this about a thousand years ago— he probably would have called her by that amusing word *my*); to the right—two other strangers, a female-number and a male-number.

A sky of blissful blue, minute, toylike suns in each of the badges, faces unclouded by the insanity of thoughts . . . Rays of light—you understand: everything made of some indivisible, radiant, smiling matter. And the rhythmic measures of the brass: "Tra-ta-ta-tam. Tra-ta-ta-tam," those were the brass steps gleaming in the sun and with each step—you climbed higher and higher, into the dizzy azure.

And then, just as had been the case that morning, at the launching site, once again I perceived, as if only then for the first time in my life—I perceived everything: the absolutely straight streets, the glass pavements shimmering with rays of light, the divine parallelepipeds of transparent dwellings, the square harmony of the grayish-blue ranks. To illustrate: it was as though not entire generations, but I—yes I alone—had conquered the old God and the old life, yes, I alone had created all of this, and I, like a tower, I was afraid to move my elbow lest the walls, cupolas, machines collapse in showering fragments . . .

And an instant later—a leap through the centuries, from + to – . I recalled (apparently,—an association by contrast)—I suddenly recalled a painting in a museum: one of their avenues from twentieth-century times, a deafening, motley, jumbled mob of people, wheels, animals, billboards, trees, colors, birds . . . And they do say that it was in fact like that—it could have been so. It seemed to me that it was so unlikely, so absurd, that I lost control and suddenly burst into laughter.

And immediately there was an echo—laughter—from the right. I turned: before my eyes—white—extraordinarily white and sharp teeth, an unfamiliar woman's face.

"Forgive me," she said, "but you were gazing about with such inspiration—like some mythological god on the seventh day of creation. It seems to me you are certain that you and nobody else created me as well. I am very flattered . . ."

All of this—without a smile, I might even say—with a certain deference (perhaps she knew that I was the builder of the INTEGRAL). Yet I could not say—in the eyes or the eyebrows—there was some manner of strange, irritating X and I could not understand it in the least, I could not give it any mathematical expression.

For some reason I grew embarrassed and with some confusion I began to justify my laughter logically. It was perfectly clear that this contrast, this impassable abyss between now and then . . .

"But why— impassable'? (What white teeth!) One can throw a small bridge—over the abyss. Just imagine to yourself: a drum, battalions, ranks—that did exist as well—and, consequently . . ."

"Yes, of course: it's clear," I cried (it was an amazing intersection of thoughts: she—almost with my very same words—what I had recorded before the walk).—You understand: even the thoughts. This was because nobody is *one*, rather *one of*. We are so one and the same . . ."

She:

"Are you certain'?"

I perceived the brows upturned at a sharp angle towards the temples—like the sharp horns of an X, again I felt bewildered for some reason; I glanced to the right, to the left—and . . .

To my right—she, slender, sharp, tensely resilient, like a whip, I-330 (now I saw her number); to the left—0-90, entirely different, all circles, with the childlike fold of skin around her wrist; and on the extremity of our foursome—an unfamiliar male number—double—curved, in the shape of the letter S. We were all different . . .

The one on the right, I-330, apparently caught my distraught look and with a sigh:

"Yes . . . Alas!"

In essence, this alas was perfectly appropriate. But again there was a certain something in her face or in her voice . . .

With an extraordinary sharpness for me—I said: "There's no alas about it. Science is advancing and clearly—if not now, then in fifty, in a hundred years . . ."

"Even all the people's noses . . ."

"Yes, the noses," I was practically shouting now. "As long as there — is whatever basis for envy . . . If I have a nose like a button, while someone else . . ."

"Well, but your nose, forgive me, is even *classical*, as they said in olden, times. And your hands there . . . No, do show me, show me your hands!" I could not bear it when people looked at my hands: they were all hairy, shaggy—some kind of absurd atavism. I stretched out my hand and—in a voice as indifferent as possible—I said:

"Apelike."

She glanced at the hands, then at my face: "But there is a most curious affinity," she seemed to be weighing me with her eyes, the little horns at the corners of her eyebrows appeared fleetingly.

"He is registered to me," 0-90 opened her mouth in pink joyfulness.

It would have been better for her to remain silent—it was completely irrelevant. In general, this dear O— . . . how could I say . . . the speed of her tongue is incorrectly designed, the speed per second of the tongue should always be slightly less than the speed per second of thought, and by no means the contrary.

At the end of the avenue, on the Accumulator Tower, the bell was striking a booming 17. The personal hour was ended. I-330 was leaving together with that S-shaped male number. He had the kind of face that inspired respect, and then I saw what seemed to be a familiar face. I had met him somewhere—but then I could not recall.

Upon leaving, I-330—still X-like—gave me a wry smile. "Come by auditorium 112 the day after tomorrow."

I shrugged my shoulders:

"If I am assigned—precisely to that auditorium you have named . . ."

She, with a kind of incomprehensible confidence: "You will be."

This woman had the same unpleasant effect on me as an insoluble, irrational component which has made a haphazard intrusion in an equation. And I was happy to be left alone with dear O—if only for a short while.

Arm-in-arm we passed four rows of avenues. At the corner she had to turn left, I—to the right.

"I would like so much to come to you today, to lower the blinds. Especially today, right now . . ." O-timidly raised her crystal-blue eyes to me.

She is amusing. Well, what could I say to her? She had been at my place only yesterday and she knew as well as I that our next sexual day was the day after tomorrow. This was simply the same case of her "premature thoughts"— as happens (at times harmfully) with a premature ignition in a motor.

Upon parting I kissed her twice . . . no, I shall be precise: three times I kissed those marvelous blue eyes, unspoiled by a single cloudlet.

Record 3
Synopsis: A Jacket / A Wall / The Book of Hourly Tables

I have looked over everything that I wrote yesterday—and I see: I did not write with sufficient clarity. That is, all of this is perfectly clear for any one of us. But how is one to know: perhaps, you, the strangers, to whom the INTEGRAL will carry my notes, perhaps, you will have read the great book of civilization only as far as the page that our ancestors did about 900 years ago. Perhaps you do not even know such ABC's as the Book of Hourly Tables, the Personal Hours, the Maternal Norm, the Green Wall, the Benefactor. It seems ridiculous to me—and at the same time very difficult to speak about all this. It would all be the same as though some writer or other, let us say, of the 20th century, were forced to explain in his novel what was meant by *jacket, apartment, wife.* But nevertheless, if his novel is translated for savages—is it really conceivable to avoid annotations concerning a *jacket?*

I am certain that a savage would look at *jacket* and think: "Well, what is that for? Merely a burden." It seems to me that you would look precisely the same way when I told you that since the time of the Two Hundred Years' War none of us has been on the other side of the Green Wall.

But, dear friends, you must do at least some thinking, it does help a great deal. After all, it is clear: all of human history, as much as we know of it, is the history of the transition from nomadic forms to increasingly sedentary ones. Does it not then follow from this that the most sedentary form of life (ours)—is at the same time the most perfect (ours). If people dashed about the earth from one end to the other, then it was only during prehistoric times when there were nations, wars, commerce, the discoveries of the various Americas. But whatever for, who needs that now?

I grant you: growing accustomed to this sedentary form did not come immediately or without difficulty. When during the time of the Two Hundred Years' War all the roads were destroyed and became overgrown with grass—for the first while it must have seemed very inconvenient to live in cities, cut off from one another by green jungles. But what of it? After man first lost his tall, he probably did not learn at once how to chase away flies without the aid of that tail. But now—can you imagine yourself—with a tail? Or: perhaps you can imagine yourself on the street—naked, without a *jacket* (it's possible that you still go strolling about in *jackets*). Here it is precisely the same thing: I cannot imagine to myself a city that is not enveloped by a Green Wall. I cannot imagine a life that is not arrayed in the figured chasubles of The Book of Hourly Tables.

The Tables . . . Right at this very moment the purple figures on a golden background are gazing sternly and tenderly into my eyes from my wall. I am involuntarily reminded of what among the ancients was called an *icon* and I feel the urge to compose verses or prayers (which is one and the same thing). Oh, why am I not a poet that I might sing in worthy praise of you, O Tables, O heart and pulse of the United State.

All of us (and, perhaps, you too), while yet children in school, read this mightiest of monuments to come down to us from ancient literature—*The Railroad Timetables*. But place even it beside The Tables—and you will see, side by side, graphite and diamond: both have one and the same thing—C, carbon,—but how eternal, how translucent, how the diamond gleams. Whose spirit would not thrill when you rush headlong with a roar through the pages of *The Railroad Timetables*. But the The Tables —actually transform each of us into the steel, six-wheeled hero of a mighty poem. Every morning, with six-wheeled precision, at precisely the same hour and at precisely the same minute,—we, millions of us, arise as one. At precisely the same hour, millions like one, we begin our work—millions like one we finish. And coalescing into a single, million-handed body, at precisely the very same second, designated by The Tables, —we raise our spoons to our mouth,—and at precisely the very same second we emerge for our walk and we proceed to the auditorium, to the hall for the Taylor exercises, and we withdraw to sleep . . .

I will be entirely frank: even we do not yet have the absolutely precise solution to the question of happiness: twice a day—from 16 to 17 and from 21 to 22 the single mighty organism dissolves into separate cells: these are what The Tables have designated as—the Personal Hours. During these hours you may see: in the rooms of some—the blinds are modestly lowered, others, to the slow steps of the March—walk in measured time along the avenue, while yet others—as I myself am doing right now—are at their desks. But I resolutely believe—let them call me an idealist and a dreamer—I believe: sooner or later—but someday we shall find a place in the general formula for these hours as well, someday all 86,400 seconds will be included in The Book of Hourly Tables.

I have had the occasion to read and hear a great deal that was improbable about those times when people were still living in a free, i.e., unorganized, wild state. But the most improbable thing always seemed to me to be precisely the following: how in those times—even a rudimentary governmental authority could permit people to live without anything resembling our Tables, without any obligatory walks, without any precise regulation of mealtimes; they would get up and go to bed whenever they took it into their heads; several historians even say that apparently in those times lights burned in the streets all night, people walked and rode along the streets all night.

I cannot comprehend any of this in the least. However restricted their intelligence might have been, all the same they should have understood that a life like that was the most genuine form of mass murder—albeit a slow one, from day to day. The state (humaneness) prohibited the outright murder of a single person and did not prohibit the partial murder of millions. To murder a single person, i.e., to decrease the sum of human lives by 50 years—that was criminal, but to decrease the sum of human lives by 50 million years—that was not criminal. Really, is that not ridiculous? Any of our ten-year-old numbers can resolve this mathematical-moral problem in half a minute; but they were incapable—with all their Kants together (because not one of those Kants could hit on the idea of constructing a system of scientific ethics, i.e., based on subtraction, addition, division, multiplication).

Moreover—is it really not absurd that a state (it dared to call itself a state!) could leave sexual life without any control. Whoever, whenever and as much as one wished . . . Completely unscientific, like animals. And like animals, blindly, they bore children. Is it not ridiculous: to know horticulture, poultry-breeding, fish-breeding (we have exact data that they knew all of this) and not know how to proceed to the ultimate step in this logical ladder: child-breeding. Not to hit upon the idea of our Maternal and Paternal Norms.

It is so ridiculous, so improbable, that now that I have written it l am afraid: what if suddenly, you the unknown readers, should take me for a malicious jokester. What if suddenly you should think that I simply wish to have my joke at your expense and I am relating the most utter rubbish with a serious face.

But first of all: I am not capable of jokes—falsehood is a secret function that enters into every joke; and secondly: the United State Science can not be mistaken. And where would any state logic be forthcoming in those times when people lived in a condition of freedom, i.e., like that of animals, apes, the herd? What could one demand of them if even in our time—from somewhere at the bottom, out of the shaggy depths,—a wild, apelike echo can still be infrequently heard?

Fortunately—only infrequently. Fortunately—this is only a minor breakdown in details: they can be repaired logically, without halting the eternal, mighty progress of the whole Machine. And for the disposal of the twisted bolt—we have the skillful, heavy hand of the Benefactor, we have the experienced eyes of the Guardians . . .

Yes, by the way, now I remember: that male number from yesterday, the double-curved one, like S,—it seems to me that I have had occasion to see him coming out of the Bureau of Guardians. Now I understand why I had that instinctive feeling of deference towards him and a kind of awkwardness when in his presence that strange number I-330 . . . I must confess that this I . . .

The bell is ringing for sleep: 22 1/2. Until tomorrow.

Record 4
Synopsis: The Savage with the Barometer / Epilepsy /If Only

Up until now everything in life had been clear to me (it is hardly by chance that I have, apparently, a certain predilection for this very word "clear"). But today . . . I do not understand.

First of all: I was actually assigned to be precisely in auditorium 112, just as she had told me. Although the probability was—

$$\frac{1,500}{10,000,000} = \frac{3}{20,000}$$

(1,500—that is the number of auditoria, 10,000,000—represents the numbers). Secondly... But better to take it in order.

The auditorium. An enormous hemisphere of glass massifs all suffused with sunlight. Circular rows of noble, globe-shaped, closely cropped heads. My heart gently skipped a beat as I looked all around. I think, I was searching: whether somewhere above the pale-blue waves of unifies a rosy crescent would be glistening—the dear lips of O—. Then suddenly salmon's extraordinarily white and sharp teeth, similar to . . . no, wrong. This evening, at 21, O- would come to me—the wish to see her here was perfectly natural.

Then—a bell. We rose, sang the Hymn of the United State—and on the stage appeared the phonolecturer gleaming with wit and a golden loudspeaker.

"Respected numbers! Archeologists recently unearthed a book from the 20th century. In it the ironical author tells of a savage and a barometer. The savage noted: every time when the barometer came to rest on *rain*—it actually rained. And since the savage felt like rain, he then began to remove the right amount of mercury so that the level stopped at rain (on the screen—a savage in feathers, shaking out the mercury: laughter). You laugh: but does it not seem to you that the European of that era is more deserving of your laughter. Like the savage, the European also wanted rain,—but rain with a capital letter, an algebraic rain. Yet he stood before the barometer like a wet hen. The savage, at least, had more daring and energy and—even though a savage—more logic: he was able to ascertain that there was a connection between effect and cause. Shaking out the mercury he was able to take the first step on that mighty road by which . . ."

At this point (I repeat: I am writing without concealing anything)—at this point I became seemingly impervious to the vivifying streams pouring forth out of the loudspeakers. It suddenly seemed to me that I had come here in vain (why *in vain* and how could I have not come once I had been assigned here?); it all seemed to me—hollow, only a shell. And with difficulty I switched my attention back on only when the phonolecturer had gone on to the main theme: to our music, to mathematical composition (the mathematician is the cause, the music is the result), to a description of the recently invented musicometer.

"By simply turning this handle, anyone of you can produce up to three sonatas in an hour. Yet how difficult that was for your ancestors to achieve. They could create only by driving themselves into fits of *inspiration*—an unknown form of epilepsy. And here is a most amusing illustration for you of what they produced,—the music of Scriabin—the 20th century. This black box (curtains parted on the stage and there—their most ancient instrument)—they called this box a piano or a *royal grand*, which shows but one more time to what extent their music . . ."

And so forth—again I do not remember, quite possibly because . . . Well, yes, I shall say it straight: because she had walked up to the *royal grand* box—I-330. No doubt I was simply struck by this unexpected appearance of her on the stage.

She was in a fantastic costume of the ancient era: a tightly fitting black dress, the white of her bare shoulders and bosom sharply defined, and undulating with her breathing that warm shadow between . . . and the blinding, almost wicked lips . . .

Her smile—a bite, directed here—below. She sat down, began to play. Wild, convulsive, motley, like their entire life in those times,—not a shadow of rational mechanicalness. And, of course, they, around me, were right: everyone was laughing. Only a few . . . but why me as well—me?

Yes, epilepsy—a spiritual illness—a pain . . . A slow, sweet pain—a bite—if only it would go deeper yet, more painfully yet. And then, slowly the Sun. But not ours, not the azure crystalline and uniform one through the glass bricks—no: a wild, soaring, scorching Sun—off with everything—rip everything into tiny shreds.

The number sitting beside me on the left glanced sideways—at me—and snickered. For some reason I have a very clear memory of that: I saw a microscopic bubble of saliva form on his lips and burst. That bubble sobered me. I was—myself again.

Like everyone else —I heard only the absurd, fussy squeaking of strings. I was laughing. I felt light and simple. The talented phonolecturer had been depicting that wild era too vividly for us—that was all there was to it.

With what pleasure I listened to our contemporary music afterwards.

(It was demonstrated in conclusion—for contrast.) The crystalline chromatic progressions of merging and diverging series—and the summarizing chords of Taylor McLauren; the full-bodied / full-toned, squarely massive passages of the Pythagorean theorem; the mournful melodies of a fading oscillatory movement; the brilliant measures alternating with Frauenhofer's lines in the pauses —the spectral analysis of the planets... What grandeur! What unwavering equilibrium: And how pitiful—totally unrestricted by anything other than wild fantasies —that willful music of the ancients...

As usual, in even ranks, four abreast, everyone exited through the wide doors of the auditorium. The familiar double-curved figure flitted past me; I nodded respectfully.

Dear O— was supposed to come in an hour. I felt pleasantly and, usefully excited. Home—quickly to the desk, I handed the duty clerk my pink ticket and received a permit for the right to use the blinds. We have this right—only for Sexual Days. Otherwise amid our transparent walls seemingly woven of sparkling air—we always live in full view, eternally washed by the light. We have nothing to hide from one another. Moreover it facilitates the burdensome and exalted labor of the Guardians. Otherwise who can say what might happen. It is possible that it was precisely those strange, opaque dwellings of the ancients that gave birth to that pitiful cellular psychology of theirs. "My [sic!] home is my castle"—it really must have cost them an effort to think that one up!

At 22 I lowered the blinds —and at that very minute O—entered slightly out of breath. She held out her tiny pink mouth to me—and her pink ticket. I tore off the coupon—and then I could not tear myself away from that pink mouth until the very last moment—22:15.

Then I showed her my *records* and I talked—very well, I thought about the beauty of the square, the cube, the straight line. She listened so enchantingly and pinkly—and suddenly from her blue eyes a tear, a second, a third,—straight onto the opened page (p. 7). The ink ran. Well, now I shall have to recopy it.

"Dear D-, if only you would—if only . . ."

Well, what *if only*? What about if only? Again her old refrain: a child. Or, perhaps, something new—concerning . . . concerning that other one? Even if it were . . . No, that would be too absurd.

[the novel continues with 36 more "Records", ed.]

(1920)

Translated by S. Cioran

Boris Andreevich Pilniak
(1894–1937

A Year in Their Life

I

To the south and north, to the east and west—in all directions for a hundred versts—lay forests and wetlands, wrapped, veiled with mosses. There were stands of tawny cedars and pines. Beneath these throve an impassable thicket of fir, alder, cherry, juniper and low-growing birch. And in the small clearings amid the brush, in the peat beds ringed by fox berries and cranberries, sunk into the moss were "wells"—terrifying, filled with reddish water, and bottomless.

The cold came in September—fifty degrees below zero. The snow lay hard and blue. For only three hours did sunlight arise; the rest of the time it was night. The sky appeared heavy and hung low over the land. There was silence; only in September did the moose roar as they battled; in December the wolves howled; the rest of the time there was silence, of a kind that can only exist in the wilderness.

On a hill by the river stood a village.

Naked, of tawny granite and white shale, worn down by water and wind, a slope led to the river. On the bank lay clumsy, tawny boats. The river was large, gloomy, cold, bristling with murky blue-black waves. Tawny huts could be seen here and there, their tall, over-hanging, shingled roofs covered with greenish moss. Their windows looked blind. Around them nets were drying. Trappers lived here. In the winter they would leave for long stretches on the taiga and there they killed game.

II

In the spring the rivers overflowed: broadly, freely and powerfully.

Heavy waves rolled along, shimmering—the body of the river—and from them spread a damp, muffled noise, troubling and troubled. The snows melted away. On the pines grew pitchy candles, and they gave off a strong smell. The sky rose higher and turned dark blue, and at twilight it was greenish-shimmery and bleakly alluring. In the taiga, after the death of winter, the foremost task of the animal kingdom was in train—birth. And all the forest-dwellers—bears, wolves, moose, red foxes, polar foxes, owls, eagle-owls—all entered into the spring-time joy of birth. Out on the river were loudly calling eider, swan, geese. In the twilight, when the sky became

green and shimmery , so that at night it might become satiny dark blue and
many-starred, when the eider and swans had quieted down, falling to sleep
for the night, and the night air, soft and warm was barely ruffled by crickets and crakes—at the ravine the girls would gather to sing of Lada and
dance round-dances. The young men would be returning from wintering
over in the taiga, and they also gathered there.

The bank fell steeply to the river. The river rustled below. And overhead
the sky unfolded. All was quiet, but at the same time one could sense life
swarming and hurrying along. At the head of the ravine, where stunted
moss and wayside grasses grew on the granite and shale, the girls would sit
in a dense cluster. They all wore bright dresses, were all strong and healthy;
they sang sad, broad, ancient songs; they gazed off somewhere into the
darkening, greenish mist. And it seemed that the girls were singing those
unforgettable, broad songs of theirs for the young men. And the young men
stood as dark, hunched silhouettes around the girls, sharply hooting and
behaving riotously, exactly like the males in the forest mating-grounds.

The gathering had its own laws.

The young men would come and choose wives, they would fight for
them and attack each other; the girls were indifferent and submitted to the
males in everything. The lads, hooting and beating each other, would fight,
make an uproar, and the victor—he would choose a wife for himself first.

And then they, he and she, would leave the gathering together.

III

Marina was twenty years old, and she went to the embankment.

Her tall, slightly heavy body was remarkably well-formed, with strong
muscles and matte-white skin. Bosom, stomach, spine, thighs and legs were
sharply defined—strongly, resiliently and in sharp relief. Her rounded,
broad bosom rose up high. She had black-heavy braids, brows and lashes.
Her eyes were black, moist, with deep pupils. Her cheeks flushed bluish-
crimson. And her lips were soft like a wild creature's, very red and full. She
always walked slowly, shifting her long, strong legs and barely moving her
springy thighs.

She came to the slope to join the girls.

The girls were singing their songs—drawn out, inviting and spare.

Marina forgot herself in the cluster of girls, threw herself onto her
back, closed her clouded eyes and also sang. The song went along, went out
in wide, radiant circles, and into it, into the song, went everything. Her eyes
closed languidly. Her lean body was gnawed by a secret pain. Her heart
contracted flutteringly, seemed to grow mute and from it, with the blood,
this muteness went into her hands and knees, weakening them, and clouded
her mind. And Marina stretched herself out passionately, grew entirely

mute, entered the song and sang: and was startled only by the aroused hooting voices of the young men.

And then, at home in her stuffy cell, Marina lay down on her bed; she
threw her arms behind her head, which made her bosom rise; she stretched
out her legs, she opened wide her dark, misty eyes; she pursed her lips and,
once again fainting with spring-time languor, lay that way for a long time.

Marina was twenty years old, and from the day of her birth she had
grown up like a thistle on the ravine—freely and alone—with the trappers,
the taiga, the ravine and the river.

IV

Demid lived on the bluff. Like the village, the bluff stood over the river.
Only the hill was higher and steeper. The taiga had crept close; the dark-
green tawny-trunked cedars and pines reached out for it with their forest
paws. You could see a good distance from here: the troubled dark river, the
water-meadow beyond it, the taiga, toothy at the horizon and dark-blue,
and the sky—low and heavy.

The house built of huge pine trunks, with its log walls and white
unadorned ceilings and floors, was hung all over with the pelts of bear, elk,
wolves, white fox, ermine. The pelts hung on the walls and lay on the floor.
On the tables there were powder, pellets, shot. In the corners were piled
nooses, snares, traps. Guns had been hung up. It smelled strongly and
sharply here, as if all the smells of the taiga had been gathered together.
There were two rooms and a kitchen.

In the middle of one of the two rooms stood a table, home-made and
big, and around it were low benches covered with bearskin. In this room
lived Demid, in the other room lived the young bear Makar.

At home Demid would lie on his bearskin bed, long and motionless,
would listen to his own large body, to how alive it was, how the strong
blood flowed through it. The bear Makar would approach him, put his
heavy paws on Demid's chest, and sniff him over in a friendly way. Demid
would scratch the bear behind the ear and one sensed that they, the man
and the bear, understood each other. The taiga would look in through the
window.

Demid was thick-set and broad-shouldered, with black eyes that were
large, calm and kind. He smelled of the taiga, healthily and strongly. He
was dressed—like all the trappers—in furs and in a coarse homespun fabric, white with a red warp. His feet were clad in tall heavy boots sewn from
deer hide, and his hands, broad and red, were covered with calluses like a
thick rind.

Makar was young, and like all young animals—clumsy. He waddled
about and often got into mischief: gnawed the nets and lines, broke the

nooses, licked at the powder. Then Demid would punish Makar—thrash him. And Makar would roll over onto his back, make innocent eyes and howl piteously.

V

Demid went to the girls on the cliff, led Marina from the cliff to his house on the bluff, and Marina became Demid's wife.

VI

In the summer the luxuriant, dark-green grasses sprang up, swiftly and succulently. During the day the sun shone from a blue and seemingly moist sky. The nights were white, and it seemed then that there was no sky at all: it had dissolved into a pale mist. The nights were short and white, all the time it was red liquid dawn—evening or morning—and shimmery mists crept over the land. Strongly, rapidly, life took its course, sensing that its days were short here.

At Demid's Marina lived in Makar's room.

Makar had been moved to Demid's room.

Makar had greeted Marina in an unfriendly way. When he saw her for the first time he set up a howl, showed his teeth, and struck her with his paw. Demid thrashed him for this and the bear quieted down. Later he and Marina became friends.

During the day Demid would go out into the taiga. Marina would remain alone.

She fixed up her room in her own way, roughly and with a sort of emphatic grace. Symmetrically she hung up the pelts and the scraps of cloth embroidered in bright red and blue, with cockerels and stags; in the corner she hung up an icon of the Mother of God; she scrubbed the floors; and her room, motley-colored and still smelling strongly of the taiga, began to resemble a forest chapel, where forest folk prayed to their gods.

In the pale-greenish twilight's, when the skyless night was coming on and only eagle-owls called in the taiga and crickets chirped by the river, Demid would come to Marina. Marina could not think—her thoughts tumbled like huge heavy boulders—slowly and clumsily. She could sense that she had surrendered everything to Husband-Demid, and through the pale, skyless nights, her body hot and redolent, thrashing about on her bearskin, she took Demid unto herself: and she gave herself over, surrendering everything to him, wanting to dissolve into him, into his strength and passion, wearing out her own.

The nights were white, shimmery, misty. There was only the night-silence of the taiga. The mists drifted. Eagle-owls and wood-doves called.

But in the morning the dawn was a red fire and a huge sun arose in the damp-blue sky. The grasses sprang up swiftly and succulently.

The summer went on, the days passed.

VII

In September it snowed.

From August on the days had started to close in, to gray, and long dark nights had sprung up. The taiga suddenly quieted, became mute and began to seem empty. The cold came and shackled the river with ice. There were very long twilights when the snow and ice on the river looked blue. At night the elk would roar as they battled. They roared so loudly and so strangely that it became frightening, and the walls shook.

In the fall Marina conceived.

One night Marina awoke before dawn. The room was stuffy because of the stove, and it smelled of bear. It had just begun to get light and on the dark walls the blue patches of the window frames were barely aglow. Somewhere near the outcrop an old elk was roaring; by the rough voice with its hissing bass notes one could tell it was an old one.

Marina sat up on her bed. Her head was spinning and she was slightly queasy. The bear was lying next to her. He was already awake and looking at Marina. His eyes glowed like quiet green fires, as if they were chinks through which was visible the sky of spring twilights, peaceful and shimmery-quiet.

Again Marina grew queasy and her head began to spin, and the fires of Makar's eyes subconsciously and deeply transformed themselves in Marina's soul into an immense, unbearable joy, with which her entire body began to tremble painfully—she had conceived. Her heart was pounding as if she had fallen into a snare, and the head-spinning sensation came on, shimmery and misty like a summer morning.

Marina arose from her bed—from her bear-skin—and quickly, with awkward-unsure steps went naked into Demid's room. Demid was asleep— she wrapped his head in her hot arms, pressed it to her broad bosom and whispered:

A child . . . I'm pregnant . . .

Little by little the night was graying and a blue light was coming through the windows. The elk had ceased to roar. In the room fluttered gray shadows. Makar came in, sighed and lay his paws on the bed. With his free hand Demid grasped the scruff of his neck and, trembling with love, said to him:

—So, Makar Ivanovich,—do you understand?

Then he added, turning to Marina:

—What do you think—does he understand? Marinka! . . . Marinka! Marinka!

Makar licked Demid's hand and intelligently and knowingly lowered his head onto his paws. The night grew gray, soon lilac stripes appeared on the snow, entered the house. Below in the ravine lay the river's blue ice, beyond it in ridges lay the taiga.

Demid did not go into the taiga on that day, and for many days thereafter.

VIII

The winter came, stayed, was passing.

The snow lay in deep layers, it was blue—night and day—and lilac during the short dawns and sunsets. The sun, pale and weak, barely rising above the horizon, would come up for three hours, far-off and alien. The rest of the time it was night. At night the northern lights shot out their shimmery arrows. The frost was a milk-white mist, sprinkling rime everywhere. There was the quiet of the wilderness, which spoke of death.

Marina's eyes had changed. Before, they had been cloudy-dark and intoxicated, now they had become astoundingly clear, peaceful-joyful, direct and calm, and a chaste modesty had appeared in them. Her thighs became broader and her belly much larger, and this had given her a certain new grace, awkward-soft and heavy, and again, a chasteness.

Marina moved about very little, sitting in her room that resembled a forest chapel where the people prayed to their gods. During the day she dealt with her simple housekeeping: lit the stove, chopped the wood, cooked the meat and the fish, skinned the animals Demid killed, tidied her clearing. In the evening—the evenings were long—Marina spun thread on her spindle and wove cloth on her loom; she was sewing for the child. And as she sewed she would think of the child, sing, and smile quietly.

Marina thought about the child—an unconquerable, strong, all-encompassing joy filled her body. Her heart would pound and an even stronger joy would arise. But about the fact that she, Marina, would give birth—suffer—there was no thought.

Demid, in the morning lilac dawns, when the round full moon stood in the south-west, would go out on skis with a rifle and a Finnish knife, into the taiga. Pines and cedars stood there, traced out in a firm, heavy pattern of snow; at their feet clustered prickly firs, juniper and alder. Silence reigned, dampened by the snow. In the dead soundless snows Demid went from trap to trap, from noose to noose, finishing off the game. He fired his rifle, and the echo would dance long in the silence. He tracked elk and wolf-packs. He went down to the river, lay in wait for beaver, caught wildly thrashing fish in the melt-holes, put out the cages. Around him was everything that he had always known. Slowly the red sun dimmed and the shimmery rays of the northern lights began to glimmer.

In the evening standing on the bluff he would gut the fish and the game, hang it up to freeze, throw the scraps to the bear, would himself eat, wash in icy water and sit down beside Marina, large, thickset, his strong legs spread wide and his hands on his knees—the room seemed crowded. He would smile peaceably and kindly.

The lamp burned. Beyond the walls lay the snows, the silence and the cold. Makar would come in and roll playfully on the floor. In the room that looked like a chapel it would grow cozy and peaceful-joyful. The walls would crackle in the frost, and darkness peered in at the frozen windows. On the walls hung the cloths sewn with red and blue, with stags and cockerels. Then Demid would arise from his bench, take Marina tenderly and firmly by the hand and lead her to bed. The lamp would die down and in the darkness would quietly burn the eyes of Makar.

Makar that winter grew up and became what a mature bear is: somber-serious, ponderous and clumsy-clever. He had a very wide, high-domed face with somber-kind eyes.

IX

In the last days of December, at Yule, when the wolves took to howling, Marina began to feel inside herself, beneath her heart, the child beginning to move. He moved about inside, tenderly and so softly, exactly as if her body was being stroked by an eiderdown cloth. Marina was filled with joy—she sensed only the small being that was inside her, who from inside her had seized her firmly, and she spoke to Demid of this in fearless, disconnected words.

At dawn the child would move there, inside. Marina would press her hands—surprisingly gentle—to her stomach, would stroke it solicitously and sing cradle songs of how her son would make a hunter who would kill in his time three hundred and a thousand stags, three hundred and a thousand bear, three hundred and again three hundred ermine, and would take to wife the first beauty of the village. And within her, barely noticeable, extraordinarily softly, the child would move.

And beyond the house, beyond bluff there were:

A misty cold, the night and the silence which spoke of death, and only from time to time would the wolves set up a howl: they would approach the outcrop, sit back on their haunches and howl to the sky, long and troublingly.

X

In the spring Marina gave birth.

In the spring the river roused itself and broadly overflowed, began to shimmer with gloomy, bristling leaden waves, the banks were covered with white flocks—swans, geese, eider. Life began again on the taiga. The animal kingdom was astir, the forest alarmingly rang out with the noise of bear, elk, wolf, fox, owl, grouse. The dark green grasses blossomed and flourished. Nights contracted and days grew longer. The twilights were pale green and shimmery, and during them on the clearing by the river, in the village the girls sang of Lada. At dawn an immense sun would arise in the damp-blue sky, to spend many spring hours traversing its celestial path. The time came for the spring festival when according to legend the sun would smile, and the people exchanged red eggs, symbols of the sun.

On that day Marina gave birth.

Her labor began in the afternoon. The vernal, large, and joyful sun came in through the window and lay in bounteous sheaves on the walls and on the hide-covered floor.

Marina was to remember only that there was savage pain, contorting and rending her body. She lay on her bearskin bed, the sun shone through the window—this she remembered. Remembered that its rays lay on the wall and floor as if pointing to the noon hour, then moved to the left, to the half-hour, to one o'clock. Then, later, everything vanished into the pain, into the contorting spasms of her belly.

When Marina came to herself it was already twilight, green and quiet. At her feet, all covered in blood, a red infant lay and cried. Nearby stood the bear and he markedly, comprehendingly and sternly looked on with his kindly-somber eyes.

At that moment Demid arrived—he cut the cord, washed the infant and put it to Marina as was proper. He gave her the child—there was a surprising degree of chaste modesty in her eyes. In Marina's arms there was a small red little being who cried incessantly. There was no more pain.

X

That night the bear left Demid. Likely, he had sensed the spring and gone out into the taiga to find himself a mate.

The bear left late, breaking down the door. It was night. On the horizon there lay a barely-noticeable strip of dawn. Somewhere far away the girls were singing of Lada. Above the ravine of tawny granite and white shale the girls sat in a dense cluster and sang, and around them—dark, hunched silhouettes—there stood the young men who had returned from over-wintering on the taiga.

(December, 1915)
Translated by A.L. and M.K.

From **The Naked Year**

CHAPTER VII
(the last, without a title)

Russia.
Revolution.
Snowstorm.

CONCLUSION:
THE LAST TRIPTYCH (notes, in essence)

INCANTATIONS

By October the wolf's young is no smaller than a good-sized dog. Silence. A bough snaps. From the ravine to the clearing—where in the daytime the lads from Black Creeks were on sawing duty —drifted the smell of decay, of mushrooms, of that autumn's moonshine. And this autumnal brew accurately proclaimed that the rains were ended: autumn would pour out gold for a week, and then, when the frosts hit, snow would fall. During Indian summer, when the hardening earth smells like spirits, over the fields Dobrynia Nikitich (he of the Golden Baldric, son of Nikita the Devil-Slayer) rides. By daylight his armor gleams like the cinnabar of aspens, the gold of the birches; the sky is blue (the strength of that deep blue, the blue of pure spirits). But at night, darkening, his armor is like burnished steel, rusted by the woods, dampened by the mists yet still tempered, sharp-edged, resonant as the first sheets of ice, starbursts of solder gleaming at the joins. Frost has settled, yet still from the ravine to the clearing drifts the smell of the last dampness and the last warmth. Towards October the young wolves leave the pack, and walk alone. A wolf came out of the clearing, in the distance the smoke from the guttering campfire circled, hovered a moment amid the felled birches and flowed down the bank to fields where the hares were trampling over the winter crops. In the black night and in the black silence one could not see beyond the dry valleys of Black Creeks. In Black Creeks, in the barns, girls began to keen their songs, and then as suddenly grew quiet, having sent their music to the autumn fields and the wood, a sorrowful shriek. Out of the woods, through the ravine, to Nikola's, to Egorka's, walked Arina. A wolf encountered her by the edge of the wood and dodged into the bushes. Arina must have seen the wolf—two points of green light flashed in the bushes—Arina did not turn aside, did not hurry her steps... In Egorka's hut, a chimneyless one, there was a smell of autumn, of healing herbs. Arina blew on the embers in the iron fire-pot, lit a candle made of wax from Egorka's beehive—it grew light in the hut, which was well-built, large, with benches along all the walls, with a gaily tiled stove. From the sleeping-shelf atop the stove protruded the heels of Egorka, the one-eyed wizard. The cock crowed midnight. The cats leapt to the floor. Egorka turned himself, hung his shaggy white head over the shelf edge; he crowed wheezily, in a sleepy voice:

"You've come?—Ah! You've come, you witch. Don't turn away-y-y, don't turn away-y-y-y, you'll be mine, I'll charm you, you witch."

"So, what then, I've come. And I'll never go away from you, you squinting devil. And I'll torture you, and I'll drink your blood, your witch-blood. I'll hound you to death, you squint-eye."

On the porch the bees droned excitedly, still free of their hive. The shadows from the candlelight ran and congealed in the corners. Again the cock crowed. Arina sat down on a bench, the kittens walked across the floor, arching their backs, leapt onto Arina's knees. Egorka jumped down from the stove—his bare feet and toes glistened like juniper bark.

"You've come?!—Ah, you've come, you witch! I'll drink your blood . . ."

"So what, then, I've come, you one-eyed devil. You've muddled me, you've got me drunk."

"Take off your boots, climb up onto the stove! Get undressed!"

Egorka bent down at Arina's feet, tugged at her boots, lifted her skirts, and Arina, in her shamelessness, did not rearrange her skirts.

"You've got me drunk, you cross-eyed devil! And you've got yourself drunk. I've brought some herbs, I put them on the porch."

"I've got myself drunk, I've got myself drunk! . . . You won't go away anywhere, you'll be mine, you won't go away anywhere, you won't go away, my girl . . ."

Dogs began barking under the shed: a wolf must have been passing by. And again the cock crowed, the third cock. The night was nearing midnight.

By the first frosts at Black Creeks they were caught up with their labor in the fields—peasant life subsides along with the earth. The women set up house at the threshing floors, and the girls, summer's harvest over, got themselves pregnant before their weddings. They didn't leave the threshing floors at night, spent their nights in the barns, huddled together. They stoked the smoky earthen barn stoves, sang till cock-crow their vigorous melodies—and likely the lads, too, the lads who went out to saw wood during the day, were huddled together near the barns in the evenings. Dobrynia moved over the fields, cast handfuls of white stars (some of them fell back onto the black earth), through the icy, autumnal firmament. The earth lay weary, silent—like the burnished steel of Dobrynia's armor, whose plates had thrown up forests of rust, whose buckles, chiming with icicles, were tarnished musty-white from the last mists of the year. In the evening the girls in the barns keened out their melodies; the lads arrived with a concertina; the girls locked the barn doors; the lads crashed in; the girls began to screech; they ran into the corners, dived into the straw; the lads gave chase, caught them, squeezed them, kissed them, embraced them. Ashes gleamed tawny brown in the belly of the stove, the smoke was blinding, the straw rustled a wintry rustle.

> *Chi-vi-li, willy-nilly, sway and swish—*
> *Grab the one that is your wish!*

a girl in a corner began to sing this soldier's song, a sign of surrender. They all went into an adjoining room, and stood solemnly in a circle. The concertina shrilled. The girls sniffed sternly.

> *Oh you storks—long-leg cranes,*
> *Missed your road and lost your ways!*

the girls began to sing.

Apart from the smoke there was a smell of trampled straw, sweat and sheepskins. The first cocks crowed in the village. A star fell above the earth.

Alexei Semenov Kniaz'kov-Kononov caught Ulianka Kononova in a dark corner on the straw, where there was a smell of straw, rye and mice. Ulianka fell down, covering her lips with her hand. Alexei knelt on her stomach, pulled her arms away, fell, thrust his hands into Ulianka's breasts. Ulianka's head rolled back—her lips were moist, salty, her breath hot, there was the bitter, sweet and drunken smell of sweat.

> *Chi-vi-li, willy-nilly . . .*

Dobrynia of the Golden Baldric scattered white stars across the icy sky, and in silence the weary earth lay itself down. The village slept—slept above the river, with woods to the right, fields to the left and behind—low to the earth, its cottages looking downwards with blind, cataract-covered windows, their thatched roofs combed like the pates of old men. The lads spent the night in the barn next to the girls'. At second cock-crow Alexei came out of the barn. The moon shone over the roof like a flickering candle, the earth was salted with hoar-frost, the ice crunched under foot, the trees stood like skeletons and the white mist crept almost imperceptibly among them. The girls' barn stood at the side, mute, straw gleaming on the threshing floor. And just after Alexei emerged, the door of the girls' barn creaked, and Ulianka came out into the moonlight. Alexei was standing in the darkness. Ulianka looked quietly around, spread her feet apart, began to urinate—in the biting autumn silence the splash of the falling stream was clearly heard. She drew a fold of her skirt over her privates, took one bow-legged step, and went off to the barn. The cocks in the yards began to sing—one, two, then many more. That night for the first time Alioshka had caught the scent of a woman, for true.

And two days before the Feast of the Intercession, at night, the first snow—a few hours' worth—fell. Earth greeted the morning with winter, with a crimson dawn. But on the heels of the snowfall came warmth, and the day grayed like an old woman, turned windy, vagrant; autumn had returned. On this day before the Feast of the Intercession, at Black Creeks the bathhouses by the creek were fired up. At dawn the girls, barefoot in the snow, their hems tucked up, hauled in the water, and the chimneyless stoves were heating all day. In the cottages the older folk raked up the ashes, gathered the smocks, and towards dusk they went in families to steam themselves—the oldsters, the men, sons-in-law, lads, mothers, wives, daughters-in-law, young girls, children. In the bathhouses there were no chimneys. In the smoke, in the steam, in the red stove-glow, white human bodies were crammed tightly together, men and women. They all washed in the same wood-ash solution, and the elderly men scrubbed everyone's backs, and they all ran down to the river for a dip, in the damp evening frost, in the cold wind.

And Alioshka Kniaz'kov on that day at dawn walked up to Nikola's to see one-eyed Egorka—the wizard. The wood at dawn was silent, misty, frightening, and the sorcerer Egorka was whispering frighteningly: "In the bathhouse, in the bathhouse, I say, in the bathhouse! . . ." The evening came, damp and cold, the wind whistled in every key and tone. In the evening Alioshka stood guard at the Kononova-Gnedoi bathhouse. A crazed young girl jumped out, naked, with disheveled plaits, rushed down to the river and from there ran up the hill to the hut, her white body dissolving in the darkness. And an old man came out twice, plunged coughing into the water, and again went off for a steaming. A mother dragged her children down to the river, clasping them under her arms. Ulianka lingered in the bathhouse alone, she was cleaning up the bathhouse. Alexei made his way to the foreroom and began whispering, in great fear, what had been whispered to him by Egor:

I, Lexei, stand with my back to the West, my face to the East, I look, I see. From the clear sky flies a fiery arrow. I pray to that arrow, I submit to that arrow, I question it: Where have you been sent, fiery arrow?—To the dark woods, to the shifting swamps, to the damp roots—Come now, fiery arrow! fly where I send you: fly to Uliana, to Kononova, strike her ardent breast, her dark liver, her passionate blood, her wide vein, her sugary lips, so that she may yearn for me, long for me in the sun, in the dawn, at the new moon, in the cold wind, in days that have passed and in days to come; that she might kiss me, Lexei Semenov, embrace me, and fornicate with me! My words are complete and contain the powers of incantation, like the mighty ocean sea, they are strong and sticky, getting stronger and stickier than isinglass, firmer and stronger than damask steel and stone. For ever and ever. Amen.

Ulianka was wiping the floor, working quickly, the muscles playing lightly on her powerful croup. Suddenly the fumes went to her head—or had the spell clouded it? She opened the door, leaned on the door jamb wearily and submissively, breathed in the cold air, smiled weakly, stretched—there was a sweet ringing in her ears, a cold, refreshing wind blew around her. From the hill her mother called out:

"Ulianka-aa! Hurry-y-y! Milk the cows!"

"Right away-y-y-y!" She began to hurry, gave the floor three or so slaps with the rag, splashing the corners. She pulled on her shirt, and, mounting the hill, began to sing mischievously:

> *I won't go to Coveside and wed,*
> *I won't be uncovered and shamed!*
> *I won't hop before times to bed—*
> *My shimmy will never be stained!"*

In the dark cow shed under the awning there was a warm smell of manure and cow sweat. The cow stood by resignedly. Ulianka squatted down, milk spurted into the pail, the cow's udders were soft, the cow sighed deeply . . .

And at the Feast of the Visitation, at Matins in the dark church among the spindle-shanked and dark-faced saints, Ulianka composed her own, simple, virgin's prayer:

"Holy Mother of God, cover the Earth with Snow, and me with a husband!"

And the snow that year fell early, the winter set in before the feast of Our Lady of Kazan.

CONVERSATIONS

The wind swept along in white snowstorms, the fields were covered with white powder, with snowdrifts, the cottages smoked with a gray smoke. Long since past was that spring when, blessed by the priest, their families riding in carts, the men had ridden off for three days to plunder the gentry's estates—that spring the gentry's nests flamed up like red roosters, burned to the ground for good. Then kerosene, matches, tea, sugar, salt, provisions, town shoes and clothes—vanished. The trains shuddered in their death throes; in their death agony the gaily colored rubles began to dance—the lane leading to the station was overgrown with roadside wild chicory-asters.

The snow fell for two days, there was a hard frost, the wood turned gray, the fields turned white, the magpies began to chatter. With the frosts, the winds, the snow, Dobrynia of the Golden Baldric went bald—the road after the first fall of snow lay soft, smooth. In that winter contagion swept persistently like a black shroud through the cottages, it poured out typhus, smallpox, rheums—and when the road was fit for sledges, the coffin makers came, they brought the coffins. The day was on its way towards dusk. Gray. The coffins were of pine, in all sizes. They lay on the sledges in heaps, one on top of another. At Black Creeks they sighted the coffin makers when they were still on the outskirts, by the outskirts the women went to meet them. The coffins were all bought up within a single hour. The coffin makers measured the women with a sazhen-long stick, and allowed a quarter extra. First to come up and talk business was the old man Kononov-Kniaz'kov.

"What's the price, then, roughly." he said. "Coffins, y'see, got to be bought . . . got to be bought—there's a scarcity of them in the town now. I need one, for the old girl, so, y'see . . . whoever'll need one.

Then Nikon's wife interrupted old Kononov, began to wave her elbows about, began talking with her elbows:

"Well, the price, then, what's the price?"

"The price—you know, it's 'taters we're after," answered the coffin maker.

"We knows you're not after money. I'll take three coffins. Otherwise, somebody dies and there's trouble. You feel easier."

"It's one thing to talk about feeling easier," interrupted Kononov. "You wait your turn, woman, I'm a bit older . . . Well then, m'dear, measure me—see what size I am, measure me. Dying—well, everything's in God's lap y'see, when it comes to dying."

The women ran about for potatoes, the coffin maker measured up, the lads swung the coffins over their heads—carried them proudly around to the cottages. In the cottages people examined at length the excellence of their coffins, measured themselves against the coffins and stood them on their porches, where it could easily be seen: who had two, who had three. The snow turned a wintry blue, a deathly blue in the frost. The cottages were lit up with pine splits, out back gates creaked and there were women's footsteps—footsteps to the barn to hay the cattle for the night. Nikon's wife invited the coffin makers to her place. Cautiously, with no chatter, the coffin makers sold the coffins. Once inside the cottage, having stabled the horses, over their tea, with their shoes off and their belts loosened—the guests turned out to be gay dogs, talkative, game for anything. Nikon Borisych, the master, the village chairman, bearded from the eyes down, was sitting by the lamp whittling splits, wedging them one after another into a clamp over the washtub, entertaining his amiable guests and talking away:

"Now, all the same we're by ourselves, alone. You die, and the coffin—there it is. You don't feed your hound before a hunt. Rebellion, all the same, that's troubled times. Soviet power—means that's it for the towns. We're just heading out to the mine to get our own salt.

Nikon's wife, in a velveteen vest and homespun skirt with lilac polka-dots, wearing an old-fashioned horned headdress, her breasts bulging like udders, her face plump as a cow's, was sitting at the loom with her shuttle clacking away. The torch burned smokily. It lit up the bearded peasant faces ranged in a circle in the semi-darkness and smoke (their eyes shone with the red glow of the split's red light). On the stove shelf, a dozen of them piled on top of each other, lay the women. In the corner behind the stove, in a pen, a calf was lazily chewing its cud. Fresh faces kept coming in—to have a look at the coffin makers. The others left—the door steamed, it reeked of the cold.

"The rail-w-a-y!" says Nikon Borisych with great scorn. "The rail-w-a-y, all t'same! I wisht it was scrapped!"

"It's hard labor and nothing but," answered Klimanov.

"We got no need of it, f'r example," asserted Grandfather Kononov. "The masters, y'see, need it to travel about to their government departments, or just for visiting. But we, y'see, are out on our own, without any bourgeoisse, I mean to say."

"The rail-w-a-y!" said Nikon Borisych. "The rail-w-a-y, all t'same, . . . We lived without it before and got by. Wh-y-y-y-y! . . . Once a year I used to make the trip to town, all t'same! . . . I'd loaf about a whole day on the platform, I'd have to untie my bundle about five times: 'What sort of goods you got, or it's the butt-end for you!' Well, we used to climb onto the roof, . . . and away we'd go . . . Stop! 'What sort of pass have you got, show me!' D'you think I'm an old woman or something?—I'd show the pass. Then I got hot under the collar. Such and such your mother, I say, I'm taking my lads to the Red Army to have a crack at the bourgeoisie, all t'same. I, I say— We're for the Bolsheviks, for the Soviets, and you, obv'ously, are Kom'nists? . . . He takes off . . . . . . all t'same it riles you up . . ."

Night. The torch burns dimly, the windows of Nikon's hut become dim, the village sleeps its nightly sleep, the white snowstorm whips up its white snows, the sky is dismal. In the hut, in the semi-dark, in a circle by the torch, in shag-tobacco smoke, sit the peasants, with beards from their eyes down (their eyes shine with a red glow).

The shag-tobacco smokes, red little fires become dim in the corners, the roof rafters crawl about in the smoke. It's stuffy, steamy for the stove-fleas on the women's bodies on the stove. And Nikon Borisych says with great severity:

"Kom'nists!" and with an energetic gesture (his eyes flashing in the torch light): —"We're for the Bolsheviks! For the Soviets! We want it our way, the Roossian way. We've been under the masters—and that's enough! The Roossian way, our way! Ourselves!

"One thing, f'r example," says Grandfather Kononov, "we've nothing against him. Let him go. And the factory lads—We've nothing against them—let them stuff the girls, f'r example, and get married, those who have a trade. But the gentry—they's at the end of the line, f'r example."

A WEDDING

Winter. December. Christmas.

The clearing. Trees, enveloped in hoar-frost and snow, gleam like blue diamonds. At dusk the last bullfinch cries out, a magpie rattles its bony rattle. And silence. Huge pine trees have been felled, and their branches lie about like enchanting carpets. Among the trees in a murk that is dark blue, like sugar-paper, night comes creeping. Its movements light and unhurried, a hare hops by. Overhead, the sky—glimpsed through the treetops like tatters bits of blue with white stars. On all sides, hidden from the sky, stand junipers and somber pines, their slender switches tangled, intertwined. Constant and disquieting, the sounds of the forest run on. The yellow logs are silent. The moon, like a live coal, rises above the far end of the clearing. And the night. The sky is low, the moon red. The wood stands like a stockade forged in iron. The wind creaks and it sounds like the creaking of rusty bolts. Eerie in the lunar murk, lopped-off branches of felled pines lie about. Gigantic hedgehogs, their branches bristle sullenly. Night.

And then at the far end of the clearing, among the piney hedgehogs, in the moonlight, a wolf sets up a howl, and the wolves celebrate their own beast-yule, a wolfish wedding. A she-wolf howled lazily and languorously, the he-wolves licked the snow with burning tongues. Their young look sternly askance. The wolves play, jump, roll into the snow, in the moonlight, in the frost. And the leader howls, howls, howls. Night. And above the village—at Christmas, at the fortune telling; in the lanes, in the forest, in the settlements; before the wedding season a bold marching song is heard:

> *Chi-vi-li, willy-nilly, sway and swish—*
> *Grab the one that is your wish!*

And on their way to a doleful wedding-eve gathering, in the name of maidenly chastity, through their tears, the maidens sing:

> *Small hope had the Mother to empty her nest—*
> *My Mother got shut of me one summer's day*

Sent me to strangers, a house far away
She banished me, seven years never to come to her.
Three years have gone since I've been with my mother,
But come the fourth summer the bird will take wing,
Light down by my Father in garden so green
His garden I'll water with many a tear,
And give over my sorrow for Mother to bear.

My mother goes walking 'round her new nest,
Calls to her children, her dear nightingales,
"Get up, darling children, my dear nightingales.
There's one in our garden that sits and weeps sore,
It must be the wretched one, our kin no more.
Eldest brother said: I will go and see.
Second brother said: Fetch the gun to me!
Youngest brother said: I will shoot her down.
Youngest brother said: I will shoot her down.

On the roof peak—a hex-horse; on the ridge—a dove; the bridal sheet, the pillow cases and the towels—embroidered with flowers, grasses, birds; and the wedding goes on, according to the ritual, embroidered with songs, with rhythm, with centuries and tradition.

A sketch: By the torch-holder is an old man, a torch burns, in the place of honor sits Uliana Makarova—a bride in a white dress. On the table a samovar, refreshments. At the table—the guests, Alexei Semyonych with the mothers-in-law and fathers-in-law.

"Eat up, my dear guests, you've traveled so far." this sternly, from the old man.

"Eat up, dear guests, you've traveled so far," this with fear and self-importance, from the mother.

"Eat up, dear guests, and you, Leksei Semionych," this is Uliana Makarova, hesitantly.

"Uliana Makarova, you haven't walked out with other lads, haven't sinned, you haven't cracked your saucer?

"No, Lexei Semionych . . . I've not been shamed . . ."

"So, kind parents, how do you reward your daughter?"

"Her reward is our parental blessing—with the icon of Our Lady of Kazan."

And the wedding, according to the ritual of centuries, is conducted above Black Creeks like a liturgy—in the thatched cottages, under the awnings, on the road, over the fields, through the snowstorm, by day and by night: it rings with songs and bells, ferments like home-brewed ale, it is painted and carved like the hex-horse at the peak of the roof—on evenings that are blue like sugar-paper. Chapter such-and-such of the Book of Rites, the first verse and further.

Verse 1.

When the mortgage is taken out, the house inspected, the terms agreed, and the party of maidens has arrived, then they bring to the groom the dowry goods which the groom redeems, and the mothers-in-law make up the bed with the blankets and pillows from the dowry with flowers and grasses and they decide on the wedding day.

Verse 2.

Verse 3.

> Oh mother—oh mother of mine!
> Why do you wish me to marry!
> To sleep with this wife I decline,—
> Where will I leave her or carry?!

> *They went to dance, they danced their feet right off,*
> *The girls and women laughed so hard—that they had a calf.*
> *Oo-oo-oo! Ahhhhhh! Ah! the cottage dances like a wench,*
> *Fidgets back and forth, yelling up to heaven.*

"Does the young girl know how to clean a chimney?"
"Does the young girl know how to bind a sheaf?"
"Does the young girl know how to build a nest?"
"They are nobles, they need rubles. Take the cheese and the cottage loaf,
        lay the money on the cloth."
"Measure the hessian, give me twenty *arshin*."

Oo-oo-oo. Ahhhh. Oooo. Eeee. In the cottage there's no room to breathe. In the cottage there's merrymaking. In the cottage there's shouting, victuals, and drink —hic!—and out of the house to the open shed they run to get a breath, chase away the sweat, gather their thoughts and strength.

Night. The stars wink lazily, in the frost. Under the shed roof, in the darkness there's a smell of manure, of cattle sweat. It's quiet. Only now and then the cattle sigh. And every quarter of an hour, with a lantern, old Aleshka's mother, the mother of young Alexei Semyonych comes—to inspect the cow. The cow is lying submissively, her snout thrust into the straw: the waters broke last night, any time now she'll calve. The old woman looks carefully, nods her head reproachfully, makes the sign of the cross over the cow: it's time, it's time, Brownie! And the cow strains. The old woman—

an age-old custom—opens up the back door to let in some fresh air. Outside the door is the empty cherry orchard, in the distance the barn and the path to the barn—covered with hay, coated with hoar-frost. And out of the darkness the grandfather speaks:

"I'll go down, I'll go down—I'll have a look. We'll need Egor Polikarpich, Egor, the squinting wizard. The cow's pining, pining, fading away, the cow . . ."

"Run, grandfather, run dear . . ."

"What do you think I'm doing? I'm going. And you stand by. It's cold."

Under the shed roof it's dark, warm. The cow is sighing heavily and lowing. The old woman strikes a light—two little hooves are sticking out . . . The old woman crosses herself and whispers . . . And grandfather trots through the fields to the forest, to Egorka. Grandfather is old, grandfather knows that if you don't leave the path the wolf, ferocious and mean in this season, can't touch you. Under the shed roof on the straw the wet calf lows and kicks. The lantern burns dimly, lights up the stakes, the partitions, the hens under the roof, the sheep in the fold. Outside there is silence, peace, but the cottage buzzes, sings, dances to every note and every string.

—And from the Book of Rites.

Verse 13. And when they drive away in the early hours and the guests disperse and in the cottage remain only the mother of the groom and the mother-in-law, the mothers-in-law undress the bride and lay her on the bed and settle themselves down over the stove. And to the young wife comes her husband and lies down beside her on the bed, embroidered with flowers and grasses and the husband sows his wife with his seed, breaking her maidenhead. And the mother and mothers-in-law see this and cross themselves.

Verse 14. And on the morning of the following day the mother and mothers-in-law take the young wife outside and cleanse her with warm water, and after the cleansing they give the water to their cattle to drink: to the cows, to the horses and sheep. And the couple drive to their dower fields and coarse songs are sung to them.

—The clearing. The trees are laden with hoar-frost and snow, motionless. Among the trees, in the gray murk, snapping twigs as he goes, the white haired grandfather goes trot-a-trot and in the blue murk, in the distance, a wolf barks. The day is white and motionless. And towards evening there is a snowstorm. And tomorrow there'll be a snowstorm. And in the snowstorm the wolves howl.

OUTSIDE THE TRIPTYCH, at the end

The day is white and motionless. And towards evening there's a snow-storm—mean, a January storm. The wolves howl.

—And white haired granddad atop the stove, white haired granddad tells his grandchildren the tale of the juicy apple: "Play, play, pipes! Comfort, dear father, my own dear mother. They ruined me, wretch that I am, in the dark forest they killed me for a silver dish, for the juicy apple." The snow-storm flails like a windmill, grinding out a powder of snowy grit, of murk, of cold. It's warm up on the stove, with the fairy tales, the fleas, the steamy bodies: "Awaken me, little father, from my deep sleep, fetch me the water of life." "And he came to the forest, dug up the earth on a flowery knoll and sprinkled a twig with the water of life, and his daughter, whose beauty none could relate, awakened from her long sleep." "Ivan Tsarevich, why did you burn my frogskin—why?"

—The forest stands sternly, a bastion, and the snowstorm batters it like a clutch of harpies. Night. Is the legend of how the bogatyrs met their death not truly the legend of the forest and the snowstorm? More and more snow-storm harpies batter the forest bastion, howling, shrieking, shouting, roar-ing like maddened women. Their dead fall, and after them rush still more harpies, they never decrease,—they multiply like dragon's heads—two grow where one is severed, and the forest stands like Ilia of Murom.

Kolomna: Nikola-Na-Posadakh
25 December, Old Style. 1920

Translated by A.L. and M.K.

C3. *The Waning of Modernism in Post-revolutionary Years*

THE WRITERS IN THE previous subsection embody dreams of alternate realities and express increasing anxiety as the years of upheaval and civil war roll over Russia. These were cataclysmic, apocalyptic times . . . At the end of Pilniak's *Naked Year*, for instance, we see Russia awaiting the return of Ilia of Murom as English dreamers awaited the return of King Arthur. These are heroes who can save the land because they are *of* it, an organic part of its past.

Enchanted flights of fancy over the Russian landscape were no longer possible after the end of the Civil War. In a materialist march to a command society, Russia's new leaders forced the populace to embrace a new kind of utopian vision, mechanized and international in scope, or, as V. I. Lenin stressed at its genesis: "I could care less about the fate of Russia—all I care about is World Revolution." But the proletarian revolution did not engulf the world in spite of Lenin's wishes, and once I. V. Stalin took command over Soviet society for over a quarter century, Russia was to face a new challenge: enunciated by the "glorious leader" himself. The inhabitants of the USSR were to frame the socialist future within the confines of one state—Russia itself. This future was to be attained by the doctrinaire destruction of most vestiges of Russia's religious and economic past, replacing these with materialist ideology and a planned economy. Anything thwarting these plans was considered treason against the state. It was increasingly dangerous to oppose the regime, especially after the beginning of the "Second Five-year Plan" in 1932, a period which also saw the creation of the *Union of Soviet Writers* along with the abolition of all free-thinking literary organizations and consequent persecution of all errant individuals. In the event, there were millions of these.

The writers chosen for this subsection—Nikolai Zabolotsky (1903-58), Daniel Kharms [Yuvachev] (1905-42), Yuri Olesha (1899-1960), and Mikhail Bulgakov (1891-1940)—stand here as representatives of the incredibly rich field of Russian poets and writers who came to prominence in the 1920s. They were a decade or two younger than Evgeny Zamiatin, the writer whose literary craft had more or less predicted the reality of political oppression they were to experience in their lives. Unlike Zamiatin, who was allowed to emigrate, many of this generation physically perished in concentration camps by the 1930s; those that survived found their energies sapped by the regime to the point that they ceased to be productive altogether, as their creative gifts were ill-suited to the now mandatory production work of socialist realism.

Given the tragic outcome of their lives, it is all the more gratifying to see in their works an incredible capacity for life-affirming humor. Liberating themselves from the lockstep march of socialist dictates, they created alternate, dreamscape worlds. We are uniting these quite different authors here to familiarize the contemporary reader with some of the less translated (except for Bulgakov) works of this period. Obliquely each of the works chosen is also connected with the concept of flight, be it the flight of fancy, the flight of an insect, flight "on the wings of love," or the flight of Bulgakov's witch-heroine, Margarita.

Most selections are also united by the years 1928-1929, the last years when free creativity was still imagined to be possible, but also the years when outright bans on free fiction began in earnest. Zabolotsky's and Olesha's short works were written in 1929, and Bulgakov's subsequently famous novel was begun in the same year. Each of the selections probes to a greater or lesser extent the meaning of historical truth and the applicability of ancient myths to the modernist context. In Bulgakov's novel, completed a decade later, such mythopoetic truths find full expression, whereas in Zabolotskys' *Signs of the Zodiac* their applicability to the modern world is far more equivocal. This uncertainty is practically erased in *Human of the Snows*, a poem composed thirty years later (1957) at the height of nuclear war anxiety. Here no hope is held out to humanity by Nature, Reason, Religion or Technology. In the Bibilical context God gave Adam the authority to name His creatures, but in this poem the Half-man Half-beast capers pointlessly around his skinned prey, spouting gibberish. In Kharms' *The Young Man who Surprised the Watchman,* a miniature of Kafkaesque brevity, literal flight is physically squashed, while the possibility of metaphoric flight to the gates of Heaven is implicitly preserved. No such gates present themselves to Kalugin, the protagonist of Kharms' *The Dream*—a victim of a society perhaps even less humane than the one imagined in Kafka's *Metamorphosis*.

In 1929 Zabolotsky, Kharms, and Olesha collaborated with eminent Formalist critics in a never completed collection entitled *Archimedes' Bath*, which was to include contributions by members of *Oberiu—The Association for Real Art* (Ob"edinenie real'nogo isskustva). Zabolotsky and Kharms had been instrumental in the 1927 founding of this, the last freely-formed Russian literary group. When Oberieu was effectively quashed in 1930, several of its participants were able to work in the somewhat marginalized area of children's literature; others perished in the purges. The fates of the two founders of Oberiu—each represented here by a couple of entries—can be said to typify what happened to the rest. Zabolotsky's collections of poetry beginning in the late twenties and continuing into the thirties were harshly attacked by the Soviet press; in 1938 he was arrested and sentenced to five years of hard labor; he was to survive into the post-Stalin years, but rarely again to write with the striking originality of the late 1920s. Kharms was arrested in 1931 on the charge that his "trans-sense" poetry was distracting the people from the task of building socialism; although he was only held for a year and released, he was increasingly under a cloud, and 1941 saw him again in prison, where he died.

Olesha's 1927 novel, *Envy*, and a series of superb short stories had earned him wide acclaim, but after 1932 Olesha published very little. Olesha's highly original and evocative imagery—representing the world "through the wrong end of binoculars" (as Nils Åke Nilsson, a connoisseur of Olesha's *oeuvre*, notes)—deftly made everyday objects seem alien or new by stirring up the "estrangement response" (ostranenie). But beyond such devices, showering his readers with an ensemble of pioneering similes, the writer contemplates in his fiction the role of human sensuality, feeling, and myth within the context of an insistently materialist, dehumanized, and demythologized world. This is evident in the miniature masterpiece newly translated for this volume, which was first published in the Moscow almanac "Earth and Factory", vol. 2. Beyond the obvious allusions to such universally recognizable topoi as the Garden of Eden, the Western reader should be aware that in naming his heroine "Lelia," Olesha is creating a feminine counterpart to the Russian Love-god, *Lel'*. In fact Lel' is of doubtful antiquity, with roots in the folkloric revival rather than in the deep past, but mention of this deity is common in the writings of Russian early nineteenth-century poets such as Derzhavin and even Pushkin, who felt the need for a native variant of the classic Love-god, *Eros*.

Our other selection from Olesha's *oeuvre* is his essay "On the Fantastic in H. G. Wells," written on the eve of WWII in 1937, which provides the reader with a rare glimpse into the autobiographic laboratory of Olesha's own growth as a writer. Moreover, the essay serves as a natural transition to the space-fantasies in the final section, predicated on the belief in the victory of technologies which would ground fantasy-making in the experienced reality of space-flight.

Selections from the writings of Mikhail Afanasievich Bulgakov (1891-1940), equally famous for his prose works and his plays, end this section. Some details of Bulgakov's biography parallel those of Russia's two greatest nineteenth-century writers who excelled in composing both fiction and drama, Nikolai Gogol and Anton Chekhov. Like the latter, Bulgakov was trained as a medical doctor and practiced this art; along with Chekhov he wrote socially relevant plays and prose works, was acclaimed in his lifetime, and died in his forties. But it is especially to Gogol that Bulgakov cultivated a life-long aesthetic allegiance. Like Gogol, Bulgakov was born and raised in Ukraine, and moved as an adult to the capitol; like Gogol he wrote satires, reworking in the process many of Gogol's themes and images, even rewriting and adapting Gogol's masterpiece, *Dead Souls*, for the contemporary stage. And just as Gogol had done before him, Bulgakov would ultimately burn some of his own manuscripts. Indeed, in tribute to his admiration of Gogol, a piece of rock which used to stand on Gogol's grave in the Donskoy cemetery was reused for Bulgakov's tomb.

Especially mindful of this comparison with Gogol, we have made our brief selections from what is arguably the twentieth-century Russian novel best known in the West, *The Master and Maragrita*. Bulgakov ultimately suggests in this novel that society founded solely on materialist values is the least desirable destiny for Man. The exhilaration of flight is present in the novel as experienced by the central protagonist Margarita, transformed into a witch by the application of a magic cream. Although reminiscent of the flights in Gogol's *Vyi* and Turgenev's *Fantoms*, Margarita's flight gives her and the reader a bird's eye view of a modern, Soviet Russia caught in a mesh of cities and their lights: the signs of "progress."

The meaning of technological progress is in doubt in the first selection of this section, *The Fatal Eggs* (an homage to Wells' *The Food of the Gods*), where Bulgakov advances the notion that technology is doomed to catastrophe in the Soviet social context. In our ealier neo-Wellsean selection, Kuprin's *Liquid Sunshine*, social bliss based on technology was undermined by the romantic woes of a single individual. In *The Fatal Eggs*, however, such failure is shown to be systemic. The ray causing the reptilian eggs to mutate, thus hatching the catastrophe, is a red ray—the hue itself an overarching symbol of everything touched by the Bolshevik regime. The significance of the machine, consistently glorified by the Communists, is embodied in their most powerful vehicle, the propaganda press: the ray's inventor, Persikov, is badgered by such publications as *Red Spark, Red Pepper, Red Projector, Red Evening Moscow, Red Raven*, etc. Under the umbrella of the color which medieval Russians had considered the most appealing of all ("Red Square," for example, originally meant "Beautiful Square") the disoriented, powerless citizens of the new command society bungle everything, sleep during working hours, and drink homerically. Bulgakov shows how, in such a society, it is no wonder mistakes are made, and a fatal "error" is, in fact, inevitable. Set in the 1920's, the story (especially chapter V) even seems prescient, given the current plausibility of a global avian plague.

The Fatal Eggs, first published in 1924 in a collection of stories titled *The Diaboliad*, was set in the years of the very near future—1928-29. But in 1929, when Bulgakov began *Master and Margarita* under the working title *The Man with a Hoof*, reality had become even bleaker than he had anticipated five years earlier. His art thus began to exploit even more seriously the concept which had been a life-long concern for Gogol as well—

the Devil and all His works. The fact that ethical concerns are of primary importance to Bulgakov is underscored by his implicit invitation to the reader to ponder the meaning of the famous exchange from Goethe's *Faust* that he chose as the novel's epigraph:

—Then who are you?
—*I am a part of the force that eternally wishes Evil
  and eternally accomplishes Good.*

In the Soviet Russia of the 1930's, with the Church decimated to the point of extinction, the only *FORCE* of any consequence was Communist rule. And if we were to read this epigraph with the plus and minus signs switched—as Bulgakov clearly wishes—the exchange unmistakably alludes to the Bolshevik regime, which trumpeted explicitly utopian notes about its Good intentions, but accomplished Evil beyond comprehension. All of Russia had essentially become a huge concentration camp, as its people were murdered in orchestrated famines and purges on a scale transcending any medieval plague. Under such circumstances metaphysical intervention was to Bulgakov the only remedy. With a Savior utterly silent in those days, he focused his artistry on the Old Testament God's "right hand"—the Devil. For reasons too complex to summarize here and in any case best discovered by reading this uniquely intriguing work itself, the Devil in the person of a gentlemanly yet sinister stage magician Woland descends on Moscow. Woland observes Soviet reality, and through his eyes we see a humanity deadened, all vital impulses wasted on banal trivialities. Satan seems to find it almost depressing that He can do no worse to Man than Man has done to himself. Accompanied by Behemoth, a huge cat packing a Browning, and Koroviev, an etiolated prankster in a checkered jacket, Woland ruthlessly and thoroughly disrupts the comfortable socialist philistinism of the Soviet capital.

The Germanic root of Woland's very name plays productively with the Latinate morphology of More's *Utopia—Which land? Where is that land? No land. Nowhere.* His diabolical realm begins to intersect with Soviet materialist space right from the first chapter. The novel begins as Berlioz, the well-paid editor of a state-sponsored literary journal, is about to explain to a colleague the historical impossibility of Jesus Christ, when Koroviev appears in midair:

> *At that moment the sultry air thickened in front of Berlioz, and wove itself into a transparent citizen of the very strangest appearance. He wore a jockey cap, and a cropped, checkered, spectral jacket . . . The citizen was nearly seven feet tall but narrow in the shoulder, incredibly thin and with a face that was, please note, derisive.*

Berlioz' life had been arranged in such a way that he was unaccustomed to unusual apparitions. Turning even paler he rubbed his eyes and exclaimed confusedly: "This can't be! . . ."

But alas, it could be, and the elongated transparent citizen, feet not touching the ground, hovered before him and swayed to the left and to the right.

Whereupon terror seized Berlioz to such an extent that he shut his eyes. And when he opened them,—he saw it had all passed off, the mirage had dissolved, the checkered individual had disappeared, and simultaneously the dull needle withdrew from his heart.

—Oof . . . what the Devil!—exclaimed the editor . . .

Such intersection never relents, as Bulgakov crafts his revenge on the regime that tormented him. The novel ultimately succeeds in turning the Soviet world, predicated on a false utopia, upside down.

Nikolai Alekseevich Zabolotsky
(1903–1958)

Signs of Zodiac

(The original, 1929 version)

Zodiac signs dim their gleaming
Over the expanse of fields,
DOG—the Animal—is dreaming,
SPARROW to Bird-dreams now yields.
Fatly buttocked water-nymphets
Fly away straight to the skies,
Firm their arms, like tree-trunk limblets,
Round their breasts, like turnip pies.
There the Witch rides on three angles
Disappearing in a whiff,
Mermaids rouse a corpse which dangles
In a dance with them—all stiff,
Wizards' pallid troops behind them
Stalk the wily common FLY,
And beyond the nearby mountain
Moon's calm face still hangs on high.

Zodiac signs dim their gleaming
Over buildings on a farm,
DOG—the Animal—is dreaming,
FISH—the Flounder—dreams disarmed.
Hear the clapper clack-clack-clack:
SPIDER dozes on a rack,
COW and FLY sleep near the hearth,
Moon still hangs above the Earth.
As the ladle of spilt water,
Hangs on high for reasons weird,
Goblin pulls a log that's tauter,
From his shaggy drooping beard.
From behind the cloud—a Siren
Bares her shapely leg apart;
And a Cannibal, desiring,
Bites off Sire's private part:

Africans and Brits thus humbled,
Witches, bedbugs, carrion—
All come flying rough-and-tumble
In a dance vulgarian.

Page of long-past generations,
Paladin of bright new Dawn:
Heed, my Mind! Such imp-creations
Seed in Man new doubts when spawned.
In this cramped-by-Nature kingdom,
Midst the want, the mud and rust,
What seek you—my King of Freedom—
In our restless Earth-born dust?

Earth's abode soars high and wayward.
Sleep! It's really late—Good night!
Reason—my poor Mind's crusader—
Dream till sunrise scales the height.
Why nurse doubts, why flinch and startle?
You and I, now day is gone,
Each half-beast and half-Immortal,
Slumber at the very portal
Of this new and vibrant Dawn.

Hear the clapper clack-clack-clack:
SPIDER dozes on a rack,
COW and FLY dream near the hearth,
Moon still hangs above the Earth.
As the ladle of spilt water,
Hangs on high while, planted deep,
Sleeps POTATO—Flora's daughter.
You should too be fast asleep!

Translated by A. L.

Human of the Snows

Word is, someplace in the Himalayas,
Reaching past the temples and retreats,
Lives, unknown to us, that Realm's pariah:
Being savage, fostered by the beasts.

Tranquil is his gait, his white pelt shaggy,
He, at times, descending from his tors,
Whirls and dances like a shaman craggy,
Hurling snowballs at the temples' doors.

Only when he hears the Buddhist elders
Piping down the wall their moaning horn,
He runs off in fear and, dazed, surrenders
To his rugged, icy mountain home.

If such tales can't be dismissed as gossip,
All that means: in this all-knowing age,
There still lives that missing—it's a toss up—
Nexus, link: half-beast, half-human sage.

Yes, it's clear, his mind has not been tempered,
His beclouded keep is not ornate:
No pagodas, schools, or idol's temples
Welcome creature-hunters at the gate.

He has no idea why beneath him,
Hidden in his mountain's catacombs,
Docile, acquiescent to their leaders,
Shimmer in the caverns—atom bombs.

Why, this Himalayan humanoidal
Hardly could discern their workings' trace,
Even if, in onrush asteroidal,
He were hurled, aflame, into deep space.

But so long as the lamenting Lamas
Chant, reflecting on his fresh-laid tracks,
Pace around, unfold their temple's drama,
Drumming on their weird, demonic clacks,

And so long as Buddha sits there, telling
Fortunes from above his navel's hub,
Yeti, in his snowdrift-laden dwelling,
Feels comparatively safe and smug.

As he skins his roebuck at the mountain's
Spring, he splutters sounds, at times—a word:
His loud laughs are nothing more than pronouns,
Shunning Adam's right to name the World.

(1957) Translated by A.L. and M.L.

Daniel [Evgeny] Kharms
(1905-1942)

The Young Man who Surprised the Watchman

"Whaddya know?" said the watchman, inspecting the fly. "You smear that thing with carpenter's glue and that's all she wrote—right? Just think! Plain old glue!"

"Hey you—boogeyman," a young man wearing yellow gloves shouted at the watchman. The watchman immediately understood that this was aimed at him, but went on looking at the fly.

"Am I talking to myself here, or what?"—the young man shouted again—"You lummox!"

The watchman squashed the fly with his thumb and, without turning his head toward the young man, said:

"What are you yelling for, you punk? I hear you anyway, no need to yell!"

The young man dusted off his trousers with his gloves and asked, now in a delicate voice:

"Please tell me, gramps, how do I get to Heaven?"

The watchman inspected the young man, first screwing up one eye, then the other, then stroked his beard, then again inspected the young man, and said:

"So what are you waiting for? Move along!"

"Excuse *me*"—said the young man—" but I've got some urgent business. Up there, they've even got a room ready for me."

"Fine, then," said the watchman. "Show me your ticket."

"A ticket? They said they'd let me in regardless," said the young man, looking the watchmen straight in the face.

"Whaddya know?" said the watchman.

"So what do you say," said the young man, "you gonna let me through?"

"Fine, then, fine," said the watchman, "go on!"

"But how do I go? Where to?" the young man asked. "I mean, I don't even know the way."

"Where you headed?" asked the watchman with a suddenly stern expression.

The young man covered his mouth with the palm of his hand and very quietly said:

"To Heaven!"

The watchman leaned forward, moving his right foot so he was standing more firmly, stared at the young man, and asked sternly:

"What are you trying to pull? Wanna make a fool of me, or what?"

The young man gave a smile, raised one of his yellow-gloved hands, waved it over his head, and—disappeared.

The watchman took a sniff of the air: there was a smell of burned feathers on it.

"Whaddya know?" said the watchman. He unbuttoned his jacket, scratched himself on the stomach, spat on the place where the young man had been standing, and slowly went back into his guardhouse.

The Dream

Kalugin fell asleep and saw a dream, like he was sitting in some bushes and a cop was walking past the bushes.

Kalugin woke up, wiped his mouth and fell asleep again, and again saw a dream, like he was walking past some bushes and in the bushes the cop had hidden himself and was sitting there.

Kalugin woke up, stuck a newspaper under his head so he wouldn't soak the pillow with drool, and fell asleep again, and again saw a dream, like he was sitting in some bushes and the cop was walking past the bushes.

Kalugin woke up, changed the newspaper, lay down, and fell asleep again. Fell asleep and again saw a dream, like he was walking past the bushes and the cop was sitting in the bushes.

Whereupon Kalugin woke up and decided to sleep no more, but he instantly did fall asleep, and saw a dream, like he was sitting behind the cop, and the bushes were walking past them.

Kalugin began to shriek and to thrash around in bed, but this time couldn't wake up.

Kalugin slept right on through four days and four nights, and—on the fifth day—he woke up so skinny that he had to take little strings and tie his boots to his legs, so they wouldn't keep falling off. In the bakery where Kalugin always bought wheat bread they didn't recognize him, and they slipped him bread that was half-rye. The Health Department, inspecting the apartments and spotting Kalugin, declared him anti-sanitary and good-for-nothing, and ordered the super to toss Kalugin out along with the trash.

Kalugin the charwoman then folded in two and tossed out—trash.

Translated by A. L. and M. K.

Yuri Olesha
(1899-1960)

LOVE

Shuvalov was waiting for Lelia in the park. It was noon of a hot day. A lizard materialized on a boulder. Shuvalov reflected: on that boulder the lizard is defenseless, you see it immediately. "Mimicry," he thought. The idea of mimicry led him to recall the chameleon.

"Just wonderful," said Shuvalov. "A chameleon was all I needed."

The lizard ran off.

Shuvalov stood up from the bench in a pique and set off briskly down the path. A fit of irritation had seized him, along with a desire to argue with someone. He came to a halt and observed, rather loudly:

"Well damn it all! Why should I be thinking about mimicry and chameleons? These thoughts are completely unnecessary to me."

He came out into a clearing and sat down on a stump. Insects were flying around. Stems were trembling. The flight-path architecture of birds, flies and beetles was invisible, but one could still somehow make out dotted lines, the shapes of arches, of bridges, towers, terraces a kind of swiftly mutating and second-by-second-disintegrating city.

"Something's taken me over," thought Shuvalov. "My sphere of perception is getting cluttered. I'm becoming an eclectic. Who's taken me over? I'm beginning to see things that aren't there."

Lelia was late. His stay in the garden stretched on. He kept strolling around. He was forced to concede the existence of many species of insect. A small bug was crawling up a plant stem. Shuvalov removed it and placed it on his open palm. Suddenly the bug's thorax fluoresced brightly. Shuvalov lost his temper.

"Damn! Another half an hour and I'll turn into a naturalist."

The plant stems were of various shapes, the leaves, the stalks; he saw blades of grass that were ridged like bamboo; he was astonished at the myriad hues displayed by what is called the turf; the many hues of the soil itself came as a complete surprise.

"I don't want to be a naturalist!" he implored. "I don't need all these random observations."

And Lelia was not yet in sight. He was already evolving some statistical conclusions, already establishing some classification categories. He could affirm that in this park trees with thick trunks and trilobate leaves predominated. He was becoming attuned to the chirr of the insects. His attention, against his own will, was being swamped by data that held no interest for him at all.

But Lelia still didn't arrive. He grew despondent and irritated. In Lelia's stead an unfamiliar man in a black hat showed up. The man took a seat next to Shuvalov on the green bench. The man sat there, a little downcast, having placed a pale hand on either knee. He was young and timid. Subsequently it became clear that the young man suffered from color-blindness. The two struck up a conversation.

"I envy you," said the young man. "They say that leaves are green. I've never seen green leaves. I'm forced to eat dark-blue pears."

"Blue is an inedible color," asserted Shuvalov. "I'd be nauseated by blue pears."

"I eat blue pears," the young man repeated mournfully.

Shuvalov started.

"Tell me," he began, "have you ever noticed that when birds are flying all around you that you get a city, imaginary lines? . . ."

"Never noticed," answered the color-blind man.

"So you perceive the entire world accurately?"

"The entire world, except for certain details of color." The color-blind man turned his pale face to Shuvalov.

"Are you in love?" he inquired.

"I'm in love," Shuvalov admitted manfully.

"Merely a little color confusion, but the rest is all normal," the color-blind man said happily. Whereupon he made a condescending gesture to his interlocutor.

"All the same, blue pears are no joke," Shuvalov reflected.

Lelia appeared in the distance. Shuvalov leapt to his feet. The color-blind man rose and, tipping his black hat, began to walk on.

"You're not a violinist, are you?" Shuvalov addressed the question to his retreating form.

"You're seeing things that aren't there," the young man replied.

Shuvalov lost his temper and shouted:

"You look like a violinist!"

The color-blind man, continuing on his way, said something or other, and Shuvalov made out:

"It's a dangerous path you're on . . ."

Lelia was approaching rapidly. He rose to meet her, took a few steps. Branches with their trilobate leaves were swaying. Shuvalov was standing in the middle of the path. The branches were rustling. She came on, greeted by a leaf ovation. The color-blind man, keeping to the right, thought: "Well, the weather is breezy," and glanced upwards, at the tree-tops. The leaves were behaving as all leaves do when agitated by a breeze. The color-blind man saw swaying blue tree-tops. Shuvalov saw green tree-tops. But Shuvalov drew an untenable inference. He thought: "The trees are greeting Lelia with an ovation." The color-blind man was mistaken, but Shuvalov was even more grossly mistaken.

"I'm seeing things that aren't there," Shuvalov repeated.

Lelia came up to him, In one hand she carried a bag of apricots. The other hand she held out to him. The world became a different place with amazing speed.

"Why are you squinting?" she asked.

"I feel like I'm wearing glasses."

Lelia took an apricot from the bag, parted its tiny buttocks and threw away the seed. The seed fell onto the grass. Shuvalov glanced over his shoulder in alarm. He glanced and saw: on the spot where the seed landed a tree had sprung up, a delicate, shimmery sapling, a miraculous parasol-shape.

"Something stupid is happening. I'm beginning to think in images. Laws no longer exist for me. In this spot five years from now an apricot tree will have grown up. Entirely possible. That would be completely scientific. But in defiance of all natural laws, I've seen that tree five years ahead of time. It's stupid. I'm turning into an idealist."

"It all comes from love," she said, oozing apricot juice.

She was sitting on the pillows, waiting for him. The bed had been pushed up against the wall. Little golden wreaths shone on the wallpaper. He approached, she embraced him. She was so young and so light that undressed, in nothing but her camisole, she seemed preternaturally naked. Their first embrace was stormy. Her little medallion flew off her chest and became entangled in her hair, like a golden almond. Shuvalov sank down towards her face slowly, as towards the face of a dying girl, sinking into the pillow.

The light was on.

"I'll turn it off," said Lelia.

Shuvalov was lying next to the wall. The corner seemed to narrow. Shuvalov traced the wallpaper pattern with his finger. He understood: this part of the wallpaper pattern, this section of wall he was lying next to, it had a double existence: an ordinary daytime one, not remarkable in any way, simple little wreaths; the other was nocturnal, perceived five minutes before you fall asleep. Abruptly emerging from the background, bits of the pattern grew in size, became more detailed and changed form. On the borders of sleep, returned to the sensations of childhood, he did not protest the transformation of familiar and rational forms, all the more since the transformation was charming: in place of volutes and wheels he saw a goat, a chef. . . .

"And here is a treble clef," said Lelia, who understood him.

"And a cha-chameleon . . . ," he lisped, falling asleep.

He awoke early in the morning. Very early. He awoke, looked around him and exclaimed out loud. A blissful sound flew from his throat. During the night the change in the world begun on the first day of their acquaintance had become complete. Morning sunlight filled the room. He saw the windowsill and on the windowsill were pots with many-hued flowers. Lelia was asleep, her back to him. She was lying all curled up, her spine was curved and you could see her vertebrae beneath the skin, a delicate reed. "A fishing pole, thought Shuvalov, a bamboo one. "On this new earth everything was charming and funny. Voices wafted through the open window. People were talking about the colorful pots on the sill.

He got up, dressed, remaining attached to earth with difficulty. Terrestrial gravity no longer existed. He had not yet mastered the laws of this new world and therefore moved about cautiously, with trepidation, afraid any sort of incautious act might produce a deafening effect. Even simply to think, simply to perceive objects was risky. What if overnight he had acquired the ability to materialize his thoughts? He had reason to suspect this. Like, for instance, his buttons that had buttoned themselves. Like, for instance, when he needed to wet the comb to smooth his hair, suddenly he heard a dripping sound. He glanced around. On the wall, in the sun's rays, an armful of Lelia's dresses shone with the colors of Montgolfier balloons.

"I'm over here," the voice of the tap emerged from the heap.

Under the heap of dresses he found the tap and the basin. A rose-colored sliver of soap was there as well. Now Shuvalov was afraid to think of anything frightening. "A tiger came into the room," he almost thought against his will, but was able to tear himself away from the thought. . . . Still, he glanced at the door in fear. A materialization did take place, but since the thought had not been fully formed, the effect was displaced and approximate: a wasp flew in the window—it was striped and blood-thirsty.

"Lelia! A tiger!" Shuvalov shrieked.

Lelia woke up. The wasp settled on a saucer. The wasp buzzed gyroscopically. Lelia leapt from the bed, the wasp flew towards her. Lelia flapped at it frantically, the wasp and her medallion circled around her. Shuvalov caught the medallion on his palm. They plotted out a battue. Lelia trapped the wasp beneath her crackling straw hat.

Shuvalov went out. They said their farewells in a draft which in this world turned out to be extraordinarily active and many-voiced. The draft blew open the doors downstairs. It sang like a laundress. It twirled the flowers on the sill, tossed Lelia's hat about, released the wasp and flung it into the lettuce. It made Lelia's hair stand on end. It whistled.

It made Lelia's camisole billow.

They parted, and, too happy to sense the stairs down and out into the courtyard. . . . Yes, he failed to sense the stairs. Then he failed to sense the stoop, the cobblestones; then he discovered it was no mirage but reality that his feet were suspended in the air, that he was flying.

"Flying on the wings of love," someone said out of a near-by window.

He flew upwards, his shirt became a crinoline, a fever-blister appeared on his lip, he flew on, snapping his fingers.

At two o'clock he arrived at the park. Worn out by love and happiness, he dozed off on the green bench. He slept, his clavicle sticking out from the collar of his unbuttoned shirt.

Along the path, slowly, hands clasped behind his back, pacing with the gravitas of a bishop and in a soutane-like garb, wearing a black hat and large dark-blue spectacles, now gazing upwards, now downwards, there came a man.

He approached and sat down next to Shuvalov.

"I am Isaac Newton," said the stranger, raising this black hat. Through the dark-blue glasses he surveyed his monochromatic world.

"How do you do," Shuvalov stammered.

The great scientist was sitting upright, cautiously, on tenterhooks. He was listening intently, ears pricked, his left index finger hovered in the air as if summoning the attention of an invisible choir, which was waiting second by second to burst into thunderous song at a signal from that finger. All nature held its breath. Shuvalov quietly hid behind the bench. Once the gravel beneath his heel gave a squeak. The renowned physicist was listening to the silence of nature. In the distance, above the clumps of greenery, as if there were an eclipse, the stars came out, and it grew cool.

"There!" Newton suddenly cried. "Do you hear?"

Without looking around he stretched out his hand, seized Shuvalov by the shirt-tail and, arising, dragged him away. They set off over the grass. The immense shoes of the physicist trampled the turf, leaving pale tracks. Ahead of them, often glancing backwards, ran the lizard. They went through a thicket which ornamented the iron frames of the scholar's spectacles with down and ladybugs. A clearing opened up. Shuvalov recognized yesterday's sapling.

"Any apricots yet?" he inquired.

"No," replied the scholar in irritation, "it's an apple tree."

The frame-work of the apple tree, its frame-work cage, airy and fragile like the frame-work of a Montgolfier dirigible, showed through a sparse covering of leaves. All was motionless and silent.

"There," said the scholar, bending down. The compression made his voice come out in a roar. "There!" he held an apple in his hand. "What does this mean?"

It was obvious that he was not accustomed to bending over: straightening up, he several times flexed his spine to relieve his vertebrae, his aged vertebral bamboo. The apple rested on the tripod of his three fingers.

"What does this mean?" he repeated, spoiling the resonance of the phrase with his non-Russian pronunciation. "Can you tell me why the apple fell?"

Shuvalov gazed at the apple as William Tell must have done.

"It's the law of gravity," he whispered. Then, after a pause, the great physicist asked:

"You, I believe, were flying today—disciple?" thus the Teacher inquired. His eyebrows rose above his spectacles.

"You, I believe, were flying today, young Marxist?"

A ladybug crawled from his finger onto the surface of the apple. Newton shifted his gaze. To him the ladybug appeared dazzlingly blue. He squinted. The insect took off from the highest point of the apple and flew away using wings it had pulled out from somewhere on its back, as if extracting a handkerchief from the pocket of a frock coat.

"You, I believe, were flying today?"

Shuvalov was silent.

"Pig," said Isaac Newton.

Shuvalov woke up.

"Pig," said Lelia, standing over him. "You're waiting for me and you go to sleep. Pig!"

She removed the ladybug from his forehead, marveling at its steel-blue thorax.

"Dammit!" He swore. "I hate you. I used to know that thing was a ladybug, and other than the fact that it was a "God's little cow," as the folk call it, I knew nothing about it. Well alright, I might also have come to the conclusion that its name was a bit anti-religious. But ever since we met something is happening to my eyes. I see blue pears and I see that that mushroom looks like a ladybug."

She tried to hug him.

"Leave me alone! Alone!" he cried. "I'm tired of this! It's embarrassing."

Shouting this he ran off like a stag. Snorting, in wild leaps he ran, shying at his own shadow, rolling his eyes. Panting, he halted. Lelia had disappeared. He decided to forget about everything. The lost world must be brought back.

"Good-bye," he sighed, "you and I will never see each other again."

He came to sit down on a slope, on a ridge with an overview of wide open space dotted with *dachas*. He was sitting at the apex of a prism, his legs dangling down one of its facets. Below him was the round umbrella of an ice-cream vendor, the entire equipage recalling for some reason an African hut.

"I am living in paradise," said the young Marxist in tones of utter defeat.

"Are you a Marxist?" the question came from nearby.

The young man in the black hat, the familiar color-blind man, was sitting right next to Shuvalov.

"Yes I am," said Shuvalov.

"Then you can't live in paradise."

The young man began to play with a twig. Shuvalov sighed.

"What can I do? The earth has become paradise."

The color-blind man whistled to himself and used the twig to scratch around inside his ear.

"Do you know," Shuvalov continued, hiccupping, "do you know what I've come to? I was flying today."

Up in the sky, at the angle of a postage stamp, a skate hovered like a dragon.

"Want me to demonstrate? Shall I fly right up there?" (He pointed to the skate.)

"No, thank you. I don't want to witness your shame."

"Yes, it's awful," Shuvalov said after a brief silence. "I do know it's awful."

"I envy you," he went on.

"Really?"

"Word of honor. What a good thing, to perceive the whole world accurately and be wrong only on a few color details, the way it is with you. You're not forced to live in paradise. For you the real world hasn't vanished. Everything is in order. But me? Just think, I'm completely sane, a materialist . . . and suddenly these criminal, anti-scientific deformations of matter and substances start happening right in front of me. . . ."

"Yes, that's awful," the color-blind man agreed. "And it's all from being in love."

Shuvalov seized his neighbor's hand with unexpected fervor.

"Listen!" he exclaimed. "I agree. You give me your iris and take my love in exchange."

The color-blind man slid down the slope and stood up.

"Excuse me," he said. "I'm pressed for time. Good-bye. Enjoy your paradise."

He found it difficult to make his way along the slope. He went bow-legged, losing any resemblance to a human being and acquiring a resemblance to a human being reflected in water. Finally he made it to level ground and strode off joyfully. Then, throwing down his twig, he called back one last time to Shuvalov:

"Give my best to Eve!"

The while, Lelia was asleep. A half an hour after the meeting with the color-blind man Shuvalov found her in the middle of the park, at its very heart. He was no naturalist, he could not classify what surrounded him: filbert, hawthorn, elder or dogrose. On all sides the branches and brush clung to him, he went on like a pedlar toting a delicate mesh of the branches that grew denser as he approached the heart of the grove. He shrugged off these nets, the leaves, petals, thorns, berries and birds that had besprinkled him.

Lelia was lying on her back, in a rose-colored dress with its bodice open. She was asleep. He could hear the membranes in her sleep-addled nose shiver. He sat down beside her.

Then he lay his head on her chest, his fingers grazed the cotton fabric, his head was resting on her damp chest, he saw her areola, rose-colored, with delicate crinkles like the foam on milk. He didn't hear the rustling, the sighs, the snapping branches.

The color-blind man popped up in a thicket of brush. The thicket held him back.

"Listen a minute," said the color-blind man. Shuvalov raised his head with its pleasure-flushed cheek.

"Don't follow me around like a dog," he said.

"Listen, I agree. Take my iris and give me your love."

"Go and eat some blue pears," was Shuvalov's answer.

Translated by A. L. and M. K.

On the Fantasy of H. G. Wells

1.

I was ten years old.

How did I come by that leaflet? I don't know.

A page from an English illustrated journal. On the glossy paper were printed small pictures of a uniform size. It seems to me now that they were tiny, the size of a postage stamp.

What did the pictures show?

Fantastic things.

I have remembered one of the illustrations my whole life. A kind of cul-de-sac in the ruins of a house. And metallic tentacles were creeping through a window, a doorsill, a break in a wall! Metallic tentacles! And a man hiding in the cul-de-sac stared at them wildly. What were the tentacles? No idea! They were sweeping the room, searching precisely for the man who was pressed to the wall and pale with terror.

How I taxed my imagination, trying to puzzle out the meaning of this spectacle!

I knew that these were not illustrations to a fairy-tale. The events in fairy-tales had all taken place in a far-off time. There were towers, or castles. Fairy-tale characters did not resemble the people around me. Princess in tiaras, kings with swords, peasants in striped stockings. But here everything was contemporary! These were the ruins of an ordinary house. Torn wallpaper. A dangling wire. A brick chimney. A pile of rubble in a corner. And the man was wearing an ordinary black suit.

This was no fairy-tale!

And I thought at the time that I was looking at a depiction of events that had really occurred. Yes, the pictures were like photographs. Small, clear, striking, with such everyday elements as a man in a suit coat and a white shirt with his tie askew.

A photograph of wonders!

If these were photographs it meant that somewhere and for some reason there had taken place a sequence of events during which a certain man had hidden in a ruined house and metallic tentacles searched for him.

What events could these be?

Everything fell into place a few years later. I read H. G. Wells' novel *The War of the Worlds*. The pictures that had so amazed me had been illustrations to that novel.

2.

Wells' true gift is his ability to describe fantastic events in a manner that makes them seem real.

He transforms the fantastic into the epic, which works only when the events depicted in it seem to represent actual happenings of recorded history. What? That once in a small English town there arrived an invisible man? I don't know how it is with other readers, but when I read *The Invisible Man* it is difficult for me to stave off the feeling—though much in it seems out of the ordinary—that I am reading an account of actual occurrences.

How did Wells achieve this verisimilitude? He understood that if a plot had to involve the fantastic then the characters had to be as real as possible. In this way he could make his imaginative invention truly work. Consider a detail from *The Invisible Man*. The invisible man has attacked a representative of the law, Colonel Adye, and is ready to shoot him. But Wells—before getting to the action—records the following detail:

> Adye moistened his lips again. He glanced away from the barrel of the revolver and saw the sea far off very blue and dark under the midday sun, the smooth green down, the white cliff of the Head and the multitudinous town, and suddenly he knew that life was very sweet.

A rich psychological profile of the colonel who is merely a secondary character in the novel, wouldn't you say? Or how about the rendering of the invisible man himself:

I went to bury [my father]. My mind was still on this research, and I did not lift a finger to save his character. I remember the funeral, the cheap coffin, the scant ceremony, the windy frost-bitten hillside, and the old college friend of his who read the service over him, a shabby, bent, black old man with a sniveling cold.

I remember walking back to the empty home, through the place that had once been a village and was now patched and tinkered by the jerry builders into the ugly likeness of a town: I remember myself as a gaunt black figure, going along the slippery, shiny pavement.

Note: the cheap coffin, the scant ceremony, the university friend suffering from a cold, a gaunt black figure stepping along the slippery pavement. What details! They accumulate gradually. At first our attention is captured solely by the implausibility of the situation itself—an invisible man! But after a few pages this fascination begins to merge with the multitude of varied feelings we customarily experience when we are following the development of human fate, as is especially true of epic.

3.

In Wells' novels there are many bicyclists. In most cases these are youths. They make their appearance just when the most curious sort of observer is needed to witness some surprising event or other. In *The First Men in the Moon* a boy-cyclist triggers the denouement.

Wells likes this image of the young cyclist a great deal. Is he perhaps recalling his youth? I don't know his biography. I believe he was apprenticed to a pharmacist. One can picture the young pharmacist-in-training careening along the roads connecting those small English towns that he was to describe with such affection in the future. The landscape of his novels consists precisely of the roads between small towns, their cottages, taverns and gardens, the flowering hedgerows, the sea glimpsed beyond the hills. What sort of landscape is this? The landscape of the cyclist.

Here is an excerpt from the novel *The Food of the Gods*. This work features gigantically proportioned animals, plants and human beings.

The day after, a cyclist riding, feet up, down the hill between Sevenoaks and Tonbridge, very narrowly missed running over a second of these giants [wasps] that was crawling across the roadway. His passage seemed to alarm it, and it rose with a noise like a sawmill. His bicycle jumped the footpath in the emotion of the moment, and when he could look back, the wasp was soaring away above the woods towards Westerham.

This passage is typical for Wells. All the novels and stories of Wells take place in a summer setting. Only in *The Invisible Man* is there much mention of mist and snow. The plot demanded it. Mist and snow rendered the invisible man visible.

In the most urgent situations Wells doesn't forget to describe a bit of honeysuckle, two butterflies chasing each other, a wicket-gate.

One might assume that the cyclist peddling between Sevenoaks and Tonbridge was none other than Wells himself. He had been taking a rest beneath a bush and saw an ordinary wasp. And he began to weave a fantasy on the theme of what might happen if gigantic wasps were to appear. In this fantasy one can sense a certain intoxication with the world:

> The most dramatic of the fifty appearances was certainly that of the wasp that visited the British Museum about midday, dropping out of the blue serene upon one of the innumerable pigeons that feed in the courtyard of that building, and flying up to the cornice to devour its victim at leisure. After that it crawled for a time over the museum roof, entered the dome of the reading-room by a skylight, buzzed about inside it for some little time—there was a stampede among the readers—and at last found another window and vanished again with a sudden silence from human observation.

What an enchanting play of imagination and with what skill is the fantasy worked out. Could one think of a more telling backdrop for the gigantic wasp up than the cupola around which it crawls? Narrative mastery is besides the point here. The point is that this fantasy is remarkably pure and born of an intoxicated view of the world.

Wells began writing at the end of the nineteenth century. *The Time Machine* appeared in 1895, *The Invisible Man* in 1897. On one re-reading of that novel I noticed a certain circumstance that had eluded me before, namely that the London depicted is still full of hansom cabs. This is still an old-world city. The automobile is not mentioned even once in this novel, in which daily life has not yet been altered by technology to the degree it would be within a decade.

Yet as soon as such changes begin to take shape Wells captures them at once. In the novel *When the Sleeper Wakes* he mentions the name of Otto Lilienthal, builder of the first glider. In essence Wells contemplates in this novel the rise of aviation. The pharmacist's apprentice became a writer but his relationship to the world remained as it had been—one of intoxication. If earlier he had conceived the idea of gigantic wasps, he now imagines amazing machines. The essence is unchanged. Machines imbue life with the elements of a new fascination, a new attraction.

And Wells has imagined a rocket on which two men make a journey to the moon. How much humor there is in *The First Men in the Moon*! However, alarm emerges through the lightheartedness. Wells contemplates the fate of a humanity living with advanced technology. *The War of the Worlds* appears. This is a novel about man and machine. For Wells man is terribly alone and the machine has become the monstrous Martian tripods, they emerge ominously in the flowering world of summer. In horror a human figure presses itself to a wall, and metallic tentacles snake towards him through the ruins.

4

In one of his last works, *The Shape of Things to Come*, Wells depicts the destruction of capitalist technology. A world war has broken out and is dragging on endlessly. Certain armed bands have begun to seize power in various countries. Using their remaining weapons these bands make war on each other. Human civilization has been razed and only fragments remain of its advanced technology. But the war goes on. Wells gives a portrait of the leader of one of these bands (an unambiguous caricature of of a fascist *fuehrer* or *duce*) who is obsessed by the idea of war—constant, eternal. War! War!

And just as the reader is prepared to believe that everything is doomed to total extinction, a report comes of an unknown world. A report that intellectual power continues to exist on earth. It would appear that amid the general destruction an ark of culture has been preserved—Basra. The last mechanics, engineers and pilots have gathered there—people of the machine and technology. Representing some knightly order of the vanished culture, which has made itself the emblem of the rebirth of the world, they fly in on planes from this far off oasis and sedate the locus of warfare with a special gas.

So ends the capitalist world. A new culture is born—the world governed by enlightened scientists and engineers—which has achieved happiness. At this point Wells returns to a pernicious idea of technocracy, which has long served him as an exit from the tangle of the capitalist world and is represented as triumphant in *The Shape of Things to Come*. His ideas are questionable in this regard. But he has seen the horrors of capitalism. After all it was he who characterized capitalistic society as suffering from a *plague of the soul*!

Translated by A. L. and M. K.

Mikhail Afanasievich Bulgakov
(1891-1940)

The Fatal Eggs

I. PROFESSOR PERSIKOV'S *Curriculum Vitae*

ON April, 16, 1928, in the evening, Persikov [Mr. Peach], professor of Zoology at the Fourth State University and director of the Zoological Institute in Moscow, entered his office at the Zoological Institute on Herzen Street. The professor switched on the frosted globe overhead and looked around.

The beginning of the terrifying catastrophe must be set precisely on that ill-fated evening, and just as precisely, Professor Vladimir Ipatievich Persikov must be considered the prime cause of this catastrophe.

He was exactly fifty-eight years old. A remarkable head shaped like a pestle, bald, with tufts of yellowish hair standing out on the sides. A smooth-shaven face with a protruding lower lip. Because of this Persikov always had a somewhat pouting expression on his face. Small, old-fashioned spectacles in a silver frame on a red nose; small, glittering eyes; tall, stoop-shouldered. He spoke in a creaking, high, croaking voice, and among his other idiosyncrasies was this: whenever he spoke of anything emphatically and with assurance, he screwed up his eyes and curled the index finger of his right hand into a hook. And since he always spoke with assurance, for his erudition in his field was utterly phenomenal, the hook appeared very often before the eyes of Professor Persikov's interlocutors. As for any topics out-side his field, i.e., zoology, embryology, anatomy, botany, and geography, Professor Persikov almost never spoke of them.

The professor did not read newspapers and did not go to the theater, and the professor's wife ran away from him in 1913 with a tenor from the Zimin Opera, leaving him the following note: "Your frogs make me shudder with intolerable loathing. I will be unhappy for the rest of my life because of them."

The professor never remarried and had no children. He was very short-tempered, but he cooled off quickly; he liked tea with cloudberries; and he lived on Prechistenka [Immaculate Street] in a five-room apartment, one room of which was occupied by his housekeeper Maria Stepanovna, a shriveled little old woman who looked after the professor like a nanny.

In 1919 the government requisitioned three of his five rooms. Then he declared to Maria Stepanovna, "If they don't cease these outrages, Maria Stepanovna, I'll leave and go abroad."

There is no doubt that had the professor realized this plan, he could easily have got settled in the department of zoology at any university in the world, since he was an absolutely first-rate scientist; and with the exception of Professors William Weccle of Cambridge and Giacomo Bartolommeo Beccari of Rome, he had no equals in the field bearing in one way or another on amphibians. Professor Persikov could lecture in four languages besides Russian, and he spoke French and German as fluently as Russian. Persikov did not carry out his intention to emigrate, and 1920 turned out to be even worse than 1919. Events kept happening one after the other. Great Nikitskaia was renamed Herzen Street. Then the clock built into the building on the corner of Herzen and Mokhovaia [Moss Street] stopped at a quarter past eleven, and finally, in the terraria at the Zoological Institute, unable to endure the perturbations of that famous year, first eight splendid specimens of the tree frog died, then fifteen ordinary toads, followed, finally, by a most remarkable specimen of the Surinam toad.

Immediately after the toads, whose deaths decimated the population of the first order of amphibians, which is properly known as tailless, the institute's permanent watchman, old Vlas, who did not belong to the class of amphibians, moved on into a better world. The cause of his death, however, was the same as that of the poor animals, and Persikov diagnosed it at once: "Lack of feed."

The scientist was absolutely right: Vlas had to be fed with flour, and the toads with mealworms, but since the former had disappeared, the latter had also vanished. Persikov tried to shift the remaining twenty specimens of the tree-frog to a diet of cockroaches, but the cockroaches had also disappeared somewhere, thus demonstrating their malicious attitude toward War Communism. And so, even the last specimens had to be tossed out into the garbage pits in the institute's courtyard.

The effect of the deaths, especially that of the Surinam toad, on Persikov is beyond description. For some reason he put the whole blame for the deaths on the current People's Commissar of Education. Standing in his hat and galoshes in the corridor of the chilly institute, Persikov spoke to his assistant, Ivanov, a most elegant gentleman with a pointed blond beard. "Why, killing him is not enough for this, Peter Stepanovich! Just what are they doing? Why, they'll ruin the institute! Eh? A singular male, an extraordinary specimen of *Pipa americana*, thirteen centimeters long . . ."

As time went on things got worse. After Vlas died, the windows of the institute froze right through, and ice-blossoms covered the inner surface of the glass. The rabbits died, then the foxes, wolves, fish, and every last one of the garter snakes. Persikov started going around in silence for whole days through; then he caught pneumonia, but did not die. When he recovered he went to the institute twice a week, and in the amphitheater, where the temperature for some reason never changed from its constant five degrees below freezing regardless of the temperature outside, wearing his galoshes, a hat with earflaps, and a woolen muffler, exhaling clouds of white steam, he read a series of lectures on "The Reptilia of the Torrid Zone" to eight students. Persikov spent the rest of his time at his place on Prechistenka, covered with a plaid shawl, lying on the sofa in his room, which was crammed to the ceiling with books, coughing, staring into the open maw of the fiery stove which Maria Stepanovna fed gilded chairs, and thinking about the Surinam toad.

But everything in this world comes to an end. Nineteen twenty and 1921 ended, and in 1922 a kind of reverse trend began. First, Pankrat appeared, to replace the late Vlas; he was still young, but he showed great promise as a zoological guard; the institute building was now beginning to be heated a little. And in the summer Persikov managed, with Pankrat's help, to catch fourteen specimens of the toad *vulgairs* in the Kliazma River. The terraria once again began to teem with life . . . In 1923 Persikov was already lecturing eight times a week—three at the institute and five at the university; in 1924 it was thirteen times a week, including the workers' schools, and in the spring of 1925 he gained notoriety by flunking seventy-six students, all of them on amphibians.

"What? How is it you don't know how amphibians differ from reptiles?" Persikov would ask. "It's simply ridiculous, young man. Amphibians have no pelvic buds. None. So, sir, you ought to be ashamed. You're a Marxist, probably?"

"Yes, a Marxist," the flunked student would answer, crushed.

"Very well, come back in the fall, please," Persikov would say politely, and then shout briskly to Pankrat, "Give me the next one!"

As amphibians come back to life after the first heavy rain following a long drought, so Professor Persikov came back to life in 1926 when the united Russo-American Company built fifteen fifteen-story houses in the center of Moscow, starting at the corner of Gazetny Lane [Newspaper Lane] and Tverskaia, and 300 eight-apartment cottages for workers on the outskirts of town, ending once and for all the terrible and ridiculous housing crisis which had so tormented Muscovites in the years 1919 to 1925.

In general, it was a remarkable summer in Persikov's life, and sometimes he rubbed his hands with a quiet and contented chuckle, recalling how he and Maria Stepanovna had been squeezed into two rooms. Now the professor had gotten all five rooms back; he had spread out, arranged his 2,500 books, his stuffed animals, diagrams, and specimens in their places, and lit the green lamp on the desk in his study.

The institute was unrecognizable too: it had been covered with a coat of cream-colored paint, water was conducted to the reptile room by a special pipeline, all ordinary glass was replaced by plate glass, five new microscopes had been sent to the institute, as had glass-topped dissecting tables, 2,000-watt lamps with indirect lighting, reflectors, and cases for the museum.

Persikov came to life, and the whole world unexpectedly learned of it in December 1926, with the publication of his pamphlet: *More on the Problem of the Propagation of the Gastropods*, 126 pp., "Bulletin of the Fourth University."

And in the fall of 1927 his major opus, 350 pages long, later translated into six languages, including Japanese: *The Embryology of the Pipidae, Spadefoot Toads, and Frogs*, State Publishing House: price, three rubles.

But in the summer of 1928 the incredible, horrible events took place . . .

II. THE COLORED HELIX

And so, the professor turned on the globe and looked around. He switched on the reflector on the long experiment table, donned a white smock, and tinkled with some instruments on the table . . .

Many of the thirty thousand mechanical carriages which sped through Moscow in 1928 darted along Herzen Street, wheels humming on the smooth paving stones; and every few minutes a trolley marked 16 or 22 or 48 or 53 rolled, grinding and clattering, from Herzen Street toward Mokhovaia. Reflections of varicolored lights were thrown on the plate-glass windows of the office, and far and high above, next to the dark, heavy cap of the Cathedral of Christ, one could see the misty, pale sickle of the moon.

But neither the moon nor Moscow's springtime din interested Professor Persikov in the slightest. He sat on a three-legged revolving stool and with fingers stained brown from tobacco, he turned the adjustment screw of the magnificent Zeiss microscope under which an ordinary undyed culture of fresh amoebas had been placed. At the moment that Persikov was shifting the magnification from five to ten thousand, the door opened slightly, a pointed little beard and a leather apron appeared, and his assistant called, "Vladimir Ipatievich, the mesentery is set up—would you like to take a look?"

Persikov nimbly slid off the stool, leaving the adjustment screw turned halfway, and slowly turning a cigarette in his fingers, he went into his assistant's office. There, on a glass table, a semi-chloroformed frog, fainting with terror and pain, was crucified on a cork plate, its translucent viscera pulled out of its bloody abdomen into the microscope.

"Very good," said Persikov, bending down to the eyepiece of the microscope.

Apparently one could see something very interesting in the frog's mesentery, where as clearly as if on one's hand living blood corpuscles were running briskly along the rivers of the vessels. Persikov forgot his amoebas and for the next hour and a half took turns with Ivanov at the microscope lens. As they were doing this both scientists kept exchanging animated comments incomprehensible to ordinary mortals.

Finally, Persikov leaned back from the microscope, announcing, "The blood is clotting, that's all there is to that."

The frog moved its head heavily, and its dimming eyes were clearly saying, "You're rotten bastards, that's what . . ."

Stretching his benumbed legs, Persikov rose, returned to his office, yawned, rubbed his permanently inflamed eyelids with his fingers, and sitting down on his stool, he glanced into the microscope, put his fingers on the adjustment screw intending to turn it—but did not turn it. With his right eye Persikov saw a blurred white disk, and in it some faint, paleoamoebas—but in the middle of the disk there was a colored volute, resembling a woman's curl. Persikov himself and hundreds of his students had seen this curl very many times, and no one had ever taken any interest in it, nor, indeed, was there any reason to. The little bundle of colored light merely interfered with observation and showed that the culture was not in focus. Therefore it was ruthlessly eliminated with a single turn of the knob, illuminating the whole field with an even white light.

The zoologist's long fingers already rested firmly on the knob, but suddenly they quivered and slid away. The reason for this was Persikov's right eye; it had suddenly become intent, amazed, and flooded with excitement. To the woe of the Republic, this was no talentless mediocrity sitting at the microscope. No, this was Professor Persikov! His entire life, all of his intellect, became concentrated in his right eye. For some five minutes of dead silence the higher being observed the lower one, tormenting and straining its eye over the part of the slide which was out of focus. Everything around was silent. Pankrat had already fallen asleep in his room off the vestibule, and only once the glass doors of the cabinets rang musically and delicately in the distance: that was Ivanov locking his office as he left. The front door groaned behind him. And it was only later that the professor's voice was heard. He was asking, no one knows whom, "What is this? I simply don't understand."

A last truck passed by on Herzen Street, shaking the old walls of the institute. The flat glass bowl with forceps in it tinkled on the table. The professor turned pale and raised his hands over the microscope like a mother over an infant threatened by danger. Now there could be no question of Persikov turning the knob, oh no, he was afraid that some outside force might push what he had seen out of the field of vision.

It was bright morning with a gold strip slanting across the cream-colored entrance to the institute when the professor left the microscope and walked up to the window on his numb feet. With trembling fingers he pressed a button, and the thick black shades shut out the morning, and the wise, learned night came back to life in the study. The sallow and inspired

Persikov spread his feet wide apart, and staring at the parquet with tearing eyes, he began: "But how can this be? Why, it's monstrous! . . . It's monstrous, gentlemen," he repeated, addressing the toads in the terrarium—but the toads were sleeping and did not answer.

He was silent for a moment, then walked to the switch, raised the shades, turned off all the lights, and peered into the microscope. His face got tense, and his bushy yellow eyebrows came together. "Uhmmm, uhmmm," he muttered. "Gone. I see. I see-e-e-e," he drawled, looking at the extinguished globe overhead madly and inspiredly. "It's very simple." And again he lowered the swishing shades, and again he lit the globe. Having glanced into the microscope, he grinned gleefully, and almost rapaciously. "I'll catch it," he said solemnly and gravely, raising his finger in the air. "I'll catch it. Maybe it's from the sun."

Again the shades rolled up. Now the sun was out. It poured across the institute walls and lay in slanting planes across the paving stones of Herzen Street. The professor looked out the window, calculating what the position of the sun would be during the day. He stepped away and returned again and again, dancing slightly, and finally he leaned over the windowsill on his stomach.

He got started on some important and mysterious work. He covered the microscope with a glass bell. Melting a chunk of sealing wax over the bluish flame of a Bunsen burner, he sealed the edges of the bell to the table, pressing down the lumps of wax with his thumb. He turned off the gas and went out, and he locked the office door with an English lock.

The institute corridors were in semidarkness. The professor made his way to Pankrat's room and knocked for a long time with no result. At last there was a sound behind the door something like the growling of a chained dog, hawking and muttering, and Pankrat appeared in a spot of light, wearing striped longjohns tied at his ankles. His eyes fixed wildly on the scientist; he was still groaning somewhat from sleep.

"Pankrat," said the professor, looking at him over his spectacles. "Forgive me for waking you up. Listen, my friend, don't go into my office this morning. I left some work out which must not be moved. Understand?"

"U-hm-m, understand," Pankrat replied, understanding nothing. He was swaying back and forth and grumbling.

"No, listen, wake up, Pankrat," said the zoologist, and he poked Pankrat lightly in the ribs, which brought a frightened look into his face and a certain shadow of awareness into his eyes. "I locked the office," continued Persikov. "So you shouldn't clean up before my return. Understand?"

"Yes, sir-r," gurgled Pankrat.

"Now that's excellent, go back to bed."

Pankrat turned, vanished behind the door, and immediately crashed back into bed, while the professor began to put his things on in the vestibule. He put on his gray summer coat and floppy hat. Then, recalling the picture in the microscope, he fixed his eyes on his galoshes and stared at the overshoes for several seconds, as if he were seeing them for the first time. Then he put on the left overshoe and tried to put the right one over it, but it would not go on.

"What a fantastic accident it was that he called me," said the scientist, "otherwise I would never have noticed it. But what does it lead to? . . . Why, the devil only knows what it might lead to!"

The professor grinned, frowned at his galoshes, removed the left one, and put on the right one. "My God! Why, one can't even imagine all the consequences." The professor contemptuously kicked away the left overshoe, which annoyed him by refusing to fit over the right, and went to the exit wearing only one. At that point he dropped his handkerchief and walked out, slamming the heavy door. On the stairs he took a long time looking for matches in his pockets, patting his sides; then he found them and headed down the street with an unlit cigarette in his lips.

Not a single person did the scientist meet all the way to the cathedral. There the professor tilted his head back and gaped at the golden cupola. The sun was sweetly licking it on one side.

"How is it I have never seen it before, such a coincidence? . . . Pfuy, what an idiot." The professor bent down and fell into thought, looking at his differently shod feet. "Hm . . . what should I do? Return to Pankrat? No, there's no waking him up. It'd be a shame to throw it away, the vile thing. I'll have to carry it." He took off the overshoe and carried it in his hand with disgust.

Three people in an old fashioned automobile turned the corner from Prechistenka. Two tipsy men and a garishly painted woman wearing silk pajamas in the latest 1928 style, sitting on their knees.

"Hey, Pops!" she cried in a low, rather hoarse voice. "Did 'ja drink up the other boot!"

"The old boy must have loaded up at the Alcazar," howled the drunk on the left, while the one on the right leaned out of the car and shouted, "Is the all-night tavern on Volkhonka open, buddy? We're headed there!"

The professor looked at them sternly above his spectacles, dropped the cigarette from his lips, and immediately forgot their existence. Slanting rays of sunshine appeared, cutting across Prechistensky Boulevard, and the helmet on the Cathedral of Christ began to flame. The sun had risen.

III. Persikov Caught It

The facts of the matter were as follows. When the professor had brought his eye of genius to that eyepiece, for the first time in his life he had paid attention to the fact that one particularly vivid and thick ray stood out in the multicolored spiral. This ray was a bright red color and it emerged from the spiral in a little sharp point, like a needle, let us say.

It is simply very bad luck that this ray fixed the skilful eye of the virtuoso for several seconds.

In it, in this ray, the professor caught sight of something which was a thousand times more significant and important than the ray itself, that fragile offshoot born accidentally of the movement of the microscope's lens and mirror. Thanks to the fact that his assistant had called the professor away, the amoebas lay about for an hour and a half subject to the action of the ray, and the result was this: while the granular amoebas outside the ray lay about limp and helpless, strange phenomena were taking place within the area where the pointed red sword lay. The red strip teemed with life. The gray amoebas, stretching out their pseudopods, strove with all their might toward the red strip, and in it they would come to life as if by sorcery. Some force infused them with the spirit of life. They crawled in flocks and fought each other for a place in the ray. Within it a frenzied (no other word can properly describe it) process of multiplication went on. Smashing and overturning all the laws that Persikov knew as well as he knew his own five fingers, the amoebas budded before his eyes with lightning speed. In the ray they split apart, and two seconds later each part became a new, fresh organism. In a few seconds these organisms attained full growth and maturity, only to immediately produce new generations in their turn. The red strip and the entire disk quickly became overcrowded, and the inevitable struggle began. The newborn ones went furiously on the attack, shredding and swallowing each other up. Among the newly-born lay corpses of those which had perished in the battle for existence. The best and strongest were victorious. And the best ones were terrifying. First, they were approximately twice the size of ordinary amoebas, and second, they were distinguished by a special viciousness and motility. Their movements were speedy, their pseudopods much longer than normal, and they used them, without exaggeration, as an octopus uses its tentacles.

The next evening, the professor, drawn and pale, studied the new generation of amoebas—without eating, keeping himself going only by smoking thick, roll-your-own cigarettes. On the third day, he shifted to the prime source—the red ray.

The gas hissed softly in the burner, again the traffic whizzed along the street, and the professor, poisoned by his hundredth cigarette, his eyes half-shut, threw himself back in his revolving chair. "Yes, everything is clear now. The ray brought them to life. It *is* a new ray, unresearched by anyone, undiscovered by anyone. The first thing to be clarified is whether it is produced only by electric light or by the sun as well," Persikov muttered to himself.

In the course of one more night this was clarified. He captured three rays in three microscopes, he obtained none from the sun, and he expressed himself thus: "We must hypothesize that it does not exist in the sun's spectrum . . . hmmm . . . in short, we must hypothesize that it can be obtained only from electric light." He looked lovingly at the frosted globe above him, thought for a moment, inspired, and invited Ivanov into his office. He told him everything and showed him the amoebas.

Assistant Professor Ivanov was astounded, completely crushed; how was it that such a simple thing as this slender arrow had never been noticed before! By anyone, dammit. Not even by him, Ivanov, himself, and this really was monstrous! "You just look! . . . Just look, Vladimir Ipatievich!" cried Ivanov, his eye gluing itself to the eyepiece in horror. "What's happening? . . . They're growing before my very eyes . . . Look, look!"

"I have been watching them for three days," Persikov replied animatedly.

Then there was a conversation between the two scientists, the idea of which may be summed up as follows: Assistant Professor Ivanov undertakes to construct a chamber with the aid of lenses and mirrors in which this ray will be produced in magnified form—and outside of the microscope. Ivanov hopes—indeed, he is absolutely sure—that this is quite simple. He will produce the ray, Vladimir Ipatievich cannot doubt that. Here there was a slight pause.

"When I publish my work, Peter Stepanovich, I will write that the chambers were constructed by you," Persikov put in, feeling that the pause needed to be resolved.

"Oh, that's not important . . . Still, of course . . ."

And the pause was instantly resolved. From that moment on, the ray utterly absorbed Ivanov too. While Persikov, losing weight and getting exhausted, was sitting all day and half the night over the microscope, Ivanov bustled around the brilliantly-lit physics laboratory juggling lenses and mirrors. A technician assisted him.

After a request was sent through the Commissariat of Education, Persikov received from Germany three parcels containing mirrors and polished lenses—biconvex, biconcave, and even convex-concave. This all ended with Ivanov finishing the construction of a chamber and actually capturing the red ray in it. And in all justice, it really was an expert job: the ray came out thick—almost four centimeters in diameter—sharp and powerful.

On the first of June the chamber was installed in Persikov's office, and avidly he began experiments with frog roe exposed to the ray. The results of these experiments were staggering. Within two days thousands of tadpoles hatched from the roe. But that is the least of it—within twenty-four hours, growing at a fantastic rate, the tadpoles developed into frogs, and they were so vicious and voracious that half of them immediately devoured the other half. Then the survivors began to spawn, ignoring all normal time-rules, and in another two days they had produced a new generation, this time without the ray, which was absolutely numberless. The devil only knows what had started in the scientist's office: the tadpoles were crawling out of the office and spreading all over the institute, in the terraria, and on the floor, from every nook and cranny, stentorian choruses began to croak as if it were a bog. Pankrat, who had always feared Persikov like fire anyway, was now experiencing only one feeling for him—mortal terror. After a week, the scientist himself began to feel he was going crazy. The institute was pervaded with the odors of ether and prussic acid, which almost poisoned Pankrat, who had taken off his mask at the wrong time. They finally managed to exterminate the teeming swamp population with poisons, and the rooms were thoroughly aired out.

Persikov said the following to Ivanov: "You know, Peter Stepanovich, the ray's effect on the deutoplasm and the ovum in general is quite remarkable."

Ivanov, who was a cool and reserved gentleman, interrupted the professor in an unusual tone. "Vladimir Ipatich, why are you discussing petty details, deutoplasm? Let's be frank—you have discovered something unprecedented!" Though it cost him obvious great effort, still Ivanov squeezed out the words: "Professor Persikov, you have discovered the ray of life!"

A faint color appeared on Persikov's pale, unshaven cheekbones. "Now, now, now," he muttered.

"You," continued Ivanov, "you will make such a name for yourself . . . It makes my head spin. Do you understand," he continued passionately, "Vladimir Ipatich, the heroes of H. G. Wells are simply push-overs compared to you . . . And I always thought his stories were fairy tales . . . Do you remember his *The Food of the Gods*?"

"Oh, that's a novel," replied Persikov.

"Why yes, good Lord, a famous one!"

"I've forgotten it," said Persikov." I remember now, I did read it, but I've forgotten it."

"How can you not remember, why, just look . . ." From the glass-topped table Ivanov picked up a dead frog of incredible size with a bloated belly and held it up by the leg. Even after death it had a malevolent expression on its face. "Why, this is monstrous!"

IV. DEACONESS DROZDOVA

God knows how it happened, whether Ivanov was to blame for it or sensational news transmits itself through the air, but everyone in gigantic, seething Moscow suddenly started talking about the ray of Professor Persikov. True, this talk was casual and very vague. The news of the miraculous discovery hopped through the glittering capital like a wounded bird, sometimes disappearing, sometimes fluttering up again, until the middle of July when a brief notice treating the ray appeared on the twentieth page of the newspaper *Izvestia*, under the heading: "Science and Technology News." It was stated obliquely that a well-known professor of the Fourth

State University had invented a ray which greatly accelerated the vital processes of lower organisms and that this ray required further study. The name, of course, was garbled and printed as "Pevsikov," [suggesting an entirely different morphology of his family name].

Ivanov brought in the newspaper and showed the notice to Persikov.

"Pevsikov," grumbled Persikov, puttering around with the chamber in his office, "where do these tattlers learn everything?"

Alas, the garbled name did not save the professor from events, and they began the very next day, immediately upsetting Persikov's whole life.

After a preliminary knock, Pankrat entered the office and handed Persikov a magnificent satiny calling card. "He's out there," Pankrat added timidly. Printed on the card in exquisite type was:

Alfred Arkadievich
Bronsky
Contributor to the Moscow Publications
Red Spark, *Red Pepper*, *Red Journal,* and *Red Projector,*
and the newspaper *Red Evening Moscow*

"Tell him to go to hell," Persikov said in a monotone, and he threw the card under the table.

Pankrat turned, walked out, and five minutes later he came back with a long-suffering face and a second specimen of the same card.

"Are you making fun of me, or what?" Persikov croaked, and he looked terrifying.

"From the GPU, the man says," answered Pankrat, turning pale.

Persikov grabbed the card with one hand, almost tearing it in half, and with the other hand he threw a pair of pincers onto the table. On the card there was a note written in curlicued handwriting: "I beg sincerely, with apologies, most esteemed professor, for you to receive me for three minutes in connection with a public matter of the press; I am also a contributor to the satirical journal *The Red Raven*, published by the GPU."

"Call him in," said Persikov, choking.

Immediately a young man with a smooth-shaven, oily face bobbed up behind Pankrat's back. The face was striking for its permanently raised eyebrows, like an Asiatic's, and the little agate eyes beneath them, which never for a second met the eyes of his interlocutor. The young man was dressed quite impeccably and fashionably: a long narrow jacket down to the knees, the widest of bell-bottomed trousers, and preternaturally wide patent-leather shoes with toes like hooves. In his hands the young man held a cane, a hat with a sharply pointed crown, and a notebook. "What do you want?" asked Persikov in a voice that made Pankrat step back behind the door immediately. "You *were* told I am busy."

Instead of answering, the young man bowed to the professor twice, once to the left and once to the right—and then his eyes wheeled all over the room, and immediately the young man made a mark in his notebook.

"I'm busy," said the professor, looking with revulsion into the guest's little eyes, but he had no effect, since the eyes were impossible to catch.

"A thousand apologies, esteemed professor, the young man began in a high-pitched voice, "for breaking in on you and taking up your precious time, but the news of your earth-shaking discovery—which has created a sensation all over the world—compels us to ask you for whatever explanations . . ."

"What kind of explanations all over the world?" Persikov whined squeakily, turning yellow. "I'm not obliged to give you any explanations or anything of the sort . . . I'm busy . . . terribly busy."

"What exactly is it you are working on?" the young man asked sweetly, making another mark in his notebook.

"Oh, I . . . why do you ask? Do you intend to publish something?"

"Yes," answered the young man, and suddenly he started scribbling furiously in his notebook.

"First of all, I have no intention of publishing anything until I complete my work—particularly in these papers of yours . . . Secondly, how do you know all this?" And Persikov suddenly felt that he was losing control.

"Is the news that you have invented a ray of new life accurate?"

"What new life?" the professor snapped angrily. "What kind of rubbish are you babbling? The ray I am working on has still not been investigated very much, and generally nothing is known about it as yet! It is possible that it may accelerate the vital processes of protoplasm."

"How much?" the young man inquired quickly. Persikov completely lost control. What a character! The devil only knows what this means! "What sort of philistine questions are these? Suppose I said, oh, a thousand times . . ."

Rapacious joy flashed through the little eyes of the young man. "It produces giant organisms?"

"Nothing of the sort! Well, true, the organisms I have obtained are larger than normal . . . Well, they do possess certain new characteristics . . . But, of course, the main thing is not the size, but the incredible speed of reproduction," said Persikov to his misfortune, and he was immediately horrified by what he had said. The young man covered a page with his writing, turned it, and scribbled on.

"But don't you write that!" Persikov said hoarsely, in desperation, already surrendering and feeling that he was in the young man's hands.

"What are you writing there?"

"Is it true that in forty-eight hours you can obtain two million tadpoles from frog roe?"

"What quantity of roe?" Persikov shouted, again infuriated. "Have you ever seen a grain of roe . . . well, let's say, of a tree frog?"

"From half a pound?" the young man asked, undaunted.

Persikov turned purple.

"Who measures it like that? Ugh! What are you talking about? Well, of course, if you took half a pound of frog roe, then . . . perhaps . . . well, hell, perhaps about that number or maybe even many more."

Diamonds began to sparkle in the young man's eyes, and in a single swoop he scratched out another page. "Is it true that this will cause a world revolution in animal husbandry?"

"What kind of newspaper question is that?" howled Persikov. "And, generally, I'm not giving you permission to write rubbish. I can see by your face that you're writing some sort of rotten trash!"

"Your photograph, professor, I beg you urgently," the young man said, slamming his notebook shut.

"What? My photograph? For your stupid little journals? To go with that devilish garbage you're scribbling there? No, no, no! . . . And I'm busy. I'll ask you to . . ."

"Even if it's an old one. And we'll return it to you instantly."

"Pankrat!" the professor shouted in a rage.

"My compliments," the young man said and vanished.

Instead of Pankrat, Persikov heard the strange rhythmic creaking of some machine behind the door, a metallic tapping across the floor, and in his office appeared a man of extraordinary bulk, dressed in a blouse and trousers made of blanket material. His left leg, a mechanical one, clicked and rattled, and in his hands he held a briefcase. His round shaven face, resembling a bulging yellow headcheese, offered an amiable smile. He bowed to the professor in military fashion and straightened up, causing his leg to twang like a spring. Persikov went numb.

"Mr. Professor," began the stranger in a pleasant, somewhat husky voice, "forgive an ordinary mortal for breaking in on your privacy."

"Are you a reporter?" asked Persikov. "Pankrat!"

"Not at all, Mr. Professor," replied the fat man. "Permit me to introduce myself: sea captain and contributor to the newspaper *Industrial News*, published by the Council of People's Commissars."

"Pankrat!" Persikov shouted hysterically, and at that instant the telephone in the corner flashed a red signal and rang softly. "Pankrat!" repeated the professor. "Hello, what is it?"

"*Verzeihen Sie, bitte, Herr Professor,*" croaked the telephone in German, "*dass ich störe. Ich bin ein Mitarbeiter des Berliner Tageblatts.*"

"Pankrat!" The professor shouted into the receiver, "*Bin momentan sehr beschäftigt und kann Sie deshalb jetzt nicht empfangen! . . . Pankrat!*"

And in the meantime the bell at the front entrance of the institute was start-ing to ring constantly.

* * *

"Nightmarish murder on Bronny Street!" howled unnatural hoarse voices twisting in and out of the thicket of lights among wheels and flashing headlights on the warm June pavement. "Nightmarish outbreak of chicken plague in the yard of Deacon Drozdov's [Deacon Thrush's] widow, with her portrait! . . . Nightmarish discovery of Professor Persikov's ray of life!"

Persikov jumped so violently that he nearly fell under the wheels of a car on Mokhovaia, and he furiously grabbed the newspaper.

"Three kopeks, citizen!" shrieked the boy, and squeezing himself into the crowd on the sidewalk, he again started howling, "*Red Evening Moscow*, discovery of x-ray."

The stunned Persikov opened the newspaper and leaned against a lamp post. From a smudged frame in the left corner of the second page there stared at him a bald man with mad, unseeing eyes and a drooping jaw—the fruit of Alfred Bronsky's artistic endeavors. "V. I. Persikov, who discovered the mysterious red ray," announced the caption under the drawing. Below it, under the heading, "World Riddle," the article began with the words: "'Sit down, please,' the venerable scientist Persikov said to us amiably . . ."

Under the article was a prominent signature: "Alfred Bronsky (Alonso)."

A greenish light flared up over the roof of the university, the fiery words *Speaking Newspaper* leapt across the sky, and a crowd immediately jammed Mokhovaia.

"'Sit down, please!!!'" a most unpleasant high-pitched voice, exactly like the voice of Alfred Bronsky, magnified a thousand times, suddenly boomed from the roof across the way, "the venerable scientist Persikov said to us amiably. 'I have long desired to acquaint the proletariat of Moscow with the results of my discovery! . . .'"

Persikov heard a quiet mechanical creaking behind his back, and some-one tugged at his sleeve. Turning around, he saw the round yellow face of the mechanical leg's owner. His eyes were wet with tears and his lips were shaking. "Me, Mr. Professor, me you refused to acquaint with the results of your amazing discovery, professor," he said sadly, and he sighed heavily, "you made me lose two smackers."

He looked gloomily at the roof of the university where the invisible Alfred was ranting in the black maw of the speaker. For some reason, Persikov suddenly felt sorry for the fat man. "I didn't say any 'sit down, please' to him!" he muttered, catching the words from the sky with hatred. He is simply a brazen scalawag, an extraordinary type! Forgive me, please, but really now—when you're working and people break in . . . I don't mean you, of course . . ."

"Perhaps, Mr. Professor, you would give me at least a description of your chamber?" the mechanical man said ingratiatingly and mournfully.

"After all, it makes no difference to you now . . ."

"In three days, such a quantity of tadpoles hatches out of half a pound of roe that it's utterly impossible to count them!" roared the invisible man in the loudspeaker.

"Too-too," shouted the cars on Mokhovaia hollowly.

"Ho, ho, ho . . . How about that! Ho, ho, ho," murmured the crowd, heads tilted back.

"What a scoundrel! Eh?" Persikov hissed to the mechanical man, trembling with indignation. "How do you like that? Why I'm going to lodge a complaint against him!"

"Outrageous," agreed the fat man.

A most dazzling violet ray struck the professor's eyes, and everything around flared up—the lamp post, a strip of block pavement, a yellow wall, curious faces.

"It's for you, professor," the fat man whispered ecstatically and hung on to the professor's sleeve like a lead weight. Something clicked rapidly in the air.

"To the devil with all of them!" Persikov exclaimed despondently, ripping through the crowd with his lead weight. "Hey, taxi! To Prechistenka!"

The beat-up old car, vintage 1924, clattered to a halt at the curb, and the professor began to climb into the landau while trying to shake loose from the fat man. "You're in my way," he hissed, covering his face with his fists against the violet light.

"Did you read it? What are they yelling about? . . . Professor Persikov and his children were found on Little Bronnaia with their throats slit! . . ." voices shouted around the crowd.

"I haven't got any children, the sons of bitches," Persikov bellowed and suddenly found himself in the focus of a black camera, which was shooting him in profile with an open mouth and furious eyes.

"Krch . . . too . . . krch . . . too," shrieked the taxi, and it lanced into the thicket of traffic.

The fat man was already sitting in the landau, crowding the professor with his body heat.

V. A CHICKEN'S TALE

In a tiny provincial town, formerly called Troitsk [Trinity] and currently Steklovsk [Glass], in the Steklov district of the Kostroma province, onto the steps of a little house on the street formerly called Cathedral and currently Personal, came out a woman wearing a kerchief and a gray dress with calico bouquets on it—and she began to sob. This woman, the widow of the former Archpriest Drozdov of the former cathedral, sobbed so loudly that soon another woman's head, in a downy woolen shawl, was stuck out the window of the house across the street, and it cried out, "What is it, Stepanovna? Another one?"

"The seventeenth!" dissolving in sobs the widow Drozdova answered.

"Oh, deary, oh dear," the woman in the shawl whimpered, and she shook her head. "Why, what is this anyway. Truly, it's the Lord in His wrath! Is she dead?"

"Just look, look, Matryona," muttered the deaconess, sobbing loudly and heavily. "Look what's happening to her!"

The gray, tilting gate slammed, a woman's bare feet padded across the dusty bumps in the street, and the deaconess, wet with tears, led Matryona to her poultry yard.

It must be said that the widow of Father Savvaty Drozdov, who had passed away in 1926 of anti-religious woes, did not give up, but started some most remarkable chicken breeding. As soon as the widow's affairs started to go uphill, such a tax was slapped on her that her chicken breeding was on the verge of terminating, had it not been for kind people. They advised the widow to inform the local authorities that she was founding a workers' cooperative chicken farm. The membership of the cooperative consisted of Drozdova herself, her faithful servant Matrioshka, and the widow's deaf niece. The widow's tax was revoked, and the chicken breeding flourished so much that by 1928 the population of the widow's dusty yard, flanked by rows of chicken coops, had increased to 250 hens, including some Cochin Chinas. The widow's eggs appeared in the Steklovsk market every Sunday; the widow's eggs were sold in Tambov, and sometimes they even appeared in the glass showcases of the store that was formerly known as "Chichkin's Cheese and Butter, Moscow."

And now a precious Brahmaputra, by count the seventeenth that morning, her tufted baby, was walking around the yard vomiting. "E . . . rr . . . url . . . url . . . ho-ho-ho," the tufted hen glugged, rolling her melancholy eyes to the sun as if she were seeing it for the last time. Cooperative member Matrioshka, was dancing before the hen in a squatting position, a cup of water in her hand.

"Here, tufted baby . . . cheep-cheep-cheep . . . drink a little water," Matrioshka pleaded, chasing the hen's beak with her cup; but the hen did not want to drink. She opened her beak wide and stretched her neck toward the sky. Then she began to vomit blood.

"Holy Jesus!" cried the guest, slapping herself on the thighs. What's going on? Nothing but gushing blood! I've *never*, may I drop on the spot, I've never seen a chicken with a stomach-ache like a human."

And these were the last words heard by the departing tufted baby. She suddenly keeled over on her side, helplessly pecked the dust a few times and turned up her eyes. Then she rolled over on her back, lifting both feet upwards, and remained motionless. Spilling the water in the cup, Matryoshka burst into a baritone wail, as did the deaconess herself, the chairman of the cooperative, and the guest leaned over to her ear and whispered, "Stepanovna, may I eat dirt, but someone's jinxed your chickens. Who's ever seen anything like it before? Why, this ain't no chicken sickness! It's that someone's hexed your chickens."

"The enemies of my life!" the deaconess cried out to the heavens. "Do they want to run me off the earth?"

A loud roosterish crow answered her words, after which a wiry bedraggled rooster tore out of a chicken coop sort of sideways, like boisterous drunk out of a tavern. He rolled his eyes back wildly at them, stamped up and down in place, spread his wings like an eagle, but did not fly off anywhere—he began to run in circles around the yard like a horse on a rope. On the third circle he stopped, overwhelmed by nausea, because he then began to cough and croak, spat bloody spots all around him, fell over, and his claws aimed toward the sun like masts. Feminine wailing filled the yard. And it was echoed by a troubled clucking, flapping, and fussing in the chicken coops.

"Well, ain't it the evil eye?" the guest asked victoriously. "Call Father Sergei; let him hold a service."

At six in the evening, when the sun lay low like a fiery face among the faces of the young sunflowers, Father Sergei, the prior of the Cathedral Church, was climbing out of his vestments after finishing the prayer service at the chicken coops. People's curious heads were stuck out over the ancient collapsing fence and peering through the cracks. The sorrowful deaconess, kissing the cross, soaked the torn canary-yellow ruble note with tears and handed it to Father Sergei, in response to which, sighing, he remarked something about, well, see how the Lord's shown us His wrath. As he was saying this, Father Sergei wore an expression which indicated that he knew very well precisely why the Lord had shown His wrath, but that he was just not saying.

After that, the crowd dispersed from the street, and since hens retire early, nobody knew that three hens and a rooster had died at the same time in the hen house of Drozdova's next-door neighbor. They vomited just like the Drozdov hens, and the only difference was that their deaths took place quietly in a locked hen house. The rooster tumbled off his perch head down and died in that position. As for the widow's hens, they died off immediately after the prayer service, and by evening her hen houses were deadly quiet—the birds lay around in heaps, stiff and cold.

When the town got up the next morning, it was stunned as if by thunder, for the affair had assumed strange and monstrous proportions. By noon only three hens were still alive on Personal Street, and those were in the last house, where the district financial inspector lived, but even they were dead by one o'clock. And by evening the town of Steklovsk was humming and buzzing like a beehive, and the dread word "plague" was sweeping through it. Drozdova's name landed in the local newspaper, *The Red Warrior,* in an article headlined "Can It Be Chicken Plague?" and from there it was carried to Moscow.

* * *

Professor Persikov's life took on a strange, restless, and disturbing character. In a word, working under such circumstances was simply impossible. The day after he had gotten rid of Alfred Bronsky, he had to disconnect his office telephone at the institute by taking the receiver off the hook, and in the evening, as he was riding the trolley home along Okhotny Row, the professor beheld himself on the roof of a huge building with a black sign on it: *WORKERS' GAZETTE.* He, the professor—crumbling and turning green and flickering—was climbing into a landau, and behind him, clutching at his sleeve, climbed a mechanical ball wearing a blanket. The professor on the white screen on the roof covered his face with his fists against a violet ray. Then a golden legend leaped out: "Professor Persikov in a car explaining his discovery to our famous reporter Captain Stepanov." And, indeed, the wavering car flicked past the Cathedral of Christ along Volkhonka, and in it the professor struggled helplessly, his physiognomy like that of a wolf at bay.

"They're some sort of devils, not men," the zoologist muttered through his teeth as he rode past.

That same day in the evening, when he returned to his place on Prechistenka, the housekeeper, Maria Stepanovna, handed the zoologist seventeen notes with telephone numbers of people who had called while he was gone, along with Maria Stepanovna's verbal declaration that she was exhausted. The professor was getting ready to tear up the notes, but stopped, because opposite one of the numbers he saw the notation "People's Commissar of Public Health."

"What's this?" the learned eccentric asked in honest bewilderment. "What's happened to them?"

At a quarter past ten the same evening the doorbell rang, and the professor was obliged to converse with a certain citizen in dazzling attire. The professor had received him because of a calling card, which stated (without first name or surname), "Plenipotentiary Chief of the Trade Departments of Foreign Embassies to the Soviet Republic."

"Why doesn't he go to hell?" growled Persikov, throwing down his magnifying glass and some diagrams on the green cloth of the table and saying to Maria Stepanovna, "Ask him here into the study, this plenipotentiary."

"What can I do for you?" Persikov asked in a tone that made the Chief wince a bit. Persikov transferred his spectacles to his forehead from the bridge of his nose, then back, and he peered at his visitor. He glittered all over with patent leather and precious stones, and a monocle rested in his right eye. "What a vile mug," Persikov thought to himself for some reason.

The guest began in a roundabout way, asked specific permission to light his cigar, in consequence of which Persikov with the greatest of reluctance invited him to sit down. The guest proceeded to make extended apologies for coming so late.

"But . . . the professor is quite impossible to catch . . . hee-hee . . . pardon . . . to find during the day" (when laughing the guest cachinnated like a hyena.)

"Yes, I'm busy!" Persikov answered so abruptly that the guest twitched a second time.

"Nevertheless, he permitted himself to disturb the famous scientist. Time is money, as they say . . . Is the cigar annoying the professor?"

"Mur-mur-mur," answered Persikov, "he permitted . . . "

"The professor *has* discovered the ray of life, hasn't he?"

"For goodness sake, what sort of life! It's all the fantasies of cheap reporters!" Persikov got excited.

"Oh no, hee-hee-hee . . . He understands perfectly the modesty which is the true adornment of all real scientists . . . But why fool around . . . There were telegrams today . . . In world capitals such as Warsaw and Riga everything about the ray is already known. Professor Persikov's name is being repeated all over the world. The world is watching Professor Persikov's work with bated breath . . . But everybody knows perfectly well the difficult position of scientists in Soviet Russia. *Entre nous soit dit . . .* There are no strangers here? . . . Alas, in this country they do not know how to appreciate scientific work, and so he would like to talk things over with the professor . . . A certain foreign state is quite unselfishly offering Professor Persikov help with his laboratory work. Why cast pearls here, as the Holy Scripture says? The said state knows how hard it was for the professor during 1919 and 1920, during this . . . hee-hee . . . revolution. Well, of course, in the strictest secrecy . . . the professor would acquaint this state with the results of his work, and in exchange it would finance the professor. For example, he constructed a chamber—now it would be interesting to become acquainted with the blueprints for this chamber . . ."

At this point the visitor drew from the inside pocket of his jacket a snow-white stack of banknotes.

"The professor can have a trifling advance, say, five thousand rubles, at this very moment . . . and there is no need to mention a receipt . . . the Plenipotentiary Trade Chief would even feel offended if the professor so much as mentioned a receipt."

"Out!!" Persikov suddenly roared so terrifyingly that the piano in the living room made a sound with its high keys.

The visitor vanished so quickly that Persikov, shaking with rage, himself began to doubt whether he had been there, or if it had been a hallucination.

"His galoshes?" Persikov howled a minute later from the hallway. "The gentleman forgot them," replied the trembling Maria Stepanovna.

"Throw them out!"

"Where can I throw them? He'll come back for them."

"Take them to the house committee. Get a receipt. I don't want a trace of those galoshes! To the committee! Let them have the spy's galoshes! . . ."

Crossing herself, Maria Stepanovna picked up the magnificent leather galoshes and carried them out to the back stairs. There she stood behind the door for a few moments, and then hid the galoshes in the pantry.

"Did you turn them in?" Persikov raged.

"I did."

"Give me the receipt!"

"But, Vladimir Ipatich. But the chairman is illiterate!"

"This. Very. Instant. I. Want. The. Receipt. Here! Let some literate son of a bitch sign for him!"

Maria Stepanovna just shook her head, went out, and came back fifteen minutes later with a note: "Received from Prof. Persikov 1 (one) pair galo. Kolesov."

"And what's this?"

"A tag, sir."

Persikov stomped all over the tag, and hid the receipt under the blotter. Then some idea darkened his sloping forehead. He rushed to the telephone, roused Pankrat at the institute, and asked him: "Is everything in order?" Pankrat growled something into the receiver, from which one could conclude that everything, in his opinion, was in order.

But Persikov calmed down only for a minute. Frowning, he clutched the telephone and jabbered into the receiver: "Give me . . . oh, whatever you call it . . . Lubianka . . . *Merci* . . . Which of you there should be told about this? . . . I have suspicious characters hanging around here in galoshes, yes . . . Professor Persikov of the Fourth University . . ."

Suddenly the conversation was abruptly disconnected and Persikov walked away, muttering some sort of swear words through his teeth.

"Are you going to have some tea, Vladimir Ipatich?" Maria Stepanovna inquired timidly, looking into the study.

"I'm not going to have any tea . . . mur-mur-mur . . . and to hell with them all . . . they've gone mad . . . I don't care."

Exactly ten minutes later the professor was receiving new guests in his study. One of them, amiable, rotund, and very polite, was wearing a modest khaki military field jacket and riding breeches. On his nose, like a crystal butterfly, perched a pince-nez. Generally, he looked like an angel in patent leather boots. The second, short and terribly gloomy, was wearing civilian clothes, but they fit in such a way that they seemed to constrain him. The third guest behaved in a peculiar manner; he did not enter the professor's study but remained in the semidark hallway. From there he had a full view of the well-lit study which was filled with billows of tobacco smoke. The face of this third visitor, who was also wearing civilian clothes, was graced with a dark pince-nez.

The two in the study wore Persikov out completely, carefully examining the calling card and interrogating him about the five thousand, and making him keep describing the earlier visitor.

"The devil only knows," grumbled Persikov. "A repulsive physiognomy. A degenerate."

"He didn't have a glass eye, did he?" the short one asked hoarsely.

"The devil only knows. But no, it isn't glass; his eyes keep darting around."

"Rubenstein?" the angel said to the short civilian softly and interrogatively. But the latter shook his head darkly.

"Rubenstein wouldn't give any money without a receipt, never," he mumbled. "This is not Rubenstein's work. This is someone bigger."

The story of the galoshes provoked a burst of the keenest interest from the guests. The angel uttered a few words into the telephone of the house office: "The State Political Administration invites the secretary of the house committee Kolesov to report at Professor Persikov's apartment with the galoshes," and Kolesov appeared in the study instantly, pale, holding the galoshes in his hands.

"Vasenka!" the angel called softly to the man who was sitting in the hall. The latter rose limply and moved into the study like an unwinding toy. His smoky glasses swallowed up his eyes.

"Well?" he asked tersely and sleepily.

"The galoshes."

The smoky eyes slid over the galoshes, and as this happened it seemed to Persikov that they were not at all sleepy; on the contrary, the eyes that flashed askance for a moment from behind the glasses were amazingly sharp. But they immediately faded out.

"Well, Vasenka?"

The man they addressed as Vasenka replied in a languid voice, "Well, what's the problem? They're Pelenzhkovsky's galoshes."

The house committee instantly lost Professor Persikov's gift. The galoshes disappeared into a newspaper. The extremely overjoyed angel in the military jacket got up, began to shake the professor's hand, and even made a little speech, the content of which boiled down to the following: "This does the professor honor. . . . The professor may rest assured . . . no one will bother him again, either at the institute or at home . . . steps will be taken . . . his chambers are quite safe."

"Could you shoot the reporters while you're at it?" Persikov asked, looking at him over his spectacles.

His question provoked a burst of merriment among his guests.

Not only the gloomy short one, but even the smoky one smiled in the hall. The angel, sparkling and glowing, explained that this was not possible.

"And who was that scalawag who came here?"

At this everyone stopped smiling, and the angel answered evasively that it was nobody, a petty swindler, not worth any attention . . . but nevertheless, he urged citizen professor to keep the evening's events in strictest secrecy, and the guests departed.

Persikov returned to his study and diagrams, but he still did not get to do any work. A fiery dot appeared on the telephone, and a female voice offered the professor a seven-room apartment if he would like to marry an interesting and hot-blooded widow. Persikov bawled into the receiver, "I advise you to go to Professor Rossolimo for treatment!" and then the telephone rang a second time.

Here Persikov was somewhat abashed because a rather well-known personage from the Kremlin was calling; he questioned Persikov sympathetically and at great length about his work and made known his wish to visit the laboratory. As he started to leave the phone, Persikov mopped his forehead, and took the receiver off the hook. At that moment there was a sudden blare of trumpets in the upstairs apartment, followed by the shrieking of the Valkyries: the director of the Woolen Fabrics Trust had tuned his radio to a Wagner concert from the Bolshoi Theater. Over the howling and crashing pouring down from the ceiling, Persikov shouted to Maria Stepanovna that he was going to take the director to court, that he was going to smash that radio, that he was going to get the hell out of Moscow, because obviously people had made it their goal to drive him out of it. He broke his magnifying glass and went to bed on the couch in his study, and he fell asleep to the gentle runs of a famous pianist that came wafting from the Bolshoi.

The surprises continued the next day too. When he got to the institute on the trolley, Persikov found an unknown citizen in a stylish green derby waiting at the entrance. He looked Persikov over closely, but addressed no questions to him, and therefore Persikov ignored him. But in the foyer, Persikov, in addition to the bewildered Pankrat, was met by a second derby which rose and greeted him courteously. "Hello there, Citizen Professor."

"What do you want?" Persikov asked menacingly, pulling off his overcoat with Pankrat's help. But the derby quickly pacified Persikov, whispering in the tenderest voice that the professor had no cause to be upset. He, the derby, was there for precisely the purpose of protecting the professor from any importunate visitors; the professor could set his mind at ease with regard not only to the doors of his study, but even to the windows. Upon which the stranger turned over the lapel of his suit coat for a moment and showed the professor a certain badge.

"Hm . . . how about that, you've really got things well set up," Persikov mumbled, and added naively, "and what will you eat here?"

At this the derby grinned and explained that he would be relieved.

The three days after this went by splendidly. The professor had two visits from the Kremlin, and one from students whom he gave examinations. Every last one of the students flunked, and from their faces it was clear that Persikov now inspired only superstitious awe in them.

"Go get jobs as trolleycar conductors! You aren't fit to study zoology," came from the office.

"Strict, eh?" the derby asked Pankrat.

"Ooh, a holy terror," answered Pankrat, "even if someone passes, he comes out reeling, poor soul. He'll be dripping with sweat. And he heads straight for a beer hall . . ."

Engrossed in these minor chores, the professor did not notice the three days pass; but on the fourth day he was recalled to reality again, and the cause of this was a thin, squeaky voice from the street. "Vladimir Ipatievich!" the voice screeched from Herzen Street into the open window of the office.

The voice was in luck: the last few days had exhausted Persikov. Just at the moment he was resting in his armchair, smoking, and staring languidly and feebly with his red-circled eyes. He could not go on. And therefore it was even with some curiosity that he looked out the window and saw Alfred Bronsky on the sidewalk. The professor immediately recognized the titled owner of the calling card by his pointed hat and notebook. Bronsky bowed to the window tenderly and deferentially.

"Oh, is it you?" the professor asked. He did not have enough energy left to get angry, and he was even curious to see what would happen next. Protected by the window, he felt safe from Alfred. The ever-present derby in the street instantly cocked an ear toward Bronsky. A most disarming smile blossomed on the latter's face.

"Just a pair of minutes, dear professor," Bronsky said, straining his voice from the sidewalk. "Only one small question, a purely zoological one. May I ask it?"

"Ask it," Persikov replied laconically and ironically, and he thought to himself, "After all, there is something American in this rascal."

"What do you have to say as for the hens, dear professor?" shouted Bronsky, folding his hands into a trumpet.

Persikov was nonplussed. He sat down on the windowsill, then got up, pressed a button, and shouted, poking his finger toward the window,

"Pankrat, let that fellow on the sidewalk in."

When Bronsky appeared in the office Persikov extended his amiability to the extent of barking, "Sit down!" at him.

And Bronsky, smiling ecstatically, sat down on the revolving stool.

"Please explain something to me," began Persikov. "Do you write there—for those papers of yours?"

"Yes, sir," Alfred replied deferentially.

"Well, it's incomprehensible to me, how you can write when you don't even know how to speak Russian correctly. What is this 'a pair of minutes' and 'as for the hens'? You probably meant to ask 'about the hens'?"

Bronsky burst out into a thin and respectful laugh. "Valentin Petrovich corrects it."

"Who's this Valentin Petrovich?"

"The head of the literary department."

"Well, all right. Besides, I am not a philologist. Let's forget your Petrovich. What is it specifically that you wish to know about hens?"

"In general everything you have to tell, professor."

Here Bronsky armed himself with a pencil. Triumphant sparks flickered in Persikov's eyes.

"You come to me in vain; I am not a specialist on the feathered beasts. You would be best off to go to Emelian Ivanovich Portugalov of the First University. I myself know extremely little."

Bronsky smiled ecstatically, giving him to understand that he understood the dear professor's joke. "Joke: little," he jotted in his notebook.

"However, if it interests you, very well. Hens, or pectinates . . . Order, *Gallinae*. Of the pheasant family . . ." Persikov began in a loud voice, looking not at Bronsky, but somewhere beyond him, where a thousand people were presumably listening, "of the pheasant family, *Phasianidae*. They are birds with fleshy combs and two lobes under the lower jaw . . . hm . . . although sometimes there is only one in the center of the chin . . . Well, what else? Wings, short and rounded. Tails of medium length, somewhat serrated, even, I would say, denticulated, the middle feathers crescent shaped . . . Pankrat, bring me Model No. 705 from the model cabinet—a cock in cross section . . . but no, you have no need of that? Pankrat, don't bring the model . . . I reiterate to you, I am not a specialist—go to Portugalov. Well, I personally am acquainted with six species of wild hens—hm . . . Portugalov knows more—in India and the Malay Archipelago. For example, the Banki rooster, or Kazintu, found in the foothills of the Himalayas, all over India, in Assam and Burma . . . Then there's the swallow-tailed rooster, or *Gallus varius*, of Lombok, Sumbawa, and Flores. On the island of Java there is a remarkable rooster, *Gallus eneus*; in southeast India, I can recommend the very beautiful *Gallus souneratti* to you. As for Ceylon, there we meet the Stanley rooster, not found anywhere else."

Bronsky sat there, his eyes bulging, scribbling.

"Anything else I can tell you?"

"I would like to know something about chicken diseases," Alfred whispered very softly.

"Hm, I'm not a specialist, you ask Portugalov . . . Still, and all . . . well, there are tapeworms, flukes, scab mites, red mange, chicken mites, poultry lice or *Mallophaga*, fleas, chicken cholera, croupous-diphtheritic inflammation of the mucous membranes . . . pneumonomycosis, tuberculosis, chicken mange—there are all sorts of diseases." There were sparks leaping in Persikov's eyes. "There can be poisoning, tumors, rickets, jaundice, rheumatism, the *Achorion schoenleinii fungus* . . . a quite interesting disease. When it breaks out little spots resembling mold form on the comb."

Bronsky wiped the sweat from his forehead with a colored handkerchief. "And what, professor, in your opinion is the cause of the present catastrophe?"

"What catastrophe?"

"What, you mean you haven't read it, professor?" Bronsky cried with surprise, and pulled out a crumpled page of *Izvestia* from his briefcase.

"I don't read newspapers," answered Persikov, grimacing.

"But why, professor?" Alfred asked tenderly.

"Because they write gibberish," Persikov answered, without thinking.

"But how about this, professor?" Bronsky whispered softly, and he unfolded the newspaper.

"What's this?" asked Persikov, and he got up from his place. Now the sparks began to leap in Bronsky's eyes. With a pointed lacquered nail he underlined a headline of incredible magnitude across the entire page:

CHICKEN PLAGUE IN THE REPUBLIC

"What?" Persikov asked, pushing his spectacles onto his forehead.

VI. MOSCOW IN JUNE OF 1928

She gleamed brightly, her lights danced, blinked, and flared on again. The white headlights of buses and the green lights of trolleys circled around Theater Square; over the former Muir and Merilis, above the tenth floor built up over it, a multicolored electric woman was jumping up and down, making up multicolored words letter by letter: WORKERS CREDIT. In the square opposite the Bolshoi, around the multicolored fountain shooting up sprays all night, a crowd was milling and rumbling. And over the Bolshoi a giant loudspeaker was booming: "The anti-chicken vaccinations at the Lefort Veterinary Institute have produced excellent results. The number . . . of chicken deaths for the day declined by half."

Then the loudspeaker changed its timbre, something rumbled in it; over the theater a green stream flashed on and off, and the loudspeaker complained in a deep bass: "Special commission set up to combat chicken plague, consisting of the People's Commissar of Public Health, the People's Commissar of Agriculture, the Chief of Animal Husbandry, Comrade Avis-Hamska, Professors Persikov and Portugalov, and Comrade Rabinovich! . . . New attempts at intervention," the speaker cachinnated and wept like a jackal, "in connection with the chicken plague!"

Theater Lane, Neglinny Prospect, and the Lubianka flamed with white and violet streaks, spraying shafts of light, howling with horns, and whirling with dust. Crowds of people pressed against the wall by the huge pages of advertisements lit by garish red reflectors.

"Under threat of the most severe penalties, the populace is forbidden to employ chicken meat or eggs as food. Private tradesmen who attempt to sell these in the markets will be subject to criminal prosecution and confiscation of all property. All citizens who own eggs must immediately surrender them at their local police precincts."

On the roof of The Worker's Gazette chickens were piled skyhigh on the screen, and greenish firemen, quivering and sparkling, were pouring kerosene on them with long hoses. Then red waves swept across the screen; unreal smoke billowed, tossed about like rags, and crept along in streams, and fiery words leaped out: "BURNING OF CHICKEN CORPSES ON THE KHODYNKA."

Among the wildly blazing show windows of the stores which worked until three in the morning (with breaks for lunch and supper) gaped the blind holes of windows boarded up under their signs: "Egg Store. Quality Guaranteed." Very often, screaming alarmingly, passing lumbering buses, hissing cars marked "MOSHEALDEPART FIRST AID" swept past the traffic policemen.

"Someone else has stuffed himself with rotten eggs," the crowd murmured.

On the Petrovsky Lines the world-renowned Empire Restaurant glittered with its green and orange lights, and on its tables, next to the portable telephones, stood cardboard signs stained with liqueurs: "By decree—no omelettes. Fresh oysters have been received." At the Ermitage, where tiny Chinese lanterns, like beads, glowed mournfully amid the artificial, cozy greenery, the singers Shrams and Karmanchikov on the eye-shattering, dazzling stage sang ditties composed by the poets Ardo and Arguiev:

Oh, Mamma, what will I do without eggs?

while their feet thundered out a tap dance.

Over the theater of the late Vsevolod Meyerhold, who died, as everyone knows, in 1927, during the staging of Pushkin's *Boris Godunov* when a platform full of naked boiars collapsed on him, there flashed a moving multicolored neon sign promulgating the writer Erendorg's play, *Chicken Croak*, produced by Meyerhold's disciple, Honored Director of the Republic Kukhterman. Next door, at the Aquarium Restaurant, scintillating with neon signs and flashing with half-naked female bodies to thunderous applause, the writer Lazer's review entitled *The Hen's Children* was being played amid the greenery of the stage. And down Tverskaia, with lanterns on either side of their heads, marched a procession of circus donkeys carrying gleaming placards. Rostand's *Chantecler* was being revived at the Korsh Theater.

Little newsboys were howling and screaming among the wheels of the automobiles: "Nightmarish discovery in a cave! Poland preparing for nightmarish war! Professor Persikov's nightmarish experiments!"

At the circus of the former Nikitin, in the greasy brown arena that smelled pleasantly of manure, the dead-white clown Bom was saying to Bim, who was dressed in a huge checkered sack, "I know why you're so sad!"

"Vhy-y?" squeaked Bim.

"You buried your eggs in the ground, and the police from the fifteenth precinct found them."

"Ha, ha, ha, ha," the circus laughed, so that the blood stopped in the veins joyfully and anguishingly—and the trapezes and the cobwebs under the shabby cupola swayed dizzily.

"Oop!" the clowns cried piercingly, and a sleek white horse carried out on its back a woman of incredible beauty, with shapely legs in scarlet tights.

Looking at no one, noticing no one, not responding to the nudging and soft and tender enticements of prostitutes, Persikov, inspired and lonely, crowned with sudden fame, was making his way along Mokhovaia toward the fiery clock at the Manège. Here, without looking around at all, engrossed in his thoughts, he bumped into a strange, old-fashioned man, painfully jamming his fingers directly against the wooden holster of a revolver hanging from the man's belt.

"Oh, damn!" squeaked Persikov. "Excuse me."

"Of course," answered the stranger in an unpleasant voice, and somehow they disentangled themselves in the middle of this human logjam. And heading for Prechistenka the professor instantly forgot the collision.

VII. FEIT

It is not known whether the Lefort Veterinary Institute's inoculations really were any good, whether the Samara roadblock detachments were skillful, whether the stringent measures taken with regard to the egg salesmen in Kaluga and Voronezh were successful, or whether the Extraordinary Commission in Moscow worked efficiently, but it is well known that two weeks after Persikov's last interview with Alfred, in a chicken way things had already been completely cleaned up in the Union of Republics. Here and there forlorn feathers still lay about in the backyards of district towns, bringing tears to the eyes of the onlookers, and in hospitals the last of the greedy people were still finishing the last spasms of bloody diarrhea and vomiting. Fortunately, human deaths were no more than a thousand in the entire Republic. Nor did any serious disorders ensue. True, a prophet had appeared briefly in Volokolamsk, proclaiming that the chicken plague had been caused by none other than the commissars, but he had no special success. In the Volokolamsk marketplace several policemen who had been confiscating chickens from the market women were beaten up, and some windows were broken in the local post and telegraph office. Luckily, the efficient Volokolamsk authorities quickly took the necessary measures as a result of which, first, the prophet ceased his activities, and second, the post office's broken windows were replaced.

Having reached Archangel and Syumkin village in the North, the plague stopped by itself, for the reason that there was nowhere for it to go—as everybody knows, there are no hens in the White Sea. It also stopped at Vladivostok, for there only the ocean is beyond that. In the far South it disappeared, petering out somewhere in the parched expanses of Ordubat, Dzhulfa, and Karabulak; and in the West it halted in an astonishing way exactly on the Polish and Rumanian borders. Perhaps the climate of these countries is different or perhaps the quarantine measures taken by the neighboring governments worked, but the fact remains that the plague went no further. The foreign press noisily and avidly discussed the unprecedented losses, while the government of the Soviet Republics, without any noise, was working tirelessly. The Special Commission to Fight the Chicken Plague was renamed the Special Commission for the Revival and Reestablishment of Chicken Breeding in the Republic and was augmented by a new Special Troika, made up of sixteen members. A "Goodpoul" office was set up, with Persikov and Portugalov as honorary assistants to the chairman. Their pictures appeared in the newspapers over titles such as "Mass Purchase of Eggs Abroad" and "Mr. Hughes Wants to Undermine the Egg Campaign." All Moscow read the stinging feuilleton by the journalist Kolechkin, which closed with the words, "Don't whet your teeth on our eggs, Mr. Hughes— you have your own!"

Professor Persikov was completely exhausted from overworking himself for the last three weeks. The chicken events disrupted his routine and put a double burden upon him. Every evening he had to work at conferences of chicken commissions, and from time to time he was obliged to endure long interviews either with Alfred Bronsky or with the mechanical fat man. He had to work with Professor Portugalov and Assistant Professors Ivanov and

Bornhart, dissecting and microscoping chickens in search of the plague bacillus, and he even had to write up a hasty pamphlet "On the Changes in Chicken Kidneys as a Result of the Plague" in three evenings.

Persikov worked in the chicken field with no special enthusiasm, and understandably so—his whole mind was filled with something else which was fundamental and important—the problem from which he had been diverted by the chicken catastrophe, i.e., the red ray. Straining still further his already shaken health, stealing hours from sleep and meals, sometimes falling asleep on the oilcloth couch in his institute office, instead of going home to Prechistenka, Persikov spent whole nights puttering with his chamber and his microscope.

By the end of July the race let up a little. The work of the renamed commission fell into a normal groove, and Persikov returned to his interrupted work. The microscopes were loaded with new cultures, and under the ray in the chamber fish and frog roe matured with fantastic speed. Specially ordered glass was brought from Konigsberg by plane, and during the last days of July mechanics laboring under Ivanov's supervision constructed two large new chambers in which the ray reached the width of a cigarette pack at its source and at its widest point—a full meter. Persikov joyfully rubbed his hands and started to prepare for some sort of mysterious and complicated experiments. To start with he talked to the People's Commission of Education on the telephone, and the receiver quacked out the warmest assurances of all possible cooperation, and then Persikov telephoned Comrade Avis-Hamska, the director of the Animal Husbandry Department of the Supreme Commission. Persikov received Avis-Hamska's warmest attention. The matter involved a large order abroad for Professor Persikov. Avis said into the telephone that he would immediately wire Berlin and New York. After this there was an inquiry from the Kremlin about how Persikov's work was progressing, and an important and affable voice asked whether Persikov needed an automobile.

"No, thank you, I prefer to ride the trolley," replied Persikov.

"But why?" the mysterious voice asked, laughing condescendingly.

In general everybody spoke to Persikov either with respect and terror, or laughing indulgently, as though he were a small, though overgrown, child.

"It's faster," Persikov replied, to which the resonant bass replied into the telephone, "Well, as you wish."

Another week passed, during which Persikov, withdrawing still further from the receding chicken problems, engrossed himself completely in the study of the ray. From the sleepless nights and overexertion his head felt light, as if it were transparent and weightless. The red circles never left his eyes now, and Persikov spent almost every night at the institute. Once he abandoned his zoological retreat to give a lecture at the huge Tsekubu Hall on Prechistenka—about his ray and its effect on the egg cell. It was a tremendous triumph for the eccentric zoologist. The applause was so thunderous that something crumbled and dropped down from the ceilings of the colonnaded hall; hissing arc lights poured light over the black dinner jackets of the Tsekubu members and the white gowns of the ladies. On the stage, on a glass-topped table next to the lectern, a moist frog as big as a cat sat on a platter, gray and breathing heavily. Many notes were thrown onto the stage. They included seven declarations of love, and Persikov tore them up. The Tsekubu chairman dragged him forcibly onto the stage to bow to the audience. Persikov bowed irritably; his hands were sweaty, and the knot of his black tie rested not beneath his chin, but behind his left ear. There amid the sounds of respiration and the mist before him were hundreds of yellow faces and white shirtfronts and suddenly the yellow holster of a revolver flashed and disappeared somewhere behind a white column. Persikov dimly perceived it, and forgot it. But as he was departing after the lecture, walking down the raspberry-colored carpet of the staircase, he suddenly felt sick. For a moment the dazzling chandelier in the vestibule turned black, and Persikov felt faint and nauseated . . . He thought he smelled something burning; it seemed to him that blood was dripping, sticky and hot, down his neck . . . And with a shaky hand the professor caught at the handrail.

"Are you sick, Vladimir Ipatich?"anxious voices flew at him from all sides.

"No, no," replied Persikov, recovering. "I am just overtired . . . yes . . . May I have a glass of water?"

It was a very sunny August day. That bothered the professor, so the shades were lowered. A reflector on a flexible stand threw a sharp beam of light onto a glass table piled with instruments and slides. Leaning against the backrest of the revolving chair in exhaustion, Persikov smoked, and his eyes, dead tired but satisfied, looked through the billows of smoke at the partly open door of the chamber where, faintly warming the already close and impure air of the office, the red sheaf of his ray lay quietly.

Someone knocked on the door.

"Well?" asked Persikov.

The door creaked softly, and Pankrat entered. He put his arms stiffly at his sides, and blanching with fear before the divinity, he said, "Mr. Professor, out there Feit has come to you."

A semblance of a smile appeared on the scientist's cheeks. He narrowed his eyes and said, "That's interesting. But I'm busy."

"He says he has an official paper from the Kremlin."

"Fate with a paper? A rare combination," uttered Persikov, adding, "oh, well, get him in here."

"Yes, sir," said Pankrat, and he disappeared through the door like an eel.

A minute later it creaked again and a man appeared on the threshold. Persikov squeaked around an his swivel chair, and, above his spectacles, fixed his eyes on the visitor over his shoulder. Persikov was very remote from life—he was not interested in it—but even Persikov was struck by the predominant, the salient characteristic of the man who had entered: he was peculiarly old-fashioned. In 1919 the man would have been entirely in place in the streets of the capital; he would have passed in 1924, in the beginning of the year—but in 1928 he was odd. At a time when even the most backward section of the proletariat—the bakers—wore ordinary jackets, and the military service jacket was a rarity in Moscow—an old-fashioned outfit irrevocably discarded by the end of 1924—the man who had entered was wearing a double-breasted leather coat, olive-green trousers, puttees, and gaiters on his legs, and at his hip a huge Mauser of antiquated make in a cracked yellow holster. His face produced the same kind of impression on Persikov that it did on everyone else—an extremely unpleasant impression. His little eyes looked at the whole world with surprise, but at the same time with assurance; there was something bumptious in the short legs with their flat feet. His face was blue from close shaving. Persikov immediately frowned. He squeaked the screw of his chair mercilessly, and looking at the man no longer over his spectacles but through them, he asked, "You have some paper? Where is it?"

The visitor was apparently overwhelmed by what he saw. Generally he had little capacity for being taken aback, but here he was taken aback. Judging by his tiny eyes, he was struck most of all by the twelve-shelved bookcase, which reached to the ceiling and was crammed with books. Then, of course, there were the chambers, in which—as though in hell—he scarlet ray flickered, diffused and magnified through the glass. And Persikov himself in the penumbra beside the sharp needle of light emitted by the reflector was sufficiently strange and majestic in his revolving chair. The visitor fixed on the professor a glance in which sparks of deference were clearly leaping through the self-assurance. He presented no paper, but said, "I am Alexander Semionovich Feit!"

"Well? So what?"

"I have been appointed director of the model Sovkhoz—the 'Red Ray' Sovkhoz," explained the visitor.

"And?"

"And so I've come to see you, comrade, with a secret memorandum."

"Interesting to learn. Make it short, if you can."

The visitor unbuttoned the lapel of his coat and pulled out an order printed on magnificent thick paper. He held it out to Persikov. Then, without invitation, he sat down on a revolving stool. "Don't jiggle the table," Persikov said with hatred.

The visitor looked around at the table in fright—at the far end, in a moist dark aperture, some sort of eyes gleamed lifelessly like emeralds. They exuded a chill.

No sooner had Persikov read the paper than he rose from his stool and rushed to the telephone. Within a few seconds he was already speaking hurriedly and with an extreme degree of irritation. "Excuse me . . . I cannot understand . . . How can this be? I . . . without my consent or advice . . . Why, the devil only knows what he'll do with it!"

Here the stranger turned on his stool, extremely insulted. "Pardon me," he began, "I am the direc . . ."

But Persikov waved him away with his hooked index finger and continued: "Excuse me, I can't understand . . . And finally, I categorically refuse. I will not sanction any experiments with eggs . . . Until I try them myself. . . ."

Something squawked and clicked in the receiver, and even from a distance one could understand that the condescending voice in the receiver was speaking to a small child. It ended with crimson Persikov slamming down the receiver and saying past it into the wall, "I wash my hands of this!"

He returned to the table, took the paper from it, read it once from top to bottom above his spectacles, then from bottom to top through them, and suddenly he yelled, "Pankrat!"

Pankrat appeared in the door as though rising up through a trap door at the opera. Persikov glanced at him and ejaculated, "Get out, Pankrat!"

And without showing the least surprise, Pankrat disappeared.

Then Persikov turned to his guest and began, "All right, sir . . . I submit. It's none of my business. And I'm not even interested."'

The professor not so much offended as amazed his guest. "But pardon me," he began, "you *are* a comrade? . . ."

"Comrade . . . comrade. . . . Is that all you know how to say?" Persikov grumbled, and fell silent.

"Well!" was written on Feit's face.

"Pard . . ."

"Now, sir, if you please," interrupted Persikov. "This is the arc light. From it you obtain, by manipulating the ocular," Persikov snapped the lid of the chamber, which resembled a camera, "a cluster which you can gather by adjusting object-lens No. 1, here, and mirror No. 2." Persikov turned off the ray, turned it on again—aimed at the floor of the asbestos chamber. "And on the floor you can place whatever you please in the ray and conduct experiments. Extremely simple, don't you think?"

Persikov meant to show irony and contempt, but his visitor did not notice, peering intently into the chamber with his glittering little eyes.

"But I warn you," Persikov went on, "one should not put one's hands in the ray, because, according to my observations, it causes growth of the epithelium—and I unfortunately have not yet been able to establish whether it is malignant or not."

Here the visitor nimbly hid his hands behind his back, dropping his leather cap, and he looked at the professor's hands. They were covered with iodine stains, and his right wrist was bandaged.

"And how do you do it, professor?"

"You can buy rubber gloves at Schwab's on Kuznetsky," the professor replied irritably. "I'm not obliged to worry about that."

Here Persikov looked up at his visitor, as though studying him through a magnifying glass. "Where are you from? Why you? In general, why you?"

Feit was finally deeply offended, "Pard . . ."

"After all, one has to know what it's all about . . . Why have you latched on to my ray? . . ."

"Because it's a matter of utmost importance."

"Oh. The utmost? In that case—Pankrat!"

And when Pankrat appeared: "Wait, I'll think it over."

And Pankrat obediently disappeared.

"I cannot understand one thing," said Persikov. "Why are such rushing and secrecy necessary?"

"You have already got me muddled, professor," Feit answered. "You know that every last chicken has died off?"

"Well, what about it?" shrieked Persikov. "Do you want to resurrect them instantly, or what? And why use a ray that has still been insufficiently studied?"

"Comrade Professor," replied Feit, "I must say, you do mix me up I am telling you that it is essential for us because they're writing a all kinds of nasty things about us abroad. Yes."

"Let them write."

"Well, you know!" Feit responded mysteriously, shaking his head.

"I'd like to know who got the idea of breeding chickens from eggs . . ."

"I did," answered Feit.

"Uhmmm . . . So . . . And why, may I inquire? Where did you hear about the characteristics of this ray.

"I attended your lecture, professor."

"I haven't done anything with eggs yet! I am just getting ready to!"

"It'll work, I swear it will," Feit said suddenly with conviction and enthusiasm. "Your ray is so famous, you could hatch elephants with it, let alone chickens."

"Tell me," uttered Persikov. "You aren't a zoologist, are you. No? A pity . . . you'd make a very bold experimenter . . . Yes, but you are risking failure. And you are just taking up my time . . ."

"We'll return your chambers."

"When?"

"Well, as soon as I breed the first group."

"How confidently you say that! Very well, sir. Pankrat!"

"I have men with me," said Feit. "And guards . . ."

By that evening Persikov's office had been desolated . . . The tables were bare. Feit's men had carried off the three large chambers, leaving the professor only the first, his own little one with which he had begun the experiments.

July twilight was settling over the institute; grayness filled it and flowed along the corridors. From the study came the sound of monotonous footsteps— this was Persikov pacing the large room from window to door without turning on the light. It was a strange thing: that evening an inexplicably dismal mood overcame both the people who inhabited the institute and the animals. The toads for some reason raised a particularly dismal concert, twittering ominously, premonitorily. Pankrat had to chase along the corridors after a garter snake that had escaped from its cage, and when he caught it, the snake looked as though it ad decided to flee wherever its eyes would lead it, if only to get away.

In the deep twilight the bell rang from Persikov's office. Pankrat appeared on the threshold and he saw a strange sight. The scientist was standing solitarily in the center of the room, looking at the tables. Pankrat coughed once and stood still.

"There, Pankrat," said Persikov, and he pointed to the bare table.

Pankrat was horrified. It seemed to him that the professor's eyes were tear-stained in the twilight. It was so extraordinary and so terrible.

"Yes, sir," Pankrat answered lugubriously, thinking, "It'd be better if you'd yell at me."

"There," repeated Persikov, and his lips quivered like a child's when his favorite toy has suddenly, for no reason, been taken away from it. "You know, my good Pankrat," Persikov went on, turning away to the window, "my wife . . . who left me fifteen years ago—she joined an operetta . . . and now it turns out she is dead . . . What a story, my dear Pankrat . . . I was sent a letter."

The toads screamed plaintively, and twilight enveloped the professor. There it is . . . night. Moscow . . . here and there outside the windows some sort of white globes began to light up . . . Pankrat, confused and in anguish held his hands straight down his sides, stiff with fear . . .

"Go, Pankrat," the professor murmured heavily, waving his hand. "Go to bed, my dear, kind Pankrat."

And night came. For some reason Pankrat ran out of the office on his tiptoes, hurried to his cranny, rummaged through the rags in the corner, pulled out a half-full bottle of Russian vodka, and gulped down almost a regular glassful in one breath. He chased it with some bread and salt, and his eyes cheered up a bit.

Later in the evening, close to midnight now, Pankrat was sitting barefoot on a bench in the dimly lit vestibule, talking to the sleepless derby on duty, and scratching his chest under the calico shirt. "It'd be better if he'd kill me, I swear . . ."

"He really was crying?" inquired the derby with curiosity.

"I swear . . . " Pankrat assured him.

"A great scientist," agreed the derby. "Obviously no frog can take the place of a wife."

"Absolutely," Pankrat agreed. Then he thought a bit and added, "I'm thinking of getting my woman permission to come out here" . . . why should she sit there in the village? Only she can't stand them snakes no how . . ."

"Sure, they're terribly nasty," agreed the derby.

From the scientist's office not a sound could be heard. And there was no light in it. No strip under the door.

VIII. Events at the Sovkhoz

There is absolutely no time of year more beautiful than mid-August in, let us say, the Smolensk province. The summer of 1928, as is well known, was one of the finest ever, with spring rains which had come at precisely the right time, a full hot sun, and a fine harvest . . . The apples were ripening in the former Sheremetiev estate . . . the woods stood green, the fields lay in yellow squares. A man becomes better in the bosom of nature. And Alexander Semionovich would not have seemed as unpleasant here as in the city. And he no longer wore that obnoxious coat. His face had a coppery tan, his unbuttoned calico shirt betrayed a chest overgrown with the thickest black hair, his legs were clad in canvas trousers. And his eyes had grown calmer and kinder.

Alexander Semionovich ran briskly down the stairs from the becolumned porch over which a sign was nailed, under a star: THE "RED RAY" SOVKHOZ. And he went straight to meet the pickup truck which had brought him three black chambers under guard.

All day Alexander Semionovich bustled around with his helpers, setting up the chambers in the former winter garden—the Sheremetiev greenhouse . . . By evening all was in readiness. A frosted white globe glowed under the glass ceiling, the chambers were arranged on bricks, and the mechanic who had come with the chambers, clicking and turning the shiny knobs, turned the mysterious red ray onto the asbestos floor of the black boxes.

Alexander Semionovich bustled around, and even climbed the ladder himself to check out the wiring.

On the following day, the same pickup returned from the station and disgorged three crates made of magnificent smooth plywood and plastered all over with labels and warnings in white letters on black backgrounds: "*Vorsicht: Eier*! Handle with care: Eggs."

"But why did they send so few?" wondered Alexander Semionovich—however, he immediately started bustling around and unpacking the eggs. The unpacking was done in the same greenhouse with the participation of: Alexander Semionovich himself; his wife Manya, a woman of extraordinary bulk; the one-eyed former gardener of the former Sheremetievs, currently working on the sovkhoz in the universal capacity of watchman; the guard, now condemned to life on the sovkhoz; and Dunia, the cleaning woman. This was not Moscow, and so the nature of everything here was simpler, friendlier, and more homely. Alexander Semionovich supervised, glancing affectionately at the crates, which looked like a really sturdy, compact present under the soft sunset light coming through the upper windows of the greenhouse. The guard, whose rifle rested peacefully by the door, broke open the clamps and metal bindings with a pair of pliers. Crackling filled the room. Dust flew. Flopping along in his sandals, Alexander Semionovich fussed around the crates.

"Take it easy," he said to the guard. "Careful. Don't you see the eggs?"

"Don't worry," the provincial warrior grunted, drilling away. "Just a second." T-r-r-r . . . and the dust flew.

The eggs turned out to be exceedingly well packed: under the wooden lid there was a layer of wax paper, then absorbent paper, then a solid layer of wood shavings, and then sawdust, in which the white tips of the eggs gleamed.

"Foreign packing," Alexander Semionovich said lovingly digging into the sawdust. "Not the way we do things here. Manya, careful, you'll break them."

"You've gotten silly, Alexander Semionovich," replied his wife. "Imagine, such gold. Do you think I've never seen eggs before? . . . Oy! What big ones!"

"Europe," said Alexander Semionovich. "Did you expect our crummy little Russian peasant eggs? . . . They must all be Brahmaputras, the devil take 'em! German . . ."

"Sure they are," confirmed the guard, admiring the eggs.

"Only I don't understand why they're dirty," Alexander Semionovich said reflectively . . . "Manya, you look after things. Have them go on with the unloading, and I'm going to make a telephone call."

And Alexander Semionovich set off for the telephone in the sovkhoz office across the yard.

That evening the telephone cracked in the office of the Zoological Institute. Professor Persikov ruffled his hair and went to the phone.

"Well?" he asked.

"The provinces calling, just a minute," the receiver replied with a soft hiss in a woman's voice.

"Well, I'm listening," Persikov said fastidiously into the black mouth of the phone.

Something clicked in it, and then a distant masculine voice anxiously spoke in his ear. "Should the eggs be washed, professor?"

"What? What is it? What are you asking?" Persikov got irritated.

"Where are you calling from?"

"From Nikolsky, Smolensk province," the receiver answered.

"I don't understand any of this. I don't know any Nikolsky. Who is this?"

"Feit," said the receiver sternly.

"What Feit? Oh, yes . . . it's you . . . so what is it you're asking?"

"Should they be washed? . . . I was sent a batch of chicken eggs from abroad . . ."

"Well?"

"They seem slimy somehow . . ."

"You're mixing something up . . . How can they be 'slimy' as you put it? Well, of course, there can be a little . . . perhaps some droppings stuck on . . . or something else . . ."

"So they shouldn't be washed?"

"Of course not . . . What are you doing—are you all ready to load the chambers with the eggs?"

"I am. Yes," replied the receiver.

"Harumph," Persikov snorted.

"So long," the receiver clicked and went silent.

"So long, Persikov repeated with hatred to Assistant Professor Ivanov. "How do you like that character, Peter Stepanovich?"

Ivanov laughed. "Was that him? I can imagine what he'll cook up with those eggs out there."

"The id . . . id . . . idiot," Persikov stuttered furiously. "Just imagine, Peter Stepanovich. Fine, it is quite possible that the ray will have the same effect on the deutoplasm of the chicken egg that it did on the plasm of the amphibians. It is quite possible that the hens will hatch. But neither you nor I can say what sort of hens they will be . . . Maybe they won't be good for a damned thing. Maybe they'll die in a day or two. Maybe they'll be inedible! Can I guarantee that they'll be able to stand on their feet? Maybe their bones will be brittle." Persikov got all excited and waved his hands, crooking his index fingers.

"Absolutely right," agreed Ivanov.

"Can you guarantee, Peter Stepanovich, that they'll produce another generation? Maybe this character will breed sterile hens. He'll drive them up to the size of a dog, and then you can wait until the second coming before they'll have any progeny."

"No one can guarantee it," agreed Ivanov.

"And what bumptiousness!" Persikov got himself even more distraught. "What indolence! And note this, I have been ordered to instruct this scoundrel." Persikov pointed to the paper delivered by Feit (it lay on the experiment table). "How am I to instruct this ignoramus, when I myself cannot say anything on the problem?"

"But was it impossible to refuse?" asked Ivanov.

Persikov turned crimson, picked up the paper, and showed it to Ivanov. The latter read it and smiled ironically.

"Um, yes," he said very significantly.

"And then, note this . . . I've been waiting for my order for two months—and there's neither hide nor hair of it. While that one is sent the eggs instantly, and generally gets all kinds of cooperation."

"He won't get a damned thing out of it, Vladimir Ipatich. And it will just end by their returning the chambers to you."

"If only they don't take too long doing it, otherwise they're holding up my experiments."

"That's what's really rotten. I have everything ready"

"Did you get the diving suits?"

"Yes, today."

Persikov calmed down somewhat, and livened up. "Hhmmm . . . I think we'll do it this way. We can seal the doors of the operating room tight and open the window . . ."

"Of course," agreed Ivanov.

"Three helmets ?"

"Three. Yes."

"Well, so . . . That means you, I, and possibly one of the students. We'll give him the third helmet."

"Greenmut's possible."

"The one who's working on the salamanders with you now? Hmmm, he's not bad . . . although, wait, last spring he couldn't describe the structure of the air bladder of the Gymnodontes," Persikov added rancorously.

"No, he's not bad . . . He's a good student," interceded Ivanov.

"We will have to go without sleep for one night," Persikov went on.

"And one more thing, Peter Stepanovich, you check the gas—otherwise the devil only knows about these so-called Goodchems—they'll send some sort of trash."

"No, no," Ivanov waved his hands. "I already tested it yesterday. We must give them their due, Vladimir Ipatich, it's excellent gas."

"On whom did you try it'?"

"On ordinary toads. You let out a little stream and they die instantly. Oh, yes, Vladimir Ipatich, we'll also do this—you write a request to the GPU, asking them to send an electric revolver."

"But I don't know how to use it."

"I'll take that on myself,"answered Ivanov. "We used to practice with one on the Kliazma, just for fun . . . there was a GPU man living next door to me. A remarkable thing. Quite extraordinary. Noiseless, kills outright from a hundred paces. We used to shoot crows . . . I don't think we even need the gas."

"Hmmm, that's a clever idea . . . Very." Persikov went to the corner of the room, picked up the receiver, and croaked, "Let me have that, oh, what d'you call it . . . Lubianka . . ."

The days got unbearably hot. One could clearly see the dense transparent heat shimmering over the fields. But the nights were marvelous, deceptive, green. The moon shone brightly, casting such beauty on the former Sheremetiev estate that it is impossible to express it in words. The sovkhoz palace gleamed as though made of sugar, the shadows trembled in the park, and the ponds were cleft into two colors—a slanting shaft of moonlight across it, and the rest, bottomless darkness. In the patches of moonlight you could easily read *Izvestia*, except for the chess column, which is printed in tiny nonpareil. But, naturally, nobody read *Izvestia* on nights like these . . . Dunia, the cleaning woman, turned up in the copse behind the sovkhoz, and as a result of some coincidence, the red-moustachioed driver of a battered sovkhoz pickup turned up there too. What they did there—remains unknown. They took shelter in the melting shadow of an elm, right on the driver's outspread leather jacket. A lamp burned in the kitchen where two gardeners were having their supper, and Madame Feit, wearing a white robe, was sitting on the becolumned veranda and dreaming as she gazed at the beautiful moon.

At ten in the evening when all of the sounds had subsided in the village of Kontsovka, situated behind the sovkhoz, the idyllic landscape was filled with the charming, delicate sounds of a flute. It is unthinkable to try to express how this suited the copses and former columns of the Sheremetiev palace. Fragile Liza from *The Queen of Spades* mingled her voice in a duet with the voice of the passionate Polina, and the melody swept up into the moonlit heights like the ghost of an old regime—old, but infinitely lovely, enchanting to the point of tears.

"Waning . . . waning . . . ," the flute sang, warbling and sighing.

The copses fell silent, and Dunia, fatal as a wood nymph, listened, her cheek pressed to the prickly, reddish masculine cheek of the driver.

"He blows good, the son of a bitch," said the driver, encircling Dunia's waist with his manly arm.

Playing the flute was none other than the sovkhoz director himself, Alexander Semionovich Feit, and we must give him his due, he played extremely well. The fact is that at one time the flute had been Alexander Semionovich's specialty. Right up until 1917 he had been a member of

Maestro Petukhov's well-known concert ensemble, whose harmonic sounds rang out every night in the lobby of the cozy Magic Dreams Cinema in the city of Yekaterinoslav. The great year of 1917, which had broken the careers of many people, had turned Alexander Semionovich onto new roads too. He abandoned the Magic Dreams and the dusty star-spangled satin in the lobby and dove into the open sea of war and revolution, exchanging his flute for a deadly Mauser. For a long time he was tossed on the waves, which cast him up now in the Crimea, now in Moscow, now in Turkestan, and even in Vladivostok. It took a revolution to bring Alexander Semionovich fully into his own. The man's true greatness was revealed, and naturally he was not meant to sit around the lobby of the Dreams. Without getting into great detail, let us say that late 1927 and early 1928 found Alexander Semionovich in Turkestan where he had, first, edited a huge newspaper and, next, as the local member of the Supreme Agricultural Commission, covered himself with glory through his remarkable work in irrigating the Turkestan territory. In 1928 Feit arrived in Moscow and got a well-deserved rest. The highest committee of the organization whose card the provincial-looking, old-fashioned man carried in his pocket with honor showed its appreciation and appointed him to a quiet and honorable post. Alas! Alas! To the misfortune of the Republic, the seething brain of Alexander Semionovich had not cooled off; in Moscow Feit ran across Persikov's discovery, and in his room at the Red Paris Hotel on Tverskaia, Alexander Semionovich conceived the idea of using Persikov's ray to replenish the chicken population of the Republic in one month. Feit's plan was heard out by the Commission on Animal Husbandry, they agreed with him, and Feit went with the thick sheet of paper to the eccentric zoologist.

The concert over the glassy waters and copses and park was already drawing to a close when suddenly something happened that interrupted it ahead of time. Namely, the dogs in Kontsovka, who should have been asleep at that hour, suddenly burst out into an incredible fit of barking which gradually turned into a general and very anguished howling. The howling, increasing in volume, flew across the fields, and this howling was suddenly answered by a chattering, million-voiced concert of frogs in all the ponds. All of this was so uncanny that for a minute it even seemed that the mysterious, witching night had grown dim.

Alexander Semionovich laid down his flute and went out onto the veranda, "Manya! Do you hear that? Those damned dogs . . . What do you think is making them so wild?"

"How should I know?" replied Manya, staring at the moon.

"You know what, Manechka, let's go and take a look at the eggs," suggested Alexander Semionovich.

"By God, Alexander Semionovich, you've gone completely nuts with your eggs and chickens. Take a little rest!"

"No, Manechka, let's go."

A bright bulb was burning in the greenhouse. Dunia also came in, face flushed and eyes flashing. Alexander Semionovich gently opened the observation panes, and everyone started peering inside the chambers. On the white asbestos floor the spotted bright-red eggs lay in even rows; the chambers were silent, and the 15,000 watt bulb overhead was hissing quietly.

"Oh, what chicks I'll hatch out of here!" Alexander Semionovich said enthusiastically, looking now into the observation slits in the side walls of the chambers, now into the wide air vents above. "You'll see. What? Won't I?"

"You know, Alexander Semionovich," said Dunia, smiling, "the peasants in Kontsovka are saying you're the Anti-Christ. Them are devilish eggs, they say. It's a sin to hatch eggs by machine. They wanted to murder you."

Alexander Semionovich shuddered and turned to his wife. His face had turned yellow. "Well, how do you like that? Such people! What can you do with people like that? Eh? Manechka, we'll have to arrange a meeting for them. Tomorrow I'll call some Party workers from the district. I'll make a speech myself. In general we'll have to do some work here . . . It's some sort of wild country . . ."

"Dark minds," said the guard, reposing on his coat at the greenhouse

The next day was marked by the strangest and most inexplicable events. In the morning, at the first flash of the sun, the copses, which usually greeted the luminary with a mighty and ceaseless twittering of birds, met it in total silence. This was noticed by absolutely everyone. As though before a storm. But there was not the slightest hint of a storm. Conversations in the sovkhoz assumed a strange, ambiguous tone, very disturbing to Alexander Semyonovich, especially because from the words of the old Kontsovka peasant nicknamed Goat's Goiter, a notorious troublemaker and smart aleck, it got spread around that, supposedly, all the birds had gathered into flocks and cleared out of Sheremetievka at dawn, heading north—which was all simply stupid. Alexander Semionovich was very upset and wasted the whole day telephoning the town of Grachevka. From there he was promised two speakers would be sent to the sovkhoz in a day or two with two topics—the international situation and the question of the "Goodpoul" Trust.

Neither was the evening without its surprises. Whether or not in the morning the woods *had* gone silent, demonstrating with utmost clarity how unpleasant an ominous absence of sound is in a forest, and whether or not all of the sparrows had cleared out of the sovkhoz yards by midday, heading somewhere else—by evening the pond in Sheremetievka *had* gone silent. This was truly astounding, since the famous croaking of the Sheremetievka frogs was quite well known to everyone for forty versts around. But now all the frogs seemed to have died out. Not a single voice came from the pond, and the sedge was soundless. It must be admitted that Alexander

Semionovich completely lost his composure. All of these events began to cause talk, and talk of a very unpleasant kind, i.e., it was behind Alexander Semionovich's back.

"It's really strange," Alexander Semionovich said to his wife at lunch. "I can't understand why those birds had to fly away."

"How should I know'?" answered Manya. "Maybe from your ray!"

"Manya, you're just a plain fool," said Alexander Semionovich, throwing down his spoon. "You're like the peasants. What has the ray got to do with it?"

"Well, I don't know. Leave me alone."

That evening the third surprise happened—the dogs at Kontsovka again started howling—and how they howled! The moonlit fields were filled with ceaseless wailing, and anguished, angry moans.

To some extent Alexander Semionovich felt rewarded by yet another surprise—a pleasant one in the greenhouse. An uninterrupted tapping began to come from the red eggs in the chambers. "Tap . . . tap . . . tap . . . tap" . . . came tapping from first one egg, then another, then yet another.

The tapping in the eggs was a triumphant tapping for Alexander Semionovich. The strange events in the woods and the pond were instantly forgotten. Everyone gathered in the greenhouse: Manya, Dunia, the watchman, and the guard, who left his rifle at the door.

"Well? What do you have to say about that?" Alexander Semionovich asked victoriously. They all pressed their ears curiously to the doors of the first chamber. "It's the chicks—tapping, with their beaks," Alexander Semionovich continued, beaming. "You say I won't hatch any chicks! Not so, my friends." And in an excess of emotion he slapped the guard on the back. "I'll hatch out such chicks you'll ooh and ah. Now I have to look sharp," he added sternly. "As soon as they begin to break through, let me know immediately."

"Right," the watchman, Dunia, and the guard answered in chorus. "Tap . . . tap . . . tap." The tapping started again, now in one, now in another egg in the first chamber. Indeed, the picture of new life being born before your eyes within the thin, translucent casings was so interesting that this whole group sat on for a long while on the empty overturned crates, watching the raspberry-colored eggs ripen in the mysterious flickering light. They broke up to go to bed rather late, after the greenish night had poured light over the sovkhoz and the surrounding countryside. It was an eerie night, one might even say terrifying, perhaps because its utter silence was broken now and then by outbursts of causeless, plaintive, and heart-rending howling from the dogs in Kontsovka. What made those damned dogs go mad was absolutely unknown.

In the morning a new unpleasantness awaited Alexander Semionovich. The guard was extremely embarrassed, put his hand over his heart, swore and made God his witness that he had not fallen asleep, but that he had noticed nothing. "It's a queer thing," the guard insisted. "I'm not to blame, Comrade Feit."

"Thank you, my heartfelt thanks," Alexander Semionovich began the roasting, "What are you thinking about, comrade'? Why were you put here? To watch! So you tell me where they've disappeared to! They've hatched, haven't they? That means they've escaped. That means you left the door open and went away to your room. I want those chicks back here—or else!"

"There's nowhere for me to go. Don't I know my job?" The warrior finally took offense. "You're blaming me for nothing, Comrade Feit!"

"Where've they gone to?"

"Well, how should I know?" the warrior got infuriated at last. "Am I supposed to be guarding them? Why am I posted here? To see that nobody filches the chambers, and I'm doing my job. Here are your chambers. But I'm not obliged by the law to go chasing after your chickens. Who knows what kind of chicks you'll hatch out of there; you probably couldn't catch them on a bicycle, maybe!"

Alexander Semionovich was somewhat taken aback, grumbled a bit more, then fell into a state of astonishment. It was indeed a strange thing. In the first chamber, which had been loaded before the others, the two eggs lying closest to the base of the ray turned out to be broken. The shell was scattered on the asbestos floor under the ray.

"What the devil?" muttered Alexander Semionovich. "The windows are shut—they couldn't have flown out through the roof!" He tilted his head back and looked up where there were several wide holes in the glass transom of the roof.

"What's wrong with you, Alexander Semionovich," Dunia cried extremely surprised. "All we need is flying chicks. They are here somewhere. Cheep . . . cheep . . . cheep," she began to call, looking in the corners of greenhouse where there were dust flowerpots, boards, and other rubbish. But no chicks responded anywhere.

All of the personnel ran about the sovkhoz yard for two hours searching for the nimble chicks, but no one found anything anywhere. The day went by in extreme agitation. The guard over the chambers was increased by one watchman, and he had been given the strictest order to look through the windows of the chambers every fifteen minutes and call Alexander Semionovich the second anything happened. The guard sat by the door, sulking, holding his rifle between his knees. Alexander Semionovich was snowed under with chores, and he did not have his lunch until almost two in the afternoon. After lunch he took an hour-long nap in the cools shade on the former ottoman of Prince Sheremetiev, drank some sovkhoz kvass, dropped by the greenhouse and made sure that everything was in perfect order there now. The old watchman was sprawled on his belly on a piece of burlap and staring, blinking, into the observation window of the first chamber. The guard was sitting alertly without leaving the door.

But there was also something new: the eggs inloaded last of all began to make a gulping and clucking sound, as if someone were sobbing inside.

"Oh, they're ripening, said Alexander Semionovich. "Getting ripe, I see it now. Did you see?" he addressed the watchman . . .

"Yes, it's a marvel," the latter replied in a completely ambiguous tone, shaking his head.

Alexander Semionovich sat by the chambers for a while, but nothing hatched in his presence; he got up, stretched, and declared that he would not leave the estate that day, he would just go down to the pond for a swim, and if anything started to happen, he was to be called immediately. He ran over to the palace to his bedroom, where two narrow spring beds with crumpled linen stood, and on the floor there was a pile of green apples and heaps of millet, prepared for the coming fledglings. He armed himself with a fluffy towel, and after a moment's thought he picked up his flute, intending to play at leisure over the unruffled waters. He walked out of the palace briskly, cut cross the sovkhoz yard, and headed down the small willow avenue toward the pond. He strode along briskly, swinging the towel and carrying the flute under his arm. The sky was pouring down heat through the willows, and his body ached and begged for water. On his right hand began a thicket of burdocks, into which he spat as he passed by; and immediately there was a rustling in the tangle of broad leaves, as though someone had started dragging a log. Feeling an unpleasant fleeting twinge in his heart, Alexander Semionovich turned his head toward the thicket and looked at it with wonder. The pond had reverberated with no sounds of any kind for two days now. The rustling ceased; the unruffled surface of the pond and the gray roof of the bathhouse flashed invitingly beyond the burdocks. Several dragonflies darted past in front of Alexander Semionovich. He was just about to turn to the wooden planks leading down to the water when the rustle in the greenery was repeated, and it was accompanied by a short hiss, as if a locomotive were discharging steam and oil. Alexander Semionovich got on guard and peered into the dense wall of weeds.

"Alexander Semionovich," his wife's voice called at that moment, and her white blouse flashed, disappeared, and flashed again in the raspberry patch. "Wait, I'll go for a swim too."

His wife hastened toward the pond, but Alexander Semionovich made no answer, all attention was riveted on the burdocks. A grayish and olive-colored log began to rise from the thicket, growing before his eyes. The log, it seemed to Alexander Semionovich, was splotched with some sort of moist yellowish spots. It began to stretch, flexing and undulating, and it stretched so high that it was above the scrubby little willow . . . Then the top of the log broke, leaned over somewhat, and over Alexander Semionovich loomed something like a Moscow electric pole in height. But this something was about three times thicker than a pole and far more beautiful, thanks to the scaly tattoo. Still comprehending noting, but his blood running cold, Alexander Semionovich looked at the summit of the terrifying pole, and his heart stopped beating for several seconds. It seemed to him that a frost had suddenly struck the August day, and it turned dim, as though he were looking at the sun through a pair of summer pants.

There turned out to be a head on the upper end of the log. It was flat, pointed, and adorned with a spherical yellow spot on an olive-green background. Lidless, open, icy, narrow eyes sat on the top of the head, and in these eyes gleamed utterly infinite malice. The head made a movement, as though pecking the air, then the pole plunged back into the burdock, and only the eyes remained, staring unblinkingly at Alexander Semionovich. The latter, bathed in sticky sweat, uttered four completely incredulous words, evoked only by terror bordering on insanity. So beautiful were those eyes among the leaves!

"What sort of joke . . ."

Then he recalled that the fakirs . . . yes . . . yes . . . India . . . a woven basket and a picture . . . They charm . . .

The head arched up again, and the body began to emerge too. Alexander Semionovich lifted the flute to his lips, squeaked hoarsely, and gasping for breath every second, he began to play the waltz from *Eugene Onegin*. The eyes in the foliage instantly began to smolder with implacable hate for the opera.

"Have you lost your mind, playing in this heat?" Manya's merry voice resounded, and out of the corner of his eye Alexander Semionovich caught sight of a white spot.

Then a sickening scream pierced through the whole sovkhoz, expanded and flew up into the sky, while the waltz hopped up and down as if it had a broken leg. The head in the thicket shot forward—its eyes left Alexander Semionovich, abandoning his soul to repentance. A snake approximately fifteen yards long and as thick as a man leaped out of the burdock like a steel spring. A cloud of dust whirled from the road and the waltz was over. The snake swept past the sovkhoz manager straight toward the white blouse down the road. Feit saw it all quite distinctly: Manya turned yellow-white, and her long hair stood up like wire a half-yard over her head. Before Feit's eyes the snake opened its maw for a moment, something like a fork flicked out of it, and as she was sinking to the dust its teeth caught Manya by the shoulder and jerked her a yard above the earth. Manya repeated her piercing death scream. The snake coiled itself into a huge screw, its tail churning up a sandstorm, and it began to crush Manya. She did not utter another sound, and Feit just heard her bones snapping. Manya's head swept up high over the earth, tenderly pressed to the snake's cheek. Blood splashed from Manya's mouth, a broken arm flipped out, and little fountains of blood spurted from under her fingernails. Then, dislocating its jaws, the snake opened its maw, slipped its head over Manya's all at once, and began to pull itself over her like a glove over a finger. Such hot breath spread all around the snake that it touched Feit's face, and its tail almost swept him off the road in the acrid dust. It was then that Feit turned gray. First the left, then the right half of his jet-black hair was covered with silver. In mortal nausea he finally tore away from the road, and seeing and hearing nothing, making the countryside resound with wild howls, he took off running . . .

IX. A LIVING MASS

Shchukin, the agent of the State Political Administration (GPU) at the Dugino Station, was a very brave man. He said thoughtfully to his assistant, redheaded Polaitis, "Oh, well, let's go. Eh? Get the motorcycle." Then he was silent for a moment, and added, turning to the man who was sitting on the bench, "Put down the flute."

But the trembling, gray-haired man on the bench in the office of the Dugino GPU did not put his flute down—he began to cry and mumble. Then Shchukin and Polaitis realized that the flute would have to be taken from him. His fingers seemed frozen to it. Shchukin, who possessed enormous strength, almost that of a circus performer, began to unbend one finger after the other, and he unbent them all. Then he put the flute on the table.

This was in the early, sunny morning the day following Manya's death.

"You will come with us," said Shchukin, addressing Alexander Semionovich. "You will show us what happened where." But Feit moved away from him in horror and covered his face with his hands in defense against a terrible vision.

"You must show us," Polaitis added sternly.

"No, let him alone. Don't you see, that man is not himself."

"Send me to Moscow," Alexander Semionovich begged, crying.

"You mean you won't return to the sovkhoz at all?"

But instead of answering, Feit again put out his hands as if to ward them off, and horror poured from his eyes.

"Well, all right," decided Shchukin. "You really aren't up to it . . . I see. The express will be arriving soon, you go ahead and take it."

Then, while the station guard was plying Alexander Semionovich with water, and the latter's teeth chattered on the blue, cracked cup, Shchukin and Polaitis held a conference. Polaitis felt that, generally, none of this had happened, and that Feit was simply mentally ill and had had a terrifying hallucination. But Shchukin tended to think that a boa constrictor had escaped from the circus which was currently performing in the town of Grachevka. Hearing their skeptical whispers, Alexander Semionovich stood up. He came to his senses somewhat, and stretching out his arms like a Biblical prophet, he said, "Listen to me. Listen. Why don't you believe me? It was there. Where do you think my wife is?"

Shchukin became silent and serious and immediately sent some sort of telegram to Grachevka. At Shchukin's order a third agent was to stay with Alexander Semionovich constantly and was to accompany him to Moscow. Meanwhile, Shchukin and Polaitis started getting ready for the expedition. All they had was one electric revolver, but just that was quite good protection. The 1927 fifty-round model, the pride of French technology, for close-range fighting, had a range of only one hundred paces, but it covered a field two meters in diameter and killed everything alive in this field. It was hard to miss. Shchukin strapped on the shiny electric toy, and Polaitis armed himself with an ordinary, twenty-five-round submachine gun, took some cartridge belts, and on a single motorcycle they rolled off toward the sovkhoz through the morning dew and chill. The motorcycle clattered off the twenty versts between the station and the sovkhoz in fifteen minutes (Feit had walked all night, crouching now and then in the roadside shrubbery in spasms of mortal terror) and the sun was really beginning to bake when the sugar-white becolumned palace flashed through the greenery on the rise—at the bottom of which meandered the Top River. Dead silence reigned all around. Near the entrance to the sovkhoz the agents passed a peasant in a cart. He was ambling slowly along, loaded with sacks, and soon he was left behind. The motorcycle swept across the bridge, and Polaitis blew the horn to call someone out. But no one responded anywhere, except for the frenzied Kontsovka dogs in the distance. Slowing down, the motorcycle drove up to the gates with their green lions. The dust-covered agents in yellow leggings jumped off, fastened the machine to the iron railing with a chain lock, and entered the yard. They were struck by the silence.

"Hey, anyone here?" Shchukin called loudly.

No one responded to his bass. The agents walked around the yard, getting more and more astonished. Polaitis frowned. Shchukin began to look more and more serious, knitting his fair eyebrows more and more. They looked through the closed window into the kitchen and saw that no one was there, but that the entire floor was strewn with white fragments of broken china.

"You know, something really has happened here. I see that now. A catastrophe," said Polaitis.

"Hey, anyone in there? Hey!" called Shchukin, but the only response was an echo from under the kitchen eaves. "What the hell," grumbled Shchukin, "it couldn't have gobbled all of them up at once. Unless they ran off. Let's go into the house."

The door to the palace with the columned porch was wide open, and inside it was completely empty. The agents even went up to the mezzanine, knocking on and opening all of the doors, but they found absolutely nothing, and they went back out to the courtyard across the deserted porch.

"Let's walk around back. To the greenhouses," decided Shchukin. "We'll go over the whole place, and we can telephone from there."

The agents walked down the brick path past the flowerbeds to the backyard, crossed it, and saw the gleaming windows of the greenhouse. "Wait just a minute," Shchukin noted in a whisper, unsnapping the pistol from his belt. Polaitis got on his guard and unslung his submachine gun. A strange and very resonant sound came from the greenhouse and from behind it. It was like the hissing of a locomotive somewhere. "Z-zau-zau . . . z-zau-zau . . . ss-s-s-s-s," the greenhouse hissed.

"Careful now," whispered Shchukin, and trying not to make noise with their heels, the agents tiptoed right up to the windows and peered into the greenhouse.

Polaitis instantly jumped back, and his face turned pale. Shchukin opened his mouth and froze with the pistol in his hand. The whole greenhouse was alive like a pile of worms. Coiling and uncoiling in knots, hissing and stretching, slithering and swaying their heads, huge snakes were crawling all over the greenhouse floor. Broken eggshells were strewn across the floor, crunching under their bodies. Overhead burned an electric bulb of huge wattage, illuminating the entire interior of the greenhouse in an eerie cinematic light. On the floor lay three dark boxes that looked like huge cameras; two of them, leaning askew, had gone out, but in the third a small, densely scarlet spot of light was still burning. Snakes of all sizes were crawling along the cables, climbing up the window frames, and twisting out through the openings in the roof. From the electric bulb itself hung a jet-black spotted snake several yards long, its head swaying near the bulb like a pendulum. Some sort of rattling clicked through the hissing sound; the greenhouse diffused a weird and rotten smell, like a pond. And the agents could just barely make out the piles of white eggs scattered in the dusty corners, and the terrible, giant, long-legged bird lying motionless near the chambers, and the corpse of a man in gray near the door, beside a rifle.

"Get back," cried Shchukin, and he started to retreat, pushing Polaitis back with his left hand and raising the pistol with his right. He managed to fire about nine times, his gun hissing and flicking greenish lightning around the greenhouse. The sounds within rose terribly in answer to Shchukin's fire; the whole greenhouse became a mass of frenzied movement, and flat heads darted through every aperture. Thunderclaps immediately began to crash over the whole sovkhoz, flashes playing on the walls. "Chakhchakh-chakh-takh," Polaitis fired, backing away. A strange quadruped was heard behind him, and Polaitis suddenly gave a terrified scream and tumbled backwards. A creature with splayed paws, a brownish-green color, a massive pointed snout, and a ridged tail resembling a lizard of terrifying dimensions, had slithered around the corner of the barn, and viciously biting through Polaitis' foot, it threw him to the ground.

"Help!" cried Polaitis, and immediately his left hand was crunched in the maw. Vainly attempting to raise his right hand, he dragged his gun along the ground. Shchukin whirled around and started dashing from side to side. He managed to fire once, but aimed wide of the mark, because he was afraid of killing his comrade. The second time he fired in the direction of the greenhouse, because a huge olive-colored snake head had appeared there among the small ones, and its body sprang straight in his direction. The shot killed the gigantic snake, and again, jumping and circling around Polaitis, already half-dead in the crocodile's maw, Shchukin was trying to aim so as to kill the terrible reptile without hitting the agent. Finally he succeeded. The electric pistol fired twice, throwing a greenish light on everything around, and the crocodile leaped, stretched out, stiffened, and released Polaitis. Blood was flowing from his sleeve, flowing from his mouth, and leaning on his sound right arm, he dragged his broken left leg along. His eyes were going dim. "Run . . . Shchukin," he murmured, sobbing.

Shchukin fired several times in the direction of the greenhouse, and several of its windows flew out. But a huge spring, olive-colored and sinuous, sprang from the basement window behind him, slithered across the yard, filling it with its enormous body, and in an instant coiled around Shchukin's legs. He was knocked to the ground, and the shiny pistol bounced to one side. Shchukin cried out mightily, then gasped for air, and then the rings covered him completely except for his head. A coil passed over his head once, tearing off his scalp, and his head cracked. No more shots were heard in the sovkhoz. Everything was drowned out by an overlying hissing sound. And in reply to it, the wind brought in the distant howling from Kontsovka, but now it was no longer possible to tell what kind of howling it was— canine or human.

X. CATASTROPHE

Bulbs were burning brightly in the office of *Izvestia*, and the fat editor at the lead table was making up the second page, using dispatch-telegrams "Around the Union of Republics." One galley caught his eye; he examined it through his pince-nez and burst out laughing. He called the proofreaders from the proof room and the makeup man and he showed them all the galley. On the narrow strip of paper was printed:

> Grachevka, Smolensk province.
> A hen which is as large as a
> horse and kicks like a stallion
> has been seen in the district.
> Instead of a tail, it has a
> bourgeois lady's feathers.

The compositors roared with laughter.

"In my day," said the editor, guffawing expansively, "when I was working for Vania Sytin on *Russkoe Slovo*," some of the men would get so smashed they'd see elephants. That's the truth. But now, it seems, they're seeing ostriches."

The proofreaders roared.

"That's probably right, it's an ostrich," said the makeup man. "Should we use it, Ivan Vonifatievich?"

"Are you crazy?" answered the editor. "I'm amazed that the secretary let it past—it's simply a drunken telegram."

"It must have been quite a bender," the compositors agreed, and the makeup man removed the communication about the ostrich from the table.

Therefore *Izvestia* came out the next day containing, as usual, a mass of interesting material, but not a hint of the Grachevka ostrich.

Assistant Professor Ivanov, who read *Izvestia* quite punctiliously, folded the paper in his office, yawned, commented, "Nothing interesting," and started putting his white smock on. A bit later the burners went on in his office and the frogs began to croak. But Professor Persikov's office was in confusion. The frightened Pankrat was standing at attention.

"I understand . . . Yes, sir," he said.

Persikov handed him an envelope sealed with wax and said, "You go directly to the Department of Animal Husbandry to that director Avis, and you tell him right out that he is a swine. Tell him that I, Professor Persikov, said so. And give him the envelope."

A fine thing, thought the pale Pankrat, and he took off with the envelope.

Persikov was raging.

"The devil only knows what's going on," he whimpered, pacing the office and rubbing his gloved hands. "It's unprecedented mockery of me and of zoology. They've been bringing piles of these damned chicken eggs, but I haven't been able to get anything essential for two months. As if it were so far to America! Eternal confusion, eternal outrage!" He began to count on his fingers: "Let's say, ten days at most to locate them . . . very well, fifteen . . . even twenty . . . then two days for air freight across the ocean, a day from London to Berlin . . . From Berlin to us . . . six hours. It's some kind of outrageous bungling!"

He attacked the telephone furiously and started to call someone. In his office everything was ready for some mysterious and highly dangerous experiments; on the table lay strips of cut paper prepared for sealing the doors, diving helmets with air hoses, and several cylinders, shiny as quicksilver, labeled: "Goodchem Trust" and "Do Not Touch." And with drawings of a skull and crossbones.

It took at least three hours for the professor to calm down and get to some minor tasks. That is what he did. He worked at the institute until eleven in the evening, and therefore he did not know anything about what was happening outside the cream-colored walls. Neither the absurd rumor that had spread through Moscow about some strange snakes nor the strange dispatch in the evening papers, shouted by newsboys, had reached him, because Assistant Professor Ivanov was at the Art Theater watching *Tsar Fyodor Ioannovich*, and therefore, there was no one to inform the professor of the news.

Around midnight Persikov came home to Prechistenka and went to bed. Before going to sleep he read in bed an English article in the magazine *News of Zoology* which he received from London. He slept and all of Moscow, which seethes until late at night, slept—and only the huge gray building in a courtyard off Tverskaia Boulevard did not sleep. The whole building was shaken by the terrific roaring and humming of *Izvestia*'s printing presses. The editor's office was in a state of incredible pandemonium. The editor, quite furious, red eyed, rushed about not knowing what to do and sending everyone to the devil's mother. The makeup man was following him around, breathing wine fumes, and saying, "Oh, well, it's not so bad, Ivan Vonifatievich, let's publish a special supplement tomorrow. We can't pull the whole issue out of the presses, you know!"

The compositors did not go home, but walked around in bunches, gathered in groups and read the telegrams that were now coming in every fifteen minutes all night long, each more peculiar and terrifying than the last. Alfred Bronsky's peaked hat flicked about in the blinding pink light flooding the press room, and the mechanical fat man screaked and limped, appearing here, there, and everywhere. The entrance doors slammed incessantly, and reporters kept appearing all night long. All twelve telephones in the press room rang constantly, and the switchboard almost automatically answered every mysterious call with "busy, busy," and the signal horns sang and sang in front of the sleepless young ladies at the switchboard.

The compositors clustered around the mechanical fat man, and the sea captain was saying to them, "They'll have to send in airplanes with gas."

"No other way," answered the compositors. "God knows what's going on out there."

Then terrible Oedipal oaths shook the air, and someone's squeaky voice screamed, "That Persikov should be shot!"

"What has Persikov to do with it?" someone answered in the crowd. "That son of a bitch on the sovkhoz—he's the one should be shot!"

"They should have posted a guard!" someone exclaimed.

"But maybe it's not the eggs at all!"

The whole building shook and hummed from the rolling presses, and the impression was created that the unprepossessing gray edifice was blazing with an electric fire.

The new day did not stop it. On the contrary, it only intensified it, even though the electricity went out. Motorcycles rolled into the asphalt yard one after the other, alternating with cars. All Moscow had awakened, and the white sheets of newspaper spread over it like birds. The sheets rustled in everyone's hands, and by eleven in the morning the newsboys had run out of papers, in spite of the fact that *Izvestia* was coming out in editions of one and a half million that month. Professor Persikov left Prechistenka by bus and arrived at the institute. There something new awaited him. In the vestibule stood wooden boxes, three in number, neatly bound with metal straps and plastered with foreign labels in German—and the labels were dominated by a single Russian inscription in chalk: "Careful—Eggs."

The professor was overwhelmed with joy. "At last!" he exclaimed. "Pankrat, break open the crates immediately and carefully, so none are crushed. They go into my office."

Pankrat immediately carried out the order, and within fifteen minutes the professor's voice began to rage in his office, which was strewn with sawdust and scraps of paper.

"What are they up to? Making fun of me, or what?" the professor howled, shaking his fists and turning the eggs in his hands. "He's some kind of animal, not an Avis. I won't allow him to laugh at me. What is this, Pankrat?"

"Eggs, sir," Pankrat answered dolefully.

"Chicken eggs, you understand, chicken eggs, the devil take them! What to hell do I need them for? Let them send them to that scalawag on his sovkhoz!"

Persikov rushed to the telephone in the corner, but he did not have time to call.

"Vladimir Ipatich! Vladimir Ipatich!" Ivanov's voice thundered from the institute corridor.

Persikov tore himself away from the phone, and Pankrat dashed aside, making way for the assistant professor. Contrary to his gentlemanly custom, the latter ran into the room without removing his gray hat, which was sitting on the back of his head. He had a newspaper in his hands.

"Do you know what's happened, Vladimir Ipatich?" he cried, waving in front of Persikov's face a sheet of paper headed *Special Supplement* and graced in the center with a brightly colored picture.

"No, but listen to what they've done!" Persikov shouted in reply, without listening. "They've decided to surprise me with chicken eggs. This Avis is an utter idiot, just look!"

Ivanov was completely dumbfounded. He stared at the opened crates in horror, then at the newspaper, and his eyes almost jumped out of his head. "So that's it! he muttered, gasping, "Now I see . . . No, Vladimir Ipatich, just take a look." He unfolded the newspaper in a flash and pointed to the colored picture with trembling fingers. It showed an olive-colored, yellow-spotted snake, coiling like a terrifying fire hose against a strange green background. It had been taken from above, from a light plane which had cautiously dived over the snake. "What would you say that is, Vladimir Ipatich?"

Persikov pushed his spectacles up onto his forehead, then slipped them over his eyes, studied the picture, and said with extreme astonishment, "What the devil! It's . . . why, it's an anaconda, a water boa!"

Ivanov threw down his hat, sat down heavily on a chair, and said, punctuating every word with a bang of his fist on the table, "Vladimir Ipatich, this anaconda is from the Smolensk province. It's something monstrous! Do you understand, that good-for-nothing has hatched snakes instead of chickens, and, do you understand, they have had progeny at the same phenomenal rate as the frogs!"

"What?" Persikov screamed, and his face turned purple. "You're joking, Peter Stepanovich . . . Where from?"

Ivanov was speechless for a moment, then he recovered his voice, and jabbing his finger at the open crate, where the tips of the white eggs gleamed in the yellow sawdust, he said, "That's where from."

"Wha-a-t!" howled Persikov, beginning to understand.

Ivanov shook both of his clenched fists quite confidently and exclaimed, "You can be sure. They sent your order for snake and ostrich eggs to the sovkhoz and the chicken eggs to you by mistake."

"My God . . . my God," Persikov repeated, and turning green in the face, he began to sink onto the revolving stool.

Pankrat stood utterly dumbfounded at the door, turned pale, and was speechless.

Ivanov jumped up, grabbed the paper, and underscoring a line with a sharp nail, he shouted into the professor's ears, "Well, they're going to have fun now. Vladimir Ipatich, you look." And he bellowed out loud, reading the first passage that caught his eye on the crumpled page, "The snakes are moving in hordes toward Mozhaisk . . . laying incredible quantities of eggs. Eggs have been seen in the Dukhovsk district . . . Crocodiles and ostriches have appeared. Special troop units . . . and detachments of the GPV halted the panic in Viazma after setting fire to the woods outside the town to stop the onslaught of the reptiles . . ."

Persikov, turning all colors, bluish-white, with insane eyes, rose from his stool and began to scream, gasping for breath, "Anaconda . . . anaconda . . . water boa! My God!" Neither Ivanov nor Pankrat had ever seen him in such a state.

The professor tore off his tie in one swoop, ripped the buttons from his shirt, turned a terrible livid purple like a man having a stroke, and staggering, with utterly glazed, glassy eyes, he dashed out somewhere. His shouts resounded under the stone archways of the institute. "Anaconda . . . anaconda," thundered the echo.

"Catch the professor!" Ivanov shrieked to Pankrat, who was dancing up and down in place with terror. "Get him some water! He's having a stroke!"

XI. BATTLE AND DEATH

The frenzied electric night was ablaze in Moscow. Every light was on, and there was not a place in any apartment where there were no lamps on with their shades removed. Not a single person slept in a single apartment anywhere in Moscow, which had a population of four million, except the youngest children. In every apartment people ate and drank whatever was at hand; in every apartment people were crying out; and every minute distorted faces looked out the windows from all floors, gazing up at the sky which was crisscrossed from all directions with search lights. Every now and then white lights flared up in the sky, casting pale, melting cones over Moscow, and they would fade and vanish. The sky hummed steadily with the drone of low-flying planes. It was especially terrible on Tverskaia-Yamskaia Street. Every ten minutes trains arrived at the Alexander Station, made up helter-skelter of freight and passenger cars of every class and even of tank cars, all covered with fear-crazed people who then rushed down Tverskaia-Yamskaia in a dense mass, riding buses, riding on the roofs of trolleys, crushing one another, and falling under the wheels. At the station, rattling, disquieting bursts of gunfire banged out every now and then over the heads of the crowd: the troops were trying to stop the panic of the demented running along the railway tracks from the Smolensk province to Moscow. Now and then the station windows flew out with a crazy light gulping sound, and all the locomotives were howling. All of the streets were strewn with discarded and trampled placards, and the same placards—under fiery red reflectors—stared down from the walls. All of them were already known to everyone, so nobody read them. They proclaimed martial law in Moscow. They threatened penalties for panic and reported that unit after unit of the Red army, armed with gas, was departing for Smolensk province. But the placards could not stop the howling night. In their apartments people were dropping and breaking dishes and flowerpots; they were running around, knocking against corners; they were packing and unpacking bundles and valises in the vain hope of making their way to Kalancha Square, to the Yaroslavl or Nikolaev stations. Alas, all stations leading to the north and east had been cordoned off by the heaviest line of infantry, and huge trucks with rocking and clanging chains, loaded to the top with crates on which sat soldiers in peaked helmets, with bayonets bristling in all directions, were carrying off the gold reserves from the cellars of the People's Commissariat of Finance and huge boxes marked "Handle with Care. Tretiakov Art Gallery." Automobiles were roaring and running all over Moscow.

Far on the horizon the sky trembled with the reflection of fires, and the thick August blackness was shaken by the continuous booming of howitzers.

Toward morning a serpent of cavalry passed through utterly sleepless Moscow, which had not put out a single light. Its thousands of hooves clattered on the pavement as it moved up Tverskaia, sweeping everything out of its path, squeezing everything else into doorways and show windows, breaking out the windows as they did so. The ends of its scarlet cowls dangled on the gray backs, and the tips of its lances pierced the sky. The milling, screaming crowd seemed to recover immediately at the sight of the serried ranks pushing forward, splitting apart the seething ocean of madness. People in the crowds on the sidewalks began to roar encouragingly:

"Long live the cavalry!" cried frenzied female voices.

"Long live!" echoed the men.

"They'll crush me! They are crushing me! . . ." someone howled somewhere.

"Help!" was shouted from the sidewalks.

Packs of cigarettes, silver coins, and watches began to fly into the ranks from the sidewalks; some women hopped down onto the pavement and risking their bones they trudged along beside the mounted columns, clutching at the stirrups and kissing them. Occasionally the voices of platoon leaders rose over the continuous clatter of hooves: "Shorten up on the reins!"

Somewhere someone began a gay and rollicking song, and the faces under the dashing scarlet caps swayed over the horses in the flickering light of neon signs. Now and then, interrupting the columns of horsemen with their uncovered faces, came strange mounted figures in strange hooded helmets, with hoses flung over their shoulders and cylinders fastened to straps across their backs. Behind them crept huge tank trucks with the longest sleeves and hoses, like fire engines, and heavy, pavement-crushing caterpillar tanks, hermetically sealed and their narrow firing slits gleaming. Also interrupting the mounted columns were cars which rolled along, solidly encased in gray armor, with the same kind of tubes protruding and with white skulls painted on their sides, inscribed: "Gas" and "Goodchem."

"Save us, brother!" the people cried from the sidewalks.

"Beat the snakes! . . . Save Moscow!"

"The mothers . . . The mothers . . . ," curses rippled through the ranks. Cigarette packs leaped through the illuminated night air, and white teeth grinned at the demented people from atop the horses. A hollow, heart-rending song began to spread through the ranks:

> . . . no ace, no queen, no jack,
> We'll beat the reptiles; without doubt,
> Four cards are plenty for this pack . . .

Rolling peals of "hurrah" rose up over this whole mass, because the rumor had spread that at the head of all the columns, on a horse, rode the aging, graying commander of the huge cavalry who had become legendary ten years before. The crowd howled and the roars of "hurrah!" "hurrah!" swept up into the sky, somewhat calming frantic hearts.

The institute was sparsely lit. Events reached it only as vague, fragmentary, distant echoes. Once a volley of shots burst fanlike under the fiery clock near the Manège: soldiers were shooting on the spot some looters who had tried to rob an apartment on Volkhonka. There was little automobile traffic on this street—it was all massing toward the railway stations. In the professor's study, where a single lamp burned dimly, casting light on the table, Persikov sat with his head in his hands, silent. Layers of smoke were floating around him. The ray in the box had gone dark. The frogs in the terraria were silent because they were already asleep. The professor was not reading or working. At one side, on a narrow strip of paper under his left elbow, lay the evening edition of news dispatches reporting that all of Smolensk was in flames, and that the artillery was shelling the Mozhaisk forest all over, sector by sector, to destroy the heaps of crocodile eggs piled in all the damp ravines. It was reported that a squadron of planes had been extremely successful near Viazma, flooding almost the entire district with gas, but that the number of human victims in the area was incalculable, because instead of abandoning the district following the rules for orderly evacuation, the people had panicked and rushed around in divided groups in all directions, at their own risk and terror. It was reported that a separate Caucasus cavalry division near Mozhaisk had won a brilliant victory over flocks of ostriches, hacking them all to pieces and destroying huge caches of ostrich eggs. In doing this the division itself had sustained insignificant losses. It was reported by the government that in case it proved impossible to halt the reptiles within two hundred versts of the capital, the latter would be evacuated in complete order. Workers and employees should maintain complete calm. The government would take the sternest measures to prevent a repetition of the Smolensk events. There, thanks to panic caused by the unexpected attack of rattlesnakes—several thousand of which appeared —the people had started hopeless, wholesale exit, leaving burning stoves— and the city began to catch fire everywhere. It was reported that Moscow had enough provisions to last for at least six months and that the Council of the Commander-in-Chief was undertaking prompt measures to fortify all apartments in order to conduct the battle with the snakes in the very streets of the capital in the event that the Red armies and air forces failed to halt the advance of the reptiles.

The professor read none of this; he stared ahead, glassy-eyed, and smoked. Besides him, there were only two other people at the institute— Pankrat and the housekeeper, Maria Stepanovna, who every now and then would break into tears. The old woman had not slept for three nights, spending them in the professor's office, where he adamantly refused to leave his only remaining, now extinguished chamber. Now Maria Stepanovna was huddled on the oilcloth couch in a shadow in the corner, and she was keeping silent in sorrowful meditation, watching the kettle with some tea for the professor coming to a boil on the tripod over the gas burner. The institute was silent, and everything happened abruptly.

From the sidewalk there was suddenly such an outburst of rancorous shouts that Maria Stepanovna started and cried out. Flashlights flickered in the street, and Pankrat's voice was heard in the vestibule. The professor was hardly aware of this noise. He raised his head for a second and muttered "Ooh . . . they're going crazy . . . What can I do now'?" And he again fell into his stupor. But it was rudely broken. The iron doors of the institute on Herzen Street began a terrible clangor, and all of the walls began to shake. Then the solid mirrored wall in the adjoining office crashed. The glass in the professor's office began to tinkle and fly to pieces, and a gray brick bounced through the window smashing the glass table. The frogs scuttled around in their terraria and set up a cry. Maria Stepanovna ran around shrieking, rushed to the professor, seized him by the hands, and shouted, "Run, Vladimir Ipatich, run!"

The professor rose from his revolving stool, straightened himself up, and curled his index finger into a little hook, his eyes recovering for an instant the old sharp glitter reminiscent of the old, inspired Persikov. "I'm not going anywhere," he pronounced. "This is simply stupidity. They are rushing around like lunatics . . . And if all Moscow has gone insane, then where can I go? And please stop screaming. What do I have to do with this. Pankrat!" he called, pressing a button.

He probably wanted Pankrat to stop all the commotion, something which generally he had never liked. But Pankrat could no longer do anything. The banging had ended with the institute doors flying open and a distant popping of shots; and then the whole stone institute shook with the thunder of running feet, shouts, and crashing windows. Maria Stepanovna clutched at Persikov's sleeve and began to drag him back; but he pushed her away, drew himself up to his full height, and just as he was, in his white lab coat, he walked out into the corridor. "Well?" he asked. The doors swung open, and the first thing to appear in them was the back of a military uniform with a red chevron and a star on the left sleeve. He was retreating from the door, through which a furious mob was surging forward, and he was firing his revolver. Then he started to run past Persikov, shouting to him, "Save yourself, professor! I can't do anything else!"

His words were answered by a shriek from Maria Stepanovna. The officer shot past Persikov, who was standing there like a white statue, and vanished in the darkness of the winding corridors at the opposite end.

People flew through the door, howling.

"Beat him! kill him!"

"Public enemy!"

"You let the snakes loose!"

Distorted faces and ripped clothing jumped through the corridors, and someone fired a shot. Sticks flashed. Persikov stepped back a little, barring the door to his office, where Maria Stepanovna was kneeling on the floor in terror; and he spread out his arms, as one crucified . . . he did not want to let the mob in, and he yelled irascibly, "This is utter lunacy . . . You are absolute wild animals. What do you want?" And he bellowed, "Get out of here!" and completed his speech with a shrill, familiar cry, "Pankrat, throw them out!"

But Pankrat could no longer throw anyone out. Pankrat, trampled and torn, his skull crushed, lay motionless in the vestibule, while more and more crowds tore past him, paying no attention to the fire of the police in the street.

A short man with crooked, apelike legs, wearing a torn jacket and a torn shirt twisted to one side, dashed out ahead of the others, leaped toward Persikov, and with a terrible blow from his stick he split open Persikov's skull. Persikov tottered and began to collapse sideways. His last words were, "Pankrat . . . Pankrat . . ."

Maria Stepanovna, who was guilty of nothing, was killed and torn to pieces in the office; the chamber in which the ray had gone out was smashed to bits, the terraria were smashed to bits, and the crazed frogs were flailed with sticks and trampled underfoot. The glass tables were dashed to pieces, the reflectors were dashed to pieces, and an hour later the institute was a mass of flames. Corpses were strewn around, cordoned off by a line of troops armed with electric pistols; and fire engines, pumping water from the hydrants, were pouring streams through all the windows, from which long, roaring tongues of flame were bursting.

XII. A Frosty *Deus ex Machina*

On the night of August 19 to 20 an unprecedented frost fell on the country, unlike anything any of its oldest inhabitants had ever seen. It came and lasted two days and two nights, bringing the thermometer down to eleven degrees below zero. Frenzied Moscow locked all doors, all windows. Only toward the end of the third day did the populace realize that the frost had saved the capital, and the boundless expanses which it governed, and on which the terrible catastrophe of 1928 had fallen. The cavalry at Mozhaisk had lost three-quarters of its complement and was near prostration, and the gas squadrons had not been able to stop the onslaught of the vile reptiles, which were moving toward Moscow in a semicircle from the West, Southwest, and South.

The frost killed them. Two days and two nights at eleven below zero had proved too much for the abominable herds, and when the frost lifted after the 20th of August, leaving nothing but dampness and wetness, leaving the air dank, leaving all the greenery blasted by the unexpected cold, there was no longer anything left to fight. The calamity was over. Woods, fields, and infinite bogs were still piled high with multicolored eggs, often covered with the strange, unearthly, unique pattern that Feit—who had vanished without a trace—had once mistaken for mud, but now these eggs were quite harmless. They were dead, the embryos within lifeless.

For a long time the infinite expanses of land were still putrescent with numberless corpses of crocodiles and snakes which had been called to life by the mysterious ray born under the eyes of genius on Herzen Street—but they were no longer dangerous; the fragile creatures of the putrescent, hot, tropical bogs had perished in two days, leaving a terrible stench, disintegration, and decay throughout the territory of three provinces.

There were long epidemics; there were widespread diseases for a long time, caused by the corpses of snakes and men; and for a long time the army combed the land, no longer equipped with gases, but with sapper gear, kerosene tanks and hoses, clearing the earth. It cleared the earth, and everything was over toward the spring of 1929.

And in the spring of 1929 Moscow again began to dance, glitter, and flash lights; and again, as before, the mechanical carriages rolled through the traffic, and the lunar sickle hung as if on a fine thread over the helmet of the Cathedral of Christ; and on the site of the two-storey institute that had burned down in August 1928, a new zoological palace rose, and Assistant Professor Ivanov directed it, but Persikov was no longer there. Never again did the persuasively hooked index finger rise before anyone's eyes, and never again was the squeaking, croaking voice heard by anyone.

The ray and the catastrophe of 1928 were long talked and written about by the whole world, but then the name of Professor Vladimir Ipatievich Persikov was shrouded in mist and sank into darkness, as did the red ray he had discovered on that April night. The ray itself was never again captured, although the elegant gentleman and now full professor, Peter Stepanovich Ivanov, had occasionally made attempts. The raging mob had smashed the first chamber on the night of Persikov's murder. Three chambers were burned up in the Nikolsky sovkhoz, the "Red Ray," during the first battle of an air squadron with the reptiles, and no one succeeded in reconstructing them. No matter how simple the combination of lenses and mirrored clusters of light had been, the combination was never achieved again, in spite of Ivanov's efforts. Evidently this required something special, besides knowledge, something which was possessed by only one man in the world—the late Professor Vladimir Ipatievich Persikov.

(Moscow, October 1924)
Translated by Carl R. Proffer; ed. by A.L. and M.K.

From The Master and Margarita

AZAZELLO'S CRÈME (From Chapter 20)

The moon hung, full, in the clear evening sky, visible through the branches of a maple. Lime-trees and acacias patterned the ground in the garden with intricate blotches. The streetlamp's three-sided aperture, open but masked by a blind, gave off a maniacal electric glow. In Margarita Nikolaevna's boudoir all the lights were on and they illuminated the complete disorder of the room. <. . . >

Margarita Nikolaevna sat before her vanity with nothing more than a bathrobe thrown over her naked body, wearing black suede slippers. The gold bracelet-watch lay before her, together with the little box she had received from Azazello, and Margarita did not shift her gaze from the face.

At times it seemed to her that the watch must be broken and the hands not in motion. But they were moving, if very slowly, as if they were sticking, and at long last the big hand reached twenty-nine minutes into the tenth hour. Margarita's heart was pounding terribly, so that she wasn't even able to reach for the box. Getting hold of herself, Margarita opened it and saw inside a greasy yellowish cream. It seemed to smell of swamp mud. With the tip of her finger Margarita smeared a small dollop of the cream on her palm, whereupon the smell of the swamp and the forest grew stronger, and then with her palm began to massage the cream into her fore-head and cheeks.

The cream was easy to work in, and, it seemed to Margarita was already evaporating. After several applications Margarita glanced in the mirror and dropped the box straight onto the watch crystal, so it was instantly covered with cracks. Margarita closed her eyes, glanced into the mirror a second time, and burst into wild laughter.

Her brows, which had been tweezed to a thread, had thickened and stretched in even black arches over eyes that had suddenly turned green. The delicate vertical wrinkle across the bridge of her nose, which had appeared in October when the Master disappeared, had faded without a trace. Gone as well were the yellowish shadows at the her temples and the two barely perceptible webs at the outer corners of her eyes. The skin on her cheeks was infused with an even rosy tint, her brow had become white and smooth, and her salon coiffure had come undone.

From the mirror the thirty-year-old Margarita was regarded by a woman of twenty, with dark naturally curly hair, who was shaking with laughter.

When she had her laugh Margarita took one bound that left the robe behind, dipped deep into light greasy cream and with strong strokes began to rub it over her body. Her body immediately became rose pink and warm. Then in an instant, as if someone had withdrawn a needle from her brain, the pain in her temple, which had ached all evening after her encounter in the Alexander Gardens, went away. The muscles in her arms and legs grew stronger, and then Margarita's body lost all its weight.

She leapt upwards and hovered in the air over the carpet, then she was slowly pulled downwards and alit.

"Hurrah for the crème, the crème!"—Margarita cried, flinging herself into an armchair.

The anointing had changed not only her external appearance. Within her now everywhere, in each tiny part, joy was seething, joy which she perceived as tiny bubbles prickling over her entire body. Margarita felt herself to be free, free of everything. Moreover she understood with all possible clarity that precisely what her morning presentiment had spoken of *had* happened, and that she was leaving the apartment and her past life forever. < . . . >

Her mind completely relieved, Margarita flew back to the bedroom and on her heels came Natasha with her arms full of things. And at once all these things, the wooden hangers with their dresses, the lace scarves, the dark-blue silk sandals with their straps and laces—all this fell to the floor, and Natasha threw up her freed hands.

"Well? How do I look?" Margarita Nikolaevna shrilled loudly.

"How can it be?" whispered Natasha, stumbling back. "How are you doing that, Margarita Nikolaevna?"

"It's the crème! Yes, the crème, the crème!" Margarita replied, pointing to the shiny gold box and twirling before the mirror.

Natasha, forgetting the crumpled dress on the floor, ran to the vanity and with greedy sparkling eyes stared at the remains of the ointment. Her lips whispered something. She turned back to Margarita and murmured, with a sort of reverence:

"And your skin? Your skin! Margarita Nikolaevna, your skin is glowing!" But then she remembered herself, ran to the dress, picked it up and began to shake it out.

"Let it be! Stop it!"—Margarita cried—"The hell with it. Throw it all out. Better yet, keep it to remember me by. I'm telling you, to remember me by. Take everything in the room!"

As if dazed, a motionless Natasha gazed at Margarita, then threw her arms around her, kissing her and crying:

"Like satin! It glows! Satin! And your eyebrows!"

Take all these rags, take the perfume, and haul it off to your trunk, hide it," cried Margarita, "but don't take the jewelry or they'll say you stole it!"

Whatever came to hand Natasha gathered up into a bundle, dresses, shoes, stockings and lingerie, and ran out of the bedroom.

Through the open window at that moment, from somewhere across the way a thunderous virtuoso waltz rang out, and one could hear the puffing of a car approaching the gates. < . . . > The car roared past. The gate banged open and footsteps were heard on the stones of the walkway.

"That's Nikolai Ivanovich, I know his walk," thought Margarita. "I must do something amusing and interesting as a farewell." < . . . >

Just then behind Margarita in the bedroom the phone rang. Margarita tore herself away from the windowsill and, forgetting Nikolai Ivanovich, seized the receiver.

"Azazello here," came through the receiver.

"Dear, dear Azazello!" cried Margarita.

"It's time. Fly away," said Azazello, and by his tone it was clear that he was pleased by Margarita's sincere, joyful outburst. "When you fly over the gates shout out—'Invisible.' First fly around a little above the city, to get used to it, then go south, away from town, and head straight for the river. They're waiting for you!"

Margarita hung up and just then, in the next room something began to thump woodenly and beat against the door. Margarita threw it open and a broom, bristles up, dancing, flew into the room. Its handle kept up a tattoo on the floorboards, it kicked and strained towards the window. Margarita shrieked in ecstasy and leapt astride it. Only then did the rider consider that in all the tumult she had forgotten to get dressed. She galloped over to the bed and seized the first thing that came to hand, some sort of light blue chemise. Waving it like a battle-flag she flew through the window. And above the garden the waltz rang out more strongly.

Margarita slid down from the windowsill and saw Nikolai Ivanovich sitting on the garden bench. He gaze was fixed on her as he listened in complete stupefaction to the cries and the din coming from the bedroom of the upstairs tenants.

"Farewell, Nikolai Ivanovich!" shouted Margarita, doing a little dance in front of him.

He moaned and moved closer, groping his way down the bench and letting his briefcase fall to the ground.

"Farewell forever! I'm flying away!" cried Margarita, drowning out the waltz. Whereupon she understood that the blouse she was holding was completely useless to her, and, laughing maliciously, she dropped it over Nikolai Ivanovich's head. Blinded, Nikolai Ivanovich tumbled from the bench onto the brick walkway.

Margarita turned to look once more at the apartment where she had been unhappy for so long, and in the glowing window she saw the face of Natasha, distorted by amazement.

"Good-bye, Natasha!" cried Margarita and shook the broom. "Invisible, Invisible!" still louder she shouted and through the branches of the maple that lashed at her face, over the gates, she flew out above the street. And in her wake flew a waltz gone mad.

The Flight (From Chapter 21)

Invisible and free! Invisible and free!—Flying the length of her own street brought Margarita to a second street, which intersected the first at a right angle. This patched, darned, crooked and long street with its fuel shop with the crooked door, where they sold kerosene by the pitcher and insecticide by the bottle, she flew over in an instant and immediately grasped that, completely free and invisible as she was, all the same she must be a bit more circumspect in her delight. It was only by some sort of miracle that she was able to brake and did not dash herself to pieces on the old crooked lamp post at the corner. Swerving away from it, Margarita grasped the broom more firmly and flew on at a slower speed, watching out for electrical wires and for signs hung out over the sidewalk. < . . . >

The street beneath her rolled and fell away. In its place beneath Margarita's feet was only an assemblage of roofs, dissected at the corners by glowing pathways. All of this unexpectedly veered to one side, and the chain of lights blurred and brightened.

Margarita made another bound, and then the whole roof assemblage fell through the earth and in its place there appeared below her a lake of trembling electric lights, and that lake made an abrupt vertical ascent and reappeared above her head, while the moon shone below her feet. Understanding that she had turned upside down, Margarita righted herself and glancing back, saw that there was no more lake, just a rosy glow on the horizon. That too disappeared in a second and Margarita saw she was alone with the moon sailing above her and to her left. Her hair had long since arranged itself in a shock, and the moonlight, whistling by, bathed her body. Judging by the fact that beneath her the two rows of scattered lights had merged into two uninterrupted lines, and by the speed of their retreat, Margarita guessed that she was flying at a monstrous speed, and was surprised she wasn't out of breath.

After another few seconds, far below, in the earthy blackness, a new dawn of electric light flared up and streamed past the flyer's feet, but it immediately turned into a ribbon of light and was swallowed up. Another few seconds, the same again.

"Cities! It's cities!" cried Margarita.

After this, two or three times she saw beneath her dimly sparkling sabres nestled in their black cases, and she understood that these were rivers.

Looking up and to the left, the flyer saw that the moon above her was streaking madly back in the direction of Moscow and at the same time in a strange way was standing still, so that clearly visible on its face was some sort of enigmatic, dark marking, a dragon, or a winged horse, its sharp muzzle turned towards the abandoned city.

At that point Margarita was seized by the idea that, really, it was useless for her to fly her broom at such a frenzied speed, that she was depriving herself of the opportunity to look at anything properly, to truly drink in the flight. Something told her that wherever she was going they would wait for her, and that she had no reason to bore herself flying at such an insane speed and altitude. Margarita pointed the broom's bristles forward, so that the handle rose and, sharply decreasing its speed, headed towards the ground. And this swoop downwards, as if on a transparent sled, gave her the very greatest pleasure. The surface grew nearer, and from what had been formless dark lees now materialized the mysteries and delights of the earth on a moonlit night. The earth rose to meet her, and Margarita was already enveloped by the scent of the greening forest. Margarita flew just above the mists rising from a dewy meadow, then over a pond. Beneath her there sang a chorus of frogs and somewhere in the distance a train whistle sounded, which for some reason troubled her heart. In a moment Margarita caught sight of it. It crawled along slowly, like a caterpillar, spitting sparks into the air. Passing it, Margarita flew over another watery mirror in which a second moon swam beneath her feet, she sank still lower went on, her feet nearly brushing the tops of immense pines.

A deep hum of rushing air became audible and began to overtake Margarita. To this noise of something speeding like a bullet there gradually accrued the sound of a woman's laughter, audible for many miles. Margarita glanced back and saw that some sort of complicated dark shape was catching up with her. Closing in on Margarita it became more distinct, making it possible to see that it was someone riding astride. And then it became perfectly distinct: Natasha was pulling up, overtaking Margarita.

Completely naked, tousled hair flying on the wind, Natasha was riding on a fat pig which clutched a briefcase in its front trotters while its rear trotters thrashed the air agonizingly. A pince-nez which had slipped off his nose dangled along side of the pig by its cord and kept winking on and off in the moonlight. His hat kept slipping over his eyes. Looking closely, Margarita recognized the pig as Nikolai Ivanovich, whereupon her own laughter pealed out above the forest, merging with Natasha's.

"Natashka!"shouted Margarita in a piercing voice. "Did you use the crème?

"Darling!!" Natasha's cries roused the slumbering piney woods."My Queen of France, I used it on his bald spot too, on him too!"

"My princess!" the pig moaned tearfully as he carried his rider at a gallop.

"Darling, Margarita Nikolaevna," screamed Natasha, cantering abreast of Margarita, "I confess, I did use the crème. We want to live and to fly the same as you. Forgive me, my lady, but I'm not going back, not for anything. Oh it's so good, Margarita Nikolaevna!—He made me an offer," here Natasha's finger poked the neck of the bewildered, panting pig, "an offer! What did you call me, eh?" she screamed, bending level with the pig's ear.

"Goddess!" he set up a wail, "I can't fly this fast. I could lose important papers, Natalia Prokofievna, I protest!"

"The hell with you and your papers!" cried Natasha with a mocking laugh.

"Really Natalia Prokofievna, somebody might hear us!" the pig moaned imploringly. < . . . >

"Margarita! Majesty! Ask them to leave me a witch! They'll do anything for you, you have the power! And Margarita replied: "Done, I promise."

"Thank you," shrieked Natasha and suddenly shouted sharply and somehow plaintively: "Hey there, hey! Faster! Faster! Get moving!"

She dug her heels into the pig's flanks, depleted by the flight, and the latter bolted so that once again the air unraveled and in an instant Natasha was already visible in the distance, then completely disappeared, and the roar of her wake dispersed.

Margarita flew on slowly as before over a deserted and unfamiliar spot, above some hills dotted with occasional boulders lying between immense lone pines. Margarita was not flying over the tops of these, but between their trunks, silvered on one side by the moon. The flyer's delicate shadow slid over the ground in front of her, the moon was now shining on Margarita's back.

Margarita felt the proximity of water and guessed that her destination was near. The pines parted and Margarita slowly floated towards a chalk cliff. Over the cliff down below, in shadow there lay a river. Mist hovered above and clung to the shrubs on the cliff, but the opposite shore was flat and low-lying. On it, beneath a lone group of spreading trees, a bonfire flickered and some sort of moving figures could be made out. It seemed to Margarita that a buzzing, raucous music emanated from the spot. Beyond it as far as the eye could reach on the silvered plain there was no other sign of life or humanity.

Translanslated by A. L. and M. K.

Section D
Pre-Soviet & Soviet Visions of Outer Space

THE HORIZONS OF the poet's eye were significantly widened by spell-binding advances in technology and an outright revolution in cosmology in the 20th century. In a mere half a century man was able to accelerate his new ability to be airborn, courtesy of the Wright brothers, to space-flight itself. With the way paved by Sputnik, "glances from heaven to earth, from earth to heaven" were soon to become accessible to ordinary mortals. Once Percival Lowell observed what he considered to be "Martian canals," the powers of astronomical observation fueled alternate paths for unchartered flights of fancy. Contact with new worlds and heretofore unknown civilizations became one of the most popular topics for an exploding literary and cinematic genre—Science Fiction—and the planet Mars was to be of particular importance in this regard, since proof of such an alien civilization seemed to have been offered by science itself. When in 1902 in France a substantial prize was offered to the person who could establish proven contact with an extraterrestrial civilization, the competition's rules specifically excluded Mars, as the existence of Martian civilization was deemed too close to an established fact.

Before close-range pictures were sent back to Earth by Mariner and the two Viking probes, the fictional allure of Mars as a setting was overwhelming and Martian novel-writing had been extremely productive ever since H. G. Wells published his classic *The War of the Worlds* in 1898. Except for those envisioned by Ray Bradbury, most western fictional Martians modelled after Wells by less well-known writers were nearly always hostile and horrific. However, their counterparts as portrayed by two important Russian writers introduced in this section, Alexander Bogdanov and Alexei Tolstoy, were humanoid and quite attractive. Bogdanov's and Tolstoy's writings are each alloted a single entry—from the *Red Planet* and *Aelita* respectively—containing excerpts from these major works devoted to Mars. It is hoped that inclusion of these self-contained episodes and chapters will stimulate the reader to seek out full texts of these novels available in English. The regrettable fact is that neither Bogdanov nor Tolstoy, (nor Platonov, for that matter, who follows them here) rated a mention in the popular *Encyclopedia of Science Fiction*,[1] although less accomplished authors did. Hence the justification for this section: to be both informative and enticing. In fact, each writer represented here had an admiring readership and exercised considerable influence in Russia. And each imagined space-flight to new frontiers in a unique way. In addition, each was born in Imperial Russia and died in the Soviet Union. A companion

---

1. *Encyclopedia of Science Fiction*, Robert Holdstock consultant ed., foreword by Isaac Asimov. Octopus Books: Baltimore, MD 1978.

volume of authors born after the revolution is, we hope, a future project.

The concept of space flight certainly had its antecedents in past fiction, especially in Jules Verne's *From the Earth to the Moon* (1865), but modern advances in aviation technology gave it an entirely new dimension, and scientists themselves responded to earlier predictions of science fiction writers. Konstantin E. Tsiolkovsky for example, evolved his concept of a multi-stage moon rocket from an inverted design of the propelling force of Verne's cannon. In addition Tsiolkovsky, in *Beyond the Planet Earth* (1898-1920), predicted artificial satellites and worked on detailed descriptions of space-stations. Despite Tsiolkovsky's penchant for Menippean satire with respect to his own ideas, his writings were hardly ground-breaking from a literary point of view. Bogdanov and Tolstoy were far more accomplished writers of fiction. Bogdanov's novel was strongest in its elaboration of space-flight itself, whereas Tolstoy's adventure sci-fi novel was especially successful with its readers in describing the Martian terrain and romances with blue-skinned Martian women. We offer our selections with these strengths in mind.

A number of minor science-fiction writers too numerous to list here appeared on the literary scene in post-revolutionary years. We submit newly translated selections from only two other Russian authors of the period— Andrei Platonov and Ivan Efremov. Platonov is best known for his novel *The Foundation Pit* (Kotlovan), completed in 1930 but published for the first time in the west in 1973, over two decades after his death. It is a dark novel reflecting Platonov's disillusionment with the notion of a glorious socialist future. We offer here a sampling of his earlier fiction. The loosely connected triad of separate stories *Descendants of the Sun, The Lunar Probe,* and *The Ether Trail* is still animated by enthusiasm for the coming "electric century." In it advanced technology and space travel transform both man and his world, ushering in a utopian age. But even this triad, which forecasts a glorious future for man as he overcomes Nature with incredible technological and scientific advances, already hints at the author's doubts regarding their desirability. It is not for nought that each of Platonov's protagonists—"giants" propelling mankind to new leaps in technology—is an engineer whose emotional life is either tragic, or absent altogether. Their romantic and domestic failures implicitly qualify the "glorious" life created by technological progress and socialism as not necessarily conducive to individual happiness or emotional fulfillment. Upon learning that one of these engineers is married, a colleague exclaims: "Married, hell! You've gotten used to sentimentality. As for me, brother, work is a more lasting legacy than children!" It is clear that Platonov, in the initial stages of his writing career undeniably enamored of science and technology, already entertained real doubts as to their benefits and their *human* cost. This hesitancy engendered stories like *Makar the Doubtful* (1929), for which Platonov was persecuted by the regime. Such persecution, renewed after WWII, made it impossible for his larger works, in which the author's attitude toward "socialist enthusiasm" became clearly satirical, from appearing in the USSR. Eventually Platonov's name, like Zamiatin's, was erased from the official history of Soviet literature.

Of the writers cited so far, only Efremov survived significantly beyond the year 1957, which heralded the Sputnik era. His influential, large-scale utopian novel, *Andromeda Nebula* (Tumannost' Andromedy), set in the far future of interstellar travel, was in fact published in book form the same year that Sputnik flew into space. Perhaps chiefly on this account he was the first post-war Soviet writer to reach legendary fame among younger Russians, ensuring that the space-travel theme would become the prevalent subject of post-war Soviet science fiction. So far his novel has existed only in a pedestrian English translation, and in offering two of its chapters we hope to remedy his near obscurity among English readers. Like Bogdanov's novel, *Andromeda* justifies the tenets of communist doctrine though space exploration. In Bogdanov's case that doctrine is unambiguously glued onto Mars, shown to have dialectically evolved into a rational society based on love of labor and gender equality, which provided an inspiring example to the visiting Earthling. In Efremov's novel, mankind *itself* is shown to have achieved space travel precisely because it has embraced the rational, scientific principles of communist doctrine—which, as it turns out, have universal appeal. As an intergalactic transmission from the humanoid civilization on *61 Cygni* has it: "Separated by space and time we are united by intellect." But if one forgets about the doctrinaire messages of both, there is much to admire in these works. There is Bogdanov's skilled use of androgyny to confirm his belief in the equality of the sexes, and his anticipation of automated production and atomic fission, and there is Efremov's ability to project the vastness of space itself. When read to the accompaniment of Sputnik's orbital beeps, *Andromeda*—with its skilled use of authentic and imagined scientific concepts—was Russia's first readable work celebrating the *fantastic* possibilities inherent in mankind's leap into space.

However tantalizing such possibilities were, a society governed solely by intellect was doomed to failure, just as Dostoevsky had predicted. About three decades after Efremov's novel, Russian society celebrated the millennium of its existence as an organized state and of its acceptance of Christianity. By that time there were signs that communist doctrine had already exhausted itself, and since then vast numbers of Russians have once again embraced the metaphysical, finding it principally in the belief system of the Orthodox church. But the seeds were there earlier. In 1963—six years after *Andromeda*—Efremov produced *The Blade's Edge*, a novel whose interest in eastern religion and yogic meditation ensured its rejection by the regime censors. The book became an underground best-seller and copies of it sold for approximately a month's salary for the average Russian, the same price as a copy of the quintessential banned classic, *The Bible*.

Alexander Alexandrovich Bogdanov
[Malinovsky]
(1873–1928)

Red Star

[*The Flight to Mars*. Abridged]

CHAPTER V: DEPARTURE

. . . My attention was involuntarily devoted to the exciting and imminent moment of our take-off. I watched the snowy surface of the lake which lay before us and a beetling granite cliff behind us, expecting a sudden shock and their sudden disappearance as we ascended. But nothing like this happened at all.

Silently, slowly, with a barely perceptible motion, the snow-covered landscape began to leave us. For several seconds I was not aware that we had risen at all.

"The rate of increase is two centimeters," said Menni.

I understood what this meant. In the first second we were to move one centimeter, in the second—three centimeters, in the third—five centimeters, in the fourth—seven centimeters; thus our speed was to be constantly changing, at an arithmetically progressive rate. Within a minute we would reach the speed of a walking man, in fifteen minutes that of an express train, and so on. < . . . > The ground was rapidly leaving us and the horizon expanding. The dark masses of the cliffs and the villages were diminishing and the outlines of the lakes could be seen as on a map. The sky was becoming constantly darker; at the same time that the dark blue band of the unfrozen sea claimed the entire western horizon my eyes began to distinguish the brighter stars even with a noon-day sun in the sky.

The very slow spinning of the spaceship around its vertical axis made it possible for us to see space in all directions.

It seemed that the horizon was rising with us and Earth's surface below us appeared as a huge slightly convex dish with decorations provided by the Earth's relief. But their outlines became more blurred, the contours flatter, and the whole landscape appeared more and more like a geographic map, sharply delimited in its center, but vague indefinite at the periphery where it was draped in a semi-transparent, bluish fog. And the sky had become absolutely black and innumerable stars, even the most minute, shown down on us with their steady unwinking light, unafraid of the sun whose rays had become painfully hot.

"Tell me, Menni, will that two-centimeter rate of increase at which we are now moving continue for our entire journey?"

"Yes," he answered, "but half way through our trip it will be reversed and every second our speed will decrease by the same measurement. Thus, although the greatest speed of the spaceship will be about 2,000 miles an hour and the average speed about 1,000 miles an hour, at the moment of arrival it will be as slight as at the beginning of our journey, and without any shock or strain we will drop onto the surface of Mars. Without this great and variable speed we would not be able to reach either Earth or Venus because at their closest point—40 million or 65 million miles respectively— at the speed of, say, one of your trains, the journey would require centuries, not months as does ours. As to the possibility of a "cannon shot" such as I have read about in one of your science fiction novels, that would be only a joke, because in accordance with the laws of mechanics, to be inside a shell when it is fired would be the same as having the shell fired at you."

"But how have you achieved such a smooth deceleration and acceleration?"

"The motive force of the spaceship is provided by a radioactive substance which we have acquired in great amounts. We have found a method for increasing its radiation by a hundred thousand times; this occurs within the motors with the help of relatively simple electrical and mechanical devices. This procedure releases an enormous amount of energy. The particles of the radiating atoms disperse, as you know, at a speed which is tens of thousands greater than that of an artillery shell. When these particles issue from the spaceship in one direction, that is, through a channel with impenetrable walls, the spaceship moves in the opposite direction, as in the recoil of a gun. In accordance with the laws of motion you can calculate that the smallest part of a milligram of such particles in a second's time is fully capable of giving our spaceship its steady and variable movement."

While we were conversing all the other Martians left the room. Menni asked me to join him for lunch in his cabin and I left with him. His cabin was located against the outer wall of the spaceship and it had a large window. We continued with our conversation. I knew that soon I would experience a new feeling of weightlessness and I asked Menni about this.

"Yes," said Menni, "although we are still attracted to the sun, this force is insignificant. Tomorrow or the day after, the influence of Earth will also be imperceptible. Thanks only to the spaceship's constantly increasing speed we will retain 1/400 or 1/500 of our former weight. When this first happens it is not easy to make the adjustment, although the change will come very slowly. As you acquire lightness, you will lose your agility and make many incorrect calculations as you move so that you will commit many clumsy errors. The pleasure of soaring through the air will be of doubtful worth. As regards unavoidable palpitation of the heart, dizziness, and nausea, Netti will be able to help you. You will also have difficulties with water and other fluids, which will escape from their containers when even slightly jarred and disperse in the form of spherical drops in the air. But we have taken strenuous efforts to prevent these inconveniences: furniture and dishes are fastened down, fluids are stored in closed containers, and there are handles and straps everywhere in case of sudden movements or falls. But you will become accustomed to these inconveniences; there is plenty of time."

Two hours had elapsed since our departure, and weight loss had already become rather perceptible, although it was still only something of a game; my body had become lighter and my movements freer, but nothing more. We had left Earth's atmosphere completely by now, but this was no cause for concern because there was an adequate supply of oxygen in our sealed airship. The segment of Earth's surface which we could see was now exactly like a geographic map—true, with a measure of distortion: larger in the center, reduced toward its edges; here and there it was covered with white puffs of clouds. In the south beyond the Mediterranean Sea, Northern Africa and Arabia could be seen rather clearly through a blue haze; on the north beyond Scandinavia the view was lost in a waste of snow and ice—only the cliffs of Spitzbergen showed dark. In the east beyond the greenish brown mass of the Urals, cut here and there by patches of snow, began a great white kingdom, at places with a greenish tint—a faint reminder of the great Siberian coniferous forests. To the west beyond the clear outlines of Central Europe the shores of England and Northern France were lost in clouds. I found myself unable to watch this grand picture for long, because the enormous void below us rapidly evoked a feeling in me close to fainting. I renewed my conversation with Menni.

"Then are you the captain of this craft?" Menni nodded and said:

"But that doesn't mean that I have the power of a commanding officer. It simply means that I have the most experience flying spaceships and my orders are accepted, the same way that I accept the astronomical calculations which Sterni makes, or as we accept Netti's medical advice because we want to retain our health and strength."

"How old is Dr. Netti? He seems very young to me."

"I don't remember, sixteen or seventeen," Menni answered with a smile.

That is about what I thought and I was astonished at such learning at his young age.

"A doctor at his age!" I burst out.

"And a proficient and experienced doctor at that," Menni added.

At the time I did not realize—and Menni intentionally said nothing about it—that Martian years were almost twice as long as ours: Mars' rotation around the sun requires 686 days and at sixteen Martian years of age Netti was about thirty years old by Earth time.

Chapter VI: The Spaceship

After breakfast Menni led me on a tour of our "craft." First we visited the engine room. It occupied the lowest floor of the spaceship directly above its flattened base, and was divided by partitions into five rooms, one in the center and four accessory rooms. The engine stood in the center of the largest room and around it on four sides were round glass-covered windows in the floor, one clear, the three others of various colors; the glass was an inch thick and very pure. At any given time we could see only a part of Earth's surface.

The heart of the engine was a vertical metal cylinder about ten feet high and two feet in diameter, made, as Menni explained to me, out of a very dense precious metal related to platinum. Within this cylinder the radiation process took place; a panel six inches thick which glowed red with heat testified powerfully to the energy released by this process. But still it was not excessively warm in the room: the entire cylinder was surrounded by a double shell of some kind of a transparent substance which insulated the surroundings from its heat; above, one of the shells was connected to pipes through which the heated air flowed in all directions to warm the spaceship.

The remainder of the engine connected in various ways with the cylinder—electric coils, batteries, dials, etc.—surrounded it in an attractive fashion and the technician on duty, thanks to a system of mirrors, could watch them all without leaving his chair.

Of the accessory rooms one was an astronomical observatory, to its left and right were rooms for water and oxygen storage, while opposed to them on the opposite side was the calculating room. In the observatory the floor and the outer wall were of polished optical glass. They were so transparent that when I walked with Menni over the catwalks and decided to glance downward, I saw nothing between me and the void below us—and I had to close my eyes to end the excruciating giddiness. I kept my eyes to the side on the devices which were located in the spaces between the catwalks on complex frameworks suspended from the room's ceiling and internal walls. The major telescope was about six feet long but with a disproportionately large lens and, apparently also, increased powers of magnification.

"We use only diamond lenses" said Menni. "They provide the largest possible field of observation."

"What is the power of that telescope?" I asked.

"About 600x," Menni answered. "But when this is inadequate, we photograph the field of observation and examine the photograph under a microscope. This method provides a magnification up to 60,000 times and more; the photographic process takes not more than a minute's time."

Menni suggested I look into the telescope to see Earth which we had abandoned. He focused the lens himself.

"We are now at a distance of about 1,200 miles," he said. "Now do you recognize what you have in front of you?"

I immediately identified the Gulf of Finland which I had navigated many times in the service of the Party . . . I could see ships at anchor. With a turn of a lever on the telescope, Menni replaced the eyepiece with a camera, then a second later he removed it in its entirety and placed it in a large piece of equipment standing to one side which turned out to be a microscope.

"We are developing and fixing the photograph in the microscope without touching the film," he explained, and after a few minor operations, a half minute later, he offered me the microscope's eyepiece. With startling clarity I saw a familiar steamship belonging to the Northern Company as though it were only a few feet away from me; the photograph seemed to have depth and natural colors although it was translucent. On the bridge stood the gray-haired captain with whom I had talked a number of times. A sailor who was lowering a large container onto the deck was caught as he moved, as well as a passenger who was pointing out something with his hand. And we were 1,200 miles away . . .

A young Martian, Sterni's aide, entered the room. He was to make a precise measurement of the distance covered by the spaceship. We did not wish to disturb him and we left for the water storage room. Here was a large container with fresh water and equipment for purifying it. A host of pipes transmitted this water throughout the spaceship.

Next came the calculating room. Here stood a multitude of machines with dials and gauges unknown to me. Sterni was working at the largest piece of equipment. A long tape stretched out of it, no doubt the results of Sterni's calculations; but the symbols on it, as on the dials, were unknown to me. I had no desire to disturb Sterni or even to talk with him. We quickly passed into the last accessory room.

This was the oxygen room in which were stored more than twenty five tons of oxide compounds from which more than 10,000 cubic yards of oxygen could be extracted when needed; that quantity was sufficient for several journeys such as ours. The equipment necessary for the extraction of the oxygen was also located here. Here, too, was stored a supply of barites and caustic potassium for removing the carbon dioxide from the air, as well as sulphur anhydrides to remove excessive moisture and harmful gases. Dr. Netti was in charge of this room.

Then we returned to the central engine room and from there in a small elevator we went straight to the spaceship's upper floor. Here was located a second observatory identical with the first one, but with a glass roof rather than a floor and larger telescopes. From this observatory we could see the other half of space as well as the planet which was our destination. Mars, slightly out of the zenith, glowed red. Menni turned a telescope on it and I could easily see the outlines of the continents, seas, and canal system which

I knew from Schiaparelli's maps. Menni photographed the planet and under the microscope a more detailed map emerged. But I could understand nothing on it without Menni's explanation: cities, forests, and lakes could only be distinguished from one another by distinctions which were imperceptible and incomprehensible to me.

"How far away are we?" I asked.

"Now we are relatively close—about sixty five million miles."

"Why isn't Mars at the observatory's zenith? Are we flying obliquely to it, and not directly?"

"Yes, we have no choice. When we left Earth as the result of inertia we retained its motive speed around the sun—about 1,200 miles an hour. But Mars' speed is only about 960 miles an hour, and if we were to fly perpendicularly to both their orbits we would hit the surface of Mars with a lateral speed of 240 miles an hour. This would be very awkward and we must select a curving route which equalizes the excess lateral speed."

"In this case how long will our route be?"

"About 120 million miles, which will require not less than two and a half months' travel time."

If I had not been a mathematician these numbers would have meant nothing to me. But now I felt almost as though I had been caught up in some nightmare and I was eager to leave the calculating room.

Six lateral compartments of the spaceship's upper segment which surrounded the observatory totally lacked windows and their ceiling, which was part of the spherical skin of the spaceship, descended to the floor. In that ceiling were located large reserves of "negative-matter" whose repulsion to the earth counter-balanced the weight of the whole spaceship.

The intermediate floors—numbers two and three—were occupied by lounges, individual laboratories, living quarters, toilets, a library, an exercise room, etc.

Netti's room was next to mine.

Chapter VII: People

My loss of weight was constantly more apparent and the increasing feeling of lightness was no longer pleasant. It was accompanied with a certain uneasiness and vague restlessness. I left for my room and lay on my bunk.

After an hour or two of immobility and serious thought I imperceptibly drifted into sleep. When I awoke Netti was sitting in my room next to the table. Involuntarily I sat up in bed, and as though something had thrown me I hit my head against the ceiling.

"You must be more careful when you weigh less than twenty pounds," Netti said in a genial voice.

He had come to see me with the special purpose of giving me advice in the case of "sea-sickness" which I already felt as the result of loss of weight. There was a special alarm in my cabin which I could employ to summon him if his help were needed.

I utilized the opportunity to talk with the young doctor—something attracted me to this appealing, very learned, but very vivacious lad. I asked how it had happened that he alone of all the Martians, with the exception of Menni, knew my language.

"There's a very simple explanation," he explained. "When we were searching for a human, Menni chose himself and me to visit your country and we spent more than a year there until we were able to conclude our business with you."

"That is to say, others were 'searching for a human' in other countries as well?"

"Certainly, they searched among all the major peoples of the world. But, as Menni foresaw, we found him first of all in your country, where people live most vigorously and vividly and where they must look to the future more than others. When we had found our human, we notified the others; they gathered together from all over the world and then we left."

"What do you really mean, when you say you were 'searching for a human' or 'found a human'? I realize that you were seeking a subject who could play a certain role, as Menni explained to me. I am very flattered to see that you chose me, but I would like to know too what you expect from me."

"I can tell you that, in general terms. We needed a human who possessed so far as it was possible the traits of good health and sturdiness, a capacity for intellectual labor, few personal ties on Earth, and a weak sense of his own individualism. Our physiologists and psychologists assumed that the transformation from your society, sharply divided by incessant internal warfare, to ours which is organized, as you would say, socialistically, would be a very difficult change for any individual and would require a very special personality. Menni decided that you came closer than anyone else."

"And did all of you accept Menni's opinion?"

"Yes, we all have complete trust in his analysis. He is a man of exceptional mental powers and insight, and he is rarely wrong. He has had more experience with humans than any of us; it was he who established our contact."

"And who was it that established the method of interplanetary communication?"

"That was the result of many individuals' labor, and not one man's. 'Negative-matter' was first obtained several decades ago. At first it was produced only in insignificant quantities, and it required the efforts of many workers to find and develop methods for producing it in large amounts. Then it was necessary to perfect a technique for obtaining a decomposing radioactive material so we would have an effective engine for our spaceship. That also required a great effort. Then, there were many problems resulting from the difficult conditions of space travel with its terrible cold and burning sunlight not tempered by Earth's atmosphere. The calculations necessary for the journey also turned out to be not an easy task and presented difficulties which no one had foreseen. In a word, former expeditions ended with the death of all their participants until Menni succeeded in organizing the first successful flight. But, now, by employing his methods we recently reached Venus, too."

"If that's so, then Menni is a great man," I added.

"Yes, if you wish to give that title to a man who can indeed work long and well."

"That's not what I meant: ordinary people, those who take instructions, can work long and well. But Menni is obviously something else: he is a genius, a creative talent who has invented something new and thus led humanity forward."

"That's not clear, and it seems to me, it's not true. Every workman is creative, but it is humanity and the world which create in that workman's form. Isn't it true that Menni possesses in his hands all the experience of the preceding generations as well as that of contemporary scientists and wasn't this the source of all of his discoveries? And wasn't it the world which granted him all the elements and the germs of his new ideas? And weren't all the stimuli for these ideas the result of a struggle between humanity and its world? Man is a person, but his work is impersonal. Sooner or later he will die with all his joys and sorrows, but his work remains as part of the vast current of life. In this respect there is no difference between workmen; the only difference is between the scale of what they have experienced and what they leave behind them."

"But isn't it true that the name of such a man as Menni will not die with him, but will remain in the memory of humanity when the names of innumerable others have disappeared without a trace?"

"The name of every man is preserved so long as those are alive who knew him. But humanity does not need the dead symbol of a person when he is no more. Without regard for persons, our learning and our art preserve what has been accomplished by the commonality. The dead weight of names from the past is useless for humanity's tradition."

"Perhaps you are right; but our feelings reject that logic. For us the names of thinkers and doers are living symbols essential for our learning, our art, and our social life. It often happens that in the struggle for ideas and accomplishments a name says more than an abstract slogan. And the names of geniuses are not a dead weight in our tradition."

"That is because the common cause of humanity is still not yet a common cause; thanks to the illusions which arise as the result of the struggle among men, it is fragmented and appears to be a cause of men and not humanity. It is as difficult for me to understand your point of view as it is for you to understand ours."

"Then for better or for worse there are no immortals among the crew. But the mortals here are among the most select, isn't that so? From among those who have 'worked long and well,' as you expressed it?"

"Yes, in general. Menni chose his comrades from thousands who wished to make the journey with him."

"And next to him, isn't Sterni perhaps the most eminent?"

"Yes, if you insist on measuring and comparing individuals. Sterni is a remarkable scientist, although of a completely different sort than Menni. He is a very gifted mathematician. He discovered an entire set of errors in the calculations which were employed to send the former expeditions to Earth, and he demonstrated that some of these errors were sufficient to destroy the projects and their participants. He discovered new methods for making such calculations and so far the results he obtained have been flawless."

"I gathered this was so from Menni's words as well as from my own first impression. But still, and I don't understand this myself, I don't know why the sight of him makes me so uneasy, and arouses a kind of unfounded antipathy. Do you have any explanation for this, doctor?"

"You see, Sterni has a great mind, but he is cold and above all, analytic. He dissects everything mercilessly and consistently but his conclusions are often narrow and sometimes extremely harsh, because his analysis of the details is not unified, and is less than the whole: you know that always where there is life the whole is more than the sum of its parts, just as a living human body is more than an assemblage of its members. As a consequence, Sterni does not understand others' moods and ideas. He is always willing to help you with your problems but he can never understand what you need. In part this is the result of his preoccupation with his work; his mind is always busy with some difficult problem or other. In this respect he is very unlike Menni: he always sees what is around him and sometimes he has been able to explain to me what I really want, or what is disturbing me, or what I long for."

"If that's so, then isn't Sterni rather hostile to the inhabitants of Earth who are so full of contradictions and inadequacies?"

"Hostile!—no; such a feeling is alien to him. But he is more skeptical than is necessary, I think. He lived in France for a half a year and wired Menni: 'Nothing here.' Perhaps he was partly right because Letta who was with him was also unable to find anyone of interest. But the characterizations he gave to the people of that country whom he met were much harsher than Letta's, and, of course, they were much more one-sided although there was nothing in them which could be called inaccurate."

"And who is this Letta you mentioned? I don't think I remember his name."

"A chemist, Menni's helper, not young, the oldest man on the space-ship. You will find him very accessible and that will be useful to you. He is gentle by nature and he understands others, although he is no psychologist like Menni. Visit him in his laboratory; he will be pleased to see you and can show you much that is interesting."

It occurred to me that we were now far from the Earth, and I wanted to look at her once more. We went to one of the accessory rooms equipped with large windows.

"Will we pass close to the moon?" I said as we walked along.

"No, the moon will remain well out of our path, and I'm sorry that this is so. I would like to see the moon up close. It seemed so strange to me from Earth—large, cold, deliberate, mysteriously serene; it is so different from our two little moons which fly so swiftly through our sky, changing their faces so rapidly like living and capricious children. True, your moon is much brighter than ours and her light is so pleasant. Your sun is brighter, too; in this respect you are much more fortunate than we. Your world is twice as bright as ours and so you don't need eyes like ours with their great pupils to collect the weak light of our days and nights."

We sat down at the window. Earth shone distantly below us like a giant sickle on which I could make out only the outlines of Western America, Northeastern Asia, a vague patch which was the Pacific Ocean and a white spot which was the Arctic. All of the Atlantic Ocean and the Old World lay in shadow; one could only surmise their existence beyond the uncertain edge of the sickle by the fact that the invisible part of Earth blotted out the stars over a great expanse of the black sky. Our curving trajectory and Earth's rotation on its axis led to this changing scene.

I looked and I was sorry that I could not see my native land where there was so much life, so many struggles, so much pain, where yesterday I had stood in the ranks with my comrades and where another was now to take my place. And my heart was filled with doubts.

"There, below us, blood is flowing," I said, and yesterday's worker is playing the role of a comfortable spectator . . ."

"Blood is flowing for the sake of a better future," Netti answered, "and for the sake of the struggle you must come to know that better future. That is why you are here—to gain that knowledge."

Involuntarily I pressed his little, almost childlike hand.

Chapter VIII: The Approach

Earth was yet further now and, as though it were languishing, it was transformed into a crescent moon accompanied by another tiny crescent, the real moon. All of us, the inhabitants of the spaceship too were trans-

formed—into some kind of fantastic acrobats who could fly without wings
and take any position in space, head to the floor or the ceiling or the walls,
almost indifferently . . . Little by little I was coming to know my new comrades and to feel more at ease in their presence.

On the second day after our departure (we continued to count the days,
although for us, of course, there were no real days and nights) on my own
initiative I dressed in Martian clothing, so I would not be so conspicuous
among the crew. True, I liked the costume for its own merits, since it was
comfortable without any useless, purely conventional features such as neckties or cuffs and allowed maximum body movement. The individual parts
of the suit were connected by small ties so that the entire costume was one
whole, but at the same time, if it were necessary, it was simple to unfasten
and remove, for example, one sleeve or both or the entire blouse. And the
manners of my fellow-travelers were like their costume: simple and with an
absence of anything that was superfluous or only decorative. They never
greeted one another, nor said farewell, nor gave thanks, nor continued a
conversation out of politeness if its end had been achieved; at the same time
they patiently provided explanations which were painstakingly set at the
level of the person with whom they were speaking and with understanding
for his personality although it might very much differ from their own.

Of course from the very first I turned to the study of their language and
they all, and particularly Netti, willingly played the role of teachers. Their
language was very unusual: in spite of the simplicity of its grammar and the
rules for word formation, some of its features gave me great difficulties. The
rules of its grammar had absolutely no exceptions and there was no such
thing as a gender, masculine, feminine or neuter; but instead all the names
of things and qualities were inflected in time. This I could not absorb.

"What could be the purpose of such forms?" I asked Netti.

"Don't you understand? In your languages you are very careful to indicate whether you consider a thing to be male or female, which is, you must
admit, of no importance at all; and as far as inanimate objects are concerned, more than strange. It's much more important whether a thing exists
at the present time or that it did at one time or will come into being. In your
language "house" is masculine, but "boat" is feminine, but in French the
reverse is true—but this has nothing to do with the state of things. When
you talk about a house which has burned down or which is yet to be built,
you employ the word in the same form as when you talk about the house
in which you live. Isn't there actually much more of a difference between a
man who is alive and a man who has died—between what is and what is
no more? You need whole words and phrases to indicate this difference—
wouldn't it be better to indicate it by adding one letter to the word itself?"

But at any rate Netti was satisfied with my powers of memory and his method of instruction was excellent and I made relatively rapid progress. This helped me in my dealings with the Martians—now I could confidently visit the entire spaceship, dropping into the rooms and laboratories of my fellow travelers and asking about anything which interested me.

The young astronomer, Enno, Sterni's aide, lively and cheerful, and still a lad, explained many things to me, obviously carried away, not so much by the measurements and formulas, of which he was a master, as by the beauty of what he was observing. I was happy to be with the young astronomer-poet; a very legitimate concern to orient myself in space gave me a constant excuse to spend time with Enno and his telescopes.

One time Enno in the greatest excitement showed me the tiny planet, Eros, a segment of whose orbit passed between the paths of Earth and Mars but which otherwise lay beyond Mars in the asteroid belt. Although at the time Eros was located 100 million miles from us, a photograph of its tiny crescent under the microscope was like a whole geographic chart, like the maps of the moon. Of course it was also as lifeless as the moon.

On another occasion, Enno photographed a flight of meteors which passed several million miles from us. The picture showed, naturally, only an indefinite haziness. At the time Enno told me that on one of the previous expeditions to Earth a spaceship was destroyed when it passed through such a flight. Astronomers who were following the spaceship in their telescopes saw how its electric lights were extinguished—and the spaceship disappear in space forever.

"The spaceship probably collided with several of these small bodies and because of the great difference in speeds they must have passed right through its walls. Then the air escaped out of it and the chill of interplanetary space froze the travelers. Now the spaceship is still flying, continuing its journey in a comet's orbit; it has left the sun forever and no one knows where it will end, a terrible craft manned by corpses."

As Enno spoke I could feel the cold of empty space invade my heart. I imagined our minute, glowing island in the midst of an endless dead sea, without any support moving at a dizzying pace with only a black void around us . . . Enno guessed how I felt.

"Menni is an excellent navigator," he said, "and Sterni makes no mistakes . . . And death . . . You've seen it before during your life . . . Death is death, nothing more." Soon the time would come when I would remember those words in my struggle with a great spiritual sickness.

I was attracted to the chemist Letta not only because of his extraordinary gentleness and sensitivity, which Netti had told me about, but also because of his enormous knowledge of the field which interested me more than any other—the nature of matter. Only Menni was better informed on this question, but I tried to have as little as possible to do with him, knowing that his time was too valuable both for science and for the interests of the expedition, so that I had no right to distract him for my own purposes. But Letta, a kind old man, was so endlessly patient with my ignorance and so helpfully explained to me the basic facts of the subject, even betraying pleasure when he did so, that I always felt quite unconstrained in his presence.

Letta began to deliver a whole series of lectures to me on the theory of matter, illustrating them with a number of experiments on the decomposition and synthesis of the elements. He had to omit a number of the relevant experiments-limiting himself to a description of them—which were violent in nature and were accompanied by an explosion or which might take that form.

During one of these lectures Menni entered the laboratory. Letta was finishing the description of a very interesting experiment and was about to begin its execution.

"Be careful," Menni told him, "I remember once when I performed it, it came to a bad end; only a trace of impurities in the substance which you are decomposing and even a weak electrical spark is enough to cause an explosion when you are heating it."

Letta wanted to abandon the experiment, but Menni, who was invariably thoughtful and considerate in his relations with me, offered to help him check the elements of the experiment; the reaction occurred without difficulty.

The next day there were to be more experiments with the same substance. It seemed to me that Letta did not take his materials out of the same container as the previous day. When he placed the retort in the electric furnace it occurred to me to say something to him. Disturbed, he immediately went to the locker where the reagents were stored, leaving the furnace and the retort on the table near the wall which was also the outer wall of the spaceship. I went with him.

Suddenly there was a deafening roar and both of us were blown against the locker with great force. This was followed by a deafening whistle and howling and the sound of breaking metal. I felt an irresistible force, like a hurricane, pulling me back toward the outer wall. I had time to seize a firmly attached strap on the locker and hung horizontally, held in that position by a powerful stream of air. Letta did the same thing.

"Hold on!" he shouted and I could hardly hear his voice in the midst of the storm.

Letta quickly looked around. His face was terribly pale, but the appearance of indecisiveness was replaced by one expressing thought and firm decision. He said only two words—I couldn't make them out, but it seemed that he was saying farewell forever-and his hands relaxed their grip.

There was a dull blow and the hurricane ceased. I felt I could release my hold and looked around. The table was completely gone and against the wall, his spine flat against the wall, stood Letta. His eyes were open wide and his face seemingly frozen. In one leap I reached the door and opened it.

A stream of warm air threw me back. Menni entered the room in a second and quickly went up to Letta.

A few seconds later the room was full. Netti entered, pushing everyone to the side and rushed to Letta. All the rest of us surrounded them in painful silence.

"Letta is dead," Menni said. "The explosion which occurred during the experiment punctured the spaceship's wall and Letta closed the aperture with his own body. The air pressure ruptured his lungs and paralyzed his heart—it was a quick death. Letta saved our guest's life—otherwise they would both have died."

Netti suddenly burst into tears.

CHAPTER IX. THE PAST—[The chapter consists of an unambiguous rehashing of history from a dialectic point of view—shown to be equally applicable to Mars and to Earth—which supposedly led the much older Martian society to a classless paradise after the building of its canals. A. L.].

CHAPTER X. ARRIVAL

Under Menni's cool hand the spaceship made its way without further mishaps toward its distant destination. I had become tolerably accustomed to conditions of weightlessness and I had mastered the major difficulties of the Martian language when Menni announced that we had completed half of our journey and had achieved our maximum speed, henceforth to decline.

At a time carefully determined by Menni, the spaceship swiftly and smoothly reversed itself. The Earth, which had been a great and brilliant sickle, then a smaller one, and then a greenish star close to a sun's disk, now left the lower half of the black sky and entered the upper half, while the red star of Mars which had shown bright above our heads was now below us.

After many days had passed, the star of Mars became a clear small disc with its two stars, its satellites, Deimos and Phobos, innocent, miniscule, undeserving of their threatening Greek names "Horror" and "Terror." The Martians were now elated and frequently visited Enno's observatory to view their native land. I too observed it but found it difficult to understand that I saw in spite of Enno's patient explanations. There was much there, in fact, which was strange to me.

The red spots were forests and meadows while the dark places were fields ready for the harvest. The cities were bluish patches—only water and snow had their familiar hues. The ebullient Enno sometimes asked me to identify what I saw in the eye-piece and my innocent misinterpretations vastly amused him and Netti; I in turn repaid them for their jokes, calling their planet a kingdom of learned owls and confused colors.

The dimensions of the red disk were constantly increasing—now it was much larger than the noticeably diminishing sun and it looked like an astronomical chart without labels. The force of gravity also was increasing which was surprisingly pleasant to me. From bright specks of light Deimos and Phobos were transfoemed into tiny, but well-defined circles.

Fifteen or twenty hours later Mars, like a flattened ball, opened out below us and with the naked eye I could see more than was shown on all our scientists' astronomical charts. Deimos glided over that round map, but Phobos was nowhere to be seen—it was on the other side of the planet.

Everyone around me was rejoicing; only I was beset by uneasy foreboding.

Closer and closer . . . No one could work any longer—they all were watching the ground below us, a different world, their native land, but for me a place of mystery and the unknown. Only Menni was absent—he was at the engine; the last hours of the journey were the most dangerous time and he had to regulate the craft's speed and verify its distance from Mars.

And what was the matter with me, the involuntary Columbus of this world, why did I feel no joy, no pride, nor even the peace of mind which dry land should have brought me after journey across the seas of the Unknown? Future events had already cast their shadow over the present...

Only two hours remained and soon we would enter the planet's atmosphere. My heart began to pound; I could not watch any longer and I went to my room. Netti followed me.

He began to talk to me, not about the present, but the past, and the distant Earth high above us.

"You will have to return there after you have completed your assignment," he said, and his words were a gentle reminder of my own courage.

We talked about assignement, its importance and its problems. Time passed for me unnoticed.

Netti looked at the chronometer. "We are there, let's go to my people!" he said.

The spaceship stopped, broad metal doors opened and fresh air streamed in. Over our heads was a clean greenish-blue sky and around us were crowds of people.

Menni and Sterni were the first to leave, carrying in their arms a transparent coffin where lay the frozen body of Letta, their dead comrade.

The others followed after them. Netti and I were the last to leave and hand in hand we made our way through the throngs of people all of whom looked like him...

[End of Part I]

Translated by Leland Fetzer

Alexei Nikolaevich Tolstoy
(1883-1945)

Aelita

[*First Contact with Martians*. ABRIDGED]

DESCENT

The silvery disc of Mars, at places apparently draped in clouds, had noticeably increased in size. Its southern cap gleamed blindingly. Near it was spread out a curving bank of haze. On the east it extended as far as the equator, while near the prime meridian it rose, bending around to skirt a brighter area and forking to make an extension at Mars' western edge.

Along the equator five dark round areas could be seen clearly. They were connected by dark lines which formed two equilateral triangles and one acute triangle. The base of the easternmost triangle was enclosed by an arching line. From its center to the extreme western point extended a second semi-circle. Several lines, points, and semi-circles were scattered to the west and east from this equatorial group. Mars' northern hemisphere was lost in haze.

Los eagerly traced that network of lines—there they were, the phenomena which had driven astronomers to distraction, constantly changing, geometric, the incomprehensible Martian canals. Now Los could distinguish under their precise outline a second system of lines, which were barely visible, as though carelessly erased. He began to make a rough sketch of them in his notebook. Suddenly the disk of Mars shuddered and swam towards the porthole. Los threw himself at the rheostats:

"We've made it. Alexei Ivanovich, we're being drawn closer, we're falling."

As the craft turned its base towards the planet, Los reduced the motive force and then turned it off completely. The reduction in speed was now less sickening. But then silence reigned, which was so painful that Gusev placed his face in his hands and covered his ears.

Los lay on the floor to watch the silvery disc increasing in size, growing, becoming ever more convex. As though from out of a black abyss it was flying towards them.

Once more Los advanced the rheostat. The craft shuddered, resisting Mars' gravitational attraction. The rate of fall declined. Now Mars filled the entire sky, became duller, and its edges curved upward like a bowl.

The final seconds were terrifying—a sickening fall. Mars filled the whole sky. Suddenly, the glass of the portholes was filmed with moisture.

The craft was slicing through clouds above a misty plain and then, roaring and rocking it slowly began to descend.

"We're landing!" Los barely had time to shout and turned off the motor. A sharp blow threw him against the wall and knocked him over. The craft settled heavily and then toppled onto its side.

* * *

Their knees trembled, their hands shook, their hearts stopped beating. Silently and quickly Los and Gusev repaired the damage to the craft's interior. Through an opening in one of the portholes they thrust a mouse, only half alive, which they had brought from the earth. The mouse revived somewhat, lifted her nose, twitched her ears, and began to groom herself. The atmosphere would support life.

Then they opened the inner door of the hatch. Los licked his lips and said in a hollow voice:

"Well, Alexei Ivanovich, my congratulations. Let's get out."

They threw off their boots and coats. Gusev strapped a Mauser to his belt (for any eventuality), laughed, and threw open the outer door.

MARS

A dark blue sky, like the sea in a storm, blinding, fathomless, was what Gusev and Los saw as they climbed out of their craft.

A flaming shaggy sun stood high over Mars. It was like the sun they had seen in St. Petersburg on a clear March day when a thawing wind had cleansed the whole sky.

"That's a bright sun they have," Gusev said and sneezed, so brilliant was the light in the deep blue sky. Their chests pounded and their temples throbbed but it was pleasant to breathe—the air was fine and dry.

The craft lay on a flat plain the color of oranges and apricots. The horizon was near—you could touch it. Under foot the soil was dry and crackling. Everywhere on the plain stood tall cacti like Menorahs casting precise lilac shadows. A light dry wind was blowing.

Los and Gusev spent much time looking around and then set off across the plain. It was extraordinarily easy to walk, although their feet sank to their ankles in the crumbling soil. As he made his way around a stout tall cactus, Los brushed it with his hand. The plant, as soon as he touched it, trembled as though in a violent wind and its brown fleshy branches reached for his hand. Gusev kicked it at the ground level and—unexpectedly—the cactus fell, driving its spines into the sand.

They walked on for half an hour or so. Before their eyes stretched the same orange plain—cacti, lilac shadows, cracked soil. Then they turned to the south and the sun stood to one side—Los had begun to look around closely, as though he was puzzled—he suddenly stopped, squatted, and pounded his knee:

"Alexei Ivanovich, this ground has been ploughed."

"What?"

In fact ploughed crumbling furrows could plainly be seen and it was obvious the cacti were growing in rows. A few steps later Gusev stumbled over a stone slab into which had been set a large bronze ring with part of a cable. Los rubbed his chin firmly and his eyes gleamed.

"Alexei Ivanovich, do you understand now?"

"I can see we're in a cultivated field."

"And what's the ring for?"

"The devil knows why they put the ring here."

"So they can moor buoys. You can see mussel shells. We're on the bottom of a canal."

Gusev placed a finger to his nostril and blew his nose. They turned to the west at right angles to the furrows. Far away above the field a large bird took to the air, its wings convulsively flapping, its body hanging like a wasp. Gusev paused, his hand on the revolver. But the bird circled, gleaming in the dark blue sky, and disappeared over the near horizon.

The cacti became taller, thicker, and more stalwart. They had to pick their way through the living, thorny grove that they formed. From under their feet darted animals which resembled common lizards, but bright orange with serrated crests. Several times in dense palmate thickets some kind of brush balls slid underfoot and threw themselves to the side. Here they walked carefully.

The cacti ceased at a sloping embankment as white as chalk. It was lined, apparently, with ancient dressed stone slabs. In cracks and between the slabs hung desiccated filaments of moss. Into one of the slabs was set the same kind of ring as had been on the field. The crested lizards basked in the warm sun.

Los and Gusev climbed the slope. From its summit they could see an undulating plain of the same apricot color, but of a lessened intensity. Here and there were scattered the crests of spreading trees like mountain pines. Here and there were piles of white stones, the marks of ruins. Far away to the northwest was a lilac range of mountains, jagged and uneven like frozen tongues of flame. On their summits snow glistened.

"We've got to go back to eat and rest," said Gusev. "We're tired out, and there's not a living soul here."

They stood for a while longer. The plain was empty and sad—their hearts sank. "Yes, let's get going," said Gusev.

Suddenly Gusev stopped:

"Look at him!"

With a practiced gesture he unfastened his holster and took out the revolver.

"Hey! you! there by the craft, you! I'll shoot!"

"Who are you shouting at, Alexei Ivanovich?"

"See there where the ship is shining."

"Yes, I see it."

"Well there, he's sitting to the right of it."

Los finally made him out and they ran stumbling towards the craft. The creature sitting next to the craft moved to one side leaping between the cacti, then he jumped into the air and opening long, webbed wings with a crackling noise, lifted off, and describing a semi-circle, soared over the men. It was the same creature which at a distance they had taken for a bird. Gusev took aim, hoping to cut down the winged animal in its flight. But Los suddenly knocked the weapon from his hand shouting:

"You're insane, it's a man!"

Starting, his mouth open, Gusev looked at the astonishing creature describing circles in the vast blue sky. Los took out his handkerchief and waved at the bird:

"Mstislav Sergeevich, be careful he doesn't drop something on us."

"Put away your revolver."

The great bird came closer. Now they could plainly see a man-like creature sitting in a saddle on the flying machine. He sat freely, his upper body in the open air. At the level of his shoulders flapped two pointed flexible wings. Below and in front of him spun a blurred disc—apparently a propeller. Behind the saddle was a forked tail with rudders. The entire craft was as mobile and flexible as a living creature.

Then he dove, approaching close to the ground with one wing dropped and the other lifted. They could see The Martian's head topped by a tight fitting hat with a tall peak. Over his eyes were glasses. His face was the color of brick, narrow, wrinkled, with a sharp nose. He opened his wide mouth and shouted something. Faster, faster, the wings flapped as he dropped, ran along the ground, and leaped from his saddle thirty paces from the men.

The Martian was as tall as a man of average height, dressed in a dark, broad jacket. His meager legs to a point above his knees were enclosed in woven sandals. With fervor he began to point at the fallen cacti. But when Los and Gusev approached closer, with agility he leaped into the saddle, shook a long warning finger at them, rose easily, hovered briefly without movement, and then once more settled onto the ground, continuing to exclaim in a piping thin voice, meanwhile pointing at the broken vegetation.

"He's crazy, he's got his feelings hurt," said Gusev, shouting at the Martian: "The hell with your damn cactus, keep shouting, and I'll settle you."

"Alexei Ivanovich, stop abusing him, he doesn't understand Russian. Sit down, otherwise he won't come any closer."

Los and Gusev sat down on the scorching ground. Los tried to show that they wanted to drink and eat. Gusev lit up and spat. For a time the Martian watched them, ceasing to shout but still threatening them with a finger as long as a pencil. Finally, he loosened a bag from his saddle, threw it in the men's direction, rose in circles to a great height, and rapidly left for the north, disappearing behind the horizon.

In the bag turned out to be two metal boxes and a wicker-bottle with some kind of beverage. Gusev opened the boxes with his knife and found in one a powerfully fragrant jelly and in the other lumps resembling Turkish Delight. Gusev smelled them.

"Ugh, the bastards eat that."

He brought food in a basket from the ship, collected dry cactus branches and lit them. A light stream of yellow smoke and the cactus turned to embers, but still gave off considerable heat. They heated a pan with corned beef and spread their food on a clean cloth. They devoured their food, only now feeling an overwhelming hunger.

The sun stood overhead, the wind fell, and it was hot. A lizard ran over the orange hummocks. Gusev threw a bit of dry bread at it. Rising onto its front legs, it lifted its triangular crowned head and froze as still as a stone.

Los asked for a cigarette, lay down, resting his cheek on his hand, lit up an, and smiled.

"Do you know, Alexei Ivanovich, how long it's been since we ate?"

"Since last evening, Mstislav Sergeevich, before take-off, when I filled up on potatoes."

"Well, my friend, we haven't eaten for twenty-three or twenty-four days."

"How long?"

"Yesterday in St. Petersburg it was August 18," said Los, "But today in St. Petersburg it's September 11; that's what I call a miracle."

"No matter what you do to me, Mstislav Sergeevich, I can't understand that."

"Well, its true that I don't understand it too well, but it's so. We took off at 7 o'clock. You can see it's two in the afternoon now. Nineteen hours ago we left the earth—according to this watch. But according to the clock which is still in my workshop about a month has passed. You've noticed that when you travel in a train, and you're asleep and the train stops, you either wake up from the unpleasant sensation or you get nauseated in your sleep. That's because when the car stops your whole body is subject to deceleration. When you lie in a moving car both your beating heart and your watch are going faster than if you were in a car which is stationary. The difference can't be measured because the rate of movement is so insignificant. But our flight is a different matter. We made half our journey at a speed close to that of light. Now that is considerably different. The beating of our hearts, the rate of movement within our watches and the movement of particles in our body cells did not change in relation to each other while we were flying through airless space—we were now in the craft, and everything within it moved in one rhythm. But, if the speed of the craft exceeded by five hundred thousand times the normal speed of a body moving on earth, then my heart rate—one beat per second, if you measure it by the clock in the craft—has increased by five hundred thousand times, that is, my heart during the flight was beating at a rate of five hundred thousand times per second, according to a clock which remained behind in St. Petersburg. Judging from my heartbeats, the movement of the hands on the watch in my pocket, and the feelings in my body, during our journey ten hours and forty minutes passed. And in fact it was ten hours and forty minutes. But judging from the heart of a St. Petersburg inhabitant and according to the movements of the hands on the clock on Peter and Paul Cathedral more than three weeks has passed from the day of our departure. As a result we will be able to build a large craft, provide for it enough food, oxygen, and Ultra-lyddite to last six months, and then to suggest to some eccentrics—'So you don't want to live in our age with wars, revolutions, and rebellions—a chaos. So you want to live a hundred years in the future? All you have to do is wait for half a year in this box, but then, what will life be like? You'll leap over a century.' And they'll have to be sent with the speed of light for a half a year into interstellar space. They'll be bored, their beards will grow, and they'll return to earth to find a golden age. And school boys will learn that a hundred years ago all Europe was shaken by wars and revolutions. The capitals of the world fell into anarchy. No one could believe in anyone or anything. The earth had never seen such misfortunes. But then in every country there came to be a core of courageous and hardy men, who called themselves "The Just." They took power and began to build a world on different new principles—justice, mercy, and the official recognition of the desire for happiness—that's particularly important, Alexei Ivanovich—happiness. And that's the way it will all be, someday."

Gusev said "Ah!", clicked his tongue, and was astonished:

"Mstislav Sergeevich, what do you think about this food—is it poisonous?" With his teeth he pulled the stopper out of the Martian's wicker bottle, tested the liquid on his tongue, and spat: "We can drink it," he swallowed and cleared his throat. "It's like Madeira, try it."

Los tasted it: the liquid was thick and sweetish with a strong nutmeg bouquet. With misgivings they drank half a bottle. He felt warmth and a peculiar buoyant energy spread through his body. But his head remained clear.

Los rose and stretched expansively. It was good, exciting, and strange to stand under another sky—unheard of, a wonder. It was as though he had been cast upon the shore of a stellar ocean, reborn into an unknown and novel life.

Gusev stowed the basket with the food in the craft, tightened down the hatch firmly, and pushed his cap to the back of his head:

"Good, Mstislav Sergeevich, I'm not sorry I came."

They decided to return once more to the embankment and walk until evening over the hilly plain. Talking spiritedly, they walked through the cacti, sometimes jumping over them with long springing leaps. The stones of the sloping embankment soon appeared white through the vegetation.

Suddenly Los stopped walking. A chill ran down his spine. Three paces away, close to the ground from out of the succulent vegetation, peered two great horse's eyes half veiled by red lids. They stared at him with demented animosity.

"What's the matter?" asked Gusev and then he also saw the eyes. Without hesitation he fired at them as the dust rose. The eyes disappeared.

"There it is!" Gusev turned and fired once more close to the ground at a creature running wildly—eight angular legs, a reddish, finely striped and stout body. It was a huge spider-like creature which on the earth is found only at the bottom of the sea. It fled into the vegetation.

AN ABANDONED HOUSE

From the embankment to the nearest grove of trees Los and Gusev made their way over reddish burned cinders, leaping across collapsing narrow canals and rounding dry ponds. Here and there in the drifted channels protruded the rusty frameworks of barges. Here and there on the dead melancholy plain gleamed convex discs, apparently hatches. They tried to lift them, but they turned out to be bolted down. The bright points of these discs stretched from the ragged mountains along the hills toward the woods and toward the ruins.

Between two hills stood the nearest woods, a grove of low-growing reddish trees with spreading flat-topped branches. Their branches were gnarled and stout, while their leaves were like fine moss and their trunks were sinewy and knotted. In a clearing between the trees hung rusted strands of barbed wire.

They entered the woods. Gusev bent low and kicked—from out of the dust flew a broken skull in which gleamed gold teeth. The air grew close. The mossy branches cast a thin shade in the windless hot air. Within a few paces they came upon another convex disc which was bolted to the base of a circular metal shaft. At the edge of the woods stood a dwelling in ruins, thick brick walls broken as though by an explosion, piles of debris, and the protruding ends of twisted metal beams.

"These buildings have been blown up, Mstislav Sergeevich, look here," said Gusev. "There was some kind of a fight here, the kind we know so well."

On a pile of rubble appeared a large spider which ran down the broken edge of a wall. Gusev fired at it. The spider leaped into the air and, spinning, fell. Then a second spider ran behind the building towards the trees, raising brown dust, and collided with the tangle of wires, struggling in it with its legs outstretched.

From the grove Gusev and Los climbed onto a hill and then descended to a second woods in which from a distance they could see brick structures and one stone building which was higher than the others and had a flat roof. Between the hill and the settlement lay several discs. Pointing at them Los said:

"Apparently those are the shafts for underground transmission lines. But it's been abandoned. The whole region's deserted."

They crawled over a tangle of barbed wire, made their way through the woods and came to a courtyard paved with large flagstones. In its midst touching the trees stood a building of strange and somber architecture. Its smooth walls tapered upwards and were topped by a massive cornice constructed of blood-dark stone. In the smooth walls were narrow and deep windows like slits. Two square columns made of the same blood-dark stone which also tapered upwards supported the carved roof of the entryway. Broad steps, as wide as the building, led to a low and massive door. Dried strands of creeping vegetation hung between the slabs of the walls. The building resembled an enormous tomb.

Gusev leaned his shoulder against a door mounted in bronze. It yielded to him. They passed through a dark vestibule and entered a many-walled high-ceilinged hall. Into it light entered through the glazed windows of an arched cupola. The hall was nearly empty. A few overthrown stools, a table with a cloth turned back on one corner and a dish with the dried remains of food, a few low couches near the walls, and on the stone floor metal containers, broken bottles, some kind of machine or tool of strange form consisting of discs, spheres, and a metal network which stood near the door—everything was covered with a layer of dust.

Dusty light from the cupola fell onto the yellowed marble-like walls. Near the ceiling, the walls were banded by a broad mosaic frieze. Obviously it represented events from ancient history—a battle between yellow-skinned and red-skinned giants, ocean waves with a human figure emerging above the waist, the same figure flying among the stars, then battle scenes, scenes from the hunt, a herd of shaggy animals driven by shepherds, scenes from domestic life, hunting, dancing, birth and death—this gloomy zone of mosaics, over the door, met a depiction of the construction of a gigantic reservoir.

"Strange, strange," repeated Los as he climbed onto the couches the better to see the mosaic, "Alexei Ivanovich, can you see the drawing of a head on those shields, what is it?"

Gusev in the meantime had found a barely noticeable door which opened to a closed staircase leading into a broad, arched corridor flooded by dusty light. Along the walls in niches stood stone and bronze statues, busts, heads, masks, and fragments of vases. Doors decorated with marble and bronze led to inside rooms.

Gusev went to inspect the lateral rooms which were low, musty, and dimly lighted. In one of them was a dry basin in which lay a dead spider. In the next was a shattered mirror which covered one of the walls, while on the floor were a pile of rotted cloth, upset furniture and chests containing fragments of clothing.

In the third room, low, hung with rugs, on a dais under a tall shaft from which streamed light stood a wide bed. From it was draped, half-extended, the skeleton of a Martian. Everywhere were the signs of a bitter struggle. In the corner lay a second skeleton, doubled up. Here in the midst of trash and rags Gusev found several objects made of a hammered heavy metal, apparently gold. They were a woman's objects, jewelry, coffers, and flasks. He took from the rotting garments on the skeleton great faceted stones which were transparent and as dark as the night, connected by a chain. Not bad loot at all.

Los inspected the statues in the corridor. Among the stone heads with their sharp noses, among the images of tiny monsters, among the painted masks, among the vases made of assembled fragments which in a strange fashion in outline and decoration were reminiscent of ancient Etruscan ware, his attention was captured by a large belted statue. It represented a naked woman with wild hair and a furious twisted face. Her pointed breasts were averted to the sides. Her head was encircled by a crown of stars, which above her brow extended into a delicate parabola, within which were enclosed two spheres: the one ruby and the other brick red ceramic. In the features of that emotional and powerful visage was something disturbingly familiar which arose from his most uncertain memories.

To one side of the statue was a small dark niche protected by a screen. Los inserted his fingers through the bars but the grating would not yield. Lighting a match, he saw in the niche on a rotted pillow, a golden mask. It was a representation of a broad-cheeked human face with serenely closed eyes. The crescent mouth smiled. The nose was pointed and aquiline. On the forehead between the eyebrows was a protuberance in the shape of a flattened honeycomb.

Los burned up half his box of matches as with increasing emotion he gazed at the mask. Not long before he left the earth he had seen photographs of masks like it discovered in the ruins of huge cities on the banks of the Niger in those regions of Africa where traces of the culture of a lost race had been found.

One of the side doors in the corridor was ajar. Los entered a long, very high room with a gallery with a stone balustrade. Below and above on the gallery were flat bookcases and shelves with tiny, thick books. Chased and with golden lettering, their spines stretched in uniform rows lining the gray walls. In some of the cabinets stood metal cylinders and in others great books bound in leather or wood. From the cabinets, from the shelves, from the dark corners of the library gazed with stony eyes the wrinkled bald heads of Martian scholars. In the room were scattered several deep chairs and cabinets on slender legs to the sides of which were attached circular screens.

Holding his breath, Los surveyed this treasure house with its odor of rot and must where spoke the wisdom of thousands of years of the Martian past with the mute tongues of books.

With soft steps he walked over to a shelf and began to open the books. Their paper was greenish, the writing angular and of a soft brownish color. One of the books with diagrams of hoisting machinery Los shoved into his pocket to be inspected at his leisure. Inserted into the metal cylinders he found yellowish rollers, hollow to the touch like bones, which were similar to phonograph cylinders, but whose outer surfaces were smooth like glass. One of these cylinders lay on the cabinet with a screen, apparently ready to be used but abandoned at the time of the destruction of the house.

Then Los opened a black bookcase and at random selected a light, puffy volume bound in leather eaten by worms and with his sleeve brushed the dust off it. Its yellow ancient pages folded fan-wise top to bottom with a continuous band of marks in zig-zag form. The pages one after another were covered with colored triangles the size of a finger-nail. They ran from left to right and the reverse in uneven lines which fell or merged. They changed in outline and color. Several pages later, among the triangles appeared colored circles which changed form and color like creatures. The triangles began to appear in figures. The merging and transformation of these colored triangular, circular, rectangular, and complex figures ran from page to page. Slowly, in Los's ears began to play an elusive, subtle, piercingly plaintive music.

He closed the book, covered his eyes with his hand and stood for a long time leaning against the book shelves, stirred and enchanted by a novel wonder—a singing book.

"Mstislav Sergeevich," Gusev's voice echoed through the house, "Come here, quick."

Los went into the corridor. At its end in a doorway Gusev stood with a frightened smile on his lips.

"Come and see what's happening."

He led Los into a narrow semi-lighted room on the far wall of which was a large square clouded mirror before which stood several stools and chairs.

"See that ball hanging on the cord, well, I thought it was gold, so I tried to pull it off, and look what happens."

Gusev pulled on the ball, the mirror became light and there appeared great terraced buildings, windows gleaming in the sunset, the waving branches of trees, and the hollow roar of a crowd filled the dark room. Over the mirror from top down advanced a winged shadow which enveloped the outlines of the city. Suddenly a fiery explosion filled the screen, a sharp crack resounded under the floor, and the clouded mirror faded.

"A short circuit, a connection has burned out," said Gusev, "And anyway, it's time to leave, Mstislav Sergeevich, soon it'll be night."

SUNDOWN

Throwing out narrow hazy wings, the blazing sun was declining.

Los and Gusev ran across the twilight expanse, now even more desolate and wild, towards the banks of the canal. The sun was rapidly departing over the distant edge of the plain and then it disappeared. A blinding scarlet glow spread from where the sun had gone down. Its sharp rays lighted up half the sky and then rapidly, rapidly it was covered by gray ash—the fire was extinguished. The sky grew dense.

In the gray sundown low on the horizon arose a great red star. It stood like an angry eye. For a few moments the darkness was full of only its gloomy rays.

But then over all the limitless sky stars began to appear, gleaming, greenish constellations—their icy rays pierced the eyes. The gloomy star as it rose blazed forth.

When they reached the embankment, Los paused and pointing at the red star said:

"The earth."

Gusev removed his cap and wiped the sweat from his brow. His head back, he looked at his distant homeland soaring among the constellations. His face was sad and pale.

And so they stood for a long time in the faint light of the stars on the canal's ancient embankment.

But then from behind the dark and precise line of the horizon appeared a bright sickle, smaller than the earth's moon, which rose over the cactused plain.

Long shadows fell from the palmate vegetation.

Gusev touched Los.

"Look behind us."

Behind them over the undulating plain above the groves and ruins stood Mars' second satellite. Its round, yellowish disc, also smaller than the earth's moon, inclined towards the ragged mountains. On the ground the metallic discs gleamed towards the hills.

"Well, night is here," whispered Gusev, "And it's like a dream."

They carefully descended from the embankment into the dark growths of cactus. From under their feet darted a shadow. A shaggy mass dashed through the patches of moonlight. There were crackling noises. Something whined, piercingly, unbearably keen. In the dead light, the leaves of the cactus stirred and gleamed. Spider webs as tough as nets touched their faces.

Suddenly, without warning a horrifying and excruciating roar split the night. Then it broke off. Everything was calm. Gusev and Los with great leaps, trembling in loathing and terror, ran across the plain through the quivering vegetation.

Finally, in the light of the ascending sickle gleamed the craft's steel skin. They had arrived. Panting, they sat down.

"Well, I'm not one for these spidery places," said Gusev, opening the hatch and crawling into the craft.

Los paused for a moment. He listened and watched. Then he saw it—between the stars soared a black, fantastic silhouette, the winged shadow of an aircraft.

LOS LOOKS AT THE EARTH

The shadow of the aircraft disappeared. Los climbed onto the exterior of his craft, lighted up a pipe, and gazed at the stars. A slight chill touched his body.

Gusev was busy inside the craft, mumbling, inspecting and hiding the objects he had found. Then he stuck his head out of the hatch:

"What do you think, Mstislav Sergeevich, it's all gold, and the gems are priceless. When I sell those things in Petersburg I'll get a barrel of money. My dimwit will sure be happy."

His head disappeared and soon he was completely silent. He was a happy man, Gusev was.

Los could not sleep, but sat blinking at the stars and sucking at his pipe. What did it all mean? How had the African masks with that separate honeycomb third eye come to Mars? And the mosaics? And the giants drowning in the sea and flying through the stars? And the sphinx heads on the shields? And the signs on the parabola—was the ruby sphere the earth and the ceramic one Mars? The sign of power over two worlds. It was incomprehensible. And the singing book? And the strange city which appeared on the clouded mirror? And then—why was this entire region desolate and deserted?

Los knocked the ash out of his pipe on his heel and once more filled it with tobacco. He wished day would come. Obviously the Martian aircraft would be spreading the word somewhere in some populated area.

Maybe they were already searching for them and the aircraft which had flown under the stars had been sent with the purpose of getting them.

Los looked at the sky. The light from the reddish star had turned pale as it was approaching the zenith, and a ray from it touched his very heart.

That sleepless night when he stood in the doorway of the shed, Los, just as now, with chill melancholy had watched Mars rise over the horizon. That was only two nights ago. Only one night separated him from the earth and its tormenting ghosts. But what a night!

The earth, the green earth, now in clouds, now in passing light, luxuriant, many-watered, so wastefully cruel to its children, drenched in hot blood, but still so beloved, his homeland . . .

Icy cold swept over him; Los saw himself clearly, sitting in the midst of an alien plain on an iron box, like a solitary devil, cast out, by the Spirit of the earth. A thousand years of the past and a thousand of the future—wasn't that the unbroken life of one body liberating itself from chaos? Perhaps that reddish sphere which was the earth soaring in stellar space—was it merely the carnal heart of the great Spirit, cast out into the millennia? A man, ephemeral, awakes for a moment of life, he, Los, alone, by his insane will had absented himself from the great Spirit, and now, like a despondent devil, despised and accursed, he sat alone in the wilderness.

It was enough to chill the heart. Solitude, solitude. Los leaped from the craft and crawled into the hatch next to the snoring Gusev. He felt better. This simple man had not betrayed his homeland, he had only flown over hill and dale to this seventh heaven where his only concern was what he could seize to take home to Masha. He slept calmly, his conscience clear.

From the heat and fatigue Los began to drowse. In his sleep he found consolation. He saw the bank of a terrestrial river, birches rustling in the wind, clouds, the sun sparkling on the water, and on the opposite shore someone in white was waving, calling, summoning him.

The powerful roar of propellers woke Los and Gusev.

THE MARTIANS

Blinding pink lines of clouds like skeins of yarn strewn from east to west filled the morning sky. Now appearing in the dark blue patches of sky, now disappearing behind the pink lines of clouds, descended, gleaming in the sun, an airship. The outline of its three masted fuselage resembled that of a Carthagenian galley. Three pairs of tapered, flexible wings extended from its sides.

The ship cut through the clouds, and dripping moisture silver, gleaming, hung over the cacti. On its stubby masts roared three vertical propellers which held it in the air. Stairways dropped from its sides and the ship came to rest on them. The propellers ceased turning.

Down the stairs ran the slight figures of the Martians. They all wore the same egg-shaped helmets and silver, loose jackets with thick collars which concealed their necks and the lower parts of their faces. In the arms of each of them was a weapon resembling a stubby rifle with a disc at the midsection.

Gusev, his head down, stood near the craft. His hand on his Mauser, he watched as the Martians fell into two ranks. Their weapons rested with their muzzles in their crooked arms.

"The bastards hold their weapons like old women," he muttered.

His arms crossed on his chest, Los stood smiling. The last to leave the ship was a Martian dressed in a black gown falling in broad folds. His bared head was bald and knobby. His beardless narrow face was sky-blue.

Wading with effort through the loose soil, he passed before the two rows of soldiers. His protruding light and cold eyes fastened on Gusev. Then he shifted his attention exclusively to Los. Coming close to the men, he lifted a puny hand in its wide sleeve and speaking in a thin brittle voice, uttered a bird-like call:

"Taltsetl."

He opened yet wider his eyes alight with cool surmise. He repeated the bird-like word and pointed commandingly at the sky. Los said:

"The earth."

"The earth," the Martians repeated with difficulty, the skin on his brow wrinkling. The knobs on his head darkened. Gusev stood, his legs apart, coughed, and said angrily:

"From Russia, we're Russians, that is, we've come to visit you, hello," he touched his cap, "Don't harm us and we won't harm you . . . Mstislav Sergeevich, he doesn't understand a thing."

The Martian's intelligent blue face was immobile, only on his bulging forehead between his eyebrows emerged a reddish spot, the result of his intellectual effort. With an easy movement of his hand he pointed at the sun and said what was to him a familiar word with its strange sound:

"Soatsr."

He pointed at the ground, opened wide his arms, as though holding a ball:

"Tuma."

He pointed at one of the soldiers standing in a semi-circle behind him, pointed at Gusev, at himself, and at Los:

"Shokho."

In this manner he named several objects and listened to their equivalents in the language of the earth. Approaching Los he solemnly touched the space between his eyebrows with his ring finger. Los inclined his head as a sign of greeting.

Gusev, after he had been touched, pulled the visor of his cap onto his forehead:

"Like dealing with wild men."

The Martian went up to the craft and with repressed attention looked at it, and then apparently having grasped its principle, with excitement he examined the huge steel egg covered with a layer of soot. Suddenly, throwing up his hands, he turned to the soldiers and began to speak to them very rapidly, lifting to the heavens his doubled fists.

"Aiu," howled the soldiers.

He placed his palm on his brow, breathed deeply, then overcome with emotion he turned to Los and now without restraint with dark moist eyes looked hard at him:

"Aiu," he said, "Aiu utara shókho, dátsia tuma géo taltsetl."

Then he covered his eyes with his hand and bowed deeply. Straightening up, he summoned a soldier, took from him a slender knife and began to scratch the craft's skin: he drew an egg, above it a roof, next to it the figure soldier. Gusev watching over his shoulder said:

"He wants to build a shelter and station here, but, Mstislav Sergeevich, I hope they don't take our things, since there are no locks on the hatches."

"Please, Alexei Ivanovich, don't be a fool."

"But there's gold. And I've been looking closely at that soldier, and I don't like what I see."

The Martian listened to this conversation with attention and respect. Los indicated by signs that he was willing to leave the craft under guard. The Martian placed a slender whistle to his wide, thin mouth and blew. From the ship someone answered with the same penetrating whistle. Then the Martian began to whistle some kind of signals. On the summit of the central and highest mast there arose, like hair, sections of slender wire which gave off crackling sparks.

The Martian indicated the way to the aircraft for Los and Gusev. The soldiers closed in and made a surrounding circle. Gusev glanced at them, smiled a crooked smile, went to their own ship, removed from it two sacks with clothes and other belongings, tightly screwed down the hatch, and pointing at it for the soldiers' benefit, slapped his Mauser, shook his finger at them and scowled. In astonishment the Martians followed his actions.

"Well, Alexei Ivanovich, I don't know whether we're guests or prisoners, but there's no place else to go," said Los, laughing, as he threw a bag over his shoulder and they stepped towards the aircraft.

On its masts the vertical propellers began to turn with a great roar. The wings dropped lower. The propellers howled. The guests—or was it prisoners?—ascended the flimsy stairway into the ship.

BEYOND THE RAGGED MOUNTAINS

The airship flew at a low altitude over Mars towards the northwest. Los and the bald Martian remained on deck. Gusev had descended into the ship's interior with the soldiers.

In the brightly lit cabin painted straw yellow he sat in a wicker chair

and for a moment observed the sharp-nosed slim soldiers who blinked their
eyes, red like birds. Then he took out his beloved tin cigarette case with its
engraving of the Kremlin's Czar-cannon—for seven years no matter where
he fought, it had never left him—slapped the Czar-cannon, and said "Let's
have a smoke, comrades," and offered them a cigaret.

The Martians shook their heads in fright. Still, one of them took a cigaret, examined it, sniffed it, and deposited it in the pocket of his white
trousers. But when Gusev lit up, the soldiers in abject fear stepped back and
whispered in their bird voices:

"Shókho, táo khávra, shókh-om."

Their reddish sharp faces watched in horror as the "shokho" inhaled
the smoke. But they too inhaled a little, became less agitated and once more
sat down beside him.

Gusev, not especially discomfited by his ignorance of the Martian language, began to tell his new friends about Russia, the war, revolution, and
his exploits, bragging without restraint:

"Gusev, that's my name. Gusev, it's from 'goose,' we've got a lot of
them on the earth, but I'll bet you've never seen anything like them. And
my first and second names are Alexei Ivanovich. I didn't command just a
regiment, but a cavalry division. I was a ferocious fighter, a terror. My tactics were simple: machine guns or no machine guns, use your saber, and I'd
say, 'Give up your positions, you sons-a-bitches,' and then attack. I've been
all cut up myself, but I don't give a damn. In our military academy there's
even a special course called 'Gusev Saber Tactics,' honest to God, don't you
believe me? They offered me a corps," with one finger Gusev pushed back
his cap and scratched behind his ear, "I'm tired of it, no, excuse me. I've
fought for seven years, let someone else have it. And then Mstislav Sergeevich
summoned me, and said 'Alexei Ivanovich, I'll never make it to Mars without you.' That's the way it was, you bet. Exactly."

The Martians listened in astonishment. One brought in a flask with a
brown and vaguely greenish liquid. Another opened canned food. From his
bag Gusev brought out a half a bottle of pure spirits transported from the
earth. The Martians drank it and murmured to one another. Gusev began
to embrace them, slapped them on the back, and became effusive. Then he
began to drag various objects out of his pockets, offering to exchange them.
Joyfully, the Martians gave him gold objects for a pocket knife, a pencil
stub, and a unique cigaret lighter made out of a spent cartridge. Soon Gusev
was on friendly terms with all of them.

In the meantime, Los, leaning his elbows on the aircraft's open railing,
surveyed the melancholy undulating plain which flowed below them. He
recognized the house which they had visited yesterday. Everywhere there
were similar ruins, clumps of trees, and the dry beds of canals.

Pointing at this desert, Los managed to express his perplexity—why was this entire region abandoned and dead? The protruding eyes of the bald Martian suddenly became malevolent. He made a sign and the ship rose, made a circle, and then flew towards the summits of the ragged mountains.

The sun rose high in the sky and the clouds disappeared. The propellers roared, the flexible wings creaked as the ship turned or rose, and the vertical propellers hummed. Los noted that besides the hum of the propellers and the whistling of the wind in the wings and the perforated masts no other sound could be heard; the motors operated silently. The motors themselves could not be seen. Only at the hub of every propeller spun a rounded box, like the housing for a dynamo, and at the tops of the forward and rear masts crackled two elliptical basket-like devices made of silvery wires.

Los asked the Martian for the names of objects which he wrote down. Then he removed the newly found book with its drawings from his pocket and asked him to produce the sounds indicated by the geometric letters. With astonishment the Martian looked at the book. Once more his eyes grew cold and his thin lips twisted with disgust. He patiently removed the book from Los's hands and threw it over the side.

Thanks to the altitude and the force of the wind Los's chest began to ache and tears came to his eyes. When he noticed this, the Martian gave a sign to descend to a lower altitude. The ship was now flying over blood-red barren crags. A winding, broad mountain range stretched from the southeast towards the northwest. The aircraft's shadow flew below them over jagged cliffs sparkling with veins of ore and metals, over towering cliffs hung with lichens, tore across misted gulfs, and shadowed in passing snow-covered peaks sparkling like diamonds, and mirrored glaciers. The area was wild and without inhabitants.

"Liziazira," said the Martian, nodding towards the mountains and exposing his little teeth gleaming in gold.

As he looked below at the cliffs which reminded him so much of a dead landscape, in a gorge he saw the twisted frame of an aircraft surrounded by fragments of silver metal. Then, from behind a ridge appeared the broken wing of a second aircraft. To the right, pierced on a granite peak, hung a third aircraft, all in fragments. Everywhere in these regions could be seen the wreckage of great wings, broken fuselages, and protruding airframes. This was a battlefield where, it seems, the demons had been cast down onto these barren heights.

Los glanced at his neighbor. The Martian sat holding his gown to his neck, quietly watching the sky. Towards the aircraft flew a line of long-winged birds. Then they rose, their yellow wings flashing against the dark sky, and turned away. Following their descent, Los saw the black water of a circular lake, lying deep within the cliffs. Curling vegetation clung to its banks. The yellow birds came to rest near the water. Waves appeared on the lake's surface, they became yet more turbulent, and then from its center rose a great stream of water which threw itself outward and then fell back.

"Soám," said the Martian solemnly.

The mountain range ended. To the northwest through transparent, vibrant heat waves could be seen a canary yellow plain with large bodies of water. The Martian raised his hand towards the hazy mysterious distant land and said with a broad smile:

"Azóra."

The aircraft rose slightly. Moist sweet air blew against their faces and sounded in their ears. Azora spread out before them as a broad shining plain. Divided by broad canals, covered with orange clumps of vegetation and bright yellow plains, Azora—the name means "Happiness"—seemed like those miniature springtime meadows which we saw in our dreams in our distant childhood.

Ships and small boats moved on the canals. Along their banks were small white houses and the small pathways of kitchen gardens. Everywhere the tiny figures of the Martians could be seen. Some were using the flat-roofed hous-es as platforms and from them soaring like bats over the canals or to the woods. Windmills spun on transparent towers. Everywhere in the meadows glittered ponds and sparkled streams of water. A marvelous land was Azora.

At the far end of the plain shimmered in the sunlight a great expanse of water towards which flowed the curving lines of all the canals. The aircraft flew in its direction and Los finally saw a large straight canal. Its distant bank was sunk in watery haze. Along a sloping stone embankment its yel-lowish turbid waters flowed slowly.

They flew for a long time. Finally at the end of the canal, the even edge of a wall began to lift itself out of the water, disappearing beyond the hori-zon. The wall grew larger in size. Now they could see in it huge dressed stones with bushes and trees growing out of the crevices. They approached a gigantic circular reservoir. It was full of water. Above its surface in many places rose the foaming crests of fountains . . .

"Ro," said the Martian, lifting his finger significantly.

Los brought a notebook from his pocket, hunted through it hastily to find a map of the lines and dots on Mars which he had made the day before. He extended the drawing to his neighbor and pointed below him at the reservoir. The Martian looked at it, frowned, understood, joyfully nodded, and with the nail of his little finger indicated one of the dots on the sketch.

Bending over the side, Los could make out two straight canals and one winding one, which, full of water, flowed out of the reservoir. So this was the secret: the round circles on Mars were reservoirs for water storage, while the triangles and semicircles were canals. But what kind of creatures could have built these cyclopean walls? Los looked at his traveling companion. The Martian stuck out his lower lip, and spread his extended arms to the sky:

"Tao khatskha utalitsitl."

Now the ship was crossing a scorched plain. On it lay the rose-colored, broad, waterless cultivated bed of a fourth canal, covered, just as though it had been sown, with regular rows of vegetation. Apparently this was one of a secondary network of canals—a pale network on the outline of Mars.

The plain became a region of low soft hills. Beyond them appeared the blue outlines of latticed towers. On the craft's middle mast the bundle of wires rose and began to scatter sparks. Beyond the hills rose more and more outlines of latticed towers and terraced buildings. A huge city emerged in a silvery shadow from the hazy sunlight. The Martian said: "Soatséra."

SOATSERA

The sky-blue outlines of Soatsera, the terraces on its flat roofs, its latticed walls covered with greenery, the oval mirrors of its ponds, and its airy towers emerged from beyond the hills, spreading further and further, lost on the hazy horizon. A number of dark objects above the city flew to meet the airship.

The cultivated canal receded towards the north. To the east of the city opened up an empty eroded plain strewn here and there with detritus. At the edge of this waste land, casting a sharp and long shadow rose the giant statue of a man, cracked and covered with lichen.

The stone figure of the naked man stood erect, his feet slightly apart, his arms held close to his narrow hips. A worked belt supported his deep chest, while his helmet with ear pieces and crowned by a pointed crest, like the fin of a fish, gleamed dully in the sun. His crescent mouth smiled on his broad-cheeked face, while his eyes were closed.

"Magatsitl," said the Martian, pointing at the sky.

Beyond the statue could be seen the enormous ruins of a reservoir and the sad outline of an aqueduct's fallen arches. Looking closely, Los understood that the stone on the plain, the pits, and the mounds were ruins of an ancient city. To the west of these ruins, a new city, Soatsera, began beyond the sparkling lake.

The black objects in the sky came closer, increasing in size. They were hundreds of Martians flying to greet them, riding on winged ships and small crafts, on birds made of canvas, and balloons. The first to meet them came close, banked sharply and hung over the ship, a shining, golden, four-winged narrow cigar-shaped object, like a dragonfly. From it showered flowers and brightly colored bits of paper which fell onto the deck of the craft, and out of it hung young, excited faces.

Los rose, and, holding onto a cable, removed his helmet—the wind lifted his white hair. From out of the cabin Gusev emerged and took a position next to him. Armloads of flowers floated towards them from out of the Martian aircraft. On the sky-blue or olive-skinned or brick-red faces of the Martians who came near to them were expressed the wildest excitement, delight, or horror.

Now, above their heads, from the front, the sides, and the rear of their slow-moving aircraft came hundreds of air ships. Here came gliding down in a balloon a fat Martian in a striped cap waving his arms. Here was a bearded face peering through a telescope. Here a sharp-nosed worried Martian, his hair flying, swung in front of the airship in a winged saddle, turning some kind of a spinning box towards Los. Here passed an open ship decorated with flowers and in it-three women's long goggle-eyed faces with blue bonnets, blue flying sleeves, and white scarves.

The song of the propellers, the roar of the wind in the craft's wings, the high-pitched whistles, the glitter of gold, the bright-colored clothing against the dark blue of the sky, and the vegetation of the parks below, now purple, now silver, now yellow, the windows of the terraced buildings which flashed in the sun—it was all like a dream. It was enough to make one's head spin. Gusev looked around, and kept repeating in a whisper:

"Look, just look . . ."

The ship flew past hanging gardens and smoothly came to rest on a large circular open space. Immediately like moths hundreds of ships, baskets, and great bird-like craft landed around it, thudding onto the white paving stone of the square. On the streets which radiated from it milled crowds of people, running, throwing flowers and bits of paper, and waving handkerchiefs.

The aircraft had landed near a tall, massive and gloomy building, like a pyramid, made of darkest red stone. On its broad stairs between square columns which tapered upwards to a distance of one-third of its height, stood a cluster of Martians. They were all in black gowns and round caps. This was, as Los was later to discover, the Supreme Council of Engineers—the highest governmental organ among the Martian nations.

Their Martian guide indicated to Los that they were to wait. Soldiers ran down the stairs and surrounded the aircraft, restraining the pressing crowds. Gusev in delight observed the tumultuous square and the bright clothing, the multitude of wings rising over their heads, the masses of grayish or dark red buildings, and the airy outlines of the towers beyond the roofs.

"Well, it's quite a city," he repeated, dancing in excitement.

On the stairs the Martians in black gowns opened their ranks. A tall, stooping Martian appeared, also dressed in black with a long, gloomy face and a long, narrow, black beard. On his cap trembled a golden crest like a fish's fin.

Descending the center of the stairs leaning on a stick he long surveyed the visitors from earth with his sunken dark eyes. Los too watched him, attentively, guardedly.

"Doesn't he know better than to stare, the devil," whispered Gusev.

Then he turned to the crowd and shouted enthusiastically: "Greetings, Martian comrades. We say hello to you and expect the best."

The dumbfounded crowd gasped, murmured, stirred, and moved closer. The gloomy Martian seized his beard with his hand, shifted his gaze to the crowd, and swept the square with his lackluster eyes. And under his glance the stormy sea of heads grew calmer. He turned to those standing on the stairway, said a few words, and raising his stick, pointed at the airship.

Immediately one of the Martians ran to the ship and softly and rapidly said something to the bald Martian who leaned to him over the side of the ship. Signal whistles were given, two soldiers ran up onto the craft, the propellers spun, and the aircraft, ponderously lifting off the square, flew over the city towards the north.

IN THE AZURE GROVE

Soatsera had disappeared far behind the hills. The airship was flying over a plain. Here and there could be seen the monotonous lines of buildings, the towers and cables of aerial tramways, mines, and loaded barges moving along narrow canals.

But then more and more frequently out of the forests rugged peaks began to lift themselves. The ship descended, flew though misted defiles, and landed on a meadow inclined towards dark and luxuriant woods.

Los and Gusev took their bags and together with their bald companion set off across the meadow downward toward the grove.

Water vapor, jetting from the lateral valves on irrigation pipes, played with rainbow colors over the curling grasses which were sparkling with moisture. A herd of compact, shaggy animals, black and white, were grazing over the slope. It was peaceful. Running waters murmured softly. A gentle wind blew.

The shaggy animals rose lazily as the men approached and made way for them, waddling their bear-like paws and averting their flat blunt muzzles. A shepherd boy in a long red shirt sat on a stone, his chin on his hand, lazily observing them as they passed. Yellow birds came to rest on the meadow, settled their wings, and shook themselves under the iridescent sprays of water. In the distance a solitary bright green crane wandered on its long legs.

They made their way to the grove. Its luxuriant pendulous branches were azure and sky-blue. The succulent celestial leaves rustled softly and the hanging branches murmured. Between the maculated trunks of the trees played the reflected light from a distant lake. A piquant and sweet sultriness in the blue grove made them slightly dizzy.

The grove was crossed by many paths strewn with orange sand. At their intersections in circular clearings stood large old sandstone statues, carved by other hands, touched by lichens. Above the undergrowth rose shattered columns and remains of cyclopean walls.

The trace turned towards the lake. Revealed now was its dark-blue mirrored surface with the reversed summit of a distant jagged mountain. The reflections of the weeping trees scarcely moved on the water. A luxuriant sun shone brightly. On the receding shoreline flanking a mossy stairway which descended into the lake were two huge sitting statues, cracked and overgrown with creeping vegetation.

On the steps emerging from the water appeared a young woman. A yellow pointed cap covered her head. She appeared to be young and slender and her complexion was pale blue against the massive figure, draped with moss, eternally smiling his dreaming smile, of the sitting Magatsitl. Then she slipped, seized a stone projection, and lifted her head.

"Aelita," whispered the Martian, covering his eyes with his sleeve and pulling Los and Gusev from the path into the grove.

Soon they emerged into a large clearing. In its midst in thick grass stood a gloomy gray house with inclined walls. From a star-shaped sandy courtyard which stood before its facade, direct paths ran across the meadow downwards towards the grove where among the trees could be seen a low brick structure.

The bald Martian whistled. From behind one corner of the house appeared a squat plump Martian in a striped gown. His crimson face looked as though it had been rubbed with a beet. Blinking in the sun he came closer, but when he perceived who they were he turned to dart back behind the corner of the house. The bald Martian spoke commandingly to him and the fat man, collapsing with fear, returned, showing a gold tooth in his otherwise toothless mouth, and led the guests into the house.

REST

The guests were led into brightly lighted small rooms which were nearly empty and which looked through narrow windows into the park. The walls of the dining room and bedrooms were lined with straw-colored mats. In the corner stood jars with miniature flowering trees. Gusev found their quarters suitable: "Like inside a basket, very nice."

The fat man in the striped gown who oversaw the house bustled about, muttered, waddled from door to door, wiped his skull with a brown cloth, and from time to time rolled his sclerotic eyes at the guests—and secretly clenched his hands in a strange manner, no doubt as a kind of a charm to ward off evil.

He ran water into a basin and led Los and Gusev each to his own bath—from the basin rose heavy clouds of steam. The touch of the hot, bubbling, light water to his immeasurably tired body was so sweet that Los almost fell asleep in the marble basin. The major-domo pulled him out by the hand.

Los barely staggered to the dining room where a table was set with a multitude of dishes with baked fish, pastries, fowl, tiny eggs and preserved fruits. The crisp rolls the size of a nut melted in his mouth.

They ate with tiny spoons. The major-domo stiffened when he saw how the men from the earth devoured the dishes of delicate foods. Gusev surrendered to his appetite, abandoned his spoon and ate with his hands, praising everything. The wine was especially good—it was white with a faint blue tint with a bouquet of earth and currants. It evaporated in the mouth and sent a fiery warmth through the veins.

After escorting his guests into their bedrooms the majordomo lingered for a longtime, fussing about, straightening the blankets and arranging the pillows. But a great and heavy sleep overwhelmed the "white giants." They breathed so heavily and snored so loudly that the windows trembled, the vegetation in the corners swayed, and the beds under their powerful bodies, so unlike those of the Martians, resounded.

Los opened his eyes. A bluish artificial light poured from the ceiling, as though from out of a cup. It was warm and pleasant in the bed. "What's happened? Where am I?" But he made no special effort to remember. "My God, how tired I am," he thought luxuriating, and closed his eyes again.

Some kind of radiant circles, as though water was flashing through azure leaves, floated into view. A premonition of astonishing joy, an expectation that soon from out of these radiant circles something was to emerge into his dream filled him with wondrous alarm.

In his drowsiness, smiling, he knitted his brows—struggling to penetrate that delicate curtain of shifting circles of sunlight. But a yet heavier sleep enveloped him like a cloud.

* * *

Los threw his legs off the bed. He sat up. For some time he sat in this position, his head down. Rising, he pulled aside a heavy blind. Beyond the narrow window burned the icy light of great stars whose unfamiliar pattern was strange and unsettling.

"Yes, yes, yes," said Los, "I'm no longer on the earth. The earth has remained behind. Icy wastes, endless space. So far to go! I'm in a new world. Well, certainly, but I'm dead. That I know. My soul is still there."

He sat on the bed. He dug his nails into his chest, over his heart. Then he lay face down.

"This is neither life nor death. My brain is alive, my body is alive. But I'm cast out. This is it, this is it—hell."

He bit the pillow so he would not cry out. He himself could not understand why for a second night he was still suffering such agonies for the earth and for himself who was now living beyond the stars. It was as though the thread of life had been torn free and his soul was struggling for life in an icy black void.

"Who's there?"

Los leaped to his feet. A ray of morning light pierced the window. The straw-lined little room was blindingly clean. Leaves murmured and birds chirped outside the window. Los rubbed his eyes and sighed. He felt alarmed but joyful.

Someone rapped once more lightly on the door. Los opened the door— in front of it stood the striped fat man holding to his stomach an armload of azure flowers sprinkled with dew:

"Aiu utara Aelita," he piped, extending the flowers.

THE CLOUDED BALL

After breakfast Gusev said:

"Mstislav Sergeevich, this won't do at all. We flew God knows how far, and look, we're sitting here in idleness. Probably they won't let us into the city—you saw how that bearded man, the dark one, frowned at us. Mstislav Sergeevich, watch out for him. His picture's hanging in my bedroom. For the time being they're giving us food and drink, but then what will happen? Drinking, eating, lying around in bathtubs, that isn't what we came for."

"Don't be in such a hurry, Alexei Ivanovich," said Los, looking at the azure flowers with their pungent and yet sweet odor. "Let's wait, look around, and they'll see that we aren't dangerous and allow us into the city."

"I don't know about you, Mstislav Sergeevich, but I didn't come here to lie around."

"Well, what do you think we ought to do?"

"It seems strange to hear that from you, Mstislav Sergeevich, maybe you've been sniffing something sweet [cocaine]."

"Do you want to quarrel with me?"

"No, I don't. But to sit around and smell flowers: that we could have done on earth. But I think since we're the first to get here, then Mars is ours now, Russian. We ought to make sure of that."

"You're a strange man, Alexei Ivanovich."

"We'll see which of us is strange." Gusev straightened his belt, shrugged and his eyes turned calculating. "It would be difficult, I know— there are only two of us. First we've got to get a document from them that says they want to become part of the Russian Federated Republic. They won't give it to us without a fight, of course, but you've already seen that everything is not right on Mars. I have a nose for that kind of thing."

"It's a revolution, then, that you want to make?"

"Hard to say, Mstislav Sergeevich, let's wait and see."

"No, please, let's get along without a revolution, Alexei Ivanovich."

"I don't care about the revolution, what I need is that document, Mstislav Sergeevich. What can we take back with us to St. Petersburg? Some kind of a dried spider, maybe? No, we'll go back and say: here's a document that says Mars has joined us. That wouldn't be like taking some province from Poland—it's a whole planet. That would make them sit up and take notice in Europe. Just gold alone, there are shiploads of it. That's the way it is, Mstislav Sergeevich."

Los looked at him pensively: it was impossible to say whether Gusev was joking or serious—his cunning guileless eyes were smiling, but somewhere in them lurked a touch of madness. Los shook his head and touching the translucent, waxen, azure petals on the great flowers said pensively:

"I've never known why I came to Mars. I flew here for the sake of flying. There were times when the visionary conquistadors equipped their ship and went off in search of new lands. Beyond the sea an unknown land would appear, the ship would enter an estuary, the Captain would remove his sweeping hat and name the country for himself: it was a glorious minute. Then he would plunder the country. Yes, you're probably right: it isn't enough to reach land—we ought to load up the ship with booty. Soon we'll be able to see the new world. And what treasures there are. Wisdom, Alexei Ivanovich, that's what we ought to take away on our ship. And your hands are itching all the time—that's not so good."

"We'll have a hard time coming to an agreement, Mstislav Sergeevich. You're not an easy man."

Los laughed:

"No, I'm only difficult with myself—we'll come to an agreement, my friend."

Someone scratched at the door. Rocking on his heels in fear and awe, the major-domo indicated with signs that they were to follow him. Los rose quickly and passed his hand over his white hair. Gusev screwed up his mustaches resolutely. Through corridors and stairways the guests walked to a distant part of the house.

The major-domo knocked at a low door. Beyond it responded a rapid, childlike voice. Los and Gusev entered a long white chamber. Sunbeams with their dancing motes fell through skylights onto a mosaic floor on which were reflected even rows of books, bronze statues standing between low cabinets, little tables on delicate pointed legs, and the clouded mirrors of screens.

Not far from the door and leaning against the bookshelves stood a young ashen-haired woman in a black dress which extended from her neck to the floor to the backs of her hands. Above her piled hair motes danced in a ray of the sun which fell like a sward into the gilded book bindings. It was the woman whom the day before the Martian had named Aelita.

Los bowed deeply to her. Aelita, without stirring, looked at him with the great pupils of her ashen eyes. Her pale blue elongated fare trembled ever so slightly. Her somewhat pert nose, her somewhat irregular mouth, were as delicate as a child's. As though she had been climbing a hill, her breast lifted lightly under the soft black folds of her dress.

"Ellio utara geo," she said in a voice delicate and soft, like music, almost a whisper, and inclined so low that the back of her head could be seen.

In response Los could only wring his hands until the knuckles cracked. Then, with effort, he said, for some reason in a voice full of ceremony:

"The visitors from earth salute you, Aelita."

He said it and blushed. Gusev said with aplomb:

"May we introduce ourselves—Colonel Gusev and the engineer, Mstislav Sergeevich Los. We have come to thank you for your hospitality."

Having heard the speech, Aelita lifted her head—her face became calmer and the pupils of her eyes contracted. She silently extended her hand with the narrow palm upwards and held it so for a brief time. It seemed to Los and Gusev that on her palm had appeared a small pale green ball. Aelita quickly reversed her palm and walked past the bookshelves into the depths of the library. Her guests followed.

Now Los could see that Aelita was as tall as his shoulder, slender and graceful like a little girl. The hem of her full dress swept over the mirrored mosaic. Turning to them, she smiled—but her eyes remained uneasy and cool.

She pointed at a leather bench which stood in a semicircular niche. Los and Gusev sat down. Then Aelita took her place near a reading table, placed her elbows on the table and began to survey her guests mildly and intently.

For a moment they all remained silent. With the passage of time Los felt tranquility and pleasure—such it was to contemplate this marvelous and strange girl. Gusev sighed and said in a whisper:

"A good lady, a very fine lady."

Then Aelita began to speak, as though she had touched a musical instrument—so magic was her voice. In phrase after phrase she repeated some kind of words. Her upper lip trembled and rose, and her ashen lashes touched. Her face was illuminated with charm and joy.

Once more she extended her hand before her, the palm upwards. Los and Gusev immediately perceived in the depths of her palm a pale green clouded ball, the size of a large apple. Shimmering, it constantly changed appearance.

Now both the guests and Aelita attentively observed the clouded opaline apple. Suddenly, its streaming markings ceased movement and dark masses appeared. As he watched it, Los cried out: on Aelita's palm lay the earth.

"Taltsetl," she said, pointed at it.

The ball began to turn slowly. Into sight came the outlines of America, then Asia's Pacific shore. Gusev became excited:

"That's us, we're Russians, that's ours," he said, poking at Siberia. The Urals appeared as curling shadow, then the thread of the lower Volga. The White Sea shore took shape.

"Here," said Los and indicated the Gulf of Finland. Aelita with surprise raised her eyes to him. The spinning of the ball ceased. Los concentrated and in his mind he saw part of a map—and immediately, as though in response to his imagination, a dark blotch appeared on the surface of the clouded ball and from it the radiating lines of railroads, a sign against a green field "St. Petersburg," and to its side the large red letter which began the word "Russia."

Aelita looked closely and covered the ball—but then it glowed through her fingers. Glancing at Los she shook her head:

"Otseo kho sua," she said, and he understood: "Concentrate and try to remember."

Then he began to recall the outlines of St. Petersburg the granite embankments, the icy blue waves of the Neva, a boat plunging through them with some kind of consumptive official as a passenger, the long arches of the Nicholas Bridge suspended in the fog, the dense smoke from the factories, the mists and clouds of a subdued sunset, a wet street, the sign of a corner store—"Tea, Sugar, and Coffee," an old cabby waiting at the corner.

Aelita, resting her chin in her hands, quietly contemplated the ball. In it passed Los's memories, at times clearly, at times shifting and blurred. There appeared a colonnade and the faint dome of St. Isaac's Cathedral, and then its place was taken by a granite stairway by the water's edge, a semi-circular bench, a sad girl sitting with an umbrella, while behind her were two sphinxes in tiaras. Then a column of figures came into view, a blueprint, and a glowing forge appeared with the morose Khokhlov fanning the coals.

For a long time Aelita observed the strange life passing before them in the ball's cloudy streamers. But then the images became confused: into them persistently intruded quite dissimilar outlines and scenes—lines of smoke, red skies, galloping horses, some kind of men who were running and falling. Then, blocking everything else, swam into view a terrible bearded face dripping blood. Gusev sighed deeply. In alarm Aelita turned to him, and then reversed her palm. The ball disappeared.

Aelita sat for a few moments, leaning on her elbows, her eyes covered with her hand. She arose, took a cylinder from a shelf, removed from it yet another ivory roller which she inserted into a table equipped with a screen. Then she pulled a cord and blue drapes swathed the upper windows in the library. She brought the table to the bench and turned a switch.

The screen became light and from its top downward appeared figures of Martians, animals, buildings, trees, and domestic objects. Aelita gave each object its name. When the figures moved and acted in unison she gave a verb. Sometimes the images were bordered with colored marks as in the singing book, and one could hear a barely audible musical phrase. Aelita named the subject.

She spoke in a low voice. Without haste pages appeared in that strange primer. In the quiet blue twilight of the library her ashen eyes followed Los, and Aelita's voice with its powerful and gentle charm penetrated his consciousness. His head spun.

Los felt that his head was clearing as though a clouded veil was lifting and new words and concepts were imprinted in his memory. This went on for a long time. Aelita ran her hand over her face, sighed and extinguished the screen. Los and Gusev sat as though in a fog.

"Go and rest," said Aelita to her guests in the language whose sounds were still strange but whose ideas had penetrated the recesses of their consciousness.

ON THE STAIRS

Seven days passed.

Later when Los recalled that period it seemed to him to be a blue twilight, an astonishing time of rest when a file of marvelous dreams passed before him in his waking hours.

Los and Gusev awoke early in the morning. After a bath and a light breakfast they went to the library. Aelita's attentive and affectionate eyes met them on its threshold. Now she spoke in the words most of which they understood. In the quiet and semi-darkness of the room and in Aelita's soft words was a mood of ineffable calm—and her eyes shone and flashed in their way and in them lurked visions. Shadows moved across the screen. Words, without effort, penetrated into their consciousness. A miracle was taking place: words which at first were only sound became penetrating ideas which emerged seemingly out of a fog and then took on the juices of life. Now when Los pronounced Aelita's name it stirred him doubly: the sadness of the first syllable "Ae-" which meant "To be seen for the last time," and the color of silver felt in the syllable "-lita" which meant "The color of the stars." And so the language of the new world like a delicate substance became part of their consciousness, firm and fast.

For seven days this process of enrichment went on. There were lessons in the morning and after sunset until midnight. Finally Aelita became obviously weary. On the eighth day no one came to wake her guests and they slept until evening.

When Los rose from his bed he could see long shadows extended from the trees. A bird called in a crystalline monotonous whistle. His head was light. He experienced a feeling of overflowing joy. Without waking Gusev, Los dressed quickly and went to the library, but no one responded to his knock. Then Los went outside for the first time in seven days.

The sloping meadow fell away towards the grove and to the low reddish buildings. In that direction, mournfully lowing, walked a herd of the clumsy, shaggy animals—khashi—which half resembled bears and half resembled cows. The low sun gilded the curling grasses—the whole meadow glowed with liquid gold. Over the lake emerald cranes passed. In the distance emerged the snowy cone of a mountain peak tinted by the sunset. Here it was also calm, the magic sadness of a day departing in peace and gold.

Los walked to the lake along the familiar path. Along both its sides stood the same weeping azure trees; he saw the same ruins through the maculated trunks of the trees, and the air was the same—fine and chilling. But it seemed to Los that now for the first time he saw that wonderful world—his eyes and ears were open and he knew the names of things.

Through the branches the lake sent its flaming reflections. But when Los came to the water the sun had already set and the fiery feathers and the tongues of easy flame of the sunset were in flight, capturing half the sky with such a golden frenzy that for a moment his heart stood still. Then quickly, quickly the fire was cloaked with ashes, the sky cleared, darkened and then the stars were ignited. Strange constellations were reflected in the water. At the lake's curving shore near the stairway rose the black silhouettes of the two stone giants, the guardians of the ages who sat with their faces lifted to the constellations. < . . . > Los watched and stood so long that his hand on the stone became numb. Then he left the statue and immediately saw Aelita on the staircase below him. She sat with her elbows on her knees, her chin on her hand. < . . . > He sat next to her on the step.

Aelita said with a trembling voice: "Why did you leave the earth?

"The woman I loved died," said Los. < . . . >

Aelita freed her hand from her cape and laid it on Los's large hand—touched it and then returned it to her cape. < . . . > Los felt pain: Aelita was so marvelously beautiful and such a dangerous pungent and sweet odor came from the water, from her cape with its hood, from her hands, her face, her breath . . .

(1922)

Translated by Leland Fetzer

Andrei Platonovich Platonov
[Klimentov]
(1899-1951)

The Sun, The Moon, and The Ether Channel

[A TRILOGY OF ABRIDGED VISIONS FROM THE FUTURE]

I. DESCENDANTS OF THE SUN
A Fantasy

He had been a tender, doleful child who loved his mother, the hand-made withy fences, the open field, and the sky above all these things. < . . . > No one could foresee what the boy would become. And he—he grew, and always more irrepressibly and alarmingly seethed within him stifled, repressed, shackled forces. He dreamed pure, blue, joyful dreams, and could not recall a single one in the morning—the early serene sunlight would greet him and everything inside him would grow quiet, fade from memory and subside. But he grew as he dreamed; the day held only flaming sunlight, wind, and the melancholy dust of the road.

He grew up in the great epoch of electricity and the restructuring of the globe. The thunder of labor shook the Earth, and no one had looked at the sky for a long time—every gaze was directed at the Earth, all hands were occupied. The radio's electromagnetic waves were whispering through the atmosphere and the interstellar ether, the challenging words of Man—the builder. Ever more insistently, unbearably, thoughts and machines were penetrating unknown, unconquered, rebellious matter and molding it into Mankind's slave.

The Principal Director of the projects reshaping the globe was the engineer Vogulov, a gray, hunched individual with flashing hate-filled eyes—it was that very same tender boy. He directed a million armies of workers who dug deep into the Earth with machines and were transforming its aspect, making it into a home for Mankind. Vogulov worked without respite, without sleep, with a burning hatred in his heart, with fury, with madness, and with a restless, unflagging genius. < . . . > His charge was to regulate the intensity and direction of the winds through changing the topology of the Earth's surface, and by digging new canals in the mountains to promote air circulation and wind flow so as to divert warm or cold ocean currents into the interior of continents by means of canals.

At first one had to invent an explosive compound of such power that an army of workers twenty or thirty thousand strong might send the Himalayas into the stratosphere. < . . . > And Vogulov found a means of super-charging light's electromagnetic waves—ultra-light—an energy that would explode back into the world, to its "normal" state with a strange, annihilating, incredible force that numbers alone could not express. Vogulov was content with this discovery, as there was enough of ultra-light energy to fashion the Earth into a home for Man.

They tested ultra-light in the Carpathians. Into a small tunnel they rolled a cart with a charge of ultra-light, then released the inhibitor which maintained the ultra-light in its abnormal state—and a flame howled over Europe, a hurricane swept through the nations, lightning began to rage in the atmosphere, and the Atlantic ocean began to heave sighs from its very depths, blanketing islands with millions of tons of water. Abysses of granite, spiraling, were borne up to the clouds. Heated to an incalculable temperature they were transmuted into the lightest of gases, and the gases were borne into the highest layers of the atmosphere, where whey somehow bonded with the ether and broke away from the Earth forever. Of the Carpathians there remained not a grain of sand as a souvenir. The Carpathians had resettled themselves in closer proximity to the stars. Vogulov's idea had transformed matter into very nearly nothing.

A month later they did the same thing in Asia with several portions of the Hingan and the Sayan ranges. And a month after that, in the Siberian tundra timid flowers were already blooming and warm caressing rains were falling; airplanes flew, trains moved in, and deep into the Earth were sunk as foundations the ponderous frames of factories.

Vogulov had at his command millions of machines and hundreds of thousands of technicians. Mankind was struggling with Nature in rage and fury. Teeth of consciousness and iron had seized upon matter and were masticating it. Working frenzy overcame Mankind. Labor intensity was raised to the limit—to go further led to the destruction of the body, the rupture of muscles, and insanity. The papers hailed the projects as if transmitting sermons. Composers with their orchestras played *The Symphony of the Will and Elemental Consciousness* in the recreation halls at mountain and canal sites; Man was rebelling against the Universe, armed not with a dream but with Consciousness and the Machine. < . . . >

Yet in rare moments of forgetfulness or ecstasy Vogulov's expanding mind would register flashes of a thought which did not belong to the present day. Only the mind and a flame of consciousness, which with time and work was growing more and more powerful, remained in Vogulov. To this point men had been dreamers, fainthearted poets in the likeness of women and sobbing children. They were incapable and unworthy of understanding the world. The horrifying clashes of matter, the whole of the monstrous, self-devouring universe, was unknown to them. What man needed was fierce intelligence, flintier and more real than matter itself, in order to comprehend the world, to descend into its very depths, fearing nothing, to traverse an entire hell of learning and labor to its end and to re-author the Universe. For this one must have hands that were more merciless and hard than the fists of that savage creator who once upon a time, in jest, had placed the stars within the vastness of space.

And Vogulov made the decision to re-create the Universe with ultra-light. < . . . > To accomplish this he invented a photo-electro-magnetic res-onating transformer; a device which transformed light's electro-magnetic waves into eveready electric current, good for powering motors. Vogulov simply "cooled" light rays received from space, impeded the infra-spec-trum, and derived waves of the necessary length and frequency. Unconsciously and to his own surprise he had solved what historically had been the greatest energy question of mankind: how to derive the greatest quantity of power with the smallest expenditure of force. The expenditure in this case was negligible—the fabrication of the resonating transformers needed to turn light into current—while the quantity of energy derived was, strictly speaking, infinite, since the universe is made up of light. The world's energy status, and therefore the economic status, were turned upside down: for mankind there dawned a truly Golden Age—the Universe was working for Man, nourishing him and making him happy.

Vogulov was compelling the Universe to work in his laboratories, fab-ricating ultra-light, in order to destroy that universe. But this was the least of it: Man was working too slowly and lazily to produce the required num-ber of resonators—millions of them—in a short time. The tempo of work had to be increased to extremes, and Vogulov inoculated the working mass-es with energy microbes. He took for this purpose an element of the infra-spectrum with its horrific impulse towards maximal status—towards light—he grew cultures and colonies, trillions of these elements, and sowed them throughout the atmosphere. And man began to die in the heat of his labors, to write books celebrating pure courage, to love as Dante had loved, and to live not years but rather days. And man did not regret this.

The first year produced one hundred cubic kilometers of ultra-light. Vogulov had thought to double the production each year, so that in a little over three years the one thousand cubic kilometers of ultra-light would be ready. Humanity lived within a hurricane. A day equaled a millennium in the produc-tion of goods. The swift, whirlwind rise of generations created an completely new type of human being—possessed of furious energy and radiant genius.

The energy microbe had made eternity unnecessary—a brief instant was enough to drain the cup of Life dry and to perceive Death as the fulfill-ment of a joyful instinct.

* * *

And no one knew the heart or the suffering of Vogulov—the Engineer. Such a heart and such a soul should not live in a human being. At twenty-two he had fallen in love with a girl who had died a week after they met. For three years Vogulov had wandered the Earth in madness and grief, he sobbed along desert roads, prayed, cursed and howled. He was so frightening that the courts ordered his destruction. He suffered and grieved so intensely that he could not die. His whole body became one wound, and began to decay. The soul within him had destroyed itself.

And then he experienced an organic catastrophe: the power of love and the energy of his heart rushed to his brain, burst his skull and engendered a brain of heretofore unseen, incredible power.

But nothing had really changed—it was only that love had been transformed into thought and thought—full of hatred and despair—was destroying the world which made it impossible to have the one thing a human being needs—the soul of another . . .

Vogulov was going to shatter the universe without fear or pity, yet aching for what was irretrievably lost, what gives Man life and what he needs—not bye and bye, but now. And Vogulov wished to create this impossible thing—now.

Only one who loves understands the Impossible, and only he desires it in deadly earnest and will make it possible, no matter the path that leads him there.

1922

II. From THE LUNAR PROBE

Kreizkopf's Plan

The Engineer Peter Kreizkopf, a miner's son, was in his nation's capitol for the first time. The whirlwind of automobiles and the roar of underground railways cast him into rapture. The city, it seemed, must be populated entirely by mechanics! But no factories were to be seen—Kreizkopf was sitting on a bench in the central park, while the factories stood on the marshes of the city's outskirts, where the canal water was piped, beyond the global aerodromes. < . . . >

The train had arrived early, but that strange city was already awake, as it never slept. Its life consisted of steadily accelerated motion. The city had no connection with nature: it was a concrete and metal oasis, closed in on itself, completely isolated and alone in the abyss of the world.

A luxurious theater built in dark matte stone attracted Kreizkopf's gaze. The theater was so large it could have been a hangar for airships. Grief pierced Peter Kreizkopf's heart: his young wife Erna, once in love with him, had remained in Karbomort, the coal town Peter had left behind. He had cautioned her: "It's not worth it to divorce, Erna. You and I have lived together for seven years. Things will get easier. I'll go to city and work on my "lunar probe"—they'll pay me well, for sure they will."

But Erna had grown tired of promises, tired of the coal mine's black fog, of Karbomort's narrow life and the monotonously identical faces of its unchanging technical personnel. She was especially tired of Peter's friends—narrow specialists who consciously considered themselves to be atoms of human knowledge. The witticism most frequently heard by Erna were the words of one of these co-workers, Mertz, "We live in order to know."

—But what you *don't* know—replied Erna— is that people *don't* live in order to know . . .

Peter understood both Erna and his friends, but they did not really understand him. Erna, an aristocrat, the daughter of an important coal-producer, Sorbonne educated, hated Peter's friends—the craftsmen, electricians and inventors who would sit in her living room and argue pointlessly with Peter until midnight. Kreizkopf knew that he had little in common with Erna: he, an autodidact and engineer by calling—and she, mistress of the latest "flowers of culture" which he understood not at all.

So Erna had left him and returned to her own circle.

Kreizkopf missed her, he had no idea what to do with himself, alone in a crowd of people.

* * *

The general bustle, the advertisements, the smell of exhaust and the roar of raging machinery magnified Kreizkof's grief tenfold. He recalled past years of his life, full of labor, faith in humanity, technical creativity and devotion to his beloved wife. Now it had all been destroyed by inexplicable factors: people had deceived and betrayed him, his work seemed worthless to them, his wife had fallen in love with someone else and begun to hate him, his creativity had brought him loneliness and poverty. [He nonetheless continues with his project, procuring the necessary government funds, ed.] < . . . >

His "lunar probe" project envisioned a transport device capable of movement in any gaseous medium within or beyond the atmosphere. A metallic sphere, loaded with the necessary weight, was to be fixed on the disk's periphery: the disk itself would have a horizontal, vertical or tangential orientation to the Earth's surface—depending on where the probe was to be sent. The disk was given a rotational speed appropriate to its destination. Upon achieving the RPM necessary for its path the sphere would obediently detach itself and head off on a path tangential to the disk by centrifugal force. The disk's safe landing was secured by the automaton in the probe itself; on approach to a hard surface current was switched off to the automaton, and a certain amount of fuel was ignited, its force directed in the same direction as the flight. The recoil resulted in a slowdown, and free fall was transformed into a smooth, safe descent. < . . . >

The flight of the Lunar Probe

Everyone who was anyone came to the launch site. < . . . > There was magnificent lighting, music, drinks, kvass and ice cream were served, hovering taxis gathered—the usual accompaniments of an unusual event. Three minutes before the stroke of midnight the disk began to rotate. The motor roared, five gigantic fans blew clouds of cold air through the rumbling, heating engine—and the air that escaped was dry, hard and white-hot, like a desert whirlwind. The oil in the machinery was cooled by icy streams from the centrifugal pumps, and even so a corrosive smoke hung about the disk and the entire installation; the housings were heating up excessively, the oil was burning on the ice. In spite of its precise mounting, the disk rumbled like a cannonade or an erupting volcano: so high was its rate of rotation. Its circumference was smoking due to air friction < . . . > [The craft's lift-off was successful, ed.]

Here are Kreizkopf's bulletins from space, in the order in which they were received:

1. Nothing to report. The dials show a coal-black sky. Stars of an incredible brightness. < . . . >

2. Numerous blue flames have passed over the probe. I have discovered no cause for this. The temperature has not risen.

3. The flight continues. I sense no motion, of course. All controls are in good order.

4. The moon seems to be falling onto my probe. A freakish fireball shot by on a parallel course with the probe. The probe has now outdistanced it.

5. The probe is progressing with sharp jolts. Strange forces are twisting its trajectory, throwing it into pockets and causing it to seriously overheat, although we must be surrounded by the ether.

6. The jolts are intensifying. I am sensing motion. The instruments buzz from the shaking. The landscape of the Universe resembles the painting by Churlionis—"The Call of the Stars" from the Cosmic Ocean.

7. The pitching continues. Stars literally ring as they speed along their courses. Naturally their motion disturbs the electromagnetic field, and my universal receiver transforms the waves into songs. Announce that I am at the source of earthly poetry: someone on Earth guessed the existence of the Star symphonies and, inspired, wrote poems. Report that the Astral Song physically exists. Also report: this is a symphony and not a cacophony. Launch as many human beings as possible into space on interplanetary craft—it is frightening, disturbing, yet everything becomes clear. Invent receivers for this astral sound.

8. The flight is now smooth—no jarring. One half of space is taken up by violet rays that flow like mist. What this is I don't know.

9. I have discovered an electromagnetic ocean.

10. There is no hope of returning to Earth, I am flying through a blue dawn. The dials indicate the electrical charge of the surrounding medium to be 800, 000 volts.

11. The moon is approaching. The charge is 2, 000, 000 volts. Darkness.

12. An abyss of electricity. My dials no longer function. Fantastic happenings. The Sun roars and small comets shriek as they speed by. You see and hear nothing through the mica of the atmosphere.

13. Meteor clouds. Judging by their brightness and electromagnetic attractivity meteors are metallic. Larger meteors are flickering like candles or lamps; I see nothing here that would cause it.

14. The electromagnetic waves among which I find myself have the property of arousing in me powerful, irrepressible, uncontrolled thoughts. I cannot deal with these promptings. I am no longer in control of my brain, although I resist it with all my strength, pouring with sweat. I am unable to think what I wish or about what I wish. I incessantly think about things I do not know; I constantly recall events—exploding nebulae, a bursting sun—all remembered as actual and real, but which I have never experienced. I am thinking of two distinct selves who await me on a stern knoll on which stand two rotten trunks, and on these there is frozen milk. I am invariably thirsty and steadfastly want to conserve my supplies. I eat a minnow, but want to eat a shark. I will attempt to conquer these thoughts which are engendered by electricity and which eat into my brain as lice do a sleeping body.

15. I have just returned from the perpendicular mountains where I saw the world of mummies lying in the careless grass . . . (The signals are incomprehensible. Academician Lesuren's notes.) All is clear: the moon is 100 kilometers away. Its influence on the brain is terrifying—I think not my thoughts, but those induced by the Moon. The foregoing is not to be considered sane. I am lying here like a pale corpse: the Moon incessantly nourishes me with white-hot intellect. It seems to me that my craft is an entity aware of itself, and that the radio is muttering to itself.

16. The Moon is passing by at a distance of 40 kilometers: wasteland, dead mineral and platinum twilight. I am passing by slowly, at no more than 50 kilometers per hour by visual reckoning.

17. The Moon has hundreds of surface chinks. From the chinks is emanating a sparse blue or green gas . . . I have mastered myself and become accustomed to this.

18. From some of the lunar chinks the gas emerges in the form of a whirlwind: is this a chemical element or the thought processes of a living being? . . . Thought processes, certainly; the Moon is a self-contained and monstrous brain.

19. I cannot determine the cause of the gaseous emissions: I believe I will open the hatch of my probe and jump out, it will be easier for me. I will go blind in the darkness of this probe, I am weary of seeing the unfolding universe only through the eyes of my dials.

20. I am heading into the gaseous clouds of the lunar emissions. Millennia have passed since the moment I was severed from Earth. Are you alive, you to whom I signal these words, do you hear me? (19 hours have passed since the moment of Kreizkopf's departure. Academician Lesuren's Notes)

21. The Moon is beneath me. My probe is descending. The surface chinks are radiating gas. I no longer hear the astral progression.

22. Tell them, tell everyone, that humans are very much mistaken. The world does not correspond to their knowledge. Do you or don't you see the catastrophe on the Milky Way: a transverse blue stream is roaring. This is not a nebula and not an asterism.

23. The probe is descending. I am opening the hatch to find myself a way out. Farewell.

(1926)

III. From the ETHER CHANNEL

[The Kirpichnikovs' quest]

Mikhail Yeremeevich Kirpichnikov was an electrical engineer and research associate in the Department of Electron Biology, established after the death of Professor F. K. Popov and based on his achievements. Ten years had passed since the death of Popov, but before Kirpichnikov could truly devote his time to the continuation of Popov's research, he had to deal with more immediate tasks. This time he was sent to the Nizhnekolymsky tundra—as a project supervisor on the construction of a vertical tunnel. The purpose of the installation was to capture the heat energy of the Earth's interior.

Kirpichnikov's family remained in Moscow, and he set out alone. The vertical thermal tunnel was an experimental project of the Yakutsk governmental council. If the results were successful, they proposed to cover the entire Arctic region of the Asian continent with a network of such tunnels; the loss of heat-energy from the tunnels would be prevented with an electrical transmission, bringing culture, productivity and a human population to the shores of the Arctic Ocean at the end of a power cord.

But the chief motive behind the tunnel works was the fact that on the plains of the tundra had been found the remains of marvelous unknown cultures and countries. The soil and subsoil of the tundra were not of continental or paleo-geological origin, but were in fact alluvial. Moreover, these alluvial deposits had covered over and entombed an entire succession of ancient human cultures. But thanks to the fact that this funereal shroud laid over the corpses of mysterious civilizations consisted of a band of permafrost, those interred and the structures they had built were preserved like provisions in a can—intact, fresh and unharmed.

Even the little that had been discovered by chance in spots where the surface of the tundra had collapsed presented material of unprecedented significance and timeless value. The corpses of four men and two women had been found there. The women's rosy cheeks and the light fragrance of their long hygienic garments had been preserved. One of the men had a book in his pocket—it was small, embellished with an elegant script; its contents were assumed to be an outline of the principles of individual immortality in a precise scientific light. The book described experiments in preventing the death of some sort of small creature with a life-span of four days. This creature's biosphere (its own food, air, body, etc.) had been subjected to the sustained influence of electromagnetic waves; moreover, each type of wave had been calibrated to destroy a particular kind of harmful microbe in the creature's body. Maintaining the experimental creature in an electromagnetically sterilized field, it was thus possible to achieve a hundred-fold increase in its life-span.

Somewhat later they uncovered a pyramidal column of an unidentifiable stone. The perfection of its form was reminiscent of a lathe-turned artifact, but the column was forty meters high with a circumference of ten meters at the base.

The human corpses had swarthy complexions, rosy lips, low but broad foreheads. They were of small stature and barrel-chested, and each face bore a calm, peaceful, almost smiling grimace. Clearly either death had come upon them suddenly or, which was more likely, death for them was a sensation and a happening completely different from what we normally experience.

These discoveries inflamed the scientific passions of the entire world, and popular opinion demanded the cultivation of the tundra, with the goal of fully restoring the ancient world that lay beneath the soil of the frozen wasteland and perhaps extended out onto the floor of the Arctic Ocean.

The passion for knowledge became a new organic sense for man, just as demanding, incisive, and rich as the faculty of sight, or love. This sense sometimes superseded the immutable laws of economics and aspirations to the material well-being of society.

Here was the real reason for the installation of the first vertical thermal tunnel in the tundra.

A system of such tunnels was to lay the foundation of the tundra's culture and economy, and thereafter serve as the key to open subterranean gates leading to an unknown but harmonious land, the discovery of which would be more significant than the invention of the first machine or Montblanc's discovery of radium.

Many scholars thus saw within the bowels of the tundra the model anticipating the scientific, cultural and industrial growth for the next one or two hundred years in an already perfected form. All that remained was to remove the layer of permafrost, and history would leap a century or two into the future, and then resume its own tempo. Imagine the savings in labor and time which would result from this free gift of two centuries! No philanthropy in the history of mankind could compare with it! It was well worth digging a two-kilometer hole in the Earth for the sake of this accomplishment.

Kirpichnikov set out for the tundra, his fists clenched in joyful anticipation, feeling the goal that had been set for him would be a global victory, a marriage of the ancient world and the present.

It was certainly not simple to construct such a fabulous shaft and sink it into the tundra—a man tortures himself and others, errs and causes others to err, perishes and is reborn—all this on account of the fact that he is scaling the wall of History and of Nature. Yet, the tunnel was built; [it followed Kirpichnikov's new design, which involved electromagnetic wave energy, and within eighteen months the inner-core heat of the Earth began to seep into the soil of tundra, melting tundra's ice . . .]. < . . . >

* * *

[On the heels of the successful completion of his tundra project (ed.)] one thing continued to challenge Kirpichnikov and propel him into agitated searches everywhere—in books, among people, and others' scientific studies—a thirst to complete the late Popov's work on artificial multiplication of electron microbes and to find the technological implementation for his ether channel idea, so that one could provide ethereal feed to the microbe's maw and accelerate thereby its life to a frenzied pace.

"The solution is simple—an electromagnetic channel . . ." Kirpichnikov muttered the last words of Popov's unfinished work from time to time, and sought in vain that phenomenon or someone else's idea which would enable him to solve the "ether channel" riddle. Kirpichnikov knew what such a channel could offer people: using ether, any natural body could be grown to any size. For example, one could take a one cubic centimeter bit of iron, hook it up to the channel, and lo and behold, this bit would grow before one's eyes to the size of Mount Ararat, as the electrons within the iron would multiply.

Despite his diligence and his attachment to this one accursed idea for years, its solution continued to escape Kirpichnikov. While working on a thermal tunnel out in the tundra, he thought of nothing else all through the long, restless, troubling polar night. One other unsolved riddle in Popov's works confused him: what made up the positive charge in the atom nucleus of the matter?

If microbes or all living bodies consist of pure negative electrons, what then is the material, and moreover positively charged, which is at the core of the tiny nucleus in the atom?

No one knew the answer. There were vague pointers to the answer and hundreds of hypotheses in scientific studies, but none of these satisfied Kirpichnikov. He was looking for a practical solution, the objective truth, and not the subjective satisfaction of the first, perhaps even brilliant, conjecture that came to hand—but one that did not fully accord with the structure of nature.

[One person possibly able to help him in his quest was Isaac Mathiessen, a friend and an engineer like himself, whom he hasn't seen since their student days. Mathiessen lives in the village of Kochubary, fortuitously close to Voloshino in the Voronezh region, his wife's beloved former place of residence and early work as a teacher. Having a good excuse for a leave after his eighteen-months absence from family in the tundra, Kirpichnikov decides to take his wife, Maria Alexandrovna, and their children to Voloshino, intending also to arrange a meeting with Mathiessen (ed.)] < . . . >

They reached Voloshino in just five days. The house where the Kirpichnikovs stayed had a cherry orchard, already bursting with buds, but not yet clothed in its white, indescribably touching attire. It continued warm. The days glowed so peacefully and happily, as if they were the morning of mankind's millennial felicity.

The next day Kirpichnikov drove to see Mathiessen. Isaac was not at all surprised to see him arrive. Understanding his puzzlement over the indifferent reception, Mathiessen explained, "I observe far newer and more original phenomena every day."

An hour later Mathiessen softened:

"Married, hell! You've gotten used to sentimentality. As for me, brother, work is a more lasting legacy than children! . . ." And Mathiessen burst out laughing, but so violently that wrinkles appeared across his bald skull. Clearly, his laughter was just as frequent as a solar eclipse.

"So, show and tell, how are you making a living, what are you doing, who are you in love with!" smiled Kirpichnikov.

"Aha, you're curious! I approve and I salute you! . . . But listen, I'll show you only the main work I'm doing, because I believe it's completed. I won't talk about the other studies—and don't ask! . . ."

"Listen, Isaac!" said Kirpichnikov, "your work on machineless technology would interest me, remember? Or have you already forgotten the problem and gotten disenchanted with it?"

Mathiessen screwed up his eyes; he wanted to needle and surprise his friend, but forgetting all this, he sighed in futility, wrinkled his face, which was accustomed to immobility, and simply answered:

"I'll show you right away, colleague Kirpichnikov!"

They crossed plantations, came out into the narrow valley of a small river, and stopped. Mathiessen straightened up, lifted his face to the horizon, as if surveying a million listeners on the slope of the hill, and declared to Kirpichnikov:

"I will tell you briefly, but you will understand: you're an electrical engineer, and this is right up your alley! Only don't interrupt: we're both in a hurry—you to your wife (Mathiessen gave his laugh again—his bald spot was roiled with wrinkles and his jaws stood open—the rest of his face did not move), and I—to the soil."

Kirpichnikov held his peace, and asked his question:

"But, Mathiessen, where is your equipment? You know I'm not here to listen to a lecture—I want to see your experiments!"

"You'll have both, Kirpichnikov, both! And all the equipment is right here. If you don't see it, it means you won't hear and you won't understand!"

"I am listening, Mathiessen!" Kirpichnikov hurried him on curtly.

"So, you're listening. Then I'm talking." Mathiessen picked up a little stone, flung it forcefully over the river, and began: "It is visible even to the naked eye that every body emits electromagnetic energy if that body is subjected to convulsive movement or to alteration. That's right, isn't it? And the radiation of a bundle of electromagnetic waves of such and such wavelength and such and such period corresponds—precisely, uniquely, individually—to each alteration. In a word, the radiation depends on the degree of alteration, of reorganization of the experimental body. Going on . . . Thought, being a process that reorganizes the brain, forces the brain to emit electromagnetic waves into space. But thought depends on what a person has concretely in mind—the nature and the degree of change in the structure of the brain also depends on that. The waves themselves depend in turn on the alteration of the brain structure. The thinking, disintegrating brain creates electromagnetic waves, and creates them distinctly in each case: depending on what thought has reorganized the brain. Everything clear, Kirpichnikov?"

"Certainly," confirmed Kirpichnikov. "Go on!"

Mathiessen sat down on a hillock, rubbed his tired eyes, and continued:

"I have found experimentally that one strictly determinate thought corresponds to each kind of wave. Of course, I'm generalizing and schematizing somewhat to facilitate your understanding. In fact it's all much more complicated. In this way. I have built a universal receiver—a resonator that picks up and records waves of any length and any period. But I will tell you that even a single, extremely insignificant and brief thought elicits an entire extremely complex system of waves.

"But nevertheless, an already known, experimentally established system of waves corresponds to an idea, for instance the "accursed power" (do you remember this pre revolutionary term?). This system will differ little from person to person.

"And so I connected my resonator-receiver with a system of relays (which open the circuit to a strong current, but which are themselves turned on by a weak current) and expediting apparatuses and mechanisms, technically complex but simple and unitary in design. But this system needs further fine-tuning and improvement. Eventually it should be distributed throughout the world for universal use. So far I've been working on a small area and for a specific range of thoughts.

"Now take a look! See, I've planted a cabbage bed over there on the other bank. You can see it's already dried up from the lack of rain. Now watch: I'm thinking clearly and even talking out loud, though talking isn't obligatory: i-r-r-i-g-a-t-e! Look at the other bank, chief! . . ."

Kirpichnikov looked at the opposite bank of the little river and immediately noticed a small irrigation pump, half-hidden by a bush, and some sort of compact instrument. Probably the resonator-receiver, Kirpichnikov guessed.

After Mathiessen had spoken the word "irrigate," the pumping unit began to operate, the pump began to draw water from the river, and small fountains, spraying tiny droplets, began to strike the entire cabbage patch from nozzle-tipped sprinklers. The sun's rainbow played in the little fountains and the entire patch began to make sounds and came alive: the pump buzzed, the moisture fizzed, the soil became saturated, and the young plants freshened.

Mathiessen and Kirpichnikov stood quietly some twenty meters from this strange independent world and observed.

"Do you see what human thought has become? The impact of intelligent will! Isn't that true?"

Mathiessen smiled dolefully with his lifeless face.

Kirpichnikov felt a hot burning current in his heart and in his brain— the same as had struck him the moment he met his future wife. And yet Kirpichnikov also was aware in himself of some kind of secret shame and silent timidity—feelings that inhere in every murderer when murder has been committed in the interests of the whole world. In Kirpichnikov's eyes, Mathiessen had clearly violated nature. And the crime was that neither Mathiessen himself nor all mankind had yet to make of themselves gems more precious than nature. To the contrary, nature was still more profound, greater, wiser, and more variegated than any human being.

Mathiessen explained:

"The whole thing is extremely simple! A human being, in this case I, is in the domain of actuating mechanisms, and his thought (for example, "irrigate") has the potential of actuating machines: this is how they are constructed. the thought—irrigate—is received by the resonator. A strictly unique system of waves corresponds to this thought. It is precisely only waves of such and such wavelength and such and such period, such as are equivalent to the thought, "irrigate," that close the circuit of those relays in the actuating mechanisms that control irrigation. That is, the circuit is directly opened there to the current and the electrical motor-pump begins to operate. Therefore, water glistens under the cabbage roots the very instant after the person's thought—irrigate.

"The purpose of high technology is to free man from working with his muscles. It will suffice to think out what would be needed for a star to change its course . . . But I want to reach the point of managing without actuating mechanisms and without any intermediaries, of acting on nature directly and without mediation—by sheer perturbation of the brain. I am sure of the success of machineless technology. I know that mere contact between man and nature—thoughts—is sufficient to control the entire substance of the world! You've understood! . . . I will explain. You see, there is a place, a core, in each body, such that if it is clicked, the entire body is yours: do whatever you like with it! And if you prick the body where necessary and when necessary, it will do what you compel it to do by itself! That's why I believe that the electromagnetic force emitted by the human brain in the course of any thinking is entirely sufficient to so prick nature that it *will* be ours! . . ."

Kirpichnikov shook Mathiessen's hand as he said good-bye, then embraced him and said with warmth and complete sincerity:

"Thanks, Isaac! Thanks, my friend! You know, there is just one other problem equal to yours! But it is still not solved, and yours is almost there . . . Good-bye! Thanks again! Everyone should work the way you do—with keen intelligence and a cool heart! So long! "

"Good-bye," answered Mathiessen, and, without taking his shoes off, started to wade to the other side of his little shallow river.

*   *   *

While Kirpichnikov was on vacation in Voloshino, a sensation shook the world. In the Bol'sheozersky tundra Professor Gomonov's expedition had unearthed two mummies: a man and a woman lay together in an embrace upon a well-preserved carpet. The carpet was light blue in color and unfigured, covered over with the soft pelt of an unknown animal. The couple lay clothed in thick, seamlessly woven fabric of dark hues, closely embroidered with depictions of a tall, elegant plant topped by a double-petaled blossom. The man was elderly, the woman young. It was likely that they were father and daughter. Their faces and bodies were like those found in the Nizhnekolymsky tundra. There was the same expression on their calm faces—a slight smile, a suggestion of pity or pensiveness—as if a warrior had conquered an impregnable marble city, but, amid the statuary, edifices, and unfamiliar structures had fallen and died from exhaustion and amazement.

The man was holding the woman close, as if to defend her peace and chastity in death. Under the carpet on which these long-dead inhabitants of the ancient tundra reposed were found two books—one was printed in the same script as the book found on the Nizhnekolymsky tundra, the other bore different characters. These characters were not letters, but a sort of ideograph system, in which each ideograph had a precise correspondence to a particular concept. There were an extraordinary number of ideographs, and in consequence five years were spent deciphering them. The book was then translated and published under the supervision of the Academy of Philological Studies. A portion of the text in the unearthed volume remained unintelligible since some sort of chemical compound, doubtless found in the carpet, had irremediably damaged the precious pages—they had blackened, and no reagent could clarify the ideographic signs they bore.

The content of the discovered works was abstract philosophy and, to a certain extent, historical sociology. Nevertheless the compositions were so profoundly interesting, both for their thematics and their brilliant style, that in the course of two months the book went through eleven editions.

Kirpichnikov ordered a copy. He was leaving no stone unturned in his single-minded search—for assistance in solving the ether channel enigma.

Returning home from his visit with Matthiesen, he had felt that something was coming together in his mind. This made him very happy, but once again it all dispersed—and Kirpichnikov saw that Matthiesen's research had only the most distant connection with his own tormenting problem.

When the book arrived Kirpichnilov plunged into it, hounded by an single idea, searching between the lines for a cryptic hint pointing to the solution of his own problem. Despite the wild improbability, the madness, of looking for help with the discovery of the ether channel in the Lakes culture, Kirpichnikov read through the works of the long-dead philosopher with bated breath.

The composition did not have the name of its author, it was called "The Songs of Aiuna." Having read it, Kirpichnikov was not struck—the composition contained nothing remarkable: "How boring," he observed. "Even out on the tundra they couldn't think sensibly! It's all love, creativity, and the soul. But where's the bread,—and where's the iron?"

* * *

Kirpichnikov got seriously depressed, as all humans inevitably do. He was already past thirty. His ether channel generators stood silent, underscoring his confusion. He ceaselessly pondered Popov's words: "Simple solution—an electromagnetic track . . ." but the result was always another conundrum. An ether feed-line into the electron eluded him. [He felt he could not go on living just for the sake of the bliss offered by marriage. Spending nights working on a solution to the Ether tract idea, he felt uneasy with the directionless comfort offered at home. Remembering another conversation with Popov, during which the latter likened Earth to a giant spaceship created for true seekers rather than home-dwellers, he simply decided to leave his sleeping family one night without saying a good by. His search for a solution to Popov's problem lead him eventually to America, where he hoped to find the secret of the composition of rose-oil, which he believed to be a substitute for the elixir of life. After some agonizing months of search he was no closer to it. Then he read by chance an ad in a Chicago daily, placed there by his wife, who begged him to come home. As he decided to go, he could not know that Mathiessen continued his research during his absence and that these dangerous experiments would soon begin to have global consequence and affect his own fate] < . . . >

* * *

The Hamburg-American Line steamship carried him at an average speed of sixty kilometers an hour. Kirpichnikov knew his wife, and was sure she would be dead unless he made it home in time. He did not grant the possibility of suicide, but what else could it be? He had heard that in ancient times people died of love. Nowadays this was merely worthy of a smile. Was it possible that his tough, daring Maria, thrilled by every triviality of life, was capable of dying of love? People don't perish from an ancient tradition—so why then would she die?

Pondering and in agony, Kirpichnikov wandered about the deck. He noticed the searchlight of a far-off ship coming toward them, and stopped.

Suddenly it got cold on the deck—a frightening northerly wind began to beat; and then a watery mass came down over the ship, and in an instant knocked people, objects, and the vessel's paraphernalia off the deck. The ship listed 45° toward the mirrored surface of the ocean. Kirpichnikov was saved by chance, when his leg got stuck in a hatch.

The air and the water thundered and howled, shifting densely about, breaking apart the ship, the atmosphere, and the ocean.

The noise of destruction and the pitiful squeal of despair before death went up. Women grabbed the legs of men and prayed for help. The men beat them about the head with their fists and saved themselves.

The catastrophe struck in an instant, and despite the great discipline and manliness of the crew, it was impossible to anything of substance to save the people and the ship.

Kirpichnikov was struck at once not by the storm itself and the blank wall of water, but by the instantaneous suddenness with which they descended. The ocean was calm and all horizons were open half a minute before their arrival. The steamship blasted all its horns, the radio gave off sparks of alarm, the rescue of passengers washed overboard began. But the storm suddenly subsided, and the ship rocked peacefully, groping about for equilibrium.

The horizon opened up; a kilometer away a European steamship was coming, shining its searchlights and speeding to the rescue.

The wet Kirpichnikov busied himself in a boat, fixing a motor that was refusing to work. He wasn't fully aware how he had ended up in the boat. But the boat had to be lowered quickly: hundreds of people were choking in the water. In a minute the motor was up and running: Kirpichnikov had cleaned off its oxidized contacts, which had caused the problem.

Kirpichnikov crawled into the boat's cabin and shouted: cast off!

At that moment an impenetrable acrid gas covered the entire ship, and Kirpichnikov could not see his hands. And just then he saw the sinking, wild, unbearably shining Sun, and through a fissure of his shearing brain he heard for an instant a Song—unclear as the pealing of the Milky Way—and regretted its brevity.

A government report placed in the *New York Times* was transmitted abroad by the *Telegraphic Agency* of the USSR:

"At 11:25 AM on 24/IX of this year, at 35°11' north lat. and 62°4 east longitude, the American passenger ship *California* (8,485 persons, including crew), and the German ship *Klara* (6,841, with crew), going to the aid of the former, sank. The precise reasons have not been determined. Both governments are conducting a detailed investigation. No one was rescued and there are no witnesses to the catastrophe. However, the chief cause of the wreck of both ships was deemed unequivocally established: a meteor of gigantic dimensions struck the *California* vertically. This meteor dragged the ship to the ocean floor; the funnel created by this sucked the *Klara* under as well.

* * *

[Mathiessen's experiment]

Mathiessen finally got dressed and went into the other room. It held a flat low table, 4 by 3 meters. Equipment had been placed on the table. Mathiessen approached the smallest device. He switched on the current and lay down on the floor. He lost lucid consciousness at once, and murderous nightmares of almost fatal power began to torment him, nearly physically destroying his brain. His blood overflowed with toxins and blackened his vessels; every ounce of Mathiessen's health, all the latent forces of his body, all his means of self-defense were mobilized and fought against the poisons carried by the blood circulating in his brain. But the brain itself lay nearly defenseless under the blows of the electromagnetic waves beating against it from the equipment on the table.

These waves aroused peculiar thoughts in Mathiessen's brain, and the thoughts were shot into the cosmos by spherical electromagnetic charges. They landed somewhere, maybe in the hinterlands of the Milky Way, in the heart of the planets, and disordered their pulse, —and the planets swerved from their orbits and died, falling and passing into oblivion, like drunken vagrants.

Mathiessen's brain was a secret machine that newly assembled the abysses of the cosmos, and the device on the table actuated this brain. A human being's everyday thoughts, the usual movements of the brain, were powerless to affect the world; this required vortices of cerebral particles,— then the storm would shake the world's substance.

Mathiessen did not know when he had begun the experiment, or what was happening on the Earth or in the heavens as a result of his new storm. He had not yet learned to control the marvelous and unreproducible structure of the electromagnetic wave which his brain had launched. The entire secret of its power resided in the unique structure of the wave; it was precisely that which hammered the world's substance in its most tender place; the pain caused it to give way. And the human brain alone could produce such complex waves only with the cooperation of the lifeless equipment.

After an hour a special clock was supposed to interrupt the current feeding the brain-exciting apparatus, and the experiment would end. But the clock had stopped: Mathiessen forgot to start it before the experiment began. The current fed the apparatus indefatigably, and the apparatus quietly hummed along in its work.

Two hours passed. Mathiessen's body melted, in proportion to the square of the time elapsed. The blood from his brain advanced like a solid lava of red corpuscle cadavers. The equilibrium within his body was disrupted. Destruction gained the upper hand over repair. The last incredible nightmare penetrated the still-living tissue of Mathiessen's brain, and the merciful blood extinguished the final image and the final suffering. Black blood burst into the brain like a storm through a ruptured vein and curbed the pulsating fighting heart. But Mathiessen's last image was full of humanity; his living, tormented mother rose before him; blood poured from her eyes, and she complained to her son of her torment.

At nine in the morning Mathiessen lay dead—with white eyes open, his nails dug into the floor in a fighting frenzy. The apparatus hummed assiduously and ceased only towards evening when the energy in the battery ran low. < . . . >

* * *

Two days later, *Izvestia* printed a notice from the Main Astronomical Observatory in the "From Around the World" section:

> "The Alpha star in the constellation, Canes Venatici, the Greyhounds, has not been seen in a clear sky for two days. An empty space, a breach, has formed in the Milky Way at the 4th distance (9th sector). It's Earth angle = 4°71'. The constellation Hercules is displaced somewhat, as a result of which the entire solar system must change the direction of its flight. Such strange phenomena, violating the eternal structure of the heavens, point to the relative brittleness and flimsiness of the cosmos itself. Stepped-up observations to uncover the causes of these anomalies are being carried out by the observatory."

In addition to this, a discussion with Academician Vetman was promised for an upcoming issue. With the exception of a brevier bulletin from Kamchatka, it did not appear from other telegrams from a quarter of the globe (the size of the USSR at that time), that Earth had suffered anything substantial from the stellar catastrophes. The bulletin noted:

> "A small celestial body, about 10 kilometers in cross-section, has landed on the mountains. Its structure is unknown. It is spheroidal in form. The body flew in at considerable speed and came smoothly to Earth on the mountaintops. Massive crystals are visible on its surface through binoculars. An expedition has been outfitted by the local Society of Amateur Naturalists for a preliminary study of the descended body. But the expedition is unable to provide quick answers: the mountains are nearly inaccessible. Planes have been ordered from Vladivostok. A small squadron of Japanese planes was observed today flying in the direction of the celestial body."

This note became a sensation the next day, and a three hundred line article was devoted to the strange event by Academician Vetman.

On the same day *Bednota* [Poverty] reported the death of agronomist engineer Mathiessen, a worker well-known in specialist circles in the field of optimal soil moisture conditions.

And the startling thought of a connection between the three notes only occurred to assistant agronomist Petropavlushkin in Kochubarov, who subscribed to both *Izvestiya* and *Bednota*: Mathiessen had died—a little planet had landed on the Kamchatka mountains—a star had gone missing and the Milky Way had burst. But who would believe such rural delirium?

Mathiessen was buried with solemnity. Nearly the entire Kochubarov agricultural commune followed his body. The tiller of the soil always loves religious pilgrims and eccentrics. The taciturn loner Mathiessen was one of these—everyone clearly sensed this in him. The last thin rim of hair on Mathiessen's bald pate fell out when clumsy hands roughly shoved his coffin. This surprised all the peasants, and they were filled with even greater pity and respect for the dead man.

Mathiessen's funeral coincided with the end of the work of the underwater expedition sent by the American and German governments to look for the sunken *California* and *Klara*, [the sinking of which his previous experiments caused] < . . . >

*   *   *

[The Aiuna]

Maria Alexandrovna did not entirely understand her husband: the goal of his sudden departure from their home was incomprehensible to her. She did not believe that a living man would trade warm, genuine happiness for the desert cold of an abstract, lonely idea. She thought that man seeks only man, and did not know that the path to man might lie through the severe frost of wild open spaces. Maria Alexandrovna assumed that just a few steps separated people.

But Mikhail left, and then died on a far-off voyage, seeking the precious jewel of his secret idea. Maria Alexandrovna knew, of course, what her husband was looking for. She understood the idea of the matter-multiplying invention. And in that field she had wanted to help her husband. She had bought him ten copies of a large opus—the translation of symbols of a book just found in the tundra, under the title "The Ultimate Discourse." Reading had probably been highly developed in Aiuna: this had been fostered by the darkness of the eight-month night and the isolation of the Aiunites' life.

During the construction of the second thermal tunnel, when Kirpichnikov had already disappeared, the builders discovered four granite slabs containing symbols carved in deep relief. The symbols were of the same pattern as those in the previously discovered book, "The Songs of Aiuna." For that reason they yielded themselves readily to translation into a modern language.

The slab-writings were probably the monument and testament of an Aiunite philosopher, but they contained ideas about the concealed substance of nature. Maria Alexandrovna, reading the entire book, found clear hints of what her husband had been seeking throughout the vacant world. A far-off dead man was helping her husband, scholar and wanderer, was aiding the happiness of the woman and mother.

And that was when Maria Alexandrovna placed the announcements in five American newspapers.

Fearful of losing the books somehow, and of not rejoining Mikhail with what would be the greatest happiness for him, she memorized the needed portions of "The Ultimate Discourse."

"Only what is living is comprehended by the living," wrote the Aiunite, "that which is dead is incomprehensible. The incredible cannot be measured by the indubitable. For that reason precisely we clearly comprehend such a remote thing as *aens* (corresponds to electrons. *Translators' and explicators' note.*) and such a nearby thing as *mamarva* (corresponds to matter. *Translators' and explicators' note.*) remains so little known to us. For that reason the former lives, as you live, while the latter is dead, like *Muiia* (unknown image. *Trans. and explic. note.*). When the *aens* stirred in the *proiia* (corresponds to atom. *Trans. and explic. note.*), we saw in this at first a mechanical force, and then with joy life was discovered in the *aens*. But the center of the *proiia*, full of *mamarva*, was a riddle for ages, until my son reliably demonstrated that the center of the *proiia* consists of those same *aens*, only dead ones. And the dead ones serve as food for the living. It was for my son to extract the core from the *proiia*, as all living *aens* had died of hunger. Thus it turned out that the center of the *proiia* is the fodder barn for living *aens* grazing around this repository of the corpses of their ancestors, to devour them. Thus simply and lambently veritably was discovered the nature of all *mamarva*. To the eternal memory of my son. May his name be eternally mourned! Eternal honor to his weary visage!"

Maria Alexandrovna knew this by heart, just as her son could recite some of his nursery rhymes.

The rest of the "The Ultimate Discourse" contained the teaching on the history of the Aiunites—about its beginning and its imminent end, when the Aiunites would find their zenith, and when all three forces—the Aiunite people, Time, and Nature—would come into harmonious consonance, and their three-fold being would begin to resound as a symphony.

This interested Maria Alexandrovna little. She was seeking the equipoise of her personal happiness and did not fully master the discoveries of the unknown Aiunite,

And only the last pages of the book made her shudder and forget herself in amazed attention.

The same thing has become possible today as existed in the infancy of my native land. At that time the abyss of the Maternal Ocean (the Arctic Ocean. *ed.*) was perturbed, and the ocean began to spill severe, freezing water mixed with clumps of ice on our land. The water departed and the ice remained. For a long time it crept over the hills of our capacious land until it wore them away, and our land became a barren plain. The best fertile soils on the hills were cut away by the ice, and the people were left on a bare field. But calamity is the best mentor, and the people's catastrophe—its organizer, if its blood is not yet made barren by long life on the Earth. So it was then: the ice destroyed the fruit-bearing land, deprived our ancestors of food and procreation, and destruction came down over the people's head. The hot ocean current which had inundated the country, began to move off to the north, and intense cold began to howl over the land where dusky argan trees had bloomed. In the north the chaos of dead ice guarded us, in the south, the forest, crammed with a dark swarm of powerful beasts, filled with the hiss of dark serpents and crossed by whole rivers of the poison, *zundra* (excrements of gigantic serpents. *ed.*). The Aiuna people, a people of bravery and respect for their fate, began to kill itself off, burying their books—the highest gift of the Aiuna—in the Earth, binding them with gold, impregnating the pages with a compound of *veniia*, that they might survive eternity and not rot away.

When half the people were subdued by death and lay as corpses, Eiia—the custodian of the books—appeared and went off to wander among the emptied roads and silent dwellings. He said: "The fertility of the soil has been taken from us, the warmth of the air is dying out, the ice is grinding down our native land and sorrow stifles the wisdom of the mind and bravery. All we have left is the sunlight. I have made an apparatus—behold it! Suffering has taught me patience, and I have known how to make fruitful use of the savage years of the people's despair. Light is the force of *mamarva* torn to pieces (mutating matter. *ed.*), light is the element of the *aens*; the power of the *aens* is crushing. My apparatus converts streams of solar *aens* into heat. And I can convert the light, not merely of the Sun, but of the Moon and the Stars into heat as well. I can obtain an enormous quantity of heat, by which it is possible to melt mountains. Now we do not need the warm ocean current to heat our land!"

Thus Eiia became the leader of Life and the source of the new history of the Aiuna. His device, which consists of complex mirrors transforming the heavens' light into heat and into the vital force of metal (probably electricity, *ed.*), even now provides the source for our life and prosperity.

The plains of our homeland burst into bloom, and new children were born. An *en* (a long period of time, ed.) had passed.

The vitality of the human organism was exhausted. Even a young man could not bring forth seed; even the most forceful intellect ceased to generate thought. The valleys of the homeland were covered by the twilight of ultimate despair—Man had come to his limit within himself—Aiuna, the Sun of our heart, was vanishing forever. The crushing power of ice was nothing in comparison—nor of the cold, or the death. Man was nourished only by self-contempt. He could neither love, nor think, nor even suffer. The sources of life had run dry in the depths of the body, because they had been drunk dry. We had mountains of food, courts of comfort, and crystalline book depositories. But there was no longer life, vitality and heat within the body, and hopes had darkened. Man was a mine, but all the ore had been worked out; only empty shafts remained.

It is fine to die on a strong boat in the wild ocean, but not to choke to death on one's food.

It was thus for a long time. A whole generation did not experience youth.

Then my son Riigo found a way out. What nature could not give, art had provided. He had kept remnants of a vital brain within himself, and told us that our destiny was ending, but one could still open a door to it—toward a new, bright tomorrow. The solution was simple: an electromagnetic channel. (*verbatim*: a tube for the vital force of metal. *ed.*). Riigo had laid a gullet to the *aens* of our dark body from space and passed streams of dead *aens* (corresponds to ether. *ed.*) along this gullet, and our body's *aens*, having received an excess of food, revived. That is how our brain, our heart, our love for woman, and our Aiuna were resurrected. But more than that: our children grew twice as fast and life pulsed in them, like a very powerful machine. All the rest—consciousness, feeling, and love—grew into fearsome poetry and frightened the fathers. History ceased to walk and began to race. And the wind of destiny beat against our unprotected face with great news of thoughts and deeds.

My son's invention, like every remarkable thing, has a prosaic face. Riigo took two *proiia* centers filled with the corpses of *aens* and placed them into one *proiia*. The living *aens* of the *proiia* then began to multiply rapidly, and the entire *proiia* grew five-fold in ten days. The reason was evident and unimpressive: the *aens* began to eat more because their store of food had doubled.

Thus my son Riigo developed whole colonies of satiated, fast-growing *aens*, multiplying unbelievably. Then he took an ordinary body—a piece of iron—and past it, just touching the iron, begin to emit a stream of satiated *aens*, reared in colonies, in the direction of the stars. The satiated *aens* did not tap the corpses of their ancestors (that is, ether.—*ed.*) for food, and they freely flowed toward the piece of iron, where the hungry *aens* awaited them. And the iron began to grow under peoples' eyes, like plants from the Earth.

Thus my son Riigo's art revived man and began to cultivate matter.

But triumph always prepares defeat.

The artificially fattened *aens*, having a stronger body, began to attack living, but natural *aens* and devour them. And since in any transformation of matter there are inevitable losses, the devoured small *aen* did not enlarge the body of the larger to the size it had itself when it was living. Such matter, here, there, and everywhere the artificially fattened *aens* (electrons—the current term will be used hereafter. *ed.*) penetrated, began to diminish. Riigo's art could not make a gullet for the entire Earth, and the matter melted. Only where the channel for the stream of electron corpses was laid (ether tract. *ed.*) did matter grow. People, the soil, and the substances of greatest importance for our life were fitted with ether tracts. The dimensions of everything else diminished; matter burnt up; we were living at the cost of the destruction of the planet.

Riigo disappeared from home. The water began to vanish from the Continental Ocean. Riigo knew the cause of the disappearance of the moisture and went out to meet the antagonist. One day a tribe of electrons, fattened and reared by him had, by the working of time and natural selection, reached the point where each electron, in terms of body volume, was the size of a cloud.

In raging fury swarms of electrons came out of the depths of the Continental Ocean, heaving like mountains in an earthquake, breathing like powerful winds. They will drink Aiuna dry, as if it were water! Riigo fell. It was impossible to bear the glance of an electron. Death from terror will be hideous, but Aiuna is beyond rescue. Riigo fell into obscurity long ago, like a stone into a well. These cosmic beasts move too slowly. But their path from *proiia* particle to living mountain advanced too quickly. I believe that they will sink into the Earth like curds, because their body is heavier than lead. Certainly Riigo did not fall to no purpose, but having resolved to conquer the unknown elementary bodies, and with the means to do so. The power of the electron is in rapid growth and the furious action of natural selection. And this is their weakness, because it clearly points to the extreme simplicity of their psyche and physiological organization, and perhaps reveals an unprotected point of vulnerability. Riigo understood this clearly, but was slain by the electron's paw, heavy as a slab of platinum . . .

Maria Alexandrovna drooped over the book. Little Egor slept, the clock struck midnight—the most fearful hour of loneliness, when all happy people are asleep.

"Is the nurturing of man really so difficult?" Maria Alexandrovna said loudly. "Is triumph really always the harbinger of defeat?"

Moscow was quiet. The last trams hurried to the depot, their contacts shooting sparks.

"Then what triumph does my husband's dismal death repay? What soul will replace for me his gloomy lost love?"

And she burned with a fervent grief and wept tears that kill the body more quickly than lost blood. Her mind tossed about in a nightmare: the hum of living murky electrons had ripped apart the wise, defenseless Aiuna, rivers of the green poison, *zundra*, flowed over the flowering tundra, and in the green fluid, sinking and choking, swam Mikhail Kirpichnikov—her only friend—lost forever.

* * *

In the Silver Forest, near the crematorium, stood a building in a delicate architectural style. It had been done as a spheroid in the image of a cosmic body held up by five powerful columns, without touching the ground. A telescopic column rose into the sky from the topmost point of the spheroid, as a sign and a threat to the dark natural world that takes away those who are alive, those who are loved and those who love—in the hope that the dead will be borne away into the universe by the power of ascending science, resurrected, and returned to the living.

This was the House of Remembrance, containing the urns with the ashes of perished men.

A woman, gray and splendid with age, entered the House with a young man. They went quietly through to the far end of the enormous hall, illuminated by the dark-blue light of memory and longing. The urns stood in a row, like candles with light snuffed-out, lighting a formerly unknown path.

Memorial plaques were attached to the urns:

Andrey Volugov, Engineer.
Perished in the underwater expedition exploring Atlantis.

There are no ashes in the urn—there is a handkerchief, soaked with his blood when he was wounded while working at the bottom of the Pacific Ocean. The handkerchief was delivered by a woman traveling with him.

Peter Kreizkopf. Builder of the first Lunar craft.

He flew to the Moon in his probe and did not return. There are no ashes in the urn. His baby clothes have been preserved. Honor to the great engineer and his brave will!

The gray-haired woman, her face surprisingly aglow, went on further with the young man. They stopped at the furthest urn.

Mikhail Kirpichnikov.
Investigator of the method for multiplying matter.

Colleague of the physicist Doctor F. K. Popov, engineer. Died on the *California* after collision with a fallen meteor. There are no ashes in the urn. His work on the feeding and cultivation of electrons and a lock of hair are preserved.

A small second plaque hung below:

He lost his wife and the soul of his friend in his search for electrons' nutrition. The son of the deceased will accomplish his father's work and return to his mother the heartfelt love squandered by the father. In memory of, and love for, the great seeker.

Age is like youth: expecting salvation in a miraculous later life. Maria Alexandrovna Kirpichnikova had expended her youth in vain; her love for her husband had become transformed into a passionate maternal feeling for her elder son, Egor, who was already twenty-five years old. The younger son, Lev, a student, was sociable, very handsome, but did not arouse the sharp feeling of tenderness, protectiveness, and hope that Egor did. Egor's face resembled his father's—lackluster, ordinary, but unusually attractive in its hidden formidability and unconscious power.

Maria Alexandrovna took Egor by the hand, like a little boy, and went toward the exit. A square gold plaque with gray platinum letters hung in the vestibule of the House of Remembrance:

> Death is present where sufficient knowledge is lacking of the physiological elements acting in the body, and destroying it.

There was an arch above the entrance to the House with the words:

> Remember with tenderness, but without suffering: Science will resurrect the dead and comfort your heart.

The woman and the young man went out into the open air. The summer Sun rejoiced above the full-blooded Earth, and the new Moscow stood before the eyes of the two—a miraculous city of powerful culture, unrelenting labor, and sensible happiness. The Sun hastened to do its work, people grinned from the surplus of their energy—they were eager in work and vigorous in love.

The Sun above their heads supplied them with everything—the same Sun that once lit the path to Mikhail Kirpichnikov in the citrus district of Riverside—the old Sun, which shines with alarming passionate joy, like a world catastrophe and the engendering of the Universe.

* * *

[Egor Kirpichnikov]

The Intellectual Toiler published the following note on January 4:

THE CENTRAL ELECTRICAL POWER STATION OF LIFE.

A young engineer, Egor Kirpichnikov, has performed some interesting experiments over a number of months on artificial ether production in Prof. Marand's ether laboratory. The idea behind engineer Kirpichnikov's work is that a high-frequency electromagnetic field kills living electrons in matter; as we know, dead electrons constitute the substance of the ether. The height of engineer Kirpichnikov's technical art can be understood from the fact that a field oscillating at no fewer than 1012 periods per second is required to kill electrons.

Kirpichnikov's high-frequency machine is the sun itself, whose light is decomposed by a complex system of interfering surfaces into its constituent energy elements: the mechanical energy of pressure, chemical energy, electrical energy, etc.

Kirpichnikov only needs electrical energy, which he concentrates in a very confined space by means of special prisms and deflectors to achieve the necessary frequency.

In essence, an electromagnetic field is a colony of electrons. By forcing this field to pulsate rapidly, Kirpichnikov has succeeded in causing the electrons making up what is called the field to die; this causes the electromagnetic field to be converted to ether—the mechanical mass of the bodies of dead electrons.

Obtaining a number of ether spaces, Kirpichnikov lowered common objects (for example, a Waterman fountain pen) into them; the volume of these bodies increased two-fold in three days.

The following process had taken place in the fountain pen: the living electrons in the substance of the fountain pen received fortified nourishment from the surrounding electron corpses and rapidly multiplied, thus increasing in volume as well. This brought about the growth of the entire substance of the fountain pen. As the living electrons continued to consume the ether, their growth and multiplication ceased.

On the basis of his studies, Kirpichnikov has established that only living electrons are generated within the sun's enormous mass; but their concentration in gigantic numbers in a relatively packed space leads to such a horrendous struggle among them for sources of nourishment that nearly all the electrons are totally destroyed. The struggle for food is responsible for the great pulsation of the sun. The physical energy of the sun has, so to speak, a social cause— the mutual competition of the electrons. The electrons in the solar mass live only several millionths of a second, as they are destroyed by more powerful opponents which, in their turn, die under the onslaught of still more powerful competitors, etc. Having scarcely managed to gobble up its enemy's corpse, the electron is now destroyed—and the next victor eats it along with the undigested clumps of the body of the previously killed electron.

The movements of the electrons in the sun are so precipitous that a vast number are forced out beyond the limits of the sun and fly into space at a speed of three hundred thousand kilometers per second, creating the effect of a beam of light. But there is such an awesome and devastating struggle taking place on the sun that all the electrons leaving the sun are dead, and are flying either according to the inertia of their motion when they were alive or to their opponent's impact.

However, Kirpichnikov is convinced that there are extremely rare exceptions—once per time zone—when an electron may be torn away from the sun alive. Then, having ether—an abundant nutritive medium—around it, it becomes the father of a new planet. Eng. Kirpichnikov proposes later on to produce large quantities of ether, primarily from the upper layers of the atmosphere bounded by the ether. The electrons are less active there, and their destruction requires less energy.

Kirpichnikov is completing his new method of artificial production of ether; the new means involves an electromagnetic channel in which a high frequency acts to kill off electrons. The electromagnetic high-frequency channel is directed from the ground to the sun, and a stream of dead electrons is formed in the channel, as in a pipe, driven by the pressure of sunlight toward the terrestrial surface.

The ether is collected at the Earth's surface, accumulated in special vessels, and then used for the nourishment of those substances whose volume one wishes to increase.

Eng. Kirpichnikov has also performed the reverse experiments. By exposing an object to the action of a high-frequency field, he has achieved, as it were, the extinction of the object and its complete disappearance. Kirpichnikov has destroyed the innermost essence of a substance, since only a living electron is a particle of matter; a dead electron, on the other hand, belongs to the ether. Kirpichnikov has changed several objects completely into ether by this means, including the Waterman pen which he had initially "fattened."

The aggregate of all of Kirpichnikov's studies reveals the titanic force of creation and destruction mankind has received from his invention.

In Kirpichnikov's opinion, by constantly supplying the terrestrial globe with ether flowing from the sun, the Earth itself will steadily increase in size and in the specific gravity of its matter. This guarantees mankind's progress and undergirds historical optimism with a physical basis.

Kirpichnikov says that he has fully copied the action of the sun in relation to the Earth in his invention, and has merely accelerated its work.

These astonishing discoveries automatically recall to memory the name of F. K. Popov, who bequeathed us his astounding work, and finally, the father of the inventor, the engineer Mikhail Kirpichnikov who died tragically and peculiarly. < . . . >

* * *

The days were not so long nor the nights so short for the dawn to break at one in the morning on the twentieth of March. That had never happened; even old men cannot remember such a thing.

But one day it did happen. Muscovites had gone home—some from the theater, some from the night shift at the factory, some simply from a long talk with a friend.

There was a concert that night at the Great Hall of the Philharmonic, performed by the famous Vienna-born pianist, Schachtmeier. His profound undersea music, filled with a strange feeling that could not be called either anguish or ecstasy, had shaken his audience. People silently went their ways from the Philharmonic, awed and rejoicing in new and unknown depths and heights of life, which Schachtmeier had expressed in the elemental language of music.

At twelve-thirty in the morning, Maks Valir, who had returned from halfway to the moon, had finished his report at the Polytechnic Museum. An error had been found in the rocket he had designed; moreover, the medium between the Earth and moon turned out to be completely different from what had been hypothesized from the Earth; so Valir had come back. The audience had been extremely excited by Valir's report; charged up by the strength of will and enthusiasm of the great attempt, it flowed with a fearful noise like lava out across Moscow. In this respect, the audiences of Valir and Schachtmeier were in sharp contrast to one another.

At that moment a dark-blue point began to shine high above Sverdlov Square. In a second it had increased in size ten-fold, and then began to emit a dark-blue spiral, silently rotating, and seemingly unwinding the coil of a blue viscous flux. One beam was slowly drawn to Earth, and its shuddering movement was visible, as if it had encountered stubbornly resisting forces and, in penetrating them, braked its progress. Finally, the column of dark-blue, lusterless, dead fire came to rest between Earth and infinity, and the blue dawn enveloped the entire sky. Instantly everyone was terrified, because all shadows had disappeared: all objects on the surface of the Earth were plunged into some mute but ever more penetrating dampness—and nothing had a shadow.

Moscow fell silent for the first time since it had been built: whoever was speaking broke off in mid-utterance; whoever had been silent made no exclamation. All movement ceased; anyone who was driving forgot to go on; anyone standing still could not recall the purpose that had been drawing him on.

Silence and the strange dark-blue glow stood alone above the Earth, embracing one another.

It was so silent that it seemed that the strange dawn sounded—in a monotone, and tenderly, as the crickets sang in our childhood.

Every voice was ringing and youthful in the spring air—a feminine voice cried out piercingly and astonishing under the columns of the Bolshoi Theater: someone's soul could not bear the strain and made an abrupt movement to conceal itself from this enchantment.

And at once all nocturnal Moscow went into motion: drivers pushed their starter buttons; pedestrians took their first step; those who had been speaking started to yell; sleepers awoke and rushed into the street; all eyes turned upward toward the sky; each brain began to throb from the excitement.

But the dark-blue dawn began to fade. Darkness inundated the horizons; the spiral curled up, stealing away into the depths of the Milky Way; it then became a brilliant rotating star, but that too melted away in the eyes of the living—and it all disappeared, like a forgotten dream. But every eye that had looked up into the sky long continued seeing the spinning dark-blue star up there.

For some reason everyone was exhauter by this event, although hardly anyone knew why.

* * *

Next morning the *Izvestia* published the following interview with engineer Kirpichnikov:

EXPLANATION OF THE NIGHT-TIME DAWN ABOVE THE WORLD.

Our correspondent got into the Prof. Marand Microbiological Laboratory after a great deal of effort. This took place at 4 AM, right after the optical phenomenon in the ether. In the laboratory the correspondent found G. M. Kirpichnikov—the well-known designer of the equipment for the multiplication of material, discoverer of the so-called "ether channel"—asleep. The correspondent did not have the temerity to awaken the tired inventor; however, the arrangement of the laboratory made it possible to see all the results of the nocturnal experiment.

Besides the equipment for the production of the ether channel and the accumulation of dead electrons, an old yellow manuscript lay on the table. The following was written on the open page: "The technicians' job is to rear iron, gold, or coal as livestock breeders rear pigs." The correspondent has not yet established to whom these words belong.

A glittering body occupied half of the experimental chamber. It appeared on inspection to be iron. The form of the ferrous body was a nearly regular cube measuring 10 x 10 x 10 meters. How such a body could have gotten into the chamber was unclear, since its windows and doors could have admitted one only half the size. One hypothesis is left—that the iron was not brought into the chamber from anywhere, but had been grown in the chamber itself. This was confirmed by the log of experiments which lay on the same table as the manuscript. The dimensions of the experimental body were written there in the hand of G. M. Kirpichnikov: "Soft iron measuring 10 x 10 x 10 centimeters, 1 h 25 min., optimal voltage." There are no further notes in the log. Thus the iron had increased in volume 100-fold in 2-3 hours. That is the power of feeding ether to electrons.

There was an even and steady noise in the chamber, which our correspondent at first ignored. After turning on the lights, our colleague discovered some sort of monster sitting on the floor near the iron mass. Intricate parts of a broken device, apparently burnt out by an electric arc, were lying alongside the unknown being. The animal was emitting a monotonous moan. The correspondent photographed it (cf. below). The animal's maximum height was one meter. Its greatest width, about half a meter. The color of its body was reddish-yellow. Its overall shape was oval. Visual and auditory organs were not seen. A huge maw with black teeth was wide open; each tooth was 3-4 centimeters in length. There are four short (1/4 meter) powerful paws with bulging muscles; the span of the paw is no less than half a meter; it ends in a single powerful finger in the shape of an elastic, gleaming prong. The animal sits on a stout powerful tail; its tip moves about, glittering with three spikes. The teeth in the open maw are notched and rotate in their sockets. This strange and fearsome being has a very solid build and gives the impression of being a living chunk of metal.

The hum of this repulsive creature was producing the noise in the laboratory: the animal was probably hungry. This, beyond doubt, was an electron artificially fattened and cultivated by Kirpichnikov.

In conclusion, the editorial board congratulates readers and the nation on the new conquest of scientific genius, and is delighted that this victory falls to the credit of a young Soviet engineer.

The artificially cultivated iron and the multiplication of matter in general will give the Soviet Union such economic and military advantages over the other, capitalist, part of the world that if capitalism had a sense of the epoch and historical intelligence, it would surrender to socialism at once, and unconditionally. But, unfortunately, imperialism has never had these valuable qualities. < . . .>

All Moscow—the new Paris of the Socialist world—was ecstatic over this note. The entire vibrant, passionate, gregarious city appeared on the streets, in the clubs, at lectures—everywhere where there was even a whiff of new information about the works of G. M. Kirpichnikov.

The day dawned sunny; the snow melted a bit; and unbelievable hope was growing in the human breast. As the sun moved toward the midday zenith, the future shone ever clearer in the brain of man, like a rainbow, like the conquest of the universe, and like the dark-blue chasm of the great soul that had embraced the chaos of the world as its bride. < . . . >

* * *

In August Maria Alexandrovna received a letter from Egor in Tokyo.

Mama. I am happy—and I've understood something. The end of my work is approaching. Only by wandering the Earth, under different rays of the sun and over different soils am I able to think. I have now understood Papa. We need *outside forces to stimulate our thoughts. These forces are scattered along the world's roadways, they must be sought, and one must place one's head and body beneath them, as under a downpour. You know what I am doing and what I seek—the root of the world, the soil of the universe, from which it grew. From ancient philosophical dreams, this has become the scientific challenge of the day. But someone is needed to do this, and I have taken it up. < . . .> I need the challenge, or else I would become weary and kill myself. Father also had this feeling; maybe it's an illness, maybe it's bad heredity from our ancestors— vagabonds and Kievan pilgrims. Don't hunt for me and don't feel sad—I'll do what I've planned to do—and then I'll return. I think about you, but my restless feet and my anxious head drive me forward. Maybe, probably, life is a perverse fact, and each breathing creature is a miracle and an exception. And then I marvel, and it's good for me to think of my dear mother and my unavenged father.   Egor"*

News of the death of Egor Kirpichnikov in prison in Buenos Aires was received in Moscow on the thirty-first of December. He was arrested along with bandits who had been robbing express trains. He fell ill with tropical malaria in prison. The whole gang was sentenced to be hanged. Since Kirpichnikov was unable to walk to the gallows, as he was sinking into a delirium before death, they gave him poison, and no longer recalling anything of life, he died.

His body, along with the hanged bandits, was thrown into the muddy Amazon and washed out into the Pacific Ocean. The gallows that stood on the very banks of the Amazon were also thrown into the river after the execution: there they floated, dragging the corpses in their deadly nooses.

In response to inquiries by the Soviet government regarding the punishment of a man who could not have been a criminal, yet who had ended up in a gang by an unknown chance, the Brazilian government replied that it had not known that Kirpichnikov was in its hands; when arrested he refused to give his name, and then he became ill, and did not ever regain consciousness during the investigation.

Maria Alexandrovna erected a new urn in the House of Remembrances at the Silver Forest, next to the urn of her husband. On it was inscribed:

"Egor Kirpichnikov. Died age 29. Inventor of the Ether Channel—disciple of F. K. Popov and his father. Eternal glory, and sorrowful memory, to the Architect of a new Nature."

(1922-1928)

Translated by Elliott Urday, A. L. and M. K.

Ivan Antonovich Efremov
(1907–1972)

The Andromeda Nebula

[ABRIDGED CHAPTERS ONE & TWO]

CHAPTER ONE:
THE IRON STAR

In the faint light emitted by the helical tube on the ceiling the rows of dials on the instrument panels had the appearance of a portrait gallery—the round dials had jovial faces, the recumbent oval physiognomies were impudently self-satisfied and the square mugs were immobile in their stupid complacency. The light—and the dark-blue, orange and green lights flickering inside the instruments—served to intensify the impression.

A big dial, glowing dull red, gazed out from the middle of the convex control desk. The girl in front of it had forgotten her chair and stood with her head bowed, her brow almost touching the glass, in the attitude of one in prayer. The red glow made her youthful face older and sterner, cast clear-cut shadows round her full lips and even made her slightly snub nose look pointed. Her thick eyebrows, knitted in a frown, looked jet black in that light and gave her eyes the despairing expression seen in the eyes of the doomed.

The faint hum of the dials was interrupted by a soft metallic click. The girl started and raised her head, straightening her tired back.

The door opened behind her, a large shadow appeared and turned into a man with abrupt and precise movements. A flood of golden light sprang up, making the girl's thick, dark-auburn hair sparkle like gold. She turned to the newcomer with a look that told both of her love for him and of her anxiety.

"Why aren't you sleeping? A hundred sleepless hours!"

"A bad example, eh?" There was a note of gaiety in his voice but he didn't smile; it was a voice marked by high metallic notes that seemed to rivet his words together.

"The others are all asleep," the girl began timidly, "and . . . don't know anything . . ." she added whispering instinctively.

"Don't be afraid to speak. Everybody else is asleep, we're the only two awake in the Cosmos and it's fifty billion kilometers to Earth—a mere *parsec* and a half!"

"And we've got fuel for just one acceleration!" There was fascinated horror in the girl's exclamation.

Erg Noor, Commander of the Cosmic Expedition # 37, reached the glowing dial in two rapid strides.

"The fifth circle!"

"Yes, we've entered the fifth . . . and . . . still nothing." The girl cast an eloquent glance at the loudspeaker of the automatic receiver.

"So obviously I have no right to sleep with so many variants and possibilities to study. A solution must be found by the end of the fifth circle."

"But that's another hundred and ten hours."

"All right, I'll go to sleep in the armchair here as soon as the effect of the *sporamin* wears off. I took it twenty-four hours ago."

The girl stood deep in thought for a time but at last, decided to speak.

"Perhaps we should decrease the radius of the circle? Suppose something's gone wrong with their transmitter?"

"Certainly not! If you reduce the radius without reducing speed you'll break up the ship. If you reduce speed you'll be left without *anameson* . . . with a parsec and a half to go at the speed of the old lunar shuttles! At that rate we'd get somewhere near our solar system in about a hundred thousand years."

"I know that. But couldn't they . . ."

"No, they couldn't. Eons ago people could be careless or could deceive each other and themselves. But not today!"

"That's not what I wanted to say." The sharpness of her retort showed that the girl was offended. "I was going to say that *Algrab* may have deviated from its course looking for us."

"It couldn't have deviated so much. It *must* have left at the time computed and agreed on. If the improbable had happened and both transmitters had been put out of action it would have had to cross the circle diametrically and we should have heard it on the planetary receiver. There's no possibility of a mistake—there it is, the rendezvous planet."

Erg Noor pointed to the mirror screens in deep niches on all four sides of the control tower. Countless stars burned in the profound blackness. A tiny gray disc, barely illuminated by a sun very far away from them, from the outer edge of the system B-7336-S + 87-A, was crossing the forward port screen.

"Our beacons are functioning well although we put them up four *independent years* ago." Erg Noor pointed to a clear-cut line of light running across a glass panel that stretched the whole length of the left-hand wall. "*Algrab* should have been here three months ago. That means," Erg Noor hesitated as though he did not wish to finish the sentence, "*Algrab* is lost!"

"But suppose it isn't, suppose it's only been damaged by a meteoroid and can't regain its speed?" objected the auburn-haired girl.

"Can't regain its speed!" repeated Erg Noor. "Isn't that the same thing? If there's a journey thousands of years long between the ship and its goal, so much the worse—instead of instantaneous death there'll be years of hopelessness for the doomed. Maybe they'll signal. If they do, we'll know . . . on Earth . . . in about six years."

With one of his impetuous movements Erg Noor pulled a folding armchair from under the table supporting the computer , a small MNU-11; the ITU electronic brain capable of any computation was not fitted in spaceships to pilot them unaided because of its great weight, size and fragility. A navigator had always to be on duty in the control tower, especially as it was impossible to plot an exact course over such terrific distances.

The commander's hands danced over the levers and buttons with the rapidity of a pianist's. The clear-cut features of his pale face were as immobile a statue's and his lofty brow, inclined stubbornly over the control desk, seemed to be challenging the elemental forces menacing that tiny world of living beings who had dared penetrate into the forbidden depths of space.

Nisa Creet, a young astronavigator on her first space flight, held her breath and kept silent as she watched Erg Noor, and the commander himself seemed oblivious of everything but his work. How cool and collected, how resourceful and full of energy was the man she loved. And she had loved him for a long time, for all of the past five years. There was no sense concealing it from him, he knew it already, Nisa could feel that. Now that this great misfortune had happened she had the tremendous joy of serving a watch with him, three months alone with him while the other members of the crew lay in deep hypnotic sleep. Another thirteen days and they, too, would be able to sleep for six months while the other two watches—the navigators, astronomers and mechanics—served their turns. The other members of the expedition, the biologists and geologists who would only have work to do when they arrived at their destination, could sleep longer, but the astronomers—theirs was the greatest strain of all!

Erg Noor rose and Nisa's train of thought was broken. "I'm going to the chartroom. You'll be able to sleep in"—he glanced at the clock showing dependent, or ship's, time—"nine hours. I'll have time for some sleep before I relieve you."

"I'm not tired, I can stay here as long as necessary—you must get some rest!"

Erg Noor frowned and was about to object but was captivated by the tenderness of her words and by the golden hazel eyes that appealed to him so trustingly; he smiled and went out without another word.

Nisa sat down in the chair, cast an accustomed glance over the instruments and was soon lost in deep meditation.

The reflector screens, through which those on the bridge could see what was happening in the surrounding expanses of space, gleamed black overhead. The lights of many-hued stars pierced the eyes like needles of fire. The spaceship was overtaking a planet whose gravity made the ship vacillate in a field of changing intensity. Magnificent but malignant stars also made wild leaps in the reflector screens. The outlines of the constellations changed with a rapidity that memory could not record.

Planet K2-2N-88, cold, lifeless, far from its sun, was known as a convenient *rendezvous* for spaceships . . . for the meeting that had not taken place. The fifth circle—Nisa could visualize her ship traveling with reduced speed around a monster circle with a radius of a billion kilometers, steadily gaining on a planet that crawled along at a snail's pace. In a hundred and ten hours the ship would complete the fifth circle—and what then? Erg Noor's tremendous brain was now strained to the utmost to find the best solution. As commander both of the expedition and the ship he could not afford mistakes. If he made a mistake, the First Class Spaceship *Tantra* with its crew of the world's most eminent scientists would never return from outer space! But Erg Noor would make no mistake.

Nisa Creet was suddenly overcome by a feeling of nausea which meant that the spaceship had deviated from its course by a tiny fraction of a degree, something possible only at the reduced speed at which they were traveling: at full speed not one of the ship's fragile human cargo would have survived. The gray mist before the girl's eyes had not yet dispersed when the nausea swept over her again, as the ship returned to its course. Delicately sensors had located a meteoroid, the greatest enemy of spaceships, in the black emptiness ahead of them and had automatically made the deviation. The ship's navigational controls (only they could carry out all adjustments with the necessary speed, since human nerves are unsuited to cosmic velocities) had taken her off her course in a millionth of a second and, the danger past, had returned her with equal speed. < . . . >

Cosmic Expedition No. 37 had been sent to the planetary system of the nearest star in The Serpent Holder (the constellation Ophiuchus) whose only inhabited planet, Zirda, had long been in communication with Earth and other worlds throughout the Great Circle. The planet had suddenly gone silent, and for over seventy years nothing more had been heard. It was Earth's duty, as the Circle planet nearest to Zirda, to find out what had happened. With this aim in view the expedition's ship had taken on board a large number of instruments and several prominent scientists, those whose nerves, after lengthy testing, had proved capable of withstanding confinement in a spaceship for several years. The ship was fueled with *anameson*; only the bare minimum had been taken, not because of its weight but because of the tremendous size of the containers in which it was stored. It was expected that supplies could be renewed on Zirda. In case something serious had happened on Zirda, Second Class Spaceship *Algrab* was to have met *Tantra* with fuel supplies, in orbit around planet K2-2N-88. < . . . >

Nisa's most vivid memory was that of a blood-red sun that had been steadily growing in their field of vision during the last months of their fourth space year. The fourth year for the inhabitants of the spaceship as it traveled at 83% of the speed of light, but on Earth seven independent years had already passed. The filters on the screens were kind to human eyes; they reduced the composition of the rays of any celestial body to what could have been seen through the dense atmosphere of Earth, with its protective screens of ozone and water vapors. The indescribable ghostly violet light of high temperature bodies was toned down to blue or white and gloomy greet-pink stars took on cheerful golden-yellow hues, like our Sun. A celestial body that burned triumphantly with bright crimson fire took on a deep, blood-red color, the hue that a terrestrial observer sees in Class M stars. The planet was much nearer to its star than Earth is to the Sun, and as the ship drew nearer to Zirda the star grew into a tremendous crimson disc that radiated massive heat energy. For two months before approaching Zirda *Tantra* had initiated attempts to contact the planet's outer space station. There was only one such station—on a small natural satellite with no atmosphere that was much nearer to Zirda than the Moon is to Earth. The spaceship continued calling when the planet was no more than thirty million kilometers away and the terrific speed of *Tantra* had been reduced to three thousand km/sec. It was Nisa's watch but all the crew were awake, sitting in anticipation in front of the bridge screens. Nisa kept hailing, increasing the power of the transmissions and sending rays out fanwise ahead of the ship. At last they saw the tiny shining dot of the satellite. The spaceship came into orbit around the planet, approaching it in a spiral and gradually adjusting its speed to that of the satellite. Soon *Tantra's* speed was the same as that of the fast-moving little satellite and it seemed as though an invisible hawser held them fast. The ship's stereo telescope scanned the surface of the satellite until the crew of *Tantra* were suddenly confronted with an unforgettable sight.

A huge, flat-topped glass building seemed to be on fire in the rays of the blood-red sun. Directly under the roof was something in the nature of an assembly hall. There a number of beings—unlike terrestrial humans but unmistakably people—were frozen into immobility. Excitedly, Pour Hyss, the astronomer of the expedition, continued to adjust the focus. The vague rows of people visible under the glass roof were absolutely motionless. Pour Hyss increased the instrument's magnification. Out of the vagueness a dais surrounded by instrument panels appeared, and on it a long table on which a man sat cross-legged facing the audience, his insane, terrifying eyes staring into the distance.

"They're dead, frozen," exclaimed Erg Noor. The spaceship continued to hover over Zirda's satellite and fourteen pairs of eyes remained fixed on that glass tomb, for such, indeed, it was. How long had the dead been sitting there in their hall of glass? The planet had broken off communication seventy years before; add the six years required for the transmission to reach Earth and three quarters of a century must have passed.

All eyes were turned on the commander. Erg Noor, his face pale, was staring into the smoky yellow atmosphere of the planet through which the lines of the mountain ranges and the glint of the sea were faintly discernible. But nothing gave the answer they had come for. "The station perished seventy-five years ago and has not been re-established! That can only mean a catastrophe on the planet. We have to enter the atmosphere, maybe even land. Everyone's here now, so I'll ask your opinion."

The only objection was raised by Pour Hyss, a man on his first space trip flight; he had replaced an experienced worker who had fallen ill just before launch. Nisa looked with indignation at his big, hawk-like nose and the ugly ears set low on his head.

"If there's been a catastrophe on the planet there's no possibility of our getting *anameson* there. If we circle the planet at low altitude we'll drain our supply of planetary fuel, and if we land we'll drain it even more. Apart from that, we don't know what happened, there could be high-level radiation that would kill us."

The other members of the expedition supported their commander. "There's no planetary radiation that can cause any problems to our shields. Weren't we sent here to find out what happened? What are we going to tell the Great Circle? It's not enough to establish the fact, we have to account for it—sorry if this sounds like a high-school lecture!" said Erg Noor and the usual metallic tones in his voice now held a note of ridicule in them. "I don't think we can get out of doing what's obviously our duty."

The upper layers of the atmosphere have a normal temperature!" exclaimed Nisa, happily, completing rapid measurements. Erg Noor smiled and began to put the ship down in a spiral, each turn slower than the last as they neared the planet surface. Zirda was somewhat smaller than Earth and no great speed was needed for a low-altitude orbit. The astronomers and the geologist checked the maps of the planet against the observations of *Tantra's* instruments. There had been no noticeable change in the outlines of continents and the seas gleamed calmly in the red sun. Nor had the mountain ranges altered from the configurations known from former photographs—but the planet was silent. < . . . > The spaceship was crossing Zirda's night disc at a speed no greater than that of a terrestrial helicopter. Below them there should have been cities, factories and ports, but not a single light showed in the pitch blackness, no matter how thoroughly the powerful stereotelescopes scanned the surface. The thunder of the spaceship cutting through the atmosphere must have been audible for dozens of miles. Another hour passed and still no light was seen. The anxious wait was becoming unbearable. Noor switched on the warning sirens hoping that their awe-inspiring howl, added to the roar of the spaceship, would be heard by the mysteriously silent inhabitants of Zirda.

A fiery light wave swept away the ominous darkness as *Tantra* reached the daylight side of the planet. Below them everything was still black. Rapidly developed and enlarged photographs showed that the surface was covered with a solid carpet of flowers something like the velvety-black poppies that grow on Earth. The masses of black poppies stretched for thousands of miles to the exclusion of all other vegetation—trees and bushes, reeds and grass. The city streets looked like the ribs of giant skeletons lying on a black carpet; metal structures formed gaping rusty wounds. Not a living being, not a tree anywhere, nothing but the black poppies!

Tantra dropped an observation beacon and again plunged into the night. Six hours later the robot reported the content of the atmosphere, the temperature, pressure and other conditions on the surface. Everything was normal for Zirda with the exception of increased radioactivity.

"What an awful tragedy!" Eon Thal, the expedition's biologist, muttered in a dull voice as he recorded the data. "They've destroyed themselves and everything on their planet!"

"How could they?" asked Nisa, hiding tears that were very near the surface. "Is it as bad as that? The ionization really isn't very high."

"It's been a long time," answered the biologist glumly. His virile Circassian face with its aquiline nose assumed a stern expression, despite his youth. "Radioactive disintegration is dangerous just because it accumulates unnoticed. For hundreds of years the total radiation could increase *corus* by *corus*; then suddenly there's a qualitative change, the genome implodes, species reproduction ceases, and on top of that you get epidemics of radiation sickness. It's happened before, more than once. The Circle knows about other disasters like this."

"Like the so-called 'Planet of the Lilac Sun'," came Erg Noor's voice from behind them.

"Whose Spectral-class A° sun, equal to 78 of our suns, provided its inhabitants with very high energy," added the morose Pour Hyss.

"Where is that planet?," asked Eon Thal. "Isn't it the one the Council intends to colonize?" "That's the one, *Algrab* was named after its star."

"The star Algrab, that's Delta Corvi," exclaimed the biologist. "But it's such a long way off!"

"Forty-six parsecs. But we're constantly increasing the power of our spaceships . . ."

The biologist nodded but muttered that it was hardly right to name a spaceship after a dead star.

"The star didn't die and the planet is still safe and sound. Before another century's out we'll plant vegetation there and settle the planet," said Erg Noor with confidence.

He had decided to perform a difficult maneuver—to change the ship's orbit from latitudinal to meridianal, sending the ship along a north-south line parallel to the planet's axis of rotation. How could they leave the planet until they were certain there were no survivors? It might be that survivors were unable to communicate with the spaceship because power installations had been wrecked and instruments damaged.

This was not the first time Nisa had seen her commander at the control panel in a moment of great responsibility. With his impenetrably expressionless face, his abrupt but always precise movements, he seemed to the astronavigator like the hero of a legend.

Again *Tantra* made her futile journey round Zirda, this time from pole to pole. In some places, especially in the temperate latitudes, there were wide belts of bare ground, a yellow haze hung over them and through it, from time to time, appeared rows of gigantic red dunes from which the wind sent up clouds of sand.

Then again came the funeral pall of black velvet poppies, the only plant that had withstood the radioactivity or had produced a mutation of its species viable under radiation.

The whole picture was clear. It was not only useless, it was even dangerous to search for the supplies of *anameson* that had, on the recommendation of the Great Circle, been laid in for visitors from other worlds. *Tantra* began slowly unwinding the spiral away from the planet. She gained a velocity of 17 km/sec using her ion engines that provided her with the speed necessary for pulling away from the dead planet. *Tantra* turned her nose towards an uninhabited system known only by its code name where projectile beacons had been thrown out and where *Algrab* should have awaited. The *anameson* engines were now switched on and in fifty-two hours they accelerated the spaceship to her normal speed of 900,000,000 km/hour. Fifteen months' journey would take them to the meeting place—eleven months of the ship-time—and the crew, with the exception of those on watch, could sleep. < . . . >

Tantra had been circling the gray planet for many days, and with each passing hour the possibility of encountering *Algrab* grew less and less likely. Something terrible loomed ahead. Erg Noor stood in the doorway with his eyes on Nisa as she sat there in meditation—her inclined head with its cap of thick hair like a luxuriant golden flower, the mischievous, boyish profile, the slightly slanting eyes that were often crinkled with repressed laughter but which were now wide open, apprehensively but courageously probing the unknown . . .

Nisa did not realize what a tremendous moral support her selfless love had become for him. Despite the long years of trial that had steeled his will-power and his senses, he tired of command, of the need to be ready at any moment to shoulder entire responsibility for the crew, the ship, and the success of the expedition. Back there on Earth such single-handed responsibility had long since been abandoned—decisions there were taken collectively by the group who had to carry them out. If anything unusual occurred on Earth you could always get advice, and consultations on the most intricate problems could be arranged. Here there was no one to consult, and spaceship commanders were granted special rights. It would have been easier if this responsibility had been for two or three years rather than the ten to fifteen that were normal for space expeditions! Erg Noor entered the bridge.

Nisa jumped up to meet him.

"I've got all the necessary data and charts," he said, "let's fire it up!"

The commander stretched himself out in his armchair and slowly turned over the thin metal sheets he had brought, calling out the coordinates, the strength of magnetic, electric and gravitational fields, the power of space-dust streams and the velocity and density of meteoroid showers. Nisa, every muscle tense with excitement, pressed the buttons and turned the knobs of the computer. Erg Noor noted a series of responses, frowned and lapsed into deep thought.

"There's a strong gravitational field in our way, the area in Scorpion with an accumulation of dark matter, near 6555CB + 11PKU," began Noor. "We can save fuel by changing course that way, towards the Serpent. In the old days they flew without engines, using the gravitational fields as accelerators."

"Can we do the same?" asked Nisa.

"No, our ships are too fast. At 5/6ths light speed, or 250,000 kilometers/second, our weight would be 12,000 times greater within a gravitation field, and that would reduce the whole expedition to dust. We can only fly like this in space, far from large accumulations of matter. If the ship enters a strong gravitational field we have to reduce speed, the stronger the field the greater the reduction."

"So there's a contradiction here," said Nisa, resting her head on her hand in a childish manner, "the stronger the gravitational field the slower we have to fly!"

"That's only true with velocities close to light speed, when the ship is like a ray of light and can only move in a straight line or along the so-called curve of equal tension."

"If I understand you, we've got to aim our *Tantra*-ray straight at the solar system."

"That's where the great difficulty of space travel comes in. It's practically impossible to aim directly at any star, even when we make all the corrective calculations we can think of. Throughout the entire flight we have to compute the accumulating error and constantly change the course of the ship, so an automatic pilot is impossible. Right now we're in a dangerous situation. There's nothing left to start another acceleration going, so any halt or even a significant deceleration means certain death. Look, the danger's here—in area 344 + 2U, which has never been explored. No stars, no inhabited planets, nothing known but the gravitational field—there's the perimeter. We'll wait for the astronomers before we make the final decision—after the fifth rotation we'll wake everybody, but in the meantime . . ." The commander massaged his temples and yawned.

"The *sporamin* is wearing off," exclaimed Nisa, "you can get some sleep!" "Good. I'll be fine right here, in this chair. What if there's a miracle . . . just one beep from them would suffice!" There was something in Erg Noor's voice that made Nisa's heart race. She wanted to take that stubborn head of his, press it to her breast and stroke his dark hair with its strands of premature gray. < . . . >

The powerful anameson engines were silent. The peace of a long night hung over the sleepy ship as though no serious danger threatened her and her inhabitants. At any moment the long-awaited call signal would be heard over the loudspeaker and the two ships would check their unbelievably rapid flight, draw closer on parallel courses and finally equalize their speeds that they would essentially be berthed side by side. A wide, tubular gallery would connect the two ships and *Tantra* would regain her tremendous strength.

Deep in her heart Nisa was calm, she had faith in her commander. Their five years of travel had not seemed either long or tiring. Especially when Nisa realized that she fell in love. . . . But even before that the absorbingly interesting observations, the electronic recordings of books, music and films gave her every opportunity to increase her knowledge, and not feel the loss of beautiful Earth, that tiny speck of dust lost in the depths of infinite darkness. Her fellow travelers were people of true erudition. And when her nerves were exhausted by a surfeit of impressions or lengthy, strenuous work, there was prolonged sleep. The sleep state was maintained by attuning the patient to hypnotic oscillations and, after certain preliminary medical treatments, long stretches of time were lost in forgetfulness, passed without leaving a trace. Nisa was now especially happy because she was near the man she loved. The only thing that troubled her was the thought that others were having a harder time, especially Erg Noor. If only she could . . . no, what could a young and still very green astronavigator do, compared with such a man! Perhaps her tenderness, her constant fund of good will, her ardent desire to give up everything in order to make his tremendous task easier—would help.

The commander woke and raised his sleep-heavy head. The instruments were humming evenly as before, there were still the occasional thuds from the planetary engines. Nisa Creet was at the instruments, bending slightly over them, the shadows of fatigue on her young face. Erg Noor cast a glance at the ship-time clock, and leapt from his deep chair in a single athletic bound.

"Fourteen hours! And you didn't wake me, Nisa! That's. . . ." Meeting her radiant glance he stopped short. "Off to bed at once!"

"May I sleep here, like you did?" asked Nisa. She had a quick meal, and dropped into the deep armchair. Her flashing hazel eyes, circled by dark rings, stealthily followed Erg Noor as he took his place at the instruments. He checked the indicators on the communications panel and then began to pace back and forth with rapid strides.

"Why aren't you sleeping?" he asked the navigator. She shook the red curls that were by then in need of clipping—women on extraterrestrial expeditions did not wear long hair. "I was thinking . . ." she began hesitantly, "just now, when we're in this great danger, I bow my head before the might and majesty of humanity, who has penetrated to the stars, far, far into the depths of space! Most of this is ordinary for you, but I'm in space for the first time. Just think of it, I'm taking part in a magnificent journey through the stars to new worlds!"

Erg Noor smiled and rubbed his forehead. "I'll have to disappoint you, or rather, show you the real measure of our so-called might. Look. . . ." He paused beside a projector and on the back wall of the bridge appeared the glittering spiral of the Galaxy. Erg Noor pointed to a ragged outer branch of the spiral comprised of sparse stars, looking like dull dust and scarcely perceptible in the surrounding darkness.

"This is a desert area in the galaxy, an outer fringe poor in light and life, and our solar system is here, and right now so are we. That branch of the galaxy stretches, as you can see, from Cygnus to Carina and, in addition to being far removed from the central zone, it contains a dark cloud, here . . . Just traveling to that branch of the Galaxy would take our *Tantra* 40,000 independent years. To cross the empty space that separates our branch from our neighbors would take 4,000 years. So you see that our flights into the depths of space are still nothing more than just marking time on our own ground, a ground with a diameter of no more than fifty light-years! We'd know very little about the Universe if it weren't for the Great Circle. Reports, images and ideas transmitted through space's unconquerable in man's brief life span reach us sooner or later, and we get to know about still more distant worlds. Knowledge is constantly piling up and the work goes on all the time!"

Nisa listened in silence.

"The first interstellar flights . . ." continued Erg Noor, still lost in thought. "Small ships with low speed and no effective shields . . . and people in those days lived only half as long as we do—that was the period of man's real greatness!"

Nisa tossed her head as she usually did when she disagreed. "And when new ways of overcoming space have been discovered and people don't just force their way through it like we do, they'll say the same about you—those were the heroes who conquered space with their primitive methods!"

The commander smiled happily and held out his hand to the girl. "They'll say it about you, too, Nisa!"

"I'm proud to be here with you!" she answered, blushing. "And I'm prepared to give up everything if I can only travel into space again and again!"

"I know that," said Erg Noor, thoughtfully, "but that's not the way everybody thinks!" Intuition gave her an insight into the thoughts of her commander. In his cabin there were two stereo portraits, splendidly done in violet-gold tones. Both were of Veda Kong, a woman of great beauty, a specialist in ancient history; eyes of the same transparent blue as the skies above Earth looked out from under long eyebrows. Tanned by the sun, smiling radiantly, she raised her hands to her ash-blonde hair. In the second picture she was seated, laughing heartily, on the bronze gun of a ship, a relic of ancient days . . .

Erg Noor lost some of his impetuosity—he sat down slowly in front of the astronavigator.

"If you only knew, Nisa, how brutally fate dealt with my dreams, there on Zirda!" he said suddenly, in a dull voice, placing his fingers cautiously on the lever controlling the *anameson* engines as though intending to accelerate the spaceship to the limit. "If Zirda hadn't been destroyed, if we had gotten our fuel," he continued, in response to her unspoken question, "I'd have led the expedition farther. That's what I arranged with the Council. Zirda would have made the necessary report to Earth and *Tantra* would have continued its journey with those who wanted to go. The others would have waited for *Algrab,* it could have gone on to Zirda after its tour of duty here."

"Who'd want to stay on Zirda?" exclaimed the girl, indignantly. "Unless Pour Hyss would. He's a great scientist though, wouldn't he be interested in gaining further knowledge?"

"And you, Nisa?"

"I'd go, of course."

"Where?" asked Erg Noor suddenly, fixing his eyes on the girl.

"Anywhere you wanted, even . . ." and she pointed to a patch of abysmal blackness between two arms of the Galaxy's starry spiral; she returned Noor's fixed stare with one equally determined, her lips slightly parted.

"Oh, not that far! You know, Nisa, my dear navigator, about eighty-five years ago, Cosmic Expedition No. 84, the 'Three-Stage Expedition' left Earth. It consisted of three spaceships carrying fuel for each other, and it took off for Lyra. The two ships that weren't carrying scientists passed their *anameson* on to the third and then came back to Earth. That's the way mountain-climbers used to reach the highest summits. Then the third ship, *Parus. . . .*"

"That's the ship that never returned!" whispered Nisa excitedly.

"That's right, *Parus* didn't return. It reached its objective but was lost on the return journey after transmitting a message. The goal was the large planetary system of *Vega,* or *Alpha Lyrae,* a bright blue star that countless generations of human eyes have admired in the northern sky. The distance to *Vega* is eight parsecs and human beings had never been that far from our

Sun. Anyway, *Parus* got there. We don't know why it was lost, a meteoroid or an irreparable malfunction. It's even possible that the ship is still traveling through space and the heroes we think are dead are still alive."

"That would be terrible!"

"It's the fate of any spaceship that can't maintain a speed approaching light speed. It's instantly separated from the home planet by thousands of years."

"What message did *Parus* send?" asked the girl.

"There wasn't much to it. It was interrupted several times and then broke off altogether. I remember every word : 'This is *Parus*. This is *Parus*, traveling twenty-six years from Vega . . . enough . . . will wai . . . Vega's four planets . . . nothing more beautiful . . . happiness. . . . '"

"But they were calling for help, they wanted to wait somewhere."

"Of course they were calling for help, otherwise they wouldn't have used up the tremendous energy needed for transmission. But nothing could be done, there wasn't another word was from *Parus*."

"They'd been on their way back for twenty-six independent years, from Vega to the Sun is thirty-one years. They must have been somewhere near us, or even nearer Earth."

"Hardly, unless, of course, they exceeded the normal speed and got close to the quantum limit. Which would have been very dangerous!"

Briefly Erg Noor explained the mathematical basis for the destructive change that takes place in matter when it approaches light speed, but he noticed that Nisa was not really listening.

"I understand all that!" she exclaimed. "I'd have realized it before if your story about the lost ship hadn't taken my mind off it. Things like that are always terrible, and you just can't accept them!"

"You recognize the main point of the transmission," said Erg Noor gloomily. "They discovered some particularly beautiful worlds. For a long time I've been dreaming of following *Parus'* course; with modern improvements we could do it with one ship. I've been living with a dream of *Vega*, the blue sun with the beautiful planets, since I was very young."

"To see worlds like that . . ." breathed Nisa, a break in her voice, "But to see them and return would take sixty terrestrial years—forty dependent . . . and that's . . . half a lifetime."

"Great achievements demand great sacrifices. For me, though, it wouldn't be a sacrifice. I've lived on Earth for a few short intervals between space flights. I was born on a spaceship, you know!"

"How could that have happened?" asked the girl in amazement.

"Expedition No. 35 consisted of four ships. My mother was astronomer on one of them. I was born half-way to the binary star MN19026 + 7AL and managed to break the conventions twice—firstly by being born on a spaceship, and secondly because I was raised and educated by my parents, not in a school. What else could they have done? When the expedition returned to Earth, I was eighteen years old. I'd learned to pilot a spaceship and had acted as astronavigator in place of one got sick. I could also do mechanical repairs on the planetary or the *anameson* engines, and all this was accepted as the Labors of Hercules I had to perform to grow up."

"I still don't understand . . ." began Nisa.

"About my mother? You'll understand when you're a little older! Although the doctors didn't know it then, the Anti-T serum didn't keep. . . . Well, never mind how—I was brought onto a bridge like this one to look at the screens with my brand-new eyes, and to watch the stars dancing up and down on them. We were on course for Lupus , where there was a binary star close to the Sun. The two dwarfs, one blue and the other orange, were hidden by a dark cloud. The first thing that registered on my consciousness was the sky over a lifeless planet, which I observed from the glass dome of a temporary space station. The planets of double stars are usually lifeless because of the irregularity of their orbits. The expedition touched down and for seven months engaged in mineral prospecting. As far as I remember there were enormous quantities of platinum, osmium and iridium. My first toys were unbelievably heavy building blocks made of iridium. And that sky, my first sky, was black and dotted with the pure lights of stars that didn't twinkle, and there were two suns of indescribable beauty, one a deep blue and the other a bright orange. I remember how their rays sometimes crossed and at those times our planet was inundated with so much wonderful green light that I shouted and sang for joy!" Erg Noor stopped. "That's enough, I've been carried away by my memories and you have to sleep."

"Go on, please do, I've never heard anything so interesting," Nisa begged him, but the commander was implacable. He brought a pulsating hypnotizer and, either because of his impelling eyes or the sleep-inducing apparatus, Nisa was soon fast asleep, and she awoke only the day before they were to enter the sixth circle. By the cold look on the commander's face Nisa Greet realized that *Algrab* had not shown up.

"You're awake just in time!" "Switch on the re-animation music and lights. For everybody!"

Nisa swiftly pressed a row of buttons, sending intermittent bursts of light and music consisting of certain of low, vibrant chords, gradually increasing in intensity, to all the cabins where members of the expedition were asleep. This initiated a gradual awakening of their inhibited nervous systems, returning them to a normal active state. Five hours later everyone gathered in the bridge; by then they had fully recovered from their sleep, eaten, and taken nerve stimulants.

They received the news of the loss of the auxiliary spaceship in various ways. As Erg Noor expected, the expedition was equal to the occasion. Not a word of despair, not a glance of fear. Pour Hyss, who had not shown himself particularly brave on Zirda, heard the news without a tremor. Louma Lasvy, the expedition's young physician, went slightly pale and furtively licked her parched lips.

"To the memory of our lost comrades!" said the commander as he switched on the screen of a projector showing *Algrab,* a photograph taken before *Tantra's* launch. All rose to their feet. On the screen, one after another, came the photographs of the seven members of *Algrab's* crew, some serious, some smiling. Erg Noor named each of them in turn and the travelers gave the farewell salute. This was the astronauts' custom . < . . . >

There was a conviction among astronauts that there existed in space certain neutral fields, or zero areas, in which all radiation and all communications sank like stones into water. Astrophysicists, however, regarded the zero areas as nothing more than the idle invention of space travelers who were, in general, inclined to monstrous fantasies.

After the sad ceremony and a very short conference, Erg Noor changed *Tantra's* course in the direction of Earth and switched on the *anameson* drive. Forty-eight hours later they were switched off again and the ship began to approach its home planet at the rate of 21,000 million kilometers per day. The journey back to the Sun would take about six terrestrial years. Everybody was busy on the bridge and in the ship's combined library and laboratory, where a new course was being computed and plotted on the charts.

The task was to fly the whole six years using *anameson* only for course corrections. In other words the spaceship had to be flown with as little deceleration as possible. Everyone was worried about the unexplored area 344 + 2U that lay between the Sun and *Tantra.* There was no way of avoiding this: on both sides of it, as far as the Sun, lay belts of free meteoroids and apart from that they would lose velocity if they redirected the ship. Two months later the flight-course computation was complete. *Tantra* began to describe a long, flat curve.

The superb ship was in excellent condition and her speed was kept within the computed limits. Now nothing but time, about four dependent years, separated the ship from its home.

Erg Noor and Nisa Greet finished their watch and, dead tired, started their period of extended sleep. Together with the two astronomers, the geologist, biologist, physician and four engineers departed into temporary forgetfulness. The watch was taken over by Pel Lynn, an experienced astronavigator on his second expedition, assisted by astronomer Ingrid Dietra and electronic engineer Kay Bear, who had volunteered to join them. Ingrid, with Pel Lynn's consent, often left for the library adjoining the bridge. She and her old friend, Kay Bear, were writing a monumental symphony, *Death of a Planet,* inspired by the tragedy of Zirda. Pel Lynn, whenever he tired of the hum of the instruments and his contemplation of the black cosmic void, left Ingrid at the control desk and plunged into the thrilling task of deciphering puzzling inscriptions from a planet in the system of the nearest stars of Centaur, whose inhabitants had mysteriously abandoned it. He believed in the success of his impossible undertaking. . . .

Twice watches were changed, the ship had drawn ten billion kilometers nearer Earth and the *anameson* engines had only been activated for a few hours.

One of Pel Lynn's watches, the fourth since *Tantra* had left the place where she was to have met *Algrab,* was coming to an end. Ingrid Dietrahad finished a calculation and turned to Pel Lynn who was watching, with melancholy mien, the constant flickering of the red arrows on the graded blue scales of the gravitation dials. The usual sluggishness of psychic reaction that not even the strongest people could avoid made itself felt during the second half of the watch. For months and years the ship had been automatically piloted along a given course. If anything untoward had happened, something that the controls were incapable of dealing with, it would have meant the loss of the ship. Human intervention could not have saved it, since the human brain, no matter bow well-trained, cannot react with the necessary alacrity.

"In my opinion we are already deep in the unknown area $344 + 2U$. The commander wanted to take over the watch himself when we got there," said Ingrid. Pel Lynn glanced up at the counter that marked off the days. "Another two days and we change watches. So far there doesn't seem to be anything to worry about. Shall we see the watch through?"

Ingrid nodded assent. Kay Bear came into the control tower from the stern of the ship and took his usual seat beside the equilibrium mechanism. Pel Lynn yawned and stood up. "I'll get some sleep for a couple of hours," he said to Ingrid. She got up obediently and went forward to the control desk.

Tantra was travelling smoothly in an absolute vacuum. Not a single meteoroid, not even at a great distance, had been registered by the supersensitive Voll Hoad detectors. The ship's course now lay somewhat to one side of' the Sun, about one and a half light-years. The screens of the forward scanners registered an astounding blackness. It seemed as though the spaceship was diving into the very heart of universal darkness. The side telescopes still showed needles of light from countless stars.

Ingrid's nerves tingled with a strange sensation of alarm. She returned to her computers and telescopes, again and again checked their readings as she mapped the unknown area. Everything was quiet but still Ingrid could not take her eyes from the malignant blackness ahead of the ship. Kay Bear noticed her anxiety and for a long time studied and listened to the instruments. "I don't see anything," he said at last, "aren't you imagining things?" "I don't know why, but that unusual blackness ahead of us both-ers me. I think our ship is diving straight into a dark nebula." < . . . >

The long shrill of a bell made them all start. Ingrid grabbed Kay Bear.

Tantra was in danger! The gravitation was double the computed figure!

The astronavigator turned pale. The unexpected had happened and an immediate decision was essential. The fate of the spaceship was in his hands. The steadily increasing gravitational pull made a reduction in speed necessary, both because of increasing weight in the ship and an apparent accumulation of solid matter in the ship's path. But after reducing speed what would they use for further acceleration? Pel Lynn clenched his teeth and turned the lever that started the ion trigger motors used for braking. Gong-like sounds disturbed the melody of the measuring dials and drowned the alarming ring of those recording the ratio of gravitational pull to velocity. The ringing ceased and the indicators showed that speed had been reduced to a safe level and was normal for the growing gravitation. But no sooner had Pel Lynn switched off the brake engines than the bells began ringing again. Obviously the spaceship was flying directly into a powerful gravitation pool which was slowing it down.

The astronavigator did not dare change the course that had been plotted with such difficulty and precision. He used the planetary engines to brake the ship again although it was already clear that there had been an error in plotting the course and that it lay through an unknown mass of matter.

"The gravitational field is truly great," said Ingrid softly, "perhaps . . ."

"We must slow down still more so as to be able to turn," exclaimed the navigator, "but what can we accelerate with after that? . . ."

There was a note of fatal hesitancy in his words. "We have already passed the zone of outer vortices," Ingrid told him, "gravitation is increasing rapidly all the time." The frequent clatter of the planet engines resounded through the ship; the electronic ship's pilot switched them on automatically as it felt a huge accumulation of solid matter in front of them. *Tantra* began to pitch and toss. No matter how much the ship's speed was reduced the people in the control tower began to lose consciousness. Ingrid fell to her knees. Pel Lynn, sitting in his chair, tried to raise a head as heavy as lead. Kay Bear experienced a mixture of unreasoning brute fear and puerile hopelessness.

The thuds of the motors increased in frequency until they merged into a continual roar—the electronic brain had taken up the struggle in place of its semi-conscious masters: it was a powerful brain but it had its limits, it could not foretell all possible complications and find a way out of unusual situations.

The tossing abated. The indicators showed that the supply of ion charges for the motors was dropping with catastrophic rapidity. As Pel Lynn came to consciousness, he realized that the strange increase of gravity was taking place so fast that urgent measures had to be taken to stop the ship and then make a complete change of course away from the black void. He turned the handle switching on the anameson engines. Four tall cylinders of boron nitride that could be seen through a slit in the control desk were lit up from inside. A bright green flame beat inside them with lightning speed, it flowed and whirled in four tight spirals. Up forward, in the nose of the spaceship, a strong magnetic field enveloped the engine jets, saving them from instantaneous destruction.

The astronavigator moved the handle farther—through the whirling green wall of light a directing ray appeared, a grayish stream of K-particles. Another movement and the gray stream was cut by a blinding flash of violet lightning, a signal that the anameson had begun its tempestuous emission. The huge bulk of the spaceship responded with an almost inaudible, unbearable, high-frequency vibration. . . .

Erg Noor had eaten the necessary amount of food and was lying half asleep enjoying the indescribably pleasurable sensation of an electric nerve massage. The veil of forgetfulness that still covered mind and body left him very slowly. The music of animation changed to a major key and to a rhythm that increased in rapidity . . .

Suddenly something evil coming from without interrupted the joy of awakening from a ninety-day sleep. Erg Noor realized that he was commander of the expedition and struggled desperately to get back to normal consciousness. At last he recognized the fact that the spaceship was being braked and that the anameson engines were switched on, all of which meant that something serious had occurred. He tried to get up. His body still would not obey his will, his legs doubled under him and he collapsed like a sack on the floor of his cabin. After some time he managed to crawl to the door and open it. Consciousness was breaking through the mist of sleep—in the corridor he rose on all fours and made his way into the control tower.

The people staring at the screens and instrument dials looked round in alarm and then ran to their commander. He was not yet able to stand but he muttered: "The screens . . . the forward screen . . . switch over to infrared . . . shut the engines!"

The borason cylinders were extinguished at the same time as the vibration of the ship's hull ceased. A gigantic star, burning with a dull reddish-brown light, appeared on the forward star-board screen. For a moment they were all flabbergasted and could not take their eyes off the enormous disc that emerged from the darkness directly ahead of the spaceship.

"Oh, what a fool!" exclaimed Pel Lynn bitterly, "I was sure we were in a dark nebula! And that's . . ."

"An iron star!" exclaimed Ingrid Dietra in horror.

Erg Noor, holding on to the back of a chair, stood up. His usually pale face had a bluish tinge to it but his eyes gleamed brightly with their usual fire.

"Yes, that's an iron star," he said slowly and the eyes of all those in the room turned to him in fear and hope, "the terror of astronauts! Nobody suspected that there would be one in this area."

"I only thought about a nebula," Pel Lynn said softly and guiltily.

"A dark nebula with such a gravitational field would contain comparatively large solid particles and *Tantra* would have been destroyed already. It would be impossible to avoid a collision in such a swarm," said the commander in a calm, firm voice.

"But these sharp gravitational changes and vortices—aren't they a direct indication of a cloud?"

"Or that the star has a planet, perhaps more than one. . . ." The astronavigator bit his lip so badly that it began to bleed. The commander nodded his head encouragingly and himself pressed the buttons to awaken the others.

"A report of observations as quickly as possible! We'll work out the gravitation contours."

The spaceship began to rock again. Something flashed across the screen with colossal speed, something of terrific size that passed behind them and disappeared.

"There's the answer, we've overtaken a planet. Hurry up, hurry up, get the work done!" The commander's glance fell on the fuel supply indicator. His hands gripped the back of the chair more tightly, he was going to say something but refrained.

CHAPTER TWO:
EPSILON TUCANAE

The faint tinkle of glass that came from the table was accompanied by orange and blue lights. Varicolored lights sparkled up and down the transparent partition. Darr Veter, Director of the Outer Stations of the Great Circle, was observing the lights on the Spiral Way. Its immense curved into the heights and scored a dull yellow line along the sea-coast. Keeping his eyes on the Way, Darr Veter stretched out his hand and turned a lever to point M, ensuring himself solitude for meditation. A great change had on that day come into his life. His successor Mven Mass, chosen by the Astronautical Council, had arrived that morning from the southern residential belt.

They would carry out his last transmission to the Circle together and then . . . it was precisely this "then" that had not yet been settled. For six years Veter had been doing a job demanding superhuman effort. This was work for which the Council selected extraordinary people, those who were distinguished by superb memories and encyclopedic knowledge. When he began to experience attacks of complete indifference to work and to life with ominous frequency— and this is one of the most serious ailments of man—Veter had been examined by Evda Nahl, a noted psychiatrist. A proven remedy—melancholy strains of minor music in a room of blue dreams saturated with pacifying waves—hadn't helped. The only thing left was to change his work and take a course of physical labor, anything that demanded daily, hourly muscular effort. His best friend, the historian Veda Kong, had offered him an opportunity to do archaeological work with her. Machines couldn't do all the excavation work, the final stage required human hands. Veda had promised him a long trip to a region of the ancient steppes where he would be close to nature.

If only Veda Kong . . . but of course, he knew the whole story. Veda was in love with Erg Noor, Member of the Astronautical Council and Commander of Cosmic Expedition No. 37. There should have been a message from Erg Noor—he should have reported from Zirda and said whether he was going farther. But since no message had come—and all space fights were computed with the greatest precision—then . . . but no, he must not think of winning Veda's love! The Vector of Friendship, that was all, that was the greatest tie that there could be between them.

Nevertheless he would go and work for her. Darr Veter moved a lever, pressed a button and the room was flooded with light. A crystal window formed one of the walls of this room situated high above land and sea, giving a view over a great distance. With a turn of another lever Darr Veter caused the window to open inwards, leaving the room open to the starry sky; the window frame blocked the lights of the Spiral Way and the buildings and lighthouses on the sea-coast.

Veter's eyes were fixed on the hands of the galactic clock with its with three concentric, subdivided rings. Information transmission in the Great Circle followed galactic time, every one hundred-thousandth of a galactic second, or once in eight days, forty-five times a year according to terrestrial time. One revolution of the Galaxy around its axis equaled one day of galactic time.

The next and, for Veter, the final transmission would be at 9 a.m. Tibetan Mean Time or at 2 a.m. at the Mediterranean Council Observatory. A little more than two hours still remained.

The instrument on the table tinkled and flashed again. A man in silky light-colored clothing appeared from behind the partition.

"We're ready to transmit and receive," he said briefly. He showed no outward signs of deference, but in his eyes one could read admiration for his Director. Darr Veter did not say a word, nor did his assistant who stood by, confident and relaxed.

"In the Cubic Hall?" asked Veter at last, and, receiving an answer in the affirmative, asked where Mven Mass was.

"He's in the Morning Freshness Room, getting tuned up after his journey and, apart from that, I think he's a little excited."

"In his place I'd be excited myself " said Darr Veter, thoughtfully. "That's how I felt six years ago.

"The assistant flushed with the effort necessary to preserve his outward calm. With all the fire of youth he was sorry for his chief, perhaps realizing that some day he too would experience the joys and sorrows of work and great responsibility. The Station Director didn't show his feelings in any way, at his age it wasn't considered decent. "When Mven Mass appears, bring him straight to me." The assistant left the room.< . . . >

Darr Veter closed the shutters and turned to meet his successor. Mven Mass entered the room with long strides. The cast of his features and his smooth, dark-brown skin revealed his African ancestry. A white mantle fell from his powerful shoulders in heavy folds. Mven Mass took both Darr Veter's hands in his strong, slender ones. The two Directors of the Outer Space Stations, the new and the old, were both very tall. Veter, whose genealogy led back to the Russian people, seemed broader and more massive than the graceful African.

"It seems to me that something important is happening today," began Mven Mass, with the trusting sincerity typical of humans in the Era of the Great Circle. Darr Veter shrugged his shoulders. "Important things are happening for three people. I'm handing over my work, you're taking over for me and Veda Kong will speak to the Universe for the first time."

"She is beautiful'" responded Mven Mass, half questioning, half affirming.

"You'll see her. By the way, there's nothing special about today's transmission. Veda will give a lecture on our history for planet KRZ 664456 + BS 3252."

Mven Mass made an astonishingly rapid mental calculation. "Constellation of the Unicorn, star Ross 614, its planetary system has been known from time immemorial but has never in any way distinguished itself. I love the old names and old words," he added with a scarcely detectable note of apology.

"The Council knows how to select people," Darr Veter thought to himself. Aloud he said:

"Then you'll get on well with Junius Antus, the Director of the Memory Banks. He calls himself the Director of the Memory Lamps. He's not thinking of the lamps they used for light in ancient days but of those first electronic devices in clumsy glass envelopes with the air pumped out of them."

Mven Mass laughed so heartily and frankly that Darr Veter could feel his liking for the man growing rapidly.

"Memory lamps! Our memory network consists of kilometers of corridors lined with billions of cells." He suddenly checked himself. "I'm letting my emotion run away with me and haven't found out about essentials. When did Ross first speak?"

"Fifty-two years ago. Since then they 've mastered the language of the Great Circle. Only four parsecs away from us. They'll receive Veda's lecture in thirteen years."

"And then?"

"After the lecture we'll go over to reception. We'll get some news from the Great Circle through our old friends."

"Through 61 Cygni?"

"Of course. Sometimes we get contact through 107 Ophiuchi, to use the old terminology."

A man in the same silvery Astronautical Council uniform worn by Veter's assistant entered the room. He was of medium height, sprightly, with an aquiline nose. People liked him for the keenly attentive glance of his jet-black eyes. The newcomer rubbed his hairless head.

"I'm Junius Antus," he said to Mven Mass. The African greeted him respectfully. The Directors of the Memory Banks exceeded everyone else in erudition. They decided what must be preserved by the data machines, and what would be sent out as general information or used by the Palaces of Creative Endeavor.

"Another *brevus,*" muttered Junius Antus, shaking hands with his new acquaintance.

"What's that?" inquired Mven Mass.

"A Latin appellation I thought up. I give that name to all those who don't live long—*vita breva,* you know—workers on the Outer Stations, pilots of the Interstellar Space Fleet, technicians at spaceship engine plants . . . And . . . er . . . you and me. We also live no more than half the allotted span. What can you do, it's more interesting. Where's Veda?"

"She intended to get here earlier," began Darr Veter. < . . . >

Suddenly Mven Mass' glance became fixed and his face began to glow with admiration. Darr Veter looked around. Unobserved by them Veda Kong had arrived and was standing beside a luminescent column. For her lecture she had donned the costume that most complements the beauty of women, a costume invented thousands of years ago, during the Great Civilization era. The heavy knot of ash-blonde hair piled high on the back of her head did not detract from her strong and graceful neck. Her smooth shoulders were bare and her neckline was cut very low to reveal a high bosom supported by a bodice of cloth of gold. A wide, short silver skirt embroidered with blue flowers, exposed bare, sun-tanned legs in slippers of cherry-colored silk. Large cherry-colored stones from Venus, set with careful crudeness in gold links, lay like roundels of flame on her soft skin, echoing the excited glow of her cheeks and delicate ear-lobes.

Mven Mass was meeting the learned historian for the first time, and he gazed at her in frank admiration.

Veda lifted her troubled eyes to Darr Veter.

"Very nice," he said in answer to his friend's unspoken question.

"I've spoken to many audiences, but not like this," she said.

"The Council is observing the custom. Communications to other planets are always read by beautiful women. This gives them an impression of the sense of the beautiful as perceived by the inhabitants of our world, and in general it tells them a lot," continued Darr Veter.

"The Council is not mistaken in its choice!" exclaimed Mven Mass.

Veda gave the African a penetrating look. "Are you a bachelor?" she asked softly and, acknowledging Mven Mass's nod of affirmation, smiled. < . . . >

"It's time. In half an hour the Great Circle will be activated!" Darr Veter took Veda Kong carefully by the arm. Accompanied by the others they went down an escalator to a deep underground chamber, the Cubic Hall, carved out of living rock.

There was little in the hall but instruments. The dull black walls looked like velvet panels divided by clean lines of crystal. Gold, green, blue and orange lights lit up the dials, signs and figures. The emerald-green points of needles trembled on black semi-circles, giving the broad walls an appearance of strained, quivering expectation. < . . . >

Darr Veter beckoned to Mven Mass and pointed to high black armchairs for the others. The African approached, walking on the balls of his feet, just as his ancestors had once walked the sun-baked savannas on the trail of huge, savage animals. Mven Mass held his breath. Out of this deeply-hidden stone vault a window would soon be opened into the endless spaces of the Cosmos and humans would unite their thoughts and their knowledge with that of their brothers in other worlds. This small group of five individuals represented terrestrial mankind to the entire Universe. And from the next day on, he, Mven Mass, would be in charge of these communications. He was to be entrusted with the control of that tremendous power. A slight shiver ran down his back. Perhaps only at that moment did he realize what a burden of responsibility he had undertaken when he accepted the Council's proposal. As he watched Darr Veter manipulating the control switches something of the admiration that burned in the eyes of Darr Veter's young assistant could be seen in his own gaze.

A deep, ominous rumble sounded, as though a huge gong had been struck. Darr Veter turned around swiftly and threw over a long lever. The gong ceased and Veda Kong saw that a narrow panel on the right-hand wall had lit up from floor to ceiling. The wall itself seemed to have disappeared into the unfathomable distance. Phantom-like outlines of a pyramidal mountain surmounted by a gigantic stone ring appeared. Below its cap of molten stone, lay patches of pure white mountain snow.

Mven Mass recognized the second highest mountain in Africa, Mount Kenya.

Again the strokes of the gong resounded through the underground chamber, putting all those present on the alert and compelling them to concentrate their thoughts.

Darr Veter indicated a handle in which a ruby eye glowed. Mven obediently turned the handle as far as it would go. All the power produced by

Earth's 1,760 gigantic power stations was concentrated on the equator, on a mountain 5,000 meters high. A multi-colored luminescence appeared over the peak, formed a sphere and then surged upwards in a spear-shaped column that pierced the very depths of the sky. Like the narrow column of a whirl-wind it remained poised over the glassy sphere, and over its surface, climbing upwards, ran a spiral of dazzlingly brilliant blue smoke.

The directed rays cut a regular channel through Earth's atmosphere that acted as a line of communication between Earth and the Outer Stations. At a height of 36,000 kilometers above Earth hung the diurnal satellite, a giant station that revolved around Earth's axis once in twenty-four hours and kept in the plane of the equator so that to all intents and purposes it stood motionless over Mount Kenya in East Africa, the point that had been selected for permanent communications with the Outer Stations. < . . . >

The narrow panel on the right went dark, a signal that the transmission channel had connected with the receiving station of the satellite. Then the gold-framed, opalescent screen lit up. In its center appeared a monstrously enlarged figure that grew clearer and then smiled broadly. This was Goor Hahn, one of the observers on the diurnal satellite, whose picture on the screen grew rapidly to fantastic proportions. He nodded and stretched out a ten-foot arm to switch on all the Outer Stations around our planet. They were linked up in one circuit by the power transmitted from Earth. The sensitive eyes of receivers scanned every quarter of the Universe. The planet of a dull red star in Monoceros had established a better contact with Satellite 57, and Goor Hahn switched over to it. This invisible contact between Earth and the planet of another star would last for three-quarters of an hour and not a moment of that valuable time could be lost.

At a sign from Darr Veter, Veda Kong stepped to a spot on a gleaming round metal dais facing the screen. Invisible rays poured down from above and noticeably deepened the her sun-bronzed skin. Computers blinked soundlessly as they translated her words into the language of the Great Circle. In thirteen years' time the receivers on the planet of the dull-red star would write down the incoming oscillations in universal symbols and, if they had them, computers would translate the symbols into the living speech of the planet's inhabitants.

"All the same it's too bad those distant beings will not be hearing the soft, melodious voice of a woman of Earth, and will not understand its expressiveness," thought Darr Veter. "Who knows how their ears are constructed, they may possess an entirely different type of hearing. But vision, which uses the range of the electromagnetic oscillations capable of penetrating the atmosphere, is almost the same throughout the Universe, and they will see the charming Veda in her flush of excitement . . .

"Darr Veter did not move his gaze from Veda's delicate ear, partly covered by a lock of hair, while he listened to her lecture.

Briefly but clearly Veda Kong spoke of the chief stages in the history of mankind. She spoke of the early epochs of man's existence, when there were numerous large and small nations that in constant conflict, owing to the economic and ideological hostility dividing their them. She spoke very briefly and called the period The Era of Disunity. People living in the era of the Great Circle were not interested in lists of the destructive wars and the horrible sufferings, nor in the so-called great rulers who filled ancient history books. More important to them were the development of productive forces and the formation of ideas, the history of art and knowledge and the struggle to create the authentic human, the ways in which the creative urge had been developed and humanity had evolved new conceptions of the world, of social relations and of the duties, rights and happiness of Mankind. These concepts had nurtured the mighty tree of communist society now flourishing over the entire planet.

During the last century of the Era of Disunity, known as The Fission Age, humanity had at last begun to understand that their misfortunes were attributable to a social structure with its origins in ancient savagery: they realized that all their strength, all the future of Mankind, lay in labor, in the correlated efforts of millions of free people, in science and a scientific way of life, something that came to be of greater importance as the population of the planet increased.

In the Fission Age the struggle between the old and new ideas became more acute and led to the division of the world into two camps. The first types of atomic energy had been discovered, but the stubbornness of those championing the old order had almost led mankind into a colossal catastrophe.

The new social system was bound to triumph, but victory was delayed by the difficulty of training people in the new spirit. Rebuilding the world along communist lines entailed a radical economic change accompanied by the disappearance of poverty, hunger and heavy, exhausting toil. < . . . >

Communist society had not been established in all countries and among all nations simultaneously. A tremendous effort had need required to eliminate the hostility and, in particular, the lies remaining from the propaganda prevalent during the Fission Age's ideological struggles. Many mistakes were made in this period as new human relations were developing. Here and there insurrections had been raised by backward people who worshipped the past and who, in their ignorance, saw a solution to humanity's difficulties in a return to that past.

"With inexorable persistence the new way of life spread over the entire earth, and the many races and nations had been united into a single friendly and wise family.

Thus began the next era, the Era of World unity, consisting of four ages—The Age of Alliance, the Age of Linguistic Disunity, the Age of Power Development and the Age of the Common Tongue.

As Man's power over nature progressed with giant steps society developed more rapidly and each new age passed more quickly than the one before.

In the ancient Utopian dreams of a happy future, great importance had been attached on Man's gradual liberation from the necessity of work. The Utopians promised Man an abundance of all he needed in exchange for a brief working day of two or three hours, with the rest of his time free to devote to doing nothing, to the *dolce far niente*. This fantasy had arisen naturally, out of Man's abhorrence of the arduous, exhausting toil of ancient days.

Humanity soon realized that happiness could only derive from labor, from a never-ceasing struggle against nature, from overcoming difficulties and the solution of ever-new problems arising as science and the economy evolve. Man needed to work to the full measure of his strength, but his labor had to be creative and in accordance with his natural talents and inclinations. And it had to be varied and changed from time to time. < . . . > Progressively expanding science embraced all aspects of life and a growing number of people came to know the joy of the creator, of the discoverer of new secrets of nature. Art played a greater part in social education and in the formation of a new way of life. Then came the most magnificent era in Man's history, the Era of Common Labor—consisting of The Age of Simplification, The Age of Realignment, The Age of the First Abundance, and The Cosmic Age. < . . . >

The frail and risky old spaceships, poor as they were, enabled us to reach the other planets of our system. Earth was encircled by a belt of artificial satellites from which scientists were able to make a close study of the Cosmos. And then, eight hundred and eight years ago, there occurred an event of such great importance that it marked a new era in the history of mankind—the Era of the Great Circle.

For a long time the human intellect had labored over the transmission of images, sounds and energy over great distances. Hundreds of thousands of the most talented scientists worked in a special organization that still bears the name of the Academy of Direct Radiation; they developed methods for the directed transmission of energy over great distances without any conductor. This became possible when ways were found to concentrate energy in non-divergent rays. The clusters of parallel rays—laser beams— then provided constant communication with the artificial satellites, and, therefore with the Cosmos. Long, long before, towards the end of the Era of Disunity, our scientists had established the fact that powerful radiation streams were inundating Earth from the Cosmos. Signals from the Cosmos transmissions from the Great Circle of the Universe were reaching us, together with radiation from other constellations and galaxies. At that time we did not understand them, although we had learned to receive the mysterious signals which we, at that time, thought to be natural radiation.

Kam Amat, an Indian scientist, got the idea of conducting experiments from the satellites with television receivers, and with infinite patience tried all possible wavelength combinations over a period of dozens of years. He caught a transmission from the planetary system of the binary star that had long been known as 61 Cygni. A man appeared on his screen—not like us but undoubtedly a man—and he pointed to an inscription made in the symbols of the Great Circle. Another ninety years passed before the inscription was deciphered and today it is inscribed in our language, the language of Earth, on a monument to Kam Amat: 'Greetings to you, our brothers, who are joining our family. Separated by space and time we are united by intellect in the Circle of Great Power.'

The language of symbols, drawings and maps used by the Great Circle proved easy to assimilate at the level of development then reached by man. In two hundred years we were able to use translation computers to converse with the planetary systems of the nearest stars and to receive and transmit whole pictures of the varied life of different worlds. We recently received an answer from the fourteen planets of Deneb, a first magnitude star and tremendous center of life in the Cygnus; it is 122 parsecs distant from us and radiates as much light as 4,800 of our suns. Intellectual development there has proceeded on different lines but has reached a very high level.

Strange pictures and symbols come from immeasurable distances, from the ancient worlds, from the globular clusters of our Galaxy and from the huge inhabited area around the Galactic Center, but we do not understand, and have not yet deciphered them. They have been recorded by our computers and passed on to the Academy of the Bounds of Knowledge, an institution that works on problems our science can as yet only hint at. We are trying to understand ideas that are millions of years ahead of us—ideas that greatly differ from ours due to life there having followed different paths of development.

Veda Kong turned away from the screen into which she had been staring as though hypnotized and cast an inquiring glance at Darr Veter. He smiled and nodded his head in approval. Veda proudly raised her head, stretched out her arms to those invisible and unknown beings who would receive her words and her image in thirteen years.

"Such is our history, such is the difficult, devious and lengthy ascent we have made to the heights of knowledge. We appeal to you—join us in the Great Circle, aid us in carrying to the ends of the tremendous Universe the gigantic power of the intellect!"

Veda's voice had a triumphant sound to it, as though it were filled with the strength of all the generations of the people of Earth who had reached such heights that they now aspired to send their thoughts beyond the bounds of their own Galaxy to other stellar islands in the Universe . . .

The bronze gong sounded as Darr Veter turned over the lever that switched off the stream of transmitted energy. The screen went dark.

The luminescent column of the conductor channel remained on the transparent panel on the right. Veda, tired and subdued, curled up in the depths of her armchair. Darr Veter turned the control desk over to Mven

Mass and leaned over his shoulder to watch him at work. The absolute silence was broken only by the faint clicks of switches opening and closing.

Suddenly the screen in the gold frame disappeared and its place was taken by unbelievable depths of space. It was the first time that Veda Kong had seen this marvel and she gasped audibly. Even those well acquainted with the method of complex light-wave interference by means of which this exceptional expanse and depth of vision was achieved found the spectacle amazing. < . . . >

The unchanging voice of the electron translator continued: "We have received a transmission from star . . ." again a long string of figures and staccato sounds, "by chance and not during the Great Circle transmission times. They have not deciphered the language of the Circle and are wasting energy transmitting during the hours of silence. We answered them during their transmission period and the result will be known in three-tenths of a second . . ." The voice broke off. The signal lamps continued to burn with the exception of the green electric eye that had gone out.

"We get these unexplained interruptions in transmission, perhaps due to the passage of the astronauts' legendary neutral fields between us," Junius Antus explained to Veda.

"Three-tenths of a galactic second—that means waiting six hundred years," muttered Darr Veter, morosely. "A lot of good that will do us!"

"As far as I can understand they are in communication with Epsilon Tucanae in the southern sky. That's ninety parsecs away from us and close to the limit of our regular communications. So far we haven't established contact with anything farther away than Deneb," Mven Mass remarked.

"But we receive the Galactic Center and the globular clusters, don't we?" asked Veda Kong.

"Irregularly, quite by chance, or through the memory machines of other members of the Great Circle that form a circuit stretching through the Galaxy," answered Mven Mass.

"Communications sent out thousands and even tens of thousands of years ago are not lost in space, but eventually reach us," said Junius Antus.

"So that means we get a picture of the life and knowledge of the peoples of other, distant worlds with great delay. For the Central Zone of the Galaxy, for example, a delay of about twenty thousand years.'"

"Yes, it doesn't matter whether they are computer records of other, nearer worlds, or whether they are received by our stations, we see the distant worlds as they were a very long time ago. We see people that have long been dead and forgotten in their own worlds." < . . . >

"The Academy of the Bounds of Knowledge is engaged in projects to overcome space, time and gravity," Darr Veter put in. "They're working on the fundamentals of the Cosmos, but they haven't even gotten as far as the experimental stage yet, and can't . . ." The green eye suddenly flashed on again and

Veda once more felt giddy as the screen opened out into endless space.

The sharply outlined edges of the image showed that it was the computer record and not a direct transmission.

At first the onlookers saw the surface of a planet, obviously as seen from an outer station, a satellite. The huge pale violet sun, spectral in the terrific heat it generated, deluged the cloud envelope of the planet's atmosphere with its penetrating rays.

"Yes, that's it, the luminary of the planet is Epsilon Tucanae, a high temperature star, class B, 78 times as bright as our Sun," whispered Mven Mass.

Darr Veter and Junius Antus nodded in agreement. The spectacle changed, the scene grew narrower and seemed to be descending to the very soil of the unknown world. The rounded domes of hills that looked as though they had been cast in bronze rose high above the surrounding country. An unknown stone or metal glowed like fire in the amazingly white light of the blue sun. Even in the imperfect apparatus used for transmission the unknown world gleamed triumphantly, with a sort of victorious magnificence.

The reflected rays produced a silver pink corona around the contours of the copper-colored hills and lay in a wide path on the slowly moving waves of a violet sea. The water, of a deep amethyst color, seemed heavy and glowed from within with red lights that looked like an accumulation of living eyes. The waves washed the massive pedestal of a gigantic statue that stood in splendid isolation far from the coast. It was a female figure carved from dark-red stone, the head thrown back and the arms extended in ecstasy towards the flaming depths of the sky. She could easily have been a daughter of Earth, the resemblance she bore to our people was no less astounding than the amazing beauty of the carving. Her body was the fulfillment of an earthly sculptor's dream; it combined great strength with inspiration in every line. The polished red stone of the statue emitted the Games of an unknown and, consequently, mysterious and attractive life.

The five people of Earth gazed in silence at that astounding new world. The only sound was a prolonged sigh that escaped the lips of Mven Mass whose every nerve had been strained in joyful anticipation from his first glance at the statue.

On the sea-coast opposite the statue, carved silver towers marked the beginning of a wide, white staircase that swept boldly over a thicket of stately trees with turquoise leaves. "They ought to ring like bells!" Darr Veter whispered in Veda's ear, pointing to the towers, and she nodded her head in agreement.

The camera of the new planet continued its steady and soundless journey into the country. For a second the five saw white walls with wide cornices through which led a portal of blue stone; the screen carried them into a high room filled with strong light. The dull, pearl-colored, grooved walls lent unusual clarity to everything in the hall. The attention of the Earth-dwellers was attracted to a group of people standing before a polished emerald panel.

The flame-red color of their skin was similar to that of the statue in the sea. It was not an unusual color for Earth—photographs preserved from ancient days recorded tribes of Central American Indians whose skin had been almost the same color, perhaps just a little lighter. There were two men and two women in the hall. They stood in pairs, differently clothed. The pair closest to the emerald panel wore short golden garments, something like elegant overalls fastened with a number of clips. The other pair wore cloaks that covered them from head to foot and were the same pearly hue as the walls. < . . . >

At this moment the pair in golden clothing moved away to the right and their place was taken by the second pair. With a movement so rapid that the eye could not follow it the cloaks were thrown aside, and two dark-red bodies gleamed like living fire against the pearl of the walls. The man held out his hands to the woman and she answered him with such a proud and dazzling smile of joy that the Earth-dwellers responded with their own involuntary smiles. And there, in the pearl hall of that immeasurably distant world, the two began a slow dance. It was probably not danced for the sake of dancing, but was something more in the nature of eurythmics, in which the dancers strive to show their perfection, the beauty of their lines and the flexibility of their bodies. A majestic and at the same time sorrowful music could be sensed in the rhythmic alternation of movement, as though the dancers were recalling the great ladder—countless unnamed victims sacrificed to the development of life that had produced Man, that beautiful and intelligent being. < . . . >

The dance was over. The young red-skinned woman came into the center of the hall and the camera focused on her alone. The red-skinned girl from the distant world turned to face her audience, her arms spread wide as though to embrace some invisible person standing before her. She threw back her head and shoulders as a woman of Earth might do in a moment of passion. Her mouth was open slightly, and her lips moved as she repeated inaudible words. So she stood, immobile, appealing, sending forth into the cold darkness of interstellar space fiery human words, an entreaty for friendship with people of other worlds. < . . . >

Mven Mass had worked on the construction of the water-supply system of a mine in Western Tibet, on the restoration of the Araucaria pine forests on the Nahebt Plateau in South America and had taken part in the annihilation of the sharks that had again appeared off the coasts of Australia. His training, his heredity and his outstanding abilities enabled him to undertake many years of persistent study to prepare himself for difficult and responsible activities. On that day, during the first hour of his new work, there had been a meeting with a world that was related to our Earth and that had brought something new to his heart. With alarm Mven Mass felt that some great depths had opened up within him, something whose existence he had never even suspected. How he craved another encounter with the planet of star Epsilon in the Tucana Constellation! . . . That was a world that seemed to have come into being by power of the best legends known to Earth-dwellers. He would never forget the red-skinned girl, her outstretched alluring arms, her tender, half-open lips! The fact that the two hundred and ninety light years dividing him from that marvelous world was a distance that could not be covered by any means known to the technicians of Earth served to strengthen rather than weaken his dream. Something new had grown up in Mven's heart, something that lived its own life and did not submit to the control of the will and cold intellect. The African had never been in love, he had been absorbed in his work almost as a hermit would be and had never experienced anything like the alarm and incomparable joy that had entered his heart during that meeting across the tremendous barrier of space and time.

(1956-7) Translated by A. L. and M. K.

On Contemporary Russian Fantasy and Science Fiction:

An Afterword by Sofya Khagi

A s Richard Stites aptly observed in *Revolutionary Dreams: Utopian Vision and Experimental Life in the Russian Revolution*, "the world of fantasy . . . reveals and evokes deep layers, archaic dreams and longings that may better describe the feelings and anxieties [of a nation] than some conventional acts of political adherence." Thus even a necessarily concise sketch of the latest trends in Russian fantastic literature will prove of value to anyone interested in the moral, cultural, and political climate of post-Soviet Russia.

Closely on the heels of the launch of *Sputnik* in 1957, the brothers Arkady and Boris Strugatsky appeared on the literary scene with their first fantastic fables. It was primarily their oeuvre which, as the writers insisted, was "about adventures of the spirit, and not of the body," that captivated the heart of the Soviet intelligentsia during the twilight decades of the Soviet state. The influence of their works which, in contrast to mainstream science fiction that was dedicated to sheer entertainment, raised somber ethical questions, remains substantial up to the present. Thus younger practitioners of the genre who claim not to have succumbed entirely to the crude realities of the post-Soviet literary market profess to be inspired by the Strugatskys.

With the advancement of Gorbachev's reforms in the mid-eighties, Russian fantastic writers (following the general trend in Russian *belles-lettres* of the perestroika years) engaged in an increasingly open attack on the mythology of the Socialist utopia. It was during this period that the genre of dystopia once again came to the forefront of fantastic literature. As the collapse of the Soviet empire seemed more and more imminent, there appeared a number of parodic treatments of the Socialist experiment. Of these, one ought to mark out Vladimir Voinovich's *Moscow 2042* (1986), a brilliantly farcical account of the protagonist's time-travel to the dilapidated totalitarian republic of Moscowrep. In contrast to his grimmer classical dystopian predecessors (Zamiatin, Huxley, Orwell), who presented disturbing accounts of triumphant totalitarianism, Voinovich portrayed a singularly inept social structure. The depicted community displays all the trademark features of Orwell's *Oceania*, but with a clownish face: "citizens worked poorly, drank heavily, and stole left and right"; "Newspeak" was travestied through the ridiculous jargon of "Komyaz"; technology was too backward to allow for any surveillance; and one could no longer write denunciations because "the paper situation was a total disaster."

One may be tempted to assume that Voinovich's hilarious rendition of a totalitarian regime at an advanced state of deterioration implied an exclusively joyful anticipation of impending social change. However, the writer did not merely debunk the corrupt social model, but also undertook to play out alternative social scenarios. It is when Voinovich devalues both back-to-nature and counter-utopian (return to the monarchical past) resolutions that one becomes aware of his darker outlook on the country's future. Alexander Kabakov's *No Return* (1989), another important dystopia of the glasnost era, revealed a similar concern with the menaces attending the looming breakdown of the Soviet state. In the novella, a scientific researcher named "Extrapolator" is forced to travel to post-perestroika Russia. He discovers that the Soviet Union has dissolved into "barbarism and idiocy," a military dictator conducts mass executions, and crazed terrorist bands are raging on the streets of Moscow.

Whether writing in a primarily satiric vein (e.g., Voinovich, M. Veller), or in a more wistful spirit (e.g., the Strugatsky brothers' later works), the Sci-Fi and fantasy writers of Gorbachev's epoch were mainly preoccupied, on one hand, with the deconstruction of Soviet utopia, and, on the other hand, with prognostications of the possible consequences of the country's breakdown. These attempts to reinterpret the past and to discern possible venues for the country's future continued after the fall of the Soviet Union. With the faith in an upcoming technological "paradise" shaken no less badly than that in the victory of Communism, and with the country in utter disarray, it became all but impossible to produce futurist eutopian fiction.

Nevertheless, some kind of an antidote to the general sentiment of despondency attending the country's chaotic transformation had to be found. It comes as no surprise, therefore, that the demythologization of the Soviet past, vigorously undertaken during the perestroika years by a host of dystopian writers, began yielding in the nineties to a nostalgic mentality. This kind of nostalgia had to do first and foremost with the glorification of old Russia and of the country's traditional moral and religious values. In terms of fantastic fiction this suggested several directions. One way was to spin out magic stories of primeval Rus', an enchanted realm of pagan deities, spell-bound beauties, and supernatural entities following in the footsteps of Tolkien and other famous fantasy writers. Marina and Sergei Diachenko's *Ritual* and *Skrut*, Nick Perumov's *Ring of Darkness* (his take on the fabled world of the Middle Earth) and *Hiervard's Chronicles*, and numerous similar patchworks of ancient history, mythology, adventure etc., published in the nineties, are representative of this trend.

A somewhat different mode of alleviating the ache occasioned by the dire economic and political circumstances of Russia's present (as well as of reassessing the country's tortuous path into the third millennium) was to engage the subgenre of alternative history. Andrei Lazarchuk, Khol'm van Zaichik, Kir Bulychev, Sergei Lukianenko, and a host of other Russian fantasts tried their hand at imagining "what would have been if. . . ." Of those, Kir Bulychev's *River Chronos* (1992) may be singled out as an epic contemplation of historical possibilities that might have taken place had the "River of Time" but slightly changed its course. One should also mention van Zaichik's (Viacheslav Rybakov's) highly popular series about the country Ordus', founded in the Middle Ages, and representing a curious symbiosis of Russian and Eastern cultures (2001-).

As the ideological control of Soviet times was replaced in the nineties by the no less tyrannical demands of the market, huge masses of hack science fiction and fantasy began to be produced. Writing such works (along with detective stories and romances) became one of the most lucrative pseudo-literary venues. At present there exists in Russia, just as in the West, a well-established industry that clones innumerable stories of spaceships, matrixes, cyber-beauties and mythical brawny proto-Slavic warriors. Simultaneously, a number of trendy younger writers have been experimenting with the genre. Given fantastic literature's probing of alternative states of consciousness, the grotesque, the absurd, and the phantasmagoric, it offers a peculiarly rewarding domain for postmodernist play. Dmitry Lipskerov's unashamedly Marquez-inspired *Forty Years of Chanddzoe* (1996) and Vladimir Sorokin's provocative, if distasteful *Blue Lard* (1999), are examples of postmodernist engagements with the genre.

The postmodernist works mentioned, though highly conspicuous on the literary market, can hardly be deemed sterling expressions of Russian fantasy. Recent years have witnessed an appearance of several productions that deserve to be placed alongside those excellent Russian and Soviet fantastic works that are gathered in this anthology. One of these works is Tatyana Tolstaya's novel *The Slynx* (2001), a first-rate dystopia that draws a striking picture of a primitive post-nuclear war society. Moscow is transformed in her novel into a feudal village inhabited by physically and mentally deformed citizens. The people, ruled by petty tyrants, survive on a diet of mice, are forbidden to have books, and are pursued by a frightening monster wandering in the forest. Like the Strugatsky brothers, as well as classical modernist dystopian writers, Tolstaya employs fantastic discourse to explore burning social, historical, and ethical issues. As her readers realize in the course of the narrative, the mythical monster of the title symbolizes the human "heart of darkness." The work is a bitter, thought-provoking meditation on Russia—past, present, and future.

No survey of recent Russian sci-fi and fantasy, however succinct, would be adequate without saying a few words about Viktor Pelevin, one of the most popular contemporary Russian writers. Pelevin's socio-metaphysical fantasies, compared by some critics to those of Mikhail Bulgakov, Abram Tertz, and even Nikolai Gogol, blend hilarious parody and the blackest absurd, supernatural twists of plot and meticulous observations of the everyday, the occult and the surreal. *Blue Lantern* (1992), his early collection of short stories, presented a darkly phantasmagoric vision of Russia during the era of *perestroika*. In the course of the nineties he published other short stories, as well as several novellas and a novel. One should mention *The Yellow Arrow,* a novelette about a train that rushes into nothingness, while uncomprehending passengers go about their mundane lives; *Omon Ra*, the story of a young Soviet astronaut, named by his father after the OMON (a special division of the Soviet police), who renamed himself Ra after the Egyptian God of the Sun; a satiric parable *The Life of Insects*; *Buddha's Little Finger,* a fascinating exploration of realities and illusions; and finally, *Generation 'P'*, a scathing *fin-de-siècle* consumer dystopia in the spirit of Huxley's *Brave New World.*

Of those works, *Omon Ra* (1992) would prove particularly pertinent for the companion volume to this anthology. Written three and a half decades after the Soviet Union dumbfounded the world with the launch of the first *Sputnik*, this is a story of a young boy dreaming of space exploration. Having undergone training, he is sent to the moon to pilot a supposedly unmanned moonwalker. There is no way for him to return to Earth. As the narrative progresses, the young protagonist gradually comes to perceive all of existence as "a life sentence in a prison car on an endless circular railroad." As for the reader, he just as gradually comes to comprehend that what seems to be on the surface a mere phantasmagoric send-up of Soviet space exploration has a greater depth to it. In Pelevin's own words, he "did not write a satire on the Soviet space program, as the book was branded both in Russia and abroad." Rather, "[this] was a novel about coming of age in a world that is absurd and terrifying. His part of this frigtening world was Russia." The novelette, thus, explores profound existential and moral concerns in the guise of science fiction. As such, it follows the time-honored tradition of the best examples of Russian fantastic literature presented in this volume.

Selected Bibliography and Suggested Readings

Aldris, Brian. *Billion Year Spree: The True History of Science Fiction*. London: Weidenfeld and Nicolson, 1973.

Amis, Kingsley. *New Maps of Hell: A Survey of SF*. NY: Arno Press, 1975.

Armstrong, John. *The Paradise Myth*. Oxford, 1969.

Baehr, Stephen L. "Utopian Literature (Sumarokov through Odoevsky c.1750–c.1850) in Victor Terras, ed. *Handbook of Russian Literature*. New Haven: Yale U.P., 1985, pp. 497–8.

———. *The Paradise Myth in Eighteenth-Century Russia: Utopian Patterns in Early Secular Russian Literature and Culture*. Stanford, CA: Stanford U.P., 1991.

Bailey, James. *Pilgrims through Space and Time: Trends and Patterns in Scientific and Utopian Fiction*. Westport, CT: Greenwood Press [1972, c1947].

Barooshian, Vahan D. *Russian Cubo-Futurism 1910–1930*. The Hague: Mouton, 1974.

Baxter, John. *Science Fiction in the Cinema*. New York: 1970.

Berneri, Marie Louise. *Journey Through Utopia*. London: 1950.

Bethea, David M. *The Shape of Apocalypse in Modern Russian Fiction*. Princeton, NJ: Princeton U.P., 1989.

Bowlt, John E. ed. *Russian Art of the Avant-Garde: Theory and Criticism, 1902–34*. NY: Viking, 1976.

Brandis, Evgenij. *Sovetskij nauchno-fantasticheskij roman*. L.: 1959.

Bretnor, Reginald, ed. *SF Today and Tomorrow: A Discursive Symposium*. Baltimore: Penguin, 1975.

Britikov, A. F. *Russkij sovetskij nauchno-fanasticheskih roman*. L: Nauka, 970.

Brown, Edward J., ed. *Major Soviet Writers: Essays in Criticism*. NY: Oxford U.P., 1973.

———. *Russian Literature Since the Revolution. Revised edition*. Cambridge: Harvard U.P., 1982.

Buchner, Hermann. *Programiertes Glück. Socialkritik in der utopischen Sowjetliteratur*. Vienna: Europa Verlag, 1970.

Carter, Lin. *Imaginary Worlds: The Art of Fantasy*. NY: Ace Books, 1971.

Carter, Paul A., *The Creation of Tomorrow: 50 Years of Magazine Science Fiction*. NY: Columbia U.P., 1977.

Clarenson, Thomas D. *Many Futures, Many Worlds: Theme and Form in Science Fiction*. Kent, Ohio: Kent State U.P., 1977.

———. *Science Fiction Criticism: an Annotated Checklist*. Kent, Ohio: Kent State U.P., 1972.

———. *SF: The Other Side of Realism; Essays on Modern Fantasy and Science Fiction*. Bowling Green, Kent, Ohio: Kent State U.P., 1971.

———. *Voices of the Future: Essays on Major Science Fiction Writers*, vols 1&2. Bowling Green, Kent, Ohio: Kent State U.P., c1976–.

Davenport, Basil. *The Science Fiction Novel: Imagination and Social Criticism*. Chicago: Advent, 2959.

de Camp, L. Sprague and Catherine Crook de Camp. *Science Fiction Handbook*. Philadelphia: Owlswick Press, 2975.

Delic-Masing, Irene. "Peredonov's Little Tear and Why Is it Shed" in Fyodor Sologub, *The Petty Demon*. Ardis, 1983.

Edwards, T. R. N. *Three Russian Writers and the Irrational, Zamyatin, Pil'niak and Bulgakov*. Cambridge: Cambridge U.P., 1982.

Elliott, Robert. *The Shape of Utopia*. Chicago, 1970.

Erlich, Victor. *Russian Formalism: History of Doctrine*. New Haven: Yale U.P., 1981.

Ermolaev, Herman. *Soviet Literary Theories 1927–1934. The Genesis of Socialist Realism*. NY: Octagon, 1977.

Foldeak, Hans. *Neure Tendenzen der sowjetischen Science Fiction*. Slavistische Beiträge 88. Münich: Otto Sagner, 1975.

Folijewski, Zbigniew. *Futurism and its Place in the Development of Modern Poetry. A Comparative Study and Anthology*. Ottawa: University of Ottawa Press, 1980.

Glad, John. *Extrapolations from Dystopia. A Critical Study of Soviet SF*. Princeton: Kingston Press, 1982

Green, Michael A. "Kheraskov and the Christian Tragedy." *California Slavic Studies* 9 (1976), p. 1–25.

Green, Roger L. *Into Other Worlds: Space Flight in Fiction from Lucian to Lewis*. NY: Arno Press, 1975.

Gunn, James. *Alternate Worlds: The Illustrated History of Science Fiction*. Englewood Cliffs, NJ: Prentice-Hall, 1975.

Gurevich, G. *Karta strany fantazij*. Moscow: Iskusstvo, 1967.

Hillegas, Mark. *The Future as Nightmare: H.G. Wells and the Anti-Utopians*. So. Illinois U.P., 1974.

Hingley, Robert. *Nightingale Fever: Russian Poets in Revolution*. NY: Knopf, 1981.

Katz, Michael R., *Dreams and the Unconscious in Nineteenth-Century Russian Fiction*. Hanover & London: Univ. Press of New England, 1984.

Kaun, Alexander. *Soviet Poets and Poetry*. Berkeley: U. of California Press, 1943.

Kern, Gary and Christopher Collins, eds. *The Serapion Brothers: A Critical Anthology of Stories and Essays*. Ann Arbor: Ardis, 2975.

Larin, Sergej. *Literature krylatoj mechty*. Moscow: 1961.

———. "Pafos sovremennoj fantastiki,: in *Chernyj stolb*, G. Malinina, ed. Moscow: 1973.

Le Guin, Ursula. *The Language of the Night: Essays on Fantasy and Science Fiction*. NY: Putnam, 1979.

Lem, Stanislaw. *Fantastyka i Futurologia*, 2 vols. Kraków: Wydawnictwo Literackie, 1973.

———. Microworlds. NY: H. B. Jovanovich, 1984.

Levitsky, Alexander. "V. F. Odoevskij's *The Year 4338*: Eutopia or Dystopia?" in A. Mandelker, ed., *The Supernatural in Slavic and Baltic Literature*. Columbus: Slavica, 1988.

———. "Utopia Literature (c. 2850-present)" in V. Terras, ed. *Handbook of Russian Literature* (Yale, 1985), pp. 498–500.

———. "Gogol, N.V.," *Encyclopedia of Folklore & Literature*. M.E. Brown & B.A. Rosenberg, eds. (Santa Barbara, Denver, Oxford: ABC-CLIO, 1998), 260–e.

———. "The Baroque Spirit of Czech Literature and the Legacy of Russian Arabesques," *Modern Czech Studies, Brown Slavic Contributions*, vo. XI. pp. 100–127.

———. "In Search of Representational Means for Inner Worlds," *Modern Czech Studies, Brown Slavic Contributions*, vo. XI. pp. 112–140.

Lewis, C. S. *Of Other Worlds*. NY: Harcourt, Brace & World 1967, c1966.

Maguire, Robert A. *Red Virgin Soil. Soviet Literature in the 1920s*. Princeton: Princeton U.P., 1968; 2nd ed. Ithaca: Cornell U.P., 1987.

Mandelker, Amy, ed. *The Supernatural in Slavic and Baltic Literature*. Columbus: Slavica, 1988.

Manuel, Frank E. ed. *Utopians and Utopian Thought*. Boston: Beacon Press, 1967.

Markov, Vladimir. *Russian Futurism. A History*. Berkeley: University of California Press, 1968.

Mirsky, D. S. Contemporary Russian Literature, 1881–1925. NY: Alfred A. Knopf 1926.

Moscowitz, Sam. *Seekers of Tomorrow: Masters of Modern SF*. Westport, CT: Hypersion Press, 1974, c1966.

Negley, Glenn. *Utopian Literature: A Bibliography*. Lawrence: The Regents Press of Kansas, 1977.

Nicolson, Marjorie. *Voyages to the Moon.*

Oulanoff, Hongor. *The Serapion Brothers.* The Hague: Mouton, 1966.

Patrick, George Z. *Popular Poetry in Soviet Russia.* Berkeley: U. of California Press, 1929.

Phillips, Delbert D. *Spook or Spoof? The Structure of the Supernatural in Russian Romantic Tales.* Washington, DC: U. P. of America, 2982.

Poggioli, Renato. *The Poets of Russia. 1890–1930.* Cambridge: Harvard U.P., 1960.

———. *The Oaten Flute. Essays on Pastoral Poetry and the Pastoral Ideal.* Cambridge: Harvard U.P., 1975.

Prédal, René. *La Cinéma Fanastique.* Paris, 1970.

Rullkötter, Bernd. *Die wiessenschaftliche Phantastik der Sowietuion. Eine vergleichende Untersuchung der spekulativen Literaure in Ost und West.* Frankfurt: H. Lang, 1974.

Rabkin, Eric. *The Fantastic in Literature.* Princeton; Princeton U.P., 1976.

Scholes, Robert. *Structural Fabulation.* Notre Dame-London: Osford U.P., 1977.

Struve, Gleb. *Russian Literature under Lenin and Stalin. 1917–1953.* Norman: U. of Oklahoma P., 1971.

Suvin, Darko. *Metamorphoses of Science Ficion: On the Poetics and History of a Literary Genre.* New Haven: Yal U.P., 1979.

———. *Russian Science Fiction 1956–74: A Bibliography.* Elizabethtown, NY: Dragon P., 1976.

Suvin, Darko & Philmus, Robert, eds., *H. G Wells and Modern Science Fiction.* Lewisburg, PA: Bucknell U.P., c1977.

Thalmann, Marianne. *The Romantic Fairy Tale. Seeds of Surrealism.* Ann Arbor: U. Michigan, 1964.

Todorov, Tsvetan. *The Fantastic: A Strutural Approach to a Literary Genre.* Cleveland: Press of Case Western Reserve University, 1973.

Tuck, Donald H. *The Encyclopedia of SF and Fantasy Through 1968.* Chicago: Advent Publishers, 1974.

Tucker, Frank H. "Soviet Science Fiction: Recent Development & Outlook" in *Russian Review* #2, 1974, pp. 189–200.

Williams, Robert C. *Artists in Revolution: Portraits of the Russian Avant-Garde, 1905–25.* Bloomington: Indiana U.P., 1977.

Yershov, Peter. *Science Fiction and Utopian Fantasy in Soviet Literature.* Research Program on the U.S.S.R., 62. NY: East European Fund, Inc., 1954.

Zavalishin, Viacheslav. *Early Soviet Writers.* NY: Praeger, 1958.

Zhiirmunsky, Viktor. "Symbolism's Successors," in *The Noise of Change*, ed. & tr. Stanley Rabinowitz. Ann Arbor: Ardis, 2985.

Collections for Further Reading:

An Anthology of Pre-revolutionary Russian Science Fiction. Leland Fetzer, ed. & tr. Ann Arbor: Artis, 1982.

An Anthology of Russian Folk Epics. James Bailey and Tatiana Ivanova, eds. & tr. Armonk, NY, London: M. E. Sharpe, 1998.

An Anthology of Russian Literature in the Soviet Period from Gorki to Pasternak. Bernard G. Guerney, et. & tr. NY: Random House, 1960.

An Anthology of Russian Romantic Prose. Carl R. Proffer. ed. Ann Arbor: Ardis, 1979

The Ardis Anthology of Russian Futurism. Carl R. and Ellendea Proffer, eds. Ann Arbor: Ardis, 1980.

The Ardis Anthology of Russian Romanticism. Christina Rydel, ed. Ann Arbor: Ardis, 1984.

A Bilingual Collection of Russian Short Stories, Vol. 1. Maurice Friedbrg, ed. NY: Random House, 1964.

A Bilingual Collection of Russian Short Stories, Vol. 2. Maurice Friedbrg, ed. NY: Random House, 1965.

Fifty Years of Russian Prose. 2 vols. Krystyna Pomorska, ed. Cambridge: MIT Press, 1971.

The Heart of the Serpent. R. Prokofieva, tr. Moscow: Foreign Languages Publishing House, n.d.

Journey Across Three Worlds. G. Evans, tr. Moscow: Mir, 1973.

Modern Russian Poetry: An Anthology with Verse Translations. Bernard G. Guerney and Merrill Sparks, eds. Indianapolis: Bobbs-Merrill, 1967.

Everything but Love. A Shkarovsky, tr. Moscow: Mir, 1973.

The Molecular Cafe. Arkady and Boris Srugatsky, intro. Moscow: Mir, 1968.

More Soviet Science Fiction. Isaac Asimov, intro. NY: Collier Books, 1967.

New Soviet Science Fiction. Theodore Sturgeon, ed. NY: Collier Books, 1980.

"Novy Mir." A Selection 1925–1967. Michael Glenny, ed. London: Jonathan Cape Ltd, 1972.

Other Worlds, Other Seas: SF Stories from Socialist Countries. Darko Suvin, ed. NY: Random, 1970.

Path into the Unknown: The Best of Soviet SF. Judith Merril, intro. NY: Delacorte Press, 1981.

The Penguin Book of Russian Short Stories. David Richards, ed. and tr. NY: Penguin, 1981.

Russian Fairy Tales. A postscript "On Russian Fairy Tales" Roman Jakobson; Norbert Guterman, tr. NY: Random (Pantheon), 1975.

Russian Literature of the Twenties: An Anthology. Intro. by Robert A. Maguire, Carl R. Proffer, Ellendea Proffer, Ronald Mayer, Mary Ann Szporluk, eds. Ann Arbor: Ardis, 1987.

Russian Literature Triquarterly. Translations, criticism, documents. See in particular: No. 1 (19710—Acmeism; No 2 (1972)—Prose of the Twenties; No. 4 (1972)—Symbolism; Nos. 12–13 (1975)—Futurism and Consructivism; No. 14 (1976)—Satire and Parody; No. 15 (1976)—Bulgakov.

Russian Poetry: The Modern Period. John Glad and Daniel Weissbort, eds. Iowa City: U. of Iowa P., 1978.

Russian Science Fiction. Mirra Ginsburg, tr. Chicago: Chicage, U.P., 1975

Russian Science Fiction 1964. Robert Magidoff, ed. NY: NYU Press, 1964.

Russian Science Fiction 1968. Robert Magidoff, ed. NY: NYU Press, 1968.

Russian Science Fiction 1969. Robert Magidoff, ed. NY: NYU Press, 1969.

Russian Stories: Bantam Dual-Language Book. Gleb Struve, ed & transl. NY: Bantham, 1961.

Soviet Science Fiction. Isaac Asimov, intro. NY: Collier Books, 1962.

Three Centuries of Russian Poetry. Nikolai Bannikov, comp. Billingual edition. Moscow: Progress, 1980.

The Ultimate Threshold: A Collection of the Finest in Soviet SF. Mirra Ginsburg, tr. NY: Penguin, 1978.

Utopian Literature. J. W. Johnson, ed. NY: Random, 1968.

Utopias. Catriona Kelly, ed. London: Penguin, 1999.

P.S. Since we were unable to offer in our volume any of the writings by Arkadi and Boris Stugatsky, all of which appeared afer *Sputnik,* we refer interested readers to he following works available in English: *Definitely Maybe: A Manuscript < . . . > Far Rainbow: The 2nd Invasion from Mars; The Final Circleof Paradise; Hard to be a God; Monday Begins on Saturday; Roadside Picnic; The Tale of the Troika; Prisoners of Power; Noon: 22nd Century; The Snail on the Slope; The Ugly Swans.*

Selected Western authors who have influenced the sense of the Fantastic in Russia before 1957:
Asimov, Isaac. *I, Robot* (1950)
Bacon Francis. *The New Atlantis* (1627)
Bellamy, Edward. *Looking Backward* (1888)
Bradbury, Ray. *The Martian Chronicles* (1946–50)
Böhme, Jacob. *The Mysterium Magnum* (1623); Collected Works (1730)

Byron, George G. *Childe Harold's Pilgrimage* (1812–18) and Don Juan (1818–24)

Cabet, Etienne. *A Voyage to Icaria* (1839–40)

Clarke, Arthur C. *Childhood's End* (1953)

Dante Alighiere. *The Divine Comedy* (1308–21)

Dickens, Charles. *A Christmas Carol* (1843) and his entrie oeuvre

Fourier, F. M. Charles. *Le Nouveau Monde Industriel* (1829–30) and his previous Garden-city utopias

Goethe, Johann Wolfg. *The Sorrows of Young Werther* (1774); *Faust* (Pt. 1, published 1898; Pt 2, published 1832)

Hegel George, W. F. *Phenomenology of Spirit* (1807) and other works

Herder, Johann G. von. *Concerning the Origin of Speech* (1772) and most of his other writings

Hoffmann, E.T.A. *The Serapion Brothers* (1819) and his entire prose oeuvre

Homer. *The Iliad* and the *Odyssey* (8th or 7th century BC)

Huxley, Aldus. *Brave New World* (1932)

Lindsay, David. *A Voyage to Arcturus* (1923)

Lem, Stanislav. *The Star Diaries* (Dzienniki Gwiazdowe)(1957)

Marlowe, Christopher. *Doctor Faustus* (1588)

Marx, Karl. *Das Kapital* (1867)

Mercier, Louis S. *The Year 2440* (*L'An 2440, rêve s'il en fut jamai*) (1771)

Meyrink, Gustav. *The Golem* (1914–5)

Milton, John. *Paradise Lost* (1667)

More, Thomas. *Utopia* (1516)

Münchhausen, KFH. *Adventures . . . of Baron Münchhausen* (1781)

Orwell, George. *Animal Farm* (1945); *1984* (1949)

Plato. *The Republic* (c. 380 BC)

Polidori, J. W. *The Vampire* (1819)

Pope, Alexander. *An Essay on Man* (1734)

Rabelais, François. *Gargantua and Pantagruel* (1534–52)

Rousseau, Jean-Jacques. *The Social Contract* (1762); *Confessions* (1782)

Schelling, F. W. J. *System of Transcendental Idealism* (1800) and other works

Scott, Walter (Sir). *The Lay of the Last Minstrel* (1805) and most of his novels

Shelley, Mary. *Frankenstein* (1818)

Stoker, Bram. *Dracula* (1897)

Swift, Jonathan. *Gulliver's Travels* (1726);

Verne, Jules. *20,000 Leagues under the Sea* (1869) and dozens of his other novels

Wells, Herbert G. *The Time Machine* (1895) and all his other major works

Additional inspiration, of course, came from the Classical Literature of Ancient Greece and Rome, the Bible, and the Scandinavian Epos.

Permissions